JAYNE ANN KRENTZ

SWEET FORTUNE

POCKET STAR BOOKS

New York   London   Toronto   Sydney   Tokyo   Singapore

An *Original* Publication of POCKET BOOKS

A Pocket Star Book published by
POCKET BOOKS, a division of Simon & Schuster Inc.
1230 Avenue of the Americas, New York, NY 10020

ISBN: 0-671-72854-7

First Pocket Books printing October 1991

10 9 8 7 6 5 4 3 2 1

POCKET STAR BOOKS and colophon are registered
trademarks of Simon & Schuster Inc.

Printed in the U.S.A.

SWEET FORTUNE

CHAPTER ONE

I can't see."

"It's all right, Mrs. Valentine. Your eyes are fine." Jessie Benedict leaned anxiously over the frail figure on the hospital bed and patted the hand that clenched the sheet. "You took a nasty fall and you've got a few cracked ribs and a concussion, but there was no harm done to your eyes. Open them and look at me."

Irene Valentine's faded blue eyes snapped open. "You don't understand, Jessie. I can't *see.*"

"But you're looking right at me. You can see it's me standing here, can't you?" Jessie was alarmed now. She raised her hand. "How many fingers am I holding up?"

"Two." Mrs. Valentine's gray head moved restlessly on the pillow. "For heaven's sake, Jessie, that's not the kind of seeing I'm talking about. Don't you understand? I can't *see.*"

Understanding dawned and Jessie's own eyes widened in shock. "Oh, no. Mrs. Valentine, are you sure? How can you tell?"

1

The elderly woman sighed and closed her eyes again. "I can't explain it." The words sounded thick and slurred now. "I just know it's gone. It's like losing your sense of smell or touch. Dear God, Jessie, it's like being *blind*. All my life it's been there, and now it's just gone."

"It's the blow on the head. It must be. As soon as you've recovered from the concussion, everything will be fine." Jessie looked down at her and thought how small and fragile Mrs. Valentine appeared when she was not wearing one of her colorful turbans or the flowing skirts and jangling necklaces she favored.

Mrs. Valentine said nothing for a minute. She lay motionless on the hospital bed, her hand still clenched around the sheet. Jessie wasn't sure if she had fallen asleep.

"Mrs. Valentine?" Jessie whispered. "Are you okay?"

"Didn't fall," Mrs. Valentine muttered heavily.

"What did you say?"

"Didn't fall down those stairs. I was pushed."

"Pushed." Jessie was horrified anew. "Are you sure? Did you tell anyone?"

"Tried to tell 'em. Wouldn't listen. They said I was all alone in the house. Jessie, what am I going to do? The office. Who's going to keep the office open?"

Jessie squared her shoulders. This was her big chance and she was not going to blow it. "I'll take care of everything, Mrs. Valentine. Don't worry about a thing. I'm your assistant, remember? Holding things together while the boss is out of the office is what assistants are for."

Irene Valentine opened her eyes again briefly and gazed at Jessie with a dubious expression. "Maybe it would be better if you just closed the office for a couple of weeks, dear. We don't have all that many clients, heaven knows."

"Nonsense," Jessie said briskly. "I'll manage just fine."

"Jessie, I'm not sure about this. You've been with me only a month. There's so much you don't know about the way I run the business."

2

A nurse bustled through the door at that moment and smiled pointedly at Jessie. "I think that's enough visiting for now, don't you? Mrs. Valentine needs her rest."

"I understand." Jessie patted the frail hand that clutched the sheet one last time. "I'll be back tomorrow, Mrs. V. Take care and try not to worry about the office. Everything's going to be just fine."

"Oh, dear." Mrs. Valentine sighed and closed her eyes again.

With one last concerned glance at the pale woman in the hospital bed, Jessie turned and walked out into the corridor. She cornered the first official-looking person she saw.

"Mrs. Valentine believes she was pushed down the stairs of her home," Jessie informed him bluntly. "Have the police been notified?"

The resident, an earnest-looking young man, smiled sympathetically. "Yes, as a matter of fact, they were. First thing this morning after she was found. I was told there was no sign of any intruder. It looks like she simply lost her balance on the top step and tumbled to the bottom. It happens, you know. A lot. Especially to older people. You can check with the cops, if you like. They'll have filed a report."

"But she seems to think there was someone in the house. Someone who deliberately pushed her."

"In cases such as this, where there's been a severe blow to the head, the patient often loses any memory of what really happened during the few minutes just before the accident."

"Is it a permanent memory loss?"

The doctor nodded. "Frequently. So even if there had been an intruder, she probably would have no real recollection of it."

"The thing is, Mrs. Valentine is a little different," Jessie began, and then decided the young man probably did not want to hear about her employer's psychic abilities. The medical establishment was notoriously unsympathetic to that sort of thing. "Never mind. Thanks, Doctor. I'll see you later."

Jessie swung around and hurried toward the elevators, her mind intent on the new responsibilities that awaited her back at the office. In a gesture that was unconscious and habitual, she reached up to push a strand of hair back behind her ears. The thick jet-black stuff was cut in a short, gleaming bob. It was angled from a wedge at her nape to a deep curve that fell in place just below her high cheekbones. Long bangs framed her faintly slanting green eyes and emphasized her delicate features, giving her an oddly exotic, almost catlike look.

The feline impression was further enhanced by her slender figure, which seemed to throb with quick energy when she was in motion, or appeared sensually relaxed when she sprawled in a chair. The black jeans, black boots, and billowing white poet's shirt that Jessie had on today suited the look.

She frowned in thought as she waited impatiently for the elevator to reach the hospital lobby. There was a lot to be done now that she was temporarily in charge of Valentine Consultations. And the first thing on the list was to cancel a previous engagement.

The thought brought both giddy relief and simultaneous disappointment. *She was off the hook for this evening.*

But she was not certain she really wanted to be off the hook.

This unpleasant and confusing mix of emotions was something she was having to deal with frequently of late, and matters were not getting better. Her intuition warned her that as long as Sam Hatchard was in her life, things were only going to get more complicated.

Jessie strode quickly down the street, her boot heels moving at a crisp pace along the sidewalk. It was a beautiful late-spring day, if one ignored the faint tinge of yellow that hung over Seattle. Smog was something nobody really

wanted to talk about in what was considered the most
beautiful and livable of cities. People tended to ignore it
when it had the audacity to appear. They preferred to talk
about the rare sunshine instead. And it was perfectly true
that the smog would disappear soon, blown away with the
next rain. Fortunately, in Seattle a rain shower was always
on the way.

The trees planted in a row along the sidewalk formed a
fresh green canopy overhead. The rapidly evolving Seattle
skyline, with its growing number of high-rise buildings, was
spread out against the sparkling backdrop of Elliott Bay.
Ferries and tankers glided like toy boats on a deep blue
pond. In the distance Jessie could barely make out the
rugged Olympic Mountains through the haze.

Jessie narrowed her eyes against the glare. She reached
into her black shoulder bag and whipped out a pair of dark
glasses. Sunny days were always disconcerting in the Pacific
Northwest.

It took Jessie about twenty minutes to cover the distance
to the quiet side street where Valentine Consultations had
its offices. The tiny firm was housed in a small two-story
brick building located several blocks from the First Hill
Hospital, where Mrs. Valentine had been taken that morning.

The outer door of the aging structure bore the legend of
Irene Valentine's business and the stylized picture of a
robin, the logo of a small, struggling computer-software-
design firm which shared the premises. Jessie opened the
door and stepped into the dim hall.

The opaque glass door on the right opened. A thin,
rumpled-looking young man in his early twenties stuck his
head out. He looked as if he had slept in his clothes, which
he probably had. He was wearing jeans, running shoes, and
a white short-sleeved shirt with a plastic pocket protector
full of pens and assorted computer implements. He peered
at her through a pair of horn-rimmed glasses, blinking

against the light. Behind him machinery hummed softly and a computer screen glowed eerily. Jessie smiled.

"Hi, Alex."

"Oh, it's you, Jessie," Alex Robin said. "I was hoping it might be a client. How's Mrs. V?"

"She's going to be okay. Bruised ribs and a concussion. The doctors want to keep her in the hospital for a couple of days, and then she's going to stay with her sister for a while. But she should be fine."

Alex scratched his head absently. His sandy hair stuck up in patches. "Poor old lady. Lucky she wasn't killed. What about her business?"

Jessie smiled confidently. "I'll be in charge while she's away."

"Is that right?" Alex blinked again. "Well, uh, good luck. Let me know if you need anything."

Jessie wrinkled her nose. "All we really need are a few new clients."

"Same here. Hey, maybe we should try advertising our combined services." Alex grinned. "Robin and Valentine: Psychic Computer Consultants."

"You know," said Jessie as she started up the stairs, "that is not a bad idea. Not bad at all. I'm going to give that some thought."

"Hold on, Jessie, I wasn't serious," Alex called after her. "I was just joking."

"Still, it has distinct possibilities," Jessie yelled back from the second level. She shoved her key into the door marked VALENTINE CONSULTATIONS. "I've already got a slogan for us. 'Intuition and Intelligence Working for You.'"

"Forget it. We'd have every weirdo in town knocking on our door."

"Who cares, as long as they pay their bills?"

"Good point."

Jessie stepped into the comfortably shabby office and tossed her shoulder bag and sunglasses down onto the faded chintz sofa. Then she crossed the room to the mammoth old-fashioned rolltop desk and grabbed the phone. Best to get this over with before she lost her nerve, she told herself.

She threw herself down into the large wooden swivel chair and propped her booted feet on the desktop. The chair squeaked in loud protest as she leaned forward to punch out the number of her father's private line at Benedict Fasteners.

"Mr. Benedict's office." The voice sounded disembodied, it was so composed and exquisitely professional.

"Hi, Grace, this is Jessie. Is Dad in?"

"Oh, hello, Jessie." Some of the professionalism leaked out of the voice and was promptly replaced by the comfortable familiarity of a longtime acquaintance. "He's here. Busy as usual and doesn't want to be disturbed. Do you need to talk to him?"

"Please. Tell him it's important."

"Just a second. I'll see what I can do." Grace put the phone on hold.

A moment later her father's graveled voice came on the line. He sounded typically impatient at the interruption.

"Jessie? I'm right in the middle of a new contract. What's up?"

"Hi, Dad." She resisted the automatic impulse to apologize for bothering him at work. Vincent Benedict was always *at work*, so any phone call was, by definition, an unwelcome interruption.

Jessie had concluded at an early age that unless she took pains to avoid it, she would end up apologizing every time she talked to her father.

"Just wanted to let you know something's come up here at the office," she said, "and I won't be able to go to dinner with Hatch and the Galloways this evening. Got a real management crisis here, Dad."

"The hell you do." Benedict's voice thundered over the phone. "You gave me your word you'd help Hatch entertain the Galloways tonight. You know damn well it's crucial for

7

you to be there. I explained that earlier this week. Galloway needs to see a united front. This is business, goddammit."

"Then you go to dinner with them." Jessie held the phone away from her ear. Nothing, literally nothing, came before business in her father's world. She had learned that the hard way as a child.

"It won't look right," Vincent roared. "Two men entertaining Ethel and George will make the whole thing look too much like a goddamned business meeting."

"For all intents and purposes, that's what it is. Be honest, Dad. If it weren't a disguised meeting of some kind, you and Hatch wouldn't be so concerned about it, would you?"

"That's not the point, Jessie. This is supposed to be casual. A social thing. You know damn well what I'm talking about. We're concluding a major deal here. Hatch needs a dinner companion and Galloway needs to see that I'm backing Hatch one hundred percent."

"But, Dad, listen . . ." Jessie was afraid she was starting to whine and stopped speaking abruptly.

It was impossible to explain to her father how much she resented being ordered out on a business date with Sam Hatchard. Vincent would not understand the objection, and neither would Hatch. Two birds were obviously being killed with one efficient stone here, after all. Hatch could pursue company business and the courtship of the president's daughter at the same time.

"Sending you along is the perfect solution," Vincent continued brusquely. "The Galloways have known you for ages. When they see my daughter with the new CEO of Benedict Fasteners, they'll be reassured that the shift in management has my full support and that nothing is going to change within the firm. This is important, Jessie. Galloway is from the old school. He likes a sense of continuity in his business relationships."

"Dad, I can't go. Mrs. Valentine was injured today. She's in the hospital."

8

"The hospital? What the hell happened?"

"She fell down a flight of stairs. I'm not sure yet just what happened. She's got a concussion and some broken ribs. She'll be out of the office for a few weeks. I'm in charge."

"Who's going to notice? You told me yourself she doesn't have a lot of clients."

"As her new assistant, I'm aiming to fix that. I'm going to develop a marketing plan to improve business."

"Jesus. I can't believe my daughter is working on a marketing plan for a fortune-teller."

"Dad, I don't want to hear any more nasty comments about my new job. I mean it."

"All right, all right. Look, Jessie, I'm sorry about Mrs. Valentine, but I don't see how that changes anything concerning tonight."

"But I'm in charge here now, Dad. Mrs. Valentine is depending on me to hold things together, and there's a ton of stuff that has to be done around here."

"Tonight?" Vincent demanded skeptically.

Jessie glanced desperately around the empty office, her eye finally falling on the blank pages of the appointment book. She tried to sound firm. "Well, yes, as a matter of fact. I'm going to be very busy getting the files in order and working up my new plan. You should understand. You've never worked anything less than a twelve-hour day in your life. Usually fourteen."

"Give me a break, Jessie. Running Benedict Fasteners is hardly the same thing as running a fortune-teller's operation."

"Don't call her a fortune-teller. She's a psychic. A genuine one. Look, Dad. This is a business I'm running here. Just like any other business." Jessie lowered her voice to an urgent, coaxing level. "So, would you do me a favor and tell Hatch I'm sort of tied up and won't be able to go with him tonight?"

"Hell, no. Tell him yourself."

"Dad, please, the guy makes me nervous. I've told you that."

"You make yourself nervous, Jessie. And for no good reason, far as I can tell. You want to stand him up tonight when he's counting on you, go ahead and stand him up. But don't expect me to do your dirty work."

"Come on, Dad. As a favor to me? I'm really swamped, and I don't have time to track him down."

"No problem tracking him down. He just walked into my office. Standing right in front of me, in fact. You can explain exactly why you want to leave him stranded without a dinner date two hours before he's set to finalize a major contract."

Jessie cringed. "Dad, no, wait, please . . ."

It was too late. Jessie closed her eyes in dismay as she heard her father put his palm over the receiver and speak to someone else in his office.

"It's Jessie," Vincent snorted. "Trying to wriggle out of dinner with the Galloways tonight. You handle it. You're the CEO around here now."

Jessie groaned as she sensed the phone being handed into other hands. She summoned up an image of those hands. They were elegant, beautifully masculine. The hands of an artist or a swordsman.

Another voice came on the line, this one as dark and quiet and infinitely deep as the still waters of a midnight sea. It sent a faint sensual chill down Jessie's spine.

"What seems to be the problem, Jessie?" Sam Hatchard asked with a frightening calmness.

Everything Hatch did or said was done calmly, coldly, and with what Jesse thought was a ruthless efficiency. On the surface it appeared the man had ice in his veins, that he was incapable of real emotion. But from the first moment she had met him, Jessie's intuition had warned her otherwise.

"Hello, Hatch." Jessie took her feet down off the desk and unconsciously began twisting the telephone cord between her fingers. She swallowed and fought to keep her tone crisp and unhurried. "Sorry to spring this on you, but something unforeseen has come up here at the office."

"How could something unforeseen come up at a psychic's office?"

Jessie blinked. If it had been anyone else besides Hatch, she would have suspected a joke. But she had decided weeks ago that the man had no sense of humor. She glowered at the wall. "I won't be able to help you entertain the Galloways tonight. My boss is in the hospital and I'm in charge around here. I've got an awful lot to do and I've really got to get going. I'll probably have to work most of the evening."

"It's a little late for me to make other plans, Jessie."

Jessie coughed to clear her throat. Her fingers clenched around the phone cord. "I apologize for that, but Mrs. Valentine is depending on me."

"There's a lot of money riding on the Galloway deal."

"Yes, I know, but—"

"George and Ethel Galloway are looking forward to seeing you again. George made a point of it. I'm not certain how they'll interpret the situation if you fail to show up tonight. They might think there's a buyout in the works or dissension between your father and me if I turn up alone."

Each word was an invisible blow, nailing shut the escape route she had hoped to use. "Look, Hatch . . ."

"If Galloway gets the idea that Benedict Fasteners is about to change hands or is in trouble, he might not want to go through with the deal. I would be extremely disappointed to lose this contract."

Jessie began to feel cornered. This was something Hatch did very, very well. She gazed around the office with a hunted sensation. "Maybe Dad could go with you?"

"That would be a little awkward, don't you think?"

The cold reasonableness of the words heightened Jessie's nervousness. Nobody on earth could make her as nervous as Sam Hatchard did. She twitched the phone cord and began swinging the swivel chair from side to side in a restless movement. "Hatch, I realize this is awfully short notice."

"And not entirely necessary, I think." Hatch's voice was very quiet now. "I'm sure Mrs. Valentine doesn't expect you to work nights."

"Well, not usually, but this is kind of an emergency."

"Is there really anything there that can't wait until tomorrow?"

Jessie stared helplessly at the pristine work surface of her desk. She had a problem with honesty. When pushed into a corner, she tended to tell the truth. "This isn't the kind of business where you can schedule things, you know."

"Jessie?"

She swallowed again. She hated it when Hatch gave her the full force of his attention. She was far too vulnerable. "Yes?"

"I was looking forward to seeing you this evening."

"What?" Jessie straightened as if she had just touched a live electrical wire. The abrupt motion snapped the phone cord taut. The instrument toppled off the desk and landed on the floor with a resounding crash. "Oh, hell."

"Sounded like you dropped the phone, Jessie," Hatch observed as he waited patiently for her to come back on the line. "Everything all right?"

"Yes. Yes, everything's fine," she gasped as she straightened the twisted cord and replaced the telephone on the desk with trembling fingers. She was furious with herself. "Look, Hatch . . ."

"I'll pick you up at seven," Hatch told her, sounding preoccupied again, which he probably was.

He frequently did two things at once, both of which were usually business-related. The present situation was a perfect example. Jessie knew that courting her definitely came under the heading of business.

"Hatch, I really can't—"

"Seven o'clock, Jessie. Now, I'm afraid you'll have to excuse me. I've got to go over some final figures on the Galloway deal with your father. Good-bye." He hung up the phone with a gentle click.

Jessie perched on the edge of the chair and stared numbly at the receiver in her hand as she listened to the whine of the dial tone. Defeated, she dumped the instrument back into its cradle and lowered her forehead onto her folded arms. She should have known there would be no easy way out of the Galloway dinner. The invitation had not been a casual one. Hatch was pursuing her. Nothing had been said yet, but it was no secret that Hatch had marriage in mind.

She was fascinated by Hatch. She might as well admit it. But she knew she dared not give in to his plans to marry her. For Hatch, the wedding would be no more than the consummation of yet another business deal. This particular contract would guarantee him a lifetime chunk of Benedict Fasteners, which was something he wanted very badly.

At the moment, courting Jessie was near the top of Hatch's list of priorities. She knew she was at least temporarily as important to him as any business maneuver in which he was presently involved. That meant she was in a very treacherous position. There was no denying her own interest in him, and on those occasions when he made her the sole focus of his attention, she was in serious danger of succumbing entirely.

A moth dancing around a flame.

Jessie closed her eyes and conjured up a picture of the man who had become her nemesis during the past two months. His personality was strongly reflected in his physical characteristics. He was built along lean, powerful, curiously graceful lines. His long-figured swordsman's hands went well with his austere, ascetic features.

She had tried to tell herself in the beginning that there was no fire beneath the cold, polite surface of the man, but she had known she was fooling herself right from the start. The problem was that, just as with warriors and saints, the fire in Hatch would never burn for any woman. It burned for an empire—the kingdom he planned to build on the cornerstone of Benedict Fasteners.

Hatch had the full support of Vincent Benedict and the

entire Benedict family for his ambitions. He had dangled an irresistible lure in front of all the Benedicts: in exchange for a chunk of the small, thriving regional business that was now Benedict Fasteners, he would take the company into the big time. Benedict Fasteners was a company based quite literally on nuts and bolts. It designed and manufactured a wide variety of products used in construction and manufacturing to hold things together. It had the potential to grow into a giant in the industry, a conglomerate that could dominate a huge market share. All it needed was a man of vision and enterprise at the helm.

Everyone in the family was convinced that Sam Hatchard was that man.

Of course, the only one who had really needed to be convinced was Vincent Benedict, the founder of the firm. And he had taken to Hatch immediately. The relationship that had developed between the two men was as profound as it was inevitable. Jessie had sensed it from the first moment she had seen her father and Hatch together in the same room. Hatch was the son her father had never had. Which might make him an excellent choice to take Benedict Fasteners into the big time but definitely made him lousy husband material, Jessie thought grimly.

Sam Hatchard was thirty-seven. Jessie had concluded that it would probably be another thirty years, if ever, before he mellowed. She was not about to give him that long. She was surely not that big a fool.

But the terrible truth, the heavy burden that weighed her down these days, was the knowledge that although she was running from Hatch, she was not running fast enough, and she knew it. The moth in her was strongly tempted to play with fire. Hatch had sensed the weakness and he was deliberately using it. It was no big secret. Everyone in the family was using it.

In one of the saner corners of her mind, Jessie was well aware that if she allowed herself to fall into Sam Hatchard's clutches she would be condemning herself to a marriage of unbearable frustration and unhappiness. She would be repeating the same mistake her mother had made in marrying Vincent Benedict. She would be tying herself to a driven man, a man who would never find room in his life for a wife and a family.

The end result of all her wallowing about in such a morass of conflicting emotions was, naturally, chaos for Jessie. For the last month, as Hatch's subtle pursuit gradually intensified, she had found herself dancing closer and closer to the flame, unable to resist, yet unable to surrender to what she knew would be disaster. It was ridiculous. She had to put a stop to the bizarre situation.

She had to learn to just say no.

The phone rang in her ear. Jessie started and jerked back in the chair. She automatically stretched a hand out toward the receiver and then hesitated, letting the answering machine take the call. There was a click, a recorded message of her own voice saying that the office was closed but that all calls would be returned as soon as possible, and then her friend Alison Kent came on the line.

Ever since Alison had become a stockbroker, her voice had taken on the upbeat cadences of a professional cheerleader. Jessie could almost see her old friend wearing a short skirt and waving a pom-pom as she made her cold calls.

"Jessie, this is Alison at Caine, Carter, and Peat. Give me a call as soon as possible. I've just found out about an incredible opportunity in a new fat-free cooking-oil product but we're going to have to move fast on this one."

Jessie sighed as the machine clicked off. For Alison, still new on the job, every deal was the opportunity of a lifetime, and Jessie always had a hard time keeping her distance. She had to admit that her initial enthusiasm had been high when she had agreed to become Alison's first real account at Caine, Carter, and Peat. Visions of making a killing had danced through her head and she had even wondered if she might have an aptitude for playing the market full-time. But a series of recent losses had given Jessie a more realistic view of Wall Street.

She dreaded returning Alison's phone call because when she did she would very likely end up buying a lot of shares in some company that wanted to market fat-free cooking oil.

The phone rang again and this time Jessie heard Lilian Benedict's voice on the answering machine. Her mother's warm, cultured tones poured over Jessie's frayed nerves like rich cream.

"Jessie? This is Lilian. Just checking to see if you'd had a chance to talk to Vincent about the loan for ExCellent Designs yet. Oh, and by the way, enjoy yourself this evening, dear. Wear the little black dress with the V in the back. It's wonderful on you. Give my best to Hatch and the Galloways. Talk to you later."

There was another click followed by a pregnant silence as Jessie contemplated the fact that even her own mother was trying to push her into the arms of Sam Hatchard.

The situation was getting out of hand. Jessie got to her feet and began to pace the office. Nobody had actually used the word "marriage" yet in her presence, but it did not require Mrs. Valentine's psychic abilities to know what everyone was thinking, including Hatch.

A month ago when Jessie had first begun to realize what was happening, she had actually laughed. She had been so certain she could handle the pressure of the crazy situation. But now she was getting scared. There was no doubt but that she was being gently, steadily, inexorably maneuvered toward an alliance that a hundred years ago would have been baldly labeled exactly what it was, a marriage of convenience.

If she was not very careful, she was going to find herself in very big trouble. People who played with fire frequently wound up in the emergency room with singed fingers.

Jessie glanced at the clock and saw with dismay that it was nearly six. She would have to hurry if she was going to get back to her apartment and get dressed before Hatch showed up on her doorstep.

Hatch was never late.

Hatch pushed the folder of computer printouts across the desk toward Vincent Benedict. "Take a look. I think you'll like what you see."

Vincent scowled impatiently at the folder. "Of course I will. You're a magician with this kind of deal. Nobody puts a contract together better than you do."

"Thanks," Hatch murmured. It was true, he was very good at putting together projects such as the one he had recently completed between Benedict Fasteners and Galloway Engineering, but it was nice to be appreciated. Especially by Vincent Benedict.

Benedict continued to frown thoughtfully across the wide expanse of desk. It occurred to Hatch that Jessie had gotten her eyes from her father. They were a curious feline green, very clear and very intelligent. But there was a vulnerable quality in Jessie's gaze that was definitely not present in her father's eyes.

Vincent was nearing sixty, a vigorous, ruggedly built man whose heavy shoulders were a legacy of his early years in the construction business. His hair was white and thinning slightly. His face had no doubt softened somewhat over the years, but the hawklike nose and square, strong jaw still reflected the image of a man who had come up in the world the hard way. This was a man who had made most of his own rules in life, but he had played by those rules. If you were honest with Vincent Benedict, he was honest with you. If you crossed him, you paid. Dearly.

Hatch understood that kind of code because he lived by it himself. He had learned it long before he'd entered the corporate world, learned it in the hardworking, hard-playing world of his youth and young manhood, a world where real labor meant working with your hands. It meant ranching, construction, driving trucks.

The code had been drummed into him on the job, and after work it had been reinforced during nights spent in smoky taverns where a man learned to drink beer instead of white wine and where he picked up basic psychology by listening to the words of country-western music.

Hatch had liked Benedict right from the start. There had been an immediate rapport between them, probably because their origins were so similar. Vincent Benedict was one of the very few men Hatch had ever met whom he actually respected; he was also one of the even fewer number whose respect Hatch wanted in return.

"Are you worried about Galloway getting cold feet tonight?" Hatch asked after a minute during which it dawned on him that Vincent was not paying close attention to the figures on the printout.

"No." Vincent drummed his fingers on the desk in an uncharacteristically restless gesture and scowled.

"Did you have some questions?" Hatch prodded, wondering what the problem was. Benedict was usually nothing if not forthright.

"No. Everything looks fine."

Hatch shrugged and opened the second folder to scan the numbers inside. He had seen the potential in Benedict Fasteners immediately when Benedict had hired Hatchard Consulting briefly for advice on doing business with a Japanese company. The company had recently opened up a plant in Washington and had wanted to use local suppliers. Most were unable to meet the quality-control demands of the Japanese. Vincent Benedict had been wise enough to see the future could be even more profitable if he found a way to do so.

Hatch had shown him the way, and in the process concluded that Benedict Fasteners was precisely the ripe, cash-rich little business he had been looking for to use as a springboard to an empire. Vincent had refused to sell outright, but had hinted there was a possibility of a deal.

Benedict had given Hatch a one-year contract as chief executive officer, during which time both men agreed to size up the situation and each other as well as the future.

The ink had hardly dried on the CEO agreement before Benedict had started playing matchmaker.

It had quickly become clear that the price tag on a share of Benedict Fasteners was ensuring the firm stayed in the family. There was only one way to do that, but by then Hatch had met Jessie Benedict and had decided the price was not too high. In fact, the whole deal appeared very neat and satisfactory all the way around.

The Galloway contract was in the bag, of course. The dinner tonight was just a social touch. It would cement the relationship and emphasize to Galloway that from now on he would be dealing with Sam Hatchard, the new CEO of Benedict Fasteners. Jessie's presence would attest to the fact that the transfer of power had Vincent's blessing.

"She says you make her nervous," Vincent growled suddenly.

Hatch looked up, his mind still on the numbers in front of him. "I beg your pardon?"

"Jessie says you make her nervous."

"Yes." Hatch returned his attention to the printout.

"Dammit, man, doesn't that bother you?"

"She'll get over it."

"Why do you make her nervous, anyway?" Vincent demanded.

Hatch glanced up again, amused. "What is this? You're not worrying about your daughter at this late date, are you? She's twenty-seven years old. She can take care of herself."

"I'm not so sure about that," Vincent muttered. "Twenty-seven years old and she still hasn't found a steady job."

Hatch smiled briefly. "She's found plenty of jobs, from what I've heard. She just hasn't stuck with any of them very long."

"She's so damn smart." Vincent's scowl deepened. "She

was always smart. But she's changed jobs so often since she got out of college that I've lost count. No direction. No goals. I can't believe she's gone to work for a goddamned fortune-teller now. It's the last straw, I tell you."

Hatch shrugged again. "Take it easy. In a month or two she'll probably quit to go to work at the zoo."

"I should be so lucky. She seems real serious about this new job with the psychic. She's been there a month already and she sounds more enthusiastic than ever. She hasn't gotten herself fired yet, and that's a bad sign. People usually start thinking about firing Jessie within a couple weeks of hiring her. Hell, she didn't even last two weeks at that damned singing-telegram job. Guess it took 'em that long to figure out she couldn't sing."

"Give her time."

Vincent eyed him suspiciously. "It doesn't bother you that she's always bouncing around? Doesn't it make her seem kind of flighty or something?"

"She'll settle down after she's married."

"How do you know?" Vincent shot back. "What do you know about women and marriage, for crying out loud?"

"I was married once."

Vincent's mouth fell open. "You were? What happened? Divorced?"

"My wife died."

Vincent was obviously stunned that Hatch, whom he'd come to think of as a friend, if not the son he'd never had, had never mentioned his previous marriage before. "Oh, Jesus. I'm sorry, Hatch."

Sam met Vincent's eyes and said, "It was a long time ago."

"Yeah, well, like I said, I'm sorry."

"Thank you." Hatch went back to studying the printout. "Stop worrying about your daughter. I'll take care of her."

"That's what I'm trying to tell you. She doesn't seem to

want you to take care of her, Hatch. She's not exactly encouraging you, is she?"

"You're wrong," Hatch said gently. "She's been very encouraging in her own way."

Vincent gave him a dumbfounded look. "She has?"

"Yes." Hatch turned a page of the printout.

"Dammit, how can you say that? What has she done to encourage you?"

"She gets very nervous around me," Hatch explained patiently.

"I know, dammit, that's what I've been telling you. What in God's name . . . ?" Vincent broke off, incredulous. "You're saying that's a good sign?"

"A very good sign."

"Are you sure about that? I've got two ex-wives and neither Connie nor Lilian was ever nervous around me," Vincent said. "Nerves of steel, those two."

"Jessie's different."

"You can say that again. Never did understand that girl."

"That's an interesting comment, given the fact that you intend to leave Benedict Fasteners to her."

"Yeah, well, she's the only one in the family I can trust enough to leave it to." Vincent snorted again. "Whatever else happens, Jessie will do what's best for the firm and the family. That's the important thing."

"But she obviously has no interest in or talent for running Benedict Fasteners," Hatch pointed out.

"Hell, that's why I brought you on board. You're the perfect solution to the problem." Vincent pinned him with a sharp look. "Aren't you?"

"Yes."

At five minutes to seven Hatch carefully eased the new silver-gray Mercedes into a space on the street in front of Jessie's Capitol Hill apartment building.

He got out of the car and automatically looked down to

check the polish on his wing-tip shoes. Then he centered the knot on his discreetly striped tie and straightened his gray jacket. Satisfied, he started toward the lobby door.

Hatch was very conscious of the sober, restrained elegance of his attire. He was careful about such details as the width and color of the stripes on his ties and the roll of the collars on his custom-made shirts. He did not pay attention to these things because of any natural interest in fashion, but because he did not want to accidentally screw up on something so basic. In the business world a lot of judgments were made based on a man's clothes.

Hatch had grown up in boots and jeans and work shirts. Even though he had been functioning successfully in the corporate environment for some time now, he still did not fully trust his own instincts when it came to appropriate dress, so he erred on the side of caution.

His wife, Olivia, had taught Hatch most of what he knew about the conservative look favored by American corporate powermongers. For that advice some part of him would always be grateful to her. That was about all he could find to thank her for after all these years.

Hatch glanced at his steel-and-gold wristwatch as he rang the buzzer at the entrance of the aging brick building.

When he had first bought the watch he had worried that it was a bit too flashy. He'd had the same qualms about the Mercedes. But both had appealed to him, not only because they were beautifully made and superbly functional but also because they represented in a very tangible way the success Hatch had made of his life. It was a success his father, a bitter, whining failure of a man, had always predicted would elude his son.

When Hatch was in a philosophical mood, which was an extremely rare event, he sometimes wondered if he had fought his way to his present level of success primarily to prove his father's predictions wrong.

The gold hands on the watch face told Hatch he was right on time. Not that it would do him much good. Jessie was inclined to be late whenever Hatch was due to pick her up. He knew from previous experience that she would be rushing frantically around the apartment collecting her keys, checking to be certain the stove was turned off, and switching on her answering machine. Anything to delay the inevitable, Hatch thought wryly.

He took his finger off the intercom button as Jessie's breathless voice finally answered.

"Who is it?"

"Hatch."

"Oh."

"Were you expecting someone else?" he asked politely.

"No, of course not. Come on in."

The door made a hissing sound as it unlatched itself, and Hatch went into the interior lobby. He took the stairs to the second floor and walked down the hall to Jessie's apartment. He knocked softly and she opened the door, peering out with a vaguely accusing frown.

"You're right on time," she muttered.

Hatch ignored the reproach in her voice. He smiled with satisfaction at the sight of her, his gaze moving appreciatively over the close-fitting little black dinner dress that skimmed her waist and stopped just below her knees. "Hello, Jessie. You look very good tonight. As usual."

And she did. But then, Jessie always looked good to him. There was a vibrant, feminine, mysterious quality about her. She made him think of witches and cats and ancient Egyptian queens.

For all its exotic quality, Jessie's face mirrored both intelligence and a deep, womanly vulnerability. Both appealed to Hatch. His response to her intellect he understood immediately. He was a man who had always preferred intelligent women. The other kind irritated him.

But his reaction to Jessie's vulnerability still surprised him. It had been a long time since he had felt protective toward a woman, and he did not remember the compulsion being nearly as intense the last time, not even back in those

23

early days with his first wife, Olivia. He could not explain to his own satisfaction just why he reacted this way to Jessie. She was, after all, an entirely different kind of woman than Olivia had been, his dead wife's opposite in many ways.

Jessie was lively and volatile, whereas Olivia had always been serene and charming. Benedict's elder daughter was proving feisty and difficult. Olivia had always been well-mannered and refined. Jessie was the sort of female who put up roadblocks for a man, even though she wanted him. Olivia had known instinctively how to cater to the male ego.

Hatch knew Jessie was going to make him wait tonight because she was annoyed at being maneuvered into the date in the first place and even more annoyed with herself for being unable to escape the net.

Olivia might have made him wait, but only for a couple of minutes, and even then just so that she could make a proper entrance. Above all, she would have understood the importance of tonight's engagement and given Hatch her full support. She had always supported him in his career.

Jessie could not have cared less about Hatch's career.

Hatch sighed inwardly as he crossed the threshold. Jessie stepped back, holding the door open. She promptly stumbled over the large iron horse that served as a doorstop. Hatch reached out and caught her arm to steady her. Her skin felt like silk and he could smell the faint spicy fragrance she was wearing.

"Damn," she said, glancing down. "Now look what's happened. I've got a run in my hose. I'll have to change."

"No problem." Hatch pretended not to hear the irritation in her voice as he closed the door softly behind himself. "I've built a few extra minutes into our schedule. We're not due at the restaurant until seven-forty-five."

She glared at him over her shoulder as she headed toward the bedroom. "You told me seven-thirty."

"I lied."

The bedroom door slammed shut behind her, but not before Hatch had had a chance to notice the deep V cut into the back of the little black dinner dress. A great deal of smooth, cream-colored skin was showing in the cut-out portion.

Hatch smiled again and glanced around the small, cozy room. He had not had occasion to spend a great deal of time in Jessie's apartment, much to his regret, but whenever he found himself in it, he was oddly intrigued by the eclectic, colorful decor.

The place reflected Jessie's constantly shifting, often whimsical interests. The furniture was basically modern and consisted of a lot of glass, black metal, and high-tech designs. There were framed posters on the walls because Jessie changed her mind too often to risk investing in expensive paintings. One could always throw a poster away when one got tired of it, she had explained when Hatch had inquired about them. Near the front window there was a low glass table with a collection of miniature cacti arranged on it. The spiny plants looked vaguely bewildered here in the damp environs of the Pacific Northwest. The last time Hatch had been in the apartment there had been ferns on the table.

There was a wall of books behind the sofa. The titles ranged from works on magic and myth to self-help volumes on how to find a creative, fulfilling career. There were none of the trendy books one often saw in a woman's apartment about how to find and keep a man, Hatch noticed. The collection of fiction covered nearly every genre from romance and suspense to horror and science fiction.

The only thing that appeared to stay constant in Jessie's world was her unswerving loyalty to her family. Hatch had observed during the past two months that she was in many ways the heart and soul of the Benedict clan.

Loyalty was something that Hatch prized highly in a woman, probably because he'd experienced so little of it from them in the past. It had become clear to him that if he embedded himself deeply enough into the Benedict family, he would enjoy the same degree of loyalty the others got from Jessie. His entire courtship strategy was based on that observation.

The phone on the glass end table warbled just as Hatch started to leaf through a book entitled *Toward a New Philosophy of Ecology*. He noticed it was a birthday gift to Jessie from her cousin David.

"Get that for me, will you, Hatch?" Jessie called from the bedroom.

Hatch picked up the phone. "Yes?"

"Hi," said a bright, bubbling voice. "This is Alison from Caine, Carter, and Peat calling for Jessie Benedict."

"Just a minute." Hatch put down the phone and went down the hall to knock on the closed door of the bedroom.

"Who is it, Hatch?"

"Sounds like a broker."

"Oh, God. Alison. At this hour? I've been ducking her calls all day." Jessie opened the door and stared at Hatch with dismayed eyes. "I thought I could avoid her until tomorrow morning. She's trying to sell me stock in some company that's making fat-free cooking oil. Do you know anything about fat-free cooking oil?"

"Only that it's probably too good to be true."

"I was afraid of that. What am I going to tell her?"

"Why don't you just say no?" Hatch inhaled the subtle scent that was emanating from her bedroom. Through the crack in the doorway he could just make out the corner of a white-quilted bed. A pair of discarded panty hose lay in seductive disarray on the white carpet.

"You don't understand," Jessie hissed in exasperation. "I can't say no to Alison. She's a friend and she's new in the business and she's working very hard to build up a list of clients. I feel I should help her."

Hatch raised his brows, went back out into the living room, and picked up the phone.

"Jessie is not interested in any shares in fat-free cooking oil," he said. He paid no attention to the burst of chirpy, chattering protest on the other end of the line as he calmly hung up the phone.

Then he turned to see Jessie staring at him from the hallway. She had a shocked, annoyed expression on her face. He smiled blandly back at her.

"It's really very easy to say no, Jessie."

"So I see. I'll be sure to remember your technique," she snapped.

CHAPTER TWO

Of course it was no problem at all for people like Sam Hatchard to say no, Jessie thought, still seething as she opened her menu in the crowded downtown restaurant. The Sam Hatchards of this world did not worry about other people's feelings or fret overmuch about what might happen when one casually said no.

Hatch was not one to concern himself with the fact that poor Alison was new in the business of selling stocks and bonds, a woman struggling to make it in a ruthless, cold-blooded, male-dominated world. He would not care that Alison desperately needed to build up her commissions if she was to hold on to her job at Caine, Carter, and Peat. He would not be bothered by the fact that Alison was a personal friend of Jessie's.

Jessie looked up, feeling Hatch's cool, emotionless topaz eyes on her. He was sitting at the opposite side of the small table, politely responding to a question from a beaming George Galloway. But even as he said something very intelligent and shrewd to George about long-term interest rates, Jessie knew part of Hatch's mind was on the problem of how to handle Jessie Benedict. She was, after all, a top priority at the moment. Almost as important as interest rates.

Jessie shivered and knew that only part of the atavistic thrill that flashed down her spine was dread. The other part was pure feminine anticipation. She scowled, feeling like an idiot, and concentrated on her menu. George Galloway was an old-fashioned kind of man. Hatch had, therefore, selected one of the few restaurants downtown that still featured a wide variety of beef on the menu. Jessie preferred seafood.

"Tell me, Jessie, dear," Ethel Galloway said brightly, "how is your mother? I haven't seen Lilian in ages."

Jessie, searching through the short list of fish dishes at the end of the menu, looked up and smiled. Ethel was in her late fifties, a plump, pleasant-faced, grandmotherly woman. She was an excellent complement to her bluff, down-to-earth husband. Jessie had known them both for years.

"Mom's fine," Jessie said. "She and Connie are really excited about expanding their interior-design firm. Business is booming."

Ethel chuckled. "Oh, yes. The design business. What do they call their firm? ExCellent Designs or something like that, isn't it? In honor of the fact that they're both ex-wives of Vincent's?"

Jessie grinned ruefully. "That's right. They always claim they found a lot more in common with each other than they ever found with my father. Dad agrees."

"And your half-sister?" Ethel continued. "Little Elizabeth. She's still doing well in school?"

Jessie's smile widened enthusiastically. She felt a rush of pride, the way she always did when she talked about Elizabeth. "Definitely. She's determined to go into scientific research of some kind. She's just finished a fascinating project dealing with the chemical analysis of a toxic-waste dump for her school's science fair. Can you imagine? Toxic-waste chemistry and she's only twelve years old."

Ethel gave Hatch a meaningful glance. "Sounds more like the proud mother than a half-sister, doesn't she? You have to understand that Jessie has had a big hand in raising Elizabeth. Connie and Lilian have been very busy with their design business for the past few years and I do believe the child spends more time with Jessie than with her mother."

"I see." Hatch studied Jessie with an unreadable expression. "I imagine Jessie would make a very good mother."

Jessie felt herself turn an embarrassing shade of red, but the Galloways didn't seem to find the remark off-base in the least.

"Well, well, well," George said, chuckling heartily as he gave Jessie a knowing look. "Sounds like things are getting serious here. Your father implied as much last time I talked to him. Are congratulations in order yet?"

"No," Jessie managed in a croaked voice as she picked up her wineglass. She took a sip and nearly choked as it went down the wrong way. Eyes watering from the strain of trying not to cough, she shot a quick glance at Hatch. He was smiling his remote, mysterious smile. He was fully aware of his impact on her. She longed to reach across the table and throttle him.

"Jessie is feeling a little pressured these days," Hatch explained gently to his guests. "It's no secret that everyone in the family is matchmaking."

"Oh, ho." Ethel gave Hatch a droll look. "So that's the way of it, then, hmm?"

Jessie wished she could count to three and vanish.

"Pretty damn obvious why they'd all want you two to get together," George observed cheerfully. "Your marriage would certainly simplify things, wouldn't it? Keep Benedict Fasteners in the family and at the same time give Vincent the man he needs to take over and move the company into the big time."

"George, really." Ethel slanted her husband a chiding glance. "You're embarrassing poor Jessie."

"Nonsense." George turned a paternal smile on Jessie. "Known her since she was a toddler, haven't I, Jessie?"

"Yes," Jessie agreed with a sigh.

"And we know, of course, that Vincent intends to leave the company to her," George concluded.

"Unfortunately, I don't particularly want it," Jessie muttered.

"But you will take it," Hatch observed quietly, "because if you don't, Vincent will either sell it when he retires or continue to run it until he drops dead at his desk. Either way, the family will lose the future potential of Benedict Fasteners, which is enormous. It could easily be worth five times what it is today within five years."

"If you're running things, that is, eh?" George gave Hatch a shrewd glance.

Hatch shrugged. "I do have a few ideas for the firm."

"Ideas that he's done a wonderful job of selling to Dad and the rest of the family. Everyone's convinced that if Hatch remains CEO, we'll all get filthy rich," Jessie said a little too sweetly. Nobody seemed to notice the sarcasm except Hatch, who merely gave her one of his faint, polite smiles.

"Everyone's right," Hatch said.

A shark, Jessie thought nervously. The man was a cold-blooded shark. The fascination she felt for him was nothing more than the instinctual interest of a deer staring into a wolf's glowing eyes.

Ethel's brows lifted. "How did you and Hatch first meet, dear?"

Jessie managed a brittle smile. "I believe we first spoke the morning he fired me from my job in Benedict's personnel department. Isn't that right, Hatch?"

Ethel and George Galloway looked at her in shock.

"He fired you?" Ethel echoed in disbelief.

"Yes, it was all very traumatic, actually." Jessie saw the faint hint of irritation in Hatch's expression and she began to warm to her topic. Getting any kind of rise out of Hatch was a victory of sorts. It happened so rarely.

"Didn't know you'd gone to work for your father," George said. "Thought you'd always avoided working for Vincent."

"I had been working there only a few weeks. Dad had insisted I at least try a job at Benedict. He claimed I owed it to him and to the family. I was between jobs at the time . . ."

"As happens so frequently in Jessie's life," Hatch murmured.

Jessie glowered at him. "I finally agreed to give Benedict a shot. It wasn't too bad, to tell you the truth. I discovered I rather liked personnel and I think I was starting to get the hang of it. But two days after Hatch was installed in the management suite, he canned me."

"Good heavens." Ethel glanced at Hatch.

"I'm sure it wasn't all that traumatic for Jessie," Hatch said calmly. "After all, she's used to getting fired. Happens regularly, doesn't it, Jessie?"

She shrugged. "I've had my share of shortsighted, old-fashioned bosses," she informed the table loftily.

Hatch nodded. "Poor bastards."

Jessie glared at him, wondering if he was actually trying for a bit of humor or if he was serious in his sympathy for the long line of managers who had preceded him in her life. She concluded he was serious. Hatch was always serious. "As I said, I was getting along fairly well in personnel. Admit it, Hatch. Most of the people I recommended for employment have made excellent employees."

"Your hire recommendations were not the problem."

George turned directly to Hatch. "So why in hell did you toss her out of Benedict?"

Hatch put down his menu. "Let's just say that Jessie is not cut out for a happy life in a corporate environment."

"Translated, that means I tended to be on the side of the

employees, rather than management, when there was a dispute," Jessie explained. "The new CEO did not approve of my approach."

George Galloway gave a muffled snort of laughter. "What did Vincent say?"

"Vincent," Hatch said, "was profoundly grateful to me for terminating Jessie's employment with Benedict Fasteners. He'd been trying to figure out a way to get rid of her since the day after he'd hired her. It took him about twenty-four hours to realize he'd made a major mistake when he'd put Jessie to work in personnel."

"I must admit it all turned out for the best, however," Jessie assured the Galloways. "A month ago I landed a terrific new position with a wonderful firm called Valentine Consultations. I feel that I've finally found my true calling in life. Mrs. Valentine says that if things work out the way she believes they will, she'll make me a full partner in the firm."

"What sort of consulting work does Valentine do?" George turned to her with a businessman's natural interest.

"You don't want to know," Hatch warned softly.

"Nonsense. Of course we want to know, don't we, Ethel?"

"Certainly," Ethel confirmed. "We're always interested in what Jessie is doing. You do lead an adventurous sort of life, my dear."

"Mrs. Valentine is a psychic," Jessie explained with a broad smile.

"Oh, Lord." Ethel rolled her eyes.

"No wonder Benedict's praying you'll marry her," George said, leaning confidentially toward Hatch. "She's getting worse."

"I'm sure it's just a phase," Hatch said imperturbably as the waiter approached.

Two hours later Jessie breathed a sigh of relief as Hatch brought his gray Mercedes to a halt outside her apartment building. She reached for the door handle before he had finished switching off the engine.

"Well, there you go, Hatch," she said, infusing her tone with a false note of good cheer. "The Galloway deal is signed, sealed, and delivered. Tell Dad I did my duty. Now, if you don't mind, I've got to run. Big day tomorrow at the office. I'm sure you'll understand."

Without glancing to his side, Hatch touched the button that locked all the doors.

Jessie heard the solid *click* and sat back, resigned to the inevitable. "There was something else you wanted?"

Hatch turned slightly in the seat and draped his arm over the wheel, one long finger idly stroking its smooth surface. She found herself staring at that finger, hypnotized by the oddly erotic gesture.

"I think," Hatch said finally, "that we need to talk. Please invite me in for tea."

Jessie jerked her gaze away from his gliding finger and shot him a sharp glance. There was just enough light coming from the streetlamp to reveal the determination in his expression. The request for tea was more like a demand. Well, he had a point. Maybe it was time they talked. They had played cat-and-mouse long enough.

"All right," she said.

Hatch released the locks and Jessie opened her door before Hatch could get around to her side of the car.

Conversation had been sparse since Jessie and Hatch had left the restaurant. It was even sparser as they went down the hall to her apartment. When they reached her door, Hatch took the key from her hand and fitted it into the lock.

Jessie stepped inside, found the light switch, and flipped it on.

Hatch reached for Jessie's burnt-orange duster. He eased it from her shoulders slowly, letting her feel the weight of his hands. She was suddenly conscious of just how much material was missing from the back of her dress.

"Would it be so bad, Jessie?" he asked quietly.

She stepped briskly away from the lightweight coat, leaving it in his fingers. "Would what be so bad?"

"You and me." He tossed the duster over the back of a chair. His eyes held hers as he shrugged out of his suit jacket.

There was no point in pretending she didn't know what he meant. Jessie turned toward the shadowed kitchen. "Yes."

"Why?" He followed her, one hand loosening the knot of his tie.

"Don't you understand, Hatch?" Jessie opened a cupboard and took down two mugs. "It would be a disaster for both of us."

"You haven't given us much of a chance yet." He took a seat at the counter, one well-shod foot hooked on the bottom rung of the kitchen stool. "Every evening we've had together, all four or five of them, has followed the same pattern as this one."

"What do you mean?"

"First, I've had to corner you and cut off all the obvious exits. Then I've had to coax you or blackmail you or lay a guilt trip on you in order to keep you from backing out at the last minute. When I do get you out to a restaurant, you spend the time baiting me. Then I take you home and you say good night downstairs and dash out of the car as if you're running off to meet another man. You call that giving us a chance?"

"Certainly makes one wonder what you see in me, doesn't it? But I guess we both know the answer to that." She switched on the kettle with a savage little twist of her fingers. "I'm Vincent Benedict's daughter."

Hatch responded only with mild curiosity to that unsubtle taunt. He smiled quizzically. "You think I'm interested in you just because of the company?"

Jessie sighed. "I think that's a big part of it."

"The company is what brought us together. And I want it very badly. But I would not marry you to get it unless I also wanted you just as badly. And I do. Want you, that is."

Jessie gasped and her hand jerked so quickly that she

scattered a spoonful of tea leaves all over the kitchen counter. "Damn."

"Relax, Jessie."

"You always have this effect on me."

"I know," he said softly.

"How can you expect me to get serious about a man who makes me feel like a complete klutz?" She put another spoonful of tea in the pot and reached for the hissing kettle.

"Jessie, please. I know there's a mutual attraction here. And we both have the best interests of Benedict Fasteners at heart. So why won't you give me a chance?"

She leaned back against the counter and eyed the tea as it steeped. "Okay, okay. I'll give you an answer but you aren't going to like it."

"Try me."

"I'll admit I'm attracted to you, but I'm not going to get involved with you, Hatch. I am not going to get serious about you. I am definitely not going to marry you, even though everyone else thinks it would be a really nifty idea."

"Because?"

She drew a deep, steadying breath. "Because you are a carbon copy of my father."

He considered that in thoughtful silence. "No," he said at last. "I'm not."

"You're right. You're worse than my father in a lot of ways. Harder. More driven. More consumed by your work. If that's possible. There's a reason my father has two ex-wives, Hatch. And the reason is not that he's a womanizer or that he's the kind of man who has to trade in older wives on younger ones in order to feel powerful and successful. The truth is, he chose good women both times he married and he knew it. He would still be married if he had his way."

"I know."

"If you ask Connie and Lilian, they'll tell you that they each married him because when he made them a top priority he was irresistible. They each left him because once he had married, he went right back to Benedict Fasteners, his true mistress."

"That's a rather juvenile, self-centered view of things, isn't it? No woman should expect to be the only focus of attention in a man's life. Running a successful business like Benedict Fasteners takes a lot of time and energy, Jessie. You know that."

"Too much time and energy, as far as I'm concerned. Connie and Lilian will both tell you they got sick and tired of trying to compete with the company. *I don't intend to make the same mistake they did.* I won't commit myself to a man for whom business will always come first."

"Jessie . . ."

"My father is a workaholic. So are you. Workaholics don't make good family men, Hatch. I know. I'm the daughter of one, remember?"

"That's a pretty extreme view."

Jessie was incensed. The man was being deliberately dense. "Don't you understand? If I ever decide to get married, I'll want a husband who cares more about me than he does about building a corporation, a man who will think it's just as important to get to his children's school plays as he does to a meeting with a client. I want a man who knows that life is short and that people—and especially family—are far more important than business."

"Calm down, Jessie, you're getting worked up."

"You wanted this little chat." She was vaguely aware her voice was rising. She picked up one of the mugs. "You asked me a question and I'm answering it. What's more, I'm not finished. In addition to a man who is not totally addicted to his job, I want one with blood instead of ice water in his veins. I want one who's got some real, honest emotions and who isn't afraid to show them. You're always so damn cool and controlled. I want a man who can—"

"That's enough, Jessie."

She broke off quickly as Hatch got to his feet. When he stepped toward her, closing the distance between them in two strides, she panicked and dropped the mug she had been clutching.

Hatch reached her just as the mug crashed on the counter-top and rolled into the sink. His artist's hands closed slowly, inevitably around her upper arms and he pulled her against him with unnerving gentleness.

"I think," Hatch said, his mouth inches from her own, "that it's the comment about having ice water instead of blood in my veins that I take exception to the most. Kiss me, Jessie."

Wide-eyed, Jessie stood very still, looking up at him. This was the first time he had ever taken her in his arms. If she kissed him, it would be the *first time*. The monumental importance of the occasion threatened to overwhelm her. She shuddered. "Hatch, I was just trying to make a point."

"Kiss me," he commanded again, his voice very soft even though his eyes were very brilliant. "Find out for yourself if it's blood or ice water that keeps me alive."

"Oh, Hatch . . ." Jessie threw caution to the winds. In that moment she knew she could not go to her grave without finding out what it was like to kiss Sam Hatchard just once. The tension she felt in his presence had been building for weeks and it had to be released.

With an anguished little cry she wrapped her arms around his neck and pulled his head down to hers. Standing on tiptoe, she crushed her mouth against his.

Her first impression was that she was peering over the rim of a volcano. Boiling lava simmered deep down in the heart of the mountain, just as her intuition had warned her. There was definitely heat here, but it was under awesome control, surrounded by layers of frozen stone. Images of banked fires and smoldering furnaces flickered in her mind.

Moth to the flame.

Hatch's mouth moved slowly on hers, taking complete control of the kiss with effortless ease. Jessie was not quite certain just when she was no longer doing the kissing but became, instead, the one being kissed.

Hatch's elegant, dangerous hands tightened on her arms as he held her against the length of him. She could feel the long, hard muscles of his upper thighs and was deeply aware of the strength in him. It compelled and fascinated everything that was feminine within her.

But overshadowing all the other impressions that were pouring in on her was a sense of Hatch's pure self-mastery.

Jessie did not know what she had been expecting, perhaps some proof that Hatch would be as cold physically as he was in every other aspect of his life. Perhaps she had hoped such a discovery would calm the storm of conflicting emotions she felt toward him.

What she found instead was infinitely more disturbing. It would have been reassuring to know that there really was no emotion buried in this man. To discover that the fire was there, just as she had suspected, but that he had complete control of it, was unsettling in the extreme.

Jessie began to tremble. Alarmed, she brought her hands up and pushed at Hatch's shoulders. He let her go at once, his gaze amused and all too knowing. The pace of his breathing was unchanged, slow and steady as ever.

Jessie stepped quickly away from him, aware that her mouth was quivering. She bit her lip in an effort to regain her self-control as she stalked to the cupboard and got down another mug.

"Well, Jessie?"

"I think you'd better go." She poured the tea with shaking fingers.

He waited a moment longer and then, without a word, he turned and walked out of the kitchen and out of the apartment.

When the door closed behind him, Jessie sagged heavily against the counter, shut her eyes, and gulped down the hot tea.

* * *

The dowdy, worried-looking woman was hovering in the hall outside the offices of Valentine Consultations the next morning when Jessie arrived for work. Jessie was so excited at the prospect of a real live client that she nearly dropped her key.

"I'm sorry," she apologized. "Have you been waiting long? I'm afraid Mrs. Valentine isn't here today, but perhaps I can help you?"

"I'm Martha Attwood," the woman said, glancing around uneasily. "I had an appointment."

"You did?" Jessie opened the door and led the way into the office. "I'm Mrs. Valentine's assistant. I don't recall setting up an appointment for you."

"I called her at home the night before last." The woman trailed slowly into the office, looking as though she expected to find crystal balls on the tables and dark, heavy drapes covering the windows. "I told her I wasn't sure if I really wanted to hire her. She said to come in this morning. Just to talk, you know."

"Certainly. Have a seat, Mrs. Attwood. Coffee?"

"No, thank you." Martha Attwood sat down on the edge of a chair, her handbag perched on her knees. She cast another anxious look around the office. "I don't really believe in this sort of thing. Bunch of silly mumbo jumbo, if you ask me. But I don't know where else to turn. I'm desperate and the police say there's nothing they can do. There's been no actual crime committed, and my daughter . . ." Her face started to crumple. "Excuse me."

Jessie sprang up from behind the desk and came around the corner to extend a box of tissues. "It's all right, Mrs. Attwood. Just take your time."

Martha Attwood sniffed several times, blew her nose, and then dropped the used tissue into her purse. "I'm so sorry. It's the stress, you know. I've been under so much of it lately."

"I understand."

"She was doing so well in college. I was so proud of her. She was studying computer science."

"Who was studying computer science?"

"My daughter. Susan. She was always so mature for her age. Even as a child. Quiet. Hardworking. Sensible. Never got into trouble. I never dreamed she'd do something like this. I feel as though she's run off and abandoned me. Just like Harry did."

"Where, exactly, has Susan gone, Mrs. Attwood?" Jessie sat down beside the woman.

"She's gone off and joined some sort of cult. It's operating here in the Northwest somewhere. At least, I think it is. Her last letter was postmarked from right here in Seattle. Dear God, I still can't believe it. How could Susan get caught up in something like that?" Mrs. Attwood reached for a fresh tissue.

"Let me get this straight, Mrs. Attwood. You know where your daughter is?"

"Not exactly. I just know she's dropped out of her studies at Butterfield College and joined DEL."

"DEL?"

"In her letter she said it stands for Dawn's Early Light. I gather it's some sort of cult that thinks the rest of us are going to poison the environment so badly that we'll all be destroyed. But the DEL people claim they can save the planet."

"I've never heard of this particular cult."

"In her last letter Susan said she wasn't free to tell me too much yet because the DEL Foundation is trying to maintain a low profile, whatever that means."

"What is she doing for the foundation?"

"I don't know," Mrs. Attwood wailed. "They're using her, somehow. I'm sure of it. God knows what they have her doing. I can't even bear to think about it. Dear heaven, she was going to get a degree in computer science. She would have had a good job, a bright future, not the sort of life I had. I just can't believe this is happening. I came to you because I didn't know where else to turn. I can't afford a private detective, which is what I really need."

Jessie frowned thoughtfully as she absently patted the woman's hand. "Why did you call Mrs. Valentine if you don't believe in her psychic abilities?"

Mrs. Attwood blew her nose again. "Because the leader of DEL, a man named Dr. Edwin Bright, is obviously some sort of charlatan. He must be. He's convinced innocent young people like my Susan that he has special powers to predict the future and that he can change it. I guess I had some vague notion that if Mrs. Valentine could find some way to expose the man, Susan might lose her faith in him."

"You're working on the theory that it takes one to know one?" Jessie asked dryly.

Mrs. Attwood nodded, looking more miserable than ever. "It occurred to me that a . . . well, a professional like Mrs. Valentine would know all the tricks a man like Bright would use to convince others he had special powers. I mean, she must have been using such tricks, herself, for years."

Jessie bristled. "I think you should understand, Mrs. Attwood, that Mrs. Valentine has a genuine talent. She is not a fraud."

"It doesn't matter to me, don't you see?" Mrs. Attwood said hastily. "Either way, she'll recognize an impostor, won't she? Be able to expose him? And I'm sure Edwin Bright is an impostor."

"I'm really not sure we can help you, Mrs. Attwood."

Mrs. Attwood clutched at Jessie's arm. "Please. I don't know where else to turn. I'll pay her to help me prove Bright is a fake. Will you tell her that? I don't have a lot of money, but I'll find some way of paying the fees. *Please.*"

Jessie felt her irritation dissolving swiftly in the face of the woman's obvious desperation. It was so hard to say no to someone who was clearly at the end of her rope. And besides, this was a potential client.

"Let me see if I understand," Jessie said carefully. "You

don't actually want to buy the services of a true psychic. You simply want Valentine Consultations to prove that this man who runs the Dawn's Early Light Foundation is a fake, right?"

"Yes. Exactly."

"Hmmm." This was something she could handle on her own, Jessie told herself with gathering excitement. The client was not even looking for a genuine psychic. A successfully completed case such as this one could open up whole new realms of possibilities for Valentine Consultations. It was the perfect place to start her new marketing program. *Valentine Consultations, Psychic Investigations.*

"Say you'll help me," Mrs. Attwood pleaded.

"You do realize that even when their leaders are exposed, people don't always lose faith in them, don't you?" Jessie felt obliged to point out. "People who need to follow a leader will make all sorts of excuses for that leader so that they can keep on following him. It's possible we could prove this Bright is a fraud but not be able to convince Susan of it. Do you understand, Mrs. Attwood?"

"Yes, yes, I understand. But I have to try. I have to get my Susan out of the clutches of DEL."

"All right," Jessie said, making her decision on a crest of rising enthusiasm. "Valentine Consultations will take the case."

Mrs. Attwood blinked in the face of Jessie's new gung-ho attitude. "Thank you." She opened her purse. "I've brought some things along. A picture of Susan. Her last letter. There isn't much. If you can think of anything else you might need, let me know."

Her first real case. Jessie picked up the photo of a shyly smiling young woman who appeared to be about twenty years old. She wore glasses and her hair was tied back in a ponytail. There was something rather innocent and naive about Susan Attwood's face. She looked as though she had grown up in a small farm town, not a city.

"I will certainly keep you informed, Mrs. Attwood. And

don't worry, I'll get started on this right away. In fact, I'm going to consult with Mrs. Valentine immediately."

"Where is Mrs. Valentine?" Martha Attwood peered through the open doorway of the inner office.

"She took a nasty fall the night before last and she's still recovering."

"Oh, dear. Will she be able to work on my, uh, case?"

"Don't you worry about a thing, Mrs. Attwood. I'm Mrs. Valentine's assistant and I'm in charge around here now."

Mrs. Attwood cleared her throat, looking vaguely alarmed. "You're sure?"

"Absolutely positive. Relax, Mrs. Attwood. I was born for this kind of thing. It's in my blood. I just know it."

Irene Valentine looked even more worried than Mrs. Attwood had appeared. She lay back on the white pillows and listened to the entire tale, shaking her head slowly back and forth.

"I don't know, Jessie. I don't like the feel of this."

Jessie stared at her in astonished delight. "The *feel* of it? You've got your psychic abilities back, then, Mrs. V?"

"No, no, I mean I just don't like the plain old ordinary human feel of it. It doesn't take any psychic ability to sense a little trouble on the horizon, my dear. Just common sense. And my common sense tells me this cult business is way out of our league."

"But, Mrs. V, just think what a case like this could do for the image of Valentine Consultations."

"This isn't the sort of thing we normally handle, Jessie, dear. You've been with me long enough to know that. We deal with people who are under a lot of stress. Or people who are confused about things. We soothe their fears of the future and give them self-confidence. We're therapists of a sort, not private detectives."

"But this is an ideal chance to expand our business," Jessie said, unwilling to give up. "Please, Mrs. V. I told the client we'd take the case. I can work on it while you're recovering. It's not like I'm going to try to fool the client. Mrs. Attwood herself said she really doesn't expect to hire someone with genuine psychic ability. She just wants someone who can prove this Bright character is a fraud. That should be easy enough to do."

"Don't count on it. Con men are extremely clever." Mrs. Valentine narrowed her eyes. "You really want to take on this case, don't you?"

"It's a great opportunity for me to prove myself to you, Mrs. V. Let me at least do a little research on the cult and this guy Bright. If it looks too big for us to handle, I'll tell Mrs. Attwood she'll have to go to someone else. What do you say?"

"If I had any sense, I'd say no."

"Mrs. V, *please*. I have a feeling about this case. I know I can handle it."

Mrs. Valentine sighed. "As it happens, I've just taken a nasty blow on the head and I'm obviously not thinking clearly at all. All right. Do a little research, dear. Find out what you can about DEL and this man named Bright." She fixed Jessie with a firm gaze. "But you are not to go any further than that on your own, understand? Keep me posted every step of the way, and please don't do anything foolish. We don't know what is involved here, and I do not want you taking any chances."

Jessie grinned, satisfied. "Don't worry, Mrs. V. I'll be careful."

"Why do I get this overwhelming sense of impending doom?"

"You must be psychic." But Jessie regretted the little joke instantly when she saw the tears in the corner of Mrs. Valentine's eyes. "Oh, God, I'm sorry, Mrs. V. I didn't mean to upset you. You *are* psychic and you will get your inner sight back when you've recovered from the fall. I know you will."

"I hope so, Jessie." Mrs. Valentine wiped away the tears and smiled mistily. "I feel as if some part of me has been amputated. It's a dreadful feeling."

"I can imagine. Do you still think you might have been pushed down those steps?"

"I don't know what to think. The doctor explained to me about how one loses one's memory after a head injury. And the police were very nice. An officer came around again this morning and assured me there was no sign of any intruder in the house. My sister says nothing was missing or out of place. I guess I just slipped and fell."

Jessie nodded. "Well, to tell you the truth, I'd rather believe it was an accident. The idea of someone deliberately pushing you gives me the creeps."

"I agree. Best change the subject. How did your date go last night?"

"It was a disaster, just as I predicted." Jessie forced a smile. "You see? I may have some psychic ability of my own, Mrs. V."

"Yes." Mrs. Valentine looked very serious suddenly. "Yes, you may, Jessie, dear. I have suspected for some time now that you have a natural, intuitive ability that you have never fully developed."

"Really?" Jessie asked, surprised.

"It's the reason I took you on as my assistant. The thing is, I can't quite figure out what sort of talent you have, dear. No offense, but there's something rather odd about the way your mind works."

"A lot of my previous employers have said something along those lines."

CHAPTER THREE

Jessie looked down at her half-sister who was standing with her in Vincent Benedict's reception area. "You ready, kid?"

Elizabeth Benedict, curly brown hair in a neat halo around her head, her serious green eyes shielded behind a set of thick-lensed glasses, grinned bashfully. She tugged on the strings in her hand. The strings were attached to several helium-filled balloons which bobbed merrily in the air above her head. "Ready."

Jessie glanced at the trim middle-aged woman sitting at the nearby desk. "His calendar's clear for lunch?"

"I cleared it, Jessie, just like I did last year for you. He doesn't have a clue."

"Thanks, Grace. We couldn't manage this without you. All right, Elizabeth, here we go." Jessie shifted the huge bouquet of cut flowers and knocked on the heavy paneled door.

"What the hell is it now, Grace?" Vincent called out irritably from the other side of the door. "I said I didn't want to be disturbed for a couple of hours."

Elizabeth's grin faded, and behind the lenses of her glasses, her young eyes took on an uncertain expression. She glanced up at her sister uneasily.

"Don't worry," Jessie advised. "You know his bark is worse than his bite. He's forgotten it's his birthday, as usual. When he realizes what's happening, he'll lighten up. Come on." Jessie pushed open the door and marched into the room.

Vincent Benedict looked up with a ferocious scowl. "What the hell? I said I didn't . . . Oh, it's you two. What are you doing here?"

"Happy Birthday, Dad." Jessie put the huge basket of flowers down squarely in the center of the desk in front of her father. "We're here to take you to lunch."

"Good God. Is it that time of the year already?" Vincent took off his glasses and gazed at the mass of balloons and flowers. His expression warmed ever so slightly as he swung his gaze back to his daughters. "Shouldn't you be in school, Elizabeth?"

"Sure," Elizabeth admitted. "But Jessie wrote a note saying I had an urgent appointment. The teachers always believe Jessie's notes."

"I have a talent for making excuses." Jessie untwisted the balloon strings from Elizabeth's fingers and reattached them to the nearest lamp. The balloons hovered over the massive desk, looking very much out of place in the solemn atmosphere of her father's office. "Nice touch, don't you think? The balloons were Elizabeth's idea."

"I figured no one else would give you balloons. Do you like 'em, Dad?" Elizabeth anxiously awaited the verdict.

Jessie caught her father's eye. It was automatic. She'd been doing it for years in this sort of situation, she reflected. She was always on the alert to make certain her father understood he was not to casually hurt Elizabeth's feelings the way he had frequently bruised her own when she was younger.

Vincent pretended to ignore the warning look as he

contemplated the balloons with a deliberate air. "Definitely a nice touch. And you're absolutely right. No one else is very likely to give me balloons for my birthday. Or flowers." He touched one of the petals. "Thank you, ladies. Now, what was this about lunch?"

"Pizza or hamburgers. Your choice." Jessie perched on the edge of the desk. "Elizabeth and I are treating."

Vincent frowned down at his desk calendar. "Better let me check my schedule. I thought I had something on for today."

Elizabeth grinned hugely. "Jessie made Grace keep your calendar clear for today, Dad."

"Is that right? A conspiracy again, eh?" Vincent raised his brows at Jessie.

"Whatever works," Jessie murmured, fingering one of the petals of a brilliant red lily.

"What the hell, it's my birthday." Vincent turned back to Elizabeth. "Pizza or hamburgers, huh? That's a tough choice. I think I'll go with the pizza."

Jessie relaxed. The battle was over. It had not been too bad this year. There had been far worse battles in the past. Maybe her father was finally mellowing. She looked at her sister. "Pizza it is. Witness a true executive decision, kid. Dad is definitely a man of action."

"Damn right," Vincent agreed as Elizabeth giggled again.

Jessie hopped off the desk. "Let's get going. We want to beat the crowd to the pizza parlor. It gets real cutthroat in there at lunchtime."

The office door swung open before Vincent could get to his feet. Everyone automatically turned around to gaze at the man filling the open doorway.

"Somebody die?" Hatch asked, his gaze resting on the bright bouquet of flowers.

"Not yet." Vincent stood up and reached for his jacket. "Just another birthday. My daughters are taking me out to lunch. Seems my calendar has been mysteriously cleared for an hour or so this afternoon."

"You can come with us, if you want," Elizabeth told Hatch shyly.

Jessie smiled loftily. "I'm sure Hatch is much too busy to join us. I'll bet he's got all sorts of megabuck deals that need his personal attention this afternoon. Isn't that right, Hatch?"

Hatch regarded her meditatively, idly tapping the folder in his hand against the door frame. "I think I could manage to get away for an hour or so. Unless Vincent would rather hog all the female company for himself?" He glanced at the older man.

"Hell, no. There's two of 'em. Enough to go around. You're welcome to join us. Jessie and Elizabeth are buying."

"In that case, how can I refuse?"

"It's pizza," Jessie warned quickly, her heart sinking. She could almost see the computer that served as Hatch's brain as it quickly reprioritized his afternoon. First things first. And item number one on his agenda was the courtship of Jessie Benedict, even if that meant taking an hour out of his precious schedule to eat pizza.

"I'll try very hard not to get any tomato sauce on my tie," Hatch said seriously.

Jessie narrowed her eyes and decided he was not joking.

"Jessie's going to tell us all about her new case," Elizabeth announced. "She's going to start work on it right away while Mrs. Valentine is in the hospital."

"Is that right?" Hatch cocked a faintly mocking brow. "Going to help some little old lady talk to the shade of the dear departed, are we? Or maybe banish a few evil spirits from a haunted health club?"

"No," said Jessie, stung by the cool sarcasm. "As a matter of fact, I'm going to help rescue a young girl who's been kidnapped by a bizarre cult."

That wiped the condescension off Hatch's face. "The hell you are!"

* * *

His first, albeit vain hope was that she had been teasing him again, deliberately baiting him the way she so often did. If that was the case, he was reluctantly willing to admit that this time she had managed to draw a reaction.

But as Hatch sat next to Elizabeth in the pizza-parlor booth and listened to Jessie talk about her new "case," he realized this was no joke. He glanced at Vincent, silently willing the older man to put his foot down. Unfortunately, although Benedict looked singularly annoyed, it was obvious he was unable to think of any barriers to put in Jessie's path other than overwhelming disapproval. Disapproval was not doing the trick.

Hatch glanced surreptitiously around. He felt out of place sitting in the garishly decorated pizza parlor. True, his and Benedict's were not the only two business suits in the restaurant, but they were definitely the two most expensive suits.

Hatch knew full well Vincent had planned to work through lunch. Benedict always had lunch sent in unless he was doing business over the meal, in which case he usually took his guests to his club. Hatch knew the basic schedule because he followed a similar one.

But today they were both sitting here eating pizza and listening to Jessie talk about a farfetched plan to rescue some idiot who'd gotten involved in a cult. As if Jessie knew anything about cults.

Jessie and Elizabeth appeared oblivious of the fact that they were not garnering any male support for the crazy scheme. Hatch watched both females down vast quantities of pizza while nattering on excitedly about just how Jessie should start her investigation.

"The library would be a good place to begin," Elizabeth said seriously. "You can check the newspaper indexes to see if there are any articles on Dawn's Early Light or its leader."

"Good idea," Jessie mumbled around a bite of pizza. She looked at her father. "I don't suppose you've ever heard anything about it, have you?"

"Hell, no," Vincent muttered. "Sounds like a bunch of damned tree-huggers. Stay out of this, Jessie. You've got absolutely no idea what you're doing."

"I'm just going to ask a few questions and see what I can turn up."

"You're supposed to be an assistant fortune-teller," Hatch pointed out coldly. "Not some sort of unlicensed private investigator. Stick to learning how to read tea leaves and crystal balls. You've got no business researching cults, much less trying to discredit their leaders. People who lead cults don't take kindly to other people trying to prove they're frauds. You could be opening up a real can of worms here."

Jessie traded a meaningful glance with her sister. "You get the feeling we're doing lunch with a couple of real corporate wet blankets, Elizabeth?"

Elizabeth grinned. "You said their main problem was that they didn't know how to have fun."

"How right I was." Jessie waved a slice of pizza at Hatch and her father. "You two better be careful or Elizabeth and I are going to walk off in a huff and stick you with the bill."

"We'll talk about this later," Hatch said evenly as he saw Vincent's mouth tighten.

"Sorry, didn't mean to bore you," Jessie drawled. "By all means, let's change the subject."

Vincent glanced at Hatch. "This is the wildest thing she's come up with yet."

"I think it sounds like fun," Elizabeth said loyally.

Hatch eyed Elizabeth thoughtfully. The girl was a little shy but certifiably brilliant. Hatch did not doubt that someday she was going to cure rare diseases or journey into remote tropical jungles in search of exotic plants. In the meantime it was obvious Jessie was struggling to make certain the younger girl built a relationship with her father.

Hatch had figured out weeks ago just what Jessie's role in the complex Benedict family was. She was the go-between who held everything together, the one who linked Vincent to the clan and the rest of the clan to Vincent. It was clear that her real job in life was holding the Benedict family together. Anything else that might come along in terms of employment was going to be strictly part-time. He wondered why none of the family, including her own father, realized that.

"Don't forget you're supposed to pick Elizabeth up at ten o'clock on Saturday to take her to the science fair," Jessie reminded Vincent.

"I won't forget. Got it on my calendar." Vincent gave his younger daughter a knowing look. "You going to win first prize again this year?"

"Maybe." Elizabeth spoke with shy confidence. Then she frowned. "Unless they give it to Eric Jerkface."

Hatch frowned curiously. "Who's Eric Jerkface?"

"The science teacher's favorite. He looks like he came right off of some television show featuring cute kids, and he knows how to kiss up to the teachers. You know what I mean?"

"Of course Hatch knows what you mean." Jessie smiled blandly at Hatch over her sister's head. "He's very familiar with that kind of corporate mentality, aren't you, Hatch?"

"Very." Hatch shot her a withering glance and turned back to Elizabeth. "What's Jerkface's project?"

"He's doing something on extraterrestrial life."

Jessie was incensed. "Nobody even knows if there is any extraterrestrial life. How can he do a project on the subject?"

"Eric Jerkface talked the teacher into it," Elizabeth explained.

"Well, the project's bound to bomb next to yours," Jessie declared. "You're going to knock the socks off the judges with your chemical analysis of a toxic-waste dump, isn't she, Dad?"

"Right," Vincent agreed readily. Then he scowled at Elizabeth. "I just hope you're not going to turn into one of those radical environmentalists."

"Ecologist, Dad, not environmentalist," Jessie said quickly. "And Elizabeth hasn't decided which scientific career she wants to pursue yet, have you, Elizabeth?"

"No. I'm still making up my mind." Elizabeth concentrated on her pizza.

"No rush, I guess. Just don't take as long to make up your mind about a career as Jessie's taking," Vincent muttered. "What's the difference between an ecologist and an environmentalist, anyway?"

Elizabeth assumed a serious, pontificating tone. "Ecology is the *science* of studying the environment. Environmentalism is the social and political movement that causes all the headlines."

"I wonder if Edwin Bright is a genuine ecologist turned con man," Jessie mused, "or just an opportunist."

"I don't see that it matters," Hatch said flatly. "Either way, you don't have any business getting involved."

"But that's just it." Jessie's smile was radiant. "This is business. I'm working for a living. I should think everyone would be pleased. Just think, I'm actually holding down a job for longer than one month."

"Save me," Vincent growled.

Jessie turned to Elizabeth. "I'll tell you something, kid, you definitely deserve first place, and if for some reason Eric Jerkface actually wins, we'll all know it was because he was the teacher's pet and got by on his looks and charm alone."

Hatch reached for the last slice of pizza. "You haven't even seen Jerkface's project."

"Doesn't matter. Elizabeth's is tons better."

Hatch smiled slightly. "I get the impression that once you choose a side, you stick to it, come hell or high water. Is that right, Jessie?"

"Jessie is nothing if not loyal." Vincent eyed his eldest daughter with a severe glare. "Sometimes to a fault."

"I don't see it as a fault," Hatch said. "I've always considered loyalty an extremely valuable commodity."

"Just another business commodity you can buy or sell, right, Hatch?" Jessie inquired coolly.

Hatch deliberately wrapped his fingers around his glass of water. It was better than wrapping them around Jessie's throat, he told himself philosophically.

Half an hour later Vincent stalked back into his office and threw himself down into the big leather chair behind the desk. He leveled a blunt finger at Hatch.

"This problem with Jessie," Vincent announced, "is all your fault."

"My fault?"

"Damn right. If you hadn't fired her when you first came on board, she'd still be working here at Benedict Fasteners instead of running around investigating weirdo cults."

"Come off it, Vincent. You were so grateful to me the day I fired her that you bought me a drink, remember? She was a loose cannon here at Benedict. Hell, she was wreaking havoc downstairs in personnel. If she'd stayed, your whole organization would have been in a shambles by now."

"It wasn't that bad."

"Oh, yes it was," Hatch shot back. "The department heads were up in arms. The word was out. Want a few extra days of sick leave? See Jessie in personnel and give her a good sob story. She'll arrange things. Want a long weekend? See Jessie in personnel and tell her your grandmother died again. Jessie will fix things up for you. Think you got overlooked for promotion because your boss secretly hates your guts? See Jessie in personnel. She'll be on your side."

Vincent winced. "Damn. It *was* getting out of hand, wasn't it?"

"Yeah. And nobody dared call her to heel because she was the boss's daughter. How long do you think that could have gone on before every last shred of corporate discipline disintegrated, Benedict?"

Vincent held up his hand. "You're right. She was a loose

cannon around here. But that doesn't change the fact that if she were still working here at Benedict she wouldn't be dealing with cults."

Hatch went to the window and stood thinking quietly for a few minutes. "Maybe you're panicking over nothing."

"I am not panicking. I am seriously concerned. And what's this 'me' business? You're just as panicked as I am. I saw the way your jaw dropped when she exploded her little bombshell about starting an investigation. First time I've ever seen you looking like you'd been caught off-guard, Hatch. I'd have gotten a good laugh out of it if we'd been talking about anything else except Jessie's damn-fool cult-busting project."

"All right, maybe you . . . maybe *we* are seriously concerned over nothing." Hatch swung around to face him. "Look, the worst that can happen is that Jessie manages to locate the headquarters of this DEL crowd and asks to see Susan Attwood. Or maybe she'll try to talk to the leader, the one they call Bright."

"So?"

"So, think about it logically, Vincent. How would you react? More than likely Jessie will be politely told to mind her own business and that will be the end of things. She's not a threat to anyone, and whoever's running the show at Dawn's Early Light will know that. They'll treat her like an annoying reporter and just stonewall her."

Vincent gave that some thought. "You're probably right. But, hell, I wish she'd stay out of it. Why can't she find a regular job like everybody else?"

"Jessie's not like everyone else." Hatch walked over to the desk and stood looking down at the huge basket of bright flowers. "Does she always bring you flowers on your birthday?"

Vincent's eyes softened as he followed Hatch's gaze. "Started a couple of years after Elizabeth was born. Connie and I were already having problems and she and Lilian were talking about going into the interior-design business together. They were spending a lot of time on the project and somehow Jessie wound up taking care of Elizabeth a lot. One day Jessie showed up here at the office with a bunch of flowers in one arm and her little sister in the other. Said she was taking me to lunch. Been the same every year since. I've sort of gotten used to it."

Hatch cautiously touched the petal of a flame-colored lily. It was as soft as gossamer silk, as brilliant as a sunrise. "Kind of strange. Giving a man flowers, I mean."

"Like I said, you get used to it."

"Nobody's ever brought me flowers."

"Don't whine about it," Vincent said with a grin. "Marry the woman and you'll probably get flowers for your birthday too. How did things go last night?"

"The Galloway deal is closed."

"Well, hell, I know that. I mean how did things go between you and my daughter?"

"I'm not going to tell you every detail of my personal life, Benedict. But I will tell you this: I found out I'm working under a serious handicap."

"What handicap?"

"She thinks I'm too much like you in some ways."

"Bullshit. That's just an excuse. Besides, she *likes* me."

Hatch remembered Jessie's quivering mouth crushed beneath his own and the feel of her arms wrapped around his neck. "She likes me too. But she doesn't think I'll make her a good husband. Says she doesn't want to marry a man who's more concerned about his work than his family."

"*Women.* They don't understand the demands of the business world. Always want to come first in a man's life. You'd think they'd figure out that companies like Benedict Fasteners don't just run themselves. I thought Jessie would have more common sense."

"Something tells me common sense is not one of Jessie's biggest virtues," Hatch said.

Vincent scowled. "Jessie's all right. Hell, what you said at lunch hit the nail on the head. She's real loyal. In the end she always does what's best for the family. You know what the real problem is here? You're still making her nervous. That's what the real problem is. You want some advice, Hatch? Stop making her nervous, goddammit."

"Advice? From a man with two ex-wives? Forget it. I'd rather muddle through this on my own." Hatch ceased stroking the scarlet lily and headed toward the door.

But on the way back down the hall to his office, Vincent's words rang in his ears. *She always does what's best for the family.* Hatch nodded in cool satisfaction. He was counting on it.

"So how did the big date go last night?" Elizabeth asked as Jessie drove her back toward her Bellevue school.

"I told you, it wasn't a date, it was a business dinner." Jessie guided her little red Toyota onto the bridge that crossed Lake Washington via Mercer Island. She kept her expression serious, trying to look as if she was having to concentrate very hard on the sparse afternoon traffic. Elizabeth knew better.

"Hey, Jessie, this is me, your very smart kid sister, remember?"

"You mean my smartass kid sister."

Elizabeth shrugged. "Everything I know, I learned from you."

"Don't blame your bad manners on me. Bad manners are usually the result of hanging out with a bad crowd. Remind me to check out your current peer group."

"You can spot them right away when we get to school. They're the ones wearing black leather jackets and safety pins in their ears. So how'd it go, Jess?"

"What do you care?"

"Are you kidding? Everybody in the family cares. Mom says the situation is very delicate." Elizabeth studied the expensive landscape of Mercer Island with a thoughtful expression. "She says the best thing that could happen for everyone is for you to marry Hatch."

"This may come as a shock, Elizabeth, but that's not really a good enough reason for me to marry him. Not that he's asked me."

Elizabeth shot her a shrewd glance. "The moms are going to want to know how last night went too."

"I'm aware of that," Jessie said through set teeth.

"What are you going to tell 'em?"

"As little as possible. It's none of their business."

Elizabeth frowned. "I don't think they see it that way. I heard Lilian talking to Glenna on the phone yesterday. She was saying they all had a 'vested interest' in this relationship. I think that was the phrase she used."

"You know what 'vested interest' means, Elizabeth?"

"There's money involved?" Elizabeth hazarded.

"You've got it." Jessie smiled without any humor. "If I marry Hatch, Benedict Fasteners stays in the family and has a good chance of going big-time. Which appears to be everyone's fondest dream." *Including Hatch's.*

"The moms say Hatch is a real corporate shark and that he'll know how to turn Benedict into a giant in the industry."

Jessie shrugged. "I wouldn't be surprised. But I can't see being married to a shark, can you? Too many teeth."

Elizabeth giggled. "Just don't let him bite you."

"I'll try to avoid it."

"Jessie?"

"Yeah?"

"What happens if you don't marry him?"

Jessie hesitated and then decided to lay it on the line. "Dad might sell the company when he retires. But my guess is that he'll never retire. He'll just continue to run it the way he has been for the past thirty years."

"Would that be so bad?"

Jessie chewed on her lower lip. "I don't think so, but everyone else seems to."

"Including Dad. You know, I think it would be kind of sad for him if you don't marry Hatch. Dad really wants Benedict Fasteners to grow, doesn't he? He's real excited about the idea."

"What is this? Are you going to lay a guilt trip on me too? I don't need anyone else pushing me into this marriage, Elizabeth."

"Sorry." Elizabeth was silent for a moment. "Do you think Hatch likes you? I mean, just you?"

"You mean me without the business attached?" Jessie thought about the kiss that had taken place in her kitchen last night. She remembered the sensation of banked fires and relentless self-control. "Maybe, Elizabeth. But with Hatch, business will always come first."

"He's started asking you out a lot these days, hasn't he? And he didn't have to go to lunch with us today. I think it was because he really wanted to be with you."

"Right now I'm a priority for Hatch. That means I'm the focus of a great deal of his attention. It wouldn't last five minutes after the wedding. Heck, we'd probably spend our honeymoon with a fax machine and a modem hooked up beside the bed so he could stay in touch with the office. Hey, don't you have soccer practice this afternoon?"

"Yep."

"I thought so. Don't forget to wear your sun-block cream."

"Geez, Jessie. I'm not a kid any longer. I won't forget."

"Sorry. What are you doing after soccer practice?"

"Jennifer and I are going to the mall to hang out with some friends."

"Alone?" Jessie asked sharply.

"No," Elizabeth said with elaborate patience. "I just told you, we're going to hang out with some friends. Jennifer's mother is going to drop us off and pick us up later."

"I don't think it's a good idea for a kid your age to be hanging out at the mall at night without an adult," Jessie said firmly.

Elizabeth giggled. "Mom and Lilian say you're overprotective."

Jessie sighed. "Maybe I am."

There was a slight pause before Elizabeth said, "Hey, Jessie?"

"Uh-huh?"

"You think Dad'll be too disappointed on Saturday if Eric Jerkface gets first place at the science fair?"

"Nope. He might be mad at the judges, because he knows how smart you are and he'll probably figure you got ripped off if you don't get first place. But he would never be disappointed in you, Elizabeth. No matter what happened. You know that, don't you?"

"Yeah, I guess so." Elizabeth relaxed. "Kind of hard on Dad, I guess, having to go through all this dumb school stuff a second time around. You and me being so far apart in age and all."

"Don't worry about it, kid," Jessie said grimly. "This is the *first* time around for him."

At five o'clock that afternoon Jessie opened the office door labeled "Dr. Glenna Ringstead, Ph.D., Clinical Psychology," and went into the softly lit waiting room. It was empty. Her aunt's secretary, a sober-looking woman with short graying hair, looked up and smiled in recognition.

"Hello, Jessie. Dr. Ringstead's just finishing up with her last patient of the day. Have a seat."

"Thanks, Laura."

The inner door opened at that moment and a woman in her late thirties emerged. She was wiping her tear-reddened eyes with a tissue. Jessie discreetly studied a print on the wall. Her aunt's waiting room always made her uneasy. The people one found in it always appeared so terribly depressed.

The patient went over to Laura and mumbled something about an appointment for the following week, paid her bill, and then left. Glenna Ringstead stepped out of her office a moment later.

Jessie's Aunt Glenna was Lilian Benedict's sister, but it

was easy to forget that fact. The two women were as different as night and day. In many ways Lilian was a lot closer to Vincent Benedict's other ex-wife than she was to her own sister.

Glenna had been married once. Lloyd Ringstead had been an accountant at Benedict Fasteners who had walked out on his wife and son years ago and never contacted them again. Jessie barely recalled her Uncle Lloyd. Her aunt had never remarried.

Glenna was an attractive woman in a severe sort of way. She was in her early fifties and she wore her silvered blond hair pinned in a no-nonsense coil that gave her the regal look of an Amazon queen. Her large black-framed glasses were something of a trademark. She had worn them for years. They went well with her trim, tailored beige suits and her air of grave authority.

"Hello, Jessie." Glenna smiled her cool, remote, professional smile. "Come on in and sit down. I assume you're not here to consult me in my professional capacity. You haven't asked for advice from me since the day I told you not to try so hard to force a relationship with your father."

"Let's see, that was when I was about fifteen years old, wasn't it? Right after Elizabeth was born." Jessie grinned cheerfully. "Don't take it personally, Aunt Glenna. I haven't taken advice from anyone else since."

"The entire family is well aware of that."

"I appreciate your taking some time to see me today. I won't keep you long, I promise." Jessie trailed after her aunt into the inner office and flopped down in a chair next to a table that held a massive box of tissues. She stuck her jeaned legs out in front of her and shoved her hands into her front pockets. Something about Glenna's depressing office triggered all her irreverent impulses.

"Don't worry about the time, Jessie."

"Thanks." Jessie glanced at the tissues sitting on the table next to her. "I guess your patients must go through a lot of these."

"Therapy can bring a lot of deep emotions to the surface," Glenna pointed out.

"Yeah, I'll bet. Mrs. Valentine keeps a big box on hand too. Amazing how clients in both of our lines of work tend to cry a lot." But at least Mrs. V's clients rarely left the office crying, Jessie thought silently.

"Speaking of your new line of work, how are things going at Valentine Consultations?" Glenna sat down behind the desk and folded her hands in front of her as if preparing to discuss a particularly troublesome form of neurosis.

"Terrific. I know how someone in your profession must feel about Mrs. Valentine, but I assure you, we're not stealing any business."

"I'm not worried about it. People who are going to a psychic are obviously not yet ready to deal with their real problems. I can wait."

"Because sooner or later they'll wind up in your office?"

Glenna nodded. "If they're serious about resolving their inner conflicts, yes. How did the date go last night?"

Jessie made a face. "Not you too, Aunt Glenna."

"That bad, is it? I suppose Lilian and Constance have already grilled you?"

"I'm afraid so. I'm trying to let everyone down easy."

Glenna studied her intently. "Then you're really not interested in Hatch?"

"Oh, sure, I'm *interested*. But I could never marry the man, Aunt Glenna. He's too much like Dad. Beating one's head against a stone wall is damn hard work. It's taken me years just to put a few dents in Dad. I'm not about to start all over again with another workaholic."

"Is that how you see Sam Hatchard?" Glenna asked seriously. "As a man who is too much like your father?"

"When it comes to his attitude toward work, yes. But that's not what I wanted to talk to you about."

"What did you want to talk about?"

"I need to know something about the psychology of cults."

63

"Cults? Religious cults?"

"Any kind of cult, I guess." Jessie recalled Susan Attwood's long, rambling letter to her mother. It had contained very little hard information, just a lot of grand promises to save the world. "The particular cult I'm interested in appears to be telling its followers that there's an environmental catastrophe on the way and the members are the only ones who have a shot at finding the secret to survival."

"The principle behind most cults is a belief that only the chosen few will be saved," Glenna mused. "The members see themselves as the only ones who are on the one true path. Everyone else will be damned. Jessie, for heaven's sake, tell me you haven't gone off the deep end this time. You're not seriously interested in joining a cult, are you?"

Jessie grinned. "Gone off the deep end? Is that technical jargon?"

Glenna sighed ruefully. "Hardly,"

"Don't fret. I'm not about to join a cult. We all know I don't take orders well."

"That's true enough. And the people who tend to join cults are people who like clear-cut rules to follow. Rules make them feel safe. They are not required to think for themselves or to make decisions. You would be surprised at how many people will cheerfully give up those rights in exchange for rules. So what is this all about?"

"Actually, I see this as a major career move for me." Jessie hunched forward in her chair and began to tell her aunt about the new case.

Ten minutes later Glenna Ringstead leaned back, looking resigned. "I suppose it won't do any good to advise you to drop this so-called 'case'?"

"I can't, Aunt Glenna. This is my big chance."

"That's what you said a year ago when you joined Exotic Catering," Glenna reminded her.

Jessie flushed. "How was I to know it was really an escort

service? I thought I was actually going to learn how to run a gourmet catering operation. It could have been the opportunity of a lifetime."

"Oh, Jessie." Glenna shook her head.

"Look, Aunt Glenna, I'm really serious about this job. I like working with Mrs. Valentine. She feels I might have genuine talent or at least a healthy dose of intuition, which she says works just as well. I'd like to prove myself useful to the firm by helping her develop a larger clientele and expand her operations."

"Jessie, this is ridiculous. You can't go on hopping from one job to another for the rest of your life. Furthermore, your choice of careers is getting more and more bizarre."

"I've found my niche this time, Aunt Glenna. I'm sure of it."

"You're much too smart to believe in this psychic nonsense."

"I think Mrs. V really does have some psychic ability."

"Jessie, really."

"Maybe it's just intuition combined with a lot of common sense. Who knows? Whatever it is, she does have a certain talent, I'm sure of it. Aunt Glenna, I love this job. I want to make a go of it. What do you say? Will you give me a few pointers on the cult mentality?"

"I can't believe I'm letting you drag me into this. This is definitely outside my field of expertise, you know."

"Hey. You're the only shrink in the family. I'll take what I can get. Oh, before I forget, how's David doing? Has he heard from any of the grad schools he applied to yet?"

Glenna picked up a gold fountain pen and examined it closely. "He's been accepted into the Department of Philosophy at Parkington College. He got the word yesterday."

"He made it into Parkington? His first choice? Aunt Glenna, that's *terrific.*"

"It's certainly what he seems to think he wants more than anything else in the world, isn't it?"

Jessie nodded with great certainty. "It's the right thing for him, Aunt Glenna. I can feel it in my bones. David was made for the academic world."

"I hope you're right." Glenna carefully put the pen down on her desk, aligning it neatly with her clipboard. "I had rather thought for a while that he would eventually join Benedict Fasteners."

"That was never a viable option for David, and you must know that as well as I do."

"Vincent did try to encourage him."

"We all know Dad was desperate for a son, and for a while he thought he could ram David into the mold. But I saw right off it would never work and I told him to stop trying to force the issue. It was hopeless."

"David was certainly very grateful to you for getting him off the hook with his uncle. He's always been somewhat in awe of Vincent. I think he might have tried to make the situation at Benedict work out if you hadn't stepped in."

"Hey, rescuing him from Dad's clutches was the least I could do."

"Yes, you're definitely the little Miss Fix-It of the Benedict clan, aren't you? Everyone in the family turns to you when someone is needed to intercede with Vincent."

Jessie's smile faded. She eyed her aunt thoughtfully. "You know as well as I do that David would have hated the corporate world. He would have been especially unhappy working for my father. David has spent enough of his life trying to please Dad and he feels he's never succeeded. He deserves a chance to pursue his own goals."

"Only time will tell if you're right, won't it?"

Jessie's intercom rang at seven-thirty the following evening. She paused on the verge of tossing an entire pound of cheese ravioli into a pot of boiling water. With a groan she wiped her hands on a dish towel and went to answer the summons.

"It's me," Hatch announced over the speaker. He sounded bone-tired.

Jessie froze in front of the speaker. "What do you want?"

"Let me in and I'll tell you."

She frowned. "Have you been drinking, Hatch?"

"No. Working."

"Figures. What are you doing here?"

"I just left Benedict for the day. Haven't had dinner yet. What about you?"

"I was just about to eat."

"Good," said Hatch. "I'll join you."

Jessie could not think of a reasonable excuse not to open the downstairs door. Then again, she chided herself, maybe she was just not trying hard enough. Something in Hatch's weary voice was sparking a decidedly dangerous flare of womanly sympathy. She tried to squelch the sensation. The last thing she could afford to risk was to go all nurturing and empathic toward a shark like Hatch.

She punched the lock release, wondering if she was doing the right thing.

Three minutes later Jessie heard footsteps out in the hall. The apartment doorbell chimed. She answered it with a sense of reluctant anticipation.

Outside in the corridor she found Hatch leaning negligently against the wall, expensive suit jacket slung over one shoulder. He looked exhausted. His dark hair was tousled as if he had been running his fingers through it and his subdued gray-and-maroon-striped tie had been loosened with a careless hand. His eyes gleamed as he looked down at her.

"Seriously, Hatch," Jessie said, holding the door open cautiously, "what do you want?"

"Seriously, Jessie," he retorted, not moving away from the wall, "what I want is to find out what it would take to get you to send me flowers."

She blinked and groped swiftly for a way to hide her startled confusion. "Well, for starters, you could make yourself useful to Valentine Consultations."

"Yeah? How?"

"Tell me how to go about investigating a cult. I've been reading like crazy for the past day and a half, but I'm getting nowhere fast."

"Hell. Are you still on that stupid Attwood case? I was afraid of that."

"If that's the best you can do, good night." She started to close the door in his face.

"Follow the money," Hatch said wearily.

"What?"

"Follow the money trail. It takes money to finance something like a cult, just like any other business. Find out how the cash comes into the organization and where it goes. Once you know that, you'll know everything."

Jessie stared at him, astounded. "Hatch, that's *brilliant.* Absolutely brilliant. Why didn't I think of that? Come on in, pour yourself a drink, sit down, and make yourself at home. We have got to have a meaningful discussion."

Ignoring the flare of surprise in Hatch's eyes, she grabbed hold of the end of his boring tie and hauled him forcibly into the apartment.

Hatch did not put up much resistance.

CHAPTER FOUR

A hissing noise from the kitchen made Jessie release her grip on Hatch's tie. "Oh, my God, the boiling water." She whirled and rushed back into the kitchen.

Hatch followed more slowly.

"There's a bottle of wine on the counter," Jessie said over her shoulder as she picked up the package of ravioli. "Go ahead and open it. And then start talking."

"About what?" Hatch tossed his jacket down and picked up the wine.

"About following the money, of course."

"Were you planning to eat that entire package of ravioli all by yourself?" He went to work on the cork, his hands working in a smooth and controlled fashion.

"Yeah, but now that you're here, I'm feeling generous. I'll let you have some." She dumped the cheese ravioli into the boiling water. "I've got some sourdough bread and enough salad to fill in the gaps. Now, what about following the money?"

"If you're not a little more subtle, I'll get the impression you only invited me to stay for dinner because you're planning to use me." The cork came out of the bottle with a small, polite pop. "Where do you keep the glasses?"

"To the right of the sink." Jessie concentrated on gently stirring the boiling ravioli. The kitchen was suddenly feeling very warm. Hatch seemed to be taking up all the available space. Predictably, she could feel a wave of klutziness coming on. She reminded herself to be careful. "And you're right. I am using you. Start talking."

"Always nice to feel wanted. Mind if I sit down first?" Hatch took one of the counter stools without waiting for permission. "Damn, I'm really beat tonight. Hell of a day." He loosened his tie a little more and took a swallow of his wine.

Jessie risked a sidelong glance and realized he was telling the truth. Hatch had definitely had a long, hard day. She firmly suppressed the little flicker of guilt that immediately assailed her. "Your own fault, Hatch. You shouldn't spend so much time at the office. You're as bad as my—"

He cut her off with an upraised palm. "Don't say it. I'm not in the mood for another comparison between me and your father. You know, this is the first time I've had a chance to see your domestic side."

"Don't blink or you'll miss it."

"I'll keep that in mind. Still, there's something appealing about seeing you standing there at the stove."

"Is that the way you like your women? Chained to the kitchen?"

"I think I'll avoid that question. Aren't you going to ask me about my hard day at the office?"

She shot him a suspicious glance, uncertain, as usual, whether or not he was trying to joke with her. He looked perfectly serious sitting there, leaning against the counter. She decided to humor him. "Did you have a hard day at the office, Hatch?"

"Yeah."

"Must have been a real pain having to stop by here and put in some additional overtime working on the big courtship, hmmm?"

"You're determined to make this as difficult as possible, aren't you?"

"I'm trying to stop it before it gets going," Jessie said bluntly. "There's no future in it." She picked up her own glass of wine and took a sip. "For either of us. We'd frustrate, irritate, and generally annoy each other to death."

"You're wrong, Jessie. I think we have got a future. And I think we can learn to coexist, provided you make some effort. Be careful with that glass. It's going to fall off the counter if you don't watch out. I don't have the energy to go over there and rescue it."

She glanced down to see that she had set the wineglass right on the edge of the white tile. Cautiously she moved it to safety. "Whew. Another disaster narrowly averted. Let's hope I don't accidentally set fire to the apartment or something equally dramatic while you're here."

"I told your father that the fact that I make you nervous is a good sign."

"Is that right? I consider it a sure indicator that we weren't meant for each other." She picked up the pot of boiling ravioli and started to dump it into a colander that was sitting in the sink. Steam gushed upward toward the ceiling. Jessie yelped as she suddenly realized just how warm the handles of the pot had gotten. *"Damn."*

"Here. Let me take that." Hatch was there beside her, moving with surprising speed for a man who claimed to be exhausted. He deftly removed the pot from her fingers. "Why didn't you use hot pads?" He set the empty pan on the stove.

"I was in a hurry." Jessie held her fingers under a stream of cold water. "I got a little careless, that's all." *Because you have a way of turning me into a nervous wreck,* she fumed silently.

"You sound as if you're blaming me. It's not my fault you forgot the pads. You ought to stop and think before you pick up a hot pan, Jessie."

She lifted her eyes heavenward. "Lord help us, he's an authority on kitchen management too. Is there no end to this man's talents? Tell me about following the money, Hatch."

"After dinner. I'm tired and I want some food before you start grilling me."

"You're just stalling," she accused as she turned off the tap and started ladling out the small salad she had made earlier.

"Right, I'm stalling." Hatch sat down at the counter again and picked up his wine. "What's that stuff?"

"Pesto sauce. I made it myself."

"I'm in luck. You can cook."

"Look, Hatch . . ."

"After dinner, okay?" He smiled his faint, unreadable smile. "I give you my word I'll tell you what I can after I've had a chance to relax."

She frowned. "Promise?"

"Word of honor."

Jessie decided she would have to be satisfied with that much. She went to the cupboard to pull down two octagonal black china plates. "All right," she continued, determined to be conciliatory now that she was going to get what she wanted. "Just how bad was your day at the office?"

Hatch narrowed his gaze in surprise. "Bad enough. We've got trouble on a construction project down in Portland. Your father and I spent the afternoon getting briefed by the engineers and the on-site manager. On top of that, your father has decided that we have to bid on a job in Spokane simply because a company called Yorland and Young is also bidding on it. I've told him the job is too small for us and not worth the effort of undercutting Y and Y's bid."

"Dad sees Yorland and Young as a competitor."

"Yeah, well, it's not. Not any longer, at any rate. We're starting to play in a different ballpark. Vincent shouldn't be fooling around with a small contract bid like that one anyway. Your father's problem is that he gets too involved in the details and doesn't pay enough attention to the big picture. That's the main reason Benedict Fasteners is still small."

"I know." Jessie shrugged. "Dad built that company from the ground up. He can't stand letting go of all the details."

"He's going to have to get used to the idea. No point hiring other people to handle things if you don't let them do their jobs." Hatch rubbed the back of his neck as he surveyed the plate being set in front of him.

Jessie sat down across from him and forked up a large ravioli. "Dad's old-fashioned when it comes to management techniques. Just like he is about wanting to keep the firm in the family."

"You don't think the company should stay in the family?"

"I don't mind the idea. I just wish he wasn't leaving it to me. I wish he'd give equal chunks of it to my cousin, David, Elizabeth, and me when he retires. But Dad won't even listen to that idea."

Hatch narrowed his eyes. "You've tried to get him to divide up Benedict Fasteners among the three of you?"

"Oh, sure. Lots of times. A lost cause. He thinks it would lead to the ultimate destruction of the company."

"He could be right," Hatch said slowly. "None of you three has the foggiest idea of how to handle the firm, which means that, inevitably, you'd have to hire someone from outside, someone who would then get his fingers into the pie. And that could spell the beginning of the end."

"I agree that none of the three of us knows how to run Benedict," Jessie snapped. "So why leave it to me?"

"Because you'll do what's best for the company and the family, won't you?" Hatch murmured. "And you won't have to hire an outsider. You'll have me to run it for you."

"You don't want to just *run* it, though, do you, Hatch? You want to own a chunk of it."

"You're right. But in turn, I'm willing to let you adopt me into the clan."

"Adopt you?" Jessie put down her fork with a clatter. *"Adopt you?"*

"Figure of speech." Hatch took another sip of wine. His long, elegant fingers slid along the tapering stem of the glass as he set it back down on the counter. "You don't have to be afraid of what will happen once your father allows me to buy into Benedict, Jessie. I'll take care of you and the company. You have my word on it."

Jessie stared at him, unable to tear her glance away from the intensity in his topaz eyes. She could almost feel his hand gliding down the length of her spine. She shivered and wondered if Mrs. Valentine was right about her having some faint smidgen of untrained psychic awareness. The very air around her seemed to be vibrating with an almost palpable aura.

The downstairs door buzzer broke the spell. Jessie jumped and her elbow struck the fork she had just put down. The implement bounced off the counter and clattered onto the floor.

"Now see what you did?" Jessie glowered at Hatch as she leapt off the stool and went to answer the summons.

Hatch ignored the fallen fork.

"Who is it?" Jessie asked into the speaker.

"Jessie, it's me. David. Got some good news."

Jessie smiled. "I think I already know what it is. But come on up and tell me anyway." She pushed the button to let him into the building and turned her head to speak to Hatch over her shoulder. "It's my cousin, David. Aunt Glenna told me he's been accepted into graduate school. Parkington College, no less."

Hatch's brows rose. "Ah, yes. David, the philosopher-wimp."

Jessie rounded on Hatch furiously. "Don't you dare call

David a wimp. That's what Dad calls him and I will not tolerate it from either of you."

"Take it easy, Jessie. I only meant—"

"It makes me sick the way you wheeling-and-dealing corporate types look down so condescendingly on the academic world. As if your way of making a living was somehow superior and more manly than teaching and studying. I swear, Hatch, if you say one insulting word to David under my roof, I'll kick you right out the door, in spite of what you may or may not know about investigating cult finances. Do you hear me?"

"I hear you. The neighbors probably do too. For the record, I don't have anything against the academic world. When I called David a wimp I was referring to his habit of asking you to go to your father for financial assistance. I'll bet graduate school is going to cost a bundle. Naturally he's come straight to you. That's what everyone else in the family does, isn't it?"

Jessie glared at him, her cheeks burning because he was hitting close to home. "I'll have you know David hasn't asked me to go to Dad for more money." Mentally she crossed her fingers and prayed that was not the reason David had decided to visit her.

"He will." Hatch forked up another ravioli just as the doorbell chimed.

Jessie swung around on her heel and marched to the door. She threw it open to reveal her cousin, an intense young man of twenty-two.

Even if one did not know about David's aspirations to pursue an academic career, one could have guessed his future from his attire. He favored jeans, slouchy tweed jackets, and black shirts. He wore round tortoiseshell frames that enhanced his look of earnest, insightful intelligence, and his unkempt blond hair gave him an air of ivory-tower innocence. Glenna had always stressed to everyone else in the family that David was a very sensitive individual.

"Come on in, David. You know Hatch, don't you?"

"We've met." David nodded tentatively at Hatch, who inclined his head coolly in return.

Neither man made an effort to shake hands. Hatch did not even get off the stool. He went back to eating ravioli, looking faintly bored.

"Glass of wine, David?" Jessie offered quickly. "To celebrate?"

"Thanks." David accepted the glass and glanced around rather diffidently for a place to sit. "Sorry to bother you, Jessie. Didn't know you had company."

"That's all right. Hatch wasn't invited either." Jessie smiled serenely, her eyes sliding away from Hatch's mock ing gaze. "We were just talking business, weren't we, Hatch?"

"In a way," Hatch agreed.

"We were definitely discussing business," Jessie said tartly. "What else would you and I have been talking about?"

"I can think of a wide variety of subjects. But they'll keep."

David glanced quickly from Hatch's face to Jessie's. "Well, this is certainly interesting. I take it the Big Plan is on track?" He sat down on the stool next to Jessie's.

"What's the Big Plan?" Jessie asked as she resumed her seat.

David raised one shoulder in an eloquent manner. "You and Hatch get married and Benedict Fasteners grows into a Giant in the Industry and the whole clan lives happily ever after. Come on, Jessie. Everyone knows the Big Plan. It's all your mother, my mother, and Elizabeth's mother talk about these days. So how's it going? Is romance in bloom?"

"To be perfectly honest, we were at each other's throats before you walked in the door, weren't we, Hatch?" Jessie tore off a slice of sourdough bread.

Hatch's gaze rested briefly on her throat. "Not quite, but

it's a tantalizing thought." He turned toward David. "I hear you're going on to graduate school in philosophy."

David nodded, looking distinctly wary. "Parkington has one of the most respected philosophy departments in the nation. It was one of the first to offer a doctorate in the philosophy of science and technology in Western civilization."

"That's your field of interest?

"Yes, as a matter of fact it is." There was a defiant note in David's tone now. "Modern science and technology is in the process of changing our world in fundamental ways. It could easily be destroying us. Just look at the depletion of the ozone layer and the effects of acid rain. Most of our thinking on the subject is straight out of the late eighteenth and early nineteenth centuries, the age of the machine. That kind of outmoded thinking has to change because we desperately need new perspectives on man and nature. That's the task of philosophy."

"And you think you can change our outmoded thinking?" Hatch asked.

"Well, maybe not yours," David admitted sarcastically. "But I have hopes for other people, like Jessie."

Sensing disaster, Jessie rushed in to divert the conversation. "David, I was absolutely thrilled when Aunt Glenna told me you'd been accepted at Parkington. I'm so pleased for you."

"Parkington's one of those fancy private colleges back East someplace, isn't it?" Hatch picked up a chunk of bread, took a bite that showed his strong white teeth, and leaned his elbows on the counter as he chewed. "Expensive."

"Well, yes, as a matter of fact." David shot an uncertain glance at Jessie, as if asking for guidance.

"David," she said firmly, "tell me something. Do you know anything about a group that calls itself DEL? It stands for Dawn's Early Light. Some sort of environmental extremist group, I think. They supposedly recruited some students from Butterfield College. Did you ever see any of them on campus?"

"DEL?" David looked thoughtful, an expression he did very well. "Yeah, I think I did hear something about it a few months ago. Led by a so-called climatologist, I think. I didn't pay too much attention. They held a couple of small group lectures and talked to some people, but they didn't hang around long. We get that kind of thing all the time around a college campus. Why?"

"I'm looking for a student at Butterfield who apparently joined DEL. Her name is Susan Attwood. Know her?"

"No. What year?"

"Sophomore, I believe."

David shook his head again. "Haven't run into her."

Jessie sighed. "I suppose it was too much to hope that you might have known her."

"There are a few thousand students at Butterfield," David pointed out. "Why are you looking for this Susan Attwood?"

"Jessie's pursuing a new career option," Hatch said. "Psychic cult-buster."

"What?" David wrinkled his intelligent brow. "Is this some sort of joke?"

"Got it first try," Hatch told him. "It's a joke. Unfortunately, Jessie's taking it seriously. No sense of humor, our Jessie."

Jessie shot Hatch an annoyed glance. "Ignore him, David. This is a serious matter. I'm trying to research DEL for a client of Mrs. Valentine's whose daughter ran off and joined the cult."

"What are you supposed to do? Get her back?"

"If possible. The client believes this Edwin Bright person has hypnotized her daughter and others somehow. She assumes he's claiming some psychic ability to forecast disaster. She wants Valentine Consultations to prove the guy is a phony."

"Sounds a little out of your line, Jessie," David remarked, helping himself to a chunk of the sourdough.

"Very observant of you," Hatch said approvingly. He was apparently surprised by such a show of intelligence. "It's way out of her line."

"Stop it, both of you," Jessie ordered. She leaned forward and folded her arms on the counter. "David, could you do me a favor and see what you can find out about DEL's activities on campus? What I'd really like is an address. There's nothing in the local-area phone books and I couldn't find anything at all in the newspaper indexes. Your mother gave me some books to read on cults in general, but I need specific information on this one."

"Well, I suppose I could ask around and see if anyone knows someone who talked to the DEL people when they were on campus. But I'm not so sure this is a good idea, Jessie."

"It's not," Hatch agreed.

"Sounds more like a job for a real private investigator," David said.

"It is," Hatch said.

"Pay no attention to him, David," Jessie instructed. "He and Dad are being extremely tiresome and depressingly downbeat about my new career. Only to be expected, I suppose. The corporate mentality, you know."

"Uh-huh. I know. Very narrow thinkers."

"How true." Jessie stifled a smile and ignored the impatient glance Hatch gave her. "Will you give me a hand, David?"

David smiled. "Sure. I'll see what I can do. But don't count on much, all right? Most of the people I know don't get involved with cults and related crap."

"Anything at all would be useful."

"All right." David glanced at his watch. "I'd better be on my way. I only stopped by to give you the good news, but since you already know it, I might as well leave you two alone." He got to his feet and flashed a quick glance at Hatch, who was finishing the last of his ravioli. "Uh, Jessie?"

"Yes?"

"Would you mind walking downstairs with me? I wanted to talk to you in private for a minute if that's okay."

"Sure." Jessie got down off the stool.

Hatch gave David a hard look. "Why don't you ask him yourself, instead of using Jessie as an intermediary?"

David flushed. "I don't understand." His glance flickered to Jessie.

"Ignore him, David. It's all one can do. I'll go downstairs with you." She hurried toward the door, chatting excitedly about Parkington in an effort to cover the awkward moment.

David was silent as they started down the stairs. "He's right, you know," he finally said on a long, drawn-out sigh.

"Who?"

"Hatchard. I did want to ask if you'd feel out the old man for me on the subject of a loan. Think he'll spring for another one? He's already made it pretty damn clear what he thinks about my going for a doctorate. Hell, he gave me a bad-enough time when he found out I'd changed my undergraduate major from business administration to philosophy."

Jessie nodded sympathetically. "I know. I'll talk to him, David. I can't promise anything."

"I realize that. But he listens to you more than he does to anyone else in the family. You're the only one who seems to be able to beard the lion in his den with any real success."

"Probably because I just keep pounding on him until his resistance is finally worn down. It's very wearing, you know. On me, I mean. I get so tired of it."

"Why bother to do it?" David asked reasonably.

"In the beginning, when I was much younger, I think I started doing it just to get some attention for myself. Later, in my teenage years, I was naive enough to think I could actually change him, make him *want* to pay more attention to his family."

"Mom says that kind of change is virtually impossible."

"She may be right. All I know is that after Elizabeth came along I got very angry at Dad. It infuriated me to see him ignoring her the same way he had always tried to ignore you and me. So I became even more aggressive about getting him to play the part of a father."

"You've had some success in terms of Elizabeth. You know, Uncle Vincent's a lot more aware of what's going on in her life than he ever was with either one of us."

"Only because I've learned a few tricks. I've formed a conspiracy with Grace, his secretary. She helps me get things onto his calendar. I nag him. I plead with him. I yell at him. And at best I've got maybe a fifty-fifty success rate. He still calls half the time at the last minute to tell me he can't make a school function because he's got a crisis at the office."

"I'll bet." David shoved his hands into his jacket pockets. "But at least he's always been around, hasn't he? He didn't just disappear the way my old man did."

"Oh, David, I know. I'm sorry for whining like this."

As always when the subject of David's father came up, Jessie was consumed with sympathy and guilt. Her cousin was right. At least Vincent Benedict had stuck around to be nagged and harangued by his elder daughter. Lloyd Ringstead had vanished, never to be seen or heard from again. David had been only four.

"Forget it. Nothing more boring than old family history."

"I suppose," Jessie agreed. "But I'll say this much for Dad. He does have some sense of what you might call patriarchal obligation. At least when it comes to money."

"Only because it's a means of controlling the rest of us," David said bitterly. "He likes being in control."

"I know that's part of it. Still, look on the bright side. I

81

think he'll probably come through with another loan for you." Jessie smiled and stood on tiptoe to give David a quick hug. "Don't worry. I'll talk to him."

"Hatchard is right. I guess I shouldn't ask you to do it. You already did enough when you convinced Uncle Vincent I was never going to be the heir apparent to Benedict Fasteners." David gave her a rueful smile. "You know, without your help I'd probably still be there busting my ass trying to please the old man. Even Mom wanted me to try harder."

"You'd have been very unhappy spending the rest of your life running Benedict Fasteners. Anybody can see that."

"Not anybody. You were the one who realized it first. Thank God for Sam Hatchard. Without him Uncle Vincent would probably be trying to mold you or Elizabeth into a corporate shark."

"I'm not sure God is the one who deserves the credit for giving us Sam Hatchard."

David grinned as he opened the lobby door. "You may be right. He's not what you'd call real angelic, is he? Don't worry, Jessie, you can handle him. My money's definitely riding on you."

"Dammit, David, this isn't some kind of sporting event," Jessie called out after him as he went through the doorway and out into the night.

But it was too late. Her cousin was already halfway down the path to the sidewalk. He lifted a hand in farewell but did not look back.

Jessie stood on the other side of the heavy glass door and stared bleakly out into the darkness for a few minutes. Then she turned and walked slowly back upstairs. She wondered how difficult it was going to be to wheedle the information she wanted out of Hatch and then get him out of her apartment. Something told her it was not going to be an easy task.

She was right. She knew she was in trouble the minute she

opened the door and saw him sprawled on the couch, sound asleep. He had not even bothered to take off his beautifully polished wing tips.

Jessie slowly closed the door and leaned back against it. If she had any sense, she told herself, she would wake him up and hustle him out the door.

She definitely should not allow him to spend the night there on the couch. It would set a dreadfully bad precedent. A man like Hatch would use that sort of precedent to his own advantage, no doubt about it. One thing always led to another. Come tomorrow morning, she would have to give him breakfast.

Too dangerous by far. When all was said and done, there would be no way of getting around the fact that he had made himself very much at home in her apartment.

Jessie moved cautiously away from the door, considering the best method of awakening him. She came to a halt beside the couch and stood looking down at Hatch for a long while. The strength and willpower that were so much a part of him did not appear the least bit diminished by sleep. By rights he should have looked a little vulnerable, but he did not.

Jessie wondered if sharks actually slept.

There was no denying the fact that Hatch did appear exhausted. The man worked much too hard. Fourteen-hour days plus courtship time on the side.

She studied the strong, tapering fingers of one supple masculine hand as it lay on the black leather cushion. Everything that compelled her and repelled her about Hatch was embodied in his graceful, dangerous, powerful hands.

With a small sigh, Jessie turned away and went to the closet to get a blanket. She was going to regret letting him stay. She just knew it. But she could not bring herself to awaken him from his exhausted slumber.

She pried off the heavy wing tips and spread the blanket over Hatch's sleeping frame.

When she had finished, she went into the kitchen and put

the dishes into the sink. Then she placed the empty wine bottle in the recycling bin Elizabeth had given her and headed for the bedroom.

Several hours later Jessie came awake on a rush of adrenaline. She sat bolt upright in bed, confused by two powerful stimuli. The phone on the bedside table was warbling loudly and there was a half-naked man standing in the open doorway of her bedroom. She did not know which had awakened her.

For a handful of seconds she could not move. She could only sit there clutching the sheet.

The phone rang again.

"Better get that," Hatch advised, one hand braced against the door frame.

Jessie blinked and reached out for the phone.

"Jessie? It's Alex. Alex Robin. I'm calling from your office. Sorry to wake you, but you might want to come on over here. I went out to get something to eat a while ago and when I got back I came upstairs to use the rest room. I found the door to Valentine Consultations open. Did you leave it unlocked?"

"No." Jessie pushed hair out of her eyes and tried to think. "No, I'm certain I locked up when I left, Alex. I'm always very careful about that."

"I know. Listen, I think someone's been inside here, but I can't be certain. Maybe you'd better check to see if anything's missing. You may want to call the cops and report a break-in. If that's what's happened." Alex paused. "Nothing's broken or anything, as far as I can tell."

"I'll be right over, Alex. Thanks."

Jessie slowly replaced the phone, her eyes on Hatch's shadowed face. She realized he was wearing only a pair of briefs. Sometime during the night he had awakened and undressed. Talk about making himself at home, she thought. Give the man an inch and he took a mile.

"I have to go over to the office. Alex, the downstairs

tenant, thinks someone might have broken in to Valentine Consultations." Jessie pushed back the covers, belatedly realizing her nightgown was hiked up around her waist. Hastily she retreated back under the sheet. "Do you mind?" she asked acidly.

"No." Hatch yawned and ran his fingers through his tousled hair. "I'll go with you. I had no idea the life of an assistant fortune-teller was so exciting. You keep worse hours than I do, Jessie."

CHAPTER FIVE

It's damn near three o'clock in the morning," Hatch muttered as he slipped the Mercedes into a space in front of the building that housed Valentine Consultations.

He was not pleased about having his first night in Jessie's apartment interrupted in this fashion. Granted, he had not been in her bed, but when he had awakened earlier and discovered he had been allowed to stay, he had known progress was finally being made. "What the hell was this Alex guy doing at the office at this hour?"

"He's a computer jockey," Jessie explained as she yanked the door handle. "He works weird hours." She jumped out of the car and dashed toward the darkened entrance of the building, fishing for her keys.

"Hold it, Jessie." Hatch got out and slammed his own car door before following her up the walk. The lady was far too impulsive. He would have to work on curbing that tendency. "Not so fast."

"Oh, for heaven's sake, Hatch. I let you come along because you insisted, but don't get the idea you're in charge around here. Save the dynamic-leadership act for Benedict Fasteners." She started to shove the key into the lock and belatedly realized the door was already open.

Before she could turn the handle, Hatch shot out a hand and clamped it over hers. The small bones of her fingers and wrist felt astonishingly delicate. "I said, not so fast," he repeated very quietly.

She glanced down at where his hand covered hers. He knew she was silently debating whether or not to test his strength. Her eyes lifted briefly to meet his, and he saw the annoyance in them. She had obviously realized she did not stand a chance of shaking off his grip.

"For Pete's sake, Hatch. The door is already unlocked. Alex must have left it that way for us."

"Fine. I'll go in first." Without waiting for a response, Hatch calmly shouldered Jessie aside and shoved open the door. He stepped over the threshold into the darkened hall and stopped, groping along the wall. He found the switch and flicked it. Nothing happened.

"What is it? What's wrong?" Jessie was trying her best to peer around him.

"The hall light is out." *A bad sign.* His instinct warned him the smartest thing to do at this point was back out of the place.

"It's been out for ages." Jessie tried impatiently to shove past Hatch's unyielding form. He did not move.

"Alex," she called over Hatch's shoulder. "Alex, are you in there? Is everything all right?"

A low groan from off to the right inside the hall was the only answer.

"Alex." Jessie panicked now, shoving furiously at Hatch. "Get out of my way, Hatch. He's hurt."

"Damn." Hatch moved slowly into the darkened interior as his eyes adjusted to the deep gloom. "I should have gone back for the flashlight."

"There's a light switch just inside his office door. I'll get it."

Quick as a cat, she darted around him the instant he ceased blocking the doorway. "Jessie, come back here."

But she was already racing for the door of the office, which was just barely visible in the shadows. A flash of anger and alarm galvanized Hatch. Jessie was not just impulsive, she clearly lacked even an iota of common sense.

He moved forward to jerk her back, but he did not have to bother halting her mad dash for the dark office. Before he could grab her, she gasped, yelped, and promptly tripped over a man's prone form lying in the middle of the hall.

"Alex."

The man on the floor groaned again and struggled to sit up. "Jessie? Is that you?"

Hatch watched as Jessie crouched beside Alex. Then he frowned as he tried to discern the outlines of whatever was housed in the darkness of the office beyond the doorway. There was no sound from within the room, but the hair on the back of his neck was stirring.

"Dear heaven." Jessie was fussing over the figure on the floor. "What on earth happened? Alex, you mustn't move until we see how badly you're injured."

"I'm okay, I think. Just got banged on the head. Didn't completely lose consciousness. Hurts like hell, though. Who did you bring with you?"

"The name's Hatchard." The sense of uneasiness grew. Restlessly Hatch stepped around Alex's feet and moved into the doorway of the office.

"The light switch is on the right," Jessie said.

The rush of thudding footsteps, however, came from the left. A body hurtled forward toward the door. Hatch had a fleeting impression of a slight, wiry form covered from head to toe in black. Something metallic glinted in the upraised fist.

"Shit." It had been years since Hatch had last confronted a man who was wielding a knife. He still remembered the occasion with great clarity. The memorable event had taken place, as such events often do, in the alley behind a tavern that catered to truckers and cowboys.

He'd thought those days of barroom brawls and dirty alley fights were behind him. Hell, he was supposed to be white-collar now, he reminded himself. He had the silk ties and handmade shirts to prove it.

After all the years that had passed since his last brawl, Hatch was vaguely surprised to find that his reactions were automatic. He feinted to the side and lashed out with his foot, catching his assailant on the leg as he went past. The blow was off-center but it was powerful enough to destroy the man's balance.

The knife glinted evilly as the attacker whipped around, struggling to regain his feet.

"Outta my way, you fucking bastard." The voice was high-pitched and raw with desperation. It was also muffled by the black cloth of a stocking mask. "Get outta my way. *I'll cut your fucking throat for you.*"

"Oh, my God, *Hatch.*" Jessie's horrified shriek filled the darkness.

Hatch followed up on the small advantage he had created by getting his attacker off-balance. He snapped out another kick and slashed at the knife arm with the edge of his hand. The blade fell from numbed gloved fingers and clattered to the floor.

There was a sharp, shrill gasp and another vicious curse. Then the assailant turned and fled through the hall, nearly colliding with Jessie. The running man leapt over Alex's prone form and vanished out the door into the night.

"Hatch, are you all right?"

"I'm okay, Jessie." A primitive surge of anger flared in Hatch as he realized his quarry was escaping. He ran out into the hall and got as far as the outer door before he realized it was hopeless.

Frustrated, he stood on the front step of the building, restlessly searching the shadows of the dark street. There was no sign of anyone, no sound of running footsteps. Nothing.

The light in Alex's office snapped on behind Hatch. Reluctantly he turned to see that Jessie was on her feet, staring at him with eyes made huge by concern.

"Are you sure you're all right?"

"Yes."

"There's a knife in here."

"He didn't get a chance to use it. I'm okay, Jessie."

"You're sure?"

"Dammit, I'm *sure.*" Hatch heard the frustrated fury in his own voice. He made a grab for his self-control and his temper. It was not an easy task. It occurred to him that he was dealing not only with the adrenaline of the short-lived battle but also with a fierce anger that was focused one hundred percent on Jessie.

Apparently the little idiot did not yet realize that if it had not been for Alex lying there on the floor, she would have dashed straight into the office and wound up being the one confronting the bastard with the knife in his hand. Hatch longed to point that out to her in an extremely blunt fashion, but told himself that now was not the time.

"What about you, Alex?" he said to the injured man.

"I'm okay too. I think. Like I said, I didn't completely lose consciousness. I've just been dazed for the past few minutes."

"I assume you're the one who called Jessie?"

"Yeah. Sorry about that." Alex found a pair of horn-rimmed glasses beside his leg and put them on. They sat somewhat crookedly on his nose. Then he gingerly touched his head. "Didn't realize anyone was still around or I would have called the cops first. I wasn't even sure there had been a break-in. Nothing seemed disturbed upstairs. Thought maybe Jessie had just left the door unlocked." He gave Hatch a questioning look. "Guess we'd better call the police now, though, huh?"

"Yes," said Hatch. "I think that would be a very logical

next step. Although I doubt there's much they'll be able to do."

Jessie swung around, clearly startled. "What do you mean? There's been a break-in and an act of violence."

Hatch gave her a pitying glance. "Jessie, get real. It happens all the time in the big city."

She frowned. "Yes, well, it's never happened to me."

"You just got lucky. Where's the phone?"

"Over on the desk near Alex's computer." She tipped her head slightly to the side. "Hatch, are you angry?"

"What the hell gave you that idea?"

Three hours later Hatch opened Jessie's refrigerator door and rummaged around inside until he found the skim milk. He closed the door and started opening cupboards until he located a box of cereal. Then he started searching for bowls and spoons.

He was putting breakfast together on his own because Jessie, who had recently emerged from the shower wearing a pair of snug-fitting black leggings and a voluminous orange sweater that fell below her hips, was not much help at the moment. She was still chattering away excitedly about the break-in. It was obvious she was viewing the whole thing as a grand adventure.

Hatch realized he was still seething. Every time he thought about what had nearly happened earlier, his gut went cold. As furious as he was, he was also vividly aware of the fact that he would have liked nothing better in that moment than to haul Jessie over to the couch and make concentrated, determined love to her.

He had wanted Jessie for some time, but never so intensely as he wanted her right now. It was the aftermath of the fight, he told himself. Rampaging hormones or something.

But deep down he knew it was because some primitive part of him actually thought that if he claimed her physically he might be able to control her in other ways. Control her so that next time she would follow orders in a crisis. Control her so that he could keep her safe.

Follow orders? Jessie Benedict? Who was he kidding?

She was sitting at the counter, blithely unaware of his precarious mood. She pushed a thick curve of witchy black hair back behind one ear and her jeweled eyes gleamed with excitement. "I suppose the cops were right," she allowed. "The guy broke into the building and started going through the upstairs offices first. When he didn't find anything valuable, he went back downstairs and discovered Alex's computer equipment." Jessie drummed her fingers on the countertop. "But I don't like it."

"Nobody *liked* it, Jessie."

"I mean, something doesn't feel right about it. I think I'll go visit Mrs. Valentine today and see what she thinks. She might have some insights into this thing."

"Jessie," Hatch said wearily, "you're not going to try to tie this break-in to your DEL case, or something equally stupid, are you?"

"Why not? I don't care what the cops said. The whole thing is very suspicious. The guy did go through the offices of Valentine Consultations first."

"The cops also said guys like that tend to go through a place in a methodical fashion. Makes sense to start upstairs and work down. Use some logic here, instead of drama, Jessie. What could he have been searching for in Valentine Consultations? You haven't discovered anything incriminating about DEL yet, and you're not likely to do so. The DEL crowd probably knows that better than anybody."

"Maybe."

He considered the stubborn, mutinous set of her mouth out of the corner of his eye as he poured milk over the cereal. "You're trying to overdramatize your Big Case, Jessie. Forget it. Waste of time."

"Oh, yeah?"

"Yes." He sat down across from her and reached for the

coffeepot. "Eat your breakfast like a good girl and then you can send me off to the office with a wifely little kiss."

Jessie scowled ferociously. "Don't get any ideas just because I let you spend the night on my couch."

"I'll keep that in mind." Hatch dug into his cereal. He was actually getting a lot of ideas, but he figured he could wait to tell her about them.

Negotiating with Jessie was a tricky business, and he had no intention of giving away too much information in advance. He waited for her to lecture him further, but when she spoke again, she surprised him with her question.

"What did you do to that jerk in Alex's office, Hatch?"

"Took out my frustrations on him."

"I mean, seriously, what did you use on him? Karate or something?"

"Nothing that fancy. Just some old-fashioned alley-fighting techniques."

"Where did you learn them?"

"In an old-fashioned alley. Look, could we change the subject? I had what is frequently referred to as a misspent youth. I'd prefer to forget it."

"Whatever you say. Still, I'm glad it was you who went into that office instead of me."

"Which brings up an interesting point," Hatch said, deciding to seize the opportunity. "The only reason you didn't go charging into that office first was that you conveniently happened to stumble over Alex. I warned you not to rush blindly into that place."

"We all know I don't take orders well, Hatch. Want some more coffee?"

"Quit trying to change the subject. You're walking on thin ice, lady. I am not in a good mood this morning."

"Oh, my. Are you going to yell at me?" She fixed him with an expression of great interest, as if waiting for a show to begin.

"I've resisted this long, I think I can manage to hold back

what would seem to be a very natural urge under the circumstances. But I wouldn't advise you to push me."

"Veiled threats. How exciting. I've never seen you quite like this, Hatch. It's a whole new you. I'll bet you're only holding back because you don't want to lose any of the territory you think you gained last night by conveniently falling asleep on my couch."

"Is that right?"

"I know exactly how your mind works, Hatch. You've weighed the pros and cons of losing your temper with me and decided that it's in your own best interests not to yell at this rather delicate stage of the game."

"You think you know me very well, don't you?"

"Well enough to know how you think." She took a swallow of coffee and wrinkled her nose. "But I'll admit I didn't realize you'd make coffee like this. It tastes like pure, refried, undiluted grounds." She tried another tentative sip. "With perhaps just a hint of old tires thrown in for body."

"I grew up on a cattle ranch. Nobody drinks weak coffee on a ranch."

A wary spark of interest lit her eyes. "You grew up on a ranch? Where was it?"

"Oregon."

"Do your folks still live there?"

"No." He wished he had kept his mouth shut, but one look at her expression told him it was too late to close the subject. She was curious. A curious Jessie Benedict was a dangerous Jessie Benedict.

On the other hand, it was gratifying to have her exhibit some real interest in him.

"Where are your parents living now?"

Hatch sighed. "When I was five my mother decided she couldn't take ranch life any longer. Or maybe it was my old man she couldn't take. Whatever, she filed for divorce and left. Went back East and married some guy who worked for an insurance firm."

Jessie's brows came together in a swift frown. "What about you?"

Hatch shrugged. "I stayed on the ranch with Dad until I was sixteen and then I left."

"You went off to college early?"

"No. I just left home early. Dad and I were not what you'd call a real father-and-son team. We didn't get along." Hatch shoved aside the memories of the weak, whining, bitterly angry man who had raised him. "Not that I was a model son, you understand. I was in trouble from the time I was nine years old. At any rate, when I left home, I lied about my age and found work on a ranch in California. Dad died in a car accident two years later."

"Then what happened?" She was riveted now.

"I went back to Oregon, sold the ranch, and used the money to pay off the bank. The place was buried in debt. My father was not much of a businessman. Hell, he wasn't much of anything. After he died I told myself I was going to prove him wrong."

"About what?"

Hatch studied his thick, dark coffee. "He had a habit of telling me I was never going to amount to anything."

"Well, he was certainly wrong about that, wasn't he?" Jessie's eyes flickered briefly to the gold-and-steel watch on his left wrist.

Hatch smiled grimly. "I guess you could say that everything I am today I owe to my old man."

"What about your mother? Is she still alive?"

"Yes."

Jessie chewed thoughtfully on her lower lip. "Ever see her?"

"Not much." Hatch swallowed another bite of cereal. "I call her every Christmas."

"That's not very often, Hatch."

Her reproachful eyes refueled his irritation. "For God's sake, Jessie, let the subject drop, will you? It's none of your business, but the fact is, she's no more interested in hearing from me than I am in hearing from her. She built a whole new life for herself back East. She's got two more sons, both lawyers, and a man who makes her a lot happier than Dad ever did."

"But what about you?"

"I haven't been real fond of her since she walked out and left me alone with that sonofabitch she married the first time around." Hatch shrugged.

"She should have taken you with her."

"Yeah, well, she didn't. I probably reminded her too much of my old man. Jessie, I do not want to discuss this any further. Is that clear?"

"Yes."

Hatch took a deep breath and made another grab for his self-control. His past was not one of his favorite topics. He glanced at his watch. "I'd better get moving. Got an early-morning meeting with the site manager on the Portland project." He stood up, automatically checking his pockets for keys and wallet. "See you this evening. I'll probably be home around seven-thirty or eight."

"Home? Are you talking about here?"

"Right."

"Now, wait just a minute, Hatch. I've got plans for today. Maybe for tonight too. You can't just move in on me."

"Sorry, Jessie. I'm in a rush. Haven't got time to argue." He took one stride that brought him around the end of the counter, kissed her lightly on the forehead before she could protest, and then headed for the door.

"Dammit, Hatch. Just because you spent last night here does not mean you're going to make a habit of it. Do you hear me?" She was on her feet, coming after him.

"We'll talk about it later, Jessie."

"Oh, yeah? Well, I've got news for you. I don't serve dinner after eight o'clock at night. If you come here that late, don't expect to get fed."

"I'll bear that in mind." He gently closed the door behind him, cutting her off in mid-tirade.

He paused a moment, smiling a little as he heard her slam the dead bolt home. Then he went down the stairs feeling reasonably satisfied. Small battles won here and there led to major victories.

At least he was now fairly certain he finally had her full attention.

Jessie might not want to admit it, but the fact that he had spent the night on her couch was a turning point in their relationship. It added a whole new layer of intimacy to things. The very fact that she had not awakened him and kicked him out last night said a lot. Probably a lot more than she wanted to acknowledge.

Sharing the adventure of the break-in at three o'clock this morning was another binding clause, however unplanned, in the contract he was forging.

All in all, Hatch decided as he walked outside and got into the Mercedes, the business of courting Jessie Benedict was finally starting to come on-line. He sensed success in the offing.

This was one merger he was definitely looking forward to consummating.

Jessie studied the notes she had made on the pad in front of her as she listened over the phone to David rattling off the information he had managed to dig up at Butterfield College.

"Good luck with that name I gave you. It's not much, but it's all I think I'll find," he said. "Frankly, most of the students here on campus weren't particularly interested in dedicating themselves to the cause of the DEL Foundation. The DEL people were basically viewed as loonies."

"Hardly surprising. Anything on Dr. Edwin Bright himself?"

"Just that the 'doctor' in front of his name is a little

suspect. Probably one of those mail-order degrees. No one seemed to know what field it was in."

"Hah. Definitely a con man. Thanks a million for the help, David." As she hung up the phone, Jessie stared at the name she'd written on the pad: Nadine Willard. She actually had a place to start. A clue. She was beginning to feel like a real live investigator.

Nadine Willard worked at an espresso café across the street from the front entrance of Butterfield College. She proved to be a thin, rather washed-out-looking young woman with pale, wary eyes, pale, lanky hair, and bad skin. But she was willing to talk if Jessie would wait until she took her break.

Jessie killed the time by ordering a cup of dark-roasted coffee and after the first sip, immediately wished she'd abstained. Her nerves promptly went into overdrive. One cup of Hatch's brew was apparently enough to last a person all day. No wonder the man was able to work fourteen-hour days.

Jessie sat fiddling with the unfinished coffee and idly studied the mix of campus types seated around her while she contemplated Mrs. Valentine's reaction to the news of the break-in. It had been, to be perfectly truthful, rather disappointing.

"Oh, dear," Mrs. V had said, looking alarmed. "I do hope that nice Alex Robin was not badly hurt."

"He's fine, Mrs. V. Back at work already," Jessie had assured her. She had realized then that Mrs. Valentine had had no enlightening psychic revelations regarding the incident and decided not to mention the remote possibility that it could have been related to the DEL case. No point upsetting the woman. A good assistant shielded one's boss from the petty little day-to-day annoyances of the job.

Jessie was getting bored enough to risk another sip of the dark-roasted coffee when she saw Nadine Willard finally coming toward her.

"Okay, I guess I can talk to you now." Nadine sat down

across from Jessie. "You wanted to know about Susan Attwood?"

"That's right. Her mother is very concerned about her going off to join DEL. Did you know Susan well?"

"No, not really. I don't think anyone did. Susan was not what you'd call real friendly. One of those computer nerds, you know? Kept to herself. She and I had a class together during the winter quarter. When DEL first showed up on campus, I went to one of the evening lectures and Susan was there. We talked a little about the whole thing afterward."

"Were you interested in joining DEL?"

Nadine shook her head. "Nah. Just curious for a while. You know. I mean, everyone knows the environment's in trouble and all, but what can you do? Susan was fascinated right from the start, though. She tried to talk me into going with her when she accepted the invitation."

"What invitation? To join the group?"

"No. It was like a tour of the DEL facilities, you know. She went out to the island and was so impressed she decided to stay and go to work for the foundation."

"Island? What island?" Jessie was getting excited now. She told herself to calm down. She had to take things step by step and make notes. Investigators always took notes. Hastily she whipped out her pad of paper and a pen.

"The DEL Foundation owns an island in the San Juans."

"A whole island?"

"Sure. It's not that big a deal, you know. There are other privately owned islands out there, I guess. At any rate, you have to have a special invitation to go ashore and see the facilities."

"Where does one get an invitation to take the tour?" Jessie asked, tapping the pen restlessly against the table.

"At a DEL lecture, I guess. But there hasn't been one around this campus for weeks now. Maybe they've been recruiting on one of the other campuses in the area." Nadine shrugged her thin, wiry shoulders.

"Damn. I don't suppose you have any brochures or

handouts left over from the lecture you attended, do you? Something with a phone number or an address on it?"

"I doubt it. I wasn't interested, so I didn't keep most of it."

"Damn," Jessie said again. "Sorry."

Nadine paused. "You can have my invitation if you want it. I'll never use it."

"What?" Jessie dropped her pen in astonishment. "You got one?"

"Sure. We all did. I kept it because Susan suggested I hang on to it, just in case I changed my mind, you know."

"Is the invitation transferable? Can anyone use it?" Jessie was having a hard time containing herself now.

Nadine frowned. "I don't see why not. There's nothing on it that identifies me. I think it just says something about the bearer and a friend being welcome to tour the facilities. There's a charge, though. A stiff one. Two hundred dollars apiece. You can write it off as a donation to the foundation, I think."

"Two hundred dollars? Apiece?" Jessie was shocked. "That's a lot of money for a tour."

"Yeah. It's one of the reasons I didn't go. Susan said they stipulate a high donation in order to discourage curiosity seekers."

Jessie made her decision. "Nadine, I will gladly pay you for the invitation." She reached for her purse and yanked it open. "How much do you want for it?"

Nadine thought about it. "I dunno. Maybe twenty bucks?"

"I'll give you fifty," Jessie said, feeling extremely magnanimous. She would put it on the expense account, she told herself. She was not so sure that account would run to the two hundred she would need to take the DEL tour. She would have to approve it with the client. But she was almost certain Mrs. Attwood would want her to go to the island.

* * *

The invitation, which was inscribed "Admit bearer and one friend," was safely tucked into Jessie's purse an hour later when she returned to the office. She was feeling inordinately pleased with herself until she saw Constance Benedict, Elizabeth's mother, waiting for her just inside the hall.

One glance at Connie's face was enough to tell Jessie that this was no casual visit.

"Hello, Connie. What on earth are you doing here?"

"I'm working on a downtown condo residence. Thought I'd stop by and see you for a few minutes before I went back over to the Eastside."

"Something wrong?" Jessie's stomach clenched suddenly. "Elizabeth's okay?"

"Yes. But I want to talk to you about her." Connie sounded grim as she followed Jessie up the stairs and into the office.

"Have a seat." Jessie motioned her to the sofa.

Constance was a few years younger than Jessie's mother. She had not had Elizabeth until she was thirty-five, nine months to the day after marrying Vincent.

After the divorce Constance had admitted she had known Vincent was probably not going to make an ideal spouse, but she had been panicked by a ticking biological clock. She had apparently regretted the marriage within a few short months.

She had stuck it out, however, until Elizabeth was nearly two. By then she had become close friends with Lilian Benedict, the only other woman in the world who really understood what it was like to be the wife of the head of Benedict Fasteners.

Constance was a strikingly handsome woman. Dark-haired and dark-eyed, she had an instinct for making the most of her dramatic coloring, just as Jessie's mother did. She favored strong colors and vivid makeup. She had a lush, full figure that somehow always looked chic and sensual

101

rather than dowdy. Today she was tightly sheathed in a short-skirted turquoise suit.

"All right, what's the problem, Connie?" Jessie sprawled in the swivel chair behind the rolltop desk and waited. She knew she would not have to sit in suspense for very long. Connie was very much like Lilian in that they both had a habit of coming straight to the point.

"Vincent called this afternoon. He left a message for me at the office."

Jessie's stomach tightened again. "And?"

"And he says to tell Elizabeth that he's very sorry but something has come up and he won't be able to take her to the school science fair."

Jessie's worst fears were confirmed. She closed her eyes as frustration and anger washed over her. *"Damn him.* Damn him, damn him, damn him. He knows how important this fair is to Elizabeth. He *promised* he'd be there."

"We all know what Vincent's promises are worth, Jessie. If you're a business associate and the promises have to do with a contract or a deal, they're solid gold. You can take them to the bank. If you're family, they're written in snow. They melt almost as soon as you have them in your hand."

"I know that. But sometimes . . ." Jessie slapped the surface of the desk with her open palm. *"Most* times, I can get him to come through. I thought that he understood this science fair was really important to Elizabeth."

"I think he does understand." Connie shrugged. "And I believe he genuinely regrets not being able to take her. It's just that with Vincent, business is always more important than anything else. Jessie, you should know that better than anyone."

Jessie winced at the accusation in Constance's words. "This is all my fault, isn't it? That's why you're here. To tell me that it's all my fault."

"Well, yes, to be perfectly blunt." Constance sighed. Her eyes held a hint of sympathy beneath the accusation. "I've warned you before that unless you can guarantee Vincent's actions, it's far kinder not to set Elizabeth up."

"I didn't set her up." But she had. Jessie knew she had done exactly that. She had set Elizabeth up for a bad fall. Guilt lanced through her, as sharp as any knife. "Oh, God, Connie. I'm so sorry."

"I realize that. But I'm beginning to think it would be better if you didn't try to create a relationship between Elizabeth and her father. Let the chips fall where they may. She'll survive it. You did."

"But it means so much to her when he takes her out for her birthday or to a school project. I don't want her growing up the way I did, with Dad as some distant, remote figure who occasionally pats her on the head and asks if she needs any money. You can't say all my efforts have been in vain, Connie. You know she has a much better relationship with him than I did at her age."

"I know. And I've been grateful for what you've managed to accomplish. But now that she's about to become a teenager, I don't know if it's wise to keep trying to arrange things between them. Teenagers take rejection and disappointment so seriously. They're so emotional at that age. She was really counting on him being at the science fair on Saturday. She's going to be badly hurt."

Jessie clenched her hand into a small fist. "Have you told Elizabeth yet?"

Constance shook her head. "No. I'll do it tonight." Her mouth twisted with brief bitterness. "By rights, I should make you do it, shouldn't I?"

"Yes." Jessie bit her lip. "Connie, this is Thursday. Give me until tomorrow to see if I can change his mind, all right?"

"It won't work. You'll just be delaying the inevitable. Vincent said this was *business,* remember?"

"Just give me a few hours."

Constance shook her head as she got to her feet and

collected her purse. "I suppose it won't make much difference if I tell Elizabeth tonight or tomorrow."

"Thanks. I'll try to make this work, Connie. I promise."

"I know you will, but . . . Oh, well. We'll see." Constance glanced around the shabby interior of Valentine Consultations. "So this is your latest career move, hmmm? When are you going to settle down and find a real job, Jessie?"

"This is a real job. Why won't anyone take it seriously?"

Constance went to the door. "Probably because of your track record. You're always getting yourself fired, remember?"

"Well, I'm not planning to get myself fired from this job. This one is going to work out. Connie?"

"Yes?"

"You promise you won't tell Elizabeth until I've had a chance to talk to Dad?"

"You're wasting your time, Jessie, but you have my word on it." Constance paused before going through the door. "By the way, how are things going with the heir to the throne?"

"Don't hold your breath. He's just like Dad. You wouldn't really want me to make the same mistake you made, would you?"

Constance frowned. "I thought matters were getting serious between you and Hatch."

"Sheer idle speculation, rumor, and gossip. Most of it started by Dad. I wouldn't marry that man if he were the last male on earth."

Constance's expression relaxed. "Good. Sounds like it's all going to work out for the best, then. I'm glad. I like Hatch, and Benedict Fasteners needs him desperately. We all do."

"Dammit, Connie, I said I wasn't going to . . ."

But further protest was useless. Constance had already closed the door behind herself.

CHAPTER SIX

At eight-thirty that evening Jessie was still sitting at the rolltop desk in the office. She finally forced herself to admit defeat. Her father had not returned any of her calls.

She had not even been able to get past Grace, Vincent's secretary, all afternoon. No, at eight-thirty it was obvious her father, who was probably still at his desk, was not answering his phone.

Jessie knew the pattern all too well. He would not get back to her now until after the weekend. Then he would apologize and explain that he had been called away on business. And everyone knew that business came first.

All the old anger and pain from her own childhood boiled within her anew. Most of the time she could keep it buried, but it had a bad habit of resurfacing whenever Elizabeth was threatened with the same rejection.

"Bastard." Jessie picked up a pen and hurled it across the room.

She listened to the pen clatter as it struck the wall and bounced on the floor. Outside the window a late-spring twilight was fading rapidly into night. It was starting to rain. At least the ugly yellow haze which had blanketed the city for the past few days had finally cleared.

Jessie got to her feet and went into the inner office. She yanked open the bottom drawer of Mrs. Valentine's small file cabinet and picked up the bottle of sherry her employer kept there for medicinal purposes.

Jessie poured a dollop of sherry into her coffee mug and replaced the bottle. She returned to the outer office, turned off the light, propped her feet on the desk, and sprawled back in the squeaky chair. She sipped the sherry slowly. For a long while she sat watching the gloom descend outside the window. It was like a black fog that seemed to be trying to seep into the office, filling every vacant corner.

"You bastard," Jessie whispered as she took another swallow of sherry.

When she heard the footsteps on the stairs, she paid no attention. It was Alex, no doubt, heading for the rest room. He would assume she had gone home for the day hours ago, as she usually did.

She waited for the footsteps to go on down the hall. But they halted, instead, on the other side of the pebbled glass. Belatedly Jessie realized she had not locked the door.

She glanced across the width of the room and saw the dark shadow of a man through the opaque glass. She held her breath, torn between getting up to lock the door and thereby betraying her presence inside the office and sitting tight and hoping he would leave.

She hesitated too long. The door opened and Hatch came into the room, his jacket hooked over his shoulder. His shirt was open at the throat and his tie hung loose around his neck.

"I take it you've changed your regular working hours?" he asked calmly.

"No."

"I see." He paused and glanced around the office. "This looks like a scene straight out of a hard-boiled-detective novel," Hatch said. "There sits our tough, alienated heroine guzzling booze from a bottle she keeps in the desk drawer. She is clearly lost in moody contemplation of the hard life of a private eye."

"I'm surprised you find time to read anything except the *Wall Street Journal*," Jessie muttered. "How did you know I was here?"

"I went to your apartment. Got there shortly before eight o'clock, I might add. Per your instructions. When you didn't show, I decided to try here."

"Very clever."

"You're in a hell of a mood, aren't you?"

"Yeah." Jessie took another swallow of sherry and did not bother to remove her feet from the desk. "I get that way sometimes."

"I see. Got any more of whatever it is you're drinking?"

"It's Mrs. Valentine's tonic. Bottom drawer of her file cabinet."

"Thanks. Don't bother getting up."

"I wasn't going to."

Hatch went into the inner office and returned with the bottle and another coffee mug. "Mrs. Valentine's tonic looks like good Spanish sherry. Is this the source of her psychic powers?"

"Bastard."

"Are we discussing me or your father?"

"Dad."

"Figured I had a fifty-fifty shot at guessing right." Hatch pulled up a chair and sat down. He put the bottle on the desk. "What's he done now?"

"He's found something more important to do than take Elizabeth to her school science fair."

"Yes. That's Saturday, isn't it?" Hatch took a long swallow of the sherry and contemplated the remainder.

Jessie snapped her head around sharply. "That's right. Saturday. What's Dad doing on Saturday that's so important he has to miss Elizabeth's big day?"

"He's going down to Portland," Hatch said. "I told you we're having some problems there."

"Damn him." She slammed the mug down onto the desk, her rage flaring high once more. "Dear God in heaven, I could strangle him for this. Elizabeth is going to be heartbroken. And he doesn't give a damn." Tears burned in her eyes. She blinked angrily.

"You're being a little hard on him, Jessie. You know he cares about Elizabeth. But this thing down in Portland is—"

"I know what it is, Hatch," she said through her teeth. "This is *business,* isn't it? *Business as usual."*

"There's a lot of money involved in the Portland project. Jobs and the company reputation are on the line too. We have to keep to the schedule."

"That's right, go ahead and defend him. You're no better than he is, are you? You'd have done the same thing in his shoes."

Hatch's fingers tightened around the mug. "Don't drag me into this. It's between you and your father."

"Not your problem, is it? But the truth is, you're on his side because you think like him. You have the same set of values, don't you? The same priorities." She narrowed her eyes. "Business always comes first. What do a twelve-year-old kid's feelings matter when there are a few thousand bucks on the line?"

"Dammit, Jessie, I'm not the one who changed his plans for Saturday. Don't blame me for this mess. You set it up and you knew as well as anyone that Vincent might alter his plans if business got in the way at the last minute."

The fact that he was right only made things worse. "Are you telling me that you wouldn't have acted the same way in the same situation?"

"Christ, Jessie, take it easy, will you?"

"Just answer me, Hatch. No, don't bother. We both know what the answer is, don't we? You would have done exactly the same thing."

"That's enough."

Jessie stared at him, astounded by the flash of raw temper. She had never seen Hatch lose his self-control like this. Until now she had found baiting him a challenge, a way of protecting herself from the attraction he held for her. But having succeeded at last in drawing a reaction, she realized she had made a mistake.

"It's true and you know it," she muttered, unwilling to back down completely.

But Hatch was already on his feet, looming over her. His hands clamped around the wooden arms of the chair. "Shut up, Jessie. I don't want to hear another word about how much I resemble your father. *I am not your father, goddammit.*"

"I know that. But you certainly could have been his son. A real chip off the old block, aren't you? You'd have gone down to Portland on Saturday, wouldn't you? Given the same situation, you'd have done what he's doing. Admit it."

"No, I damn well would not have gone down to Portland," Hatch told her, his voice a dangerously soft snarl. His eyes glittered in the gloom. "Not if I'd promised a little girl I would take her to a science fair instead. I do not break my promises, Jessie. If I make a commitment, I keep it. Remember that."

"Let me up, Hatch." Her lower lip was trembling. She could feel it. Out of long habit she caught it between her teeth to still it.

"Why? Am I making you nervous?"

"Yes, dammit, you are."

"Tough."

"Hatch, stop it." Jessie drew her legs quickly up underneath her and stood in the chair. She teetered there for a few seconds and then she stepped over the arm of the chair and onto the desktop. She glared down at Hatch, feeling a little safer in this position.

Hatch straightened, reaching for her with his powerful, dangerous hands. "Come here."

"Hatch, no. Don't you dare touch me, do you hear me?" Jessie sidled backward until the backs of her knees came up against the rows of little cubbyholes that lined the top of the desk.

"I hear you. But I don't feel like listening to you just now." His hands closed around her waist and he lifted her effortlessly down off the desk.

"Hatch."

He lowered her feet to the floor, gripped her upper arms, and pulled her against his hard length. "I've had it with you lumping me into the same category as your father. From now on, Jessie, you're going to start seeing me as an individual. I'm me, Sam Hatchard, not a clone of Vincent Benedict. I make my own decisions and I do my own thinking and I make my own commitments. And I damn sure keep those commitments."

"Hatch, listen to me, I'm not confusing you with my father. Believe me, that is not the issue. I'm just saying you have the same list of priorities and I don't like the list."

He cut off her frantic defense in mid-sentence by covering her trembling mouth with his own. Jessie froze beneath the onslaught of his kiss. The argument she was composing went out of her head in an instant. She sagged against Hatch as her knees gave way.

Jessie could hardly breathe. She was ablaze already. The soul-searing sensuality of the kiss shook her to the core, calling forth a response that dazed her. A liquid heat was pooling in her lower body, intense and compelling.

"Say my name, Jessie." The command was rough against her soft mouth. "Say it, dammit."

"Hatch. Please, Hatch. Please." She wrapped her arms

around his neck, clinging to him as the desire swirled in her blood.

When her feet left the floor again she thought she had fallen over the edge of a volcano. But a moment later she felt the sofa cushions beneath her back and dimly realized that Hatch had carried her across the room. His wicked, beautiful hands were moving over her, yanking at the buttons of her shirt.

She felt his fingers glide over her breast and she cried out. The weight of him came down on top of her. Instinctively she raised one knee and discovered she was already cradling him between her thighs.

All the torment and uncertainty of the past few weeks coalesced into a driving need to find out what lay at the heart of this whirlpool in which she found herself.

Jessie heard her shoes hit the floor. She heard the zipper of her jeans sliding downward, felt the denim being pulled away along with her panties.

When Hatch's fingers found the hot core of her she would have screamed if she'd had the breath to do it. As it was, she had to content herself with wrapping herself even more tightly around him and lifting her hips in a way that pleaded for a more intimate union.

"You want me, don't you, Jessie? As much as I want you. Say it."

"I want you. I've wanted you from the beginning." She caught his earlobe between her teeth and bit. Hard. "And you knew it, damn you."

"I knew it. You were making me crazy." Hatch retaliated for what she had done to his ear by taking one taut nipple between his lips.

Another wave of shimmering excitement and need washed through Jessie. When Hatch pulled slightly away, she moaned in protest and tried to drag him back.

"Just give me a second." His voice was ragged with desire. He yanked open his shirt but did not bother to take it off.

Instead his hand went straight to the fastening of his pants, jerking at the belt and zipper. He pulled a small plastic packet out of one pocket, ripped it open with his teeth, and then reached down again.

Then he was on top of her once more, crushing her into the cushions.

"Put your legs around me, Jessie. Tight."

She did so, following his commands blindly. She felt him at the entrance of her body, poised and ready. Every muscle in his back was rigid with sexual tension. Jessie sucked in her breath as she sensed the size of him.

He started to push himself into her, and she dug her nails into his shoulders. She breathed deeply.

"Jessie. Jessie, look at me."

She opened her eyes warily and gazed up at him through her lashes. The lines of his face were starkly etched, his eyes brilliant as he entered her.

She knew she had driven him over some internal precipice and that she probably should have been afraid. But something that was wild and powerfully feminine deep within her gloried in the knowledge.

He pushed harder against her, easing himself into her. "So tight. Hot and tight. *Jessie.*" He surged forward suddenly, thrusting deeply and completely into the moist, clinging heat of her.

Jessie gasped as he filled her. She shut her eyes as her body struggled to adjust itself to the glorious invasion. She did not dare move yet.

Hatch groaned heavily and went still. "Damn, you feel good. I knew it would be good but I . . . Jessie, did I hurt you?"

She licked her lips. "I'm all right." Her fingers bit deeper into the muscles of his shoulders as she moved her hips in a tentative fashion.

"Oh, Christ."

Whatever self-control Hatch still retained evaporated beneath the gentle, cautious movement of her thighs. His arms closed around her so tightly Jessie wondered if she would ever be free again. He began moving swiftly, each thrust more forceful than the last.

Then Jessie felt his wonderful fingers sliding down between their bodies, felt him search out the sweet spot between her legs, and suddenly she was no longer a moth dancing around a flame, but part of the fire itself.

"Oh, my God, Hatch. Hatch. *Please.*"

"Jessie."

Hatch surged forward one last time, his gritty shout of satisfaction muffled against her mouth. And then he collapsed against her, his body damp and heavy and satiated.

Hatch stirred and opened his eyes when he realized Jessie was starting to wriggle beneath him. "Can't you lie still?" he muttered.

"You're getting heavy."

She was probably right. She was so soft and delicate compared to him, and he was no doubt crushing her into the faded cushions. But, damn, it felt good just to lie here on top of her, breathing in the scents of her moist body and of their recent lovemaking. A deep awareness of the intimacy of the moment flowed through him, making him loath to move.

He looked down at her and thought he saw the same cautious awareness in her cat-green eyes. He also saw uncertainty and wariness mirrored there. From now on she would take him very seriously. Hatch smiled slightly.

"I didn't think we'd go nuclear quite so fast," he said, not without satisfaction.

"But you were prepared for any eventuality, weren't you?" Tears appeared at the edges of her beautiful eyes.

Hatch was startled. He reminded himself that Jessie was an emotional creature. He framed her face gently between his palms. "I've wanted you from the beginning. You knew it. The tension was always there between us. It was just a matter of time."

"I suppose you think this changes everything." She

113

blinked back the tears, clearly struggling for an air of cool challenge. She failed miserably.

"I suppose I do." He brushed his mouth across hers. "I'll take care of Saturday, Jessie."

She scowled. "What are you talking about?"

"Like I said, I'll take care of it. You can call Constance and tell her that Vincent will be escorting Elizabeth to the science fair."

Jessie's eyes widened. "Just how do you plan to make that happen?"

He shrugged. "I'm the CEO of Benedict Fasteners, remember?"

"Yes, but my father is president. And nobody gives my father orders."

"I can handle Vincent." Hatch sat up reluctantly, unable to tear his gaze away from the slender, naked length of her. He watched her blush beneath his scrutiny, and he smiled again. Her breasts shifted enticingly as she leaned over the edge of the sofa and groped for her clothing.

"Why?" she demanded in a small, tight little voice as she held her shirt up like a shield in front of her breasts.

"Why what?" Deprived of the sight of her breasts, he stared lingeringly at the moist hair between her legs.

"You know what I'm talking about." She waved a hand helplessly in the air.

He raised his eyes to meet hers. "That's a dumb question. We were bound to wind up in bed sooner or later. I was planning on later, but you couldn't resist pushing me, could you? And for some crazy reason, I let you push me right over the edge tonight. This wasn't the way I had planned things, honey. I wanted to do it right. Flowers and champagne. The whole works."

"I wasn't talking about . . . about what just happened. I meant why are you suddenly offering to get Dad to the science fair?"

"Oh, that." Hatch shrugged. "Maybe I want you to learn

something about me. Something more than what you seem to think you already know."

"I see." She clutched the shirt more tightly to her throat and stared up at him. Her catlike eyes were narrowed with ill-concealed anxiety. "It's not because I let you do what you just did, is it? Is this your notion of compensating me for a toss in the hay? Because if it is, you can just bloody well forget it."

"I think it's safe to say that you don't have one single shred of psychic ability, Jessie. If you did, you'd have known better than to make an asinine statement like that. Put your clothes on. We'll go out and get something to eat." Hatch knew that earlier, before she had emptied him of the sexual tension that had been gnawing at him for weeks, he probably would have been enraged by the accusation. Now, however, he was feeling too lazy and satisfied to take any real offense.

"I'm not hungry."

"I am. Starving, in fact." He grinned slowly down at her, aware of a happy, exuberant sensation that he had not felt in a long time. "Trust me. You'll feel much better after you've had something to eat and a chance to get back into fighting form. You're just temporarily dazed, that's all."

He was right, just as he had known he would be. By the time they had dressed and he had walked her down the street to a nearby café, Jessie was well on the road to recovery. She started to chat conversationally about a wide variety of subjects. They all had one thing in common. They did not touch on the subject of their relationship.

Later, as Hatch parked his car in front of her apartment, it dawned on him exactly what tactic she had decided to employ in order to deal with the new situation between them. He switched off the engine and sat back to study her in the shadows.

"I'll be damned," he said, amused. "You're just going to pretend it never happened, aren't you? You disappoint me, Jessie. I didn't think you'd take the coward's way out."

"What did you expect me to do?" she flared. "Throw myself all over you and beg you to marry me?"

He considered that. "No, probably not. But I didn't think you'd try to ignore the whole thing either. What are you going to do the next time we make love? Act like it's all a huge surprise?"

"Don't get the idea I intend to make a habit out of that sort of idiotic incident." She slung the strap of her bag over her shoulder and reached for the door handle. "It's not as if I don't have other, more important things going on in my life."

He reached out and flicked the door-lock button, trapping her. "Such as?"

She sat back in the seat and crossed her arms beneath her breasts. "Such as the investigation I'm conducting. I suppose you've forgotten about that, haven't you? You never did bother to tell me about following the money."

"Haven't had a chance," he pointed out. "We've been a little busy today, haven't we? What with getting up at three in the morning to investigate break-ins and making love on your office sofa."

She shot him a quick searching glance. "Tell me now."

"About the money? There's not a whole lot to tell until we know more about DEL. The first thing to find out is how they finance the operation."

"Donations, apparently." She chewed on her lower lip. "I might know more when I get back from visiting their headquarters."

She could not have jolted him more if she had dropped a live grenade into his lap. "Visiting their headquarters?" Hatch shot out a hand and caught her chin, turning her so that she had to meet his eyes. "What the hell are you talking about now?"

She shooed his hand away and smiled rather smugly. "I've been working today, Hatch. With David's help I tracked down someone who knew Susan Attwood, a young woman named Nadine Willard. She and Susan had both attended

116

one of the lectures DEL gave to interested students at Butterfield College, and Nadine just happened to have an extra invitation to visit DEL headquarters. She said anyone who had one could probably go see the place. It's on an island in the San Juans."

"And you're going to go up there? By yourself?"

"Why not?"

"Are you crazy?"

"Probably, or I wouldn't have found myself flat on my back on Mrs. V's office sofa an hour ago."

Hatch was incensed all over again. He could not believe the effect this woman had on him. Deliberately he clamped down his ironclad self-control and forced himself to speak coldly and quietly.

"You are not going up there alone. I absolutely forbid it." He got a sinking sensation in his gut when Jessie's smile turned even more smug.

"Want to come with me and see if you can spot the money trail?" she inquired softly. "The invitation is for the bearer and a friend."

"Now, hold on just one damn minute," Hatch ordered, already reeling under the implications.

"You could always think of it as a mini-vacation, Hatch. I'll bet you haven't taken a vacation in ages, have you?"

"Dammit, Jessie." Hatch realized he desperately needed time. "Look, you're not to do anything at all until I get back from Portland, understand?"

"Portland? You're going down there?" she asked quickly.

"Somebody has to go, Jessie. I told you it was important. Since your father already has a previous commitment, that leaves me. In the meantime, I want your word of honor you won't traipse off to the San Juans alone while I'm out of town."

"Well . . ."

"Let me make that clearer," he said coolly. "You're not getting out of this car tonight until I have your promise not to leave Seattle without me."

"Since you feel that strongly about it, I suppose I can wait." She gave him a triumphant look. "As it happens, I'm going to the science fair too. I won't be going anywhere until Monday. One other thing. The tour requires a two-hundred-dollar donation to the foundation."

"Two hundred dollars? Dammit to hell, Jessie . . ."

"The price of doing business," she murmured blandly. "Even psychic investigators have expenses. Maybe you can put it on your gold card."

"Damn."

Hatch did not trust himself to say another word as he walked Jessie to her door and saw her safely inside her apartment. Still smoldering with pure masculine outrage, he went back outside to his car, got in, and drove to the offices of Benedict Fasteners.

If he was going to Portland on Saturday, he needed to review some files tonight. He would deal with Jessie when he returned.

He would have to deal with Vincent Benedict first thing in the morning, however.

Hatch did not look forward to either project.

Two hundred dollars? Just to keep an eye on Jessie?

"Damn."

"What the hell are you talking about, Hatch?" Benedict's bushy white brows met in a solid line above his glowering eyes.

"You heard me. I'm going down to Portland in your place." Hatch noticed that the birthday flowers on the desk were wilting quickly. They would not last much longer. He wondered why Benedict had not ordered them thrown into the garbage. "You've promised to take Elizabeth to the science fair, remember?"

"Jesus. Of course I remember. But this problem in Portland has gotten too big to handle over the phone. It has to be taken care of in person as soon as possible. You know

118

that. We agreed on it. What the devil's gotten into you, Hatch?"

Hatch planted both hands flat on the surface of Benedict's desk and leaned forward. "I promised Jessie you would take Elizabeth to the science fair. It means a lot to her. Not to mention Elizabeth."

"So what? This is business. These things happen. Both my girls understand that."

"You still don't get it, do you, Benedict? I made Jessie a promise. She needs to learn that when I make a promise, I keep it. If I don't come through on this one, you can probably kiss off any possibility of a marriage between me and your daughter."

"Goddammit, you're serious, aren't you?" Benedict looked appalled.

"Real serious. Better sort out your priorities here, Vincent. You know damn well I can handle the problem in Portland."

"That's not the point. You're needed here. We've got that situation with the bid on the Spokane project to deal with, remember? Or have you forgotten Yorland and Young?"

"We can finesse that for a few days. For the record, I still don't think it's worth the effort anyway."

"Is that right? Well, I happen to want that contract."

"I'll get it for you if it means that much to you," Hatch said impatiently. "But in the meantime, let's get it clear that you are going to take your daughter to the science fair tomorrow."

Vincent snorted and sank back in his chair, brows still beetled. "You sure Jessie won't understand?"

"Oh, she'll understand, all right. She'll understand only too well." Hatch bit out each word. "What she'll understand is that if I don't keep this promise, I'm just what she thinks I am."

"Which is?"

"Too much like you."

"*Women.* What the hell's the matter with 'em anyway? Their priorities are all screwed up. They don't understand how the real world works."

"I've got news for you, Benedict. Women do not think the same way men do. Unfortunate, but true." Hatch straightened, removing his hands from the desk. He was satisfied he had made his point. "Have a good time watching Elizabeth win first place tomorrow."

Vincent sighed. "Hope you know what you're doing."

"I usually do. That's why you hired me in the first place, remember?"

"Should have known this would happen," Vincent said glumly.

"What would happen?"

"Should have known you'd be giving me orders by now," Vincent said. "Knew it wouldn't take you long to take over completely. You just make damn certain you marry that gal of mine. Hear me?"

"I hear you."

Hatch plucked a scarlet lily from the fading bouquet on the desk and carried it back to his own office. He sat down behind his desk and studied the delicate flower for a long while.

Benedict was right. They had just arrived at a subtle turning point in their relationship. Hatch had given the older man orders and Vincent Benedict had taken them. Hatch knew his hold on Benedict Fasteners was more secure than ever.

His hold on Jessie Benedict, however, was still far too tenuous.

He stared at the scarlet lily and remembered the expression on Jessie's face when she had climaxed in his arms.

CHAPTER SEVEN

Eric Jerkface did not win first place at the science fair. When the award was handed out it went to a grinning Elizabeth Benedict. Her father was standing proudly beside her when the film crew took the shots for the evening news. Jessie was so excited she could hardly contain herself. Constance, looking sophisticated in a white suit that clung to every full curve, smiled with delight.

"Are you going to tell me how you pulled off this little miracle?" Constance murmured in Jessie's ear under cover of a round of applause. "I can't believe you got Vincent here. He made that business down in Portland sound more important than the Second Coming."

"Don't thank me, Connie. We owe this one to Hatch."

"He did it for you, didn't he?" Constance slid her a speculative glance.

"Who? Hatch? Umm, yes. I believe he did."

"You don't sound overly thrilled. It was a lovely gesture, Jessie."

"The thing is, Connie, men like Hatch don't make lovely gestures unless there's a price tag attached."

"Such cynicism is unbecoming in a young woman, my dear. It's only us tough old broads who get to indulge in that kind of thing."

"What do I get to indulge in?" Jessie asked.

"Safe sex, if you're lucky. And if you would stop being so damn picky. Your mother's starting to worry about you, you know. Lilian says she did not raise you to go into a convent."

Jessie felt herself turning a vivid shade of red as memories of the previous night on Mrs. Valentine's sofa burned through her mind again. "For heaven's sake, Connie."

"Well, well, well." Constance gave her a warm, approving glance. "Congratulations. I assume we have Hatch to thank for that blush too?"

Jessie fought for composure. "As I said, Connie, when men like Hatch make lovely gestures, there's usually a price tag attached."

"Take some advice from a tough old broad. Pay the price. By the way, speaking of the cost of doing business these days, I know this isn't exactly the time or place to ask, but have you had a chance to talk to Vincent about another little loan for ExCellent Designs?"

Jessie groaned silently. "No, not really. I've been a little busy lately, Connie. I'll say something to him as soon as I get a chance."

"Thanks." Constance smiled at her in gratitude. "Lilian and I would approach him ourselves, but those kinds of conversations always turn into screaming matches between the three of us. You know your father when it comes to money. He won't give it out unless there are strings attached. He likes to control people that way. You're the only one who seems to be able to talk him into being reasonable on the subject."

"Only because I go on screaming longer than you or Lilian," Jessie pointed out morosely.

The film crew was hovering over Elizabeth as she did her best to explain her chemical analysis of a toxic-waste dump to a reporter who wanted it summed up in a thirty-second sound bite. Jessie rushed forward as soon as the reporter was finished and hugged her sister tightly.

"I knew you'd do it, kid. You were fabulous. Wasn't she, Dad?"

"Damn good job, Lizzie." Vincent gazed down on his younger daughter with genuine paternal pride. "I can't say I'm surprised, though. You are one smart little cookie, aren't you? I'll bet it comes from my side of the family."

Elizabeth turned pink and her grin grew wider. "I knew you'd be here today, Dad. Mom said you might not be able to make it at the last minute, but I knew you'd be here."

Constance Benedict gave her daughter a hug and then stood on tiptoe to brush her ex-husband's cheek with a quick, affectionate kiss. "Thanks for coming, Vince," she murmured.

Vincent caught Jessie's eye. "Wouldn't have missed it," he said heartily. Jessie gave him a cool smile in return and turned back to congratulate her sister again.

Fifteen minutes after the conclusion of the awards ceremony, Elizabeth scurried off to admire a friend's project and Constance stopped to chat with an acquaintance. Vincent came up beside Jessie, who was watching a small robot buzz around a tabletop.

"Still mad at me?" he asked, his eyes on the robot.

"Let's not talk about it, okay? You're here. That's the bottom line, as they say in the business world."

Vincent exhaled heavily. "I'm sorry, Jessie. I wanted to be here. I'd planned on it. You know that. It was just that we ran into problems down in Portland."

"I know, Dad. Forget it. Like I said, you're here."

"Only because you sicced Hatch on me."

"I didn't sic him on you. He took it upon himself to make you show today."

"Hell, you got what you wanted. I can understand why you're a little upset with me, but why don't you sound more thrilled with Hatch?"

Jessie watched the robot roll to the edge of the table and

halt as if by magic. "Probably because I know how his mind works. He'll figure I owe him for this."

"Maybe you do. There's a price tag attached to everything in this world." Vincent followed her gaze as she watched the robot make a hundred-and-eighty-degree turn and scoot to the other side of the table. "Tell me the truth, Jessie. How do you really feel about the man?"

"What have my feelings got to do with it? All you care about is marrying me off to him so you can keep the company in the family and watch Hatch take it big-time, right? Don't go all paternal and concerned on me now, Dad. We know each other too well for that kind of nonsense."

"Goddammit, you may not believe this, but I want you to be happy, Jessie. The thing is, I think you and Hatch can make a go of it. There's something about the two of you. When you're in the same room together I can almost see the sparks."

"That's probably just the two of us sharpening our knives for battle."

"Come on, Jessie. This is your old man, remember? I know you well enough to be sure you aren't exactly indifferent to Hatch. I'll never forget the day he fired you. You came out of that office looking shell-shocked, like you'd just done ten rounds with a lion."

"Shark," Jessie corrected. "And it wasn't that big a deal. I've been fired before, Dad."

"Hell, I know that. You've made a career out of getting fired. But somehow in the past you've always come out of it looking as if you were the one who had fired your boss, instead of vice versa. This was the first time I'd ever seen you look like you'd actually lost a battle. That's when I knew for sure it could work between you and Hatch."

Jessie gritted her teeth. "You're not exactly the world's leading authority on what it takes to create a successful long-term relationship, Dad."

"You don't have to spell it out. I know damn well I haven't

been a good role model in the husband-and-father department. Who knows how I would have turned out if Lilian or Connie had been more like you? They both gave up on me, you know. Lost patience somewhere along the line. But you, you're a fighter. You keep after what you want. And you've got Hatch while he's still young. You can work on him, can't you?"

"Young? The man's thirty-seven years old."

"Prime of life. I'll tell you something, Jessie. From where I stand these days, thirty-seven looks damn young. And he's got the guts and the brains it takes to make Benedict Fasteners very, very big."

"What makes you so sure he's got what it takes?"

Vincent grinned. "Partly my own instincts and partly his track record."

"I figure the instinct part is based on the fact that he's a lot like you."

"Now, Jessie, that's not true. Fact is, our management styles are damn different. Hatch has got all kinds of ideas for the company I'd never have approved if he hadn't talked me into them. He's got what they like to call *vision,* if you know what I mean."

"Vision?"

"Yeah, you know. He's aware of new management stuff like concurrent engineering and design. He knows how to deal with foreign markets. He thinks big. Me, I'm a more basic kind of guy. Hatch says I get bogged down in the details, and he's right. Takes vision to pull a company into the big time."

Jessie gave him a speculative glance. "So what makes his track record so impressive?"

"Well, for one thing, he's come up the hard way. No one ever gave him a handout. He's tough. A real fighter. The kind of guy you like to have at your back in a barroom brawl, if you know what I mean. Should have seen what he did to a company called Patterson-Finley a few years back."

Jessie got an odd sensation in the pit of her stomach, although she had never heard of Patterson-Finley. "What, exactly, did he do to it?"

"He was a consultant to one of its smaller rivals. Engineered a takeover bid for them designed to gain controlling interest in Patterson-Finley. It was brilliantly handled. Patterson-Finley never knew what hit 'em. Put up one hell of a fight, naturally, but Hatch sliced 'em into bloody ribbons. When it was all over, Patterson-Finley damned near ceased to exist. It was a wholly owned subsidiary of the smaller firm."

"I think I know why people call him a shark."

"Damn right," Benedict said proudly.

"Tell me, Dad. If you had it to do over again, would you have allowed some woman to work a few changes on you back when you were thirty-seven?"

"Who knows?" Vincent's eyes rested on Elizabeth's brown head and his expression softened slightly. "Sometimes I think maybe I missed some of the important stuff with you."

"Ah, well, I wouldn't waste too much time worrying about it, if I were you. After all, it couldn't be helped, could it?" Jessie smiled sweetly. "You had a business to run."

"Better watch it, Jessie," Vincent retorted. "Men don't take kindly to sharp-tongued females. You're liable to end up an old maid if you aren't careful."

"That's a thought." Jessie deliberately widened her eyes in innocent inquiry. "Think I can scare Hatch off with my sharp tongue?"

"No, but you might piss him off. And that, my darling daughter, you might seriously regret. Say, are you sure that all this interest in ecology isn't going to turn Elizabeth into one of those damn radical tree-huggers?"

"Dad, I've got news for you. We're relying on tree-huggers like Elizabeth to save the world."

* * *

When the downstairs door buzzer sounded at one o'clock that morning, Jessie came awake with a start. She sat blinking in the darkness for a moment, orienting herself. The buzzer screeched again and she pushed back the covers.

Barefoot, she padded out of the bedroom and into the living room. "Who is it?" she asked, pressing the intercom button.

"Jessie, it's after midnight. Who the hell do you think it is?"

"Hatch. What on earth are you doing here at this hour?"

"You know damn well what I'm doing here. Let me in. It's cold out here and I'm likely to get mugged any minute."

Jessie tried to think clearly, failed, and ended up pushing the release button. Then she rushed back into the bedroom to grab a robe.

She was running a brush through her short hair when the doorbell chimed. Aware of a dangerous sense of anticipation mingled with a curious dread, she went to answer it.

Hatch was standing in the hall, looking as if he'd had a long day followed by an even longer drive. He was in his shirtsleeves and he was carrying his jacket and a bulging briefcase. His eyes gleamed at the sight of her in her robe and slippers.

"So how did we do at the science fair?" he asked as Jessie stood staring up at him.

She forgot her trepidation entirely and gave him a glowing smile. "We won. Elizabeth was thrilled. Dad was thrilled. Connie was thrilled. I was thrilled. Everyone was thrilled. Reporters came and they even took film of Elizabeth and Dad for the evening news. I saw it at five-thirty. It was wonderful. Elizabeth looked so happy standing there with her father beside her as she accepted the award. You made her day."

"Good. Glad it all worked out okay."

"Okay? It was much better than *okay*. It was wonderful." Without stopping to think, Jessie threw herself impulsively

127

against Hatch, wrapped her arms around him, and brushed her mouth lightly over his. "Thank you. We owe it all to you."

"You're welcome." Hatch dropped the suitcase at his feet and clamped his hands around Jessie's waist. His palms slid warmly up her back, holding her tightly to him while he took advantage of the situation to deepen the kiss.

Jessie told herself she should probably struggle. She did not want Hatch getting the idea that he could show up on her doorstep at any time of the day or night and expect such a warm welcome. But somehow she could not bring herself to fight him off tonight. His mouth felt too good on hers, deliberate and sure, with a controlled eroticism that set her nerves tingling. He wanted her and, heaven help her, she wanted him.

It was Hatch who broke off the kiss. "I'd better get in out of the hall before one of your neighbors decides to see what's happening." He released her with obvious reluctance in order to pick up the briefcase and move on into the room.

Jessie stepped back, quashing the tide of sensual longing that he had elicited with his kiss. She searched frantically for something appropriate to say. She just knew he had read far too much into that greeting at the door. He was already making himself at home, hanging his jacket in the closet and stowing the briefcase on the floor beneath it. When he sat down on the couch and started to take off his shoes, she panicked.

Out of hand, she thought. Things were definitely getting out of hand. Give Hatch an inch and he clearly felt he could take a mile. And she had given him a great deal more than an inch, she reminded herself.

"How did things go in Portland?" she managed to ask politely while she clutched the lapels of her robe and wondered what to do next.

Hatch gave her a hooded glance as he unlaced his other shoe. "Under control again. We're back on schedule."

"Oh. Good." She glanced over her shoulder into the kitchen. "Uh, did you want a cup of coffee or anything?"

"Nope. All I want is bed. It's a four-hour drive down to Portland. I left at four this morning. Spent the whole day until nine o'clock this evening chewing on everyone involved in that project and then I got into my car and drove four hours to get back here." He stood up and started toward her, unbuttoning his shirt en route. "I'm beat."

"I see. Well, then, you'll probably want to go straight home to your place and get some sleep." She gave him a bright little smile.

"You're right about one thing, at least. I want to get some sleep."

He scooped her up in his arms, carried her into the bedroom, and tossed her lightly down onto the bed. He leaned over her as he tugged the robe free and dropped it on a chair.

Jessie lay back against the pillows and watched with a deep, disturbing hunger as he stripped off the rest of his clothing. She might as well face it, she told herself. She was not going to kick him out. Not tonight, at any rate.

"You can make the coffee in the morning," Hatch said as he got into bed wearing only a pair of briefs. "Just be sure you make it strong."

He turned on his side, facing her, and anchored her with a possessive arm around her waist. She could feel the sinewy muscles of his forearm pushing lightly against the soft weight of her breasts. In an agony of anticipation, Jessie waited for his wonderful, powerful hand to glide down her hip and over her thigh.

Nothing happened.

Jessie looked closer and noticed Hatch's astonishingly dark lashes lying against his high cheekbones. His breathing was slow and even. He was already asleep.

She touched his shoulder gently, knowing she was at least partially responsible for his exhaustion tonight. He had done it for her, she realized. She had to remind herself that his motives had certainly not been entirely altruistic. She was temporarily a high priority for Sam Hatchard. He was willing to indulge her to a certain extent while he courted her.

Still, he had come through in a way she had never expected. He had made a commitment and he had kept it. He had even taken on her father in order to make good on a promise to her. Jessie had to admit she did not know any other man on the face of the earth who could have pulled off the feat of getting Vincent Benedict to the school fair today.

"I hope," she whispered into the darkness, "that you don't think you can just show up like this and fall into my bed any night you happen to feel like it."

"Now, where would I get an idea like that?" Hatch asked without opening his eyes.

Hatch awoke the next morning, inhaled the womanly fragrance of the white sheets, and exhaled with satisfaction as he realized he was finally in Jessie's bed.

Another turning point, he decided, pleased. Another victory in the small, important war they were waging.

Hatch reached for Jessie and found the other side of the bed empty. He groaned and opened his eyes. A rain-drenched daylight was filtering through the slanted blinds and the aroma of coffee wafted in from the kitchen.

Some victory. A whole night in Jessie's bed and he had not even managed to make love to her while there.

Maybe he was working too hard lately.

Hatch shoved back the covers and sat up slowly. He glanced around with deep interest, enjoying the intimate sensation of being in Jessie's bedroom. Her robe still lay on the chair. The mirrored closet door was open, revealing a colorful array of clothing. A selection of loafers, running shoes, sandals, and high heels were scattered carelessly on the closet floor.

Jessie was obviously not a fanatic about neatness. Just as

well, Hatch told himself as he went into the bathroom. Neither was he.

The small tiled room was still steamy from Jessie's recent shower. Hatch opened the sliding glass door and stood gazing at the collection of items arranged on the ledge beside the shower handle. There were a variety of shampoo bottles and soaps, a woman's razor, and a long-handled back brush. The scent was fresh and flowery.

When he got into the shower, Hatch felt as if he were invading some very private, very female place. It made him acutely conscious of his maleness and of how alien that maleness was here in this female sanctuary.

The sense of possessiveness that rippled through him as he stood there in Jessie's shower made Hatch's mouth twist in a faint, wry smile. Everything felt right, somehow, as if he had been waiting a long time for this moment.

When he emerged from the bedroom twenty minutes later he found Jessie sitting at the kitchen counter with the morning paper. She glanced up quickly as he came into the room and he caught the flash of nervousness in her eyes just before her elbow struck the coffee cup that was sitting next to her.

The cup went spinning across the counter. Hatch watched with interest as it teetered precariously on the edge and then went over the side. As Jessie stared in dismay, he reached out and caught the empty cup before it hit the floor.

"Another cup of coffee?" Hatch asked calmly as he picked up the pot and poured one for himself.

"Yes, please." She carefully refolded the paper.

"Anything exciting in the headlines?" He sat down across from her and grimaced as he tasted the weak brew.

"There's another article about the damage being done to the earth's ozone layer by pollutants." Jessie frowned. "You know, I can see why people would be attracted to a cult that focused on saving the world from environmental disaster. The issue has the same awful sense of impending doom that the thought of global war has. Don't forget, there was a time when everyone wanted to build a bomb shelter in his backyard."

"Speaking of which, have you given up that damn-fool idea of using the invitation to visit DEL headquarters?" Hatch asked without much real hope.

"Of course not. I'm going to phone and make the arrangements first thing tomorrow morning." She eyed him warily. "Are you still going to insist on going up there with me?"

"I don't see that I have much option."

"Sure you do. You can decide to let me go alone."

"No way, Jessie. We don't know what you're getting into. You're not going up there alone, and that's final."

"It'll probably take a couple of days," she pointed out. "That's a heck of a long time to stay away from Benedict Fasteners. The company might fall apart without you."

"Don't you think I know that? Stop trying to talk me out of going with you. You aren't going alone."

"What about the company?"

"I'll leave your father in charge. He's run it for the past thirty years. No reason he can't handle it for a couple more days."

"I suppose you've got a point." She frowned. "Are you going into the office? It's Sunday."

"There are some things I have to clear up if I'm going to be out of town for a couple of days."

"I see. Are you really sure you can afford to take the time off?"

He raised his brows. "Don't bother trying to get rid of me, honey. I'm here to stay."

She bit her lip. "Hatch, we have to talk about this."

"The trip to the San Juans?"

"No, *this*. You. Here. In my kitchen at eight o'clock in the morning." She drew a deep breath. "If we're going to have an affair or something, we need to set a few ground rules."

"We're not having an affair." Hatch got to his feet and carried his cup over to the sink.

"What do you call this business of showing up on my

doorstep at one in the morning and spending the night?" she demanded.

"I call it being engaged to be married." He caught her chin on the heel of his hand and gave her a quick, hard kiss. Then he headed for the closet where he had left his jacket and briefcase.

"Hatch, wait. Don't you dare walk out of here before we've had a chance to discuss this. Hatch, come back here. I mean it. I swear, if you don't come right back here I'm going to . . . Oh, damn."

He gently closed the door behind him as he went out into the hall.

Hatch was not in the least surprised to find Vincent in his office on Sunday morning. The older man almost always came in on the weekends, just as Hatch did. Benedict looked up, scowling when Hatch stuck his head around the door to announce his presence in the building.

"Where the hell have you been?" Vincent rapped out. "I've been calling you since seven-thirty this morning to find out how things went down in Portland."

"Things went fine down in Portland. Next time you can't reach me at my place, try Jessie's."

Benedict blinked and then started to turn a strange shade of red. "You spent the night with her? You're sleeping with my Jessie?"

"Better get used to the idea, Benedict. I'm going to marry her, remember?"

"You damn well better marry her now or I'll get out my shotgun." Vincent drummed his fingers on the desk and narrowed his gaze. "I suppose this is a sign the courtship is going okay?"

"I like to think of it that way. Before I forget, I'll be gone for a couple of days this week. Jessie and I are going up to the San Juans while she investigates her psychic cult case. You're in charge while I'm out of town. Don't run us into Chapter Eleven, okay?"

"For Christ's sake, Hatch. You're the CEO around here. You can't just take off like this."

"Not much point being the boss if you can't take a couple of days off when you feel like it, is there?" Hatch growled.

"Goddammit, this DEL thing is crazy. Don't waste your time on it."

"No choice. Jessie's decided to waste her time on it, so that means I've got to waste some of mine. You don't want her going into that mess alone, do you?"

"Hell, no. I don't want her going at all."

"She's made up her mind. So I'm going along to ride shotgun."

Vincent glowered at him. "Strikes me she's got you running around in circles. If you can't control her any better than this, I'm not so sure you're the right man for her after all."

Hatch's fingers clamped around the edge of the door. He smiled thinly. "Stay out of this, Benedict. I'm in charge around here, remember?"

"I can cancel your contract anytime, and don't you forget it."

"You won't do that. Not as long as you're getting what you want. And so far, I'm giving you exactly what you want. Oh, yeah, congratulations on Elizabeth's first-place win in the science fair."

"Yeah. Thanks." Vincent nodded proudly. "The kid gets her smarts from my side of the family."

Jessie lounged in the chair next to her mother and watched Lilian methodically try on twelve different pairs of shoes. The saleswoman who had brought out the dozen boxes did not seem in the least dismayed by the prospect of a customer who wanted to try on so many different styles. Lilian Benedict was a regular at the big downtown department store's shoe salon. She never left without buying at least one pair.

"You're serious about this nonsense of going up to the San

Juans to look at some cult headquarters?" Lilian frowned thoughtfully at the pair of patent-leather heels she was considering.

"Afraid so," Jessie said cheerfully. "I don't like those. The spectator pumps look better on you."

The truth was, almost anything Lilian tried on looked good. She had the same innate style that Constance had. Lilian was a few years older than Constance but she kept her dark hair tinted close to its original ebony shade, allowing only a few dramatic traces of silver to show. Her full, womanly figure was still amazingly firm and her fine bone structure ensured that her look of exotic sophistication would hold up beautifully until she was a hundred.

Jessie had frequently wondered about the similarities between Lilian and Constance. They were so much alike, not only in their physical appearance but also in the way they thought and acted. Connie, rather than Glenna, could have been Lilian's sister. Both women found her observation amusing.

"What did you expect?" Lilian had once said to Jessie. "Men are creatures of habit. They're attracted to the same sort of woman over and over again. Second wives often resemble first wives, and they often have a lot in common."

Jessie watched her mother try on the spectator pumps again. "Hatch insists on going up to the island with me."

"That's reassuring. When do you leave?"

"Tomorrow morning. I called the phone number on the invitation card this morning. The person who answered was very helpful. Sounded very professional. We take a ferry to one of the nearby islands. The DEL people will pick us up in a seaplane and fly us to New Dawn Island."

"New Dawn Island?"

"That's what they call it," Jessie said. "Apparently they own it, so I guess they can call it anything they want."

"Sounds completely screwy to me." Lilian shook her head over a pair of red heels the saleswoman was offering.

"We'll be given a tour that lasts a couple of hours and then flown back to the island where we spent the night. That's all there is to it." Jessie shook her head regretfully. "I'm not sure how much I can possibly learn about Susan Attwood's fate or the leader of this DEL thing in just a couple of hours. But at least it's a starting point."

"Well, I suppose there's really nothing to worry about. Hatch should be able to take care of anything that comes up. He's a very competent sort of man, isn't he?"

"Uh, yes. In some ways."

Lilian gave her a sly smile. "I get the impression the big romance is heating up rapidly. Connie says she thinks you and Hatch are already sleeping together."

"That's what I like about this family. Absolutely no privacy."

Lilian chuckled. "You know as well as I do that we're all hoping you and Hatch will work it out."

"I'm not so sure Aunt Glenna feels that way."

"Nonsense. Glenna knows that a marriage between you and Hatch would be the best thing for all concerned. It's the only viable solution to the situation."

Jessie gazed broodingly at the pair of Italian leather sandals her mother had on at that moment. "Doesn't it strike you that it's a bit strange that Hatch is thirty-seven years old and still single?"

Lilian flashed her a look of genuine surprise. "Didn't anyone tell you he was married once?"

Jessie stared at her, dumbfounded. "No. No one mentioned that little fact." Least of all, Hatch. "Divorced?"

"Widowed, I think. Connie told me about it. She said Vince mentioned it in passing a few days ago."

"Widowed. I see." Jessie absorbed that bit of information slowly, examining it from every angle. "I wonder why Hatch never told me about his first wife."

"I gather she died several years ago. Don't fret about it, Jessie. I'm sure he'll tell you all about his first marriage in his own good time."

Jessie rested her elbows on the arms of the chair and laced

her fingers together. She stared sightlessly at a display of glittery evening shoes and contemplated the many similarities she had often observed between Constance and Lilian.

Men are creatures of habit. Second wives often resemble first wives.

Jessie felt a small chill go down her spine. "I hope I don't look like her," she whispered, not realizing she had spoken aloud.

Her mother gave her a sharp glance. "What are you talking about?"

"Hatch's first wife. I hope I don't resemble her. I wouldn't want to be a stand-in for a ghost."

Lilian frowned. "For heaven's sake, Jessie. There's no need to get carried away with the dramatics of the situation."

"Right. This is business, isn't it?"

"You know, I'm amazed you got Hatch to agree to take a couple of days off just to go up to the San Juans with you," Lilian said in an obvious attempt to redirect the conversation.

Jessie stared gloomily at the evening shoes. "No big deal when you think about it. Like I said, it's business."

CHAPTER EIGHT

Mrs. Valentine, ensconced in an old-fashioned rocking chair in the living room of her sister's Victorian-style house on Monday afternoon was looking appreciably improved. But her expression of welcome turned to one of dismay as Jessie concluded her report.

"You're going to go up there? To the headquarters of these DEL people? Oh, dear, Jessie, I don't think that's a good idea at all. Not at all."

"Don't worry," Jessie said soothingly. "I won't be alone. Hatch will be with me. And we're just going to look the place over. We're not going to try to rescue Susan Attwood or anything. Remember, we're only trying to find some evidence that Bright is a phony."

"Oh, dear," Mrs. Valentine said again. Her fingers toyed nervously with a deck of tarot cards in her lap. "Have you told Mrs. Attwood?"

"Of course." Jessie recalled the conversation with Martha Attwood that had taken place earlier. Mrs. Attwood had been very excited that something concrete was finally going to happen. "She's very anxious for a report. Her main concern is to find out if her daughter is on the island. I'm not sure we'll be able to do that, but we might get lucky. Hatch and I are just going to play it by ear."

"Oh, dear." Mrs. Valentine's gaze sharpened abruptly and her hand stilled on the cards. "Jessie, I'm getting a feeling about this situation. A real feeling. Do you understand?"

"A psychic sort of feeling? Mrs. V, that's wonderful. Maybe you're getting back some of your natural ability."

Mrs. Valentine shook her head in frustration. "It's not that clear. Not like these things were before I fell down the stairs. But I think there's something dangerous in all this. I can sense that much. Jessie, I do not like this. Not one bit. I think it would be better if you don't go to the island."

"But, Mrs. Valentine, all I'm going to do is get a look at what's going on up there at the DEL headquarters. And I've already promised Mrs. Attwood I'll go."

Mrs. Valentine sighed heavily. "Then promise me one thing."

"Of course, Mrs. V. What is it?"

"That you will not do anything rash. Promise me you will stay with Sam Hatchard at all times. He does not strike me as a rash or reckless man. I think we can rely on his good sense." But Mrs. Valentine did not appear completely certain of that analysis.

Jessie's Aunt Glenna phoned to put in her two cents' worth on Monday evening.

"Lilian tells me you've tracked down this DEL outfit and you're going up to take a look at the headquarters tomorrow," Glenna Ringstead said in a disapproving tone. "Do you really think that's a good idea, Jessie?"

"I'm not going alone, Hatch will be with me." Jessie was learning that using Hatch's name was rather like waving a talisman in front of all the people who had serious doubts about the expedition to the island. They all seemed to calm down a little when they found out he was going to be going along.

"I see." There was a distinct pause on the other end of the line. "I assume that the relationship between you and Hatch has taken a more serious turn, then?"

"Uh-huh." Jessie did not know what else to add. She glanced at the clock and saw that it was already after seven. She wondered if Hatch had left the office yet. "But don't get too excited, Aunt Glenna. I admit I'm attracted to the man, but can you honestly see me marrying him? It would never work."

"No," Glenna said quietly. "It wouldn't. As much as everyone would like to have you marry Sam Hatchard, I have to admit it would probably be a disaster for you, emotionally."

Jessie clamped her fingers more tightly around the phone and swallowed heavily. It occurred to her that her aunt's response was not what she had wanted to hear. Had she actually been hoping Aunt Glenna would, like everyone else, blindly reassure her that things could work between herself and Hatch? "Well, I've got to pack. I'll talk to you when I get back, Aunt Glenna. And thanks for recommending all those books on cults. I've learned a lot."

"You're welcome."

The roar of the seaplane's prop engines made conversation virtually impossible. Jessie peered out the window as the pilot eased the craft down into the cove and taxied toward the floating dock. The headquarters of the Dawn's Early Light Foundation did not look at all like the sort of facility she had been expecting to house a group of strong-minded environmentalists.

The pilot, a young man in his early twenties dressed in a spiffy blue-and-white uniform and wearing an engaging grin, chuckled as he shut down the engines. "Not quite what you anticipated, I'll bet. Most visitors are surprised. I guess they expect us to be living in caves and munching on roots and berries."

"Well, I certainly didn't expect anything as plush as this,"

Jessie admitted, surveying the magnificent old mansion that overlooked the cove. "Did you, Hatch?"

Hatch shrugged as he opened the cabin door and stepped out onto the gently bobbing dock. "Who knew what we'd find up here? Bunch of weirdos running around trying to save the world."

Jessie smiled apologetically at the pilot. "Don't pay any attention to him. He's a confirmed skeptic. I'm afraid I'm guilty of more or less dragging him up here today."

"Sure. I understand. A lot of the people I fly in here are skeptical at first. Your guides are on their way. Enjoy your tour." The pilot smiled his charming smile again. He stood with his booted feet braced slightly against the motion of the dock, the breeze ruffling his sandy hair.

He looked extremely dashing in his crisp uniform, Jessie thought. He certainly had the build for it. Jessie eyed the broad shoulders and chest and wondered if he lifted weights as a hobby. With his breezy, all-American good looks and smile, he could have been any corporate pilot working for any private business anywhere. The name engraved on his name tag was Hoffman.

"When does this famous tour begin?" Hatch demanded, glancing at his watch. "Haven't got all day, you know."

Jessie winced in embarrassment and shot another apologetic glance at Hoffman. "Please, dear," she murmured, doing her best to sound like a placating wife, "don't be so impatient. It's a lovely day and I'm sure we're going to enjoy the visit."

"Enjoy myself? Don't be an idiot. If I wanted to enjoy myself, I'd have gone fishing. I wouldn't have agreed to waste my time up here."

"Yes, dear." Jessie hid a quick smile. Hatch was putting on an act, of course. But he was awfully good at it and she suspected he was well and truly into the role. Probably because he really did think this jaunt was a waste of time and effort.

It had been Hatch's idea to adopt the facade of a married

couple. "It'll be sort of like playing good-cop/bad-cop," he'd explained on the drive up from Seattle. "You'll be the gullible, easily influenced, weak-brained little wifey who buys into the whole save-the-world scene."

"Thanks. What part do you get to play?"

"I will be the cynical, jaded, tough-minded husband who has to be convinced."

"You don't think it'll work if we reverse the roles?" Jessie suggested dryly. "I could play the cynical, jaded, tough-minded wife and you could play the gullible, easily influenced, weak-brained husband."

"Are you kidding? You're a natural for your part, already. You're the one who can't say no to anyone, remember? If it hadn't been for me, you'd probably own a couple of hundred shares of a company that makes fat-free cooking oil by now."

"You know something, Hatch? If that company's stock goes up in the next six months, I'm going to hold you personally responsible for reimbursing me for whatever profits I don't make."

He'd smiled faintly. "What happens if the stock goes down?"

"Why, then, I'll be forever grateful, of course."

"I could live with that."

The trip had gone smoothly until this point, Jessie reflected as she watched two figures come down the path toward the cove. It had been almost like setting out on a mini-vacation with Hatch. She'd felt a flash of pure sensual anticipation as she'd watched him load their overnight bags into the trunk of his Mercedes. *She was going off to spend a night with her lover.*

She was having an affair.

"Affair" was the only word she could come up with to describe Hatch's role in her life at the moment. She refused to call their relationship an "engagement" as Hatch insisted on doing and she could not bear to think of it as a one-night stand. That left "affair."

"I'll introduce you to your guides," Hoffman, the pilot, said cheerfully as a man and woman from the mansion stepped onto the bobbing dock. "This is Rick Landis and Sherry Smith. Rick, Sherry, meet Mr. and Mrs. Hatchard."

Jessie nodded politely. "How do you do? We really appreciate your taking the time to tour us around your facility."

"Glad you could make it," Rick Landis said, smiling respectfully at Hatch. He had the same sort of open, easy charm the pilot displayed. His dark hair was trimmed in a short, clean-cut style and he was wearing the same blue slacks and military-style white shirt that comprised the pilot's uniform. He looked to be about the same age as Hoffman, somewhere in his mid-twenties, perhaps. And he appeared to be in the same excellent physical shape.

"Didn't have much choice," Hatch muttered, fleshing out his disgruntled-husband role nicely. "Wife insisted on this little jaunt. Had my way, we'd have gone to Orcas for a couple of days instead."

"Oh, I think you'll find our little island is even more lovely than Orcas Island," Sherry Smith said earnestly. A young woman, no more than nineteen or twenty at the most, she seemed much more intense than either Hoffman or Landis. She was also quite attractive, Jessie could not help but notice. Her hair was long and honey-colored and the blue-and-white outfit she was wearing showed off her narrow waist and flaring hips.

"It's certainly beautiful here," Jessie gushed, as if anxious to make up for her surly husband. She made a show of surveying the scenery, which consisted of the cove, a rocky beach, and the old mansion. A thick forest of green, mostly pine and fir, rose up behind the great house. "Just lovely." She batted her lashes at Hatch. "Isn't it, dear?"

Hatch slanted her a wry glance. "It's okay. Can we get on with this four-hundred-dollar tour? I'd like to get back to our inn in time for dinner."

"By all means," Landis said. "I'm sure that after the tour

143

you'll feel the four-hundred-dollar donation to the DEL Foundation has gone to a terrific cause. Follow us, please." He turned and led the way back up the path toward the mansion.

"I'll give you some quick background first," Sherry said. "The island was originally owned by a timber baron who made his fortune back in the early nineteen hundreds. He had this beautiful house built as a retreat and as a place to entertain his guests."

"How did DEL get the place?" Hatch asked.

"It was donated to the foundation a few months ago by the last surviving member of the family. Dr. Bright took advantage of the offer to move his headquarters here. The previous owner was a strong supporter of DEL."

"Was?" Hatch glanced at her.

"She was a very old woman," Sherry said sadly. "She died not long after she had put DEL in her will."

"Kind of appropriate, isn't it?" Jessie murmured. "Using a timber baron's old home as the base for an environmentalist operation. Poetic justice."

Landis chuckled. "Not quite. But I'll explain that part later. The general routine is to start with a video presentation of the work of DEL." He opened the front door of the huge house and ushered his visitors into a vast paneled hall. "The show will give you an overview of what we're doing."

"No offense," Hatch muttered as he followed Jessie into a small auditorium, "but I'd have thought a bunch of radical environmentalists would have wanted something a little more environmentally efficient than this old pile of stones. Must cost you a fortune to heat it in the winter."

Sherry shook her head sadly as she handed him a plastic cup of coffee. "I'm afraid that, like most people, you don't really understand what DEL is all about yet. But you will soon."

Jessie eyed the cup of coffee Sherry was offering. "I'll admit I didn't expect to see anyone up here using plastic cups."

Landis nodded, his handsome face turning more serious. "I understand what you must be thinking. Have a seat and let me run the video. That should give you a good idea of what DEL is really doing."

Jessie sat down beside Hatch in one of the plush auditorium seats. She glanced around quickly as the lights were dimmed.

"Know what this reminds me of?" Hatch asked under cover of a rousing musical score that heralded the film.

"What?"

"The kind of expensive presentation prospective clients get when they fall into the clutches of some slick real-estate-investment outfit."

Jessie scowled in the darkness. "Hush. They'll hear you."

Hatch shrugged and sat back as the show began. A deep, concerned, masculine voice filled the room:

Most of the scientific community is well aware that the environment is on the verge of disaster. It will be a disaster every bit as catastrophic as the nuclear winter that would be caused by a third world war. Each day the radioactive waste piles up in our oceans. Acid rain destroys our agricultural lands. The destruction of rain forests threatens the very air we breathe.

The ultimate fate of our planet is no longer a matter of debate. All that can be debated now is the timing of that fate and the method of saving ourselves from it.

"Pretty fancy graphics," Hatch observed softly as the music swelled again. "Someone hired a first-class ad agency to put this show together."

The narrator's voice rose again, this time sounding confident and reassuring:

One man, an expert in computer programming, climatology, and ecology, has studied the problem more intensely than most. His name is Dr. Edwin Bright. And he is the founder of Dawn's Early Light. Meet the one individual who can make it possible for you and me to survive the disaster that is already on its way.

145

The scene on the film was of the cove in front of the DEL mansion. The camera zoomed in to show a man dressed in well-cut blue trousers and a crisp white shirt standing on the dock. He was gazing past the camera, out toward the horizon, as if he could see something extremely important approaching.

Jessie leaned forward to study the film more closely. Dr. Edwin Bright appeared to be in his late forties and there was no denying the camera loved him. He looked very, very good on film.

He was a striking individual with rugged features, closely cut brown hair, and vivid blue eyes. A pair of steel-framed aviator-style glasses gave him an air of serious intelligence coupled with a bold, decisive, almost military look. When he finally turned toward the camera, his eyes met the lens unflinchingly, as if he could see past it to the audience. The vivid intensity of his gaze was mesmerizing. Jessie remembered what David had reported about the man being extremely charismatic.

"Looks like one of those characters on television who will offer to save your soul if you'll just send him the contents of your bank account," Hatch muttered.

"Shush. I told you, Rick or Sherry will hear you."

Dr. Bright agrees with his fellow scientists on many points. However, he has run his own computer forecasts based on his own calculations. He has simulated climatological events over the next fifty years. There is little doubt that environmental disaster is inevitable. Dr. Bright's estimate of the timing of this disaster differs from many in the scientific community.

According to Bright's carefully constructed programs and calculations, that disaster will overtake us much sooner than most people predict. It will very likely strike within the next ten to fifteen years.

Edwin Bright also disagrees with his associates in the scientific community and with the radical environmentalists on the subject of how to survive this disaster.

Edwin Bright looked straight into the camera and spoke for the first time. His voice was rich, measured and imbued with almost hypnotic intensity:

It is technology that got us into this environmental mess, Bright said grimly, *"and it is technology that will save us. I'm afraid it is far too late to employ conservation measures, in spite of what the liberal extremists tell us. Switching from plastic to paper bags at the supermarket is like trying to plug a leak in a dam with a Band-Aid. In any event, we cannot go back to some primitive time before the invention of electricity or antibiotics. To do so would be to deny the very thing that makes us human, the very thing that can save us, namely our intelligence. Such a retreat into the past is unthinkable. It is, to put it bluntly, too late to return to that world of early death and periodic famine that our ancestors endured. We do not have enough time to reverse our economy or change our life-styles drastically enough to forestall the cataclysm.*

Jessie glanced down at the cup in her hand. "I guess that philosophy explains the plastic. Why bother trying to recycle when the damage has already been done and there's no time left to clean it up anyway?"

"Convenient sort of theory," Hatch murmured. "Bound to appeal to a lot of people. Lets 'em have their cake and eat it too."

But there is hope, Edwin Bright continued in a strong, reassuring voice. *And that hope lies with the work of the Dawn's Early Light Foundation. Here at DEL we are attacking the problem the way real Americans have always attacked their problems: with the power of modern science and technology and with good old American-style know-how. My friends, we are making great progress. With your help, we can continue our important work. But time is short. I urge you to give what you can now, today, to the cause. Without your support, we can do little. With it, we can save the world.*

The narrator took over once more as the camera went high for an aerial shot of the island:

You may be surprised to know that much of the technology

*needed to save our world already exists. Part of the work of
the DEL Foundation is to correlate data on that existing
technology and find ways of employing it effectively. We
cannot wait for the world governments to do this. They are
too bogged down in red tape and bureaucracy. Only private
enterprise has the ability to react to this kind of crisis.
Farsighted Americans believe in private enterprise and they
support it because they know it works. We hope you will help
us.*

Jessie listened to the rest of the filmed lecture and realized
ruefully that she wanted to believe that somehow DEL
really could save the world with existing technology. It was
reassuring and inspiring to think that the tools were already
available and all it took was a master plan to put them into
use. She had to remind herself that Dr. Edwin Bright was
probably nothing more than a fast-talking salesman.

The music swelled once more as the film came to a stirring
conclusion. The lights brightened slowly in the auditorium
as the film came to an end.

"I imagine you've both got a lot of questions," Landis
said as he got to his feet.

"Right," said Hatch. "For starters I'd like to know how
the hell this Edwin Bright came up with his time frame for
the total destruction of the environment. Ten to fifteen years
is a damn short prediction. Everything else I've read says
we'll have longer to solve the problem than that."

"Good question," Landis agreed gravely. "Let's go downstairs to the computer room and I'll show you how we do
Bright's calculations."

Sherry Smith fell in behind Jessie as Landis led the way
down a darkly paneled hallway. He paused once to open a
door briefly.

A hum of voices greeted Jessie as she glanced inside what
must have originally been the mansion's formal dining
room. Banks of telephones and desks were set up in a long
row. They were manned by several men and women who all
appeared to be in their early twenties. It was not difficult to

figure out what was happening. Jessie focused on the voices of the nearest telephone operators while she scanned the room for anyone who looked like Susan Attwood.

"Yes, sir, Mr. Williamson, we've made enormous progress and we're now dealing with a major corporation on a contract to mass-produce the machine. It will go into production next month and will be available to all of the nation's cities and towns within eighteen months. The profit potential on this is enormous. It is an affordable product and will be mass-produced. You will easily triple your investment in the next eighteen months. Can we count on your donation?"

The operator reminded Jessie of her friend Alison, the stockbroker. She caught Hatch's sardonic eye and realized he was thinking the same thing.

One of the other operators was selling something else.

"As I explained," the vivacious, earnest young woman was saying to the person on the other end of the line, "the Bright Vaporizer totally eliminates all garbage via a chemical process. The end product is pure, clean oxygen. It will eliminate the need for landfills, ocean dumping, and every other kind of garbage facility. All we need is a little more financial help from you. If you can see your way clear to donate a minimum of five thousand dollars, you will be considered a registered investor and thus a potential stockholder. You will share in the profits, which are guaranteed to double every six months for the next five years."

Landis quietly closed the door and went on down the hall to a stone staircase. "The original owner of the mansion had a huge basement built down here," he explained as he started to descend the stairs. "We've turned it into our computer facility. Dr. Bright runs all of his programs on the computers you'll see here. Those programs are being constantly updated with all kinds of information, including the latest climate information and reports of accidental releases of radiation, toxic spills, and such."

"The programs are almost unbelievably complex," Sherry

149

confided. "We chart the amount of rain forest destroyed each day, the quantity of pollutants being released into the atmosphere from all major manufacturing plants around the world, as well as concentrations of natural gases from such things as volcanic eruptions. Then we do our projections, using the past several thousand years of the earth's climate history."

"And that's just the tip of the iceberg, as they say." Landis smiled as he reached the bottom of the staircase and opened a door in the narrow hall. "A whole different kind of research is done to pull together all the information we can get on existing technology, including the work of small private inventors around the nation and material buried in our country's research labs."

Jessie heard the unmistakable high-pitched whine of computer machinery. She moved to the doorway and stood looking into the windowless room. Hatch came up behind her and studied the scene over the top of her head.

"Hell of an operation," he said, sounding impressed for the first time.

That was an understatement, Jessie decided. A row of computer terminals occupied one long table. Three intent young people, who all reminded her of Alex Robin, crouched in front of the screens. They were so entranced with what they were doing that they did not even glance toward the door.

Fax machines, printers, telephones, and computer modems were sprinkled around the room. The gray concrete walls were almost entirely covered in huge world maps. Charts and bound printouts lay everywhere. In addition to the three people at the computer consoles, there were two other people in the room. They were women who appeared to be about the same age as Susan Attwood. But neither of them looked like Jessie's client's daughter.

"You're welcome to go in and take a closer look," Sherry said encouragingly.

Hatch nodded brusquely and moved on into the room,

followed closely by Jessie. He came to a halt in front of one of the computer screens and studied the display. It showed several rows of numbers.

"What are we looking at?" Hatch asked the man hovering over the keyboard.

"Climate data on northern Europe that goes back two hundred years. I'm using it to run projections for the next fifty years." The young man did not look up. He pushed a button and the numbers on the screen flickered and altered as if by magic. "You can see the warming trend is accelerating rapidly."

Hatch nodded and moved on to the next screen, where the operator explained he was charting seismic activity.

"Dr. Bright believes there will be some major shifts in the tectonic plates due to the recent increased activity of some volcanoes," the man said. "Volcanoes affect the climate in some unusual ways."

Jessie stared at the screen and recalled something Elizabeth had mentioned recently. "What about the destruction of the rain forests?"

"A major problem. But Bright has done a lot of thinking in that area and has come up with some interesting solutions. His main work is in climatology. You know, the ozone layer, global warming tendencies, that kind of thing. In fact he phoned an hour ago and said to double-check some recent projections. He's got some new data that say there might be even less time than we think."

"I see." Jessie began to feel genuinely uneasy. It occurred to her that everything about the DEL operation looked extremely credible. "Where is Edwin Bright?"

"In Texas, I think," the young man said. "He's talking to a scientist there who's come up with a way to seed clouds with a chemical that can neutralize acid rain. Bright wants to help him rush through a patent."

"There is so little time left," Sherry whispered softly.

"Yeah." Hatch tossed his empty coffee cup into the nearest waste can, which was overflowing with discarded computer printouts. "Would someone mind pointing me toward the men's room?"

"Sure. There's one just down the hall." Sherry smiled at him. "I'll show you."

"Appreciate it." Hatch ignored Jessie's annoyed glance as he followed the young woman out the door.

Jessie watched him leave and then turned to Landis with what she hoped was an innocent, curious expression. "I'll have to admit I'm very impressed by all the computers and technology here, but I was under the impression Dr. Bright was more than just a brilliant scientist. The person who gave me the invitation implied he had certain . . ." She hesitated. ". . . certain *abilities.*"

Landis nodded, his eyes meditative. "You're referring to the rumor that Bright has psychic powers, aren't you?"

"Is that all it is? A rumor?"

Landis drew her out of the computer room and shut the door on the high-pitched hum. "I suppose it depends on how you look at it. Dr. Bright is a very brilliant man with an incredible ability to assimilate vast amounts of raw data and come up with forecasts and projections. His brain is virtually a computer. To some people that might make him look like he actually has psychic powers. But he does not encourage anyone to believe that."

"I guess I was misinformed." Jessie remembered that Mrs. Attwood had only assumed Bright was using claims of psychic abilities to influence people such as her daughter.

"And where do you draw the line between natural human ability and real psychic ability, anyway?" Landis asked in a reasonable tone. "Everyone accepts the idea of intuition, and a lot of people pride themselves on the accuracy of their hunches. But if someone has an extraordinary amount of intuitive ability, as Dr. Bright does, people tend to label it a psychic gift."

"Good point. I see what you mean." Jessie wondered if that was what Mrs. Valentine actually had, a keen intuitive ability and nothing more. "You appear to have quite a large staff."

"Only about fifteen people in all. They come to us because they're genuinely concerned with environmental issues and because they believe in our nation's proved ability to find technological solutions to problems. They stay with us because they believe Dr. Bright holds out the best hope for finding answers. We certainly hope you and Mr. Hatchard can see your way clear to assist our work with a donation."

Jessie started to respond to that but closed her mouth when she caught sight of Hatch returning from his foray to the men's room. Sherry Smith was walking down the hall beside him, her pretty face more intent than ever as she talked. Hatch was frowning thoughtfully as he listened. Jessie found herself strangely irritated by the air of intimacy surrounding the two. She turned back to Landis and smiled politely as she took refuge in a traditional wifely excuse.

"About your request for another donation. I always discuss major decisions like that with my husband, Mr. Landis."

"Of course, Mrs. Hatchard." Landis smiled his charming smile and motioned toward the staircase. "Shall we continue our tour?"

CHAPTER NINE

Jessie swirled the liqueur in the balloon glass and ducked her head to inhale the pleasant fragrance. She was feeling cozy and warm and replete. Outside the small restaurant a steady rain was falling. The meal she and Hatch had just concluded had been excellent. There was a fire burning in the hearth of the little dining room and the place was half-full of quietly talking people who were obviously enjoying themselves.

Jessie and Hatch had gone back to the inn after returning from the DEL tour, changed clothes, and walked to the restaurant. It had not been raining then, although the threat had been apparent. Hatch had said little during dinner. He appeared to be lost in thought.

For once Jessie had not felt like baiting him. She had been content, instead, to luxuriate in the unfamiliar sense of companionship. It was gratifying somehow to know they were both mulling over their shared adventure of the afternoon.

The trip had established a new bond between them, she thought. They had something in common now in addition to the undeniable physical attraction, something that had nothing to do with Benedict Fasteners. For the first time she had a glimmer of hope about the future of their relationship.

It was just barely possible that she and Hatch might be able to establish a meaningful communication, she told herself wistfully. The fact that Hatch was obviously concentrating on her investigation tonight was a good sign. He was clearly capable of taking a genuine interest in her work.

Maybe Hatch's devotion to his own career was not quite so single-minded as her father's after all. Maybe he just needed to be lured away from his desk from time to time. Maybe with a bit of coaxing he could learn to develop the playful side of his nature, learn to pause and relax, learn to stop and smell the roses.

Jessie risked a quick assessing glance at her dinner partner as he signed the bill and pocketed his credit card. He was, for Hatch, almost casually dressed this evening. In other words, that meant he was not wearing a business suit. He had on a richly textured charcoal-gray jacket over a white shirt and a pair of black trousers. Instead of his usual discreetly striped silk tie, he was wearing one with little dots all over it. The man had obviously thrown all caution to the winds when he had packed for this trip.

Hatch glanced up and saw her watching him. She smiled warmly and waited expectantly for him to comment on some conclusion he had arrived at concerning DEL, or at least to note what a pleasant evening this had been.

"Damn," Hatch said, frowning slightly, "I wonder if Gresham got his status report in to Vincent this afternoon. If he didn't, I'll hand him his head on a platter when I get back. I've had it with that guy. We're on a critical path with that Portland project. Nobody involved in it can miss even one more deadline."

"Gosh, Hatch, that's about the most romantic thing anyone has ever said to me after a cozy little dinner for two in front of the fire. I could just swoon."

He gave her a blank look for about one and a half seconds.

Then her comment appeared to register. He got to his feet. "If you're not feeling well, we'd better get back to the inn."

"Don't worry. I feel just fine." She wrinkled her nose at him but said nothing more as he steered her toward the door. So much for the assumption that he had been dwelling on her project or her presence. His mind had been on Benedict Fasteners after all.

A few minutes later they stepped out into the misty rain and walked in silence back toward the little waterfront inn where they were staying. Hatch held the black umbrella over both of them and Jessie stayed close to his side.

The street through the center of the small island village was nearly deserted. A single streetlight marked the intersection with the road that led down to the harbor, but other than that there was little illumination. Jessie linked her arm through Hatch's, enjoying the size and strength of him there in the wet darkness. She thought of the bed waiting for them at the inn. Perhaps there was no long-term future for them, but there was the affair.

"Hatch?"

"Yes?"

"Would you mind if I asked you a rather personal question?"

"Depends on the question."

Jessie drew a steadying breath. "Do I look like her?"

"Like who?"

"Your wife?"

The muscles of his arm tightened beneath her fingers. "Hell, no."

"You're sure?"

"Of course I'm sure. What a damn-fool thing to ask. What brought this on? Who told you I'd been married in the first place? Your father?"

"No. I'm sorry, Hatch. I shouldn't have said anything."

"Well, now you've said something, you might as well finish it."

Jessie studied the wet pavement ahead. "I was talking to

my mother. She mentioned that you had been married and that you had lost your wife. That led sort of naturally into a discussion of how men tend to look for the same things in a second wife that they looked for in a first wife. Which led to the observation that she and Connie are very much alike. Mom says men are creatures of habit. Especially when it comes to women. They're attracted to the same types, if you see what I mean, and—"

"I think that's enough, Jessie."

She closed her mouth abruptly, aware that she had begun to ramble. "Sorry."

"You're not anything like her."

"Oh." Jessie experienced a strong sense of relief.

"She had blond hair and blue eyes."

"I see. Pretty, I imagine."

Hatch hesitated. "Yes. Well, in a different way than you are." He was silent for another beat. "She was taller than you."

"Ah."

Hatch shrugged. "That's about it," he said gruffly. "What else did you want to know?"

"Nothing."

"Good." He sounded relieved.

"What was she like?"

"What the hell does that mean?"

"Was she nice?"

"Dammit, Jessie."

"Did you love her very much?" She knew she should quit while she was ahead, but for some reason she could not seem to stop herself. The questions bubbled to the surface, demanding answers.

Hatch came to a halt and pulled Jessie around to face him. In the rain-streaked light that was coming through a nearby cottage window she could see that his face was harder-edged and bleaker than usual. Jessie wished she had kept her mouth shut.

"Jessie . . ."

"I'm sorry, Hatch," she whispered. "Let's just forget it, shall we? It's none of my business. I know that."

He shook his head slowly. "I know you better than that, Jessie. You won't be able to forget it now that you've started thinking about it. You're going to chew on it and fret about it and spin all kinds of questions about it."

She closed her eyes, knowing he was right. "I won't say another word about her. I promise."

"Sure. And if I believe that, you've got a bridge you can sell me, right?" He sighed. "I thought I loved her when I married her. She was everything I needed and wanted in a wife. And she was just as ambitious for me as I was. She was beautiful and understanding and supportive. She was born into the world I was moving into and she knew how to function in that environment. I was on my way up and she was going with me, the perfect corporate wife."

"Hatch, please, don't."

"She worked as hard to help me build my career as I did. She entertained my business associates on short notice. She saw to it we joined the right country club. She never complained when I was called out of town on a business trip. She understood about the demands of my job. She never made a fuss when I was late for dinner or too tired to make love to her."

"Hatch, I really don't want to talk about this any more."

"Neither do I. But you brought it up, so I'll finish it. To make a long story short, we were very happy together for about four years. I had a good position in a fast-moving company. Our future was all mapped out. I thought it was time to talk about having kids. She thought we should wait a little longer. Then a couple of things happened at once."

"What things?"

"The company I was working for was the object of a hostile takeover. When the bloodletting was over, I was out of a job along with most of management. Not unusual in a takeover situation. Olivia took the news badly, though. We were almost back to square one as far as she was concerned."

"And she had a hard time dealing with that?"

"Let's just say she was not particularly interested in starting over from scratch, and I couldn't blame her. I wasn't real thrilled with the idea, myself, but I had confidence that I could do it. I believed in myself, but she didn't. We quarreled a lot. She blamed me for the mess. And then she died in a car accident."

Jessie could feel tears burning in her eyes. "Hatch, I'm so sorry."

"It was rough. I was pretty well out of it for a while after the funeral. Which probably explains why it took me so long to find the note she had left before she got into the car for the last time."

Jessie's insides clenched as she suddenly realized where all this might be leading. "What was in the note?"

"She told me she couldn't tie herself to a loser. She had her future to consider and she was filing for divorce. She planned to marry a friend of mine. Someone I had worked with at the company, someone I had trusted. He had landed on his feet after the takeover. Gone to work as a vice-president for the new owner."

"Oh, Hatch."

"Apparently he and Olivia had been having an affair for six months prior to the accident. The day she was killed, she was leaving to meet him. Olivia said in her note she hoped I understood."

"My God." Jessie had not felt this thoroughly miserable for a long time. "I'm sorry," she said again, unable to think of anything else. "I'm so sorry, Hatch."

"I figured out a lot of things after I read that damned note. I understood at last why she had been so reluctant to talk about babies. She hadn't wanted to get pregnant until she had decided whether or not she would be leaving me."

Jessie could feel his fingers biting into her arms through

the fabric of her jacket. She lifted her hand and touched his cheek. "Please, Hatch. Don't say anything more about it. I should never have asked about her."

His mouth tightened. "You're getting wet. It's damn stupid for us to be standing around out here in the rain."

"Yes."

He took her arm again and started walking. "Anything else you want to know about me? I'd rather get the question-and-answer phase over as fast as possible."

She had a thousand questions but she could not bring herself to ask a single one of them at that moment. "I guess I'm not very good at this sort of thing."

"You might not be good." His mouth quirked wryly. "But something tells me you'll be persistent. Are you sure you don't have any more questions?"

"I'm sure." She reached up to pull the lapels of her jacket closed. "Feels like it's getting colder, doesn't it?"

"Not particularly. You're probably just getting wetter."

"No, it's more than that. It is colder. Or something." A small ripple of awareness went down her spine. Instinctively she glanced behind her. There was nothing to see but the dark, rain-washed street. A car's headlights briefly speared the night behind them and then vanished.

"Something wrong, Jessie?"

"No. For a minute I thought there was someone else around."

Hatch glanced back. "I don't see anyone. Even if there were, it wouldn't be anything to worry about. This isn't exactly downtown Seattle."

"True." She shook off her uneasiness. "What did you think about our tour this afternoon? You haven't even mentioned it since we got back."

"I don't know what to think yet. I want to take a closer look at something I picked up at the mansion first," Hatch said. "Maybe have someone else look at it too."

Jessie glanced up quizzically. "What on earth did you pick up? I didn't see you carrying anything."

"I'll show you when we get back to the room."

"Do you think there's any chance DEL is for real?"

"No," Hatch said flatly. "It's a scam, pure and simple. What we saw today was a first-class boiler-room operation. One constructed with lots of fancy window dressing to impress the suckers."

"I was afraid of that. You know, in a way, I was almost hoping it was for real."

"Jessie, there are no easy fixes for the environmental problems we're facing. Just ask Elizabeth or David."

"I know. Just wishful thinking. You have to admit that all those computer screens full of climate projections and stuff looked awfully convincing. I talked to Landis when you went to the men's room."

"I'll bet he hinted he'd like a sizable donation."

"Well, yes. But more important, I tried to get him to tell me whether or not Bright claims psychic powers. He said some people could interpret the man's combination of intelligence and intuition that way, but he made it clear Bright makes no overt claims to having psychic abilities."

"Smart. Let the sucker think what he wants to think, and play to it. I'm not so sure he'd need to claim psychic gifts anyway. Not to attract the kind of young, hopeful people we saw working at the mansion. They're more than willing to be seduced by the quick-fix promises we heard on that video. And the promise of cashing in on the profits that will be made from all the magic machines supposedly being invented."

"Yes. Bright's pitch is terrific, isn't it? Save the world and make a fortune at the same time. Who could resist?"

"There's a sucker born every minute, Jessie. Just keep in mind how hard it was for you to say no to your stockbroker friend."

"Let's leave Alison out of this. Just how dedicated do you think that staff of Bright's is?"

"Some of them are certainly dedicated enough to offer to

sleep with the prospective sucker in exchange for a sizable donation," Hatch said.

"What? She didn't." Jessie was incensed. "Did she?"

"Ummm."

"What kind of an answer is that? Did that little Sherry Smith try to seduce you or not? Just what were you doing down there in the men's room, anyhow?" Jessie started to demand further explanations, but the odd rippling sensation shot through her nerve endings again. She glanced over her shoulder.

"What's wrong now?" Hatch asked.

"I know this is going to sound crazy, but I don't think we're alone out here."

"We're almost at the inn," he said soothingly. "Just another block."

"Have you ever had the feeling someone was following you?" She quickened her steps, straining to see the lights of the inn through the rain.

"I'm a businessman, remember? Every time I look over my shoulder, someone's gaining on me. Goes with the territory."

"I'm not joking, Hatch. This is making me very nervous. There's somebody back there. I know it."

"Probably a local resident on his way home from the same restaurant."

Hatch sounded as calm as ever, but Jessie felt the new alertness in him. He obligingly quickened his step to match hers.

A moment later they were safely back in the warm, inviting lobby of the small bed-and-breakfast inn where they had booked a room. Two guests who were playing checkers in front of the fire looked up and nodded as Jessie and Hatch went past on their way to the stairs.

Jessie was relieved when she stepped into the bedroom and watched Hatch close and lock the door. She shook the rain off her jacket and hung it up in the tiny closet. "I think that visit to DEL must have made me more nervous than

I realized. Better show me what you picked up on the tour."

"I've got it right here." Hatch pulled a piece of paper out of his inside pocket.

Jessie took it from him as he hung up his jacket and took off his tie. She unfolded it carefully and found herself staring down at one page of a large-size computer printout. It was covered with numbers. "Where did you get this?"

"From the trashcan in the men's room. One of the things about computers is that they tend to produce a hell of a lot of paper. It's tough to control the garbage, even under the tightest security conditions. Someone's always accidentally tossing a few pages into the nearest trashcan." Hatch sat down in the one chair in the room and stretched out his legs.

Jessie sank down onto the bed, stunned. "You went through the trash in the men's room? That's why you asked directions to it? Good grief, Hatch. Whatever made you decide to do that?"

"I wanted a sample of whatever those computer operators were printing out. I was curious to see if it was the same kind of data we were being shown on the screens."

"Is it?" Jessie studied the array of numbers on the printout.

"No. What you're looking at there looks very much like a financial spread sheet, not climate forecasts."

"A spread sheet." Jessie glanced up again. "That would fit with a real scam, wouldn't it?"

"It would fit with a lot of scenarios. That page of data doesn't prove anything, one way or the other. A legitimate foundation would have to track its financial picture just like any other corporation. We need more information before we can get a handle on what's going on at DEL headquarters."

"How do we get more details?"

Hatch contemplated her for a long moment. "For starters, I suggest we have someone who knows computers and computer programs take a look at what's on that piece of paper."

"Why? What will it tell someone else that it won't tell you?"

Hatch appeared to hesitate again before making up his mind to explain further. "If someone who was very good with computers took a look at that page of printout, he might, just might, mind you, be able to use some of the information on it to do a little discreet hacking."

Jessie stared at him uncomprehendingly for a moment, and then realization struck. "Of course. Hatch, that's a wonderful idea. Absolutely brilliant. If we got a hacker to break into the DEL computers, we could see what they're really doing. We could at least find out if their scientific research is for real or just a cover, couldn't we?"

"Possibly. If we got lucky. And if we knew someone we could trust to do the hacking for us."

"But that's just it. We do know someone. Alex Robin would be perfect. He's desperate for work. And he'd be terribly discreet."

Hatch shook his head over her sudden enthusiasm and regarded her with a brooding expression. "Jessie, this is tricky territory. You know that as well as I do."

"If DEL is on the up-and-up, we'll back off immediately. I'll tell Mrs. Attwood that the foundation is legitimate and suggest she try some other approach to getting Susan back. But if DEL is running a scam and we can prove it, then she'll have the kind of information she needs to do something. She can go to the police or the papers and have Bright exposed, just as she wants to do."

"It's a job for a genuine private investigator or an investigative reporter, not an assistant fortune-teller."

"Now, don't be so negative, Hatch. We're not ready to turn this over to someone else yet." Jessie carefully refolded the piece of computer paper and leaned over to drop it into her purse. "We'll try to get more information first. When we have proof, we'll let Mrs. Attwood decide how she wants to handle things. Hatch, I really appreciate this. More than I can say."

"Yeah?"

She nodded seriously. "Definitely. I'll admit I had a few doubts about bringing you along on this trip, but you've certainly proved your usefulness."

"I can't tell you what that means to me."

Jessie scowled at him, wondering, as she frequently did, if he was making a wry joke. She decided once again that he was dead serious. "I couldn't have gotten this far without you, and I truly am grateful. You've given us the first strong lead we've had since I tracked down the invitation that got us into DEL."

"That's something else I've been meaning to talk to you about."

"The invitation? What about it."

Hatch gave her a level look. "Does it strike you that we got hold of that invitation very easily? Maybe too easily?"

"It wasn't easy. I had to work at it. And David helped. It was just my good luck that he attends Butterfield College and was able to find Nadine Willard."

"Jessie, we tough, cynical business types don't like to trust in things like good luck. I'm wondering why DEL went to the effort of laying on that little show for us today with almost no questions asked."

"I don't see what was so strange about it. After all, they're in the business of drumming up big donations."

"Why didn't they arrange to have a whole bunch of potential suckers make the trip at the same time? Why go out of their way to accommodate our schedule? Sending that plane over here to pick us up wasn't cheap."

Jessie paused, struck by those observations. "I see what you mean. You think maybe they're suspicious of us?"

"I don't know what to think yet. But I do know I don't like it. Not one damn bit of it."

"This is getting a tad complicated, isn't it?" Jessie mused.

"A tad."

"But it's kind of exciting in a way too. This is a heck of a lot more interesting than my last job."

"What was your last . . . ? Uh, right. You were working for Benedict Fasteners, weren't you?"

"Don't look so glum, Hatch. Things could be worse. If circumstances had been slightly different, I'd still be working for you."

"I know I should look on the bright side, but somehow it's hard to do that at the moment."

Jessie eyed him cautiously. "Was that supposed to be humorous by any chance?"

"You think I lack a sense of humor, among other funloving attributes, don't you?"

"Let's just say the subject is open to question."

"Would it make things simpler if I told you I am extremely serious about taking you to bed tonight?"

Jessie jumped to her feet and in the process accidentally knocked over a small candy dish that was sitting on the table beside the bed. It fell to the floor with a crash.

"Oh, hell," she muttered, bending down to pick it up. At least it hadn't broken. She knew she should be grateful for small favors. Setting the heavy glass dish back down on the table, she stalked to the window.

"Why do I make you nervous, Jessie?"

"I don't know." She took a handful of the curtain and crushed it between her fingers as she studied the rainy darkness outside the window. "Why are you so sure you and I could have some kind of genuinely meaningful long-term committed relationship?"

"I never thought about having a genuinely meaningful long-term committed relationship. I was thinking more along the lines of a marriage."

"See? That's exactly what I mean when I say I can never tell if you're making a joke or if you're serious. It's very disconcerting. Why don't you just answer my question? What makes you think you and I could make a go of it?"

Hatch appeared to turn that question over in his mind for a long moment before he said, "Things feel right with you."

"Right? What do you mean, 'right'?"

He shrugged. "I think it would work out. The two of us, I mean."

She crushed the curtain more tightly in her clenched fist. "But what do you want from a . . . a relationship, Hatch?" She simply could not bring herself to say the word "marriage."

"The usual things. A loyal wife. Kids. I'm thirty-seven years old, Jessie. I want to have children. Put down some roots. I grew up on a ranch, remember? Part of me still wants to feel like I belong to a place. I know I won't have that feeling until I've established a home and family of my own. It's time."

"You sound as if you're listening to some sort of biological clock."

His mouth curved briefly. "Did you think only women had internal clocks?"

"I guess I hadn't thought much about biological clocks at all. Even my own." She sighed. "I would definitely not make you a good, supportive, corporate president's wife. You know that, don't you? I would nag you if you didn't come home on time in the evenings. I would yell at you if you took too many business trips. I would show up at the office and cause a scene if you canceled an outing with one of the children because of a business appointment."

"I know."

She spun around. "Then why in heaven's name do you want to marry me? Are you that eager to get your hands on Benedict Fasteners?"

"No."

"Then give me one good reason," she challenged, feeling oddly desperate. "Why me instead of someone else? Someone who wouldn't give you a hard time about your work?"

Hatch got slowly, deliberately to his feet, his eyes never leaving hers. He moved toward her until he was standing directly in front of her. Then he caught her face between rough palms and brushed his mouth lightly, possessively across hers. "Because I know I can trust you."

Her eyes widened. "Trust me?"

"You might yell at me, nag me, annoy me, infuriate me. But I am almost certain you would never lie to me. And I know I'll have your loyalty because I'll always be tied to Benedict Fasteners and therefore to your family. I'm going to make myself a part of your world, Jessie. You're very loyal to the people in your world, aren't you?"

She stared up at him. "Is loyalty so important to you?"

"I do not think you would have an affair with my best friend. I do not think you would run off with him and leave me a goddamned note telling me you hoped I understood. If you are angry or hurt or feeling neglected, I think you'll complain directly to management, not go behind my back and cry on some other man's shoulder."

"Complain to management." Her lip quivered. "Oh, Hatch. What am I going to do with you?"

"Right now all you have to do is go to bed with me."

She inhaled sharply and gave a tiny little whimper of desire as he cupped her breasts. Her arms stole softly around his waist and she leaned her head against his shoulder.

"I've decided we might as well try having an affair," she mumbled into his shirt.

He almost laughed out loud at that ridiculous statement. But he managed to control his initial reaction and merely smiled into her hair as he unfastened her skirt. "Do you think we can handle an affair?"

"Well, we're two healthy single people who happen to be very strongly attracted to each other. Neither one of us is the type to get involved in one-night stands." She lifted her head and frowned up at him in the darkness. "Are we?"

"No. I've never been particularly interested in one-night stands," he assured her. "The risk/reward ratio is badly skewed. Frankly, I've never considered them cost-effective."

He heard her swallow a choked little laugh, and her arms tightened around his waist. "Hatch, you are impossible."

"You, on the other hand, are very, very lovely," he breathed as her skirt fell to the floor.

He moved his hands over her, enthralled by the gentle contour of her back and the flare of her hips. He slipped his fingers inside her panties and eased them down until they followed the skirt to her ankles. Then, with a sigh of sheer masculine pleasure he cupped her buttocks and squeezed carefully. She shivered.

The small shudder of unmistakable desire that rippled through her was intoxicating. Hatch did not wait any longer. He leaned over and pulled down the covers of the bed. Then he picked her up in his arms and put her on the sheets.

He undressed impatiently, unable to take his eyes off her as she lay waiting for him. He was fascinated with the dark outline of her nipples, the tiny hollow in her gently curved belly, and the triangular thicket of hair that concealed her deepest feminine secrets.

He was already fully aroused by the time he got out of the

CHAPTER TEN

Hatch watched the sweet, wistful longing in Jessie's eyes as he reached out and turned off the light. She wanted him. But then, he had understood that almost from the start. It was the primary reason he had been willing to be patient in his pursuit. A man could afford patience when he knew the end was not in doubt. He would not rush her into marriage.

But after having had a taste of her in bed, he could no longer resign himself to patience in that department. A man had his limits.

Hatch curved his hands around her shoulders, enjoying the delicate, womanly feel of her. She did not pull away. His eyes met hers in the shadows and, as always, he was drawn into the depths of that wide, luminous gaze. He let his hands slide down to the row of buttons below the collar of her silk shirt.

The shirt parted easily as he slowly worked his way down to the waistband of the long, flared skirt. Hatch took a deep breath as he slid his fingers inside the opening and found the warm, scented softness of her skin. His thumb touched the front clasp of her lacy little bra and he unclipped it.

last of his clothes. His body felt taut and strong and powerful. Jessie did this to him, he thought in awe. She made him feel this way. He could not wait to bury himself in her tight, humid sheath.

"I promised myself that this time we'd take it slow." He came down onto the bed beside her and drew her toward him.

"Did you?" Her eyes were shimmering with wonder and sensual excitement. She stroked his arm and touched his hip lightly, fleetingly. Her legs shifted restlessly on the sheet.

"I let you push me too fast last time." He bent his head to kiss the soft, vulnerable hollow of her throat.

Her eyes widened in instant outrage. "Now, just a minute here. I did not push you into making love to me in Mrs. V's office. How dare you blame me for that? You were the one who pushed me into doing it right there on her sofa, of all places."

He slowly combed his fingers through the crisp hair between her legs, aware of the welcoming scent of her. "You might as well face it, sweetheart. You have the power to push me over the edge."

"Hah. I don't believe that for a minute."

"I didn't either. Until I found myself taking you right there on Mrs. Valentine's office sofa." He kissed one tight, firm nipple. "That kind of power is a dangerous thing, Jessie. Be careful how you use it. Who knows where we'll be the next time you push me too far?"

She shivered again as he forced his knee gently between her legs, opening her to his touch. He sucked in his breath, clamping down what was left of his self-control when he realized she was already wet. "Jessie, honey. Jessie, touch me."

She kissed his chest as her fingers floated lightly down to curve around his throbbing shaft. Hatch thought he would explode then and there.

"So much for taking it slow this time," he muttered. He

rolled onto his back and pulled her down on top of him. She knelt astride his hips, her lips parted in sensual wonder. She cradled him in both hands, openly marveling.

"What's so funny?" she demanded in a husky voice as she glanced up suddenly.

Hatch realized he was grinning widely. "Something about the way you're looking at me." It occurred to him that he had never seen such a look of discovery and delight on a woman's face. He had never been wanted in quite this way. It was wildly exhilarating. Pleasure and a very primitive satisfaction rushed through him like a shot of adrenaline.

"Hatch," she whispered, "I truly do not understand any of this."

"Don't worry. You're doing just fine." He tested himself against her, letting her feel the extent of his arousal.

"I don't mean this." She stroked him lightly and smiled in delight when Hatch caught his breath in an undeniable, starkly passionate response. "I mean, why is it you who can do this to me? I know this sounds trite, but the truth is, you really aren't my type at all."

"Why don't you stop trying to analyze it and just put me inside you where we both can feel it?" He reached down between her legs and drew his finger through the slick, wet moisture there. Then he guided himself inside her. He heard her take a deep breath as he pushed himself carefully into the snug passage.

When he was partway inside he clamped his hands around her waist and lowered her slowly down over the full length of him.

"Hatch."

"You fit me so perfectly. So damn good." He could feel her clinging to him, sucking him deeper, holding him prisoner there inside her. Again he had to will himself not to give into the temptation of an early release. It was all he could do to wait while he used his fingers to bring her to her own peak.

She began to move on him, cautiously at first. He watched

her expression through narrowed eyes, enthralled by her responsiveness. He was right. No woman had ever responded to him with such complete and such sensual abandon. She made him feel powerful; the most powerful man on the face of the earth.

He had never reacted to a woman's touch with such violent need.

He let her set the pace as long as possible. But when he felt her start to tighten around him, he lost what was left of his willpower. He had to end this sweet torture or go out of his mind.

Deliberately he tried to insert his finger into her alongside his engorged manhood. There was no room. He had known there would not be, of course. She was already stretched too far, filled too completely with him. But when he added the extra bit of pressure there at the sensitive entrance, she gasped. Her eyes widened briefly and then she shuddered and went over the edge.

"Hatch. Oh, my God, *Hatch.*"

He locked his arms around her, swallowing her soft, keening little scream of ecstasy as he thrust himself once more straight to the core of her. "Yes, Jessie. Hold me. *Hold me.*"

In that moment he could not have said exactly what it was he wanted from her, but he knew he needed it more than he had ever needed anything in his life. When she collapsed in a soft little heap on top of him he thought he had it.

For a while, at least.

Hatch did not know how long he had been asleep. But he awakened because some sixth sense alerted him to the fact that Jessie had left the bed. He turned over and opened his eyes.

"Jessie?"

She was standing at the window, still nude. He could just barely make out the shape of her gently curving breasts in the pale, watery moonlight. As he watched, she put her face

173

closer to the glass, and he realized she was staring down into the parking lot of the inn.

"Hatch, there's somebody out there."

He yawned. "Probably some guest getting back late from dinner. Come back to bed, honey."

"No, I think he's trying to break into your car."

"The hell he is." Hatch shoved back the covers and came off the bed in one swift movement. A split second later he was at the window, following Jessie's gaze. She was right. A lone figure was hovering near the passenger door of the Mercedes. There was just enough light coming from the weak yellow porch lamp to reveal an object in the man's hand. Even as they watched, the figure raised his arm.

"He's going to smash the window," Jessie said in horror.

"Sonofabitch." Hatch unlatched the bedroom window. He vaulted up onto the sill and stepped out on the ledge.

"No, wait, what are you doing? Hatch, come back here. You're in your shorts, for heaven's sake. Wait until I call the police. For goodness' sake, *Hatch.*"

Hatch swore softly as he saw the figure near the car look up at the sound of Jessie's voice. The man was wearing a stocking mask. "Dammit, Jessie, he heard you. He'll get away."

Hatch stepped down onto the porch roof and in two strides reached the edge. Crouching low, he took a firm grip, swung himself over the side, and lowered himself down onto the porch railing. His bare feet touched the wooden surface and he was grateful there were no splinters.

But he was too late. Light, rapid footsteps sounded on the pavement of the small parking lot. Hatch knew he had lost his quarry even as he leapt from the railing onto the ground. He winced as he felt a pebble dig into his sole. He caught a glimpse of the black-clad figure disappearing around the corner of the inn.

"Shit."

Hatch started after the dark figure but gave up when he realized he was running on sharp gravel. Pursuit was useless.

His bare feet would be torn to shreds. His only chance of getting his hands on the jerk had been the element of surprise, which Jessie had ruined.

Hatch swore again as he limped back to examine the Mercedes. He surveyed the windows anxiously and ran a questing hand along the pristine silver-gray fender. He relaxed a little when he realized that no damage had been done.

The dealer had told him the new state-of-the-art alarm system Hatch had ordered would be available for installation at the end of the month. Hatch decided he'd call when he got back to Seattle and see if he could speed up the delivery date. No place was crime-free these days. It was a damned disgrace when a man could not even park his car out in the open on a quiet little island.

"Hatch. *Hatch.* For heaven's sake, Hatch."

He glanced up to see Jessie leaning out the window. She was clutching his trousers. He opened his mouth to chew her out for having caused the commotion that enabled the man to get away. Then he promptly closed it again as it occurred to him that he was standing around in his briefs in a public parking lot.

"Shit." Hatch grimly held up one hand. Jessie bundled up the trousers and pitched them down to him.

Hatch was adjusting his zipper when a light went on in the room next to the one he and Jessie were using. A plump bald man wearing a T-shirt stuck his head out and glowered down at Hatch.

"What the hell's going on down there? We're trying to sleep up here. You want to get drunk and cause trouble, go somewhere else, you bum."

"I'll do that," Hatch said.

He went up the porch steps, found the front-door key in the pocket of his trousers, and let himself into the darkened lobby.

Jessie was waiting anxiously inside the room. She had put on her robe but her hair was still pleasantly tousled from sleep. Her obvious concern for him was gratifying. Almost gratifying enough to make him forget that she had been the reason the would-be vandal had gotten away.

"Are you all right?" She fussed around him as he lowered himself into the chair.

"Hell, yes."

She frowned as she sank down onto the bed across from him. "Is something wrong?"

"Dammit, Jessie, I nearly had him. If you hadn't started yelling about calling the cops, I would have had him."

"Hatch, it's only a car."

"Only a car? *Only a car?* Do you know what that model costs? Do you know how long I waited for it to be delivered? Maybe you come from the kind of background where beautiful things like that get taken for granted, but I don't."

"Hatch, calm down. Believe me, I appreciate the value of your car. But I value you more than I do your Mercedes. Be reasonable. In this day and age you can't just go around confronting criminals. It's very dangerous. He might have had a gun." She paused. "Or a knife. Like last time."

Hatch went very still. "What are you talking about?"

She hesitated. "I'm not sure if I should say this or not because it will only upset you and if you get too upset, you're liable to start lecturing me again and I don't want you ruining everything, if you see what I mean."

Hatch came up out of the chair, took one step over to the bed, reached down, and hauled her to her feet. "What the hell are you talking about?"

She touched the tip of her tongue to the corner of her mouth. "Well . . ."

"Dammit, Jessie."

"Okay, okay, I'll tell you, but you mustn't get too concerned, because I'm probably wrong."

"Wrong about what?" He tightened his grip on her shoulders.

"About the fact that the guy you just chased off in the parking lot reminded me a bit of the one who broke into

Mrs. V's offices and tried to steal Alex's computer equipment."

Hatch felt himself go cold. "Christ. Are you sure?"

She shook her head quickly. "No, how could I be certain? The man was wearing a stocking mask each time, remember? But there was something about his build. Slight. Wiry. I don't know, Hatch. It was just a feeling. Sort of like the one that made me get out of bed and look out the window in the first place."

"That settles it." Hatch released her and went across the room to check the lock on the door.

"Settles what?"

"You're through playing big-time psychic investigator. This case of yours is developing too many angles and I don't like any of them. I'm declaring it closed, as of now."

Her mouth dropped open in shock. And then outrage kindled in her eyes. "You can't do that. This is my case. I've got a client. And I've got all sorts of new leads to follow. I'm not about to stop my investigation on your orders."

"Look, Jessie, this is no longer a game, understand? I was willing to indulge you for a while because it all seemed relatively safe."

"Indulge me? Is that how you saw it?" She stared at him in gathering fury. "Thanks a lot, Sam Hatchard. I had a hunch that was your attitude but I was willing to give you the benefit of the doubt after you found that computer-printout page for me. You had me almost convinced you were taking my new job seriously, that you were actually interested in my project."

"I am taking it seriously. That's why I'm calling a halt to it."

"You can't stop me from continuing this investigation."

He exhaled heavily and absently rubbed the back of his neck while he tried to think of a better way to deal with her anger. "Be reasonable, Jessie. You know for certain now that you're not dealing with a fake psychic. Edwin Bright is most likely running some kind of scam, from the looks of things.

But he's not seducing his followers by pretending he has psychic abilities. Report that to Mrs. Attwood and you'll have done your job. She needs a real private investigator if she wants to carry this any further."

"At dinner you implied you were willing to help me finish this investigation," Jessie reminded him through clenched teeth.

"Yeah, well, that was when I thought we could play with it a bit longer and keep you happy. But the possibility that some guy is following you around means the fun and games are over."

"Dammit, Hatch, we don't know it was the same man. In all likelihood it wasn't. I knew I shouldn't have said anything."

"Well, you did, so that's that."

"I will not tolerate this condescending attitude toward my new career."

That remark inflamed him further. "I'm not being condescending, I'm being careful. Someone's got to exercise a little common sense around here, and it sure doesn't look like you're going to be the one to do it, does it?"

"If that's the way you're going to be, you're off the case."

He lifted his eyes briefly toward the ceiling in silent supplication. "Case? What case? This isn't a *case*, it's another calculated effort by you to drive some poor innocent employer crazy. Mrs. Valentine has my sincerest sympathy. I know just how she's going to feel when she finds out what's happening."

"Is that right?"

"Damn right. She's going to realize she's got a loose cannon on board, just like every other one of your past employers has eventually been forced to realize. Come to think of it, this proves she's a fraud herself. If she had any real psychic powers she would have known better than to hire you in the first place."

"A loose cannon."

Hatch knew he'd gone too far. She was furious. "Dammit, Jessie, I never meant to say that. I'm sorry. Look, I'm just trying to make a point here."

A violent pounding on the wall that adjoined their room silenced Hatch immediately. He felt himself turning a dull red as the voice of the plump bald man next door boomed through the barrier.

"If you two don't shut the fuck up in there, I'm calling the manager, goddammit. You hear me?"

Jessie glared at Hatch in satisfaction. "Yes, Hatch, why don't you shut up? You're disturbing the neighbors. You're going to get us kicked out of here."

"I don't believe this." He raked a hand through his hair, stunned at his own loss of control. Then he surged to his feet and started to pace the small room. "I am in a hotel room at one o'clock in the morning engaging in a domestic quarrel with a woman who thinks she's some kind of psychic private investigator. I ought to have my head examined."

"I'm sure Aunt Glenna would be glad to do it for you at the usual family discount."

He swung around, his voice very soft as he leveled a finger at her. "I don't want to hear another word about your damned case until morning. Got that?"

Her chin came up and her eyes glittered in anticipation of the next act of rebellion.

"Jessie, I swear if you give me any more grief tonight, I won't give a damn about disturbing the neighbors," he said very quietly.

"Is that a threat?"

"It's a promise. Close your mouth and get back into bed."

"Or else what?" She looked at him expectantly.

"Christ, lady, you don't know when to quit, do you? *Or else* I will put you in that bed myself. And I won't care if you scream the place down while I do it. That should have the idiot next door calling the manager in no time. I'll let you do all the explaining as they kick us out of here."

She flushed. "Honestly, Hatch."

"Yes, honestly, Jessie. *Get back into bed.*"

She got back into bed without a word.

Hatch took off his trousers and got in beside her, not touching her. He was aware of how stiffly she was lying next to him and decided she was probably staring at the ceiling, just as he was. Moments crept past.

"Hatch?"

"Yeah?"

"It would never have worked anyway." She sounded oddly sad rather than angry.

"Your job as a psychic detective? I could have told you that."

"No. I meant us. You and me. A long-term, committed relationship. It would never have worked. You can see that for yourself now, can't you? We'd be at each other's throats all the time."

"It'll work," he muttered, still too angry and frustrated at her obstinacy to risk letting himself get dragged into a detailed discussion of just how it was going to work. In his present precarious mood he was likely to say a lot of things that would only add fuel to the fire. He had his self-control back and he intended to keep it.

"But, Hatch—"

"Go to sleep, Jessie."

She sighed wistfully, turned her back to him, and curled up in a pathetic little ball. A few minutes later Hatch was sure he heard a suspicious sniff. He did not say anything. When he heard another, similar sound he rolled onto his side so that he was facing her back. Then he reached out and pulled her tightly against him, snuggling her into his warmth.

She resisted silently at first and then acquiesced without a murmur. A few minutes later he was sure she was asleep.

Hatch lay awake for a long while, contemplating the fact that he had never allowed a woman to undermine his self-control the way Jessie had. One minute he was making love to her, the next he was involved in an argument that was loud enough to wake the neighbors. That kind of scene would never have happened with Olivia.

Hatch grinned briefly in the darkness and pulled Jessie closer.

The full ramifications of the argument that had taken place in the middle of the night did not sink in until Jessie emerged from the tiny bath the next morning. She came to a halt in the middle of the room, staring at Hatch; who was buckling his belt.

"Oh, my God. This is a bed-and-breakfast place." It was the first time she had spoken to him since she had awakened.

He quirked one brow as he checked for his wallet. "So what?"

She glowered at him. "So we can't possibly go downstairs to breakfast."

"We paid for it. Might as well eat it."

"Hatch, we *can't.* That man from next door and his wife will be in the dining room. And who knows about the people from the room on the other side of us or across the hall? I couldn't possibly face them. Not after that scene we conducted last night."

"We?"

"You were as involved in it as I was. Don't you dare try to wriggle out of this. Hatch, I wouldn't be able to eat a bite, knowing they all heard us last night."

He studied her in silence for a long moment, giving no indication whatsoever about what he was thinking. Then he astonished her with the briefest of rueful grins. "You and me both, babe. Let's get the hell out of here before we run into the neighbors."

Their mutual interest in conducting a hasty exit from the scene of the debacle succeeded in reestablishing communications between them. Jessie realized they were both wary of starting another argument, however, and they did not say a whole lot to each other on the drive back to Seattle. The silence was cautious but not hostile.

Jessie did make one or two efforts to introduce the subject of the investigation of Dawn's Early Light, but did not pursue them when she ran up against a stony response.

It was not until he had carried her overnight case to her front door and seen her safely inside that Hatch finally brought up the topic himself.

"Jessie, I meant it last night when I told you I want you to forget this stupid investigation. Tell Mrs. Attwood you've done all you can. Let her go another route."

He did not wait for her to restart the argument. He simply turned and went back out the door after putting down her bag.

"Hatch, I told you . . ." She broke off to hurry after him as he headed for the stairs. "Wait. Where are you going?"

"To the office. It's only the middle of the afternoon. I've got work to do."

"I should have known," she muttered. She folded her arms under her breasts and leaned against the door frame.

Hatch glanced back once. "See you for dinner. I'll probably be a little late."

"Hold it. I am not altering my life-style to suit your schedule, Mr. Hatchard."

"I recently altered mine to suit yours."

He was gone before she could think of a response. With a muffled groan of disgust Jessie unfolded her arms, closed the door, and stalked over to the phone. She had a duty to call Susan Attwood's mother.

The phone was answered midway through the first ring. Mrs. Attwood's voice sounded very tense.

"Yes?"

"Mrs. Attwood?"

"Yes. Who is this? Is this the lady from Valentine Consultations?"

"Right. Jessie Benedict. I wanted to report back to you on the results of my trip to DEL headquarters."

"Thank God you called. I've been trying to get hold of you."

The shrill edge in the woman's voice alarmed Jessie. "Is something wrong, Mrs. Attwood?"

"No. That is, something has happened. I've changed my mind. Yes, that's it. I've changed my mind. I don't want a silly psychic involved in this. I don't know what got into me, going to you like that. I want you to stop work on this thing right away. Do you hear me?"

"I hear you, Mrs. Attwood, but I don't understand. Don't you want to locate Susan?"

"It's all right. Everything's fine. Just . . . just a misunderstanding on my part. I panicked, that's all. Now, I want you to stop your investigation immediately. I am not going to pay you for any work on my behalf. Is that quite clear?"

"Perfectly clear, Mrs. Attwood." Jessie spoke very gently. "There is the little matter of the four hundred dollars and travel expenses which you did approve the other day, however."

"No. Not one red cent. You should never have gone up there. You're not a real detective."

"But, Mrs. Attwood—"

"Just stay out of this."

Jessie held the phone away from her ear as Mrs. Attwood slammed down the receiver.

CHAPTER ELEVEN

What do you think, Alex? Can you use some of the information on these to get into the DEL computers for me?" Jessie handed him the page of computer printout Hatch had filched from the men's room at DEL headquarters.

"Maybe." Alex studied the printout in the dim light. It was only four in the afternoon but, as usual, he had the shades drawn in his office to create the perpetual twilight he favored. The glow of the computer screen in front of him reflected off the lenses of his glasses.

Alex's working area was a dump site. Candy wrappers, cans of soda, and open bags of potato chips took up every spare inch that was not already occupied by a computer printout or a container of disks.

"Looks like there are a couple of things I could try," Alex mused. "Possible access codes and stuff. You said there was a lot of climatalogical data coming in on his computers. He's probably got an open line into a couple of standard weather data bases. If he has, he's vulnerable. I can probably find him. What do you want to look for?"

"I'm not certain. Financial stuff, I guess. I was hoping Hatch would help me with this. He knows about this kind of thing and could direct us. But he's turned snake mean just because of a minor little incident up in the San Juans."

"How minor?"

"Someone tried to break into his Mercedes. It shook him."

"No shit? That Mercedes he drives? I don't blame him," Alex said with great feeling. "You know what that model goes for these days?"

"It's just a car, Alex."

"That's not just a car. It's one beautiful machine."

"As it happens, the car is just fine. But we'll have to go ahead without Hatch. Now, what I'm trying to find out here is if DEL is a legitimate operation or if it's a scam."

"Why bother?" Alex frowned down at the printout. "If this client of yours took you off the project, why keep working on it?"

Jessie tapped one fingernail lightly on the surface of his cluttered desk. "I'm not sure, to tell you the truth. It's just a feeling I have."

"A feeling about what?"

"About Susan Attwood. I think her mother may have been right. She was sucked into something and she's being used somehow. I have a funny feeling she may be in real trouble."

"Intuition, huh?"

"That's as good a word for it as any."

Alex nodded. "Okay, I'll see what I can do with this."

"You don't mind?"

He grinned, his eyes gleaming with enthusiasm. "Heck, no. This looks like fun."

"I'll pay you."

"How? Your client fired you, remember?"

"We'll work out something. You certainly shouldn't have to do this for free. Mind if I watch?"

"Nope. But this kind of thing can take a while."

Jessie sighed, thinking of Hatch's irritation with her and

how likely he was to spend the entire evening at the office. She did not know if he would even show up at all at her apartment this evening. "I'm not doing anything else tonight."

"Let's see what we've got here." Alex turned toward the computer and went to work.

Hatch flipped absently through a month-old magazine he'd found lying on the table in Dr. Glenna Ringstead's office. He was beginning to regret agreeing to meet Jessie's aunt this afternoon. But when his secretary had informed him that Dr. Ringstead had called earlier in the day and asked to see him, he had decided to be accommodating.

He glanced at his watch for the third time in ten minutes. The secretary seated in the small office frowned reprovingly at him.

"Dr. Ringstead is just finishing up some notes. She'll be with you in a minute."

Hatch nodded, thinking privately that he'd give Glenna five more minutes, max. He had better things to do than hang around a shrink's office. The place made him uneasy.

He tossed aside the magazine and got to his feet. "Mind if I use your phone?"

The secretary shook her head quickly. "No, of course not. Go right ahead."

Hatch pulled the instrument around to face him and punched out Jessie's home number. Still no answer. He tried her office and got the same lack of response. He had been unable to get hold of her since he'd left her at her apartment earlier in the day. He was wondering whether to try Elizabeth's home number to see if she'd gone to visit her, when the inner door of Glenna's office opened.

"Hello, Hatch. Sorry to keep you waiting. I appreciate your taking the time to stop by this afternoon." Glenna stood back, smiling her cool, distant smile. "Come in."

"What's the problem, Glenna?" Hatch walked past her

and examined the softly lit room where she dealt with her patients. He liked it even less than he did the outer office.

"I would have come to see you at your office but, frankly, I didn't want to risk running into Jessie's father. Vincent would be bound to ask what I was doing there, and since this concerns Jessie, I'd rather not get involved in explanations."

"This is about Jessie?" Hatch's sense of uneasiness grew.

"I'm afraid so. Won't you sit down?"

He glanced at the chair. It was situated near a table that held a large box of tissues. He did not like the look of it. "No, thanks. I haven't got much time, Glenna."

"Yes, of course. You're such a busy man. Just like Vincent." She gave him a knowing, superior sort of smile and sat down behind her desk. She folded her hands primly in front of her on the surface of the polished wood. "This is going to be a little difficult to start, Hatch. Please bear with me."

Hatch made a bid for patience. He could see the woman was not having an easy time with this. "Suppose you start with Jessie."

"Yes. Jessie." Glenna paused, looking past him toward a subtle pastel print that hung on the wall. "I am extremely fond of her, Hatch. I have known her since she was born."

"I'm aware of that."

"She has always had a difficult niche to fill in our rather unusual extended family. That has come about primarily because, although she has frequently quarreled with her father, she is the only one who can really deal with him on a consistent basis. He is an extremely difficult man. Do you understand what I'm saying?"

"Sure. She's willing to tackle him when no one else has got the guts to do it. The others have come to depend on her to intercede on their behalf when they want something from Benedict. She does it because she's very loyal to the rest of you and to Vincent. Real simple."

Glenna sighed. "That's putting it a bit crudely, but

essentially you're correct. That's how it works. Vincent Benedict likes to maintain a strong sense of control. He does it in this family by holding all the purse strings."

"The interesting part," Hatch said meaningfully, "is that Jessie never asks Vincent for anything for herself, does she?"

"That's where you're wrong. She got into her present role in the first place precisely because she was seeking something from Vincent. As a young girl she wanted her father's attention and love. God knows, Vincent has never given much of himself emotionally to others. He was a distant, rather remote figure all during Jessie's childhood. So she adopted a role that gave her a way to force him to pay attention to her. In all fairness, it was about the only role available to her."

"So Jessie sets herself up as everyone else's champion in order to get his attention?" Hatch eyed Glenna curiously.

"Yes. She's been doing it so long, it's grown into a pattern of behavior for her. One she does not know how to break."

"The end result is that she's held the whole bunch of you together in some sort of family. What's the point of this little chat, Glenna?"

"I'm trying to explain how and why Jessie got herself trapped in this difficult, anxiety-producing relationship with her father." Glenna hesitated. "And the reason I'm spelling it out is that, as convenient as it would be for everyone concerned, the last thing she needs is another, similar relationship with a husband."

Hatch finally understood. He fought down a surge of raw anger. "You're talking about me, I assume?"

"Yes, I'm afraid so. In all good conscience, I must tell you it would be very unfair to push her into marriage with you. And she's so accustomed to going to bat for the rest of the family that she's liable to let us do just that. In the end she might very well ruin her own life to try to please the family."

"Tell me something, Glenna, just what kind of husband do you think Jessie needs?"

"What she needs and wants is someone who is the exact opposite of her father. A gentle, supportive, nurturing man who is capable of love and friendship. A man who will be family-oriented, not one who will be focused entirely on his work. I am sorry to have to say this, Hatch, but the truth is, you would be very wrong for her. With you she would be repeating the destructive pattern she has established with her father. I'm asking you to think about that before you push Jessie into a permanent relationship. If you care for her at all, you will let her go."

"Let go of Jessie? Don't hold your breath." The cold rage was simmering in his gut now. It was all Hatch could do not to pick up the nearest object and hurl it against the wall. He managed to maintain his outward calm, however, as he started for the door. "I've got news for you, Dr. Ringstead. You may have a Ph.D. but you don't know what the hell you're talking about. I'll make Jessie a damned good husband."

He got out of the office without slamming any doors, but it was a close call.

Let go of Jessie? The woman was crazy. Hatch knew he had never wanted anything as much in his life as he wanted Jessie Benedict.

A few minutes later he was out on the downtown sidewalk in front of Glenna's office. It was five-thirty and the streets were crowded with people heading home or to the nearest bar. He found a phone inside a department store and tried Jessie's home number once more.

Still no answer.

Hatch swore softly as he hung up the phone.

Ringstead was wrong. He was exactly the kind of man Jessie needed and wanted. Hell, she would walk all over one of those sweet, supportive, gentle types. She and her aunt might think that was what she wanted, but Hatch was sure she'd be frustrated within six weeks if she actually got her hands on that kind of husband. Jessie needed someone who was as strong-willed as she was, someone she respected. Someone who could protect her, not only from her own reckless streak but also from the demands of her family.

It did not take a doctorate in psychology to figure out something as basic as that, Hatch decided grimly. It was a quite simple man-woman thing.

Vincent was waiting for him when he got back to his office. He was standing in the hall outside Hatch's door. He scowled and waved a file folder.

"Where the hell have you been? What's going on around here, anyway? Lately you've been away from your desk more than you've been behind it. How the devil do you expect to run this company if you go gallivanting off whenever you get the urge?"

"Back off, Benedict. I am not in a good mood." Hatch pushed past the other man and went on into his office.

Vincent followed, still waving the file folder. "You know what this is? It's a report from the construction firm we hired to build the new warehouse for us. The doors arrived today and the damned things don't fit. Can you believe it? They're all going to have to go back."

"Benedict, that's a problem that someone on a much lower level than you should be handling. I've told you before, you've got to learn to stay out of the details and concentrate on the big picture."

"A whole set of doors that don't fit happens to be a very big picture, goddammit. And there's something else we need to deal with. The Spokane project. We're going to lose out to Yorland and Young if you're not careful."

"No loss." Hatch sat down behind his desk.

"No loss? Dammit, I want that contract. You said you could get it."

"I can and I will if you're dead set on it, but I still think it's not worth the effort. We don't need it. We're moving into much bigger projects now. Leave the penny-ante stuff to companies like Y and Y."

Benedict started to argue further and then halted abruptly. "Jesus. You're really pissed about something, aren't you?"

"You could say that, yes."

Benedict's eyes narrowed. "You still having problems with my daughter?"

"Nothing I can't handle."

"Then what's the situation here? Where have you been for the past hour, anyway?"

"Talking to Glenna Ringstead."

"Jesus." Vincent sat down abruptly and heaved a weary sigh. "No wonder you're pissed. That woman has a way of getting a man's back up without half-trying, doesn't she?"

Hatch heard the odd note in Benedict's voice and glanced up quickly. "I take it you've tangled with her?"

"Once or twice."

"She try to lecture you about Jessie?"

"Sometimes."

Hatch lost what little was left of his patience. "Benedict, I don't need any obscure remarks. If you've got something to say, say it."

Vincent massaged his temples and sighed again. "Glenna and I, we sort of, you know, got involved for a while."

"Involved?" Hatch was startled in spite of himself. "You and Glenna had an affair? That's hard to believe."

"You're telling me. It was a long time ago. Right after Lilian and I got divorced. Lloyd Ringstead had taken off for parts unknown a short while earlier. It was just one of those things, you know? I was feeling low and so was Glenna. We got together one night and started commiserating. Drank too much. Sort of fell into bed. It happened a couple more times and then we both realized we were acting like fools."

"I'll be damned. Somehow I don't see you and Glenna together at all."

"Neither did we when we came to our senses. Like I said, it was just one of those things." Benedict shifted uncomfortably in his chair. "I never mentioned it to Lilian or anyone else. Neither did Glenna, as far as I know. We were both kind of embarrassed about the whole thing."

"Had she gone back to school to get her doctorate at that point?" Hatch asked.

Benedict shook his head. "No. But she talked to me about it while we were seeing each other. I told her to go ahead, and offered to help pay for it. Hell, David was just a little guy at the time and his old man was gone. Lloyd had worked for me here at Benedict. A damned smart accountant. But I knew Glenna and the kid didn't have any money. And Glenna was Jessie's aunt, for Christ's sake. And I'd slept with her. I dunno. I guess I just felt like I owed her something."

"I'll be damned," Hatch said again.

"I'll tell you one thing. I liked her better before she got that degree in psychology," Vincent confided. "You know, I tried to sort of help David along now and then. But I don't think I did too good a job."

"Hey, he's graduating from college and he hasn't done any jail time. What more can you ask? I've known worse father figures."

Vincent's brows rose. "Yeah? Like who?"

"My own," Hatch said dryly. "A real SOB."

Vincent gave him a thoughtful look. "I'll bet mine could have given yours lessons. That is, if he'd stuck around long enough to bother—walked out when I was eight. Never saw him again."

Hatch nodded. "Sometimes it's better if a kid's father doesn't stick around."

"Yeah. Sometimes. But sometimes I kind of wished I'd had a chance to show the bastard I made something of myself. You know what I mean?"

"I know what you mean," Hatch said.

Hatch did not know whether to be worried or furious when he rang Jessie's buzzer at eight that evening and got no answer. He tried leaning on the button for a while but it was useless. If she was upstairs in her apartment, she was not answering the summons.

He walked back toward his car and stood looking up at the darkened window of her bedroom. On a hunch, he decided to drive to her office.

Ten minutes later he found a parking place on the street in front of Valentine Consultations. One glance told him that the lights were off in the upstairs office.

It occurred to him that she was deliberately avoiding him. He was mentally going through a list of places where she might possibly be at that hour when he remembered Alex Robin. The first step in tracking Jessie down was to ask Robin if he'd seen her that afternoon. Hatch got out of the Mercedes and went to the front door of the office building.

The door was locked but he was close enough to see the faint green glow in the crack of the blinds. He raised his hand and pounded heavily on the outer door.

A moment later Jessie appeared in the doorway. "What in the world? Oh, it's you, Hatch."

He eyed her from head to toe, taking in the tight faded jeans and silver-studded denim work shirt. As he studied her in pointed silence, she nervously combed her hair back behind her ears with her fingers.

"You weren't at home," he said finally.

She stepped back from the door. "Alex and I are busy. If you want to be entertained, you'll have to go somewhere else."

"Damn. I should have known. You gave that printout to Robin, didn't you?" Hatch moved into the hall and strode toward the door of the inner office. Jessie hurried after him.

Alex was hunched over his terminal. He did not bother to look up. "Hey, Hatchard. Sorry about what almost happened to your Mercedes."

"It was a near thing," Hatch admitted gruffly.

"Know how you must have felt. Going to get an alarm?"

"It's on order. For all the good it will do."

Alex nodded. "Ain't that the truth? Anyway, I'm glad you're here. Want to show you something."

"I don't think Hatch is interested in what we've found," Jessie said stiffly.

Hatch threw her a grim glance. "Want to bet?" He turned back to Robin. "Well? What have you got?"

"DEL has two major data bases. One is a financial program and the other is this climate-forecasting thing." Alex stabbed a button on the keyboard. "Take a look."

Hatch watched as rows of numbers moved across the screen. "A spread sheet. You're into the financial data base?"

"One of the programs, at least. There's a lot of information here," Alex said slowly. "Maybe even enough to help us figure out where the money's really going. I could use some professional advice."

"Dammit, I'm not going to help you follow that trail. I told Jessie I want her out of this thing."

Alex's mouth curved ruefully. "So did her client."

"What?" Hatch turned his head to confront her. "You talked to Mrs. Attwood?"

"That's right." Jessie picked up a half-finished carton of takeout potato salad and forked up a bite. "She told me she wanted me to stop the investigation."

Hatch raised his brows. "Interesting. You, naturally, are going full steam ahead."

Jessie shot him a quick glance and then returned her attention to her food. "I think something happened to frighten Mrs. Attwood."

"Then she should go straight to the police," Hatch said flatly.

"Probably. But I don't think she will. She was scared, Hatch. I could feel it. I suspect that someone from DEL warned her off. She said it had all been a misunderstanding. But I don't believe a word of it."

"Christ." Hatch shook his head, knowing a losing battle when he saw one. "So what are you two up to here?"

"Just poking around," Alex explained. "Trying to find out what's going on at DEL. Our main goal at the moment is to see if we can find out anything at all about the money. But I'm also curious about this climate program they're running." He punched some more keys.

"Why?"

"I've got a buddy up at the university who's into this kind of thing. I know for a fact his programs aren't projecting any ten-to-fifteen-year disaster scenarios. I'd like to see what he says about these DEL projections. I'm going to download them onto some diskettes and have him take a look."

Jessie spoke up around a mouthful of potato salad. "We want to see if they're genuine scientific projections or some kind of fake theories designed to fool potential investors."

Hatch groaned. "What are you going to do if you do manage to prove the program is a deliberate fraud?"

"Well, I suppose we could go to the authorities with the information," Jessie said slowly, obviously thinking through the situation. "After all, fraud is fraud. We can at least get DEL closed down."

"And how is that going to help Susan Attwood?" Hatch asked quietly. "If she's a part of this fraud, she's guilty of a crime. Do you really want to push things that far?"

Jessie gave him a stubborn look. "I just want to see if she's working with DEL of her own free will or if she's been duped. Please try to understand, Hatch. I can't seem to let this go now. I've gone too far with it. I have this feeling that there's something terribly wrong and that my client's daughter is in some kind of danger."

"You've been playing psychic investigator too long." Hatch turned back to Alex. "Can you do this without alerting anyone on the other end?"

"I think so," Alex said confidently.

"No footprints that would lead anyone back here to you and Jessie?" Hatch clarified, wanting to be absolutely certain on that point.

"Heck, no." Alex pulled his attention away from the screen long enough to squint briefly up at Hatch. "Does this mean you're going to help us?"

"It doesn't look like I've got a whole hell of a lot of choice, does it?"

Something clattered to the floor behind Hatch. He turned his head in time to see Jessie bending down to pick up the plastic fork she had just dropped.

"Want some potato salad?" she asked brightly.

A long time later Jessie stirred amid the tangle of sheets, stretched out one bare foot, and encountered Hatch's leg. "You awake?"

"Yes."

"I've been thinking," she said softly.

"About what?"

"About you. I haven't thanked you yet for staying on the case. I know you're not exactly thrilled with the idea of me pursuing the investigation."

"That's a mild way of putting it."

"Well, thanks anyway," she mumbled.

"Jessie?"

"Uh-huh?"

"Your Aunt Glenna talked to me today."

"Good grief. Why on earth did she do that?"

"She wanted to point out that I'm really not the kind of man you should marry. Even if it would be convenient for all concerned."

Jessie was startled to find herself annoyed. "Aunt Glenna said that?"

"Yes."

"I know Aunt Glenna means well, but sometimes she thinks that because she's got a degree in psychology she knows what's best for the rest of us. It can be irritating."

"But you agree with her, don't you? You told me yourself that I'm not the kind of man you would ever marry."

"Let's not get into that subject, Hatch. It's nearly three in the morning."

He grunted. "Did you know that your aunt and your father once had a brief affair?"

"Really?" Jessie was wide-awake now. "Are you sure?"

"Vincent told me about it this afternoon. He implied that was one of the reasons he helped her pay her way when she went back to college. He felt he owed her something."

"I'm stunned." Jessie sat up against the pillows and wrapped her arms around her updrawn knees. "I can't believe those two would ever get together in a million years."

"Why not?"

"Well, for one thing, she doesn't seem like his type. She's not colorful and sophisticated and outgoing like Constance and Lilian. She's not oriented toward art and design, the way they are. She's so serious all the time. And so clinical, if you know what I mean."

"The affair didn't last long. Your father implied he was at a low point because of the divorce from Lilian and Glenna was getting over being abandoned by her husband. One thing led to another. Then, according to Vincent, they both came to their senses."

Jessie turned that over in her mind. "I can see how it would happen. But it still seems strange, somehow."

"I agree."

"I wonder if Mom knows."

"I doubt it. Vincent said he never told her or anyone else, and he doesn't think Glenna did either. I got the feeling they both regretted the whole thing."

"Strange how you can know the members of your own family for so many years and still not know their secrets," Jessie mused.

Hatch turned toward her, his face unreadable in the deep shadows. "Your aunt talked about you today."

"Is that right?"

"She says you've become the intermediary between your father and the rest of the family because you're the only one willing to tackle him."

Jessie shrugged. "You've said the same thing."

"Yeah. But I don't have a Ph.D. in psychology to back me up. It was interesting hearing my diagnosis confirmed by a professional."

"Oh, for heaven's sake, Hatch. You make me sound like some sort of nut case just because I'm the only one who ever figured out how to deal with Vincent Benedict."

"I didn't mean that. And you're not the only one who can handle him. I can deal with him too."

She slanted him an assessing glance. "That's true. I figured that was because you're so much like him that you understand how his mind works."

"Maybe that applies to you too."

"I'm not anything like him," she protested.

"No? You're just as mule-headed stubborn as he is, for one thing. I can personally testify to that."

Jessie got annoyed. "It's not the same thing at all."

"It's okay, Jessie. I'm mule-headed stubborn too. But that's not my point."

"What is your point?"

"After I talked to Glenna today I got to thinking about us and I want to make sure we have something real clear here. Whatever else happens, I want you to swear to me that you will not let yourself get pushed, urged, bullied, or otherwise forced into marriage with me in order to protect, defend, or placate anyone in your family. Agreed?"

"I've already told you, I have no intention of marrying you."

"I know what you told me, but I happen to think the outcome is going to be a little different. I just want to make certain that when you do marry me, you do it for the right reasons, not because you feel you have to do what's best for the family."

A soft warmth welled up in her. He looked so serious, she thought. "You're the kind of man who usually doesn't worry too much about the means as long as you get the end you want," she noted carefully.

"In this case," he told her as he pulled her into his arms, "I definitely care about both."

"What are you trying to tell me, Hatch?" she whispered, her fingertips braced against his shoulders.

"That I want you to marry me because you damn well can't resist me," he muttered, his mouth moving on her throat. "I want you to marry me because I did such a hell of a good job seducing you and making you fall head over heels in love with me. Got that?"

She caught her breath as she felt his body hardening rapidly under hers. "Yes. Yes, Hatch, I've got it." She waited for him to volunteer the fact that he loved her, but he did not say the words that might have made the difference. And in that fragile moment she was afraid to ask for them.

"Swear?" Hatch prodded.

"I swear. If I ever do agree to marry you, it will be because I love you. But, Hatch?"

"Uh-huh?" He was nibbling at her earlobe now.

"I still have no intention of marrying you."

"I haven't finished this damned courtship yet."

CHAPTER TWELVE

Vincent Benedict was simmering. The initial explosion had dissolved into the customary roiling boil, which in turn was now all the way down to the mild, bubbling simmer.

Jessie was familiar with the pattern. She'd dealt with it all her life. Her father definitely had a problem with money, especially when it came to giving any of it away.

It was not that he was an ungenerous man; quite the opposite. Over the years Vincent had doled out thousands to his clan. But Constance and Lilian were right: he liked to attach strings. He liked to make certain the receivers were properly grateful and that they kept him posted on where every dime went. He felt free to make loud judgments on whether or not the money was being well-spent. He criticized, approved, or grumbled about what the recipient did with the money. And always he wanted everyone to remember where it had originated. Jessie routinely fielded the grumbles and complaints from both sides.

"Jesus H. Christ, those two women are never satisfied," Vincent roared. He slammed a palm down on his desk and regarded Jessie with a baleful gaze. "They're like sponges, always soaking up more of my cash."

"Dad, you know that's not true." Jessie was slouched low in the chair across from her father. She had her legs stretched out in front of her and her thumbs hooked loosely in the pockets of her jeans. She was wearing a snug-fitting, long-sleeved black dance leotard with the jeans, and her hair was caught back behind one ear with a large silver clip.

"The hell it isn't true. What happened to all that cash I gave Connie and Lilian two years ago to open that damn furniture store?"

"It's not exactly a furniture store, Dad, it's more of a showroom they use to give ideas to their clients. Now they want to expand it. Turn it into a design store. They're going to specialize in avant-garde European furniture styles."

"What's wrong with American furniture?" Vincent pointed to the wide mahogany desk in front of him. "Nothing wrong with good, solid American furniture."

"Dad, Connie and Lilian do not have a lot of clients who are into Early American."

"I'll tell you something, Jessie. That European crap is for the birds. I had one of those silly little Italian lamps in here for a few weeks and the damn thing broke."

"Only because you tried to bend it in a direction it was never intended to go." Jessie remembered the lamp. It had been a delicate device. Too delicate for her father's big hands. "And your opinion of Italian furniture has got nothing to do with the issue. The fact is that a lot of people like that style. Connie and Lilian cater to that crowd."

"Probably the same crowd that eats sushi and pays good money to watch films that have subtitles," Vincent grumbled.

"You hit the nail on the head when you said it's a crowd that pays good money for what it wants. Come on, Dad, you're a businessman. You know a business person has to

201

cater to the client's taste. That's all the moms want to do. They've been very successful up to this point, and you know you're proud of them. Why not finance another expansion for them?"

"They treat me like I'm some kind of bank."

"You want them to go to a real bank instead?"

"Hell, no." Vincent turned a dangerous shade of red at that suggestion. "Damned interest rates are sky-high again. Like throwing money down the drain. Can't trust bankers, either. They won't stand by you. First hint of trouble and they call in the loans."

Jessie grinned. "And besides, if the moms went to a bank, you wouldn't have a license to complain, would you? Be honest, Dad. You like controlling the purse strings in this family."

"Somebody has to do it. God knows they all go through money like it was water. No common sense. No appreciation for the hard work involved."

"You know that's not true. The rest of us just aren't as tightfisted about it as you are."

"Yeah, well, maybe that comes from never having had to do without. Men like Hatch and me, we know what it's like to do without." Vincent narrowed his eyes. "How come you never ask me for money?"

Jessie widened her eyes in mocking innocence. "Are you crazy? There would be too many strings attached, and you know it. You'd hound me constantly, asking me what I was doing with it, where I'd invested it, what I was buying with it. You'd probably want weekly and monthly reports. No, thanks."

"You know your problem, Jessie, girl? You're too damn independent. Too blasted stubborn for your own good. When are you going to marry Hatch?"

Jessie blinked. "Don't hold your breath."

"You're sleeping with the man, dammit. He told me so himself. If you can sleep with him, you can damn sure marry him."

"I'll have to talk to him about kissing and telling. Gentlemen aren't supposed to do that."

The door opened behind her and Hatch's voice cut in on the argument. "What's this about gentlemen?"

Jessie looked over her shoulder. "Dad says you've been chatting about my love life. I was telling him that gentlemen don't do that."

"I believe I was making an unrelated point at the time," Hatch said as he came into the room and shut the door behind him. In spite of the calm response, there was a faint tinge of ruddy color high on his cheekbones. "I was telling him not to interfere in our private life, as I recall. Isn't that right, Benedict?"

Vincent scowled at him and then turned back to Jessie. "Forget that. What, exactly, is the status between you two?"

"You'll be the first to know when we've got it settled." Hatch lounged against Vincent's desk, folded his arms, and regarded Jessie with a cool, searching gaze. His eyes skimmed over the tight black leotard that fit her like a glove. He frowned with disapproval. "What are you doing here?"

"Having a little father-daughter chat," she murmured.

Vincent snorted. "She's trying to talk me into giving Lilian and Connie twenty grand to expand their business."

"I see." Hatch did not take his eyes off Jessie. "Have you already made your pitch?"

"Yep," said Jessie. "And since Dad has already changed the subject, I assume he's going to go for it, aren't you, Dad?"

"Hell, I suppose I'll have to. If I don't, those two will end up in the clutches of some smooth-talking banker who'll charge 'em an arm and a leg in interest."

Jessie clamped her hands around the arms of the chair and pushed herself to her feet. "Thanks, Dad. I'll give them the good word. I'm sure they'll be properly grateful and will keep perfect records on how they spend every cent." She gave Hatch a challenging smile. "You'll probably be late getting home tonight as usual, won't you?"

Annoyance sparked in his gaze. "Probably. I've got some figures to go over with your father."

"Hey, don't worry about it," Jessie said airily, starting for the door. "I'll be working late myself. Alex and I are making real headway on our investigation."

Vincent's expression became thunderous again. "Investigation? Are you still fooling around with that cult thing? I thought that nonsense was finished. Hatch said the guy was running some kind of scam, not a cult, and that your so-called client called off the investigation."

"Things have changed," Jessie said.

"What things, dammit?"

"I'll explain it all to you later, Benedict." Hatch straightened away from the desk and went toward Jessie. "I'd like a word with you before you take off, Jessie."

"Sure. 'Bye, Dad."

Jessie winced as Hatch's hand closed firmly around her upper arm. But other than slanting him a reproachful look, she said nothing as he steered her through the outer office and into the hall.

He stopped when he was out of earshot of the secretaries and released Jessie near a potted palm. Coolly, deliberately, he planted one hand on the wall beside her right ear and leaned in close. The pose was deliberately intimidating. It was one of the many things he did well, Jessie reflected. She started to push her hair back and discovered it was already held back by the clip.

"I don't want you doing any more of this," Hatch stated softly.

She groaned. "Hatch, we've been through all the arguments. I've told you, I can't just halt the Attwood case. At least not until I'm satisfied Susan Attwood is all right."

"I am not talking about that damned case," Hatch bit out. "I am referring to what you were doing there inside your father's office. This business of letting the entire family use you to get what they want from Benedict is going to stop.

Whoever wants to ask him for something can damn well ask for it in person. You're no longer the intermediary. Clear?"

She sighed. "Hatch, you don't understand."

"The hell I don't. Just say no, Jessie. Remember?"

"Easy for you to say."

"You'll learn how. All it takes is a little practice. I won't have them using you anymore, Jessie. I mean it. I don't want you doing those kinds of favors for any of them. Not your mother or Connie or David or your Aunt Glenna. Enough is enough."

"But it's easier for me to deal with him, Hatch. Don't you see? I've always done it. I know how to do it."

"The others can damn well learn if it's important enough to them."

She shook her head sadly. "That's just it. It might not be important enough to them."

Hatch stared at her. "What the hell are you talking about?"

Jessie looked up at him, willing him to understand. "I'm afraid they'll all give up on him if they're forced to deal with him directly. After all, Connie and Lilian both gave up on him while they were married to him. David got so resentful and frustrated trying to please him that he finally stopped talking to him. Aunt Glenna says it's a waste of time trying to forge a relationship with Dad. But it's not. Not entirely."

"What you mean is that you've managed to keep some kind of bond established among all of you by doing all the diplomatic work. Jessie, that's wrong."

"Is it?" she demanded softly. "At least this way he's got some kind of family ties and the rest of us have some kind of contact with him. Maybe it hasn't been exactly *Father Knows Best* around here, but at least we've all had a relationship of some sort. It could have been worse, you know. He could have done what David's father did and just disappeared from our lives altogether."

"Christ, what a mess." Hatch's eyes glittered. "Jessie, I

don't want you holding the whole thing together by yourself any longer. With the exception of Elizabeth, they're all adults. They can deal with their own problems."

"I'm supposed to just step out of the picture, is that it?"

"Yeah. That's it."

"This is my family, Hatch. Give me one good reason why I should do what you want," she hissed.

"I thought I'd already explained this part. I want to be damn sure that when you marry me you're not doing it solely for the benefit of the Benedict-Ringstead clan."

"And I've already told you, I have no intention of marrying you." But the protest sounded weak, even to her own ears.

"We'll save that argument for another time. Right now I want to make sure you understand that you're out of the intermediary business. Let the other Benedicts and Ringsteads fend for themselves."

"But I've already promised David I'd ask Dad about financing grad school."

"I'll handle David."

"You'll handle him? Hatch, you barely know him. You haven't been around our family long enough to figure out how to deal with this kind of thing. David's very sensitive."

"So am I," Hatch snarled softly, slapping his other hand against the wall on the other side of her head. "You just haven't bothered to take much notice, what with being too busy worrying about everybody else's sensitive nature. One last time. I want to make damn sure I'm not being married so that David and his mother and the moms and your sister are all being taken care of by you as per usual. Got that?"

"You're about as sensitive as a rhino. And stop talking about marriage. We're having an affair and that's as far as it's going to go." Jessie tried to duck out from under one of his arms and managed to blunder straight into the potted palm. The plant and Jessie both began to topple to the side.

With a muttered oath Hatch caught both palm and woman before they sprawled ignominiously on the floor. He steadied the plant and held Jessie's arm as she spit out a palm leaf.

"I want your word on this, Jessie. I mean it."

"Look, Hatch . . ."

"I said, I want your guarantee not to play go-between for everyone in the family, at least until our relationship has been finalized," he repeated through tightly clenched teeth.

"Finalized?" For a split second, standing there, looking up at him, Jessie felt disoriented. A strange, familiar sense of need hovered just at the edge of her awareness, not her own need, she realized, but something Hatch was experiencing.

"You know what I'm talking about." Once more he put his hand on the wall behind her and leaned in close.

"This is intimidation, Hatch." She was breathless and confused all of a sudden. *Hatch needed her?*

"Damn right. Come on, Jessie, stop wasting my time and your own."

"All right, I promise." The words were out before she had quite realized she was going to say them.

Hatch nodded once, satisfied. "I'll see you at dinner tonight." His fist dropped away from the wall. With one last warning glance he swung around on his heel and stalked back toward Vincent Benedict's office.

Jessie walked toward the elevators on trembling legs. She must have gone crazy there for a minute. She had stood up to him on the matter of the Attwood case. But she'd collapsed completely on this issue. It made no sense.

She sincerely hoped she was not turning into a wimp.

Forty-five minutes later, Jessie parked her car in front of the low, modern building that housed the offices of ExCellent Designs. She opened the car door and got out slowly, not particularly looking forward to the meeting that lay ahead.

Downtown Bellevue was humming with its usual assortment of BMW's and well-dressed suburbanites. Jessie always felt as if she had crossed some sort of international border when she drove over one of the bridges that linked the Eastside with Seattle.

Over here everything always looked clean and trendy and expensive. In Seattle the high-fashion shops and restaurants competed for space with the gritty elements that had characterized real cities since the dawn of time.

Connie glanced up from the design plan she was perusing on her desk when Jessie opened the office door. She smiled. "Hello, Jessie. Is this good news or bad news?"

"A little of both."

Connie made a face. "Better save it until your mother gets here, then. She just went out to get us some coffee. Ah, here she is."

"Hi, Jessie." Lilian Benedict walked into the office carrying two cups of latte. "This is a surprise. I assume you've got some news for us?"

"Dad will give you the money for the expansion," Jessie said, sinking down into one of the exotically shaped black leather-mesh chairs.

"Fabulous. I knew you could talk him into it. Any serious catches this time?" Lilian removed the top from her latte.

"No, but I had a little trouble with Hatch over the arrangement."

"With Hatch?" Constance stared at her in astonishment. "Why is Hatch involved in this?"

"He's not, actually. He just thinks he is. To put it briefly, he got very annoyed that I was doing the asking. I don't think he likes me going to Dad with requests like yours."

"But this is a personal matter between us and Vince." Lilian frowned. "Does he think the money comes directly out of Benedict Fasteners or something?"

"No, it's not that." Jessie shifted slightly in the chair, trying to find a comfortable position. Her father was right. Some of this European design stuff looked better than it felt. "It's me being in the middle that bothers him for some reason. I explained to him that I'm used to dealing with

Dad, but Hatch doesn't understand exactly how things work, if you see what I mean."

Lilian and Constance exchanged glances.

"I think we see," Lilian said dryly.

Constance sighed and sat back in her chair. Her long mauve nails traced the rim of the cup she was holding. "He's quite right, you know. We have all tended to let you handle Vincent for us, by and large. You have a knack for it."

"Ummm, true." Lilian studied her daughter. "I wonder why Hatch is interested in that fact."

"I think he believes I'm being used," Jessie said carefully.

Lilian's expression tightened into one of deep concern. "Do you feel used, dear?"

Jessie glanced out the window. "No. I did it of my own free will. It was just the way things were. A pattern, as Aunt Glenna would probably say. I guess I felt that as long as I was running back and forth between everyone else in the family and Dad, we were all still linked, somehow. Still a family."

"Well, it worked, after a fashion," Constance murmured. "We're all living amicably enough in the same region and we're all on speaking terms, except possibly David. Vince has been difficult, but, on the whole, reasonably fair when it comes to money. And if it hadn't been for you, I doubt that Elizabeth would have nearly as much contact with her father as she does have. I think he would have drifted away from her and everyone else if it hadn't been for you, Jessie."

Lilian nodded. "Vincent is like a Missouri mule. You have to keep hitting him over the head with a big stick to get his attention. But when you do have it, he's a decent man."

"I've been the stick," Jessie said.

"For better or worse, I'm afraid so," her mother agreed. "In a very real way, you've been what Glenna likes to call the caretaker in the family, haven't you? The one who holds things together."

"I think Aunt Glenna calls it being the family enabler," Jessie muttered.

Lilian frowned. "I'm not sure I like the fancy new words the psychologists use these days to describe the old nurturing skills. They demean them somehow. And I'm not at all sure 'enabler' is the right word here anyway. But it's obvious Hatch now wants you out of the role, whatever it is."

"He says he doesn't want me marrying him because I'm under pressure to do so," Jessie said slowly.

Constance pounced on that remark. "He's asked you, then?"

"No, not exactly. He's just sort of assumed we'll get married. You know how men like that operate. They're like generals. They set a goal and they just keep driving toward it until they've achieved their objective."

Lilian eyed her curiously. "Does that strange expression on your face mean you're contemplating the same objective Hatch has in mind? Are you finally thinking seriously about marriage?"

"No, dammit, I am not. I seem to be involved in an affair with him, but that's as far as it's going to go."

"But, Jessie, why?" Constance stared at her, perplexed. "If you like him enough to have an affair with him, why not marry him?"

Jessie looked away and suddenly she was crying. "Dammit, I will *not* spend the rest of my life fighting for a man's love. That's one pattern I will not repeat."

"Jessie. Oh, Jessie, honey, don't cry." Lilian leapt to her feet and stepped around her desk to crouch beside Jessie's chair. She put her arms around her and held her close, rocking her gently the way she had when Jessie had been a child and Vincent Benedict had canceled yet another outing on account of business. "It's all right, dear. It's going to be all right."

Jessie groped blindly for a tissue, disgusted with her loss of control and frightened by what it signified about the depth of her feelings for Hatch.

There was silence in the office for a while. Jessie blinked back the tears and blew her nose a couple of times. Then she gave her mother a watery smile. "Sorry. I've been under a lot of pressure lately."

"Being in love can do that," Constance observed gently. "It's quite all right, Jessie. Your mother and I understand. Every woman understands."

"I'm not going to marry him, you know." Jessie wiped her eyes, crushed the tissue, and hurled it into the stylish black cylinder that served as a trashcan. "I am going to enjoy an affair with him for as long as it lasts and then I will walk away. It's highly probable he will walk away first when it finally dawns on him that he's not going to get what he wants."

"You really believe he wants to marry you only because of Benedict Fasteners?" Lilian asked quietly.

"No," Jessie admitted. "It's a hell of a lot more complicated than that. He admires Dad. Wants to please him. And then there's the business angle. We all know that marrying me would be an excellent business move for him. And I admit, there's a physical attraction. I think what it boils down to is that he's satisfied with the package deal."

"Jessie, I think Hatch's feelings run a lot more deeply than that. Whatever else he is, he's simply not a superficial kind of man. Even I know that much about him," Lilian said firmly.

"He doesn't say he loves me," Jessie sniffed sadly. "He says he thinks he can trust me. Says he thinks I'll be loyal. His first wife was running off to meet another man when she was killed, you know. His mother left him and his father when Hatch was only five. Loyalty is very important to Hatch. A lot more important than love, I think. I'm not sure he'll ever trust in love again."

"Frankly, it sounds like the two of you have an excellent basis for a relationship, Jessie," Constance stated.

"Trust and attraction and a couple of good business reasons are apparently enough for Hatch. But they're not enough for me."

Lilian pursed her lips thoughtfully as she got to her feet.

"Are you sure you're not romanticizing this whole thing a bit too much, Jessie? You're twenty-seven, not seventeen. How much can you realistically expect from a man?"

Constance nodded. "Your mother's right, Jessie. You're old enough not to need rose-colored glasses. I hate to break this to you, but having trust and physical attraction between yourself and a man is about as good as it gets. A lot of women never get that much. What are you holding out for?"

"I don't know," Jessie whispered.

The office door opened and Elizabeth ambled into the room. Her brown hair was anchored with two colorful clips and her glasses were slightly askew on her small nose.

"Hi, everybody. What's going on?"

"Hi, Elizabeth." Jessie blinked back the remaining moisture in her eyes. "I'm just sitting here sobbing my heart out for no good reason."

"PMS, huh?"

Constance groaned. "This is what comes of sex education in the schools."

"I didn't hear about that at school. I heard about it from you," Elizabeth informed her mother. She sauntered over to Jessie. "I bet you're crying on account of Hatch, aren't you?"

"Afraid so," Jessie said.

"Why don't you just punch him out instead?"

"That would probably be a much more satisfying approach to the problem," Jessie said. "But he happens to be a lot bigger than I am."

"I don't think he'd hit you back," Elizabeth said, thoughtful. "At least, not very hard."

"Of course he wouldn't hit me back. Which is exactly why I can't start pounding on him," Jessie explained patiently. "It wouldn't be fair, you see. He couldn't retaliate in the same way."

"So what does that leave?" Elizabeth asked.

"I don't know," Jessie said. "I'm still trying to figure that out."

"What it leaves," Lilian said deliberately, "is common sense."

Constance smiled. "We know you'll do the right thing, dear. You always have."

Somewhere halfway across the bridge it came to Jessie that what she wanted from Sam Hatchard was proof that he could love her enough to choose her over Benedict Fasteners or anything else on the face of the planet if it ever came to that.

But Constance and Lilian were right. It was totally unrealistic to even contemplate such a scenario. What could she do? Tell him she would marry him if he walked away from the business arrangement he'd made with her father? That would be blackmail. Even if he did it, he would be disgusted with her for demanding such a sacrifice when there was no legitimate need for it. And she would be disgusted with herself for doing it.

As she had told Elizabeth, a woman had to fight fair.

A small, distinct sense of dread washed over her. There was a dark gray fog lying just beyond the edge of her awareness, as if the future held some bleak danger.

If this was what it was like to have premonitions or intuition or some other psychic ability, Jessie decided, she did not care for the sensation.

Hatch let himself warily into Jessie's apartment at eight o'clock that evening. He was not certain what kind of welcome to expect after the scene that had taken place in the hall outside Vincent's office door that afternoon.

He got a strong hint about what was in store when Jessie barely glanced up from the couch where she lay reading a book.

"Hi," she said without looking up from her book.

"Hello." Hatch closed the door and set down his briefcase. He noticed the lights were off in the kitchen. "Did you want to go out to get a bite to eat?"

"I already ate an hour ago. I told you, I don't serve dinner this late."

"I see." Hatch realized he was starving. "Any leftovers?"

"It was ravioli again. You weren't here, so I ate the whole package. You can't expect me to hold dinner for you, Hatch. Not when you don't even bother to call and let me know you'll be late."

Hatch felt a wave of chagrin. "I don't think of eight o'clock as being real late."

"I do."

"It's been a long time since I had to call home to tell someone I'd be late for dinner. Guess I'm out of the habit."

"Uh-huh. Well, don't let it worry you." Jessie turned the page in her book. "You don't have to account for all your time to me. We're just sleeping together. It's not like we're married or anything."

"You're really pissed about this, aren't you?"

"No, just realistic."

He winced inwardly and walked over to the couch to stand looking down at her. "Would it help if I said it won't happen again?"

She slanted him an uncertain look out of the corner of her eye. She was obviously taken aback by the offer. "Is that a promise?"

He hunkered down beside her, not touching her. "It's a promise, Jessie."

She sat there gnawing on her lower lip for a while and Hatch knew she was recalling all the similar promises her father had given her over the years. Casual, meaningless promises that nine times out of ten wound up being broken.

"I guess I could make you a peanut-butter sandwich or something," she said, tossing aside her book. She got to her feet and headed for the kitchen.

Hatch heaved a silent sigh of relief and followed. He knew he had come very close to disaster that time. And all because he had been a little late for dinner.

"Jessie, one more time for the record. I am not a carbon copy of your father. I don't break my promises."

She glanced up, her eyes meeting his over the refrigerator door. "I know."

Hatch realized they had just passed a major milestone. He was grinning like an idiot. "Say that again."

"Say what again? I know?" She opened the peanut-butter jar and reached for a knife.

"The whole thing. Say you know I am not a carbon copy of your father and that you know I don't break my promises."

She swirled the knife inside the jar of peanut butter. "I know you are not a carbon copy of my father and I know you don't break your promises."

"Damn right," Hatch said. "I'm glad we got that much straightened out. You got any bread for that peanut butter or do I have to eat it off the knife?"

CHAPTER THIRTEEN

The phone rang that evening just as Jessie was reaching for her nightgown.

"Hello?"

"Jessie, it's me, Alex." Robin's voice was bubbling with excitement. "Listen, you're never going to believe this, but I think I've found Susan Attwood."

"You *what?*" Jessie sat down abruptly on the edge of the bed, clutching the nightgown. Hatch came out of the bathroom and eyed her questioningly.

"It's true, Jessie," Alex said quickly. "I've been watching to see what kind of passwords and access codes are being used to enter the different files. One of the codes is matched with the name Attwood. She's updating the climate program right now. Plugging in some new temperature numbers. And that reminds me, I've got something else to tell you. My friend at the university got back to me a half-hour ago."

"And?"

"First, he knew something about Edwin Bright. Said the guy is one of those characters in the scientific community who always operate way out in left field. He hadn't heard much about him in recent years. Bright's theories and calculations are not accepted by any reputable people."

"Ah hah."

"Second, he said that it was clear that some of the important numbers in this climate-projection program are phony. Says Bright must be making them up. He also implied it wouldn't be the first time."

"Do you think Susan is helping him produce misleading data?"

"No." Alex sounded defensive suddenly. "I think it's more likely she's just inputting numbers that he's given her."

Hatch came over to the bed, his expression intent. "Is that Robin?"

"Just a second, Alex." Jessie looked up at Hatch. "He thinks he's found Susan. She's on the computer right now, running a climate program."

"Ask him if he can communicate with her through the computer."

"I heard what Hatch just asked," Alex said. "Tell him I can do that. Want me to get her attention now?"

Jessie gripped the phone. "He says he can do it. Hatch, this is so exciting. I'm going to have him try to contact her right now."

Hatch shook his head. "No. Tell him to wait until you and I can get over to the office. I want to think this through for a few minutes."

Alex spoke in Jessie's ear. "I heard him. See you two in a bit."

Jessie heard the phone go dead on the other end of the line. "I can't believe this." She leapt off the bed, hurling the nightgown into a corner. She grabbed her jeans. "What a break. We can talk to her in person. Come on, Hatch, let's go."

"I hope Robin laid in his usual supply of junk food. That peanut-butter sandwich didn't go far."

Twenty minutes later Jessie and the two men were

crowded around the computer screen. Somehow Hatch seemed to have taken command of the situation, much to her annoyance. Jessie was not quite certain how it had happened. She suspected it had to do with his natural leadership talents and with the fact that Alex, being a man, was automatically inclined to take orders from another male. It was extremely irritating, but there did not seem to be much she could do about it at the moment. The important thing was to make contact with Susan Attwood.

"Don't give her any idea of who you are or where you are," Hatch told Alex. "Just let her think that you're a concerned environmentalist who's also a hacker. Maybe someone who's involved in climate-projection programs and who's heard about Bright's calculations and wants to review them. And for Christ's sake, don't give her anything that can be traced back here. Understand?"

"Sure, Hatch." Alex eagerly started punching keys on the board. "I'll start by questioning the data she's trying to input. She won't be alarmed, just confused at first. She'll think it's the computer querying the information she's feeding it. When she starts responding, I'll ease into letting her know there's a real person asking."

Alex's initial query trickled out across the bottom of the screen. Jessie read it over his shoulder:

New temperature ranges for arctic quadrant do not match projections. Please explain source.

"What if the query pops up on someone else's screen?" Jessie asked.

"There's no one else on-line right now. It's the middle of the night, don't forget. She's working the late shift alone." Alex studied the response he had gotten from Susan.

Source is Bright calculation. The words appeared above Alex's on the top half of the screen.

Calculation not correct, Alex typed.

Please explain.

"She's confused, and no wonder," Alex said. "The program she's working with is not written to be interactive on this level. Up until now it's just accepted whatever numbers it gets and crunched them."

"Okay," Hatch said slowly. "Let her know you're here."

Am concerned about projections produced by this program. They don't match my own, Alex typed.

Who are you?

Alex hesitated and then typed, *Green.*

Are you with DEL?

No. Concerned about same subject. Wrong data extremely dangerous, Alex typed.

Show me the differences between your calculations and ours.

"We're in luck," Alex said confidently. "She's the naturally curious type, like most computer junkies. She wants to solve the puzzle before she does anything else. Attagirl, Susan. I'd do exactly the same thing, especially in the middle of the night when there's nothing better to do. I think you and I are two of a kind." He hunched over the keyboard and started typing furiously.

Jessie glanced at Hatch and smiled wryly. Hatch shrugged and reached for the bag of potato chips that was lying on the desk next to the computer. They both sat there munching while Alex lured Susan Attwood into an extended conversation about data errors and bad projections.

Have recently been concerned about this myself, Susan finally admitted several minutes later.

Hatch put down the bag of potato chips. "Bingo," he said softly.

"Told you she was bright." Alex looked proud, as if Susan were his protégée. "Smart enough to know something was wrong."

"Ask her if she's ever worked with the financial program," Hatch ordered.

"If I do that, she'll know we're interested in the money as well as the climate stuff," Alex warned.

Jessie finally took a hand. "Tell her you stumbled over the other program while looking for this one and that you were curious about the projects the foundation is financing."

"And tell her," Hatch added swiftly, "that the money doesn't look like it's going into normal research-and-development costs. See if she's had any concerns about those transactions."

Jessie whipped around in her chair to stare at Hatch in astonishment. "You never said anything about the R-and-D stuff looking strange."

He shrugged again. "I'm not sure what is happening. I just know it isn't a normal R-and-D spread sheet."

"You could have said something."

"I'd already told you the whole thing was probably some sort of scam. This is nothing new. I'm just fine-tuning my theories now."

Alex broke in quickly. "If you two would stop squabbling, we might get some more answers from Susan. Okay, Hatch, you want me to ask directly about offshore accounts?"

"Something tells me we should be a little more subtle than that," Jessie muttered, still annoyed.

"Jessie's right. Just ask her why the financial-management program doesn't look right and see what she says."

Alex obediently typed in the question. There was a long pause before the answer came back on the top half of the screen:

Who are you, Green? Please tell me.

"She's getting nervous," Jessie said. "I think it's time to tell her the whole truth."

"I agree," Alex said.

"You're liable to scare her off completely if you do," Hatch warned.

Jessie shook her head, staring intently at the screen. Her intuition was guiding her now. "No. She's already scared. And not because of us. Let's find out what's really going on here. Alex, ask her if she feels safe working for DEL."

"Just like that?"

"Yes. Hurry." Jessie was feeling a sense of urgency. She leaned forward to peer over Alex's shoulder.

"All right, go ahead," Hatch said slowly, after giving Jessie a speculative glance. "Start the question with her first name."

Susan, are you safe where you are?

Jessie held her breath and realized that Alex was doing the same thing as they waited for a response. Only Hatch still looked calm.

I'm not sure. I'm getting scared, Green. Please tell me who you are.

"Tell her," Jessie said, "that we've been looking for her and if she wants to leave DEL, we'll help her. Tell her that her mother is very worried."

"Tell her that her mother is also scared," Hatch put in thoughtfully. "That should do it."

Jessie nodded. "Good idea. Susan may not know that Mrs. Attwood has been threatened."

"Has she?" Alex asked, surprised.

Jessie nodded grimly. "Yes, I'm sure of it."

The response from Susan came immediately. *Is my mother all right? Have been told I may not contact her until after my training period is finished.*

"Tell her that Mrs. Attwood will not talk to me about the problem. Tell her I'm very worried about her," Jessie said.

Alex started to type in the words, but before he could get halfway through the sentence, Susan started typing something of her own.

Clear screen. Someone coming.

In a stroke Alex wiped everything off his own screen and sat back in his chair with a low groan of frustration. "She's in trouble."

"Looks like it," Hatch agreed quietly. "But we don't have any idea of how much trouble. She might just be getting nervous. Wants to come home. Afraid to admit she's made a mistake."

"I think," Jessie said slowly, "that it's more serious than that. I think she's in real danger."

Hatch and Alex looked at her.

"How do you know that?" Hatch finally asked.

Jessie shook her head, helpless to explain the sense of urgency that was growing stronger by the minute. "Just a feeling I've got." She jumped to her feet. "I'm going to go see Mrs. Valentine. With any luck, she'll have recovered some of her ability. Maybe she can tell me if I'm right in thinking Susan's in trouble."

"Jessie, it's midnight," Hatch pointed out.

"Mrs. V will understand. Do you want to come with me, Hatch?"

"I don't think I've got much choice," he muttered, standing up reluctantly.

"I'll keep an eye on things here," Alex said. "I won't attempt to contact Susan. I'll just monitor the screen in case she decides to try to find me again. If she puts out a query, I'll respond."

Jessie glanced back once from the door. Alex was sitting in front of his screen, gazing into the green glow with worried eyes.

There was another screen glowing in the living room of Mrs. Valentine's sister. A television screen.

Mrs. Valentine, wearing an old robe and slippers, answered the doorbell on the first chime. "Oh, there you are, Jessie, dear. Come in. I've been expecting you. Hello, Mr. Hatchard. So nice to see you again."

"Hello, Mrs. Valentine," Hatch said. "Sorry about the late-night visit."

"Don't worry about it. As I said, I was expecting you."

Jessie threw her arms around her boss and hugged her tightly. "You were expecting us? Mrs. V, does that mean you've recovered your psychic abilities?"

"What little ability I had seems to have begun returning," Mrs. Valentine said modestly. "Won't you sit down? My sister has already gone to bed. I was just watching TV until you arrived."

"This is wonderful, Mrs. V." Jessie sat down on the old sofa. "Isn't it, Hatch?"

"It's interesting," Hatch said coolly.

"Don't mind him, Mrs. V. He's a born skeptic. Now, let me tell you why I'm here at this hour."

"Something to do with Susan Attwood, I imagine." Mrs. Valentine looked resigned.

"Mrs. V, you *are* getting back your powers. This is wonderful."

"Simple deduction, I'm afraid." Mrs. Valentine smiled. "I couldn't imagine anything else that would have you so agitated. Better tell me everything."

"Right."

Jessie plunged into a full account, including the fact that Alex Robin had managed to contact Susan. Hatch added a few desultory comments on the probability of a scam being run by the Dawn's Early Light Foundation.

"We're starting to get very concerned about Susan's safety, Mrs. V," Jessie concluded a few minutes later. "I wanted to consult with you before we did anything else."

Mrs. V gazed at the television screen for a long while. Then she turned her head to meet Jessie's anxious eyes. "I think, my dear, that you are right to be concerned about poor Susan."

"I was afraid of that. We've got to do something."

"Perhaps you should call the police," Mrs. Valentine suggested. "This sort of thing should be turned over to them, don't you think?"

"Good idea," Hatch agreed.

"I'm not so sure," Jessie said slowly. "For one thing, we don't have any real evidence that she's in danger. Susan hasn't exactly asked for rescue. I think we should ask her what she wants us to do." She stood up abruptly. "Come on, Hatch. Let's go. No point keeping Mrs. V up any later. She's confirmed my worst fears."

"I do wish you would turn this over to the proper authorities, dear." Mrs. Valentine looked anxious.

"That's just it, Mrs. V, there are no proper authorities. Not yet, at any rate. We don't have any proof of a crime or even any evidence of danger to Susan. Don't worry, we can handle this," Jessie assured her.

"Oh, my goodness." Mrs. Valentine trailed after them to the door. She frowned as Jessie walked out onto the old-fashioned porch. "Jessie, dear . . ."

"Yes, Mrs. V?"

"You will be careful, whatever you do, won't you?"

"Of course. But it's Susan Attwood who's in danger, not me."

"I'm not so sure about that." Mrs. Valentine glanced at Hatch. "You'll take care of her, won't you." It was more of a statement than a question.

"Yes," Hatch said quietly. "I'll take care of her."

Mrs. Valentine looked somewhat relieved. "Oh, well, then, perhaps it will all be okay. But I'm really not certain I like this new aspect of our business. Not certain at all."

"I don't blame you, Mrs. Valentine," Hatch said. "Any way you slice it, there's no doubt but that Valentine Consultations is headed in new directions."

"Oh, dear," said Mrs. Valentine.

Jessie dialed Alex's number just before she climbed into bed. It was answered on the first ring.

"Heard anything more from her, Alex?"

"No. I think she's lying low."

"When's her next shift on the computer?"

"Tomorrow night. If she maintains her present schedule."

"Maybe she'll talk to us then," Jessie said.

"Unless they've gotten so suspicious they've removed her from the job," Alex said glumly.

Jessie put down the phone and turned to look at Hatch, who was lying back against the pillows, his hands behind his head. He was naked to the waist and the covers were bunched around his hips, exposing the broad, smoothly muscled expanse of his chest.

"I'm really worried, Hatch."

"I know you are." He gave her a small wry smile. "Come to bed and get some sleep. There's nothing more you can do tonight."

Jessie went over to the bed and crawled in beside him. The heat of his body enveloped her as he pulled her close.

"Hatch?"

"Uh-huh?"

"I'm glad you're helping me out on this case. I get the feeling I'm in a little over my head."

"You think you're in over your head now? Just wait until this is all over and I bill you for my services."

"Hatch, are you serious?"

"I'm always serious."

At one o'clock the next afternoon, Hatch grabbed his jacket and started for the door of his office.

"I'll be out for the next couple of hours," he said to his secretary as he went past her desk.

"Yes, Mr. Hatchard."

Twenty-five minutes later Hatch was waiting outside a classroom at Butterfield College. David Ringstead sauntered out of the room behind fifteen other students. He looked startled to see Hatch.

"What are you doing here?" David demanded. Then he frowned in sudden alarm. "Is anything wrong? Is Mom all right?"

"Nothing's wrong. I wanted to talk to you and I figured this would be the easiest way to do it. Can we go someplace where we can get a cup of coffee?"

"Why?"

"I told you. I want to talk to you."

David shrugged. "All right. There's an espresso bar across the street."

"Fine."

"Mind telling me what this is all about?"

"It's about money," Hatch said easily.

"Shit." David shoved his hands into the back pockets of his jeans. "You're here to tell me the old bastard won't finance grad school, right? Why you? Why didn't Jessie come?"

"That's a lot of conclusions to jump to without knowing any facts. But I guess that's what philosophers arc trained to do, isn't it? No wonder they have a hard time finding jobs outside the academic world."

"Shit."

Hatch sighed as he pushed open the door of the espresso bar. "Look on the bright side. I'm buying."

A pale, lanky-haired young woman behind the counter smiled wanly at David.

"Hi, David. How's it going?" she asked.

"Fine. You?"

"Okay, I guess. What will you have?"

"Latte," said David.

She turned in mute question to Hatch.

"Coffee," Hatch said. "Plain coffee."

They stood in silence while the young woman went to work at the gleaming espresso machine. When she handed them their cups, Hatch led the way to a corner table in the nearly empty café.

"Friend of yours?" Hatch asked idly, nodding faintly toward the wiry woman who was now busy cleaning up around the machine. Her washed-out blond hair swung forward, shielding her bad complexion.

"Not exactly. Met her when I was asking around for information on DEL."

Hatch slid the young woman a second glance. "That's Nadine Willard?"

"Yeah." David sipped the foam off his latte. "Now, suppose you stop messing with my head and just tell me what all this is about."

"No problem. It's real simple, David. I don't want you

pressuring Jessie to go to her father for money for grad school. Got that?"

David scowled. "What is it with you, anyway? What do you care about something that's just between Jessie and me?"

"I want Jessie out of the loop."

"The loop?"

"Right. The loop. From now on, anyone who wants something from Vincent Benedict can go and ask for it himself, directly. You don't use Jessie anymore."

David's expression tightened into a sullen frown. He sat back and stuck his legs out under the small table. "Jessie's never minded handling the old bastard for the rest of us."

"I mind."

"No offense, but who the fuck cares if you mind?"

Hatch took a taste of his coffee. "Put it this way, David. If you try to use Jessie to run interference for you, I will personally squelch any possibility you might have of getting money out of Vincent Benedict. Believe me, I can do it. Benedict and I think alike. I know just how to convince him that you shouldn't be given one more dime for your education."

"You're a real son of a bitch, aren't you?"

"I can be," Hatch agreed.

"Mom said she was afraid something like this would happen."

"Something like what?" Hatch eyed him curiously.

David lifted one shoulder in resignation. "That things would change. She said the old bastard was going to try to create a son for himself by getting one to marry into the family. She said if he succeeded, we'd all lose in the end. Looks like this is the start of it."

"You seem to be missing the point here, David. I did not say you couldn't try to talk Benedict into anything you want. Just don't use Jessie to do it for you."

"She's the only one who can deal with him. Everybody knows that."

"Have you ever tried dealing with him yourself?"

"Shit, yes." David slammed his half-finished cup down on the table. He turned fierce eyes on Hatch. "You think I haven't tried to please the old man? Hell, I spent most of my life trying to be the son everyone said he wanted. Ever since I was a little kid, I tried to be a macho, hard-charging type for his sake."

"Is that right?"

"Yeah, it is damn sure right." David leaned forward. His hands circled his cup in a crushing grip. "I went out for football because of him. Spent eight weeks in a cast when I broke a leg because some idiot linebacker fell on top of me. I got a job on a fishing boat one summer because Benedict said I was a wimp and needed to toughen up. I hated it. The smell was awful. And the endless piles of dead and dying fish made me sick to my stomach. I still can't bring myself to eat fish."

"David—"

"I've studied karate for years, trying to prove to Uncle Vincent I was made of the right stuff. Mom and the old bastard decided I should get to know the family business, so I tried working construction one summer." David shook his head at the bitter memory. "Should have seen my coworkers. Their idea of a good time was getting off work and heading straight for the nearest tavern. Their idea of intellectual conversation was a detailed discussion of the tits on the latest Playmate of the month."

"I know the type," Hatch said dryly, thinking back to his own younger days.

"Then, in sheer desperation, Mom convinced Uncle Vincent to let me try working in the head office."

"I take it that didn't work either."

"Hell, no. I couldn't do anything right. The old bastard was always yelling at me. Said I lacked the instincts for running a company like Benedict Fasteners. I started taking business-administration classes so I could develop the instincts, and he just laughed. He said no fancy college classes would ever give me what I needed. He said I just wasn't tough enough to follow in his shoes. And you know something? He was right."

"Benedict can be a little rough on people," Hatch admitted. No wonder Jessie had wound up running interference between David and her father. With her soft heart, she must have felt sick about the failure of that relationship.

"Yeah, well, as far as I was concerned, that last bit was the end. I walked away from Benedict Fasteners without a backward glance. Told Mom to forget trying to make me into a chip off the old Benedict block. Hell, I didn't even have any Benedict blood in me. I was a Ringstead. Why should I go out of my way to please the old man? Jessie was right."

"About what?"

"She told me I wasn't meant for the business world. She said I should go off and do what I wanted to do, not what someone else wanted me to do. I'll never forget the night she sat me down and said that to me. It was like she'd set me free somehow, you know? Everything was a lot clearer after that."

"So you switched your major from business administration to philosophy?"

"You got it." David swallowed the last of his latte.

"You're no longer interested in trying to please Benedict," Hatch observed slowly. "But you're more than willing to take money from him to finance your education?"

"Damned right. Bastard owes it to me."

"How do you figure that?"

David looked at him in disgust. "Don't you know? My father helped him build Benedict Fasteners."

"What the hell are you talking about?"

"My father used to work for Benedict back in the old days. He was an accountant. He pretty much set up the business, got it on its feet. He virtually created the little empire Uncle Vincent owns today." There was a hint of pride in David's voice now. "If it hadn't been for my father,

Mom said, Benedict would have gone under back at the beginning. The old bastard didn't know anything about business in those days. All he knew was construction."

"He knows a hell of a lot about business now," Hatch observed.

"So he learned. Mostly from my father, the way I see it. Took advantage of my dad. And when he didn't need Dad anymore, he fired him."

"Fired him? Are you sure?"

David gave him a disgusted look. "Of course I'm sure. Mom told me all about it. Benedict used Dad up and got rid of him rather than make him an equal partner in the business, the way he should have. My father wasn't like Benedict. He was an intellectual type, you know? Not a shark. Getting fired was hard on him. He just split."

"You remember all this? You couldn't have been more than a small boy."

"Of course I don't remember all of it. I've figured most of it out from little things Mom and Benedict and Connie and Lilian have let slip over the years. The bottom line is, Uncle Vincent owes me, just like Mom says."

"Christ," Hatch muttered. "Nothing like airing a few family secrets." He sat in silence for a while, thinking.

"You finished with this little man-to-man chat?" David asked. "If so, I've got another class in fifteen minutes."

"Just one more thing, David."

"Yeah?"

"I happen to think you're a lot tougher than your father was. The fact that you put up with all the hassle from Benedict over the years and then chucked the whole scene to find your own path tells me that."

"So?"

"So I think you've got what it takes to go to Benedict yourself and ask for the loan for grad school." Hatch swallowed the last of his coffee and got to his feet. "You want to make the old bastard pay for what he did to your father? Go ahead. Make him pay through the nose. Take every last dime you can pry out of him and spend it on a degree in philosophy. You couldn't ask for a better revenge, believe me."

"Yeah, that did occur to me. He really can't stand the idea of me getting a degree in philosophy," David agreed with grim satisfaction.

"Just make sure you take your revenge all by yourself," Hatch concluded quietly. "Don't involve Jessie in it."

David looked up swiftly. "Mom always said it was easier for Jessie to get the money from Benedict."

"Not anymore. I'm in the way now. Besides. Take it from me, David, vengeance is a lot sweeter when you take it in person. That's my little bit of philosophical wisdom for the day. Based on a lot of real-life experience. Think about it."

Hatch went out the door and walked to where he had parked the Mercedes.

CHAPTER FOURTEEN

I hope you did the right thing. I'm not so sure about this, Hatch. I just don't know." Jessie twiddled her fork in her penne pasta and sun-dried tomatoes and gazed uncertainly at Hatch.

"Stop worrying about it. It's done and that's the end of it." Hatch tore off a slice of bread from the loaf in the basket and sank his teeth into it.

The noise from the evening dinner crowd sharing the cozy restaurant with Jessie and Hatch was a contented hum. The food being served at the tables was typical Northwest-style cuisine, which meant intriguing and innovative combinations of fresh fish, pasta, and vegetables.

"I don't know." Jessie gazed moodily down into her pasta as if it were a particularly cloudy crystal ball. "Maybe you shouldn't have been so hard on him. I've told you David's very sensitive."

"I don't give a damn about his sensitivity," Hatch muttered. "I just want to make sure that from now on he does his own dirty work."

"He and Dad don't get along very well. I've told you that. They barely even speak to each other."

"You of all people should know it's not necessary to get along well with Vincent in order to deal with him. You've just got to have some staying power. It's up to David now. If he wants the cash for grad school, he can ask for it himself. You're out of it. No more rescue operations on behalf of the family."

"You're making up new rules for me and the others based on the way you like to do things. That's not fair, Hatch. The rest of us don't work the same way."

"I don't care how the rest of the clan works. I just want you out of the loop. At least for a while."

"What gives you the right to interfere in my life this way?"

"I don't see it as interference. I see it as cutting through a few of the knots in which you've got yourself tangled."

Jessie was speechless for an instant. "You have an incredible audacity, Hatch. Cutting through the knots, my foot. As if you knew what you were doing. You're not some kind of professional family counselor."

"Damn right I'm not. But I learned a long time ago that it's usually easier to cut through a knot than it is to unravel it."

"Stop talking about knots," she snapped.

"All right. What would you like to talk about? Our forthcoming engagement?"

She tensed instantly, the way she always did when he mentioned marriage. "We don't have any concrete plans for an engagement."

"Maybe we'd better make some," he mused. "I'm beginning to think we've been fooling around long enough."

Jessie felt goaded. "Maybe I like fooling around. Maybe I'd be content to fool around forever. Did you ever consider that possibility? The situation isn't bad the way it stands now. Not for me, at any rate. I'm getting the best of both worlds. All the advantages of an affair and none of the disadvantages of marriage."

"So you're just using me, is that it?" He gave her a thoughtful look. "Should I start withholding sex in order to prod you into marriage?"

Jessie flushed warmly. She glanced quickly to the right and then to the left, trying to ascertain if anyone at a neighboring table had overheard the remark. Then she glowered at Hatch. "Is that supposed to be a joke?"

"No. I have no sense of humor, remember?"

Jessie stopped fiddling with her fork and picked up the knife instead. She began tracing small agitated triangles on the tablecloth. "I'm not so sure about that."

"Is that right?" Hatch munched on a clam. "What changed your mind?"

"I haven't changed my mind. Not yet, at any rate." She raised her chin. "But I am reconsidering the issue."

"How about doing something a little more productive?"

"Such as?" she asked.

"Such as setting a date for a wedding."

"So you can get it on your calendar?" she retorted. "Get the big day properly scheduled into your busy life? Are you sure you can make time for a honeymoon? We're talking two whole weeks here, Hatch. That's the traditional length of time, I believe. Are you sure you can stay away from the office that long?"

"It's amazing how much work you can get done in a hotel room if you bring along the right equipment," he said seriously. "What with fax machines and modems and laptop computers, a man can take his office with him these days."

"There isn't going to be any wedding." The knife Jessie had been using to draw little patterns in the tablecloth suddenly jumped out of her fingers and teetered on the edge of the table. She watched in dismay as it toppled over the edge. It landed on the carpet in merciful silence. When she glanced up to meet Hatch's gaze she thought she saw a cool satisfaction in his eyes.

"It's not funny," she muttered.

"I know."

She was incensed. "I'll bet you do think it's funny, don't you?"

"No. How could I, with my nonexistent or, at best, extremely limited sense of humor?" he asked reasonably. "Forget the knife, Jessie. The waiter will bring you another one. Tell me something."

"What?"

"Do you still think I'm incapable of giving our marriage the amount of attention it would need?"

"After that crack about bringing along a fax machine and a modem on your honeymoon, what else am I supposed to think?"

"I give you my word of honor they won't get in the way," he said earnestly. "I work very efficiently."

Jessie stared at him. He *was* teasing her. She was almost certain of it. And she was rising to the bait like a well-trained little fish. She forced herself to relax before she dropped anything else on the floor.

"Come on, Jessie. Tell me the truth. I'm not nearly as much like your father as you thought back at the beginning. Right?"

"Okay, I admit it. You're turning out to be a very different sort of man, even though you've got a lot of the same workaholic tendencies. My father would never have helped me figure out what's happening to Susan Attwood." *Or gone out of his way to keep Elizabeth from being disappointed at the science fair. Or worried very much about my motives for marrying you,* she added silently. *Not that I am going to marry you,* she corrected herself immediately.

"So I'm not such a bad guy, after all? I think we're making some progress here."

"Maybe we are. I have to tell you something, Hatch. I'm not sure you're right to try to yank me out of the family loop, as you call it, but I will say that no one has ever tried to rescue me from anything before. It's kind of a novel experience."

Hatch started to smile slowly, but before he could say anything else a bird-faced woman with frizzy gray hair and tiny half-glasses perched on her beak of a nose stopped beside the table.

"*Jessie*. Jessie Benedict, it is you. I thought it was when I saw you from over there." She nodded toward a booth on the other side of the crowded restaurant. "Haven't seen you in ages. How is everything going? Did you find another job?"

Jessie looked up, recognizing the woman at once. It was hard to forget someone who had once fired you. "Hello, Mavis. Nice to see you again. Mavis, this is Sam Hatchard. Call him Hatch. Hatch, meet Mavis Fairley. You and Mavis have a lot in common, Hatch."

"We do?" Hatch was already on his feet, acknowledging the introduction with grave politeness.

"Do we, indeed?" Mavis echoed brightly, waving him graciously back into his seat. "And what would that be, I wonder? Are you by any chance in the health-food business?"

"No. I'm in nuts and bolts."

"Hatch is the new CEO at Benedict Fasteners," Jessie explained. "And what you both have in common," she added with a benign smile, "is that you've each had occasion to fire me."

"Oh, dear." Mavis looked instantly concerned. "Not another unfortunate job situation, Jessie?"

"Afraid so."

"She was wreaking havoc in her father's company," Hatch said matter-of-factly. "What kind of damage did she do to your firm?"

"To be perfectly blunt, she was driving off customers right and left. She managed my downtown store for a while. I'm in health foods, as I said, and sales began plummeting almost immediately after she took over. She was being a bit too straightforward with the customers, if you take my meaning."

"I think I get the point." Hatch's brow rose. "A little too honest, Jessie?"

"I simply told them the truth about the products they were buying and sent a few of them who looked particularly ill to a doctor. That's all," Jessie stated.

"It was enough to butcher my bottom line within a month," Mavis confided to Hatch. "She was so nice, and such an enthusiastic person, though. I really hated to let her go, but business is business."

Hatch nodded in complete understanding. "Believe me, I know the feeling, Mavis. Business is business."

For some reason that struck Jessie as funny. She started laughing and could not stop. Hatch smiled in quiet satisfaction.

The next morning Jessie walked into the small building housing Valentine Consultations with a sense of impending disaster weighing on her. As soon as she opened the front door of the building she saw the green glow seeping out from the cracked doorway of Alex's office. She pushed open the door and glanced inside.

The place was in its usual state of disarray. Alex, his head cradled on his folded arms, was fast asleep amid the clutter of empty soda cans and pizza cartons. He stirred as Jessie stepped into the room.

"Did you spend the whole night here, Alex?"

"Hi." He yawned, rubbed his eyes, and reached for his glasses. "Yeah. I was here all night. Started talking to Susan. After she went off-line, I fell asleep."

"You contacted Susan again? Is she all right?"

"She's starting to sound real scared, Jessie. Said she thinks she's being watched. I told her that I'd get her off that island anytime she wants."

"No kidding?" Jessie sat down in the chair next to his. "What did she say to that?"

"She panicked. Said absolutely no police."

"Hmmm." Jessie glanced at the screen and saw the words that had appeared on the top half. "Is that her last message?"

Alex frowned. "No, I cleared the screen after her last one. Holy shit." He leaned closer, alarmed. "That's a new one. She must have sent it to me while I was asleep."

Jessie leaned forward to read. It was the longest message she had yet seen from Susan Attwood.

I'm really getting scared, Green. I want out of here. I think I saw data I shouldn't have seen. Please come and get me. The cove on the eastern side of the island. There's a buoy marking it. Please be there in a boat at midnight tonight. Green? Green, are you still there? I hope you get this last message. I've got to get out of here. Good-bye, Green. Please, no cops. I'm so afraid. I just want to get away from here. I hope you're still there, Green.

"Holy shit," Alex said again. He surged up out of the chair. "We've got to rescue her."

"Of course we do." Jessie glanced at her watch. "We'll have to get moving. It'll take time to get to the islands and arrange to rent a boat. Do you know how to operate one?"

"No. Damn." Alex swung around, his eyes frantic. "We've got to find someone who knows how to pilot a boat. Someone who can keep his mouth shut."

Jessie thought for a moment. "My cousin, David, spent a few months on a fishing boat up in Alaska. He knows about boats."

"Think he'd help us?"

"I think so. I'll call him." Jessie reached for the phone.

"After you get hold of him, you'd better call Hatch," Alex said.

Jessie winced. "He's going to explode when he hears what we're planning to do."

* * *

She was right. Hatch exploded.

"I don't know how I let you three talk me into this. I must be going crazy." Hatch stood at the helm of the small cruiser as David let it drift silently toward the buoy that marked the small cove. The heavily forested island rose like a great black blot against the starry sky.

It was close to midnight and there was a moon. The night air was crisp and there was no fog. When they had gotten near the island David had shut off the running lights, eased back the throttle, and used the lights from the mansion as a guide. The buoy had been right where Susan Attwood had said it would be. A good twenty-minute walk from the house. Maybe longer, given the rough terrain.

Hatch had been uneasy since Jessie had phoned him that morning. If he had not known better, he'd have thought he'd developed a few psychic abilities himself lately. But it was nothing that fancy or complicated. Just his common sense trying frantically to reassert itself.

"We couldn't call the cops in on this," Alex said from the back of the boat, where he sat beside Jessie. "I promised Susan."

"He's right, Hatch. She seemed to think she would be in even more danger if we called in the authorities," Jessie said. "She just wants off that island."

"What can go wrong?" David asked in reasonable tones, his attention on the entrance to the cove. "We just go in, pick her up, and leave. Piece of cake."

Hatch heard the thread of excitement in David's voice and groaned. "Haven't you three learned yet that anything that can go wrong *will* go wrong?"

"Come on, Hatch," Jessie said in bracing tones. "Don't be such a spoilsport. David's right. We just get in and get out. No problem."

"I'll remember that." Hatch looked at her. All four of them were wearing dark clothes, on his instructions. But the attire definitely did the most for Jessie. She looked like a sexy little cat burglar in her tight black pullover sweater and black jeans. He suddenly wished she were anywhere but here, somewhere *safe*.

"Ready?" asked David. "Here we go."

"No." Hatch gazed at the cove, straining to see something, anything, in the thick darkness ahead of him. The sense of wrongness was heavier than ever. "Not here. It's just a little too damn obvious. Let's put in somewhere else along the shore."

"But this is the spot, I'm sure of it," David said.

Hatch nodded. "I know it is. But let's see if there's another place we can go in. We can hike back overland to the cove and see if she's waiting where she's supposed to be waiting."

Alex left his seat and rushed forward. "We're wasting time. Susan will be scared and cold. We've got to get her out of there."

"If she's there, we'll find her," Hatch assured him. "Sit down, Robin. Let's go, David."

David shrugged and fed the engines a bit more power. The boat churned quietly through the cold black water. A few minutes later they were out of sight of the cove.

"What about here?" David asked, indicating another small indentation in the shoreline that was just barely visible in the moonlight. "We can tie up to those rocks and walk back to the cove."

Hatch studied the natural jetty formed by a rocky outcropping. "All right. Let's try it."

David eased the craft slowly and carefully toward the rocks. He called out soft directions to Alex and Jessie, who scurried to obey.

A few minutes later the boat was bobbing gently next to the jetty. Alex jumped out to secure it with a line.

David turned to Hatch. "Okay, boss. We're all set."

Hatch set his jaw. Now came the hard part. He turned to Jessie. "Alex, David, and I will go ashore and find Susan. Jessie, you will stay here with the boat."

The mutiny was immediate and expected.

"No way," Jessie snapped. "I'm coming with the rest of you."

"I want you to stay here," Hatch said in his most reasonable tones. "That way, if something happens, you can go for help."

"Nothing's going to happen. We're just going to get Susan and leave."

"Leaving you behind is what's known as Plan B," Hatch said.

"I'm the one who organized Plan A. I have a right to be a part of it." Jessie looked at the other two men. "I'm going with you."

David glanced swiftly at Hatch and then shook his head at Jessie. "He's right, Jess. Somebody should stay here."

"Yeah," said Alex, nodding in agreement. "Makes sense."

"Then one of you stay here," she retorted. "You're trying to leave me behind because I'm the only female in the crowd, and I won't have it."

Hatch got out of the boat. "We're wasting time. You're staying here, Jessie. If we're not back in fifteen minutes, you radio for help."

"I don't know how to use the radio."

"Show her how to call for help, David."

David nodded and began giving concise instructions. Jessie listened but she looked distinctly annoyed. When she finally muttered reluctantly that she understood, David leapt out of the boat to join Alex and Hatch. They all stood there gazing down at her, a united masculine front.

Jessie scowled up at them, her hands on her hips. "This is my big case and you three are taking over. It's not fair."

Hatch felt a pang of guilt that lasted no more than two seconds. "They also serve who only sit and wait," he reminded her.

"Get out of here before I fire the lot of you."

"Right. We're on our way." Hatch started off immediately, followed by the other two.

The night breeze rustled overhead in the boughs of the

trees. Water slapped softly at the rocky shoreline. The soft sounds muffled their footsteps. Hatch glanced back once or twice, making certain Jessie had obeyed orders. She and the boat were soon out of sight as the three men moved into the thickly wooded landscape.

It did not take long to reach the cove. Hatch put out a hand, silently halting the others as they reached the point where the trees thinned out. Not caring for the sparse cover in that region, he motioned Alex and David toward a jumble of tree-shrouded boulders. There they crouched, concealed amidst the drooping branches and disordered rocks, and scanned the beach.

A tiny, blond figure dressed in jeans and a sweater huddled near the water's edge. She carried a computer-printout-size folder under her arm. Her back was to them as she anxiously searched the dark horizon.

"There she is," Alex said triumphantly. "*Susan*. Over here."

"Shut up," Hatch snarled softly, making a grab for Alex's arm. But Alex eluded him. He broke out of the trees and raced toward the figure.

The blond whirled around. She was wearing glasses. Definitely Susan Attwood.

"Green? Is that you?"

"Yeah, it's me. Green. I mean, Alex."

"Dammit, Robin, come back here, you ass," Hatch muttered under his breath, knowing that it was too late to stop the younger man.

"I think he's in love," David murmured. "Kind of touching, isn't it?"

"Kind of stupid, is what it is." Hatch watched as the pair on the beach dashed toward each other, arms outstretched. "Looks like something out of a television commercial. All we can do now is hope Susan is here alone."

"Hey, you don't think this is some sort of setup, do you?" David asked.

"How should I know? I'm in the nuts-and-bolts business. This isn't exactly my field of expertise." But he'd seen enough street fighting, both in and out of the corporate world, to know that it always paid to keep an ace in the hole.

The couple on the beach were embracing now. Hatch could not hear what was being said but he was relieved when Alex turned Susan toward the trees and started forward.

"Here they come," David observed, drawing back deeper into the shadows. "We'll be out of here in a couple more minutes."

But at that instant a dark figure stepped out of the trees on the far side of the cove. He had his arm extended and there was no mistaking the object in his fist. The gun glinted in the moonlight.

"That's far enough, you two," Rick Landis announced. "Hold it right there."

"Damn," Hatch whispered. He felt David freeze beside him.

"Christ, who's that?" David asked in the softest of voices.

"One of Bright's people. A guy named Landis. I had a feeling he was more than a tour guide." Hatch watched intently as Landis moved closer to his captives. "I knew this was not a good idea. Why in hell did I let Jessie talk me into this?"

"Don't feel too bad about it," David said consolingly. "Jessie can be very persuasive."

"Yeah, I know. Come on."

"What are we going to do? Go for help?" David followed as Hatch faded back into the forest.

"I have a nasty feeling that by the time we got the authorities here, Susan and Robin would have disappeared."

"So what do we do?"

Hatch made an executive decision. "Something simple and straightforward, I think. This is the shortest route back toward the mansion. We wait until they go past us and then one of us jumps down on top of Landis and bashes his head in."

David considered that. "Who does the bashing?"

Hatch shot his companion a sidelong glance and made another executive decision. "You're the one who studied karate."

"Damn." David sounded both thrilled and appalled. "I sure as hell never tried to use it on anybody."

"Did you learn enough to drop that guy?"

"Well, yeah. Maybe. Theoretically. Under the right circumstances. Like I said, I've never been in a real fight."

"This won't be a real fight. If we do this right, Landis won't know you're on top of him until it's all over."

"What are you going to do?" David asked softly.

"What I do best: supervise. And keep an eye out for a guy named Hoffman."

"Who's he?"

"Someone who reminded me a lot of Landis. Quiet."

"Come on, you two," Landis was saying in a loud voice. "Let's move. We haven't got all night."

Susan's response was soft and tearful on the night air. "Please let us go. I won't tell anyone a thing. I promise. I just want to get away from here."

"Too late for that now, you stupid little bitch. You should have stuck to inputting the data and not gone snooping."

"Stop threatening her," Alex said fiercely, placing himself squarely in front of Susan.

"You must be the famous Green, huh? We figured you had to be a hacker. Nobody else could have gotten into that data base. Bright was worried for a while that you might be someone dangerous. But when Susan here started making arrangements for the dramatic rescue at midnight, we knew we weren't dealing with the cops. Just an amateur."

Hatch prayed Alex would have the sense not to mention the fact that he had not come here alone tonight.

"What are you going to do with us?" Alex demanded.

"The boss has a few questions to ask you. After that, I think it's safe to say we won't need either of you around anymore."

"Don't you dare hurt Alex," Susan wailed. "He was just trying to help me."

"It's all right, Susan," Alex said soothingly. "He won't hurt either of us."

"Give me a break," Landis said. "You're both dead meat. You think Bright can afford to let you live after what you found out, Susie, baby?"

"I told you I wouldn't tell anyone. Please, Landis. Let us go."

"Shut the fuck up and move. Back to the house."

Hatch glanced back at David, silently telling him to be ready as the other three started toward the pile of boulders. Landis was making his captives keep as close to the shoreline as possible, Hatch noted with relief. That route would bring them past the jumble of boulders where he and David were hiding.

With one last reassuring nod at David, Hatch faded back into the trees. *An ace in the hole.*

Hatch sensed David's nervousness as the younger man flattened himself against a boulder, but he also sensed the determination in him. David was going to do his part, come hell or high water. Jessie's cousin was no wimp.

David waited until Alex and Susan had gone past. Then Landis was below him, cursing as he pushed aside a swaying branch.

David did not hesitate. He came down off the boulder feetfirst.

The gun Landis had been holding went off. The shot roared through the woods, louder than thunder on the night air. It was followed by a heavy thudding sound and a stifled shout that faded out quickly.

Silence descended.

The hair on the back of Hatch's neck stirred. He glanced

to his right and saw a lone figure slither out from a heavy veil of tree limbs. Moonlight glinted on the gun in his hand.

Hoffman.

The pilot was being cautious, waiting to assess the situation before he moved in.

"Hey, Hatch," David called, his voice infused with the euphoria of the victorious male. "I got him. It's okay. Come on out. *I got him.*"

The figure Hatch was watching froze, the gun still aimed in the general direction of the activity. But it was obvious the second armed man now realized there was another presence in the woods. He started to turn, nervously searching the undergrowth.

Hatch knew it was the only chance he was going to get. Hoffman had started his scan from the wrong direction.

Hatch launched himself forward. He struck solid flesh and threw a short, savage punch. The gunman choked on a groan, dropped the gun, and reeled forward. Hatch went in low and hit him a second time. Hoffman collapsed on the damp ground.

"Hatch?" David burst forth from a small stand of trees. "You okay? What's going on here?" He halted abruptly when he saw the man on the ground.

"His name is Hoffman," Hatch said. "He's a buddy of the one you just took out. These two must have comprised Bright's security force."

"What are we going to do with them?" David asked, glancing back over his shoulder.

"Leave them here. I don't want to drag them all the way back to the boat, that's for sure." Hatch scooped up the gun Hoffman had dropped. "Everything go all right back there?"

"Yeah." David's voice filled with excitement once again. "Landis is out cold. Shit. I never thought that karate stuff would really work." He was obviously awed at his own success.

Hatch gave him a faint grin as they moved back through the trees. "Nice job. You can cover my back anytime."

"Thanks." David's grin spread from ear to ear. "All right. Hey, it's a deal. Anytime."

"You guys okay?" Alex demanded as Hatch and David reached them. He had a protective arm wrapped around Susan's shoulders. Susan was whimpering softly.

"We're fine." Hatch shoved Hoffman's gun into his belt and handed Landis' to Alex, who did the same. "Now we all get back to the boat. Fast."

"You didn't tell me you had anyone else with you, Alex," Susan murmured to Robin.

"There wasn't time to explain. That bastard with the gun appeared out of nowhere," Alex said.

"I should have known you'd have it all planned out," Susan said admiringly. "You're so brilliant, Alex."

"Kind of a rough plan, but it was the best I could do on the spur of the moment," Alex said modestly.

David slid Hatch a knowing look. "I told you the man's in love," he muttered.

"You pegged it. Let's get moving here." Hatch realized that the sense of urgency he was experiencing had not diminished. If anything, it had grown stronger in the past few minutes.

This was absolutely the last time he was going to let Jessie talk him into one of her crazy schemes, he vowed silently. The woman was a menace to herself and others. She needed to be kept on a tight leash, and from here on out, Hatch intended to do exactly that.

He kept that glowing promise before him like a talisman as he followed the others through the trees back to the little cove where Jessie and the boat were waiting.

Less than five minutes later, just as they were moving out of the trees and onto the rocky beach, a familiar voice split the night air.

"Don't come any closer," Jessie yelled. "He's got a gun."

But it was too late. Alex, Susan, and David had already moved out into the open. Hatch alone was still shielded by the thick foliage as he took in the scene on the shore.

247

Jessie was standing helplessly in the gently bobbing boat. Edwin Bright had one arm around her throat. In his other hand he held a gun to her head.

"By all means, let's have your friends come a little closer, my dear," Edwin Bright said loudly.

CHAPTER FIFTEEN

What happened to Landis and Hoffman?" Bright called from the boat.

"We left them back there in the woods," David answered with astonishing calm.

"Who are you?" Bright demanded impatiently.

"A friend of Jessie's."

"The one they call Hatchard?"

David was silent.

"Answer me," Bright roared, "or I'll put a bullet through her head."

"No," David finally said, offering no further explanation.

"Dammit, where's Hatchard?" Bright yelled. "I know he's the one behind all this, the one who screwed this thing up. Where the hell is he?"

"Dead," David said, improvising with laudable speed. "Landis got him. Didn't you hear the gunshot?"

"*Dead?*" Jessie's shriek pierced the air. "*No*, he can't be dead. I'd know if he were dead." She jerked backward and forward in a frantic, violent motion that, added to the swaying action of the boat, was more than enough to take both her and Bright off-balance.

"Watch it, you bitch, we're going over," Bright shouted, scrambling to retain his balance. It was too late. He released Jessie in an effort to save himself from toppling over the edge of the bobbing boat.

But Jessie's momentum was too strong. She lost her footing and fell backward, flailing wildly. Bright tried to dodge her arm and could not. It caught him across the throat and she carried him with her as she went into the water.

Jessie screamed again just as she hit the cold water. Bright plunged in beside her, swearing furiously.

Hatch raced out of the trees and ran past the others, who were staring at the scene in stunned amazement. He dashed along the rocky jetty, leapt into the boat, and peered over the side.

"Jessie."

Jessie was bobbing in the water, her dark hair plastered to her scalp. She pushed wet tendrils out of her eyes and looked up at him with a glowing smile. "I knew you were alive."

Hatch ignored Bright, who was sputtering and gasping next to her. He leaned down, caught Jessie's raised hands, and hauled her straight up out of the black water and into the boat.

"That water's damn cold," Alex said as he stepped into the boat. "It'll kill a person in less than thirty minutes. Better get her into one of the blankets."

"He's right." David jumped into the boat and opened a locker. He dragged out a blanket. "Jessie, get your clothes off and get into this. You'll be okay. You were in the water only a couple of minutes."

Jessie nodded, already beginning to shiver violently. "My God, I'm cold." She grabbed the blanket, pulled it around her, and started to strip off her jeans underneath it.

"Hey, goddammit, help me," Bright shouted from the water. When no one responded, he struck out for shore.

The splashing caught Hatch's attention. "David, untie the

boat. Keep it between Bright and the shore. I want to talk to him."

David's brows rose but he said nothing. He and Alex quickly untied the boat and let it drift gently between Bright and the shoreline, blocking escape from the bone-chilling water.

"Goddammit, you can't do this," Bright yelled, floundering desperately. "Get me out of here. I'll freeze."

Hatch planted both hands on the hull and looked down at Bright. "Actually, that's not a bad idea."

"Are you crazy? You'll be killing me. People die of hypothermia out here all the time," Bright screamed.

"He's right," Jessie observed. "It's amazing how fast hypothermia sets in. A few minutes in this water followed by a few minutes standing around in the cold air and it's all over. He's been in that water several minutes already."

Hatch glanced at Alex. "Think he could make it safely back to the house on his own?"

Alex frowned consideringly. "Doubt it. Ambient temperature is in the forties now, and it's a good twenty-, twenty-five-minute hike. He's been in that water long enough to start the hypothermic process. Yeah, I'd say getting back to the house on his own is starting to look real iffy."

"You can't do this," Bright wailed in panic and despair.

"Swim to shore," Hatch told Bright. "I'll meet you there with a blanket. You tell me a few things I want to know and I'll let you have the blanket. Refuse to talk and I'll take my blanket and go home."

The threat was a virtual death sentence and everyone knew it, including Bright. He struck out for shore.

Hatch took one of the blankets and vaulted out of the boat onto the rocks. "Wait here," he said to the others.

He did not hurry to the rescue. When he reached the shoreline, Bright was already out of the water, hugging himself as shudder after shudder went through him. He had lost his glasses in the fall overboard and he peered at Hatch with slitted eyes.

"Give me that blanket," Bright hissed.

Hatch stopped a few feet away. "First you tell me a little bit about the operation."

Bright's eyes widened slightly. "What are you, some kind of pro? What happened to Hoffman and Landis, anyway?"

"They're both out of the picture. Talk, Bright. You'll never make it back to the mansion alive without this blanket."

"Fuck off."

"Suit yourself." Hatch turned and started back toward the boat.

"Wait, you bastard," Bright said through chattering teeth. "You can't leave me like this."

Hatch glanced back over his shoulder. "I don't see why not."

"Shit. I could die out here."

"That's not my problem, is it?"

Bright stared at him. "Dammit, what's going on? I know you're a pro. You must be. The girl's mother hire you?"

"I'm just a businessman, Bright."

"Businessman, hell. Who are you, goddammit? Who hired you?"

"You know that woman you were holding the gun on a few minutes ago?"

"What about her?" Bright snarled.

"You might say I did it for her. She's the lady I'm going to marry."

"Shit."

"Now you probably have a clearer understanding of why I don't have any real ethical problem with the idea of you freezing to death out here." Hatch turned and started once more toward the boat.

"Stop, goddammit, I'm coming with you." Bright staggered forward. "You've got to take me with you. I don't think I can make it back to the house. I'm freezing."

Hatch paused, thoughtful. Then he shook his head. "No, I don't think it's worth taking you with us. If I thought you might talk to the authorities, I'd say yes, but something tells me you won't say a word."

"I said wait, you bastard. I'll talk." Bright was clearly desperate now.

Hatch dangled the blanket in front of him. "Prove it. Tell me something real interesting."

"Like what?"

"Like which offshore bank you're using. Tell me where the money goes. Explain how you divert it. Little things like that. Convince me. And then show me something that looks like proof."

Edwin Bright glowered sullenly at him in the moonlight. And then another racking shudder went through him. Without a word he reached into his pocket and pulled out a dripping wallet. He held it out to Hatch.

"There's a list of accounts in there," Bright muttered through chattering lips. "And a key to a safe at the mansion."

"That sounds promising." Hatch handed over the blanket while he started going through Edwin Bright's wallet.

Bright clutched at the blanket and started to strip off his clothes. "I was right, wasn't I? You are a pro. Government or private?"

"Private. Very private." Hatch found several interesting items in Edwin Bright's wallet, including the list and the key. "Tell me something else now. Was that one of your people who broke into Valentine Consultations?"

Bright stepped out of his pants. "Yeah. We knew Attwood's mother had just hired that damned fortune-teller to find her daughter. We needed to know how much Valentine knew."

"How about after we took our scenic tour of the facilities? Was that one of your people who tried to break into my car?"

"We couldn't figure out how you were involved. We were trying to get a fix on you. The idea was to search the car. Look, this was just a good scam. Nobody was supposed to get hurt."

"Is that right?"

"Hell, yes. I didn't want trouble. But I've got a major investment in this operation. I've run it twice already back East and made a fortune. The idea is to get in and get out. Find a place to set up shop, recruit a few kids from the local college campus to man the phones and computers and put on the show. Then we make the pitch and wait for the money to roll in. I don't hang around. Two or three months is plenty of time to get set up and rake the cream off the top."

"Why try it here?"

"Hell, everybody knows the Northwest is hot for the environment. Everyone around here wants to save it. Besides, an old lady back East who had already forked over a hundred grand died and left the foundation this island. It was too good an opportunity to pass up. But I figured to sell the place in a few weeks, dump the kids, and head for the next location."

Hatch nodded. "Well, I think that about does it. Thanks for wrapping up a few of the loose ends for me." He started toward the boat again.

"Wait, goddammit. You've got to take me with you. I won't make it if I have to walk back to the mansion alone. I'm too damn cold, even with this blanket. I need warm liquids."

"All right. If you can make it to the boat, you can come with us. But don't get any bright ideas like trying to intimidate Susan, or I'll throw you overboard. I doubt the fish will even notice one more load of toxic waste in the Sound."

"Is that supposed to be funny?" Bright asked through clenched teeth.

254

"No. I don't have a sense of humor. Just ask anyone."

"Shit. I knew you were a pro."

Jessie was euphoric. The adventure had ended on a note of shining success and she could not wait to tell Mrs. Valentine every detail.

The police had taken statements and dispatched a boat to New Dawn Island to see what was going on there. Bright was in the local hospital under guard. He was being treated for the early stages of hypothermia. He was already demanding a lawyer.

The computer printout Susan Attwood had brought with her, as well as the list and key from Bright's wallet, was in safekeeping in the hands of the police. Susan had phoned her mother from the police station and Mrs. Attwood had broken down in tears of relief. She had explained that a man who fitted Hoffman's description had told her that her daughter would disappear forever if she did not call off the investigation.

Jessie was already mentally preparing her report to Mrs. Valentine. She knew her boss was going to be thrilled with the results of the case. Business would be flowing into Valentine Consultations as soon as the story hit the newspapers.

But now was the time for celebration.

Jessie sat tailor-fashion in the middle of the bed and gazed happily around at her little group of intrepid adventurers. They were gathered together in a room at the same inn where she and Hatch had stayed on the occasion of their first visit to Edwin Bright's island. Several cans of soda recently purchased from the inn's vending machine had been opened and were bubbling freely. Bags of potato chips were being passed around. It was a festive sight.

"I want to thank you all for what you did tonight," Jessie said. "Valentine Consultations is deeply grateful for your assistance on this case." She raised her glass of cola toward

Alex. "First, to Alex, for cracking the computer and making contact with Susan."

"To Alex," David said grandly.

"To Alex." Susan Attwood blushed rosily and looked at Alex as if he were the reincarnation of Albert Einstein.

Hatch, sprawled in the chair near the window, took a swallow of cola and nodded at Alex. "Hell of a job, Robin."

"Thanks. It was nothing." Alex was flushed with pride and embarrassment. His eyes kept straying to Susan's admiring gaze. "Anytime you need help on a case, Jessie, just let me know."

"Why, thank you, Alex." Jessie beamed fondly at him. Then she raised her glass in David's direction. "To David, who has shown he is that rarest of all beings, a philosopher who is also a man of action. A true Renaissance man."

"I wouldn't go that far," David muttered, turning almost as red as Alex. But he was grinning hugely.

"To David," Alex intoned. "I owe you one, friend, for what you did to that jerk who was holding a gun on Susan."

"Yes," Susan said shyly. "Thank you, David. You were wonderful. Almost as wonderful as Alex."

Hatch took another swallow of cola. "I told you that you didn't need anyone running interference for you, Ringstead. You can do your own dirty work just fine."

David met his eyes. "So you did."

"To Susan," Jessie continued, hoisting her glass again. "Who bravely got out of the mansion with the proof of Edwin Bright's fraud."

"To Susan." Alex gazed at her with pride and longing in his eyes.

"To Susan." David held up his glass.

Hatch munched and nodded at Susan. "Bringing that printout showing Bright's financial setup was a stroke of genius, Susan. The authorities are going to have a field day."

"It was nothing." Susan blushed again. "I just wish I hadn't been such a gullible idiot in the first place."

Alex touched her hand. "Don't blame yourself, Susan. You had only the best intentions."

"The others I worked with there at the mansion were innocent too, for the most part." Susan glanced anxiously around the room. "The people who manned the telephones, as well as the computer operators and programmers. We all believed in Edwin Bright. We thought he was a true genius who was being deliberately ignored by the establishment because his predictions were so alarming. And you know how the government is about bad news."

"Nobody likes to hear talk of disaster," David agreed. "It's easier to kill the messenger than deal with the real problem."

Susan nodded sadly. "Those of us who went to work for Bright thought we were dealing with the real problem. We believed the climate forecasts were accurate and we thought the money was needed desperately for Bright's technology-development plan. I'd started having some doubts, but it wasn't until Alex contacted me and pointed out the anomalies in the forecast data that I really questioned what was going on. Then I stumbled over a record of Bright's scam back East and knew for sure something was wrong."

"I wouldn't worry about the others," Hatch said. "The authorities will probably only go after Bright."

"Fortunately, the people who got conned into working for Bright are all basically data-oriented," Alex said. "Show them where the data are wrong and they'll buy into the truth. They're not the type to follow Bright blindly, as if he were some guru. Not when they've seen the facts."

Susan nodded soberly. "I think that's true. Edwin Bright is a charismatic man, but without solid data to back up his claims, no one I know is going to follow him."

"Not everyone who worked for Bright got conned," Hatch said thoughtfully. "A few of them were in it for the money. Landis and Hoffman, for example. Not exactly your average wide-eyed innocents."

David gave him a sharp glance. "You think there might be more hired muscle like Landis and Hoffman running around?"

Hatch shrugged. "How would I know? I'm a businessman, not a detective. But there was a lot of money involved. It just seems remotely possible that if Bright had those two on the payroll, he might have had others."

Susan frowned. "If he did, I never saw them on the island."

"That's reassuring." Hatch took another swallow of cola.

"I'm sure the authorities will pick up everyone involved very quickly," Jessie declared crisply, although she couldn't meet Hatch's eyes. "Now, then, your attention, please." She tapped the edge of her glass with her fingernail. "I have one more toast to make before we conclude this celebration. To Hatch. Without whose unflagging zeal and noble leadership this mission would never have been accomplished."

A cheer went up around the room.

"Don't forget to mention my gold card," Hatch said. "You used it to get the guy down at the marina to rent you a boat in the middle of the night, remember?"

"To Hatch's gold card," Jessie repeated dutifully. It was a joke. She was sure of it. In fact, she was almost positive. It *had* to be a joke.

"To Hatch's gold card."

"To Hatch's gold card."

Hatch met Jessie's laughing eyes and smiled coolly. "One more toast," he said softly. "To Jessie. Who is going to marry me. Soon. Aren't you, Jessie?"

A sudden silence descended on the room. Jessie froze, her glass halfway to her lips. Her gaze collided with Hatch's and she was unable to look away. She loved him. And just look what he had gone through for her sake. Surely no man would go through all that unless he cared at least a little. She took a deep breath.

"Yes," Jessie said.

This time the cheer that went up shook the paintings on the walls and rattled the glassware on the end table. Hatch gazed at Jessie with deep satisfaction as Alex and David whooped in approval.

"About time," Hatch said softly.

A loud pounding began on the other side of the adjoining wall. A man's voice yelled from the next room.

"For Christ's sake, will you hold it down in there? We're trying to get some sleep."

Hatch groaned, shut his eyes, and sank deeper into his chair.

Jessie grinned. "This makes the second time poor Hatch has nearly been kicked out of here," she explained to the others. "Guess we better not come here on our honeymoon, huh, Hatch? A little too embarrassing for you."

"I never even considered this inn for our honeymoon," Hatch muttered without opening his eyes. "No telephones in the rooms. That means no business calls, no modem hookup, and no way to run a fax machine. How could I function?"

Jessie hurled a pillow at him while the others dissolved into laughter.

A long while later Jessie emerged from the bathroom to find that Hatch was already in bed. He had turned out the light. She could see him waiting for her in the shadows, his broad shoulders dark against the snowy pillows. His eyes glittered with a masculine anticipation that sent a delightful chill down her spine.

A wave of shyness threatened to overwhelm her as she went slowly toward him. This was the first time she had been truly alone with Hatch since the others had retired to their own rooms a short while ago. It was the first time she had been alone with him since agreeing to marry him.

"What's the matter, Jessie?" His voice was deep and dark. "Nervous now that everyone else has gone?"

"No, of course not. Why should I be nervous?" At that moment Jessie stubbed her toe against the leg of the chair, tripped, and sprawled across the bed. Mortified, she buried her face in the blanket. "Good grief, how can I marry a man who turns me into a walking disaster?"

"The same way I can marry a woman who gets me into situations where I wind up running around in the woods in the middle of the night playing hide-and-seek with people who carry guns," Hatch said. "Very carefully."

Jessie tried to stifle a laugh and failed. "That was a joke. I know it was."

"You're wrong. I meant every word. In fact, I have never been more serious in my life." Hatch pulled her up so that she lay beside him on the pillows. His expression was very intent as he speared his fingers through her hair and gripped the back of her head. "We're engaged now, Jessie. It's official."

"Yes." She knew her lower lip was quivering. She could feel it. A sense of desperation tore through her. "Hatch, I love you."

"I'm glad." He covered her mouth with his own and rolled her onto her back, crushing her into the bedclothes. "I want you to love me, Jessie. I want it very, very much," he muttered against her lips. Then he deepened the kiss. His tongue invaded her mouth.

Jessie felt herself plunging into deep water for the second time that night. But this time the water was warm, not icy. Her arms went around Hatch's shoulders as the weight of him bore her downward. For long moments she was caught up in the spell of his lovemaking, unable to think of the future or the past, longing only to please and be pleased, to satisfy and be satisfied.

She slitted her eyes briefly when she became aware of Hatch's hand gliding down the length of her, lifting the hem of her nightgown. Then his fingers were on the insides of her thighs and she sucked in her breath.

He parted her, moistening his fingers in the sweet, liquid warmth he had drawn forth. His lips found her nipples through the fabric of the gown as he touched her intimately. When she lifted herself against his hand and cried out softly, he groaned.

"Touch me," he muttered. "Yes. There. Hold me. God, Jessie. *Yes.*"

He was naked beneath the sheets, his body heavy with arousal. She curled her fingers around him and felt the drop of moisture at the broad, blunt tip of his manhood.

"Hang on." He took a deep breath and pulled away from her, groping for something on the nightstand. "Give me a second. I've got it here, somewhere."

She opened her eyes again and saw the stark need on his face. Lightly, wonderingly, she touched his cheek. "You said you wanted children."

"Yes. Damn. *Yes.* Jessie, are you sure?"

"I'm sure. I think, with a little practice, you would make a very good father, Hatch."

He stopped groping for the condom and pushed her flat on her back once more. His mouth captured hers in a kiss of searing need as he surged heavily into her warmth.

Hatch lay awake for a long while after Jessie fell asleep in his arms. One hand crooked behind his head, he watched the patterns on the ceiling and thought about the future.

He was not in the clear yet and he knew it, even if Jessie did think everything was tied up with a neat pink bow. Hatch understood that the potential for disaster still loomed. It was his way to calculate the odds and to take risks when the time was right. He had learned the hard way to do it in his personal life just as he did it in business.

He knew he had done a good job of cementing his future with Jessie by deliberately linking himself to Benedict Fasteners and the entire Benedict clan. He had been as thorough as possible about the task. Jessie was devoted to her family and he was rapidly becoming a part of the family. Everything was under control so long as nothing forced Jessie to have to choose between him and the rest of the clan.

The last thing Hatch wanted was for Jessie to ever have to make such a choice.

Hatch did not kid himself on that score. He knew that if Jessie were ever placed in a position where she had to choose between him and her family, the odds were not going to be in his favor. For Jessie, family would always come first.

And the family was bound by Benedict Fasteners.

The control of the company was the key.

Hatch turned the problem over in his mind a few more times. He did not like uncertainties. This was not the first time he had contemplated a method of getting Jessie out from under the responsibility she faced. He was definitely vulnerable as long as she had the long-term duty of looking after the firm for the rest of the family.

Hatch examined the plan he had been working on for the past few days. It was almost time to implement it. There was some risk involved, but he was fairly certain it was minimal now. With every day that passed he was more in control of the company and of his relationship with Jessie. With every passing day he was more certain that Vincent Benedict trusted him.

Hatch knew it was time to make the final move in this high-stakes game he was playing with his own future.

It was nearly dawn when Jessie stirred in the depths of the tangled bedding. She brought her elbow, which had somehow gotten caught in an awkward position above her head, down by her side. She collided with something solid.

"Oooph." Hatch winced.

"Sorry." Jessie propped herself up to look down at him in concern. "Did I hurt you?"

"That's supposed to be my line." He touched his side with tentative fingers. "But since you ask, I think I'm going to survive. Damn. Is it morning already?"

"Afraid so. I wouldn't worry about it. We've got a while yet before everyone heads downstairs for breakfast."

"Good. I need some more sleep. I've had a very hard night."

She chuckled. "Yes, I know."

He looked offended. "I was speaking in the literal sense."

"So was I."

Hatch sighed. "For the record, I would just like to point out that the worst hours I have ever worked in my life were the ones I just put in for Valentine Consultations. Remember that the next time you complain that I'm a little late getting home in the evening."

"Now, wait just one minute here—"

"Forget it. I don't feel like pursuing this conversation. Let's change the topic."

"To what?"

"To our engagement."

"What about it?" Jessie asked.

"You seem to have thrown yourself somewhat wholeheartedly into the thing," he pointed out carefully. "It was your idea to forget the protection last night, wasn't it?"

"Yes. Are you sorry?"

"Good God, no." He reached out and pulled her down across his chest. "Jessie, I know you've had your doubts about marrying me, but I promise you I'll do my best to make certain you don't regret this."

"I'll see that you do. Your best, that is."

Hatch smiled ruefully. "Yeah, you probably will. Nag, nag, nag."

"You got it." She squirmed into a more comfortable position. "Hatch?"

"Hmmm?" His fingers toyed with her hair, pushing it back behind her ears.

"I've been thinking about David."

"What about him?"

"He's different somehow. I can feel it."

Hatch smiled fleetingly. "Your famous intuition?"

263

"I think so," she said quite seriously. "It's because of you, isn't it?"

"Me?"

"You made him an important part of the rescue operation."

"I didn't *make* him an important part. He was an important part."

"He wasn't the only one in the crowd who knew how to fight," Jessie said gently.

Hatch shrugged. "David needed to know he could handle himself in a fight if he had to. He's been trying to prove himself to Vincent since he was a kid. But a man doesn't start growing up until he realizes that the only one he has to prove himself to is himself. I offered him a way to do that. Lucky I did, or we'd never have known about Hoffman being in those woods until it was too late."

"Very profound, Hatch."

"You like that, huh? Well, I've got something else even more profound to say to you."

Jessie tipped her head to one side at the new note in his voice. "And that is?"

"I think it might be best if you quit Valentine Consultations."

"Quit my job?" Jessie jerked herself upward and off the bed and stood glaring down at him. "Are you out of your mind? This is the best job I've ever had."

"I don't want you involved in any more rescue operations like the one last night." Hatch sat up slowly and put both feet flat on the floor. "And I'm afraid that when the news hits the papers, people who've lost kids to cults will be flocking to Valentine Consultations. You'll want to rescue each and every one of them. It's too dangerous. I won't have it."

"Hatch, it won't be like that. This was a fluke case."

"You can say that again. But the longer you live, the more you realize there are a lot of flukish things in this world. Jessie, I don't want to argue about this."

"Good. Because I don't want to argue about it either." She turned and stomped into the bathroom, slamming the door behind her.

Half an hour later they joined the others downstairs in the breakfast room. The dining area smelled strongly of freshly brewed coffee, pancakes, eggs, and frying bacon. Alex, Susan, and David were already occupying one of the large tables. They looked up expectantly as Jessie and Hatch entered the room.

"Uh-oh," David murmured, his eyes on Jessie's set face. "Do I detect trouble in upper management already?"

"Jessie has always had a problem fitting into the corporate hierarchy," Hatch said as he sat down and picked up the menu.

"He means I don't take orders well." Jessie slanted Hatch a fulminating glance.

"She'll learn," Hatch said easily.

CHAPTER SIXTEEN

So do you love him or what?" Elizabeth leaned over the railing and peered down into the murky green depths of Elliott Bay. Sea gulls bobbed on the water, searching out french fries and other discarded edibles from an assortment of plastic cups, paper, and litter that floated on the surface.

The Seattle waterfront with its shops, restaurants, and aquarium was only sparsely crowded this afternoon. A few tourists were strolling along on the sidewalk behind Elizabeth and Jessie and there were some joggers heading toward the park at the far end of the promenade.

"Of course I love him. Why else would I agree to marry him?" Jessie frowned down at the trash that marred the beautiful bay.

"Because everyone in the family wants you to?"

"I'd do a lot for this family, Elizabeth, but I would not marry someone just to keep everyone happy."

"Aunt Glenna says sometimes people do weird stuff just to please relatives."

"I wouldn't do anything that weird," Jessie assured her.

"Don't worry about me, kid. I'm not doing this for you or David or the moms. I'm doing it for me."

The sun sparkled on the lenses of Elizabeth's glasses as she looked up. Her small face was screwed into an expression of serious concern. "You're sure?"

"I'm sure."

"What changed your mind about Hatch? You told me you couldn't ever marry him."

"That was before I got to know him better."

Elizabeth nodded. "You mean you've decided he's not like Dad after all?"

Jessie smiled to herself. "No. Whatever else he is, he is definitely not like any other man I've ever met."

"Well, if you're sure you know what you're doing, I guess it's okay." Elizabeth stepped back from the railing. "You want to go through the aquarium now?"

"Sure."

"You ever miss your old job there?"

Jessie made a face. "Not in the least. Something about cutting up plain ordinary fish to feed to fancy exotic fish just didn't appeal to me. Seemed a little unfair, somehow."

Elizabeth grinned. "They let you go because you kept wanting to rescue the plain ordinary fish, didn't they?"

"Aquarium work was obviously not a good career path for me."

"You think working for Mrs. Valentine is a good career for you? The moms say they hope you'll settle down and find a real job after you marry Hatch."

Jessie recalled the argument she and Hatch had had on that subject. Not another word had been spoken concerning her career at Valentine Consultations since they had all returned from the San Juans yesterday afternoon. But she knew Hatch better than to think he was going to let the matter drop.

"I don't know why everyone's complaining about my working for Mrs. V," Jessie muttered. "It's obvious I'm at last in an upwardly mobile position. Business is going to boom in a few days when word gets out about the Attwood case."

"Have you finished your report for Mrs. Valentine?"

"Not yet. I'm still working on it. I want it to be really impressive. This case is going to totally revitalize Valentine Consultations and I want to be sure she appreciates the brilliance of the way I handled it as well as the new marketing potential of the firm."

Elizabeth giggled and then was silent for a moment as she glanced down over the railing once more. "You know, I wonder what Elliott Bay was like before people started throwing garbage into it."

"Spectacular." Jessie looked out toward the majestic Olympics. When one viewed it from a distance, the sound was as beautiful as it must have been two or three hundred years ago. "It still is spectacular. It just needs to be cleaned up, and that's going to take some hard work and a lot of money. There aren't any easy answers and there's still so much we don't know about ecology and the environment."

"I can sort of see why people got excited about what Edwin Bright was selling."

"So can I," Jessie said. "Too bad it wasn't for real."

Later that afternoon Jessie bounded up the sidewalk and into the downstairs hall of her office building. As usual there was a green glow emanating from Alex's office. She poked her head inside and smiled at the sight of Susan Attwood and Alex huddled together in front of the computer.

"What are you two working on?" Jessie asked.

"Hi, Jessie." Susan smiled shyly.

Alex glanced over his shoulder, squinting against the glare from the hall. "Oh, hi, Jessie. Susan and I are going through some more of the DEL files for the authorities. You've got a visitor upstairs."

"Wow. A new client? Already? Word travels fast."

"Don't get excited. It's your Aunt Glenna."

Jessie wrinkled her nose. "Come to ask me if I really understand the full ramifications of what I'm doing by getting myself engaged to Hatch. I suppose I'd better reassure her. At least she didn't summon me to her office to interrogate me this time."

Alex shrugged and turned back to the computer screen. "Let Hatch handle her if she gives you a hard time. He's good at handling things."

Susan nodded soberly. "Yes. Why don't you do that?"

"I can handle my own family, thank you very much." Jessie made a face at the back of Alex's head and closed the door.

It struck her as she stalked up the stairs that everyone appeared to have forgotten she was the one who had organized the rescue of Susan Attwood. She should have thought twice about letting Hatch go along on the mission. That was the problem with a natural leader. He gave orders naturally and people naturally tended to follow them. Afterward he got all the credit. Naturally. Nobody recalled who the real brains of the operations had been.

Aunt Glenna was standing at the window gazing down at the sidewalk below when Jessie pushed open the door and walked into the office. She was dressed in a crisp, sober gray suit with a pale blue blouse and low businesslike pumps. When she turned her head Jessie could see that her eyes looked even more serious than usual behind the lenses of her black-framed glasses.

"There you are, Jessie. Your friend downstairs let me in." Glenna glanced at her watch. "I can't stay long."

"Have a seat, Aunt Glenna." Jessie dropped into the chair behind the rolltop desk and decided to take the offensive. "I expect you're here to congratulate me on my engagement."

Glenna did not move from her position near the window. "There's no need to be facetious, Jessie," she said gently.

"Sorry."

"I am naturally concerned that you know what you are doing. There has been a great deal of pressure on you from the rest of the family to go through with this marriage."

Jessie smiled and leaned back in the squeaky chair. She picked up a pencil and began tapping the point on the desk. "It's all right, Aunt Glenna. I promise you, I've come to this decision all by myself. I know what I'm doing and I'm not doing it to please the family. I appreciate your concern, though."

Glenna nodded slowly. "I was afraid of that. You're doing it for yourself, aren't you?"

"Yes."

"I had begun to suspect that."

Jessie scowled. "Suspect it?"

"It's strange, really. But I never thought you were the type to become obsessed with your role as Vincent's heir. I always believed it had been thrust upon you and was basically unwelcome. I assumed, based on the patterns of early childhood, that your tendency to be an enabler had motivated you to accept the role, but I never actually thought you wanted it. I never thought the money and the power meant that much to you."

"Money and power? What are you talking about?"

"I always saw you as trapped. I actually felt sorry for you, you know. I wanted to help you set yourself free. But now it's obvious that you're in this position willingly."

Jessie sat forward abruptly, shocked. "Aunt Glenna, what is this all about? I'm not marrying Hatch in order to get control of the company. The last thing I want is control of Benedict Fasteners."

"Are you certain of that, Jessie? Have you looked deep within and asked yourself why you really want to marry Sam Hatchard? Isn't it just possible that you've grown to like your position in the family? That what started out as a way of forcing Vincent to bond with his family has now become a means of exercising power?"

Jessie's eyes widened. "You're crazy, Aunt Glenna." She realized what she had just said and flushed in embarrassment. "I'm sorry, I didn't mean that literally."

"Jessie, ask yourself if the real reason you're marrying Hatchard isn't that you think you'll be able to control the company through him. You can have it all this way, can't you? The power that goes with being Vincent's heir and none of the responsibility for actually managing Benedict Fasteners."

"For heaven's sake." Jessie tossed the pencil down on the desk. "Even if I was marrying to secure my position as Dad's heir, I'd be a fool to think I could control the company through Hatch. Nobody controls Hatch."

"That's probably true. But you may have deluded yourself into thinking you can control him. You may think you can manipulate him the way you've learned to manipulate your father."

"I don't manipulate Dad."

"Of course you do. You're the only one who can, and everyone in the family knows it. That's why you've become the intermediary for everyone else." Glenna's voice was still remote and detached. The psychological authoritarian of the Benedict clan was pronouncing judgment.

"On the rare occasions when he listens," Jessie concluded crisply, "I can sometimes get Dad to pay attention and do the right thing. But that's only because I'm willing to dig in and go toe to toe with him. You know as well as I do that sometimes even that's not enough."

"It's worked for the most part, though, hasn't it, Jessie? You have the real power in this family. He's made you his sole heir. We all go through you when we want something from Vincent. To keep and consolidate that power, all you have to do is marry the consort Vincent has handpicked for you. I should have realized all along that you were maneuvering toward your own goal." Glenna started for the door.

"Aunt Glenna, wait. I don't understand what this is all

about. Why are you so upset about my marrying Hatch? This way the company stays in the family and has a chance to go big, just as you and the moms have always wanted."

"Don't be ridiculous. I am not upset."

"Yes, you are. I can feel it." Jessie jumped to her feet behind the desk.

"I simply want you to analyze your own motives in this."

"I am marrying Hatch because I love him."

"Nonsense. Don't be so bloody trite, Jessie. No one marries for love. That's just a label we slap on other, more fundamental drives: power, money, control, security, sex, family pressure. Those are the real reasons people marry. Do yourself a favor and decide which of them are the reasons you're engaged to Sam Hatchard."

"*I love him.*"

"Really?" Glenna was amused in a distant sort of way. "And does he love you?"

Jessie went still. "I think so. Yes. Of course he does."

"Has he told you he loves you?"

Jessie lifted her chin. "That's a very personal question, Aunt Glenna. I don't have to answer it."

"No, you don't. Not to me, at any rate. A word of advice, Jessie. Be very cautious if Sam Hatchard ever does tell you he loves you because a man like that will do whatever he has to do, say whatever he has to say, crush whomever he has to crush, in order to get what he wants. And he wants Benedict Fasteners. Even if he has to use you to get it."

"Dammit, that's not true."

"Unfortunately for all of us, Vincent has made it true. No one can stop you from marrying Sam Hatchard, Jessie. But I wonder how long you can spin out your fantasies. How long will you be able to convince yourself that Hatchard would have married you if Benedict Fasteners hadn't been your dowry?"

"Aunt Glenna, that's unfair."

"I'm sorry, Jessie. I'm a doctor, not a fortune-teller who

looks into a crystal ball and tells people what they want to hear the way your Mrs. Valentine does. I'm trained to understand and assess people's motives, even if they choose to lie to themselves or others about them."

Glenna went out the door and closed it very gently behind her.

"Hold it right there, Aunt Glenna." Jessie darted around the end of the desk and threw open the door. She flew to the staircase railing and leaned over to call after her aunt. "What's your motive in all this? Why are you so damned angry at the way things are turning out?"

"I never wanted things to turn out this way." Glenna did not look up as she descended the stairs.

"Why not? You wanted Benedict Fasteners to stay in the family. You've said so."

Glenna stopped on the bottom stair and swung around. For the first time her face lost its controlled, aloof expression. Anger blazed for an instant in her eyes and her mouth was pinched with rage. "Yes, I want Benedict Fasteners to stay in the family. Of course I do. The future potential of the firm is enormous. *But it should have gone to the rightful heir, not to you.*"

"The rightful heir?" Jessie instinctively stepped back from the rail, appalled by the fury in her normally self-contained aunt. "Whom are you talking about?"

"I'm talking about David, damn you. David should have inherited Benedict Fasteners. *Vincent owed me that much.*"

Glenna whirled and strode quickly out the downstairs door. The glass in it trembled as she slammed it shut behind her.

Jessie finally tracked her mother down in a stylish waterfront condominium where Lilian was supervising a bevy of craftspeople.

"No, no, I do not want the track lighting extended into the sitting area. The small room is supposed to be a library."

Lilian frowned intently over a set of blueprints while the electrician waited patiently. "Did you bring the fixtures for the kitchen?"

"They're downstairs in the truck," the man said. "I'll bring them up after I get this damned fancy Erector set installed in the ceiling."

"Fine. Remember, I want to approve the kitchen fixtures before they go in."

"Right."

Lilian stepped back to join Jessie. She kept her eyes on the electrician as he began setting out his tools. The smell of fresh paint emanated from a bedroom. "You've got to watch these people like a hawk. Turn your back for one second and they've put in the wrong fixtures or painted a wall white when you've distinctly ordered taupe. Then they try to convince you to accept the mistake."

"Mom, I've got to talk to you."

"I didn't think you were here because you've decided to pursue a career in interior design. What's the problem? Worrying about wedding plans already? I told you Connie and I would handle it for you. We're thinking of coral and cream for the colors. What do you think?"

"I think it sounds fine as long as you don't try to stuff Hatch into a coral tux. Listen, Mom, this is serious. I had a weird visit from Aunt Glenna this afternoon."

"Is that right?" Lilian frowned at the electrician. "Please don't start any work until you put down drop cloths. This wooden flooring was just put in a few weeks ago and it cost my client a fortune. I don't want it nicked."

The electrician obediently started to put down drop cloths. Lilian glanced at Jessie.

"What were you saying about Glenna?"

"She was very upset. Came to see me at my office."

"That is a little unusual for Glenna, isn't it? What did she want?"

"I got the feeling she wanted me to call off the wedding," Jessie said bluntly.

That got Lilian's attention. "Is she out of her mind?"

"I kind of wondered about that myself. But I think she was just plain angry."

"About what? Everyone in the family wants this marriage."

"Aunt Glenna said she thought Dad should have left the company to David."

There was a prolonged silence from Lilian. She kept her gaze on the electrician, but it was obvious she was thinking about something besides track lighting. "Interesting. David has absolutely no talent whatsoever for managing a large business like Benedict."

"Neither do I."

"That's not entirely true, dear. You had the absolutely brilliant ability to attract Sam Hatchard, who is fully capable of running it."

"Thanks, Mom. You really know how to make a daughter feel special. Why not just come right out and say Dad is using me to buy himself the son he always wanted. One who can take Benedict and expand it into a 'giant in the industry'?"

"Don't be silly, dear."

"Does it bother you to think that Hatch might be marrying me in order to get control of the company?"

"No, not in the least. The company is forever tied to you, and you are tied to the family. By marrying you, he is actually marrying into both the company and the family. We're assimilating him, if you see what I mean. It's going to work out just fine. In any event, I like Hatch. And it's about time you married someone. Why not him?"

Jessie decided not to pursue that useless line of discussion. "Mom, why does Aunt Glenna feel so strongly about David having a right to Benedict?"

Lilian sighed. "I suppose it all goes back to when Lloyd Ringstead disappeared. Glenna and your father had a brief affair."

"You know about that?"

275

"Of course. I'm not an idiot. It didn't last long, for obvious reasons. Anyone could see they weren't suited to each other. I never said anything because there was no point. Vincent and I had just gotten our divorce and Glenna was trying to deal with the trauma of Lloyd's having vanished into thin air. I suppose Vince and Glenna comforted each other for a time."

"Is it possible David is, well, more than my cousin?" Jessie asked hesitantly.

Lilian blinked in astonishment. "Are you asking me if David could possibly be Vincent's son?"

"I guess so. Aunt Glenna seems to feel very strongly about Dad owing her something."

"The answer about David is no," Lilian said firmly. Then she frowned thoughtfully. "At least, I think the answer is no. If he were your half-brother that would mean there were actually two affairs between Glenna and Vince, one a few years before Lloyd vanished. David was four when his father left, remember."

"True. But it's not an impossible scenario. If Glenna and Dad got it on once, they might have gotten it on twice."

"Frankly, if Glenna thought she could press a paternity suit, she would have done so by now. And it wouldn't have been necessary in the first place."

"Because Dad would have been more than willing to claim David if he thought he was his son?"

"Exactly. Vince has always wanted a son."

"I think you're right," Jessie said slowly. "So why does Aunt Glenna think she has such a big claim on Dad?"

Lilian shrugged. "Must have been that brief affair they shared all those years ago. Some women don't know how to let go."

Jessie awakened in the middle of the night, aware that something was wrong. It took her a minute or two to realize that Hatch had left the bed. She lay without opening her eyes, listening for noises from the bathroom. When there were none, she listened for noises from the kitchen.

When the ominous stillness became oppressive, she finally lifted her lashes. The first thing she noticed was the faint glow of light coming from the living room. She glanced at the bedside clock and saw that it was nearly two in the morning.

Pushing back the covers, she got out of bed, pulled on a robe, and traipsed toward the door. A niggling suspicion was gnawing at her. She paused in the hallway when she saw Hatch sitting at the kitchen counter. He had put on his trousers, but no shirt. His bare feet were hooked over the bottom rung of the stool. His briefcase was open on the floor at his feet. Papers and computer printouts were scattered across the top of the counter. He was punching numbers into a small calculator.

Jessie leaned against the wall, arms folded beneath her breasts. "Couldn't sleep?"

He glanced up, eyes hooded and watchful. "I didn't know you were awake."

"Obviously." She straightened away from the wall and ambled slowly over to the counter. "It's all right, you know. You could have just told me earlier this evening you had to work on some papers after dinner. I'm not a total fanatic about your schedule."

"Yes, you are."

She scowled at him as she opened the refrigerator door and started rummaging around inside. "Not true. I accept the fact that there will be the odd occasion when your work requires some overtime. I can tolerate a reasonable amount. After all, as you pointed out, look what my job requires in the way of unusual hours. There I was having to run around at midnight up in the San Juans." She closed the refrigerator door and carried a plate of cream cheese over to the counter.

"Let's not start making comparisons between my job and yours." Hatch eyed the cream cheese. "What are you doing?"

"Fixing a little midnight snack. As long as I'm up, I might as well eat. Want a bagel?" She hovered near the toaster oven, bagel in hand.

"All right."

Jessie smiled benignly and popped the bagels beneath the broiler. "Now, then, suppose you tell me what was so terribly important you had to sneak around in the middle of the night to work on it?"

"First tell me how mad you are."

She looked at him innocently. "Not mad at all."

He looked unconvinced. "Okay. I had an idea on a new approach to use on this bid your father wants to make to undercut Yorland and Young. Thought I'd crunch the numbers and see how it looked."

"Dad really wants to get that Spokane contract, doesn't he?"

"Yes."

"It's personal, you know."

"No, I didn't know," Hatch said, looking at her with new interest. "But I was beginning to wonder. This thing just isn't big enough to bother with unless there are extenuating circumstances."

Jessie checked the bagels and decided they were ready. She opened the toaster-oven door. "Yorland and Young pulled a fast one on Benedict Fasteners a couple of years ago. Walked off with an important contract that Dad felt should have been his. He just wants revenge, that's all."

Hatch nodded thoughtfully. "I can understand that."

"I rather thought you would." Jessie plunked the hot bagels down on a plate and carried them over to the counter. She sat down across from Hatch. "I'll try not to get cream cheese on your important stuff."

"Appreciate that." Hatch watched her slather cream cheese on a bagel.

"So how did you get to be such a big authority on revenge? Who taught you to understand my father's point of view?"

"It's not important," Hatch said softly. "It was all over a long time ago."

"Oh, yeah?" She eyed him with interest. "So what company did you squash or beat out or otherwise get even with?"

"A company called Patterson-Finley. It was an engineering firm."

Jessie stared at him, remembering the day of the science fair when her father had bragged about how Hatch had crushed the company in a hostile takeover bid. "That takeover was a personal act of vengeance on your part? What did you have against Patterson-Finley? What had it ever done to you?"

Hatch looked at her. "I'm not sure now is a good time to go into this."

"I've got news for you. You're not going to get a better time. I want to know the whole story and I want to know it now."

Hatch leaned his elbows on the counter. "You're really going to make a demanding sort of wife, aren't you?"

She chuckled. "Better get used to it. So, what was the deal with Patterson-Finley?"

Hatch was silent for a long moment. Then he shrugged. "The man my wife was going to meet on the day she was killed?"

"Yes?"

"His name was Roy Patterson."

Jessie nearly choked on her bagel. "The same Patterson as the one in Patterson-Finley?"

"Right. Now, if that's the end of your questions, I'll finish off these numbers and get back to bed."

Jessie watched as he returned to the calculator. "Was it worth it?" she asked.

"Tearing apart Patterson-Finley? Yes." He did not look up.

"He was your best friend, wasn't he?" she whispered. "And he was running off with your wife. You must have loved her very much to exact that kind of vengeance."

"Whatever I once felt for her died when I found her note saying she was leaving me because I was a loser and she needed to be with a winner."

Jessie considered that. "Nobody goes after revenge the way you did unless he feels very intensely about a woman."

"You don't understand revenge, Jessie. It's best cold, like the old saying has it, not hot. At least for me it is. It's not an act of passion."

"Just a business thing, is that it?"

Hatch nodded slowly. "You could say that. Yes. A business thing."

"Bull." She got to her feet and started back toward the hall that led to the bedroom. "You loved her and when you lost her it tore your heart out. You went after your vengeance with everything that was left in you." She paused in the doorway. "Tell me something, Hatch. Will you ever take that kind of risk again? Will you ever let yourself love again? Or is a long-term, committed relationship called marriage all I'm ever going to get from you?"

"Jessie." His voice was a dark growl of warning.

"What?" She'd turned back toward her room.

"You know there's more to it than that."

"No," she said. "I don't know that. Sometimes I delude myself into thinking there's more to it than that. But other times I wake up alone in the middle of the night and I panic. Because I don't know for certain, you see. I love you. But I don't know if you love me."

"Dammit, Jessie."

"Good night, Hatch."

She went back into the bedroom and crawled into bed, curling into herself.

"Jessie."

She turned her head just far enough to see him filling the doorway. Wordlessly she watched him walk toward the bed. His fingers were busy at the fastening of his trousers.

"You know there's more to it than that," Hatch said again as he got into bed beside her. He was already fully aroused.

"No."

"Yes." He pulled her into his arms, his mouth rough and heavy on hers. "Yes, dammit. There's a hell of a lot more to it than that."

"Yes," she whispered. There had to be a lot more to it than that. She was banking her entire future on the possibility that he could one day tell her he loved her.

CHAPTER SEVENTEEN

There was nothing quite like the sense of pride, satisfaction, and accomplishment one got from a job well done, Jessie decided. She gazed down at the neatly typed five-page report that lay on top of the desk. It was truly a thing of beauty. Mrs. Valentine was going to be extremely impressed.

Alex had let Jessie use the word-processing program on his computer to assure a crisp, polished finish to the report. Both right and left margins were justified, the spelling was letter-perfect, and the prose was in a businesslike style.

Jessie had stopped at an office-supply store on the way to work to buy a handsome report binder in order to add a further touch of professionalism.

No doubt about it, Valentine Consultations was never going to be the same. A new era had arrived for the psychic-consulting business. The morning papers had broken the news of the DEL case and Jessie knew the phone was going to start ringing off the hook at any minute.

She looked up expectantly when she heard a familiar tread on the stairs. A moment later the office door opened and Mrs. Valentine walked in wearing her professional attire. She had on a dark green turban, a wide-sleeved green paisley blouse, and a long green skirt that fell to her ankles. The usual assortment of beads and chains covered her bosom, tinkling merrily as she came through the door. She had a newspaper tucked under one arm.

"Mrs. V, you look great. How are you feeling?"

"Fine, dear. Just fine. I can see again, if you know what I mean. Such a relief."

Jessie smiled happily. "I'm so glad, Mrs. V. Go on into your office. The tea is almost ready. I'll bring it right in."

"Thank you, dear. I could use a cup of tea." Mrs. Valentine unfolded the newspaper as she headed for the inner office.

Jessie hurried over to the tea tray and spooned tea into the pot. She hummed cheerfully as she reached for the kettle of boiling water. When all was ready, she arranged the pot and two delicate cups on the tray, added a tiny bowl of sugar cubes and a spoon, and picked up the tray.

On the way past the rolltop desk she paused long enough to place the neatly bound Attwood report on the tray. Then she entered Mrs. Valentine's private office.

Mrs. Valentine had the newspaper spread out on top of her consulting table. Her reading glasses were perched on her nose and she was deep into the front-page story.

Jessie glanced at the headlines as she set down the tea tray. She grinned with satisfaction. "Local Psychic Exposes Multimillion Scam."

"Oh, my." Mrs. Valentine read carefully to the end of the last paragraph and then turned to the next page to continue. "Oh, my goodness."

Jessie could hardly contain her excitement. She hovered on the other side of the desk with eager impatience until Mrs. Valentine had finally finished the article. When her employer eventually closed the newspaper and sat back in her chair, looking somewhat stunned, Jessie could not wait any longer.

"Well, Mrs. V? What do you think? Valentine Consultations is going to be famous. People will be beating down our door. We'll be scheduling appointments weeks in advance. This is going to be the most important psychic-consultation agency in the city, maybe in the whole state."

"Jessie, dear . . ."

"I've been doing some planning. We'll probably have to take on additional staff to deal with the paperwork, but that's okay. I've had some experience in personnel work. I'll handle that end of it."

"Jessie . . ."

"But I'm wondering if we shouldn't get another psychic to work with you." Jessie frowned in thought and began to pace the office. "We're going to be awfully busy and I don't think we can depend too much on my abilities. The truth is, much as I hate to admit it, I don't think I have any real psychic talent. I'm much more suited for management."

"Jessie, there is something we must discuss, dear."

"I'm going to speak to Mom and Connie about coming up with some sketches for a redo of the interior design of the office too."

"Something important, Jessie, dear . . ."

"We want the place to look businesslike, yet charming and a bit otherworldly. Successful, yet unconcerned with success, if you know what I mean."

"Jessie . . ."

"We may eventually have to look for larger office space. But we can wait for that, don't you think?"

"Jessie, I'm afraid I'm going to have to let you go, dear."

"Also, I was thinking it might be a good idea to . . . What did you say?" Jessie came to an abrupt halt and stood staring down at Mrs. Valentine. "Mrs. V, you can't mean that."

Mrs. Valentine heaved a massive sigh. "I am so sorry, dear. You know I'm extremely fond of you. You're a delight to have around the place. But I'm afraid Valentine Consultations is, uh, too small an operation to warrant an assistant."

Jessie gripped the edge of the desk with both hands. "But

that's just it, Mrs. V. It won't be a small operation once these headlines hit the streets. The phone will be ringing off the hook. We're going to go *big*."

"That's precisely what I'm afraid of, dear. I never meant Valentine Consultations to go big. I liked it the way it was. Just a small, pleasant little business I could run by myself. I had doubts the day I hired you, but I liked you so much, I overcame my premonitions of trouble. You'd think I, of all people, should have known better. Now look what's happened. You've ruined everything. I may have to close entirely until the excitement dies down."

"Mrs. V, are you firing me?"

Mrs. Valentine sighed again. "I'm afraid so, dear. Don't worry, I shall be happy to give you a good reference."

The telephone on the rolltop desk started to ring.

Hatch paused briefly at Grace's desk before going on into Vincent Benedict's office. "Hold all his calls until I come out, will you, Grace? No interruptions."

"Yes, Mr. Hatchard." Grace smiled. "By the way, I saw the full story of your adventure with Jessie in the morning papers. It sounds as if it was all terribly exciting."

"That's one way of describing it." Hatch went on past the desk and into the inner sanctum.

Benedict looked up, frowning in disapproval at the unannounced visit. "I'm in the middle of something, Hatch. Is this important?"

"Very." Hatch put down the file he had brought with him and went over to the coffeepot to pour himself a cup. He carried the coffee back across the room and leaned against the edge of Vincent's massive desk. "Seen the morning papers?"

"Goddamn right, I saw the morning papers." Vincent tossed down his pen and leaned back in his chair. "When you told me what had happened up there in the San Juans, you left out a few minor details, didn't you?"

Hatch shrugged. "A few."

"I'm damn glad that nonsense is over."

"So am I."

Vincent paused and slanted Hatch a speculative glance. "David really clobber that guy?"

"Knocked him cold with a karate punch. Saved the day. We probably wouldn't have gotten out of that mess alive without him."

"I'll be damned." Vincent nodded, quietly pleased. "Maybe he'll be okay. Maybe he's going to turn out different than Lloyd, after all."

"Maybe it's time you gave him credit for being his own man."

"Yeah. Maybe." Vincent picked up his pen. "Like I said, I'm glad the whole thing is finished. But I'm holding you personally responsible to see to it that Jessie doesn't get herself into any more scrapes like that one."

"I'll do my best."

Vincent eyed him. "Speaking of Jessie, you two set a date yet?"

"No. But we're going to make the formal announcement of our engagement on Friday evening. Jessie said she was going to book a table at her favorite restaurant, the one down in the Market. Everyone in the family is invited. Even you."

Vincent grinned. "Reckon I can make that." He pulled his calendar across the desk and jotted a note on Friday's date. Then he leaned back in his chair again. "You in here to talk business or just pass the time of day?"

"Business." Hatch sipped coffee meditatively. "There are a few things that need to be cleared up before Friday."

"You're talking about buying into Benedict Fasteners, aren't you? Don't blame you for wanting to get the deal done. You've waited long enough."

"It's a little more complicated than my share of the deal, Vincent. There are a few other people involved."

Vincent scowled. "What the hell are you talking about now?"

"I'll lay it out in plain, simple terms. We can go over the details later. I want you to agree to divide the company into four equal parts, Benedict. One-fourth goes to David, one-fourth to Elizabeth, and one-fourth to Jessie. I'll buy the last quarter and I'll run the business."

Vincent's mouth dropped open. For an instant he was obviously speechless. When his voice returned, it came out in a full-throated roar. *"Are you out of your head?* Break up Benedict Fasteners? After all the sweat I've put into this company?"

"I'm not talking about breaking it up. I'm talking about keeping it in the family, just like you've always intended. But this way all the involved parties own a piece of it. That gives them a vested interest."

Vincent slammed his fist down on a stack of papers. "None of them knows a goddamn thing about running a company like Benedict Fasteners."

"That's what you've got me on board for, remember?"

"Jesus, man, you don't know what you're saying. Give David a chunk of this company and there's no telling what kind of trouble he'll start. He's always blamed me for Lloyd running off. And the boy has no common sense. He's going to study philosophy, for crying out loud. The kid's a flaming liberal with radical notions about the environment and things like that. He'd make all kinds of trouble for me if he owned a quarter of the business."

"I can handle David." Hatch took another swallow of coffee. He was fully prepared to weather the storm. He had expected nothing less when he had walked into Vincent's office. When it was all over, Benedict would calm down and agree to his plans.

"You think you can handle David, huh? Well, what about his mother? Glenna's an iron maiden, pal. She's bitter and she's weird. There's no telling what she would do if she got her hands on David's shares."

"David's not a kid any longer. The very fact that he's opted for grad school is proof that he's willing to take a stand against his mother. She wanted him to stay here at Benedict."

"You're wrong. Giving a piece of Benedict to that side of the family would be inviting disaster. And what about Elizabeth? She's just a kid. Twelve years old, for Christ's sake. You can't go turning over a quarter of this company to a twelve-year-old kid. What if Connie remarries? The new guy might try to get involved in the company and he could use Elizabeth's shares to do it."

"You're her father, remember? You can retain control of her quarter until she comes of age. Or you can make Jessie the trustee until then."

"And then what? That's less than ten years away," Benedict raged. "With the plans you've got, the firm will be three times the size it is now. Maybe bigger. Elizabeth will be dissecting rats' brains or something for a living. You want some ivory-tower research scientist trying to make business decisions for one-fourth of this outfit? She won't know what the hell she's doing."

"I have a hunch Elizabeth will be content to let Jessie guide her when it comes to making decisions for Benedict."

"Jessie? That's a joke. Jessie doesn't know beans about running this show either."

Hatch smiled faintly. "But Jessie will be married to me, remember? She'll let me make all the decisions for Benedict Fasteners. I'll be running the show, just like you planned all along."

"Except that half of the ownership will be in other hands. No, I won't have this company torn into little pieces, dammit."

"Not little pieces. Big pieces. Pieces which I will control either directly or indirectly."

"You can't be certain of retaining control of things if you've got three other owners involved. They could outvote you if they got together and decided to go in a different direction."

"There's a risk, I'll admit it. But I know your family, Vincent. The risk is a small one. I can deal with it."

"You don't know that, goddammit." Benedict pounded the table once more and shot to his feet. "There's no way to be certain you can stay in command if you've got the company divided up into quarters."

"I'm willing to chance it."

"Well, I'm not," Vincent shouted. "I've seen plenty of family-owned companies torn to shreds this way. It won't happen here."

Hatch looked down into his coffee. "You don't have a choice, Benedict."

"What the frigging hell does that mean? Of course I've got a choice. I say we don't split things up and that's final."

"Not if you want me to marry Jessie and run your company, it isn't."

Suddenly the office was silent. For a minute Vincent stared at Hatch, mouth agape. Then he sat down, clearly stunned.

"Are you telling me you won't marry Jessie unless I agree to cut up Benedict Fasteners?" Vincent asked, as if trying to make certain he had understood.

"I didn't say that. I'll marry her, all right. But I won't buy into Benedict and I won't stick around here to run it for you. I'll take Jessie and leave the state. We'll start over somewhere else. Oregon, maybe."

"Bullshit. I'll cut Jessie off without one red cent."

Hatch nodded. "Just as well. Because if you did go ahead and leave the company to her, I'd make sure she divided it up when she took possession."

"The hell you would," Benedict said softly, too softly, his eyes shrewd and angry. "You're bluffing."

"Have I ever lied to you, Benedict? Either agree to portion the company out among David, Elizabeth, Jessie, and me or forget the whole deal. I'll take Jessie and leave town."

"She won't go with you, you sonofabitch."

This was the tricky part, Hatch knew. Now he was bluffing for all he was worth. Everything was riding on his poker-playing skills. His fingers tightened on the coffee cup. "She will, you know. She loves me."

"You make her nervous. She told me so herself."

"She'll still come with me, Benedict."

"Bullshit. Not if she knows you're walking away from Benedict Fasteners," Vincent snarled. "That woman may be featherbrained about some things, but she knows her duty to her family. She won't walk away from her own people. Everyone depends on her, and she knows it."

"Everyone had better stop depending on her, then, because things are going to be different around here."

"They sure as hell are." Vincent's eyes narrowed shrewdly. "I'm canceling your contract, Hatchard. Effective right now. You're *fired,* you sonofabitch. Get out of here. You've got one hour to clean out your desk."

For an instant Hatch thought he had not heard correctly. This was not the result he had calculated. Dazed, he covered his shock by getting to his feet and slowly putting the empty coffee cup down on the desk. Without a word he headed toward the door.

"Goddammit, Hatchard, you ever change your mind and get your common sense back, you know where to find me," Vincent yelled after him.

"I won't change my mind. By the way, that file I left on your desk is the final breakdown on the Spokane job. You can undercut Yorland and Young with that bid and Benedict can still make a small profit. But my professional advice is to forget it. It's not worth it."

"Goddammit, Hatch . . ."

Hatch went out the door and closed it quietly. He stood still for a minute, adjusting to the one-hundred-and-eighty-degree turn his life had just taken.

"Mr. Hatchard?" Grace's voice was laced with concern. "Are you all right?"

Hatch forced himself to focus on her. "Call my secretary, will you, Grace?"

"Certainly, sir. What should I tell her?"

"Tell her to pack up my desk. Have everything sent to my apartment. I won't be coming back to the office."

Grace stared at him in astonishment. "You're leaving us, Mr. Hatchard?"

"It looks that way." He gave her a rueful smile as he walked to the elevators. "I've just been fired."

"Mr. Hatchard . . ." The telephone in Grace's hand dropped onto the desk with a loud crash.

Hatch stood at the window of his high-rise apartment and stared out at Elliott Bay. It was a terrific view and he wondered why he had not spent more time in the front room admiring it.

The answer to that was simple. Jessie's place had always seemed so much cozier and more inviting, more like home.

He tore his gaze away from the view and glanced around the place he had rented shortly after moving to Seattle. It was in pristine order, of course. Everything was in its proper place. There was not a speck of dust anywhere. The cleaning service he'd hired saw to that. Damned place looked as though no one actually lived in it.

He had not even unpacked a lot of his things, he reflected. There had not been time. From the moment he'd arrived he had been immersed in work and in the roller-coaster business of courting Jessie. His apartment looked more like a hotel room than a private residence.

Fired.

It was hard to believe it was all over. Hard to believe everything he had been working toward had just gone up in smoke. Hard to believe that Vincent Benedict had called his bluff.

Impossible to believe he was going to lose Jessie.

Hatch had been so certain he could force the older man

into splitting up the company, so confident of his own ability to deal with Vincent Benedict. He should have known right from the start that Benedict was too tough and too wily and too damn stubborn to get maneuvered into doing anything he did not want to do.

Hatch had played poker with an old pro and he had lost. He had risked everything on a bluff.

And threatening to take Jessie away had been nothing more than a bluff. Hatch told himself he should have known Benedict would be too savvy to fall for it. It was crazy to think Jessie would actually walk away from her family and her self-imposed responsibilities to go off with a man who made her nervous. Her first loyalty was to the clan. He had known that from the beginning. Hell, he'd used that knowledge to maneuver her into a relationship with him.

It was crazy to believe she would run off with a man she had agreed to marry in the first place only because everyone around her was urging her to do so. A man whose main attribute was that he was Vincent Benedict's handpicked candidate to take over the operation of Benedict Fasteners.

Hatch did not delude himself. He had been in this position once before and he knew how the chips would fall. Jessie was not Olivia. He was fairly certain she genuinely cared for him. But the fact that she had convinced herself she was in love with him would hardly be enough to make her run off with him when everything else in the relationship went sour.

Hatch told himself he had to be realistic about the situation. He had to see it from a woman's point of view.

Running off with him would mean leaving everything Jessie held dear. It would mean leaving Elizabeth. It would mean leaving Seattle. It would mean abdicating her loving responsibility to her family and her duty to Benedict Fasteners.

It would mean casting her fate with a man who would be essentially starting over. Women, Hatch knew from experience, rarely did dumb things like that in real life.

He glanced at the liquor cabinet and thought about pouring himself a drink. He needed one badly.

He decided to wait until he had seen Jessie. He would need one even more after that.

Outside the lobby door of Jessie's apartment house, Hatch leaned on the buzzer. He had the key Jessie had given him, but for some reason he did not want to use it. He was not coming home from work this time. He was paying a last visit.

"Yes?" Jessie's voice sounded odd through the speaker.

"It's me."

She did not say anything more, but a second later a hissing noise told him the lock had been released. Hatch pushed open the door, walked inside, and started up the stairs.

He glanced around and realized how familiar it all seemed. He had gotten accustomed to coming here at the end of each day. He had gotten to like the idea of knowing Jessie would be waiting for him with a glass of wine and that there would be mouth-watering smells coming from the kitchen.

It was easy to see why there was a strong instinct in men to keep women in the home. They had a way of making things much more comfortable for a man.

Not that any man would ever be successful in keeping Jessie barefoot and pregnant, he thought wryly.

Pregnant.

The possibility of getting Jessie pregnant hung tantalizingly in the air. If she were pregnant, she might feel compelled to marry him, after all.

But he did not want her to be forced into that kind of decision, he told himself, trying to be noble.

On the other hand, it just might work. Jessie felt so strongly about the importance of fatherhood. She had spent most of her life building bonds between Vincent and his family. The last thing she would want to do was deny her own child its father.

But the odds of getting her pregnant before she found out what had happened this afternoon were staggeringly against him. They had, after all, been making love without protection for only two days. If he kept his mouth shut tonight, he might get one more shot at it, but the odds were still bad. And his luck had not been running well lately.

Jessie opened the door for him on the second level. She had her hair slicked back behind her ears and she was dressed in a black jumpsuit. He saw the anxiety leap into her eyes the instant she got a good look at him.

"Hatch, is something wrong?"

She did not know anything yet. Now was the time to keep his mouth shut. Give himself one more chance in bed with her. Maybe stack the odds a little more in his favor. But, hell, she had always been honest with him. He owed her honesty in return.

"Your father fired me today." He was surprised at how calm the simple words sounded. Hatch stood there in the doorway waiting for the devastating reaction and wondered what he would do without this woman in his life. He could not seem to think that far ahead. All he could do was wait for the blow.

"He fired you?" Jessie finally got her mouth closed. "Dad canceled your contract with Benedict?"

"Yes."

"You're unemployed?"

Hatch nodded, propping one shoulder against the door-jamb. He shoved his hands into his pockets. "Looks that way."

"You won't be running Benedict Fasteners?"

"No." He drew a breath. "I'll be leaving Seattle soon. I'll be starting over somewhere else. Oregon, maybe. Or Arizona. I just stopped by to tell you."

"Hatch, this is incredible. I can't believe it." She blinked and then her green eyes filled with mirth. She started to giggle, and the giggle turned into full-blown laughter. "Oh, my God. We've finally got something in common."

Hatch frowned, at a loss to understand what was happening. "Jessie?"

"I got fired today too."

Hatch looked at her. "What?"

"You heard me," Jessie got out between gasps for air. "Mrs. V fired me. Said she didn't like the direction I was taking Valentine Consultations. Said she would give me nice references. Oh, my God, this is so funny. You and me both fired on the same day. I can't believe it."

"Somehow I hadn't seen it in a funny light."

Jessie blinked away the moisture the laughter had brought to her eyes and gulped in air. "No, of course not. You poor thing. I'll bet you've never been through this before, have you?"

"There was one other time," he reminded her deliberately.

She nodded, reaching out to yank him through the door. "That's right. I'd almost forgotten. Back when you were married to Olivia and your company got taken over." She closed the door behind him and threw the dead bolt. "Still, that was years ago. You haven't had my vast experience with the situation. Come on in and I'll show you how it's done."

Hatch felt as if he had just fallen down the rabbit hole. Nothing seemed to be going according to the script. "How what's done?"

"How you celebrate getting fired, of course. Since you've had such limited experience, I'll guide you through it. First, you sit down." She pushed him onto a stool in front of the counter.

"What happens next?"

"Why, next you open a bottle of champagne, of course. As soon as I left the office this morning, I bought one. I stuck it in the refrigerator hours ago." She opened the refrigerator door and grabbed the bottle sitting on the top shelf. "This is the real thing, you know. From France, not California. I splurged. I always do when I get fired."

"I see."

"Personally," she said as she peeled back the wire that held the cork in place, "I vote for Oregon. I've been to Arizona, though, and it's very nice. We can go there if you think we should. But it would be easier for Elizabeth to visit if we went to Oregon. On the other hand, I guess we really can't be too picky, can we? I mean, both of us being unemployed and all."

The cork came out of the bottle with a bang, striking the ceiling. Champagne started to billow forth, threatening to cascade all over the kitchen floor.

Hatch reached out, took the bottle from Jessie's hands, and quickly poured the sparkling liquid into the glasses.

Then he grabbed Jessie and pulled her into his arms. She went into them willingly, laughter and love gleaming in her eyes.

CHAPTER EIGHTEEN

"Does this mean," Hatch asked carefully a few minutes later as he slowly released her, "that you still view us as being engaged?"

Jessie picked up her champagne glass and shot him a startled glance over the rim. "Are you trying to wriggle out of the engagement?"

"Hell, no."

"Aunt Glenna said you might."

"Might what?"

"Might lose interest in me if I didn't bring Benedict Fasteners along as my dowry."

Hatch was annoyed. "What a coincidence. I was wondering if you'd lose interest in me if marrying me meant losing Benedict Fasteners. Your father says he's going to cut you off without a cent, by the way. I don't think I mentioned that, did I?"

"That's Dad for you. He's so engrossed with the bottom line that he just naturally assumes it's everyone else's first consideration too. How did it happen, Hatch?"

"Me getting myself fired? I gambled. Tried to bluff an old poker player, and he called. I should have known better." He thought about that. "Hell, I did know better. I realized there was a risk. But I had to take it."

"Why?"

"I wanted to cut a few more of the knots that keep you tap-dancing between your father and the rest of the family. I thought that if I could arrange for Elizabeth and David to each get a quarter of the company, you'd be out of the loop permanently."

"Out of the loop?"

"That was Plan A. Split up the company among the logical heirs and let me buy a quarter of it. That would put everyone on a more or less equal footing. No one would be dependent on you to make certain they got their fair share of the inheritance. The moms would stop pressuring you, and maybe a chunk of the company for David would appease Glenna. You would no longer feel like you had to hold the whole thing together all by yourself."

Jessie's mouth fell open in amazement. "You tried to make Dad give us all an equal portion of Benedict Fasteners?"

"Yeah. Like I said, that was Plan A. Seemed like a good idea at the time."

"Dad has never been willing to even listen to that idea. I told you that. Lord knows I tried it out on him a few times in the past. He's been absolutely nonnegotiable on the subject. Seems to think it might tear the company apart."

"I told him to trust me to hold things together. Obviously he didn't."

Jessie propped her elbow on the counter and balanced her chin on the heel of her palm. "What made you decide to push him so hard if you knew you might lose everything in the process?"

Hatch met her eyes. "I told you, I was just trying to get some of the family pressure off you."

She started to smile. "There's more to it than that, isn't there? You wanted to prove to yourself I'd marry you even if I didn't have to. Hatch, that's so sweet."

"*Sweet?* Christ, lady, it is anything but sweet. It's a full-scale financial disaster. Talk about shooting myself in the foot."

She bit her lip. "Are you really upset about losing Benedict Fasteners?"

"No, dammit. I can live without Benedict. But I don't think it's sunk in yet that you've lost it too, if you marry me."

"Big deal."

"Cutting you off from your inheritance," he continued evenly, "also effectively cuts you off from your primary role in the family."

"I'm no longer the intermediary, as you called it," Jessie said slowly, nodding in comprehension. "It's going to feel a little strange at first."

"Better be prepared to feel more than just a little strange," he growled. "You don't seem to understand that everyone is going to be madder than hell. They're all going to feel threatened now. Marry me, and everyone's share of the big pie they were all counting on is at risk."

"Why? What do you think Dad will do now?"

"Who knows? Vincent will either sell the company outright or he'll continue to run it as he has been running it. Either way, the family can kiss off the idea of taking Benedict Fasteners into the fast lane."

"Dad loves that company. I can't see him selling out."

"I can. He doesn't like being pushed around any more than I do. He's fully capable of selling it just to prove he can't be manipulated. He's into revenge, in case you haven't noticed. Look what I've gone through to beat out Yorland and Young for him, just because the company once undercut him on a contract."

"True. And you, of all people, understand vengeance, don't you?"

Hatch sighed. "Yes. I do. And even if he doesn't sell, he won't be able to turn Benedict Fasteners into what everyone wants it to become. The firm is thirty years out-of-date and so is Vincent's management style. He won't be able to revitalize the company unless he gets someone like me on board. He knows that. I doubt he'll bring himself to trust anyone like me again."

"Which means that Benedict Fasteners will stay a small-time regional business. I don't think that's such a bad fate."

"Everyone else sure as hell will, including your father. They've had the carrot dangled in front of them now and they won't forget what was once within reach. They're going to blame you for depriving them of it. I'm sorry, Jessie."

"I'm not." She was quiet for a minute. "Tell me, just out of curiosity, did Dad leave you a way back?"

Hatch smiled wryly. "Sure. All I have to do is come to my senses, crawl back, and tell him we'll do things his way."

Jessie looked surprised. "He said that? He ought to know you'd never go back on those terms."

Hatch lifted one shoulder in dismissal. "It was probably all he could think of on the spur of the moment. When he recovers from the shock, he'll turn the pressure on you. So will everyone else."

"Let 'em. I've already made my decision."

He still did not completely understand what was happening here. "Why?" he asked bluntly.

"Because I love you, of course. I told you that."

"Yeah, I know you said that, but—"

She silenced him by putting her fingertips over his mouth. "Do you love me?"

He allowed himself to think about it for the first time. "Hell, I guess so. I wouldn't have gone through all this otherwise."

She wrinkled her nose. "Be still, my beating heart. Let's try this from another angle. Would you have given up your chunk of Benedict Fasteners and the future you've got planned for it and for yourself for the sake of any other woman of your acquaintance?"

"Of course not." He swallowed champagne and hid a slow grin.

"Then say it, damn you."

He smiled into her eyes, finally beginning to relax for the first time that day. "Jessie, I love you."

Her own smile widened happily. "Was it worth it? Losing everything for love?"

A great weight seemed to be lifting from his shoulders. "Is that what I just did?"

"Uh-huh."

"You tell me if it was worth it," he said softly.

"Yes. Most definitely yes."

"Yes," he repeated. "Most definitely yes." He took the wineglass from her hand and set it down on the counter next to his own. Then he got to his feet and scooped her off the stool and into his arms.

"Lord," she whispered, eyes filling with passion as he carried her toward the bedroom. "I just wish I had a staircase. This would be so much more romantic if you carried me up a staircase, don't you think?"

"No. At my age a man has to consider his lower back," Hatch said seriously.

She punched his shoulder. "That was a joke. Darn it, this time I know that was meant to be funny. Wasn't it?"

Hatch started to chuckle. The next minute he was laughing out loud, a deep, full-throated roar of a laugh that came from far down in his chest. And as his own triumphant mirth echoed in the white bedroom, he realized he could not remember the last time he had allowed himself to surrender to sheer, unadulterated happiness.

Hatch woke from a pleasant, dozing sleep and felt the soft warmth of Jessie's body curled into his own. Her sweetly curved derriere was nestled against his thighs, and his hand cupped one rounded breast. A nipple thrust into his palm. Hatch squeezed gently.

Jessie shifted against him. "You rang?"

He chuckled and kissed her shoulder. "Just wanted to see if you were still awake."

"Ummm. Actually, I've been thinking. I know how much you counted on getting your paws on Benedict Fasteners."

"I'd rather have my paws on you."

She smiled and turned her head on the pillow to look at him. "That's nice and it certainly represents a drastic reordering of your personal priorities, for which I am extremely grateful. However, I also feel a little guilty about all this."

Some of Hatch's good mood started to slip. "Don't say that, Jessie. You've got nothing to feel guilty about. If anyone should be feeling guilty, it's me. In one fell swoop I've just changed your whole life."

"You mustn't say that." She touched his cheek gently. "As far as I'm concerned, that one fell swoop proved for certain that you loved me and I shall treasure the memory forever."

"Then what are you thinking about so seriously?"

"I could try talking to Dad for you," she said. "See if I can get him to climb down off his high horse. I know neither one of you is the type to back down. You're both so stubborn. But maybe if I sort of mediated things, I could find a compromise for both of you."

"Try it and I'll paddle your butt so hard you won't sit down for a week."

She blinked. "I beg your pardon?"

"You heard me. Jessie, this is between your father and me. You are not involved. Got that?"

"But I am involved."

"No. You said yourself, you've already made your decision. You're going to marry me, right?"

"Yes, of course, but—"

"Then you've made your choice. Your first loyalty is to me now, not your family."

"Yes."

"You aren't going to play go-between this time, honey. I won't let you. You're on my side of the fence and you're not going to try to straddle it. I don't need you to rescue me. All I need or want is you. Got that?"

She smiled mistily, her fingers splayed on his bare chest. "Got it. You know, I think that's about the nicest thing anyone has ever said to me."

He grinned. "You mean threatening to paddle your backside?"

She yanked on a handful of chest hair and looked satisfied when he winced. "No, I meant the part about needing and wanting me. Just me. Not me because I can act as an intermediary or because I can get something for you from Dad or because I can smooth things over and hold it all together. But me, just because I'm me."

"Remember that, okay?" He slid his hand down over her thigh.

"Okay."

"Jessie?" His fingers were tangled in the nest of hair between her legs now.

"Uh-huh?"

"You're sure about wanting to have my baby?"

"I'm sure. I think you'll make a good father, Hatch."

"Thank you for trusting me that much. I know what that decision means to you." He kissed her throat and pushed his leg between hers. The womanly scent of her body filled his head. He was already hard. "No one has ever trusted me as much as you do. Walking away with me will mean starting over, you know."

"I know. I don't have a lot of money saved, but I've got some. We can sell one of the cars. I hate to say this, but it should probably be the Mercedes."

"Damn."

She patted his arm sympathetically. "On the plus side, I'm very good at finding jobs."

He moved on top of her, cradled her head between his

hands, and smiled down at her. "It's not going to be too bad. I've got the stake I was planning to use to buy into Benedict Fasteners. I'll use it to start up another management-consulting business. I've done it once. I can do it again."

"I know."

"Most of the money will have to go into the new business, though. There won't be a lot left over. Not for a while."

"Don't worry about it." Jessie stroked his shoulders. "I'm not. I know you can make it work, Hatch."

He looked down at her glowing face and was filled with a deep sense of wonder and awe. "Where have you been all my life?"

"Waiting for you." She drew him down to her, wrapping her legs around his waist and her arms around his neck.

Hatch entered her with a slow, aching tenderness, letting her pull him deep within her body. He watched the desire grow in her eyes and knew a sense of completeness that he had never felt before in his life.

Nothing else really mattered, he decided. Not the uncertainties that lay ahead, not the loss of the bright, successful future he had been planning at Benedict Fasteners.

Nothing mattered except Jessie and the baby they were going to make together.

"I'm going to be one hell of a father for our kid, Jessie." It was a vow as binding as any oath he would ever take.

"Yes. I know."

"But I'll be an even better husband."

"I know." She smiled brilliantly up at him. "And don't worry. Maybe we can find a way to keep the Mercedes."

"Damn right we will."

Elizabeth finished paying for the book on famous women scientists, picked up the paper sack, and turned from the counter to join Jessie.

"I'm ready. You want to go look at clothes now?" Elizabeth glanced up inquiringly as they left the bookstore and ambled out into the crowded shopping mall.

"Nope. I don't want to be tempted," Jessie said, feeling extremely noble and virtuous and terribly thrifty. "Hatch and I will have to watch every penny for a while until he can get his new business established."

"Does this mean the big wedding production is off?"

"Afraid so. Don't worry, you'll still get to be my attendant. We'll just be cutting back on some of the extras. Like serving a large buffet to three hundred wedding guests, the way the moms had planned."

"I'm still going to get to wear the dress Mom picked out for me? And the little hat?"

"Definitely. Hatch and I will probably just wear jeans, naturally, but you can wear the fancy bridesmaid's dress. No problem."

Elizabeth slanted her a speculative glance to see if Jessie was teasing her. "Thanks. I can hardly wait. What about the engagement party?"

"Oh, it's still on for Friday night. Hatch refused to let me cancel it. Said we weren't so hard-up that we couldn't celebrate the engagement. It won't cost all that much, anyway, if only you and David show up. Do me a favor and don't order the lobster, okay?"

"It's going to seem strange, just David and me there."

"I know," Jessie said quietly. "But we'll all have a good time."

Elizabeth looked away, apparently studying a window display. "I'm going to miss you, Jessie."

Jessie put her arm around her shoulders and hugged her. "I'm going to miss you too. But you'll be able to come and visit us as often as you want."

"Hatch won't mind?"

"No. He won't mind."

"Do you think you'll go all the way to Arizona?"

"Hatch isn't sure yet. A lot depends on where he thinks the best prospects are for his new business."

"I hope you just go to Portland. I could get down to Portland on the train as often as I wanted."

Jessie took a deep breath and blinked back the moisture in her eyes. "I sort of hope we go to Portland too. But either way, it will be all right, kid. I promise you."

"Everything's going to change, isn't it?"

"I'm afraid so."

"I hope you're going to be real happy with Hatch." Elizabeth turned her face upward again, revealing the tears behind her glasses. "I want you to be happy, Jessie."

The tears in Jessie's own eyes spilled over. "Thank you, Elizabeth. Thank you very much." Jessie pulled her into her arms and the two of them stood in the middle of the mall and cried until a security guard finally stopped and asked if anything was wrong.

Jessie and Elizabeth shook their heads and walked outside to where Jessie's car was parked in the garage.

Lilian and Constance were both waiting in the office of ExCellent Designs when Jessie drove up with Elizabeth. Elizabeth grimaced when she opened the office door. She glanced back over her shoulder. "Watch out, Jessie. They're both going to let you have it."

Constance frowned at her daughter. "Why don't you run outside and amuse yourself, Elizabeth? Lilian and I want to talk to Jessie."

"Sure, Mom." Elizabeth gave Jessie a sympathetic glance on her way back out the door. A brief silence followed as it closed behind her.

"Well, Jessie." Lilian regarded her daughter with a straightforward, serious expression from the other side of her desk. "Why don't you tell us what this is all about?"

Jessie shrugged and sat down in one of the uncomfortable Italian chairs. "There's not much to tell. The engagement party's still on for Friday. Hatch and I haven't set the wedding date yet, but it will be soon. We'll probably be moving to either Portland or Phoenix. That's about all the information I have at the moment. Stay tuned. Film at eleven."

"This is hardly a joking matter." Constance leaned forward and folded her arms on her desk. "Is the deal between Hatch and Vincent really off?"

"Yes. Hatch made it a condition that the company had to be equally divided among him, David, Elizabeth, and me. Dad wouldn't go for it."

"For God's sake, we all know he wouldn't go for that kind of arrangement. We've been trying to get him to do it for years." Constance slapped the desk. "Damn that man."

"Who? Vincent or Hatch?" Lilian asked dryly.

"Both of them," Constance muttered.

"The question," Lilian murmured, "is what are we going to do now?"

"Nothing," Jessie stated.

Lilian shook her head. "Jessie, you've got to be realistic about this. There is simply too much at stake. You can't just opt out of this mess now."

"I'm not exactly opting out. I've made a choice."

"The wrong one," Constance snapped. She sighed. "Jessie, be reasonable. You've said yourself that your feelings for Hatch are uncertain."

"I never said that. They're very certain now. I've made my decision, Connie. I'm sorry if it's not the one you think I should have made, but it's the one I want to make."

"There are a lot of futures at stake here," Connie shot back. "My daughter's income from Benedict Fasteners is in jeopardy. So is yours and David's. You can't just walk out."

"Yes, I can." Jessie smiled gently. "I'll tell you something. It's really not as hard as I thought it would be. Besides, let's get real here. Nobody's going to starve. You may not get as rich as you once thought you would when you assumed Benedict was going to become a giant in the industry, but things won't be all that bad."

"Are you kidding?" Constance looked appalled. "Without you around to handle Vincent, there's no telling how bad things will get."

Lilian nodded. "She's right, Jessie. Things could get very

nasty. Vincent will make us beg for every penny. You know what he's like."

"So don't ask for a cent. That'll drive him crazy in no time," Jessie suggested dryly. "He likes the sense of control he gets from holding the purse strings. My advice is to cut the strings."

"Easier said than done," Lilian said quietly. "When I think of what Benedict Fasteners could have become . . ." She let the words trail off.

"You're talking about cutting off the strings of my daughter's potential inheritance which could be huge if Benedict goes big," Constance pointed out.

"Elizabeth will do all right. It was never Dad's money she needed. It was Dad's love and attention."

"Well, she'll get even less of that now that you're going to be leaving, won't she?" Constance pointed out.

"There's your own inheritance to be considered too, Jessie." Lilian gave her a chiding glance. "It's easy enough now to say you're going to chuck it all for love, but how will you feel five years from now when you've got children of your own?"

"I would like my children to know their grandfather," Jessie said. "But they won't need his money. And neither will I." She stood up and slung her shoulder bag over her arm.

"Jessie," Lilian said quickly, "think about this. You've been unsure of your feelings for Hatch all along. Don't rush into anything now. Give yourself time. Consider all the ramifications. You don't know what Hatch's motives are in all this. He might think he can use you against Vincent somehow."

"No. He's not going to use me. He loves me." Jessie smiled. "For myself, not because I'm useful. If anything, I've probably caused Hatch more trouble than anyone he's ever run into before in his entire life."

"What are you talking about?" Lilian demanded.

"Look at it from his point of view, Mom. I dragged him into a crazy adventure. He nearly got killed because of me. He's lost his chance to make Benedict Fasteners the cornerstone of the empire he'd planned to build when he decided to rescue me from my role in the family. And now he's going to be more or less starting over financially because of me."

"You're looking at this from a skewed perspective."

"I'm not so sure about that." Jessie went to the door and paused, her hand on the knob. "When you think about it, he's really given me one heck of a courtship, hasn't he? Obviously the man is in love."

"Jessie, we're just asking you to be reasonable about this," Lilian cut in swiftly. "What if Vincent is mad enough to sell out? Even if he doesn't, we all know the company needs to be modernized if it's to stay competitive, and Vincent can't do it. The chance to turn Benedict Fasteners into a corporate giant is too important to let slip away."

"You'd need Hatch to do it, and Dad fired Hatch," Jessie reminded her.

"But you could fix it, dammit." Constance threw up her hands in exasperation. "You can deal with Vincent. Get him to see reason. Get Hatch to see reason."

"Dad would make Hatch crawl."

"It's called compromise, dammit," Constance shouted.

"It's called pride," Jessie said. "If Dad and Hatch are ever going to find a way to work together, one of them will have to back down. And I can tell you right now, it won't be Hatch."

"You know it won't be Vincent," Lilian warned.

Jessie nodded. She knew her father as well as anyone. "I know. Oh, by the way, you're both invited to the engagement party on Friday evening."

"You can't really expect us to help you celebrate this fiasco of an engagement, Jessie," Constance muttered.

Lilian frowned at her daughter. "Go home and think it over, Jessie. Think it over very carefully. You don't want to abandon your family for a man who is so unreasonable he'll walk out on a multimillion-dollar future."

Things felt a little eerie, Jessie thought later as she parked her car in front of her apartment building and got out. She had the oddest sensation of impending disaster again, rather like the feeling she'd had about the Attwood case.

It was probably caused by the array of changes she was confronting in her life. After all, a great deal had happened at once. She had been fired from a job she had really thought was going to work out. She had gotten engaged to be married. She had become the cause of a lot of serious tension in the family, when normally she was the one who smoothed things over for everyone.

Her life was undergoing a tremendous upheaval, she reminded herself. It was probably normal to feel vaguely uneasy and perhaps even threatened. She reached into the backseat for the two sacks of groceries she had just bought at the supermarket. Grasping one in each arm, she backed out of the car.

Jessie heard the roar of the suddenly accelerating engine just as she closed the car door. Automatically she glanced to the right to look down the normally quiet street.

The dark brown car was no more than a few yards away, still accelerating rapidly. It was coming straight toward her.

Jessie screamed and dropped the two sacks of groceries. In a split-second calculation she realized she could never make it across the street in time.

She did the only thing she could do. She pressed herself flat against the side of her own car, praying the driver would at least see and try to avoid the vehicle, even if he had not seen her.

The brown car whooshed past so close that Jessie's purse caught on the fender. The bag sailed into the air and landed yards away. She felt a rush of wind sucking at her, got a glimpse of windows tinted so dark it was impossible to see the driver, and then it was all over.

All over and she was still in one piece. Barely.

Jessie nearly collapsed as she peeled herself away from her car. The vehicle that had almost run her down was already squealing around the corner, vanishing from sight.

"Damn drunk drivers," an old woman on the sidewalk yelled in sympathy. "They oughta get 'em all off the road once and for all. Take away their cars, I say."

Jessie just looked at her.

She was still staring blankly at the groceries scattered across the street when Hatch's Mercedes pulled into the empty parking space behind her car a few minutes later.

Seeing the scattered groceries, he was out of the car in a flash, racing toward her.

"Jessie?"

She almost fell into his arms. Nothing had ever felt so strong and reassuringly secure as Hatch did in that moment.

CHAPTER NINETEEN

Y ou're sure you're okay?" Hatch asked for what must have been the fiftieth time.

"I'm okay. Honest. Just a little shaken up." Jessie sat at the kitchen counter gripping the cup of hot tea he had just made for her. "Calm down, Hatch. It was just one of those things. I should have been more careful getting out of the car."

"Damn right, you should have been more careful."

Jessie cocked a brow at him. "Do I detect a lessening in the degree of sympathy you feel? Is this where you start lecturing?"

"Now that the shock is over, I'm entitled to start lecturing." Hatch leaned back against the sink, his arms folded, eyes hooded. "Christ. Next time you get out of a car, look behind you. Got that?"

"Believe me, I'm not likely to forget it."

"I just wish that old lady on the sidewalk had gotten a license plate."

"There wasn't time, Hatch. I'm telling you, it was all over in a matter of seconds. Everything happened so fast."

"And you didn't get a look at the driver?"

Jessie shook her head. "I told you, tinted windows. Not that I would have had time to take notes anyway. I was too busy trying to meld myself to the metal of my car. There's nothing to report to the police except that a brown car nearly hit me. Unfortunately, that sort of thing happens to innocent people all the time. All a person can do is be careful."

"Remember that." Hatch fell silent. His gaze turned brooding.

"Hatch?"

"Yeah?"

"What are you thinking?"

"About a few things."

"That certainly clarifies the issue," Jessie muttered. "Let's have it. What's going on in that convoluted brain of yours?"

"I was just thinking that the police haven't picked up the DEL guy who broke into your office and tried to get into my car. They're investigating Edwin Bright and they've got Landis and Hoffman, but what if there was another one running around?"

Jessie's eyes widened. "You don't think he'd be after me, do you?"

"Probably not," Hatch said a little too quickly. "If he exists, and if he's got any sense, he's skipped town. And even if he was dumb enough to still be around, he'd be more likely to go after Susan Attwood. She's the one who's supplying most of the hard evidence against Bright."

"True. Do you think we ought to call Susan and Alex?"

Hatch chewed on that. "The thing is, it really doesn't make any sense for that jerk to still be in the picture. Assuming there is a jerk, he was just hired muscle. If he was smart enough to escape the police net, he should be smart enough to be long gone. But it can't hurt to call Robin. I'll tell him to keep an eye on Susan and to lock his doors and stay out of dark alleys for the next few days."

"What are you going to do?"

Hatch smiled grimly. "Keep an eye on you and make sure you lock the doors and stay out of dark alleys for a while."

Jessie was not particularly surprised to get the summons from her father the next morning on her answering machine. The message was gruff and betrayed no hint of any emotion except anger.

"I want to talk to you ASAP. Not at the office. I'm going home early. Come by the house around five."

At five that afternoon Jessie dutifully went up the steps of the big white house in which she had been raised. The Queen Anne neighborhood was one of the nicest in Seattle, the homes large, expensive, and well-maintained. The house to which Vincent Benedict had brought two brides was an old one with a graceful garden. A professional took care of the flowers. Jessie's father had no interest in gardening.

Vincent answered the doorbell with a glass of whiskey in his hand. He glowered at his daughter.

"About time you got here." His gaze went past her to where Hatch's Mercedes was parked at the curb. Hatch was leaning against the fender, idly studying the tree-lined street. He did not glance at the doorway. "What the hell's that bastard doing here?"

"Keeping an eye on me."

Vincent's face turned red. "What in damnation for? Is he afraid I'll make you see sense?"

"Not exactly." Jessie walked on into the hall and headed for the living room.

Vincent closed the door and followed her. "Wait just a blasted minute. Did Hatch send you in here to argue his side of this thing?"

"I'm here because you asked me to stop by, remember? It's only five o'clock, Dad. Hours before your usual quitting time. I assume we are about to discuss something on a par with World War III?" Jessie examined the garden outside the bay windows. It was as pristine and perfect as the rest of the house. Nothing was out of place. It was a house in which nobody really lived. Her father came here only to sleep and change his clothes. He *lived* at Benedict Fasteners. He always had.

"You know damn well what we're going to discuss. Jessie, things have blown up in our faces."

"Not my face. I'm strictly on the sidelines this time." She sat down on the arm of one of the cream-colored chairs Constance had bought while she was in residence. The furniture in the room was about equally divided between Lilian's selections and Constance's. Everything meshed beautifully, which spoke volumes about the relationship between Vincent's two ex-wives.

"Don't give me that crap about being on the sidelines. In this family, you're never on the sidelines. You're always right square in the middle. You want something to drink?"

"No, thanks. I promised Hatch I wouldn't stay long."

"Hatch. That sonofabitch. I just wish to God I'd known what a viper I was bringing into my nest when I hired him."

Jessie raised her chin. "Watch it, Dad. You're talking about the man I'm going to marry. The future father of your grandchildren."

"Jesus. You can't marry him, Jessie. That's just it. At least not until he comes to his senses and backs off. He's gone crazy, wanting me to split up the company. This whole thing has gone far enough, and you're the only one who can end it."

"What do you want me to do?"

"Do what you usually do, dammit." Vincent waved the hand that held the whiskey glass. "Fix it. Make everybody calm down and do the reasonable thing."

"In this case the reasonable thing means make everybody do what you want, right?"

"It so happens that what I want is the best thing for the company and therefore the best thing for the family," Vincent growled.

"Hatch doesn't think so."

"Who gives a damn what that man thinks?"

"I do." Jessie smiled. "And I'm sorry, Dad, but this time I can't fix things. I can't even try."

"Why the hell not?"

"Well, for starters, Hatch has threatened to paddle me if I try to mediate between the two of you."

"Threatened you?" Vincent's head came around swiftly, eyes glittering with rage. "That sonofabitch has threatened to beat my little girl? I'll tear him apart, by God. I'll rip him to shreds."

"Relax. You know as well as I do that Hatch would never hurt me," Jessie said.

"No, I damn well do not know that. I don't know what to expect from Sam Hatchard now. I thought I knew that man, but I was obviously wrong. He's turned on me, Jessie. Like the shark he is."

Jessie raised her eyes heavenward. "Give me a break, Dad. That's a gross exaggeration and you know it."

"So fix it, dammit. Do something. You can't go running off with him."

"Why not?"

"Because the company needs him and the family needs you, that's why not."

"I'm sorry, Dad. But this is something you're going to have to fix on your own." Jessie got to her feet and walked over to him. She stood on tiptoe and brushed her lips against his cheek.

"What about the family?" Vincent rasped as she turned to leave.

"I love all of you, but you're forcing me to make a choice. I've made it."

"Jessie, wait, goddammit. Come back here." Vincent's voice was ragged. "Don't you see? If you leave, I'll lose all of 'em. Elizabeth, David, Connie, and Lilian. You're the only thing that keeps them tied to me. You and Benedict Fasteners."

"I'm sorry, Dad, but I don't want to go on doing the job alone anymore. You're going to have to help."

"I won't let Hatch tear apart everything I've worked to build," Vincent bellowed. "Do you hear me? I won't let him do it, Jessie. I can't."

"Dad, if you want it all—me, the family, and the bright future you see for the company—you're going to have to trust Hatch as if he really were your son." Jessie walked down the hall toward the front door. She paused before opening it. "By the way, you're invited to our engagement party. Seven-thirty tomorrow evening. I gave Grace the name of the restaurant, just in case."

"Don't be expecting me, goddammit. I won't sanction this . . . this damn engagement."

"I only invited family," Jessie said gently. "So I'm not expecting a big turnout at all."

Out on the street Hatch watched with interest as a light green Buick pulled in to the curb and Glenna Ringstead got out. She had her hair in its familiar tight coil and she was wearing her usual formal gray suit and black pumps. She did not immediately see Hatch lounging against the Mercedes fender. It was obvious she was concentrating on her mission to Vincent Benedict's house.

Hatch wondered how she had known that Vincent was home at this time of day.

"Hello, Glenna."

Glenna whipped around, startled amazement registering on her handsome features. "Hatchard. What are you doing here?"

"Jessie's inside talking to her father. She'll be out soon. I don't think they've got a lot to say to each other."

Glenna's eyes narrowed. "It's true, then? You and Vincent have quarreled and Jessie's running off with you?"

"Somehow when the bride is twenty-seven and the groom is staring forty in the face, 'running off' doesn't seem like quite the right description. That sounds more like two high-school kids eloping."

Glenna looked impatient. "But you are going to marry her?"

"Yes. I'm going to marry her."

"And Vincent did fire you?"

"I was told to clean out my desk and be out of the building within an hour. Didn't even get two weeks' notice, which Jessie tells me is standard. She ought to know."

Glenna's eyes brightened with rare satisfaction. "I knew it wouldn't work. I told Vincent all along that he was making a mistake bringing you into the company. He didn't need you to take Benedict Fasteners to the top. All he had to do was train David to follow in his footsteps. Now maybe he'll see reason."

Hatch shrugged. "Something tells me David is never going to want the job."

"He will. He just needed a little time to grow up and mature. Now that you're out of the picture, it's only logical for Vincent to give my son another chance. He owes David that much, and he knows it. I'm going to tell him so."

"I wouldn't count on it, Glenna. David's not cut out for the corporate world. Jessie's right. He'll be much happier in an academic environment."

"Jessie doesn't know what she's talking about. How could she? She's had no training in psychology, no advanced degrees of any kind. She can't even hold on to a job, for God's sake. Yet she thinks she knows what's best for everyone. It's about time she got out of the way. Without her around we're all going to be a great deal better off."

Hatch raised his brows. "Think so?"

"I know so." Glenna turned and strode up the walk.

The door opened and Jessie emerged from the house just as her aunt started up the steps. Her eyes flickered with surprise.

"Hi, Aunt Glenna. What are you doing here?"

"I've come to see your father."

"Right. Well, I hope you can make it to the engagement party tomorrow night. Seven-thirty."

Glenna nodded stiffly. "I'll be there."

"Good."

Hatch straightened away from the fender as Jessie came down the steps. He opened the car door for her. "You okay?"

"Yes."

"You sure?"

"Yes, I'm sure." She smiled wearily up at him as she slid into the front seat. "It's strange how people box themselves into little corners and won't come out, even though it's in their own best interests to do so, isn't it?"

"People get into patterns, like you said. Patterns are hard to break."

"Aunt Glenna was the one who first pointed out the patterns in people's lives to me."

"Speaking of Glenna . . ." Hatch glanced back toward the house. The front door was just closing. Hatch shut the car door and went around to get behind the wheel.

"What about Aunt Glenna?" Jessie asked as he turned the key in the ignition.

"She seems to think she's finally gotten what she's apparently wanted all along."

"Me out of the picture?" Jessie asked shrewdly. "Yes, I know." She gazed back at the closed door of the big white house as the Mercedes pulled away from the curb. "I hope she's happy now."

"Something tells me that woman is never going to be happy for long," Hatch observed. "But I'll give you odds she'll come to the engagement party to celebrate this turn of events."

The waiter took in the five faces seated at the table that had been set for eight. He cleared his throat as he handed out menus. "Are we still waiting for the other members of the party, sir?" he said to Hatch.

Jessie bit her lip and Hatch glanced at his watch. In

addition to herself and Hatch, only Aunt Glenna, David, and Elizabeth had arrived at the restaurant for the engagement party.

"I don't think there's much point waiting any longer," Hatch said. "It looks like they won't be joining us, after all. Bring out the champagne and that bottle of sparkling water."

"Yes, sir. I'll be right back." The waiter moved off through the crowded dining room.

Elizabeth stared at Hatch, her eyes wide with curiosity. "I can't believe you both got fired on the same day."

"Must have been fate," Hatch murmured.

David grinned. "Sounds more like bad luck to me."

"Same thing." The corner of Hatch's mouth kicked up as he traded a look with the younger man.

Glenna gave Jessie a cool, remote, oddly satisfied smile. "I'm sure it's all for the best."

David glanced toward the door. "Looks like the old bastard is going to stand you up, Jessie. You know, somehow I thought he'd at least put in an appearance."

"He's not real happy with me right now," Jessie said quietly.

"It's the moms I don't understand," Elizabeth said. "I told them they should come, even if they were mad at you. But they said you were making the biggest mistake of your life and that you were going to cause everyone a whole lot of trouble and be real sorry later. They said they couldn't be a part of it."

"Maybe in time they'll understand that I had to do it," Jessie said, her eyes going to Hatch. He smiled at her and grasped her hand under the table.

"So, where are you two going to wind up living?" David asked quickly, obviously determined to turn the conversation into less troubling channels.

"Portland, probably," Hatch said.

Elizabeth brightened. "Good. That's not far away at all."

Hatch grinned. "That's why I decided to take Jessie there

instead of Phoenix. We wanted to be someplace where you could come and visit easily."

"Thanks." Elizabeth looked at her sister. "Like I said, I can come down on the train."

"It's going to work out just fine," Jessie said firmly.

The waiter returned with the champagne and the sparkling water. Everyone watched attentively as he went through the ritual of opening the wine and pouring it. When he had left the table, Hatch picked up his glass.

"We're here tonight to make my engagement to Jessie official. I'd like to thank everyone—"

"Hold it," David broke in, his eyes on the door of the restaurant. "We've got more guests."

Jessie and the others turned to look toward the entrance. Lilian and Constance stood there, handing their coats to the hostess.

"It's the moms," Elizabeth announced gleefully. "They came after all!"

Jessie realized she was suddenly feeling a little more relaxed and happy. She smiled at her mother as Lilian moved toward the table. Lilian smiled back ruefully.

"Hello, Mother, Connie," Jessie said softly. "I'm glad you could make it after all."

"You're just in time to join us in a toast." Hatch got to his feet and held out a chair.

"So I see," Lilian murmured, her eyes on her daughter.

Elizabeth grinned up at Constance as David rose to seat her. "Hi, Mom. I'm sure glad you two decided to come. We missed you guys."

"Well, it was fairly obvious you were going to go ahead without us," Constance said in her usual pragmatic fashion. "Didn't seem much point in ignoring the whole thing. If Hatch is determined to carry Jessie off, I suppose we're all going to have to learn to adjust to the situation."

"We are, of course, overwhelmed by your gracious acceptance of the situation, Mrs. Benedict," Hatch said.

"We're here, aren't we?" Lilian retorted.

"Yes, you are, Mrs. Benedict," Hatch allowed. "And we appreciate it. I think. Have some champagne."

Glenna gave Constance and Lilian a distant but approving glance. "On the whole, I think it was a good idea for the two of you to put in an appearance. Failure to be supportive at times like this can cause irreparable damage to the parent-child relationship later on."

"I don't think they need your approval, Mom," David said in an undertone. "They're here because they care about Jessie just as much as everyone else does. Even if they do think she's making a mistake."

"How true," Constance drawled. Then she smiled at Hatch. "I do hope you find a job soon. Lord knows Jessie isn't a reliable means of support. She can't hold a position longer than six months."

Jessie grinned. "Hey, I resent that. I may not be able to hold a job, but I can sure find them. I've found more jobs than you can count."

Lilian groaned. "That's the truth." She turned to Hatch. "Well? Have you got anything lined up yet?"

"I'm still figuring out how to collect unemployment," Hatch murmured. "It's rather complicated. I had no idea there was so much paperwork involved. But if I don't get it sorted out fairly soon, there's always welfare."

"Unemployment? Welfare? You mean you haven't even started looking for another job? And you're going to marry my daughter?" Lilian stared at him, clearly aghast.

"Relax, Mom." Jessie chuckled. "That was a joke. Hatch has a little trouble with jokes. Or maybe I should say people have a problem with Hatch's sense of humor."

Lilian rolled her eyes and looked at Constance for backup. "Just what I need. A son-in-law with a warped sense of humor."

"Better than one with no sense of humor at all," Constance pointed out.

"Come on, you guys," Elizabeth interrupted. She seized her glass of orange sparkling water. "We were just about to drink a toast to Hatch and Jessie. I've never gotten to drink a toast before."

Hatch picked up his glass. "Let's try this again. We are here tonight to officially announce the fact that Jessie and I plan to marry as soon as possible. I thank you all for being here to celebrate this momentous event with us. I know it isn't easy for some among you to accept this situation, but who the hell cares? This is the way it's going to be. First, to my lovely, loyal, beloved Jessie."

Jessie blushed warmly under Hatch's searing gaze. There was so much love and possessiveness in his eyes that she trembled under the onslaught. A deep certainty welled up within her. There was no doubt about it. She was doing the right thing.

Everyone at the table was in the process of hoisting his or her glass when David halted the toast for a second time. Once again his eyes were on the restaurant entrance. "Wait," he said softly. "We've got one more late arrival."

"Who on earth?" Frowning, Glenna turned her head to glance toward the door.

"Well, for heaven's sake. Who would have guessed?" Lilian shook her head in silent wonder.

"I'll be damned," Constance stated, her eyes warm.

"I always knew he was as stubborn as a rogue elephant," Hatch said with cool satisfaction. "But I never said he was stupid."

Jessie was already on her feet, Elizabeth right behind her. They both raced toward the big man standing near the hostess's desk.

"Dad." Jessie reached Vincent first and wrapped her arms around his waist, laughing joyously. "I'm so glad you came."

"What the hell else could I do, Jessie? You're my daughter. And if you insist on marrying that stubborn sonofabitch, then I guess he and I had better find a way to get along."

Elizabeth clung to Vincent's arm and grinned up at her

father as he bent to kiss her cheek. "I knew you'd come, Dad. Just like I knew you'd come to watch me when I won first prize at the science fair."

Vincent smiled benevolently down at his offspring and then looked at the curious hostess. "My daughters," he explained proudly. "The elder one's getting engaged tonight."

"Yes, sir." The hostess smiled. "Congratulations. I believe everyone at the table is waiting for you."

Jessie led the way back to the big table and took her seat beside Hatch as Elizabeth plunked herself down in her own chair. Hatch got to his feet and eyed Vincent.

"Glad you could make it, Benedict."

"Always said you were a damned marauding shark." Vincent sat down between Lilian and Constance, who each leaned over to give him an affectionate peck on the cheek. "Should have known once you made up your mind to have my daughter, nothing short of the crack of doom could have stopped you."

"You were right." Hatch sat down again.

An odd, charged silence descended on the table. Jessie was acutely aware of the strange tension flowing around her. It was as if everyone was waiting for the other shoe to drop.

Hatch and Vincent continued to eye each other across the width of the table, reminding Jessie of two gunslingers outside a saloon at high noon.

"The thing you got to remember about sharks," Vincent said slowly, "is that they bite."

"That's why we have teeth," Hatch explained.

"And God knows, if Benedict Fasteners is ever going to have a shot at moving into the big time," Vincent continued "it'll need a shark with a lot of teeth in charge. I'm reinstating your contract, as of now, Hatch."

An audible collective gasp could be heard from almost everyone at the table.

"It's not quite that simple," Hatch reminded him gently.

"There's the little matter of splitting up the company among Jessie, Elizabeth, David, and me."

"Hell, I know that." Vincent scowled at him. "I wouldn't be here tonight if I wasn't agreeing to that part of the deal."

Jessie sat back in her chair, limp with relief as cheers of delight went up around the table. These were followed by an exuberant whooping shout from David. Heads turned in the restaurant.

"Well," Constance said with deep satisfaction as the clamor died down, "I'm pleased you've decided to be reasonable about this after all, Vince. Didn't think you had it in you."

Lilian smiled at her ex-husband and patted his hand. "Congratulations, Vince. You're doing the right thing."

"Way to go, Dad." Elizabeth was grinning from ear to ear. "Now Jessie can stay here in Seattle."

"Hatch was right." David looked at Vincent. "You might be stubborn as all hell, but you're not entirely stupid."

"Thank you, David." Vincent slanted him a wry glance.

"What if," Hatch said coolly, his expression unreadable, "I decide I don't want to go back to work for you?"

Another audible gasp was heard. This time everyone turned to stare at Hatch, who did not appear to notice that he was now the focus of attention.

Vincent smiled grimly, looking very sharklike himself. He picked up the bottle of champagne and poured himself a glass. "Why, then, I'll just have to sue you for breach of contract, won't I?"

Hatch allowed himself a slow grin. "You'd do it, too, wouldn't you, you sonofabitch."

"In about two seconds," Vincent agreed equably.

"Then it looks like I'll be going back to work at Benedict Fasteners," Hatch said. Under the table his hand closed fiercely around Jessie's. "And the company will have some new owners."

She turned her head to look at him, realization dawning

slowly as she saw the cool triumph in his gaze. Then she started to laugh. Everyone stared at her in astonishment.

"Honest to God, Hatch, if you tell me you planned it this way, I swear I'll dump the rest of this champagne over your head," Jessie managed to get out between giggles.

Hatch smiled and pulled her close long enough to cover her mouth in a quick, hard kiss. "Sometimes a man just gets lucky."

The scraping of a chair on the far side of the table broke through Jessie's euphoria. She turned to see Glenna rising to her feet in a quick, jerky movement. Her aunt's face was twisted with rage.

"No," Glenna said forcefully. "No, this isn't right. It's not right, I tell you."

The shocking sight of Glenna Ringstead looking nearly out of control held everyone at the table spellbound.

"It should have been David," Glenna hissed through set teeth. "It should have been my son you put in charge, Vincent. The company should go to him. *All of it.* Not just a quarter, but all of it. He deserved it after what you did to his father. Damn you. Damn you to hell. *It's not right.*"

Before anyone could respond, Glenna whirled around, still moving in a stiff, unnatural manner, and fled toward the door.

It was David who broke the stunned silence that followed. He looked at Vincent. "Don't you think it's time you told me just what you did do to my father?"

Vincent's sigh was one of deep resignation. "Maybe it is. I think you can handle it, David. I didn't always think that way, but now . . ." He flicked a glance at Hatch. "Now I have a feeling you can."

CHAPTER TWENTY

You want the God's honest truth, David?" Vincent asked.

"Yes."

"Your father was one of the smartest men I've ever met. Your mother was right: back at the beginning, I depended on him. Without his abilities I would never have gotten Benedict Fasteners off the ground. I knew construction and I thought I knew the industry, but I didn't know much about running a business."

"And my father did?"

"He sure did. Like I said, he was real smart that way. But two years after we finally started turning a decent profit, Lloyd nearly stole the company blind."

David stared at him. "He *what?*"

"He embezzled over three hundred thousand dollars before I realized what was going on. That was a lot of money back then. Hell, still is. Benedict Fasteners nearly went under."

David shook his head, looking stunned. *"No.* I don't believe it."

"You asked for the truth and I'm giving it to you. Straight. Man-to-man. No more chocolate-candy coating to make it palatable, like your mother always wanted me to do."

David's expression was nearly blank. "But Mom always said he was brilliant."

"He was. Your father was a brilliant, lying, cheating thief. And when I found out what he was doing, I fired his ass. Gave him a choice between clearing out and going to jail. He cleared out. Glenna decided not to go with him. Couldn't blame her. What kind of future would the two of you have had with a man like that?"

"Mother always said you owed us," David said in a dazed voice.

"When your dad left I told her I'd see to it that you and she never suffered. Told her I felt I owed her that much because of what Lloyd had contributed to the company in the early days. And because she was Lilian's sister and . . . well, there were other reasons." Vincent glanced uneasily at his two ex-wives, who were watching him with rapt attention. "Like I said, I felt I owed her."

"Why didn't anyone ever tell me the full truth?" David demanded tightly.

Vincent shrugged. "In the beginning it was because you were too young to understand. And because Glenna wanted the truth kept from everyone in the family. I went along with it. But I think that over the years she sort of chose to forget what really happened."

"She just focused on how much her husband had done for the company back at the beginning and on the fact that you owed her," Lilian said. "That explains a lot about her possessiveness toward you and the firm."

"And why she always felt David should have inherited," Constance added thoughtfully.

"I can't believe you never told me the truth." David shook his head in bewilderment. "I can't believe you kept that kind of secret for so long."

"A boy doesn't need to hear that kind of thing about his father," Hatch said quietly.

"Yeah," said Vincent. "Doesn't do a kid any good to know his old man was a complete bastard. Sort of makes things harder than they are already. Just ask Hatch. Or me."

"Why am I getting the full truth now?" David looked straight at Vincent. "Because I asked for it?"

"Nah." Vincent picked up his champagne glass. "I've been sitting on that secret for years. Could have taken it to my grave. I'm telling you the facts now because I think you can handle 'em, in spite of what your mother says about you being so goddamned sensitive."

"What makes you think that?"

"Hatch here told me you pulled your own weight when you went along on that stupid trip to rescue the Attwood girl. And you didn't send Jessie to ask me for money for grad school, like I was expecting you to do. All things considered, I figure you've turned into a man. You don't need protecting anymore."

Hatch shrugged into his jacket and picked up his briefcase. He gave Jessie a very serious look as he paused to kiss her good-bye at the door of her apartment. "Try to stay out of trouble while I'm gone."

"You betcha." She smiled beatifically up at him and batted her eyelashes.

Hatch groaned. "Why do I even bother to ask?" He kissed her soundly. "I should be back by ten tonight unless the flight is late."

"Sure you don't want to stay over in Spokane and come back in the morning?"

"No, I do not want to spend the night in a hotel room in Spokane when I can spend it here in your bed." Hatch scowled and glanced at his watch. "I just want to get this damn contract signed, sealed, and delivered before the wedding so I can enjoy my honeymoon."

"This is that dippy little contract that Dad's so proud of stealing out from under Yorland and Young?"

"Right. And if I don't get it out of the way, your father will be calling me every day we're away, asking me when I'm going to come back and handle it."

"Knowing Dad, that's probably true. Don't worry about me. I'll just be sitting here patiently waiting by the hearth with your pipe and slippers."

"The hell you will. You're going to cook yourself an entire pound of ravioli and eat it all."

"Look at it this way: after an entire pound of ravioli, I'm not likely to get into any kind of trouble." She laced her arms around his neck. "I love you, Hatch—wing tips, boring tie, and all."

His smile was slow and sexy. "Is that right?"

"Uh-huh."

"Must be because I'm so damn good in bed."

"Must be."

"Just as well. Because I love you too, even if you can't hold a job." He kissed her nose and then he kissed her mouth, hard.

And then he was gone.

It was much later that day, right after she'd eaten the pound of ravioli for dinner, in fact, that Jessie started to feel restless and uneasy. The sense of wrongness was so acute she could hardly stand it. She glanced at the clock. Hatch was not due home for another three hours.

"I wish you were here, Hatch."

Jessie tried to read, but all she could think about was how badly she wanted Hatch to be home.

The phone rang shortly after eight. Jessie pounced on it, although she could not have said why.

"Hello?"

"Jessie, dear, is that you?"

Jessie exhaled a sigh of relief. "Oh, hello, Mrs. V. Yes, it's me. How are you?"

"Fine, dear. I was just sitting here watching television and I had a sudden urge to call and see if you were . . . well, all right."

"I'm just fine, Mrs. V."

"Good. I'm afraid I just had one of my little spells of uneasiness and it seemed to have something to do with you. Dear me, I do hope that blow on the head hasn't made my inner vision unreliable."

"I appreciate your concern, Mrs. V. Is, uh, everything going all right at the office?"

"I've had to close it until things die down. I plan to reopen in a few weeks when everyone's forgotten the Attwood case. Do you know, though, I'm going to miss you. Have you found a new job?"

"Not yet, Mrs. V. But I'm sure something will turn up. It always does."

The phone rang again at nine o'clock, just as the long, slow twilight of late spring was fading into night. Jessie grabbed the instrument a second time.

The voice was that of a woman and it sounded disturbingly familiar. But it was impossible to identify because she was apparently speaking through a cloth. The message was short and to the point.

"If you ever want to see your precious Elizabeth alive again, you will come to the new Benedict warehouse now. If you tell anyone or bring anyone with you, the child dies. You have thirty minutes."

Nausea welled up out of nowhere. Jessie's knees went out from under her and she nearly collapsed on the sofa. Frantically she tried to remember Elizabeth's schedule for Monday evenings. Was there a soccer game tonight? She could not recall. Blindly she dialed Connie's number. There was no answer. She tried the office of ExCellent Designs. Again no answer. Then she glanced at the clock.

Twenty-eight minutes left of the thirty she had been given. There was no time to see if Elizabeth was safe, no time to determine if the call was a cruel hoax. No time to do anything but get to the new warehouse in the south end of town.

Jessie grabbed her car keys and rushed to the door.

She nearly fell down the stairs in her haste to reach the car. Outside on the street she fumbled desperately with the keys. She had just gotten the door open when she felt herself pinned by a pair of blinding headlights.

Memories of nearly being run down a few days earlier brought another wave of panic to Jessie's throat. But even as she turned to run she realized the car was pulling in to the curb behind her Toyota, and then she saw that it was Hatch's Mercedes. Jessie ran toward it.

"*Hatch.* She's got Elizabeth. I have thirty minutes to get there. No, about twenty-five now. Oh, God."

Hatch was out of the car, moving swiftly toward her. "Who's got her? What are you talking about?"

"I don't know," Jessie sobbed. "A woman, I think. Maybe someone I know. But her voice was disguised. She just called. She's taken Elizabeth to the new Benedict warehouse. Told me if I didn't come alone, she'd kill her."

"We'll take your car because she'll be expecting it. Get in. I'll drive."

"She says I have to go alone. Hatch, I'm so scared."

"Just get into the car. We'll figure this out on the way."

He was already pushing her into her car, getting in beside her, and starting the engine. Jessie tried to collect her wild thoughts. Something struck her suddenly.

"What are you doing home an hour early?"

"I caught an early flight."

"But why?"

"Damned if I know," Hatch said. "A couple of hours ago I just had a feeling I wanted to get home sooner than I'd planned. I made some excuses to the people I was dealing with, phoned the airport, and got on an earlier flight."

"Thank God. Hatch, I'm so afraid."

"You said it was a woman's voice?"

"Yes. I'm sure of it. Muffled, but it sounded vaguely familiar. Do you think . . . ?" Jessie could not bring herself to finish the question.

"That it was Glenna who called? I don't know, Jessie. But we have to face the fact that it's a possibility."

"I can't believe it. Why would she do such a thing?"

"You know why." His mouth tightened as he guided the Toyota onto the freeway that sliced the city in half. "A part of her still thinks that everything should have gone to David. I wonder if she's finally flipped completely and decided that the best method of ensuring that David inherits everything is to get you and Elizabeth out of the way."

"No. She wouldn't kill Elizabeth. She would not do such a thing."

"We don't really know what she'd do, Jessie. There's a lot of old anger buried in her. A lot of bitterness. What happened at the engagement party the other night might have been too much for her. Took away her last hope. Might have pushed her over the edge."

Jessie shook her head, unwilling to believe such a possibility. "I've known her all my life. I just can't believe Aunt Glenna would go this far. I won't believe it until I see it for myself. Hatch, what are we going to do?"

"Give me a minute to think about the layout of the new warehouse. I took a look at the plans last week. Thanks to your father's outdated management style, the doors were rehung last week and we started moving inventory into the place. There should be a lot of cover inside the building by now, what with equipment and product stored in there." Hatch fell silent beside her, his face set in forbidding lines.

A few minutes later he turned off the freeway and drove into a dark, silent warehouse district in the south end of the city. Buildings loomed, their windows unlit for the most part. Huge trucks were parked for the night near loading docks. The streets were empty.

"Hatch? We're almost there."

"I know." He glanced at his watch. "I'll get out at the next corner and cut through those two buildings over there. That will bring me into the back of the warehouse."

"How will you get inside?"

"I know the security-system code. Your father and I chose it together so we could both memorize it."

"How would Aunt Glenna get it?"

"Hell, she's family, isn't she? And she's smart."

"That's true. You want me to drive straight up to the front entrance?"

"Right. But stay in the car. Let her know you're there but don't make it easy for her. She'll have to think about her next move, and that should give me some time to act. Glenna's not a professional kidnapper and she's got a very rigid personality. My guess is she won't know what to do if things don't go exactly according to plan. Still, we don't want to push her too far. She's obviously unstable."

"We're assuming it is Aunt Glenna."

"I'm afraid she's the logical candidate. But that's in our favor. It won't be easy for her to kill Elizabeth. We'll have some negotiating time." Hatch stopped the car a moment later and got out. He closed the door and leaned down to speak through the open window as Jessie slid into the driver's seat.

"Remember. Stay in the car. Keep the engine running. If she calls to you, pretend you can't hear her."

"All right." Jessie's fingers trembled on the steering wheel. She watched as Hatch vanished down an alley between two darkened buildings. His dark gray suit blended perfectly into the shadows. Then she turned the corner and drove toward the warehouse.

There was no sign of life around the entrance of the building. But one of the front doors was open, revealing a gaping darkness inside. Jessie brought the car to a halt, leaving the engine running as Hatch had instructed. She waited.

Long moments passed in terrifying silence. Jessie began to

wonder if Glenna or whoever it was inside had realized she was there. The thirty minutes were up.

Fearing that the kidnapper might think she had not followed orders and would do something violent, Jessie cracked open the car door. She had to get out and see what was happening.

At that moment a familiar voice shouted at her from the gloom of the open doorway.

"Jessie." Elizabeth's small figure came pelting out of the building. "Jessie, watch out."

"Elizabeth." Jessie was out of the car without even pausing to think. She ran toward Elizabeth, instinctively grabbing her arm and jerking her off to one side of the entrance. Something told her to get her sister out of the direct line of sight.

An instant later a shot crackled through the darkness. It shattered the awful stillness that cloaked the warehouse.

"Jessie, she pushed me out here to get you out of the car. She's got a gun."

"I can't believe she'd actually shoot us. I just can't believe it." Jessie dragged Elizabeth farther away from the main entrance, deep into the shadows around the corner of the building.

Elizabeth clung to her hand. "What are we going to do?"

"Hush." Jessie pressed herself back against the wall of the building, trying to listen. She held her sister close to her side. "Hatch is here," she whispered in Elizabeth's ear.

"Geez. That's a relief."

"You think I couldn't have handled this on my own?" Jessie muttered.

"Nothing personal, but something tells me Hatch is better at this kind of thing."

"Something tells me you're right."

Another shot echoed through the night, and then a vast silence descended on the warehouse. Jessie and Elizabeth held their breaths.

A moment later Jessie heard footsteps coming around the

corner of the building. It was the familiar, solid-sounding tread of a pair of wing tips.

"Jessie? Elizabeth? It's all over."

"Hatch."

Both sisters ran to him and Hatch opened his arms to catch them both close for a moment.

"I think," Hatch said after a while, "that you'd better come and take a look at the kidnapper, Jessie."

Jessie closed her eyes, steeling herself. "Yes, I guess I'd better. What am I going to tell Mom? And David?"

"Not too much, if I were you." Hatch's voice was wry as he led the way back into the warehouse and turned on a workman's light.

Jessie stared down at the familiar wiry figure lying unconscious on the floor. A stocking mask lay crumpled beside her pale face.

"Nadine Willard."

"You know her?" Elizabeth asked curiously. "She tried to tell me you did when she grabbed me in the rest room at the mall, but I didn't believe her. Then she pulled that gun out of her purse and made me go with her. She even knew how to deactivate the security system. She cut some wire and did some things with a pair of pliers."

"Yes, I know her," Jessie said, meeting Hatch's eyes with a sense of chagrin. "I vote we don't ever tell anyone about our earlier suspicions."

"I agree," Hatch said dryly. "Dr. Ringstead would no doubt diagnose us both as severely paranoid."

"She was working for Edwin Bright all along," Jessie explained to Lilian, Constance, and Elizabeth two days later in the offices of ExCellent Designs. "A real dedicated type. The kind Aunt Glenna told me got lured into cults. She idolized Bright. Thought he was some kind of savior."

"And he used her," Constance said.

Jessie nodded. "She had a strange background. Grew up in a rough neighborhood and got into gangs and drugs at an early age. Had some trouble with the law when she was caught breaking into houses. But she seemed to have straightened out. She got her GED, got into Butterfield, and was holding down a job."

"And then she got involved with Bright?" Lilian asked.

"The police say he used her as sort of an inside person to screen the people he was recruiting. She was the one who broke into Mrs. Valentine's office and later tried to get into Hatch's car. She was trying to find out how far our investigation had gone and whether or not we were a genuine threat to DEL."

"And when she realized it was all over for Bright, she decided to try to get rid of the people who could testify against him. Starting with you." Lilian shuddered.

"Her first try was the night she nearly ran me down. She was fanatically devoted to Bright. She was going to try to kill all of us involved in the case. She started with me because she blamed me for having carried on the investigation in the first place." Jessie paused. "She had actually tried to stop things right at the beginning."

Constance looked at her. "What do you mean?"

"Mrs. Valentine called to say she recognized her picture in this morning's paper. Nadine is the one who pushed her down that flight of stairs."

Lilian shuddered. "She'd found out that Mrs. Attwood had gone to her?"

Jessie nodded. "Nadine apparently believed in Mrs. V's powers and was afraid that a true psychic might be able to hurt Edwin Bright's cause. Nobody worried about me for a while, until it became apparent I was determined to pursue the case. Then things got complicated. Bright told her to let Hatch and me come on out to the island so that Landis and Hoffman could assess the situation."

"But they still weren't overly concerned until they found out Susan had been contacted," Constance concluded.

"Right."

Constance laced her fingers together on top of her desk

and looked at Elizabeth. "I hope you understand that you are never again going to go to the mall with your friends. From now on out, one of us goes with you or you don't go."

"Ah, Mom," Elizabeth muttered.

Jessie patted her hand consolingly. "Don't worry, Elizabeth. I'll go with you whenever you want. The way I figure it, I owe you about a hundred trips to the mall."

"Fat lot of good that will do," Elizabeth complained. "Hatch won't let you out alone now either."

Jessie grinned. "He's a little overanxious these days, but I expect he'll relax after the wedding."

"Who's overanxious?" Hatch asked as he came through the door with several cups of coffee. He glanced around at the smiling faces of the four women. Then he shrugged. "You finish telling them the story, Jessie?"

"I told them everything."

"Good. Then we can get out of here." He glanced at his watch. "I've got a lot of work to do before we leave on our honeymoon."

A month later Jessie awoke in the pink-and-white bridal suite of the luxurious beachfront hotel. Outside the lanai window, sunlight danced on the incredibly blue tropical sea. She stirred, aware of Hatch's strong, solid warmth beside her. His arm lay across her breasts, his face buried in the pillow beside her.

For a long moment Jessie reveled silently in the perfection of the Hawaiian morning and the promise of the future that stretched out before her.

The wedding had been hastily planned but had gone off without a hitch, thanks to Lilian and Constance. Elizabeth had been adorable in her bridesmaid attire. Nobody had tried to stuff Hatch into a coral tuxedo. He had waited for her at the altar in austere black and white and it had suited him perfectly. Her father had walked Jessie down the aisle and handed her over, with an expression of deep satisfaction, to the man he had personally chosen for her.

Vincent had danced with his ex-wives at the reception, clearly enjoying himself in a way that surprised everyone who knew him. He did not excuse himself to make a single phone call to check in at the office.

Nor did Hatch.

"What's so funny?" Hatch shifted slightly, opening his eyes. The sexy, hungry memories of the night were reflected in his gaze.

Jessie turned in his arms. "I was just thinking that you haven't made one phone call or sent a single fax since we got here."

"We've only been here a day. Give me time."

"I'm going to slap your wrists if I see you reach for the phone." Jessie propped herself up on one elbow. "Happy, Mr. Hatchard?"

"Yes. Definitely yes." He ducked his head to kiss the tip of one rosy breast.

"It went well, didn't it?"

"The wedding?" He kissed the other nipple. "It went fine. If you overlook the way your father was bragging to everyone about how he had found your husband for you."

Jessie laughed and then sighed as Hatch slid his leg between her thighs. "I'm willing to give him some credit."

"What about giving me the credit? I took one look at you and knew I was the right man for you."

"True. You know, I'm going to be embarrassed every time I look Aunt Glenna in the face. Thank heaven she doesn't know what we thought on the way to rescuing Elizabeth. I was afraid she wouldn't come to the wedding."

"David had a long talk with her. Told her he knew everything and that he was satisfied and she should be too." Hatch's hand closed over her thigh, clenching gently.

"David certainly seems to be getting along much better with Dad these days." Jessie's legs shifted restlessly on the sheet.

"Ummm." Hatch was kissing her throat now.

"Did I tell you what Dad said to me at the reception?"

"No."

"He said it was time I stopped fooling around working for other people." Jessie inhaled sharply as Hatch's fingers moved to her inner thigh. "He said I was never going to be happy unless I was my own boss. Said I was a lot like him in that respect."

"Yeah?"

"Hatch, you're not listening. It's my future I'm trying to discuss here. I've been doing some thinking, and I've got an idea for starting up my own business."

"I'm your future," Hatch informed her, unabashed at his own arrogance. He lowered himself along the length of her, eyes gleaming in the morning light. "And you're mine. Any further discussion on the subject is hereby tabled until later. There is another matter on the agenda that needs to be taken care of first. Priorities, Mrs. Hatchard. Always remember, one must stick to priorities."

She looked up at him through her lashes and wrapped her arms around his neck. "God, I love it when you play chief executive officer."

Three months later Hatch looked up from a financial summary as Vincent Benedict stormed into his office and tossed a file onto the desk.

"Have you seen those contract terms? Personnel just sent them up for review. They're outrageous. Absolutely outrageous. Dammit, Hatch, what the hell are you going to do about her? She's gone berserk."

"I assume we are discussing Jessie?" Hatch opened the file and glanced at the proposed contract from a temporary employment agency called Intuitive Services. The owner and sole proprietor of the firm was one Jessie Benedict Hatchard. The company slogan was spelled out on the letterhead: "We Anticipate Your Short-Term Personnel Requirements."

"Damn right we're discussing Jessie."

Hatch glanced at the terms of the contract and scowled.

Jessie was asking for a year-long contract to supply software design services to Benedict Fasteners. She was featuring two exceptionally talented programmers and designers named Alex Robin and Susan Attwood. "You're right. She's asking too much. Tell personnel to keep negotiating."

"Won't do any good," Vincent said, looking glum. "They tell me this is her final offer."

"Then tell them to call off the deal."

Vincent looked shocked. "But this is Jessie's first big contract. I want her to have it."

"If she's going to run her own business, she's going to have to learn to be more competitive when she goes after a contract."

"Dammit, man, this is *Jessie*. Your wife. My daughter. Don't you want her to make this temporary-employment-agency thing work? It's ideal for her. The first decent career move she's ever made. Hell, no one knows more about short-term employment than Jessie."

"I agree." Hatch leaned back in his chair and eyed Vincent with amusement. "And I don't doubt for one minute that she'll make the business fly. She's got a lot of you in her."

"Don't you think we ought to give her the contract? We need a couple of good computer jockeys on board to design those new financial programs. You said so yourself."

"I know. But if we let her lock us into these terms, we'll never be able to get out of them. Tell personnel to try again, and if they can't get her to lower the cost, tell them to kill the deal. She'll learn fast."

Vincent heaved a sigh. "You're probably right."

Hatch grinned. "You know I'm right. Hey, this was all your idea, remember? Don't worry. It'll work out."

"I hope so. I want to see her make a go of this agency of hers." Vincent narrowed his eyes shrewdly. "Don't suppose you could, uh, sort of talk to her tonight?"

Hatch laughed and shook his head. "Impossible. Jessie has this strict rule, you see. No business after I get home from work." He glanced at the clock. "And speaking of home, it looks like it's about time to call it a day."

Vincent frowned. "It's only five-thirty."

"I know." Hatch stood up and put on the jacket of his conservative pin-striped suit. "I've got to get moving. Jessie and I are involved in a major project and I don't want to be late."

"What major project?"

"Planning the baby's bedroom." Hatch stroked the scarlet petals of a brilliant lily in the bouquet on his desk. Jessie had sent the flowers to the office that morning in honor of the third month of their marriage. "Your grandkid will be here in another five months, Benedict. See you in the morning. Oh, and don't forget dinner at our place on Saturday night. Elizabeth will be there. And be on time. Jessie has another rule. If you're late, you don't eat."

Hatch went out of the office and headed home to where Jessie and the really important part of his life were waiting.

Her Next Romantic Adventure!

JAYNE ANN KRENTZ

PERFECT PARTNERS

SHE JUST INHERITED
HIS COMPANY.
HE WANTS TO GET IT BACK.
EXECUTIVE ACTION:
A TAKEOVER OF THE HEART!

POCKET
B O O K S

Coming from Pocket Books
May 1992

431

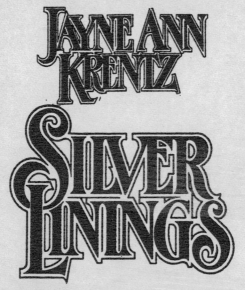

THE PENGUIN BOOK OF
ITALIAN VERSE

INTRODUCED AND EDITED BY
GEORGE R. KAY

*

WITH PLAIN PROSE TRANSLATIONS
OF EACH POEM

PENGUIN BOOKS

Penguin Books Ltd, Harmondsworth, Middlesex
U.S.A.: Penguin Books Inc., 3300 Clipper Mill Road, Baltimore 11, Md
AUSTRALIA: Penguin Books Pty Ltd, 762 Whitehorse Road,
Mitcham, Victoria

—

First published 1958
Reprinted 1960

Made and printed in Great Britain
by Richard Clay & Company, Ltd,
Bungay, Suffolk

GENERAL EDITOR'S FOREWORD

THE purpose of these Penguin books of verse in the chief European languages is to make a fair selection of the world's finest poetry available to readers who could not, but for the translations at the foot of each page, approach it without dictionaries and a slow plodding from line to line. They offer even to those with fair linguistic knowledge the readiest introduction to each country's lyrical inheritance, and a sound base from which to make further explorations. The anthologist too gains a considerable advantage from this method, since he can choose much more freely among medieval, dialect, and difficult modern poems when he knows that all the reader's problems can be solved by a glance at the bottom of the page.

But these anthologies are not intended only for those with a command of languages. They should appeal also to the adventurous who, for sheer love of poetry, will attack a poem in a tongue almost unknown to them, guided only by their previous reading and some Latin or French. In this way, if they are willing to start with a careful word for word comparison, they will soon dispense with the English, and read a poem by Petrarch, Campanella, or Montale, by Garcilaso, Góngora, or Lorca, straight through. Even German poetry can be approached in this unorthodox way. Something will, of course, always be lost, but not so much as will be gained.

The selections in each book have been made by the anthologist alone. But all alike reflect contemporary trends in taste, and include only poetry that can be read for pleasure. No specimens have been included for their historical interest, or to represent some particular school or phase of literary history.

J. M. COHEN

THE PENGUIN
FOREIGN VERSE ANTHOLOGIES

The following foreign verse anthologies have already been published in this series:

TABLE OF CONTENTS

*

ix

TABLE OF CONTENTS

TABLE OF CONTENTS

FAZIO DEGLI UBERTI (1310–70). The single work given in this poet's name has a fine turn of phrase – *Soave va in guisa di pavone...*

GIOVANNI BOCCACCIO (1313–75). Boccaccio wrote poems, as well as wonderful prose, and in the best of them his originality shows a new face. Particularly touching is the sonnet written after he had learned, at a distance of months, of Petrarch's death: *caro signor mio* – his great friend, his collaborator in hastening the Renaissance.

FRANCO SACCHETTI (1335?–1400). Sacchetti's shorter poems stir like the Greek lyric, and close as mildly. In his poetry, even more than in Petrarch's, the medieval city with its darkened streets, on which the Madonna of Dante and his friends appeared like a sudden star, is left behind, and the country, which seems so fresh and clean and new, welcomes the poet.

MATTEO MARIO BOIARDO (1434–94). Boiardo's most famous work is the *Orlando innamorato*, a fantastic saga with Childe Roland as hero. It has passages of brilliant freshness, a quality found in the best of his short poems as well.

LORENZO DE MEDICI (1449–92). The greatest member of the family in which the vital sap 'mounted to the higher branches' so remarkably. Gifted statesman, befriender rather than patron of artists like Leonardo and Michelangelo, the intelligent companion of such Renaissance wits as Politian, Ficino, Pico della Mirandola, Lorenzo was also the poet whose 'songs for dances' have all the charm of the dance.

ANGELO POLIZIANO (1454–94). The distinguished Latin scholar, close friend of Lorenzo, and, like him, a most natural poet in the Italian tongue. He too wrote 'songs for dances', wonderfully easy compositions that rival Lorenzo's own; and in the space of a day threw off the *Orfeo*, a lively ballad-play for the Carnival, today considered the first libretto in the real sense of the word.

TABLE OF CONTENTS

LUDOVICO ARIOSTO (1474–1533). Ariosto is a great name in Italian poetry, but his shorter poems, with few exceptions, lack the satisfying oneness. The *Capitolo* given is a thing of warm breath, but, to know Ariosto's range, the reader must open the *Orlando furioso*, and be caught up with Angelica as she gallops away into that vivid, fantastic world.

MICHELANGELO BUONARROTI (1475–1564). Michelangelo's wrestle with his own desires has given his sonnets their form; always nervous, sometimes too muscular from the struggle. The unhappiness incidental to his devotions (the majority of his love poems are to the good-looking young Roman, Tommaso Cavalieri: the others to the unassailably virtuous Vittoria Colonna) does much to determine their tone, a questioning, light-begging tone. But if the poet can call both Christ and Cavalieri 'my dear Lord', and ask the selfsame help from God and Vittoria Colonna, it is always Love he serves. The lines *In me la morte, in te la vita mia* are fittingly untitled.

VITTORIA COLONNA (1490–1547). This excellent lady recorded her love for her husband in numerous sonnets, several of which speak to everyone.

GASPARA STAMPA (1523–54). Little more than a girl, she fell in love with Collatino, conte di Collalto, and her poems have caught the reflection of the violence with which she burned. The whole story of her passion is told in a long series of sonnets – from first maddening to professed disillusion. The beating heart is never far beneath.

TORQUATO TASSO (1544–95). After he fell in love with Laura Peperara, Tasso wrote madrigals and songs which for cadence, cunning simplicity, tenderness, and pause are incomparable. The unhappy, uncertain life of his after years is too involved to be summarized; but it was right that he should die outside Rome, before they could crown him with a partisan or patronizing laurel.

GIORDANO BRUNO (1548–1600). Bruno illustrated parts of his challenging philosophy in sonnets, and these give a sense of the cosmic journey, the soul launched towards the infinite, as no other poetry does. The Romantics have not his swift directness. As a poet he is virtually unknown in this country. As a philosopher, the interest which began when he discussed with Philip Sidney, Fulke Greville, and their friends at London, and continued in Coleridge's awareness of him as a 'dynamic' thinker, has hardly come to full recognition.

TOMMASO CAMPANELLA (1568–1639). The great friar of the Counter Reformation who suffered much for the reasonableness of his faith and his impassioned conviction that religion was still catholic. The dangers, the assurances, the despairs, and ecstasies his soul knew breathe in the madrigals of his *Cantica*, grouped into 'Psalms' that can be compared to the divine Psalms of David.

GIOVAN BATTISTA MARINO (1569–1625). Marino has suffered much for hearsay judgements of his gift and use of it. His ease of melody, his twining of images to give works of curious, sensuous delight, are not the devices of a pallid Arcadian. Marino could describe, frankly and with humour, a love-encounter with some shepherdess who was no empty classic name. And Marino could see himself as he was. Witness the singing lines to *L'amore incostante*.

PIETRO METASTASIO (1698–1782). The flower of the Arcadian sports. That *Libertà* should be freedom from a woman, and that this should be rhymed in fifty different ways is a comment upon the spirit of the age – neatly caught by Metastasio in the sonnet on the *Olimpiade*. That the long poem holds us, or, rather, makes us move with it, although itself it hardly moves, is a tribute to his mastery. Even Thomas Gray thought him a great lyric poet.

UGO FOSCOLO (1778–1827). Foscolo's life speaks of generosity and impulsiveness: a forthright, combative spirit that won him no few loves and enemies. His campaigning with Napoleon's armies, his quick disillusionment with the man as 'Emperor', his daring addresses for the Italian cause during the weeks of his professorship at Pavia, his flight to exile in Switzerland and then England, these experiences meant a life at the centre of his time – what many of his foreign contemporaries longed for in the depths of their Romantic souls. Few of the Englishmen he met appreciated his genius. We gladly remember Hobhouse's tribute, that Foscolo never uttered a commonplace, and Lord Holland's gift of a favourite wine as the poet lay dying. His memory grows in brightness.

GIOSUÈ CARDUCCI (1835–1907). Carducci's preoccupation
with political small-life and a pedestrian strain of thinking that
was twin to it, often came in his way when he wished to write
poetry. He would cut at the tame followers of Manzoni in the
very act of mounting Pegasus: he would indulge week-end reflections about the simple life just after he had summoned up
the love of his youth, the vivid *Maria bionda*. In his shorter
poems and a few long sustained pieces like *Alla stazione in una
mattina d'autunno* (remarkable both for its broken sincerity
and its shadowiness – early Impressionist), he shows the fullness of his gift.

GIOVANNI PASCOLI (1855–1912). Pascoli is among the first
of minor poets. His gift is so evident (listen to the *cader fragile*
of the leaves in *Novembre*): and yet the reader is impelled to
demand something more as soon as the shadowy music passes.
His ear for words that lull is almost as exquisite as Tasso's, but
his melancholy does not stem from some uncertainty in his
time. The bereavements he suffered left him to gentle sadness
and, inevitably, to the desire for a quiet life. They also did
much to shape his modest, wondering poetry.

GABRIELE D'ANNUNZIO (1863–1938). D'Annunzio's
poetry is to be rescued from that grotesque, encrusted mauso-
leum, his complete works. The small body that emerges shows
irresistible youth, a maturer, questioning sensuality, and always a vigour, not unshadowed by the Romantic's dissatis-
faction with the world and its promises.

DINO CAMPANA (1885–1932). Campana was outspanned by
D'Annunzio in years, not in achievement. He left only two
collections of poems: *Canti orfici* and *Quaderno*. These give a
fair impression of the man: devil-ridden, though his phantoms
are no more than mildly evil; self-driven from theme to theme
as he, in his waking life, was from one place to another; bearing an unforgettable identity. At times his poems share the de-
fects of D'Annunzio's poorer work, the baroque excesses of
sweetness and violence. But the best of them set the reader
trembling with a new, half-recognized experience.

GIUSEPPE UNGARETTI (1888–   ). Ungaretti's poetry
was born before the 1914–18 war, but it came of age in the
middle of it, when he was a soldier. The tremendous pressures

that the new style of warfare put upon individualities – and Ungaretti's is a rare one – forced poetry from him: the long, spare forms, the short, clean-broken utterances we associate with his name. Some of these poems, *I fiumi* for instance, have a dazzling completeness about them, and defy comparison with all but the very best of his later works. But *La pietà* and a few from *Il dolore* can take their place by the diamonds of his first conceiving.

EUGENIO MONTALE (1896–   ). Montale's poetry is in itself a life. It can be said to 'come like leaves to the tree'. He found himself early as a poet. Before the First World War, when he was still a youth, he had already come alive on the Ligurian coast where he spent his summers, the Liguria of Esterina. So it was that, after the war, in which his voice was muffled, he could return to the Mediterranean, and meet himself again. *Ossi di seppia* (1925) was followed by *La casa dei doganieri* (1932) which was then incorporated in *Le occasioni* (1939), just as *Finisterre* (1943) now becomes the first part of *La bufera e altro* (1956). These volumes enclose some forty years of poetry, and no small share of Europe's best today.

SALVATORE QUASIMODO (1901–   ). Quasimodo brings us the luxurious harmonies of the South which, in Italian poetry of the past, has meant the sickly as well as the exquisite. He looks to Tasso as his ideal. Tasso himself erred this way. But Quasimodo's own lyric form – *quasi un madrigale* – has given something new to Italian poetry. Occasionally he romanticises his childhood Sicily, looking back at it from misty Milan; but in poems like *Lettera alla madre* or *Vento a Tìndari* he is finely moving.

INTRODUCTION

THIS is a good moment for putting together an anthology of
Italian poetry. Today we are beginning to see the importance of
Italy's living poets, because the best of these are older men who
have already given us a substantial body of works. We can look
at the achievement-to-date of Eugenio Montale, of Giuseppe Ungaretti, of Salvatore Quasimodo, against the background of all
Italian poetry, and their contribution in turn throws a new light
on what has gone before. The river has taken another bend. From
this point the whole course looks different. As I write, Montale's
new volume *La bufera e altro* is being put out in the bookshops,
and I remember with gratitude that, thanks to the poet's kindness in lending me a typescript, I have managed to include something from these *recentissime* in the present collection.

So this book really grows from its last part of all. It is modern
taste and modern questionings which have determined my selection. Similarly it has been in translating the works of the last
forty years (reputedly so difficult, though the essays, or rather
articles, written to illustrate this are much more obscure) that I
have learned how far a literal translator of poetry can help the
reader with small knowledge of the language. He reports faith-
fully, he may at times be obliged to choose one interpretation
rather than another, but he should stop short of explanation.
Again, however cleanly he may deliver the poet's meaning into
his own tongue, he does not pretend to transmit to the understanding the poetic shock with which his original is charged.
These translations, then, should serve to make Italy's lyric
wealth accessible to all who value poetry; and to those who are
already acquainted with the various *Rime*, something new will, I
hope, be shown.

To find Saint Francis listed as the first Italian poet will probably surprise those who have only glanced at Italian literature
before. This placing is no innovation of mine. Numerous collections published in Italy begin with his inspired hymn. It is not
given this honour here for its art or supposed lack of art – its

'primitive charm', as some would say, a weak recommendation, little more suggestive than the popular adjective 'nice'. Saint Francis comes first because, already in his distant time, he displays the virtues of the best Italian poets. He is simple, passionate, meaningful. His words are marked by an unspectacular urgency. Yet he commands our wonder, and not only when he says that God is to be praised for 'our sister, bodily death'. From Saint Francis, too, we learn something of the character of the masters of Italian poetry. They are great individuals who have dominated the word, each in his own special way. They are never professionals of verse.

Italian poetry is the work of individuals who in their own lives were original and who, to translate an expression, 'breathed more deeply' than other men. But these poets have not always grown in isolation. Lone Leopardi, the born stranger, stands today as the figure of the Italian poet. His is only half the story. To illustrate this from the earliest age – immediately after Saint Francis another solitary religious emerged, Iacopone da Todi, himself a Franciscan. He stands alone, in torment, in joy, in quiet gladness – *Fiorito è Cristo nella carne pura*. But contemporary with Jacopone the first 'school' of poets was gathering in the South, in Sicily. And however much 'school' may suggest one style or a common programme, the important ones in Italian poetry have never been more than groups of individuals.

The names of the leading Sicilians, Rinaldo d'Aquino, Giacomino Pugliese, Giacomo da Lentini, are constellated about that of the great emperor, Frederick II, himself a poet. A distinctive poetic accent gives them a family likeness. So, too, does the way they sing of love. In fact, no poets have ever revealed a greater intimacy with love as it is known to lovers. Rinaldo d'Aquino can write, with perfect sympathy, poems for the woman's voice: take that wonderful complaint, *Già mai non mi conforto*. But perhaps the Sicilian gift of knowing both voices, both hearts of love is best displayed in the popular *contrasto* (or 'contest in words') by Cielo d'Alcamo – a window dialogue, the most natural thing in the world. No one could say that these two works, or any of the best Sicilian poems, were 'essays in a style'. The accent may be the same in all, the voices are quite different.

With the Tuscan poets the reader's impression could be that they form a school in the accepted sense of the word. Their colours are easily recognized. They accept much of their imagery in common. Each gazes at his lady with adoring fixity. But where they have liberated themselves from their own conventions, the Tuscans are far more original than the Sicilians. In some of them the creative moment illuminates a few poems only. Lapo Gianni would be simply an excellent craftsman if he had not written a piece like his wonderful day-dream *Amor, eo chero mia donna in domino*. But two poets stand out, high above the others, like towers overshadowing a compact medieval city: a major poet and a great one: Guido Cavalcanti and Dante. The poet who wrote sonnets such as *Chi è questa che ven* and the incomparable *Perch'i' no' spero di tornar giammai* is still the companion, after these seven hundred years, of the one who wrote the *Vita nuova* and the Divine Comedy.

Dante's originality is as astonishing as his achievement. As a young man he put himself to school with Guido Guinizelli, regarding himself as a follower of Bologna's 'sage of love'. But no word of the story of his youthful heart, the *Vita nuova*, is prompted. In middle age Dante was overtaken by a new passion, when he lost his heart to a mere girl and was rejected. The experience was violent. It caught and shook him by the neck. No part of the poetic language he had mastered could adequately suggest it. Dante found new words, a new way of speaking: *Così nel mio parlar voglio esser aspro / com'è ne li atti questa bella petra*. This, certainly, is what it is to be a poet.

I have included several of the poems to the 'young girl of stone' in the present selection. They are not generally known in this country, even to readers for whom Dante is the one Italian poet. With Petrarch, by contrast, no neglected works have still to be honoured. Complete editions of his poems have been made and read from his own life-time to the present day, and much has been translated, meantime, into English. The reader has simply to try what readers through six centuries have known and admired. The wonder is that, in reading Petrarch, the sense of discovery never fails us. The simplicity, the new devices with which he expressed devotion to Laura lay hold of us as they did of his contemporaries and successors. We see why he was universally recognized while he lived. When they crowned him with laurel on the Capitol hill, it was no idle ceremony. We see why generations of would-be poets longed to write sonnets, *canzoni*, poems, as he had done – 'Frances Petrarke the Laureat hight'.

Petrarch left poems that are almost perfect (what finer setting of a thought is to be found than *Di pensier in pensier, di monte in monte?*); and his example dazzled. This is particularly true of the sonnet and *canzone*. Before his time these forms were still growing. The Tuscans did not take them as the Sicilians had shaped them. But once Petrarch's sonnets and *canzoni* came to be known, the forms themselves were thought of as Petrarchan. So we should not be surprised if, in all the works of his imitators, we find little innocence of vision. They only wanted a likeness of their great original. They had nothing to add. Nor is it strange that the new impulses in Italian poetry should come in forms that Petrarch had not 'appropriated': the *ballata* and the madrigal.

The moment for the *ballata* came in Florence during the early Renaissance. *Ballata* is best translated 'song for a dance', a sort of composition that, always popular, was especially so during Carnival, when the procession, cars and people, wound through the streets. The *canti carnescialeschi* of that time move with a new, a pagan abandon, but they move with grace. They are not rough-spun folk-song, because the masters of the form were not crude rhymers, but Lorenzo de' Medici, lord of the city, and Angelo Poliziano, a leading scholar of the time. These public men composed their words in the intervals of pressing duties; and, by a happy chance, gave them just the lightness, simplicity, fire that have kept them glowing to this day. How Lorenzo and

Politian enjoyed these entertainments of theirs is shown by a wood-cut of the time that depicts them looking on, while some girls dance, fair as the Graces, singing one of their songs. Lorenzo seems to be saying to his friend:

> *Queste ninfe ed altra gente*
> *son allegre tuttavia.*
> *Chi vuol esser lieta, sia:*
> *di doman non c'è certezza.*

Lorenzo's shining time, like his own song, was for a moment, no more. In his contemporary Boiardo the lyric also wakes: beautifully fresh, original. Little follows for another two generations. Ariosto's poetry, we see, is in the idyllic pauses of his long verse-tale about Roland: and it is not until Tasso writes, a century or so after the Florentine days, that the short poem finds another master.

The madrigals and other lyrics by Tasso offer a pleasure quite unlike that of the Carnival songs. They have risen in the isolated lover. They could never be taken up by the crowd, though they ask to be sung, so pure is the line of verbal melody in them. Tasso is the most musical of Italian poets. But we would wrong him if we saw him merely as the best of courtly song-writers. The very unrestraint, the recurrent sadness of his short poems betray some quarrel deep within him. In fact, it is his life and work that show how the 'heavy change' that followed the Reformation and the Catholic reaction to it affected one who was, first and last, a poet; how, after he had written his youthful poems, among them the *Aminta*, a charming pastoral entertainment with a hint of the elegaic about it, he felt he must undertake an epic defence of Christendom, and gave us the irresolute and troubled *Gerusalemme liberata*. The best poems of his contemporaries lets us see how great individuals, Michelangelo Buonarroti, Gaspara Stampa, to name two, used poetry more as a kind of diary to record how they suffered, and gladly burned (the phoenix is their image), in the new era of uncertainty. Greatest of all, in a sense, is Campanella, the friar who could accept prison, torture, oblivion, from his church and still write:

La dubbia guerra fa le virtù conte.
Breve è verso l'eterno ogn'altro tempo,
e nulla è più leggier ch'un grato peso.
Porto dell'amor mio l'imago in fronte,
sicuro d'arrivar lieto per tempo,
ove io senza parlar sia sempre inteso.

Tasso's younger contemporary, Marino, went further with curious images or 'conceits', wrote with a musicality hardly less enchanting, could suggest a most caressing pleasure (look at *L'Amore incostante*) but, as a poet, stops there. If we pass over his followers, the *Marinisti*, who are occasionally rewarding to the lover of pure style, little that can be called poetry is met with in the next two hundred years or so. Take Metastasio, the delight of the eighteenth century. His quatrains move quite perfectly, turning upon themselves with the precise and fluid movement of the brass weights revolving in a six-day clock. But what does he sing? Liberty. And what does he mean? Freedom from a woman he has doted upon. His own work can be of a seductive monotony, but, as an influence, he proved more disastrous than Marino. Not before Foscolo – great Ugo – is the small, dulcet, chiming tone lost to Italian poetry, as if it had never been. Parini and Alfieri seem, in their shorter poems, too conscious of what they are writing against.

Already in Foscolo's gallant odes *A Luigia Pallavicini* and *All'amica risanata*, the eighteenth century is behind us. Their form is still, in a sense, neo-classic, but although Foscolo handles it correctly, and even enhances the flattering style, we have the feeling that he is playing: brilliantly, not without some heat of passion, but, first and last, to show that, as a poet, he can make a far more taking bow than any of his betters. Turn to the sonnets. The impression is different. Here an unquiet strength rises and strains at the fourteen lines. It strains at them as long as they follow the honoured pattern set by Petrarch. Once Foscolo leaves this for a sonnet of his own making, something swift and incandescent is created. How the lines *A Zante* speed to their fateful end – *illacrimata sepoltura*! But sonnets could not, in the end, contain his more powerful impulses to poetry. Only in the surges of *De' Sepolcri* that gather and lunge forward until they touch their glittering horizon – *finchè il Sole | risplenderà su le sciagure umane* –, does he give his utmost as a poet.

Foscolo's Italian, with its inversions and lengthy constructions, occasionally presents difficulties to the foreign reader and to the native one as well – much as Milton's English does. The extreme instance is the image in that verse of *A Luigia Pallavicini* beginning *Tal nel lavacro immersa*. That takes unravelling. At points like this the reader will probably turn to the translation for more support than ever, but he must turn back to the original and catch the true Foscolian phrase: *O bella Musa, ove sei tu? Non sento/spirar l'ambrosia…*: …*te beata gridai…*: *e pianto, ed inni, e delle Parche il canto*: …*l'isolette | stupefatte l'udiro ed i continenti*: the whole of that perfect lyric, *Io dal mio poggio*, to give just a few examples.

If Foscolo's style of expression calls for close appreciation, so in a more special way does Leopardi's. Here the question is no longer of difficulty of language. The English reader is asked instead to see the rightness of Leopardi's phrase, the simple finality of his forms, the purity of his line: in *L'infinito*, the wonderfully youthful *Sera del dì di festa*, in *Silvia*, the passage about the stars in *Il canto notturno*, or the unearthly description of Pompei in *La ginestra*, and that poem's tender close. It is in the last-named work that Leopardi shows the modern temper – which does not break through even once in Foscolo's *De' sepolcri*, though the poem's import is perfectly 'modern'. He is willing to discuss, refute, observe life; but he still thirsts for some sublimer touch – all in one and the same poem. Clearly it was because Leopardi was too modern that he did not become a master for his contemporaries or those in the century following.

This is the background to modern Italian poetry. Leopardi was not recognized in his day for the supreme poet that he is: the century after him was spanned by three who were much less inspired, Carducci, Pascoli, D'Annunzio: and, then, with the vivid disintegration of Campana, the new age opens. As I write,

Montale's newest volume, *La bufera e altro*, is propped on the bookshop counters. The printing is not of the finest and the book may not look impressive, but I, for one, feel that this is, for now and the future, a memorable production. The poet who had already given us *Falsetto*, *Delta*, the series of *Mediterraneo* and *Motteti*, *La casa dei doganieri*, has added to these richly, and in one poem at least, *L'Anguilla*, seems to have mounted higher than ever – like the *anguilla* itself, thrashing its way upstream in defiant joy. This is a good moment for Italian poetry.

G.R.K.

Rome, October 1956

My first decision with this anthology was to choose no quotations from longer works – the *Commedia*, *Trionfi*, *Orlando*, *Gerusalemme*, and so on. The poets who have suffered most for this are Ariosto, who did not master shorter forms, and Vicenzo Monti, whose tracts of blank-verse include such excellent passages. For texts I have trusted, in the absence of one complete series of definitive editions, to the best of the series: Laterza, the handsome new Ricciardo Ricciardi, the older, red-bound Rizzolis, at times to the *Classici Italiani*, not to mention numerous other best editions for single poets. My practice with the earlier schools, Sicilians and Tuscans, has been to adopt the clean spelling of the Bianchi Govoni volumes (*La magna curia* and *Il dolce stil nuovo*), neither modernized nor fussily authentic. Coming to the moderns, I might have included younger men than Quasimodo, but Italian poetry, after the three, is an anarchic province; though I think highly of works by Maria Luisa Spaziani, Vittorio Gasparini and those new Sicilians, Bartolo Cataffi, Enrico de' Miceli, and Michele Spina. Of Italian anthologies, my favourites have long been Bontempelli's *Lirica italiana* (1182–1837) and Spagnoletti's *Antologia della poesia italiana 1909–1949*, and these have doubtless influenced some of my minor decisions.

My first acknowledgements must be to Dr Antonia Sansica Stott, the kind tutor who saw and trained my interest in Italian poetry, giving me both the books I mention, each at the right moment: to my other Italian masters at Edinburgh University, John Purves, whose *First Book of Italian Verse* is still the best student introduction to the poetic subtleties of the language, and Doctor Mario Manlio Rossi, philosopher and liveliest of teachers. Latterly I have been greatly helped, particularly with my Montale translations, by Dr Filippo Donini of the Italian Institute in London. My debt to him in the present instance is immeasurable. If it had not been for Dr Donini, I would never have had the chance of undertaking the present work. I must thank others of the Institute, its director, Count Morra, Miss Lucia Pallavicini, Mr Mallia, who were so kind in affording me books, information, every kind of facility, even during the holiday month of August: Mrs A. Walker and Magda King for valuable assistance with typing: Rafaele Fernando Squirru and the Reverend Doctor Alexander King for timely aid: J. M. Cohen for suggestions in the later stages. Lastly I would record my friends in Italy: Carlo Candi, the sculptor, who years ago in Florence let me hear *Ed è subito sera* and *Mattina* for the first time: those who, the other day, lent me books – the painters Angelo Verga and Giorgio de Gaspari, the distinguished critic, Marco Valsecchi: the others interested in my work, be they of Piazza Roma in Bibbiena or Signora Lina's *Giamaica* in Milan.

The following publishing-houses are to be thanked for permission to print modern Italian works: Nicola Zanichelli of Bologna for Carducci's poems; Vallecchi of Florence for Campana's; and Arnoldo Mondadori of Milan for those of Pascoli, D'Annunzio, Ungaretti, Quasimodo, and the earlier Montale.

In preparing this reprint I have been specially indebted, for suggestions, to C. A. McCormick of Melbourne University and the poet Cammillo Pennati, whom I gratefully thank.

THE PENGUIN BOOK OF
ITALIAN VERSE

SAN FRANCESCO

Cantico delle creature

Aʟᴛɪssɪᴍᴜ, onnipotente, bon Signore
tue so le laude la gloria e l'honore
et onne benedictione.
Ad te solo, Altissimo, se confano
et nullu homo ene dignu te mentovare.

Laudato sie, mi Signore, cun tutte le tue creature
spetialmente messor lo frate sole
lo qual jorna et allumini noi per loi.
Et ellu è bellu e radiante cun grande splendore
de te, altissimo, porta significatione.

Laudato si', mi Signore, per sora luna e le stelle,
in celu l'ai formate clarite et pretiose et belle.

Laudato si', mi Signore, per frate vento
et per aere et nubilo et sereno et onne tempo,
per lo quale a le tue creature dai sustentamento.

Canticle of All Created Things

Lᴏʀᴅ, most high, almighty, good, yours are the praises, the glory, and the honour, and every blessing. To you alone, most high, do they fittingly belong, and no man is worthy to mention you.

Be praised, my Lord, with all your creatures, especially master brother sun, who brings day, and you give us light by him. And he is fair and radiant with a great shining – he draws his meaning, most high, from you.

Be praised, my Lord, for sister moon and the stars, in heaven you have made them clear and precious and lovely.

Be praised, my Lord, for brother wind and for the air, cloudy and fair and in all weathers – by which you give sustenance to your creatures.

Laudato si', mi Signore, per sor'aqua
la quale è multo utile et humile et pretiosa et casta.

Laudato si', mi Signore, per frate focu
per lo quale ennallumini la nocte
et ello è bello et iocundo et robustoso et forte.

Laudato si', mi Signore, per sora nostra matre terra,
la quale ne sustenta et governa
et produce diversi fructi con coloriti fiori et herba.

Laudato si', mi Signore, per quelli che perdonano per lo
    tuo amore
et sostengo infirmitate et tribulatione,
beati quelli che sosterranno in pace
ca da te, altissimo, sirano incoronati.

Laudato si', mi Signore, per sora nostra morte corporale
da la quale nullu homo vivente po scappare,
guai a quelli che morranno ne le peccata mortali,
beati quelli che trovarà ne le tue sanctissime voluntati
ca la morte secunda nol farrà male.

Be praised, my Lord, for sister water, who is very useful and
humble and rare and chaste.
Be praised, my Lord, for brother fire, by whom you illuminate
the night, and he is comely and joyful and vigorous and strong.
Be praised, my Lord, for sister our mother earth, who maintains
and governs us and puts forth different fruits with coloured flowers
and grass.
Be praised, my Lord, for those who forgive because of your love
and bear infirmity and trials; blessed are those who will bear in
peace, for by you, most high, they will be crowned.
Be praised, my Lord, for sister our bodily death, from which no
living man can escape; woe to those who die in mortal sin; blessed
are those whom it will find living by your most holy wishes, for
the second death will do them no harm.

Laudate et benedicete mi Signore et rengratiate
et serviteli cun grande humilitate.

IACOPONE DA TODI

De la diversità de contemplazione de croce

– Fuggo la croce che me devora,
la sua calura non posso portare.

Non posso portare sì grande calore
che getta la croce: fuggendo vo amore;
non trovo loco, ca porto nel core
la remembranza me fa consumare. –

– Frate, co fuggi la sua delettanza?
io vo chirendo la sua amistanza;
parme che facci grande vilanza
de gir fugendo lo suo delettare. –

– Frate io fuggo, chè io son ferito:
venuto m'è 'l colpo, e 'l cor m'ha partito;
non par che senti de quel c'ho sentito,
però non par che ne sacci parlare. –

Praise and bless my Lord and give thanks to him and serve him
with great humility.

Of the Various Ways of Contemplating the Cross

'I flee the cross which devours me, I cannot bear its heat.

'I cannot bear a heat as great as that the cross sends out: I keep
flying from love; I find no refuge, for I bear the memory in my
heart and that consumes me.'

'Brother, why do you fly its delightfulness? I keep asking for its
friendship; it seems that you do a very base wrong to keep fleeing
its power to delight.'

'Brother, I flee because I am wounded: the blow has fallen on me
and split my heart; it does not seem that you feel what I feel, because you do not seem to be capable of talking of it.'

— Frate, io sì trovo la croce fiorita,
de soi pensieri me sono vestita;
non ce trovai ancora ferita,
'nante m'è gioia lo suo delettare. —

— Ed io la trovo piena de sagitte
ch'escon del lato; nel cor me son fitte:
el balestrier en ver me l'ha diritte,
on arme ch'aggio me fa perforare. —

— Io ero cieco ed or veggio luce:
questo m'avenne per sguardo de cruce;
ella me guida, chè gaio m'aduce,
e senza lei son en tormentare. —

— E me la luce sì m'ha acecato:
tanto lustrore de lei me fo dato,
che me fa gire co abacinato,
c'ha li bel occhi e non pote mirare. —

— Io posso parlar, che stato so muto,
e questo ella croce sì m'è apparuto:

'Brother, I find the cross so flourishing, that I have clothed myself with its thoughts: I do not find I am wounded in this, rather is
its sweetness my joy.'

'And I find it full of arrows that fly out from its side; they have
stuck in my heart: the bowman has aimed them at me, and shot
them through every piece of armour I have.'

'I was blind and now I see the light: this has come about from
my gazing on the cross; it leads me, that blithely leads me on, and
without it I am in torment.'

'And the light has equally blinded me: it shone so strongly upon
me, that it makes me go about like those blind people who have fine
eyes and cannot gaze.'

'I can talk who have been dumb, and it is because of the way this

tanto de lei sì aggio sentuto,
ch'a molta gente ne pos predicare. –

– E me fatt'ha muto, che fui parlatore:
en sì grande abisso entrat 'è el mio core,
ch'io non trovo quasi auditore
con chi ne possa de ciò ragionare. –

– Io era morto ed or aggio vita,
e questo è la croce sì m'è apparita:
parme esser morto de la partita
ed aggio vita nel suo demorare. –

– Ed io non so morto, ma faccio el tratto,
e Dio lo volesse ch'el fosse ratto!
star sempremai en estremo fatto
e non poterme mai liberare! –

– Frate, la croce m'è delettamento:
nollo dir mai ch'en lei sia tormento;
forsa non èi al suo giognemento
che tu la vogli per sposa abracciare. –

cross appeared to me: I have felt so much from it, that I can declare this to many people.'

'And it has made me dumb who was such a talker: my heart has come into so great an abyss, that I can hardly find a listener with whom to speak of this.'

'I was dead and now have life, and it is because of the way this cross appeared to me: I seem to be dead at its leaving me, and I have life in its sojourning.'

'And I am not dead, but suffer the last spasms, and God grant that they may be over quick! always in extremities and never able to free myself!'

'Brother, the cross is my delight: never say it is torment for you; perhaps you are not in union with the cross that you want to embrace as your bride.'

– Tu stai al caldo, ma io sto nel fuoco:
a te è diletto, ma io tutto cuoco;
con la fornace trovar non pò loco:
se non c'èi entrato non sai quegn' è stare.

– Frate, tu parli che io non t'entendo,
como l'amor gir vòi fugendo:
questo tuo stato verrìa conoscendo
se tu el me potessi en cuore splanare. –

– Frate, el tuo stato è en sapor de gusto:
ma io c'ho bevuto, portar non pò el musto;
non aggio cerchio che sia tanto tusto
che la fortuna non faccia alentare. –

Del iubilo del core che esce in voce

O IUBILO del core, · che fai cantar d'amore!

Quando iubilo se scalda, · sì fa l'uomo cantare;
e la lengua barbaglia · e non sa que parlare:
dentro non pò celare, · tanto è grande el dolzore!

⸱You are in the heat, but I stand in the fire: it is delight to you, but I am quite roasted; I can find no refuge with this furnace: if you have not entered it, you do not know what it is to stay there.'
'Brother, you speak in a way I don't understand, of how you wish to keep fleeing from love: I should like to know your state, if you could lay it open to my heart.'
'Brother, your state takes the form of joy: but I who have drunk, cannot bear the taste of must; I have no hoop that is so stout that my ferment does not loosen it.'

Of the Heart's Rejoicing which Comes Forth in the Voice

O REJOICING of the heart that makes us sing from love.
When rejoicing warms, it makes man sing; and the tongue babbles and does not know what to say; this joy cannot be hid within, so very great is its sweetness.

Quando iubilo è acceso, · sì fa l'omo clamare;
lo cor d'amore è preso · che nol pò comportare:
stridendo el fa gridare, · e non vergogna allore.

Quando iubilo ha preso · lo cor enamorato,
la gente l'ha en deriso, · pensando suo parlato,
parlando smesurato · de que sente calore.

O iubil, dolce gaudio, · ched entri ne la mente,
lo cor deventa savio · celar suo convenente:
non può esser soffrente · che non faccia clamore.

Chi non ha constumanza · te reputa empazito,
vedendo svalianza · com omo ch'è desvanito:
dentro lo cor ferito · non se sente de fuore.

When rejoicing is in flame, it makes man cry out; his heart is
seized with love, so that he cannot bear it: it makes him shout out
piercingly and he is not then ashamed.

When rejoicing has possessed the heart in love, people hold a
man in derision, thinking of his speech, for he speaks beyond all
measure of what he feels inflaming him.

O rejoicing, sweet joy, that comes into the mind, the heart grows
wise in hiding its state: it cannot bear to the point of not making
itself heard.

He who has no acquaintance with this considers you mad, seeing
your distractedness, like that of a man out of his senses: the
wounded heart does not feel what is outside it.

Pianto de la madonna de la passione del figliolo Iesù Cristo

NUNZIO

Donna del paradiso,
lo tuo filgiolo è priso · Iesù Cristo beato.

Accurre, donna, e vide · che la gente l'allide!
credo che llo s'occide, · tanto l'on flagellato.

VERGINE

Como esser porria, · che non fece mai follia,
Cristo, la spene mia, · omo l'avesse pigliato?

NUNZIO

Madonna, egli è traduto: · Iuda sì l'ha venduto,
trenta denari n'ha 'vuto, · fatto n'ha gran mercato.

VERGINE

Succurri, Magdalena: · gionta m'è adosso piena!
Cristo figlio se mena, · como m'è annunziato!

Lament of the Virgin at the Suffering of Her Son Jesus Christ

MESSENGER: Lady of Paradise, your son is taken, blessed Jesus
Christ. Run, woman, and see for the people strike him. I believe
he is being killed, they have so whipped him.

THE VIRGIN: How could this be when he never did wrong? Christ,
my hope, how could any one have seized him?

MESSENGER: Lady, he is betrayed: Judas has sold him, he has had
thirty pieces of silver for it, he has struck a great bargain.

THE VIRGIN: Help, Magdalen, pain has come upon me! Christ,
my son, is being led along, as was foretold me.

8

NUNZIO

Succurri, Madonna, aiuta! · ch'al tuo figlio se sputa
e la gente lo muta: · hanlo dato a Pilato.

VERGINE

O Pilato, non fare · lo figlio mio tormentare:
ch'io te posso mostrare · como a torto è accusato.

TURBA

Crucifige, crucifige! · Omo che se fa rege,
secondo nostra lege, · contradice al senato.

VERGINE

Priego che m'entendàti, · nel mio dolor pensàti:
forsa mò ve mutati · da quel ch'avete pensato.

NUNZIO

Tràgon fuor li ladroni · che sian suoi compagnoni:

TURBA

De spine se coroni! · chè rege s'è chiamato.

MESSENGER: Help, lady, lend aid! for they spit upon your son,
and the people push him along: they have given him to Pilate.
THE VIRGIN: O Pilate, do not cause my son to be tormented: for
I can show you how wrongly he is accused.
THE CROWD: Crucify, crucify! A man who makes himself king, by
our law, defies the senate.
THE VIRGIN: I beg you to hear me, think of my grief: perhaps
even now you begin to have misgivings.
MESSENGER: They are dragging out the thieves to be his companions.
THE CROWD: Let him be crowned with thorns! he who called
himself king.

VERGINE

O figlio, figlio, figlio! · figlio, amoroso giglio,
figlio, chi dà consiglio · al cor mio angustiato?

Figlio, occhi giocondi, · figlio, co non respondi?
figlio, perchè t'ascondi · dal petto ove se' lattato?

NUNZIO

Madonna, ecco la cruce, · che la gente l'aduce,
ove la vera luce · dèi essere levato.

VERGINE

O croce, que farai? · el figlio mio torrai?
e que ci aponerai, · chè non ha en sè peccato?

NUNZIO

Succurri, piena de doglia: · chè 'l tuo figliuol se spoglia,
e la gente par che voglia · che sia en croce chiavato.

VERGINE

Se glie tollete 'l vestire, · lassatemel vedire
come 'l crudel ferire · tutto l'ha 'nsanguinato.

THE VIRGIN: O my son, son, son! my son, lovesome lily, who
will counsel my heart in anguish?
   Son, joyful eyes, son, why do you not answer? Son, why do
you hide from the breast that has suckled you?
MESSENGER: Lady, here is the cross, being brought by the people,
upon which the true light is to be raised.
THE VIRGIN: O cross, what will you do? Will you take my son?
And what will you charge him with, since he has no sin in him?
MESSENGER: O help, thou full of grief: for thy son is being
stripped, and the people seem to wish that he be nailed to the
cross.
THE VIRGIN: If they have taken off his clothes, let me see—how the
cruel wounding has stained him all with blood.

NUNZIO

Donna, la man gli è presa · e nella croce gli è stesa:
con un bollon gli è fesa, · tanto ci l'on ficcato!

L'altra mano se prende, · nella croce se stende,
e lo dolor s'accende, · che più è multiplicato.

Donna, li piè se prenno · e chiavellanse al lenno:
onne iontura aprenno · tutto l'han desnodato.

VERGINE

Ed io comencio el corrotto: · Figliolo, mio deporto,
figlio, chi me t'ha morto, · figlio mio delicato?

Meglio averìen fatto · che'l cor m'avesser tratto,
che, nella croce tratto, · starce desciliato.

CRISTO

Mamma, o' sei venuta? · mortal me dài feruta,
chè 'l tuo pianger me stuta, · che 'l veggio sì afferrato.

MESSENGER: Lady, his hand has been taken and stretched upon
the cross; it is pierced through by a nail, in such a way have they
fixed him! The other hand is taken, and is being stretched upon
the cross, and the pain burns that is ever more multiplied. Lady,
his feet are taken and nailed to the wood; every joint is opened,
they have so wrenched him.

THE VIRGIN: And I shall begin the lament: son, my comfort, son,
who has made you dead to me, my delicate son?
    They would have done better to have taken out my heart,
than for it to be torn there, set upon the cross.

CHRIST: Mother, why have you come? You give me a mortal
wound, since your weeping casts me down when I see it gripping
you so.

VERGINE

Figlio, che m'agio anvito, · figlio, patre e marito,
figlio, chi t'ha ferito? · figlio, chi t'ha spogliato?

CRISTO

Mamma, perchè te lagni? · voglio che tu remagni,
che serve i miei compagni · ch'al mondo agio acquistato.

VERGINE

Figlio, questo non dire: · voglio teco morire,
non me voglio partire, · fin che mo m'esce 'l fiato.

Ch'una agiam sepultura, · figlio de mamma scura!
trovarse en affrantura · matre e figlio affogato.

CRISTO

Mamma, col core affletto, · entro a le man te metto
de Ioanne, mio eletto; · sia il tuo figlio appellato.

Ioanne, esta mia mate · tollela en caritate:
aggine pietate, · ca lo core ha forato.

THE VIRGIN: My son, I have good cause, son, father, and husband,
son, who has wounded you? my son, who has stripped you?
CHRIST: Mother, why do you lament? I want you to stay behind
and care for the companions whom I have gained in the world.
THE VIRGIN: My son, do not say that: I want to die with you, I do
not want to leave you, until, in a little while, my breath leaves
me.
Let us have one burial, son of a darkened mother! Let mother
and son be found overcome by anguish.
CHRIST: Mother, with a stricken heart I put you into the hands of
John, my chosen: let him be called your son.
John, keep this my mother in all love: have pity on her, for
her heart has been pierced.

VERGINE

Figlio, l'alma t'è uscita, · figlio de la smarrita,
figlio de la sparita, · figlio attossicato!

Figlio bianco e vermiglio, · figlio senza simiglio,
figlio, a chi m'apiglio? · figlio, pur m'hai lassato.

Figlio bianco e biondo, · figlio, volto iocondo,
figlio, perchè t'ha el mondo, · figlio, cusì sprezato?

Figlio, dolce e piacente, · figlio de la dolente,
figlio, hatte la gente · malamente tratto!

O Ioanne, figlio novello, · morto è lo tuo fratello:
sentito aggio 'l coltello · che fo profetizato,

che morto ha figlio e mate · de dura morte afferrate:
trovarse abracciate · mate e figlio abracciato.

De la incarnazione del verbo divino

FIORITO è Cristo nella carne pura:
or se ralegri l'umana natura.

THE VIRGIN: My son, your soul has gone, son of the lost woman,
son of the lifeless one, son who have been poisoned.

My son, white and red, son without compare, son, whom
shall I hold to? son, you have left me then?

My son, white and fair, son of joyful face, son, why has the
world so despised you?

My son, sweet and pleasant, son of the grieving one, son, the
people have used you wickedly.

O John, my new son, your brother is dead: I have felt the
blade that was prophesied,

Which has killed son and mother, both seized by hard death:
let them be found embraced, mother and son embraced.

Of the Incarnation of the Divine Word

CHRIST has flowered in the pure flesh: now let human nature
rejoice.

Natura umana, quanto eri scurata,
ch'al secco fieno tu eri arsimigliata!
Ma lo tuo sposo t'ha renovellata!
or non sie ingrata · de tale amadore.

Tal amador è fior de puritade,
nato nel campo de verginitade:
egli è lo giglio de l'umanitade,
de suavitate · e de perfetto odore.

Odor divino da ciel n'ha recato,
da quel giardino là ove era piantato:
esso Dio dal Padre beato
ce fo mandato · conserto de fiore.

Fior de Nazzareth si fece chiamare,
de la Giesse virgo vuols pullulare:
nel tempo del fior se volse mostrare,
per confermare · lo suo grande amore.

Amore immenso e carità infinita
m'ha demostrato Cristo, la mia vita;
prese umanitate in deità unita:
gioia compita · n'aggio e grande onore.

Human nature, you were so darkened that you had become like
burnt hay! But your bridegroom has renewed you: do not be ungrateful for such a lover.

Such a lover is the flower of purity, born in the field of virginity:
he is the lily of humankind, of sweetness, and of perfect fragrance.

Divine fragrance he has brought us from heaven, from the garden where he was planted: this God was sent to us from the blessed
Father, a twining of flowers.

He took the name Flower of Nazareth, in the Virgin of Jesse he
chose to stir: in the season of flowers he chose to grow, to testify
his great love.

Christ, my life, has shown me immense love and infinite charity;
he has taken humanity upon himself, joined to his godhead: this
gives me full joy and great honour.

Onor con umiltà volse recepere:
con solennità la turba fe' venire,
la via e la cittade refiorire
tutta, e reverire · lui como Signore.

Signor venerato con gran reverenza,
poi condannato de grave sentenza:
popolo mutato senza providenza,
per molta amenza · cadesti in errore.

Error prendesti contra veritade
quando lo facesti viola de viltade:
la rosa rossa de penalitate
per caritade · remutò el colore.

Color natural ch'avea de bellezza
molta in viltade prese lividezza:
sua suavitade portò amarezza,
tornò in bassezza · lo suo gran valore.

Valor potente fo umiliato,
quel fiore aulente tra piè conculcato,
de spine pungente tutto circundato,
e fu velato · lo grande splendore.

He chose to receive honour with humility: solemnly he made the
crowd come to him, the ways and the populace reflower together,
and revere him as Lord.

Lord venerated with a great reverence, and then condemned to a
grievous penalty: o people, inconstant and without vision, you fell
into error through great stupidity.

You took error's part against truth when, reviling him, you left
his flesh purple with bruises: the red rose changed its colour in
suffering for love.

The natural colour of beauty he had took on dire lividness when
he was reviled: he bore bitterness sweetly, and let his great worth
be humiliated.

Mighty worth was brought low, that breathing flower was
trampled underfoot, surrounded by piercing thorns, and its great
splendour covered.

Splendor che illustra onne tenebroso
fo oscurato per dolor penoso,
e lo suo lume tutto fo renchioso
en un sepolcro · nell'orto del fiore.

Lo fior reposto giacque e sì dormìo;
renacque tosto e resurressìo,
beato corpo e puro refiorìo,
ed apparìo · con grande fulgore.

Fulgore ameno apparìo nell'orto
a Magdalena che 'l piangea morto,
e del gran pianto donògli conforto,
sì che fo absorto · l'amoroso core.

Lo core confortò agli suoi fratelli,
e resuscitò molti fior novelli,
e demorò nello giardin con elli,
con quelli agnelli · cantando d'amore.

Con amor reformasti Tomaso non credente,
quando li mostrasti li tuoi fiori aulente,
quali reservasti, o rosa rubente:
sì che incontinente · gridò con fervore.

Splendour that lightens any shade was darkened by painful grief, and all his light was obscured in a sepulchre in the flower-garden.

The flower placed there lay and slept; it soon came to life again and arose, blessed body and pure reflowering, and appeared with great brightness.

A kindly brightness appeared to Magdalen in the garden who lamented him as dead, and comforted her in her great weeping so that her loving heart was rapt.

Her heart comforted the brethren, and raised up many new flowers, and stayed in the garden with them, with those lambs singing for love.

With love you remade doubting Thomas, when you showed him the fragrant flowers which you kept, o glowing rose: so that at once he cried with fervour.

Fervore amoroso ebbe inebriato,
lo cor gioioso fo esilarato:
quando glorioso t'ebbe contemplato,
allora t'ebbe vocato · Dio e signore.

Signor de gloria sopra al ciel salisti,
con voce sonora degli angeli ascendisti:
con segni di vittoria al Padre redisti,
e resedisti · in sedia ad onore.

Onor ne donasti a servi veraci,
la via demostrasti a li tuoi sequaci:
lo spirito mandasti acciò che infiammati
fussero i sequaci · con perfetto ardore.

Como è somma sapienzia essere reputato pazo per l'amor
de Cristo

Senno me pare e cortesia · empazir per lo bel Messia.

Ello me sa sì gran sapere · a chi per Dio vol empazire,
en Parige non se vidde · ancor sì gran filosofia.

Loving fervour had made him drunk, his joyous heart was ex-
hilarated: when he looked upon you in your glory, he cried – my
Lord and my God.

Lord of Glory, you ascended to heaven, went up to the ringing
voice of angels: you returned to the Father with symbols of victory, and sat again in the place of honour.

You gave honour to your true servants, showed the way to your
followers: sent the Spirit so that your followers were inflamed with
a perfect ardour.

That it Is the Highest Wisdom to Be Thought Mad for
Love of Christ

Sense and nobleness it seems to me, to go mad for the fair Messiah.

It seems to me great wisdom in a man if he wish to go mad for
God, no philosophy so great as this has yet been seen in Paris.

Chi per Cristo va empazato, · par afflitto e tribulato:
ma è maestro conventato · en natura e teologia.

Chi per Cristo ne va pazo, · a la gente sì par matto;
chi non ha provato el fatto, · pare che sia fuor de la via.

Chi vol entrare en questa scola, · troverà dottrina nova:
la pazia, chi non la prova, · già non sa que ben se sia.

Chi vol entrar en questa danza, · trova amor d'esme-
    suranza:
cento dì de perdonanza · a chi li dice villania.

Ma chi va cercando onore, · non è degno del suo amore,
chè Iesù fra doi latrone · en mezo la croce staìa.

Ma chi cerca per vergogna, · ben me par che cetto iogna:
ià, non vada più a Bologna · a 'mparar altra mastria.

He who goes mad for Christ seems afflicted and in tribulation:
but he is an exalted master of nature and theology.

He who goes mad for Christ, certainly seems insane to people;
it seems that he is off the road to whoever has not experienced the
state.

He who wishes to enter this school, will discover new learning:
he who has not experienced madness does not yet know what it is
exactly.

He who wishes to come into this dance will find unbounded
love: a hundred days' indulgence to whoever reviles him.

But he who goes seeking honour is not worthy of His love, for
Jesus stayed upon the cross between two thieves.

But he who seeks in humbleness, will arrive quickly, I am sure:
let him not go to Bologna any more to learn another doctrine.

FEDERIGO II

Oi lasso! non pensai
sì forte mi parisse
lo dipartire da Madonna mia;
ca poi che m'alontai,
ben paria ch'eo morisse,
membrando di sua dolze compagnia;
e giammai tanta pena non durai
se non quando a la nave adimorai.
Ed or mi crio morire certamente,
se da lei non ritorno prestamente.

Tutto quanto eo vio
sì forte mi dispiace,
che non mi lassa in posa in nessun loco;
sì mi stringe el disio,
che non posso aver pace,
e fami reo parere riso e gioco:
membrandomi suo' dolzi 'nsegnamenti,
tutti diporti m'escono di menti;
e non mi vanto ch'eo disdotto sia,
se non là ov'è la dolze donna mia.

ALAS! I did not think that leaving my Lady would cast me down
like this; for since I took myself away, it has truly seemed that I've
died, remembering her sweet society; and I have never endured
such pain unless it was when I was aboard ship. And now I believe
I shall die indeed, if I do not speedily go back to where she is.

Everything I see repels me so strongly that it leaves me no rest in
any place; desire so oppresses me that I can enjoy no peace, and it
makes laughter and sport wrong for me: remembering her sweet
graces, every pleasure goes from my mind: and I do not claim to
know delight, except where my sweet lady is.

O Deo, como fui matto,
quando mi dipartivi
là ov'era stato in tanta dignitate!
Ed io caro l'accatto,
e scioglio como nivi,
pensando c'altri l'aia 'm potestate!
Ed e' mi pare mille anni la dia
ched eo ritorni a voi, Madonna mia;
lo reo pensero sì forte m'atassa,
che rider nè giucare non mi lassa.

Canzonetta gioiosa,
va a la fior di Soria,
a quella c'à in prigione lo mio core:
di' a la più amorosa
ca per sua cortesia
si rimembri de lo suo servidore,
quello che per suo amore va penando
mentre non faccia tutto 'l suo comando;
e priegalami per la sua bontate
ch'ella mi degia tener lealtate.

O God, how mad I was when I left the place where I had lived in such eminence! And I am paying dearly for it, and melt like snow, when I think that some one else may have her in his power! And the day when I may return to you, my Lady, seems a thousand years away; that evil thought so poisons me, that it does not let me laugh or sport.

Joyous song, go to the flower of Syria, to her who keeps my heart in prison: tell her, the most loving of all, to remember her servant in her courtesy, him who keeps suffering for love of her as long as he cannot be entirely at her command; and beg her in her goodness to keep faith with me.

GIACOMO DA LENTINI

MERAVILLOSAMENTE
un amor mi distringe · e soven ad ogn'ora,
com omo che ten mente
in altra parte e pinge · la simile pintura.
Così, bella, facc'eo:
dentr'a lo core meo · porto la tua figura.

In cor par ch'eo vi porte
pinta como parete, · e non pare di fore.
O Deo, co mi par forte!
Non so se lo savete · com'io v'amo a bon core;
ca son sì vergognoso
ch'eo pur vi guardo ascoso · e non vi mostro amore.

Avendo gran disio
dipinsi una pintura, · bella, voi simigliante;
e quando voi non vio,
guardo in quella figura · e par ch'eo v'agia avante,
sì com om che si crede
salvarsi per sua fede, · ancor non vegia inante.

A LOVE has seized on me wonderfully and makes me remember at
all times, like a man who has his mind elsewhere and keeps painting
the one picture. So is it with me, my fair: within my heart I bear
your image.

It seems I bear you in my heart, painted as you look, and that this
does not appear outwardly. O God, how hard this seems! I cannot
tell if you know with what a good heart I love you: for I am so
hesitant that I even look at you in a covert way, and do not show
you love.

Feeling great desire, I painted a picture, my fair, your likeness;
and when I do not see you, I look upon that image, and it seems
that I have you before me, like a man who thinks to save himself by
his faith, although he does not see before him.

Al cor m'arde una doglia
com om che tene 'l foco · a lo suo seno ascoso,
e quando più lo 'nvoglia
alora arde più loco · e non po' stare incluso;
similemente eo ardo
quando passo e non guardo · a voi, viso amoroso.

Se siete, quando passo,
in ver voi non mi giro, · bella, per risguardare.
Andando, ad ogne passo
gittone uno sospiro · che mi facie angosciare.
E certo bene angoscio,
c'a pena mi conoscio, · tanto forte mi pare.

Assai v'aggio laudata,
Madonna, in molte parte, · di belleze c'avete.
Non so se v'è contato
ch'eo lo faccia per arte, · chè voi ve ne dolete.
Sacciatelo per singna,
zo ch'e' vòi dire a lingua · quando voi mi vedete.

In my heart a sorrow burns, I am like a man who keeps fire hidden in his bosom, which the more he wraps it round, burns the more fiercely, and cannot be contained; similarly do I burn when I pass and do not look at you, o face of love.

If you are there, I do not turn towards you to gaze, as I pass, my fair. At each step I take, I heave a sigh that puts me in agony. And truly I suffer agony, for I hardly know myself, the feeling seems so strong.

Much have I praised you, in many places, my Lady, for the beauty that is yours. I cannot tell if it is clear to you that I do it with a purpose, since you are distressed by it. Learn from the signs that appear in me when you look, what I wish to say with my lips.

Canzonetta novella,
va e canta nova cosa; · levati da maitino
davanti a la più bella
fiore d'ogn'amorosa, · bionda più c'auro fino.
Lo vostro amor ch'è caro
donatelo al Notaro · ch'è nato da Lentino.

Io m'agio posto in core a Dio servire
com'io potesse gire in paradiso,
all'auto loco c'agio audito dire
si mantiene sollazo, gioco e riso:
sanza Madonna non vi voria gire,
quella c'à blonda testa e claro viso,
chè sanza lei non poteria gaudire,
estando da la mia donna diviso.

Ma no lo dico a tale intendimento
perch'io peccato ci volesse fare,
se non veder lo suo bel portamento,
lo bel viso e lo morbido sguardare:
chè lo mi teria 'n gran consolamento,
vegiendo la mia donna in ghiora stare.

My newborn song, go and sing something new; rise up in the morning and go before the loveliest, the flower of all loving women, more finely fair than gold: 'give your love that is dear to the Notary who was born at Lentino'.

I HAVE set my heart to serving God so that I may go to Paradise, to the holy place where, as I have heard, there is always entertainment, play, and laughter: without my lady I would not want to go there, she who has the fair hair and clear brow, as without her I could not rejoice, being separated from my lady.

But I do not say this with the intention of committing a sin, if I do not see her graceful mien, her lovely face, and soft gaze: for it would keep me in great contentment to see my lady standing there in glory.

RINALDO D'AQUINO

Già mai non mi conforto
nè mi vo' ralegrare,
le navi sono al porto
e vogliono colare:
vassene lo più giente
in terra d'oltra mare,
oi me lassa, dolente,
como deg'io fare?

Vassen 'n altra contrata
e nol mi manda a dire,
io rimangno ingannata;
tanti son li sospire
che mi fanno gran guerra
la notte co' la dia!
Nè in cielo ned in terra
non mi pare ch'io sia.

O Santus, santus Deo
che 'n la Vergin venisti,
tu guarda l'amor meo
poi da me 'l dipartisti.

I'LL never more take comfort, nor do I wish to be gay. The ships are at the roadstead, and they want to set sail. The gentlest man is going away, to a land beyond the sea. Alas, wearied and sorrowing, what am I to do?

He's going to another country, and he did not let me know. I have been deceived and left; how thick come the sighs that wage war on me both night and day. And I seem to be neither in heaven nor on earth.

Holy, holy God who came in the Virgin, watch over my love

Oit alta potestate,
temuta e dottata,
la dolze mi' amore
ti sia raccomandata!

La crocie salva giente
e me facie disviare,
la crocie m' fa dolente:
non mi val Dio pregare.
Oi, crocie pellegrina,
perchè m'ài sì distrutta?
oimè, lassa tapina,
ch'io ardo e 'nciendo tutta.

Lo 'mperador com pacie
tutto 'l mondo mantene
ed a me guerra facie:
m'à tolta la mia spene.
Oit alta potestate
temuta e dottata,
la mia dolze amore
vi sia raccomandata.

now that you have sent him away from me. O high, dread, awful power, may my sweet love enjoy thy care.

The cross saves people and makes me lose my way, the cross makes me sorrowful: praying to God is of no avail. O, excellent cross, why have you destroyed me so? O wearied and wretched woman, for I altogether burn and flame.

The Emperor keeps the whole world at peace and makes war upon me: he has taken my dear hope away. O high, dread, awful power, may my sweet love enjoy your care.

Quando crocie pigliao
cierto nol mi pensai,
quel che tanto m'amao,
ed i' lui tanto amai,
ch'io ne fui batuta
e messa in presgionia
e in cielata tenuta
per tutta vita mia!

Le navi so' a le celle,
'm bon or possan andare,
e la mia amor con elle
la giente che v'à andare.
Oi Padre Criatore,
a porto le conducie,
chè vanno a servidore
de la tua santa crucie.

Però priego, Dolcietto,
che sai la pena mia,
che men facie un sonetto
e mandilo in Soria,
ch'io non posso abentare
la notte nè la dia:
in terra d'oltra mare
istà la vita mia

His becoming a Crusader was so unexpected, he who loved me so much, and I loved him so much that I was beaten for it and put into prison and kept in confinement – for life!

The ships are at the roadsteads, and they can soon depart, and my love with them, the people who are to go. Father Creator, lead them to safe port who go in service to thy holy cross.

So I beg you, Sweetling, who know my grief, to write a sonnet and send it to Syria, as I can have no peace neither by night nor by day: my true love is now in a land beyond the seas.

Ormai quando flore · e mostrano verdura
le prata e la rivera,
li ausei fanno isbaldore · dentro da la frondura
cantando in lor manera,
infra la primavera · che vene presente
frescamente · sì frondita
ciasuno invita · d'aver gioja intera.

Confortami d'amore · l'aulimento dei fiori
e 'l canto de li auselli.
Quando lo giorno appare · sento li dolci amori
e li versi novelli
che fan sì dolci e belli · e divisati
lor trovati · a provasione;
a gran tençone · stan per li arbuscelli.

Quando l'aloda intendo · e 'l rusignuol vernare,
d'amor lo cor m'afina,
e magiormente intendo · ch'è llegno d'altr'affare,
che d'arder non rifina.
Vedendo quell'ombrina · del fresco bosco,
ben cognosco · c'acortamente
serà gaudente · l'amor che m'inchina.

Now when meadow and bank show flower and greenery, the birds make merry among the leaves, singing in their different ways, while spring that comes here freshly, so leafy, invites each one to have joy entire.

The scent breathed by the flowers and the song of birds encourage me to love. When day appears I hear their sweet loves and the new songs which they make so sweet and fine and their rhyming diversified in rivalry; they vie with one another greatly among the bushes.

When I hear the lark and the nightingale first warbling, my heart is purified with love, and I know better than ever then that it is wood of another sort that does not stop burning. Seeing that little shade of fresh woodland, I am sure that the love that bends me will be joyful in a subtle way.

China, ch'eo sono amata · e giamai non amai;
ma 'l tempo m'inamora
e fami star pensata · d'aver merzè ormai
d'un fante che m'adora,
e sacio che tortura · per me sostene
e gran pene; · l'un cor mi dice
che si disdice · e l'altro m'incora.

Però prego l'amore · che m'intenda e mi svollia
come la follia vento,
che no mi facie fore · quel che presio mi tollia,
e stia di me contento.
Quelli c'à intendimento · d'avere intera
gioja e cera · del mio amore
senza romore, · nonde à compimento.

GUIDERDONE aspetto avire
da voi, donna, cui servire
non m'è noia;
ancor che mi siate altera,
sempre spero d'avere intera
d'amor gioia.

Bent, since I am loved and have never loved: but the season fills
me with sweetness, so that I think of taking pity now on a youth
who adores me, and I know that he bears torture and great pains for
me; one part of my heart tells me to deny and the other sets me on.

So I pray love for him to understand me and bend my will as
wind does the leaf, and not to do anything publicly that will
cheapen me, and to be content with me. A man who thinks of having the bloom and joy of my love by stealth will not have his way.

I EXPECT a reward from you, my lady, whom to serve is no burden
for me; although you are haughty, still I hope to have complete joy

28

Non vivo in disperanza,
ancor che mi diffidi
la vostra disdegnanza;
ca spesse volte vidi, · ed è provato,
omo di poco affare
pervenire in gran loco,
s'ello sape avanzare,
moltiplicar lo poco · conquistato.

In disperanza non mi gietto,
ch'io medesmo m'imprometto
d'aver bene:
di bon core è la leanza
ch'i' vi porto, e la speranza
mi mantene.
Però non mi scoragio
d'Amor che m'à distretto:
sì com'omo salvagio,
faragio, ch'el' è detto · ch'ello facie:
per lo reo tempo ride,
sperando che poi pèra
la laida ara che vide:
di donna troppo fera · spero pacie.

of love. I do not live in despair, although your disdain daunts me;
for often have I seen (it is common experience) a man of small
means attain a great place, if he knows how to take advantage and
multiply the little gained.

I'm not thrown into despair, for I promise myself much. I preserve my loyalty to you cheerfully, and hope sustains me.   So I do
not despond because of Love which has caught me fast; I shall act
like a savage – as it is said he acts: he laughs at the evil weather,
hoping the sullen clouds he has seen will pass away: I hope for
peace from a too cruel fair.

S'io pur spero in allegranza,
fina donna, pietanza
in voi si mova;
fina donna, non siate
fera, poi tanta bieltate
in voi si trova.
Ca donna c'à belleze
ed è sanza pietade,
com'omo è, c'à richeze
e usa scarsitade · di ciò c'ave:
se non è bene apreso
nè dritto nè insegnato,
da ogn'omo n'è ripreso,
onuto e dispregiato · e posto a grave.

Donna mia, ch'io non perisca!
s'io vi prego, non v'incrisca
mia preghera:
le belleze ch'en voi pare
mi distringie e lo sguardare
de la ciera.
La figura piagiente
lo core mi diranca:
quando vi tegno mente,
lo spirito mi manca · e torna in ghiaccio.

If I still trust in joy, fine lady, let pity stir in you; fine lady, do not be fierce with me, since you have so much beauty in you. For a woman who is beautiful and without pity is like a man who has riches but practises meanness with what he has: if he is not well advised, or right or enlightened, he is reproved for it by every man, and shamed and despised and put in a sorry position.

My lady, do not let me perish! If I pray to you, may my prayer not displease you: the beauty that shows in you and the very way you look have caught me fast. Your pleasant face lays waste my heart: when I think of you, my spirit fails and turns to ice. Nor am

Nè mica mi spaventa
l'amoroso volere
di ciò che m'ardenta,
ch'io no lo posso avere · ond'io mi sfaccio.

GIACOMINO PUGLIESE

La dolze ciera piagente
e li amorosi semblanti
lo cor m'allegra e la mente
quando mi pare davanti,
sì volentieri la vio
quella cui eo amai;
la bocca ch'eo basciai
ancor l'astetto e disio!

L'aulente bocca e le menne
de lo petto ciercai,
fra le mie braza la tenne;
basciando mi dimandai:
«Messer, se venite a gire,
non facciate adimoranza,
chè non esti bona usanza
lassar l'amore e partire.»

I in the least scared in my passionate desire for what burns me – I
am undone because it is not mine.

Her sweet and pleasant face and her loving expression delight
my heart and mind when she comes before me; so readily I look on
her whom I have loved; I still desire and long for the mouth I
kissed.
    I sought her fragrant mouth and both her breasts, I held her in
my arms; kissing, she asked me: 'Sir, if you call in passing, do not
stay, for it is not mannerly to leave love and depart.'

Allotta ch'eo mi partivi
e dissi: «A Deo v'accomando»
la bella guardò 'nver mivi,
sospirava lagrimiando;
tant'erano li sospiri
ch'a pena mi rispondia:
e la dolze donna mia
non mi lassava partiri.

Eo non fùivi sì lontano
che lo meo amor v'ubriasse,
nè non credo che Tristano
Isaotta tanto amasse.
Quando vio venir l'aulente,
infra le donne apariri,
lo cor mi trae di martiri
e ralegrami la mente.

Isplendiente
stella d'albore
e piagiente
donna d'amore!

Then when I separated from her and said, 'I commend you to
God', that fair one looked towards me, sighing and weeping; so
frequent were her sighs that she hardly answered me: that sweet
fair of mine did not let me leave.

I was not so far away that my love had left me, and I do not
think that Tristan loved Iseult as much. When I see that fragrant
one appear among the women, my heart leads me from sufferings
and my mind rejoices.

Shining star of dawn and pleasant mistress!

Bella, 'l mio core, · c'ài in tua ballìa
non si diparte · da voi, in fidanza;
or ti rimembri, · bella, la dia
che noi fermammo · la dolze amanza.

    Bella, or ti sia
    a rimembranza
    la dolze dia
    e l'alegranza,

che in diportanza · istava con vui:
Basciando dicia: · «Anima mia,
lo dolze amore · ch'è 'ntra noi dui,
non falsiasse · cosa che sia.»

    Lo tuo splendore
    mi à priso,
    di gioia d'amore
    mi à conquiso,

sì che non auso · da voi partire
e non faria · se Dio volesse:
ben mi poria · doblar martire
se fallimento · 'nver voi facesse.

My heart, that you have in your keeping, my fair, does not leave you, in faith: remember now, my fair, the day when we affirmed our sweet love.

My fair, let that sweet day now come back to you and the joy when I stayed dallying with you: kissing, I said to you: 'My soul, the sweet love that is between us two would not prove false for anything that is.'

Your brightness has so taken me, has overcome me with joy of love

so that I dare not leave you, and I would not if God were to will it: well might He double my torments if I really failed you.

Donna valente,
la mia vita
per voi, più gente,
è ismarita:

la dolze aita · è conforto
membrando ch'èite · a lo mio brazo,
quando scendesti · a me in diporto
per la finestra · de lo palazo.

Alor t'ei, bella,
in mia ballìa,
rosa novella,
per me temìa.

Di voi, amorosa, · presi vengianza:
o in fide rosa, · fosti patuta!
Se 'n ballìa avesse · e Spagna e Franza
non averìa · sì rica tenuta.

Quand'io partìa
da voi, intando
dicivi a mia
in sospirando:

Rare woman, my life has gone astray for pleasant you:

My sweet help is my comfort in remembering that I had you in my arms, my fair, when you slipped down to me in delight from the window of your high house.

Then, my fair, I had you in my power, new rose, you feared because of me.

I took revenge upon you, loving creature: o rose indeed, you suffered! If I had in my power Spain and France, I would not have so rich an estate.

When I took myself from you, you said the while with sighs:

«Se vai, meo sire · fai dimoranza
ve' ch'io m'arendo · e faccio altra vita,
giamai non entro · in gioco e danza,
ma sto rinchiusa · più che romita.»

Or vi sia a mente,
Madonna mia,
che 'ntra la gente
v'èi in ballìa.

Lo vostro core · non falsiasse:
di me vi sia · ben rimembranza.
Tu sai, amore, · pene ch'io trasse:
chi ne diparte · more in tristanza!

Chi ne diparte,
fiore di rosa,
non abbia parte
di buona cosa,

chè Deo fecie amore · dolcie e fino.
Di due amanti · che amar di core,
canta asai · versi Giacomino
e' che si parte · di reo amore.

'If you go, my lord, and stay away, see if I do not give myself up
and lead a different life, never enter into game or dance, but live
more cloistered than a nun.'

Now remember, mistress mine, that I am the one who had you in
his power.

Do not let your heart be false: let the memory of me stay with
you. You know, love, the pains I have undergone: let him who
parts us die in sadness!

Let whoever parts us, flower of the rose, have no part in anything good,

since God made sweet and tempered love. Giacomino, he who
shuns wicked love, rhymes out many lines for two lovers who have
loved with all their hearts.

Morte, perchè m'ài fatta sì gran guerra
che m'ài tolta Madonna, ond'io mi doglio?
La fior de le bellezze mort'ài 'n terra,
per che lo mondo non amo nè voglio.
Villana morte, che non ài pietanza,
disparti amore e togli l'allegranza
e dài cordoglio.
La mia alegranza post'ài in gran tristanza,
chè m'ài tolto la gioia e l'alegranza
ch'aver soglio.

Sollea aver sollazo e gioco e riso
più che null'altro cavalier che sia;
or n'è gita Madonna in Paradiso:
portòne la dolze speranza mia,
lasciòmi in pene e con sospiri e pianti,
levòmi da sollazo, gioco e canti
e compagnia;
or no la vegio, nè le sto davanti
e non mi mostra li dolzi sembianti
che far solìa.

Death, why have you waged so great a war against me, taking my
lady from me, at which I grieve? You have killed the flower of the
beauties of earth, so that I no longer love nor desire the world. Base
death, who have no pity, you divide love, take away delight and
give sorrowing. You have turned my delight to great sadness, for
you have taken away the joy and delight I used to have.

I used to enjoy ease and sport and laughter, more than any other
knight living; now my lady has gone to Paradise, she has borne
away my sweet hopes, left me in pain, sighing and weeping, plucked
me from ease, sport and songs and company: now I do not see her,
nor stand before her, and she does not show me the sweet looks
she was wont to.

Oi Deo, perchè m'ài posto in tale iranza?
ch'io son smaruto, non so ove mi sia,
che m'ài levata la dolze speranza.
Partit'ài la più dolze compagnia,
che sia in nulla parte, ciò m'è aviso.
Oimè, Madonna, chi tene tuo viso
in sua ballìa?
lo vostro insegnamento dond'è miso?
e lo tuo franco cor chi lo mi à priso,
o donna mia?

Ov'è Madonna e lo suo insegnamento,
la sua bellezza e la gran canoscianza,
lo dolze riso e lo bel parlamento,
gli ochi e la boca e la bella sembianza,
lo adornamento e la sua cortesia?
Madonna, per cui stava tutavia
in alegranza,
or no la vegio nè notte, nè dia,
e non m'abella, sì com' far solia,
in sua sembianza.

O God, why have you set me in such wrath? I am bewildered, not knowing where I am, for you have taken away my sweet hope. You have taken the sweetest company that can ever be, I am sure. O my Lady, who has your face in his keeping? your influence, where is it turned? And who has robbed me of your generous heart, O my love?

Where is my Lady and her influence, her beauty and great wit, her sweet laugh and lovely speech, her eyes and mouth and her comely appearance, her grace and courtesy? My Lady, for whose sake I spent my days in gladness, I no longer see by night or day, and I am not ennobled, as I was wont to be, in her gaze.

Se fosse mio lo regno d'Ungaria,
con Greza e la Magna infino in Franza,
lo gran tesoro di Santa Sofia,
nom poria ristorar sì gran perdanza
come fu in quella dia che si n'andao.
Madonna de sta vita trapassao,
con gran tristanza
sospiri e pene e pianti mi lasciao,
e giamai nulla gioia mi mandao
per confortanza.

Se fosse al meo voler, donna, di voi,
diciesse a Dio sovran, che tuto face,
che giorno e notte istessimo amboduoi.
Or sia voler di Dio, da c'a lui piace.
Membro e ricordo quand'era con mico,
sovente m'apellava «dolze amico»,
ed or nol face,
poi Dio la prese e menolla con sico.
La sua verute sia, bella, con tico
e la sua pace.

If the kingdom of Hungary were mine, with Greece and Germany all the way to France, the great treasure of Santa Sophia, they would not make good the great loss it was the day she went away. My Lady passed on from this life, with great sadness, sighs, and pain and tears she left me, and never sent me any joy to comfort me.

If your being were in my hands, lady, I would say to God the king, who orders all things, that we should stay together day and night. Now let it be as God wills, since it pleases him. I remember and dwell on the time she was with me, she often called me 'sweet friend', and now she does not, since God took her and led her away with him. His goodness be with you, my fair, and his peace.

PIER DELLA VIGNA

AMORE, in cui disio ed ò speranza,
di voi, bella, m'à dato guiderdone;
guardomi infin che vegna la speranza,
pur aspetando bon tempo e stagione:
com'om ch'è in mare ed à spene di gire,
quando vede lo tempo ed ello spanna,
e giamai la speranza no lo 'nganna:
così faccio, Madonna, in voi venire.

Or potess'eo venire a voi, amorosa,
come larone ascoso e non paresse!
be 'l mi teria in gioia aventurosa,
se l'amor tanto bene mi faciesse.
Sì bel parlante, donna, con voi fora,
e direi come v'amai lungiamente
più ca Piramo Tisbia dolzemente,
ed ameragio infin ch'eo vivo ancora.

Vostro amor è che mi tene in disio,
e donami speranza con gran gioia,
ch'eo non curo s'io dollio od ò martiro
membrando l'ora ched io vegno a voi;

LOVE, in whom I wish and hope, has given me, my fair, the reward of you. I save myself, awaiting good weather and season, until hope becomes real: as a man who is on the seas trusts to make way when he sees the weather for it, and spreads his sails, and that hope never deceives him; I do the same, my Lady, to come to you.

If I could come to you now, loving creature, like an undercover thief and never be seen! It would be such luck and joy for me, if love were to do me so great a favour. I would be so eloquent, love, and tell you I have loved you long, more sweetly than Pyramus, Thisbe, and I will love you as long as I live.

It is love of you that makes me desire, and gives me hope accompanied with great joy, for I do not care if I sorrow and suffer while I can think of the moment when I shall come to you; for if I delay

ca s'io troppo dimoro, aulente lena,
pare ch'io pera, e voi me perderete.
Adunque, bella, se ben mi volete,
guardate ch'eo no mora in vostra spera.

In vostra spera vivo, donna mia,
e lo mio core adesso a voi dimando,
e l'ora tardi mi pare che sia
che fino amore a vostro cor mi manda;
e guardo tempo che mi sia a piaciere
e spanda le mie vele inver voi, rosa,
e prendo porto là 've si riposa
lo meo core al vostro insegnamento.

Mia canzonetta, porta esti compianti
a quella c'à 'n balìa lo meo core,
e le mie pene contale davanti
e dille com eo moro per su' amore,
e mandimi per suo messaggio a dire
com io conforti l'amor ch'i' lei porto;
e s'io ver lei feci alcuno torto,
donimi penitenza al suo valore.

too long, o fragrant breath, it seems I die, and that you will lose
me. So, my fair, if you love me, watch lest I die hoping for you.

I live hoping for you, my lady, and now I ask my heart back
from you, and it seems late for fine love to bring me to your heart;
and I watch for the time that will favour my hope, when I may
spread my sails towards you, rose, and harbour where my heart
rests under your sway.

My little song, bear these complaints to her who has my heart in
her power, and lay my sufferings before her and tell her how I am
dying for love of her, and let her send a message to tell how I am to
console the love I bear her, and if I have done her any wrong, let
her impose penance upon me according to her worth.

CIELO D'ALCAMO

Contrasto

«R o s a fresca aulentissima · c'apar' inver la state,
le donne ti disiano · pulzelle e maritate,
trami d'esti focora · se t'este a bolontate.
  Per te non aio abento notte e dia,
  penzando pur di voi, Madonna mia.»

«Se di meve trabagliti, · follia lo ti fa fare.
Lo mar potresti arompere · a' venti asemenare,
l'abere d'esto secolo · tutto quanto asembrare:
  avèreme non pòteri a esto monno.
  Avanti li cavelli m'aritonno.»

«Se li cavelli artoniti · avanti foss'io morto,
ca i' sì mi perdera · lo solaccio e diporto.
Quando ci passo e vejoti · rosa fresca de l'orto,
  bono conforto donimi tut'ore:
  poniamo che s'ajunga nostro amore.»

Contest in Words (between a man and a woman, the man
speaking first)

'R o s e, fresh and most fragrant, that appears about the summertime, the women envy you, the young and the married, bring me out
of this fire, if it please you. For you I have no rest, night or day, as
I think of you always, my lady.'
  'If you worry yourself for my sake, folly makes you do so. You
might delve the sea and sow the wind, bring together all the wealth
of temporality: you could not have me in this world. I would shave
off my hair first.'
  'If you are to shave off your hair, may I be dead first, for then I
should lose all solace and delight. When I pass by and see you,
fresh rose of the garden, you give me great comfort at all times:
what do you say to joining ourselves in love?'

«Che nostro amore ajungasi · non boglio m'atalenti.
Se ti ci trova pàremo · cogli altri miei parenti,
guarda non t'arigolgano · questi forti correnti.
    Como ti sappe bona la venuta,
    consiglio che ti guardi a la partuta.»

«Se i tuoi parenti trovammi · e che mi pozzon fari?
Una difensa mettoci · di dumilia agostari,
Non mi tocàra padreto · per quanto avere à 'm Bari,
    Vive lo 'mperadore, graz' a Deo!
    Intendi, bella, quel che ti dico eo?»

«Tu me no lasci vivere · nè sera nè maitino.
Donna mi son di perperi · d'auro massamotino.
Se tanto aver donassemi · quanto à lo Saladino
    e per ajunta quant'à lo Soldano,
    tocàreme nom pòteri la mano.»

«Molte sono le femine · c'ànno dura la testa,
e l'omo com parabole · l'adimina e amonesta:
tanto intorno percàzala · fin che l'à in sua podesta.

'I won't have you persuading me to join ourselves in love. If my father and relatives find you here, watch that they do not lay hold of you: they are good runners. As the road here was well known to you, I advise you to look to the road away.'

'If your relatives find me here, what can they do to me? They'll risk a fine of two thousand Augustans, so your father will not touch me for all the wealth there is in Bari: long live the Emperor, thanks be to God! Do you understand what I mean, my fair?'

'You will not let me be, morning or evening. I am a woman of Greek coin and Arabian gold. If you were to bring me as much substance as Saladin has with what the Sultan has to boot, you should not touch my hand.'

'Many are the women who have hard heads, and man masters them and controls them with his words: pursues them until he has

Femina d'omo non si può tenere:
guardati, bella, pur di ripentere.»

«Ch'eo me ne pentesse · davanti foss'io aucisa,
ca nulla bona femina · per me fosse riprisa!
Aersera passastici, · còremo, a la distisa,
   Acquestiti riposo, canzoneri:
   le tue paràole a me non piaccion gueri.»

«Doi! quante son le schiantora · che m'ài mise a lo core,
e solo pur penzànnone: · la dia quanno vo fore!
Femina d'esto secolo · non amai tanto ancore,
   quant'amo teve, rosa invidiata:
   ben credo che mi fosti distinata.»

«Se distinata fosseti · caderia de l'alteze,
che male messe forano · en teve mie belleze.
Se tanto addivenissemi · tagliàrami le treze,
   e comsore m'arenno a una magione,
   avanti che m'artocchi 'n la persone.»

them in his power. Woman cannot keep herself from man: watch,
my fair, you may be repentant yet.'
   'I repent! first let me be killed, so that no good woman may be
reproved for my sake. Last night, you kept passing this way, take a
rest, minstrel: your words do not please me one bit.'
   'Ah, how many wounds have you inflicted on my heart, as I
know when I am alone and think! – but when I go out by day! I
never yet loved a woman in this world as I love you, coveted rose:
I do believe you were destined for me.'
   'If I were destined for you, I should fall from on high, for ill
would my beauties be entrusted to you. If that were to happen to
me, I should cut all my hair and enter a religious house as a sister,
before you touched my person.'

«Se tu comsore arenneti, · donna col viso cleri,
a lo mostero vènoci · e rènnomi confreri.
Per tanta prova vèncere · faràlo volonteri.
   Con teco stao la sera e lo maitino:
   besogn'è ch'io ti tenga al meo dimino.»

«Boimè, tapina misera, · com'ao reo distinato!
Gieso Cristo l'altissimo · del tutto m'è airato:
conciepistimi a abàttere · in omo blestiemato!
   Cerca la terra ch'este granne assai,
   chiù bella donna di me troverai.»

«Ciercat'aio Calabria · Toscana e Lombardia,
Puglia, Costantinopoli · Gienoa, Pisa, Soria,
Lamagna e Babilonia, · e tuta Barberia:
   donna non ci trovai tanto cortese,
   perchè sovrana di meve te prese.»

«Poi tanto trabagliastiti · facioti meo pregheri
che tu vadi adomànimi · a mia mare e a mon peri.
Se dare mi ti degnano, · menami a lo mosteri,

'If you make yourself a sister, lady of the clear brow, I will go to the monastery and offer myself as a friar. To win you by so great a trial, I will submit willingly. I will stay with you evening and morning: I must have you in my power.'

'Alas! miserable creature, what an evil fate is mine! Jesus Christ on high is altogether angered against me: you have brought me forth to encounter a man self-damned! Search the earth which is large enough, you will find a woman more beautiful than I.'

'I have searched Calabria, Tuscany and Lombardy, Puglia, Constantinople, Genoa, Pisa, Syria, Germany, and Babylon, and all Barbary: I have not found a woman so gracious. I have taken you to be my queen.'

'As you have endured so much for my sake, I shall request this of you: that you go and ask for me from my mother and father: if

e sposami davanti de la jenti,
e poi farò li tuo comannamenti.»

«Di ciò che dici, vitama, · neiente non ti bale,
ca de le tuo' parabole · fatto n'ò ponti e scale.
Penne penzasti metere, · sonti cadute l'ale;
e dato t'aio la bolta sotana.
Dunque, se pòi, teniti villana.»

«En paura non metermi · di nullo manganiello:
istomi 'n esta groria · d'esto forte castiello.
Prezo le tue parabole · meno che d'un zitiello.
Se tu no' levi e vaitine di quaci,
se tu ci fosse morto ben mi chiaci.»

«Dunque voresti, vitama, · ca per te fosse strutto?
Se morto essere deboci · od intagliato tutto,
di quaci non mi mosera · se non ài de lo frutto
lo quale stao ne lo tuo jardino:
disiolo la sera e lo maitino.»

they deign to give me to you, lead me to the monastery and marry
me before the world, and then I shall do your bidding.'

'Nothing of what you say, my life, will do you any good, for I
have made a ladder and bridge of your words. You thought to put
out feathers, your wings have fallen; and I have battered down your
defences. Then save yourself, country girl, if you can.'

'You do not frighten me with any engine of war: I stay in the
fastness of this strong castle. I value your words less than a boy's.
If you do not stir and go away from here, I should like to see you
dead.'

'So, my life, you would have me destroyed for you? If I must
meet my death, be cut to pieces, I shall not move from here until
I have the fruit that is in your garden; I long for it morning and
evening.'

«Di quel frutto non àbero · conti nè cabalieri
molto lo disiano · marchesi e justizieri,
avere nonde pòtero, · gironde molto feri.
   Intendi bene ciò che bole dire?
   Men'este di mill'onze lo tuo avire!»

«Molti son li garofani · ma non che salma 'ndai.
Bella, non dispregiaremi · s'avanti non m'assai!
Se vento è im proda e girasi · e giungeti a le prai,
   a rimembrare t'ao este parole:
   ca d'esta animella assai mi dole.»

«Macàra se doleseti · ca cadesse angosciato,
la giente ci corresoro · da traverso e da lato,
tutt'a meve diciessono : · Acorri esto malnato!
   Non ti degnàra porgiere la mano
   per quanto avere à 'l Papa e lo Soldano.»

«Deo lo volesse, vitama, · te fosse morto in casa!
L'arma n'anderia cònsola · ca dì e notte pantasa.
La jente ti chaimàrano : · Oi perjura malvasa,

'Lords and knights have had none of that fruit; marquises and
justices have much desired it, they could not have it, and went away
angered. Do you understand just what I mean? Your substance is
less than a thousand gold ounces.'
   'Many are the carnations, but you haven't a bushel of them. My
fair, do not despise me before you try me! If the wind is against
your prow and turns and you come to shore, you will have these
words to remember. I am sorely stricken for this little soul of
yours.'
   'Supposing you were so stricken that you fell in anguish, and
people ran from this side and that, and everyone said to me: Help
this wretch! I would not condescend to stretch my hand to you, for
all the wealth the Pope and Sultan have.'
   'Pray God my life, that I should die in your house! My soul
would be comforted that wanders day and night: people would cry

46

c'ài morto l'omo in càsata, traita!
Sanz'onni colpo levimi la vita.»

«Se tu no' levi e vàtine   co la maladizione,
li frati miei ti trovano · dentro chissa magione.
Bello, ben lo mi sofero · perdici la persone;
    c'a meve se' venuto a sormonare:
    parente ned amico non t'ave a aitare.»

«A meve non aitano · amici nè parenti:
istrano mi son, càrama · enfra esta bona jenti.
Or fa un anno, vitama, · ch'entrata mi se' 'n menti.
    Di canno ti vististi lo majuto,
    bella, da quello jorno son feruto.»

«Ai, tanno namorastiti, · ahi Juda lo traito!
como se fosse porpore, · iscarlato o sciamito?
S'a le Vangelie jurimi · che mi si' a marito,
    avereme non poteri a esto monno.
    Avanti in mare jittomi al perfonno.»

at you: O evil and foresworn, who have killed that man in your
house, traitress. You take my life without a blow.'
    'If you don't stir and go away with my curse upon your head,
my brothers may find you in this house. My handsome friend, if
you are to lose your life, I could well bear it; you have come to
harangue me: you have neither relative nor friend to help you.'
    'Neither friends nor relatives aid me: I am a stranger, my life,
among these good people. It is a year now since you came into my
mind. From the time I saw you in your brocade dress, my fair, since
then have I been wounded.'
    'What, you fell in love for that, O Judas the traitor, as if it were
the purple, scarlet, or samite? If you swear on the gospels you will
be my husband, you shall not have me in this world. I had sooner
throw myself into the depths of the sea.'

«Se tu nel mare jititi, · donna cortese e fina,
dereto mi ti misera · per tuta la marina,
e poi c'anegasseti · trobàrati a la rina;
 solo per questa cosa adimpretare:
 con teco m'aio a jiungiere a pecare.»

«Segnomi in Patre e 'n Filio · ed in santo Matteo!
So ca non se' tu retico · o figlio di giudeo,
e cotale parabole · non udì dire anch'eo!
 Mortasi la femina a lo 'ntutto
 perdeci lo sabore e lo disdutto.»

«Ben lo saccio, càrama; · altro non pozzo fare!
Se quisso non arcomplimi, · lassone lo cantare.
Fallo, mia donna, plazati, · chè bene lo puoi fare!
 Ancora tu nomm'ami, molto t'amo,
 sì preso m'ài como lo pesce a l'amo.»

«Sazzo che m'ami, e amoti · di core paladino.
Levati suso e vatene, · tornaci a lo matino,
Se ciò che dico faciemi, · di bon cor t'amo e fino.

'If you throw yourself into the sea, my gracious, fine lady, I shall keep myself behind you through all its breadth, and when you have drowned, I shall find you on the sand only to win this: that I join myself with you in sin.'

'I sign myself in the name of the Father, the Son, and Saint Matthew! I know you are not a heretic or the son of a Jew, but I have never heard such words. Once a woman is dead, she loses flavour and delightfulness altogether.'

'I know that perfectly well, dearest; I can do nothing else! If you do not grant me my will, I leave off singing. Do it, lady, be pleased to, as you can perfectly well. Even if you don't love me, I love you greatly. You have taken me like a fish with the hook.'

'I know that you love me, and I love you with perfect heart. Rise up and go, come back in the morning. If you do what I say, I

Quisso t'imprometto eo sanza faglia:
te' la mia fede che m'ài in tua baglia.»

«Per zo che dici, càrama, · neiente non mi muvo.
Inanti prenni e scannami: · tolli esto cortel nuvo.
Esto fatto far potesi · inanti scalfi un uovo:
  Arcompli mi' talento, amica bella,
  chè l'arma co lo core mi s'infella.»

«Ben sazzo, l'arma doleti, · com'omo c'ave arsura.
Esto fatto non potesi · per null'altra misura.
Se non a le Vangelie, · che mo ti dico, jura,
  avere me non puoi in tua podesta:
  innanti prenni e tagliami la testa.»

«L'Evangiele, càrama? · ca io le porto in sino!
A lo mostero presile: · non ci era lo patrino.
Sovr'esto libro juroti · mai non ti vegno mino.
  Arcompli mi' talento in caritate
  che l'arma me ne sta in suttilitate.»

shall love you with a good and gentle heart. This I promise without deception: keep faith with me for you have me in your power.'

'I am not moving in the least for all you say. First take and finish me: draw this new knife. It can be done quicker than you peel an egg. Fulfill my desire, fair mistress, for soul and heart are filling me with bitterness.'

'I know perfectly well, your soul torments you, like a man who suffers from a burn. This thing cannot be done in any other way — if you do not swear on the Gospel, as I tell you now, you cannot possess me. First take me and cut off my head.'

'The Gospel, dearest? I have it here in my bosom! I took it from the monastery: the priest wasn't there. Upon this book I swear never to fail you. Do what I want for mercy's sake, as my soul grows faint at all this.'

«Meo sire, poi jurastimi · eo tuta quanna incenno.
Sono a la tua presenza · da voi non mi difenno.
S'eo minespreso àioti, · merzè, a voi m'arrenno.
    A lo letto ne gimo a la bon'ura,
    chè chissà cosa n'è data in ventura.»

ANONIMO

PÀRTITE, amore, adeo,
chè troppo ce se' stato;
lo maitino è sonato,
giorno mi par che sia.

Pàrtite, amore, adeo,
che non fossi trovato
in sì fina cellata
come nui semo stati.
Or me bacia, occhio meo;
tosto sia l'andata
tenendo la tornata
come d'innamorati,
sì che per spesso usato
nostra gioia renovi,
nostro stato non trovi
la mala gelosia.

'My lord, since you have sworn to me, I am all on fire. I am with you, and do not defend myself from you. If I have slighted you, pardon, I surrender to you. Let us to bed speedily, for who knows what the future holds for us.'

LEAVE, my love, farewell, for you have tarried too long; morning has rung, I think it is full day.

Leave, my love, farewell, lest you be found in so fine a retreat as we have been in. Now kiss me, apple of my eye; let your going be quick, looking to the return, as lovers do, so that our joy, often proved, may be renewed, let our sweet state encounter no evil jealousy.

Pàrtite, amore, adeo,
e vanne tostamente,
ch'ogni tua cosa t'aggio
parecchiata in presente.

FOR de la bella caiba · fugge lo lusignolo.
Piange lo fantino · però che non trova
lo so usilino · ne la gaiba nova,
e dice con duolo: · chi gli avrì l'usolo?
e dice con duolo: · chi gli avrì l'usolo?
E in un boschetto · se mise ad andare
sentì l'osoletto · sì dolce cantare.
– Oi bel lusignolo · torne nel mio brolo
oi bel lusignolo · torna nel mio brolo.

Leave, my love, farewell, and go speedily away, for I have made
everything of yours ready for you.

OUT from the fine cage flies the nightingale. The little child is crying because he does not find his little bird in the new cage, and he
says with grief: who opened the door for him? and he says with
grief: who opened the door for him? And he started walking in a
little wood, he heard the fledgling that so sweetly sang. O lovely
nightingale, come back into my garden: O lovely nightingale,
come back into my garden.

TAPINA oi me, ch'amava uno sparviero,
amaval tanto ch'io me ne moria;
a lo richiamo ben m'era manero
ed umque troppo pascer nol dovia.
Or è montato e salito sì altero
assai più alto che far non solia,
ed è assiso dentro a un verziero,
un'altra donna lo tene in balia.

Isparver mio, ch'io t'aveo nodrito,
sonaglio d'oro ti facea portare
perchè dell'ucellar fosse più ardito;
or se' salito siccome lo mare,
ed a' rotti li geti e se' fuggito,
quando eri fermo nel tuo ucellare.

COMPIUTA DONZELLA

A LA stagion che il mondo foglia e fiora
accresce gioia a tutt'i fini amanti;
vanno insieme a li giardini allora
che gli augelletti fanno dolci canti:

MISERABLE that I am, I loved a sparrow-hawk, loved him so much that I was dying for love of him: he was very obedient to my call, and I never had to give him too much. Now he has flown up and mounted so proudly, higher far than he used to do, and he has perched in a garden, another woman keeps him in.

Sparrow-hawk mine, I have fed you, I gave you a bell of gold to wear, so that you might be bolder in your hawking. Now you have risen up like the sea, and have broken your chains, and have flown when you were secure in your preserve.

IN the season when the world puts out leaf and flower, the joy of gentle lovers grows; they go to the gardens together when the little birds make sweet song: all feeling people fall in love, and each

la franca gente tutta s'innamora,
ed in servir ciascun traggesi inanti,
ed ogni damigella in gioi' dimora;
a me n'abbondan marrimenti e pianti.

Ca lo mio padre m'ha messa in errore
e tenemi sovente in forte doglia:
donar mi vuole, a mia forza, segnore.
Ed io di ciò non ho disio nè voglia,
e 'n gran tormento vivo a tutte l'ore:
però non mi rallegra fior nè foglia.

GUIDO GUINIZELLI

Vedut' ho la lucente stella diana,
ch'appare anzi che 'l giorno rend'albore,
c'ha preso forma di figura umana,
sovr'ogn'altra mi par che dea spendore;
viso di neve colorato in grana
occhi lucenti gai e pien d'amore;
non credo che nel mondo sia cristiana
sì piena di beltate e di valore.

man passes his days in doing service, and every maiden lives in joy; but my bitterness and tears are multiplied.

For my father has wronged me, and often keeps me in deep anguish: he wishes to give me a husband against my will. And I have no wish or desire for that, and spend every hour in great torment: so that no joy comes to me from either flower or leaf.

I HAVE seen the shining star of morning which shows before day yields its first light, and which has taken the shape of a human being, I think she gives more brightness than any other. Face like snow tinged with red, shining eyes that are gay and full of love; I do not believe that in the world there is a Christian girl so full of beauty and worth.

Ed io da lo su' amor son assalito
con sì fera battaglia di sospiri
ch'avanti a lei di dir non seri' ardito:
così conoscess'ella i miei disiri,
chè, senza dir, di lei seria servito
per la pietà ch'avrebbe de' martiri.

I' vo' del ver la mia donna laudare
ed assembrargli la rosa e lo giglio:
più che la stella diana splende e pare,
e ciò ch'è lassù bello a lei somiglio.
Verde rivera a lei rassembro e l'aire,
tutti color di fior, giallo e vermiglio,
oro e azzurro e ricche gioi' per dare,
medesmo Amor per lei raffina miglio.

Passa per via adorna e sì gentile;
ch'abbassa orgoglio a cui dona salute
e fa 'l di nostra fè se non la crede;
e non si pò appressar omo ch'è vile;
ancor vi dico c'ha maggior vertute:
null'om pò mal pensar fin che la vede.

And I am beset by love of her with so fierce a battle of sighs that I would not dare say anything in her presence. Then, would that she knew my desires, so that, without speaking, I should be requited by the pity she would take upon my torments.

I WISH to praise my lady most truly and compare her to the rose and the lily: she appears, outshining the morning star, and I liken to her what is lovely on high. I compare green banks and the air to her, all colours of flowers, yellow and crimson, gold and blue and rich jewels to be offered, love itself is made purer through her.

She goes by, comely and so gentle, that she humbles the pride of whom she greets and makes him of our faith if he does not already believe it; and no man who is base can approach; and more, I tell you she has greater power: no man can think evil from the time he has seen her.

GUIDO CAVALCANTI

Avete 'n voi li fiori e la verdura
e ciò che luce od è bello a vedere;
risplende più che sol vostra figura,
chi voi non vede mai non può valere.
In questo mondo non ha creatura
sì piena di bieltà nè di piacere:
e chi d'amor si teme, l'assicura
vostro bel viso a tanto in sè volere.

Le donne che vi fanno compagnia,
assai mi piaccion per lo vostro amore:
ed i' le prego, per lor cortesia,
che qual più puote, più vi faccia onore,
ed aggia cara vostra segnoria,
perchè di tutte siete la migliore.

Chi è questa che ven, ch'ogn'om la mira,
e fa tremar di chiaritate l'a're,
e mena seco Amor, sì che parlare
null'omo pote, ma ciascun sospira?

You have in you the flowers and all green things and what shines or is fair to see; your face is more resplendent than the sun, he who does not see you can never know your worth. In this world there is no creature so full of beauty or of pleasantness: and he who fears love, is reassured by your lovely face so as to desire as much in himself.

The women who accompany you, are dear to me because of your loving regard: and I beg them, in their courtesy, that the one who best can, should do you most honour, and hold your sovereignty dear, because of them all you are the best.

Who is this who comes, that every man looks on her, who makes the air tremble with brightness, and brings Love with her, so that no man can speak, but each one sighs? O, just how she looks when

Deh, che rassembla quando li occhi gira,
dical Amor, ch'i' no 'l savria contare:
cotanto d'umiltà donna mi pare,
che ciascun'altra inver' di lei chiam'ira.

Non si porìa contar la sua piagenza,
ch'a lei s'inchina ogni gentil vertute,
e la beltate per sua dea la mostra.
Non fu sì alta già la mente nostra,
e non si pose in noi tanta salute,
che propriamente n'aviam canoscenza.

FRESCA rosa novella,
piacente Primavera,
per prata e per rivera
gaiamente cantando,
vostro fin pregio mando · a la verdura.

Lo vostro pregio fino
in gio' si rinovelli
da grandi e da zitelli
per ciascuno cammino;

she glances round, let love say, for I could never describe it: she
seems so much a woman of modesty, that every other one beside
her is to be called a thing of wrath.

Her pleasantness could not be described, since every gentle
virtue bends to her, and beauty shows her for its goddess. Our
minds have never been so exalted, nor have we in ourselves so
much grace, that we can ever rightly have knowledge of this.

FRESH new rose, delighting Spring, gaily singing by meadow and
bank, I declare your rare gifts to the greenery.

Let your rare gifts be celebrated anew by grown men and youths

e càntine gli augelli
ciascuno in suo latino
da sera e da matino
su li verdi arbuscelli.
Tutto lo mondo canti
(poi che lo tempo vène)
sì come si convene,
vostr'altezza pregiata;
chè siete angelicata · criatura.

Angelica sembianza
in voi, donna, riposa;
Dio, quanto aventurosa
fue la mia disianza!
Vostra cera gioiosa,
poi che passa e avanza
natura e costumanza,
ben è mirabil cosa.
Fra lor le donne dea
vi chiaman come siete:
tanto adorna parete
ch'eo non saccio contare;
e chi poria pensare · oltr'a natura?

and let birds sing of them, each in his own tongue, evening and morning, in the green bushes. Let the whole world sing (now that the time is come), as is right, of your valued excellence; for you are an angelic creature.

The likeness of an angel is in you, my lady; God, how lucky my desire was! Your glad look is certainly a wonderful thing when it surpasses both nature and wont. Among themselves the women call you goddess, as indeed you are: you appear so favoured that I cannot describe it; and who could think beyond nature?

Oltr'a natura umana
vostra fina piagenza
fece Dio, per essenza
che voi foste sovrana:
per che vostra parvenza
ver' me non sia lontana;
or non mi sia villana
la dolce provedenza.
E se vi pare oltraggio
ch'ad amarvi sia dato,
non sia da voi blasmato:
chè solo Amor mi sforza,
contra cui non val forza · nè misura.

O DONNA mia, non vedestù colui
che 'n su lo core mi tenea la mano,
quando ti rispondea fiochetto e piano
per la temenza delli colpi sui?
Elli fu Amore che, trovando nui,
meco restette che venia lontano,
à guisa d'un arcier presto soriano,
acconcio sol per uccider altrui.

God made your fine comeliness above human nature so that you should be queen: so do not let your look be distant to me; do not let your sweet benevolence be rude to me. And if you think it an outrage that I should be given to loving you, do not let me be blamed by you: for Love alone forces me on, against whom neither strength nor moderation has any power.

O MY lady, did you not see him who held his hand upon my hear when I answered you, feeble and low for fear of his blows? He was Love who, on discovering us, stayed with me since he came from afar, in the form of a swift Syrian archer, girded only to kill people.

E trasse poi de gli occhi tuoi sospiri,
i quai mi saettò nel cor sì forte,
ch'i' mi partii sbigottito fuggendo.
Allor m'apparve di sicur la Morte
accompagnata di quelli martiri
che soglion consumare altrui piangendo.

Era in penser d'amor quand'i' trovai
due foresette nove;
l'un cantava: «E' piove
gioco d'amore in nui.»

Era la vista lor tanto soave
e tanto queta, cortese ed umìle
ch'i' dissi lor: «Vo' portate la chiave
di ciascuna vertù alta e gentile.
Deh, foresette, no m'abbiate a vile
per lo colpo ch'io porto:
questo cor mi fu morto,
poi che 'n Tolosa fui.»

And he drew sighs from your eyes then, which he shot so violently into my heart that I fled terrified. Then suddenly Death appeared to me accompanied by those agonies that are wont to consume us in weeping.

I was deep in thoughts of love when I came upon two young
country girls; one was singing: 'Joy of love rains upon us.'
   Their look was so sweet and so calm, courteous and modest that
I said to them: 'You have the key of every high and gentle virtue.
O, country girls, do not despise me for the wound I bear: this heart
has been dead to me, since I was in Toulouse.'

Elle con gli occhi lor si volser tanto,
che vider come 'l cor era ferito
e come un spiritel nato di pianto
era per mezzo de lo colpo uscito.
Poi che mi vider così sbigottito,
disse l'una che rise:
«Guarda come conquise
forza d'amor costui!»

L'altra pietosa, piena di mercede,
fatta di gioco, in figura d'Amore,
disse: «Il tuo colpo, che nel cor si vede,
fu tratto d'occhi di troppo valore,
che dentro vi lasciaro uno splendore
ch'i' nol posso mirare;
dimmi se ricordare
di quegli occhi ti pui.»

Alla dura questione e paurosa
la qual mi fece questa foresetta,
i' dissi: «E' mi ricorda che 'n Tolosa
donna m'apparve accordellata istretta,

They turned their eyes so, that they saw how my heart was wounded and how a little spirit born of tears had come out from the wound itself. When they saw I was so frightened, one of them said, laughing: 'See how the power of love has overcome this man!'

The other pitying, full of mercy, made for joy, in the form of Love, said: 'The wound, which is seen in your heart, came from eyes of too great power, which left a splendour within that I cannot gaze at; tell me if you can remember those eyes.'

To the hard and fearful question which this country girl put to me, I said: 'I remember in Toulouse a woman appeared before me,

la quale Amor chiamava la Mandetta:
giunse sì presta e forte
che 'n fin dentro, la morte,
mi colpir gli occhi sui.»

Molto cortesemente mi rispose
quella che di me prima aveva riso;
disse: «La donna che nel cor ti pose
co' la forza d'Amor tutto 'l su' viso,
dentro per li occhi ti mirò sì fiso,
ch'Amor fece apparire.
Se t'è greve 'l soffrire
raccomàndati a lui.»

Vanne a Tolosa, ballatetta mia,
ed entra quetamente a la Dorata:
ed ivi chiama che, per cortesia
d'alcuna bella donna, sia menata
dinanzi a quella di cui t'ho pregata;
e s'ella ti riceve,
dille con voce leve:
«Per merzè vegno a vui».

tightly laced, whom Love called la Mandetta: she came so quick
and strong that her eyes struck me inwardly and deep, to the point
of death.'

She who had first laughed at me replied most courteously; she
said: 'The woman who, with the power of Love, impressed all her
features upon your heart gazed so fixedly through your eyes that
she made Love come there. If your suffering is heavy, turn to him.'

Go to Toulouse, my little song, and quietly enter the 'Gilded'
church: and there ask aloud for some lovely woman, in her kindness, to take you before her about whom I have charged you; if she
will see you, tell her in a low voice: 'I come to you for mercy.'

PERCH'I' no spero di tornar giammai,
ballatetta, in Toscana,
va tu, leggera e piana,
dritt'a la donna mia,
che per sua cortesia
ti farà molto onore.

Tu porterai novelle di sospiri,
piene di doglia e di molta paura;
ma guarda che persona non ti miri
che sia nemica di gentil natura;
chè certo per la mia disaventura
tu saresti contesa,
tanto da lei ripresa,
che mi sarebbe agnoscia;
dopo la morte poscia,
pianto e novel dolore.

Tu senti, ballatetta, che la morte
mi stringe sì che vita m'abbandona,
e senti come 'l cor si sbatte forte
per quel che ciascun spirito ragiona.
Tanto è distrutta già la mia persona

SINCE I do not hope to return ever, little song, go, lightly and quiet, to Tuscany, straight to my lady, who, in her courtesy, will do you much honour.

You will carry tidings of sighs, tidings full of pain and great fear: but watch that no one sees you who is hostile to a gentle nature; as certainly, to my misfortune you would be opposed, and so reproved by her, that it would be agony for me; then, after death, weeping and fresh grief.

You feel, little song, that death grapples me so that life deserts me, and feel how my heart beats strong because of what every spirit in me says. So much of my being is destroyed already that I

ch'i' non posso soffrire:
se tu mi vuo' servire,
mena l'anima teco,
molto di ciò ti preco,
quando uscirà del core.

Deh, ballatetta, alla tua amistate
quest'anima che trema raccomando:
menala teco nella sua pietate
a quella bella donna a cui ti mando.
Deh, ballatetta, dille sospirando,
quando le se' presente:
«Questa vostra servente
vien per istar con vui,
partita da colui
che fu servo d'amore.»

Tu, voce sbigottita e deboletta,
ch'esci piangendo de lo cor dolente,
coll'anima e con questa ballatetta
va ragionando della strutta mente.
Voi troverete una donna piacente

can suffer no more: if you wish to help me, take my soul with you,
I beg you fervently, when it has left my heart.

O, little song, I commend to your friendship this soul that
trembles: take it with you in its misery to the lovely woman to
whom I send you. O, little song, tell her with sighs, when you are
before her: 'This your servant has come to live with you, having
left him who was the servant of love.'

You, frightened, small-weakened voice, that come weeping from
the heart that grieves, go with my soul and with this little song and
tell of my mind destroyed. You will find a pleasant woman of so

di sì dolce intelletto,
che vi sarà diletto
davanti starle ognora.
Anima, e tu l'adora
sempre nel su' valore.

LAPO GIANNI

Dolc'è 'l pensier che mi notrica il core
d'una giovane donna che disia,
per cui si fè gentil l'anima mia,
poichè sposata la congiunse Amore.

I' non posso leggeramente trare
il novo esemplo ched ella simiglia
quest'angela che par di ciel venuta;
d'Amor sorella mi sembr'al parlare
ed ogni su' atterello è maraviglia:
beata l'alma che questa saluta!
In colei si può dir che sia piovuta
allegrezza, speranza e gioi' compita
ed ogni rama di virtù fiorita,
la qual procede dal su' gran valore.

---

sweet an understanding, that it will be a delight for you all to stay
by her always. My soul, adore her for ever in her worthiness.

Sweet is the thought which my heart nourishes, of a young
woman whom I desire, for whom my soul has been ennobled, since
Love took her in marriage.
   I cannot easily evoke the so new image that this angel who seems
to have come from heaven resembles; she seems Love's sister by
her speech and every least gesture of hers is a marvel: blessed is the
soul this woman greets! To her, it can be said, has gladness flowed,
hope and joy entire, and every flowering branch of virtue, which
comes from her great worth.

Il nobile intelletto ched i' porto
per questa gioven donna ch'è apparita,
mi fa spregiar viltate e villania;
e 'l dolce ragionar mi dà conforto
ch' i' fe' con lei de l'amorosa vita,
essendo già in sua nova signoria.
Ella mi fè tanta di cortesia
che no sdegnò mio soave parlare;
ond'i' voglio Amor dolce ringraziare
che mi fè degno di cotanto onore.

Com'i' son scritto nel libro d'amore
conterai, ballatetta, in cortesia,
quando tu vederai la donna mia;
poi che di lei fui fatto servidore.

AMOR, eo chero mia donna in domìno,
l'Arno balsamo fino,
le mura di Firenze inargentate,
le rughe di cristallo lastricate,
fortezze alte, merlate,

The gentle mind I have because of this young woman who has
appeared makes me scorn vileness and base dealings; and the sweet
converse I had with her about the life of love, when I was fresh to
her service, comforts me. She showed me such courtesy that she
did not scorn my soft talking; so that I want to thank sweet Love
who made me worthy of so great an honour.

As I am inscribed in the book of Love, my song, you will tell
your tale with courtesy, when you see my lady; since I have been
made her servant.

LOVE, I ask to have my mistress in my power, for the Arno to be
fine balsam, the walls of Florence silvered, the streets paved with
crystal, high, battlemented fortresses, every Italian to be my bonds-

mio fedel fosse ciaschedun latino;
il mondo 'n pace, securo 'l cammino;
non mi noccia vicino;
e l'aira temperata verno e state;
e mille donne e donzelle adornate,
sempre d'amor pregiate,
meco cantasser la sera e 'l mattino;
e giardin fruttuosi di gran giro,
con grande uccellagione,
pien di condotti d'acqua e cacciagione;
bel mi trovasse come fu Assalone;
Sansone pareggiasse e Salomone;
servaggi de barone;
sonar viole, chitarre e canzone;
poscia dover entrar nel ciel empiro.
Giovane sana allegra e secura
fosse mia vita fin che 'l mondo dura.

CINO DA PISTOIA

Io guardo per li prati ogni fior bianco,
per rimembranza di quel che mi face
sì vago di sospir ch'io ne chieggo anco.

---

man; the world at peace, the roads free; no neighbour harming me; the air mild both summer and winter; a thousand comely women made more beautiful by love, to sing with me night and morning; and flourishing gardens of great compass, with great preserve of fowl, full of little channels and hunting places; I ask to be as handsome as Absalom; equal Samson and Solomon; with barons for servants; with playing of viols, guitars, and songs; then to be sure of entering highest heaven: as that my life should be young, healthy, happy, and secure, as long as the world lasts.

I LOOK at every white flower through the fields, remembering what makes me so eager to sigh that I ask for more.

E' mi rimembra de la bianca parte
che fa col verdebrun la bella taglia,
la qual vestio Amore
nel tempo che, guardando Vener Marte,
con quell sua saetta che più taglia
mi diè per mezzo il core:
e quando l'aura move il bianco fiore,
rimembro de' begli occhi il dolce bianco
per cui lo mio desir mai non fie stanco.

Io fui 'n su l'alto e 'n sul beato monte,
ch'i' adorai, baciando il santo sasso;
e caddi 'n su di quella pietra, lasso,
ove l' Onestà pose la sua fronte,
e che là chiuse d'ogni vertù 'l fonte
quel giorno che di morte acerbo passo
fece la donna de lo meo cor, lasso!
già piena tutta d'adornezze conte.

I remember the white part of her dress which, with the dark-green, makes up its fair shape, which Love donned at the season when, Mars and Venus gazing, he struck me through the heart with the arrow that cuts deepest: and when the breeze moves the white flower, I remember the sweet whites of her lovely eyes for which my desire will never falter.

I WAS upon the high and blessed mountain, which I worshipped, kissing the holy stone; and fell upon that headstone, weary, where Honesty laid her forehead, and which shut off the fountainhead of every virtue that day when the woman of my heart went through death's bitter pass, alas! she who was once full of every brighter charm.

Quivi chiamai a questa guisa Amore:
– Dolce mio iddio, fa che qui mi traggia
la morte a sè, chè qui giace 'l mio core. –
Ma poi che non m'intese 'l mio Signore,
mi dipartii, pur chiamando Selvaggia:
l'alpe passai con voce di dolore.

CECCO ANGIOLIERI

– Accorri accorri accorri, uom, a la strada!
– Che ha', fi' de la putta? – I' son rubato.
– Chi t'ha rubato? – Una, che par che rada
come rasoi', sì m'ha netto lasciato.
– Or come non le davi de la spada?
– I' dare' anzi a me. – Or se' 'mpazzato?
– Non so; che 'l dà? – Così mi par che vada:
or t'avess'ella cieco, sciagurato! –

– E vedi che ne pare a que' che 'l sanno?
– Di' quel, che tu mi rubi. – Or va' con Dio!
– Ma ando pian, ch' i' vo' pianger lo danno.

There I called on Love in this manner: 'My sweet god, let death
take me here, since my heart lies here.' But when my Lord did not
hear me, I left, still calling on Selvaggia: I passed over the mountain with the voice of grief.

'Run, run, run, man, along that street!' 'What's wrong, whore-
son?' 'I've been robbed.' 'Who robbed you?' 'A woman, who
shears like a razor, she's left me so bare.' 'Well, why didn't you
have at her with your sword?' 'I'd sooner turn it on myself.' 'Are
you mad?' 'I don't know; what makes you think so?' 'The way
you are going on: it's as good as if she had blinded you, you
wretch!'
'See how it appears to people who understand?' 'Let them know
that you rob me.' 'O go away!' 'I'm going, but slowly, for I must

– Che ti diparti? – Con animo rio.
– Tu abbi 'l danno con tutto 'l malanno!
– Or chi m'ha morto? – E che diavol sacc'io? –

MALEDETTO e distrutto sia da Dio
lo primo punto, ch'io innamorai
di quella, che dilettasi di guai
darmi, ed ogn'altro sollazzo ha in oblio;
e si fa tanto tormento esser mio,
che 'n corpo d'uom non ne fu tanto mai:
e non le pare aver fatto anco assai,
tant'è 'l su' cor giude', pessimo e rio.

E non pensa se non com'ella possa
far a me cosa, che mi scoppi'l cuore:
di questa oppinion ma' non fu mossa.
E di lei non mi posso gittar fuore,
tant'ho la ment' abbarbagliat'e grossa,
c'ho men sentor, che non ha l'uom, che mòre.

weep my loss.' 'How do you leave me?' 'In bad heart.' 'Well, you can suffer your "loss" and every illness with it, for all I care!' 'Who is killing me now?' 'How the devil should I know?'

MAY God curse and destroy the first moment that I fell in love with her who takes pleasure in bringing me woes, and is oblivious of every other delight; and causes me so much torment, that never before was there so much in the body of man: and she doesn't seem to think she has done much yet, so pitiless, evil, and utterly bad is her heart.

And she thinks of nothing but how she may do things that will break my heart: she has never been budged from this fixed idea. And I cannot get beyond her reach, my mind is so bedazzled and stupefied, that I have less feeling in me than a dying man.

S' i' fosse foco, arderei 'l mondo;
s' i' fosse vento, lo tempesterei;
s' i' fosse acqua, i' l'annegherei;
s' i' fosse Dio, mandereil' en profondo;
s' i' fosse papa, sare' allor giocondo,
che tutt' i cristiani imbrigherei;
s' i' fosse 'mperator, sa' che farei?
A tutti mozzarei lo capo a tondo.

S' i' fosse morte, andarei da mio padre;
s' i' fosse vita, fuggirei da lui:
similmente farìa da mi' madre.
S' i' fosse Cecco, com' i' sono e fui,
torrei le donne giovani e leggiadre:
e vecchie e laide lasserei altrui.

TRE cose solamente mi so' in grado,
le quali posso non ben ben fornire:
ciò è la donna, la taverna e 'l dado;
queste mi fanno 'l cuor lieto sentire.

IF I were fire, I'd burn up the world; if I were wind, I'd storm it;
if I were water, I'd drown it; if I were God, I'd send it into the
abyss; if I were Pope, then I'd be happy, for I'd cheat all the
Christians; if I were emperor, 'know what I'd do? I'd chop off
everyone's head.

    If I were death, I would go to my father; if I were life, I'd fly
from him: likewise would I do with my mother. If I were Cecco, as
I am and was, I would take the women who are young and gay, and
leave the old and ugly to other men.

THREE things only please me, which I cannot easily provide: that
is, women, the tavern, and dicing; these gladden my heart. But I

Ma sì me le convèn usar di rado,
chè la mie borsa mi mett'al mentire;
e, quando mi sovvien, tutto mi sbrado,
ch' i' perdo per moneta 'l mie disire.

E dico: – Dato li sia d'una lancia! –
Ciò a mi' padre, che mi tien si magro,
che tornare' senza logro di Francia.
Trarl' un denai' di man serìa più agro,
la man di pasqua, che si dà la mancia,
che far pigliar la gru ad un bozzagro!

FOLGORE DA SAN GIMIGNANO

De gennaio

I' DOTO voi nel mese de gennaio
corte con fochi di salette accese,
camere e letta d'ogni bello arnese,
lenzuol de seta e copertoi di vaio;
tregèa, confetti e mescere arazzaio,
vestiti di doagio e di rascese,
e 'n questo modo stare a le difese,
mova sirocco garbino e rovaio.

am obliged to indulge them so rarely, for my purse makes me put them away from me; and, when I think of this, I rage at losing my pleasures for money.

And I say: – let him get it with a lance! – that is, my father, who keeps me so meagrely, that I would come back from far France with never an enticement. Getting one coin from his hand, on Easter morning, too, when largess is general, would be harder than taking a crane with a mousing-hawk.

For January

I MAKE you a present in the month of January of a courtyard with fires kindled with straw, rooms, and beds with every fine furnishing, silk sheets, and coverlets of vair; sugared nuts, sweets, and sparkling wine, clothes of Douai and Rascia, and in this way you would be fortified, should the Sirocco, the South-West, or the North wind blow.

Uscir di for'alcuna volta il giorno
gittando de la neve bella e bianca
a le donzelle che staran da torno;
e quando fosse la compagna stanca
a questa corte facciase ritorno
e si riposi la brigata franca.

D'aprile

D'APRIL vi dono la gentil campagna
tutta fiorita di bell'erba fresca,
fontane d'acqua che non vi rincresca,
donne e donzelle per vostra compagna;
ambianti palafren, destrier di Spagna
e gente costumata a la francesca,
cantar danzar a la provenzalesca
con istormenti novi d'Alemagna.

E da torno vi sia molti giardini
e giachita vi sia ogni persona,
ciascun con reverenza adori e 'nchini
a quel gentil ch'ò dato la corona
de pietre preziose le più fini
ch'à 'l presto Gianni o 'l re di Babilona.

Going out several times in the day, to throw the lovely white snow at the girls who are standing about; and when the company was tired, they would return to this court, and the generous band find rest.

For April

FOR April I give you the gentle countryside all flowering with fresh grass, fountains of water that will not displease you, women and girls for company; nimble horses, chargers from Spain, and people dressed in the French style, singing and dancing in the manner of Provence, with new instruments from Germany.

And round about there will be many gardens, and everyone will be stretched out at ease there, each will worship and bow with reverence to that gentle one to whom I have given the crown of precious stones, the finest that Prester John or the King of Babylon has.

Di maggio

Di maggio sì vi do molti cavagli
e tutti quanti siano affrenatori,
portanti tutti, dritti corritori,
pettorali e testiere con sonagli;
bandiere e coverte a molti 'ntagli
di zendadi e di tutti li colori,
le targhe a modo degli armeggiatori,
viole rose e fior c'ogni uom abbagli;

Rompere e fiaccar bigordi e lance
e piover da finestre e da balconi
en giù ghirlande e 'n su melerance;
e pulcellette giovene e garzoni
baciarsi ne la bocca e ne le guance,
d'amor e di goder vi si ragioni.

Di giugno

Di giugno dòvi una montagnetta
coverta di bellissimi arboscelli,
con trenta ville e dodici castelli
che siano entorno ad una cittadetta;

For May

For May I give you this – many horses and all of them will be manageable, each trained, with upright riders, breast- and head-pieces, with bells; flags, and other trappings in silk and all colours, shields in the style of the jousters, violets, roses, and other flowers to dazzle everyone;

and there will be breaking and shattering of jousting-spears and lances, and from windows and balconies will rain garlands, and oranges fly up in the air; and young maids and youths kissing one another on the mouth and on the cheeks, and everyone intent on loving and enjoying.

For June

For June I give you a small mountain covered with fairest trees, with thirty country-houses and twelve castles standing about a little

ch'abbia nel mezzó una so' fontanetta
e faccia mille rami e fiumicelli,
ferendo per giardini e praticelli
e rinfrescando la minuta erbetta.

Aranci cedri dattili e lumìe
e tutte l'altre frutte savorose
empergolate siano per le vie;
e le gente vi sian tutte amorose,
e faccianvisi tante cortesie
ch'a tutto 'l mondo siano graziose.

DANTE ALIGHIERI

A CIASCUN'ALMA presa e gentil core
nel cui cospetto ven lo dir presente,
in ciò che mi rescrivan suo parvente,
salute in lor segnor, cioè Amore.
Già eran quasi che atterzate l'ore
del tempo che onne stella n'è lucente,
quando m'apparve Amor subitamente,
cui essenza membrar mi dà orrore.

city; that has in its midst a sweet fountain and turns this into a
thousand branches and little streams striking through gardens and
meads, and freshening the tiny grass.

Oranges, lemons, dates, and limes, and all other succulent fruits,
would overarch the walks at the roadside; and everyone be ready
for love, and pay one another many fine compliments there which
should delight everyone.

To every soul possessed and gentle heart into whose gaze the present words come, greetings in the name of their lord, that is Love,
that they may write me in return their opinion of this. The hours of
the time when every star is shining were almost passed by a third,
when Love suddenly appeared to me in a form which is horrifying
to recall.

Allegro mi sembrava Amor tenendo
meo core in mano, e ne le braccia avea
madonna involta in un drappo dormendo.
Poi la svegliava, e d'esto core ardendo
lei paventosa umilmente pascea:
appresso gir lo ne vedea piangendo.

O voi che per la via d'Amor passate,
attendete e guardate
s'elli è dolore alcun, quanto 'l mio, grave;
e prego sol ch'audir mi sofferiate,
e poi imaginate
s'io son d'ogni tormento ostale e chiave.
Amor, non già per mia poca bontate,
ma per sua nobiltate,
mi pose in vita sì dolce e soave,
ch'io mi sentia dir dietro spesse fiate:
«Deo, per qual dignitate
così leggiadro questi lo core have?»

Happy Love seemed holding my heart in his hand, and in his
arms he had my lady wrapped in a mantle, asleep. Then he woke
her, and submissively, in fear, she ate this heart that burned; there-
after I saw him go away weeping.

O you who pass along the way of Love, pause and see if there is
any grief as heavy as mine, and I ask you only to give me a hearing,
and then consider if I am not the abode and key of every anguish.
Love (not in the least for my slight worth, but in his nobleness) set
me in a life so delightful and sweet that I heard people say behind
me many times: 'God, by what grace is that man's heart so lightsome?'

Or ho perduta tutta mia baldanza,
che si movea d'amoroso tesoro;
ond'io pover dimoro,
in guisa che di dir mi ven dottanza.
Sì che volendo far come coloro
che per vergogna celan lor mancanza,
di fuor mostro allegranza,
e dentro da lo core struggo e ploro.

Donne ch'avete intelletto d'amore,
i' vo' con voi de la mia donna dire,
non perch'io creda sua laude finire,
ma ragionar per isfogar la mente.
Io dico che pensando il suo valore,
Amor sì dolce mi si fa sentire,
che s'io allora non perdessi ardire,
farei parlando innamorar la gente.
E io non vo' parlar sì altamente,
ch'io divenisse per temenza vile;
ma tratterò del suo stato gentile
a respetto di lei leggeramente,
donne e donzelle amorose, con vui,
chè non è cosa da parlarne altrui.

Now I have lost all the easy pride that came from my loving treasure, and I am left so poor that a fear to speak has come upon me. So that wishing to do as those who hide what they lack from shame, I show gladness outwardly, and in my heart am torn and weep.

Ladies who have an understanding of love, I wish to speak with you of my lady, not because I think to exhaust her praise, but only to talk so as to unburden my mind. I tell you that when I think of her worth, Love makes himself known to me so sweetly, that if I did not then lose heart, I should make everyone fall in love simply by talking. And I do not wish to speak so exaltedly that I become faint-hearted from fear, but I shall treat of her gentle condition lightly out of respect for her, loving women and maids, with you, since it is not a thing to talk of with others.

Angelo clama in divino intelleto
e dice: «Sire, nel mondo si vede
maraviglia ne l'atto che procede
d'un'anima che 'nfin qua su risplende.»
Lo cielo, che non have altro difetto
che d'aver lei, al suo segnor la chiede,
e ciascun santo ne grida merzede.
Sola Pietà nostra parte difende,
che parla Dio, che di madonna intende:
«Diletti miei, or sofferite in pace
che vostra spene sia quanto me piace
là 'v'è alcun che perder lei s'attende,
e che dirà ne lo inferno: – O mal nati,
io vidi la speranza de' beati.»

Madonna è disiata in sommo cielo:
or voi di sua virtù farvi savere.
Dico, qual vuol gentil donna parere
vada con lei, che quando va per via,
gitta nei cor villani Amore un gelo:
per che onne lor pensero agghiaccia e pere;
e qual soffrisse di starla a veder
diverria nobil cosa, o si morria.

An angel exclaims in the Divine Intelligence and says: 'Lord, a marvel is seen on earth in the grace that comes from a soul that shines up to this height.' Heaven, which has no other blemish but to want her, asks her from its lord, and each saint cries out for this boon. Only Pity takes our part, speaking in God, who comprehends my lady: 'Dearly beloved, suffer in peace, for, however much your hope is pleasing to me, there is one down there who is soon to lose her, and who will say in hell: "O you evil-born, I have seen the hope of the blessed." '

My lady is desired in highest heaven; make yourselves acquainted with her virtue then. I say whoever of you wants to appear as a gentle woman, let her go with her, as when she goes along the street, Love throws a frost upon every base heart, so that every thought of theirs freezes and perishes; and whoever could bear to stand and gaze at her would become a noble thing, or die. And

E quando trova alcun che degno sia
di veder lei, quei prova sua vertute,
chè li avvien, ciò che li dona, in salute,
e sì l'umilia, ch'ogni offesa oblia.
Ancor l'ha Dio per maggior grazia dato
che non pò mal finir chi l'ha parlato.

Dice di lei Amor: «Cosa mortale
come esser pò sì adorna e sì pura,»
Poi la reguarda, e fra se stesso giura
che Dio ne 'ntenda di far cosa nova.
Color di perle ha quasi, in forma quale
convene a donna aver, non for misura:
ella è quanto de ben pò far natura;
per esemplo di lei bieltà si prova.
De li occhi suoi, come ch'ella li mova,
escono spiriti d'amore inflammati,
che feron li occhi a qual che allor la guati,
e passan sì che 'l cor ciascun retrova:
voi le vedete Amor pinto nel viso,
là 've non pote alcun mirarla fiso.

when Love finds one who is worthy to look upon her, that man
feels her power so that it comes to him (as she grants it) as a gift of
grace, and so humbles him that he forgets everything hurtful. God
has also granted as a greater blessing that whoever speaks to her
cannot end badly.

Love says of her: 'How can any mortal thing be so comely and
so pure?' Then he looks at her, and swears in himself that God intended in her to create something new. She has the colour almost
of the pearl, in the degree that is right for a woman to have, not
beyond measure: she is the sum of goodness that Nature can make;
beauty is proved by her being. From her eyes, when she moves
them, come flaming spirits of love which wound the eyes of whoever looks at them then, and they penetrate so that each one finds
out the heart. You see Love painted on her face there where no one
can look at her steadily.

Canzone, io so che tu girai parlando
a donne assai, quand'io t'avrò avanzata.
Or t'ammonisco, perch'io t'ho allevata
per figliuola d'Amor giovane e piana,
che là 've giugni tu dichi pregando:
«Insegnatemi gir, ch'io son mandata
a quella di cui laude so' adornata.»
E se non vuoli andar sì come vana,
non restare ove sia gente villana:
ingegnati, se puoi, d'esser palese
solo con donne o con omo cortese,
che ti merranno là per via tostana.
Tu troverai Amor con esso lei;
raccomandami a lui come tu dei.

Tanto gentile e tanto onesta pare
la donna mia quand'ella altrui saluta,
ch'ogne lingua deven tremando muta,
e li occhi no l'ardiscon di guardare.

My song, I know you will go about speaking to many women when I have once sped you. Now I enjoin you, because I have brought you up as the simple, young daughter of Love, to make this request in whatever place you come to: 'Show me where to go, as I am being sent to that fair whose praise adorns me.' And if you do not want to go about like a vain thing, do not stay where they are low people: contrive, if you can, to be open only with women and courteous men, who will lead you by the quick way. You will find Love and with him her; remind him of me as you ought.

My lady is so gentle and modest when she greets others that every tongue trembles and is still, and eyes do not dare to look upon

Ella si va, sentendosi laudare,
benignamente d'umiltà vestuta;
e par che sia una cosa venuta
da cielo in terra a miracol mostrare.

Mostrasi sì piacente a chi la mira,
che dà per li occhi una dolcezza al core,
che 'ntender no la può chi no la prova:
e par che de la sua labbia si mova
un spirito soave pien d'amore,
che va dicendo a l'anima: «Sospira».

Deh peregrini che pensosi andate,
forse di cosa che non v'è presente,
venite voi da sì lontana gente,
com'a la vista voi ne dimostrate,
che non piangete quando voi passate
per lo suo mezzo la città dolente,
come quelle persone che neente
par che intendesser la sua gravitate?

her. She passes, hearing herself praised, dressed most kindly with
humility; and it seems that she is a thing come upon earth from
heaven to show forth a miracle.

She shows herself so pleasant to whoever gazes at her, that
through the eyes she gives a sweetness to the heart which no one
can comprehend who has not known it: and it seems that from her
face moves a sweet spirit full of love that goes to the soul with the
words: 'O sigh.'

O pilgrims who go by thoughtful, perhaps because of something
that is not present to you here, do you come from so far a people as
by your look you show, that you do not weep as you pass through
the middle of the sorrowing city, like those who, it seems, do not
at all understand its heavy grief?

Se voi restate per volerlo audire,
certo lo cor de' sospiri mi dice
che lagrimando n'uscirete pui.
Ell'ha perduta la sua beatrice;
e le parole ch'om di lei pò dire
hanno vertù di far piangere altrui.

OLTRE la spera che più larga gira
passa 'l sospiro ch'esce del mio core;
intelligenza nova, che l'Amore
piangendo mette in lui, pur su lo tira.
Quand'elli è giunto là dove disira,
vede una donna, che riceve onore,
e luce sì, che per lo suo splendore
lo peregrino spirito la mira.

Vedela tal, che quando 'l mi ridice,
io no lo intendo, sì parla sottile
al cor dolente, che lo fa parlare.
So io che parla di quella gentile,
però che spesso ricorda Beatrice,
sì ch'io lo 'ntendo ben, donne mie care.

If you pause wishing to hear what it is, certainly, my heart of signs tells me, you will leave it then in tears. It has lost its 'Blessing One'; and the things that men can say of her have the power to make everyone weep.

BEYOND the sphere which most widely wheels, passes the sigh that comes from my heart; new understanding which Love weepingly instils into him, draws him upward still. When he has reached the place he wishes for, he sees a woman, who is visited with honour, and so shines, that this far-travelled spirit wonders at her brightness.

He sees her in such a guise that when he repeats this to me, I do not understand, he speaks so darkly to the sorrowing heart, which makes him speak. I know that he speaks of that gentle one because often he recalls Beatrice, so that I understand him well, my dear ladies.

Guido, i' vorrei che tu e Lapo ed io
fossimo presi per incantamento
e messi in un vasel, ch'ad ogni vento
per mare andasse al voler vostro e mio;
sì che fortuna od altro tempo rio
non ci potesse dare impedimento,
anzi, vivendo sempre in un talento,
di stare insieme crescesse 'l disio.

E monna Vanna e monna Lagia poi
con quella ch'è sul numer de le trenta
con noi ponesse il buono incantatore:
e quivi ragionar sempre d'amore,
e ciascuna di lor fosse contenta,
sì come i' credo che saremmo noi.

Per una ghirlandetta
ch'io vidi, mi farà
sospirare ogni fiore.

Guido, I would that you and Lapo and I could be taken up by a spell and put in a ship, that went through the sea with every wind, as you and I wished; so that neither tempest nor other evil weather could oppose us, but rather, living always in the one desire, the wish to stay together would grow.

And then the good enchanter would put with us my lady Vanna and my lady Lagia and the one who is to be found at the number thirty: and then to converse always of love, and might each of them be happy, as I believe we ourselves would be.

Because of a garland I have seen, every flower will make me sigh.

I' vidi a mia donna portare
ghirlandetta di fior gentile,
e sovr'a lei vidi volare
un angiolel d'amore umile;
e 'n suo cantar sottile
dicea: – Chi mi vedrà
lauderà 'l mio signore. –

Se io sarò là dove sia
Fioretta mia bella e gentile,
allor dirò a la donna mia
che port'in testa i miei sospire:
– Ma' per crescer disire
una donna verrà
coronata da Amore? –

Le parolette mie novelle
che di fiori fatto han ballata,
per leggiadria ci hanno tolt'elle
una vesta ch'altrui fu data.
Però siate pregata,
qual uom la canterà,
che li facciate onore.

I saw my lady wearing a garland of gentle flowers, and above it
I saw a humble little angel of love flying: and in his fine singing he
said: 'He who sees me will praise my lord.'

If I am in some place and Fioretta, my gentle fair, is present, then
shall I say to my lady who bears my sighs upon her head: ' To
make desire grow, will a lady never come crowned with Love? '

These newborn words of mine which have made a song of
flowers, have stolen, out of gaiety, a dress that was given to others.
But you are desired to honour them whenever this song is heard.

— I' mi son pargoletta bella e nova,
che son venuta per mostrare altrui
de le bellezze del loco ond'io fui.

I' fui del cielo, e tornerovvi ancora
per dar de la mia luce altrui diletto;
e chi mi vede e non se ne innamora
d'amor non averà mai intelletto,
chè non mi fu in piacer alcun disdetto
quando natura mi chiese a Colui
che volle, donne, accompagnarmi a vui.

Ciascuna stella ne li occhi mi piove
del lume suo e de la sua vertute;
le mie bellezze sono al mondo nove,
però che di là su mi son venute:
le quai non posson esser canosciute
se non da canoscenza d'omo, in cui
Amor si metta per piacer altrui. —

'I AM a young girl, beautiful and new, who have come to show
people the beauties of the place whence I am.
  'I was in heaven, and I shall return there again to give others delight with my shining; and whoever sees me without falling in love
will never have an understanding of love, for no pleasantness was
denied me when nature asked for me from Him who wished, ladies,
to make me of your company.
  'Every star rains its light upon my eyes and its influence; my
beauties are new to the world, because they have come to me from
on high: nor can they be known except to the discerning of a man
in whom Love resides at another's pleasure.'

Queste parole si leggon nel viso
d'un'angioletta che ci è apparita:
e io che per veder lei mirai fiso,
ne sono a rischio di perder la vita;
però ch'io ricevetti tal ferita
da un ch'io vidi dentro a li occhi sui,
ch'i' vo piangendo, e non m'achetai pui.

Io son venuto al punto de la rota
che l'orizzonte, quando il sol si corca,
ci partorisce il geminato cielo,
e la stella d'amor ci sta remota
per lo raggio lucente che la 'nforca
sì di traverso, che le si fa velo;
e quel pianeta che conforta il gelo
si mostra tutto a noi per lo grand'arco
nel qual ciascun di sette fa poca ombra:
e però non disgombra
un sol penser d'amore, ond'io son carco,
la mente mia, ch'è più dura che petra
in tener forte imagine di petra.

These words are to be read in the face of an angel who has appeared to us: and I, who gazed fixedly upon her, am in danger of losing my life; because I had such a wound from one whom I saw within her eyes, that I keep weeping and have not calmed myself since.

I HAVE come to the point of the circle where the horizon, when the sun goes to rest, gives birth to the Twin-governed sky, and the star of love is far from us because of the shining ray which crosses it, so as to make a veil; and that planet which cheers the frost appears to us through the great curve in which each of the Seven casts little shade: and yet my mind does not clear itself of a single thought of love, which presses upon me, for it is harder than a stone in firmly preserving an image of stone.

Levasi de la rena d'Etiopia
lo vento peregrin che l'aere turba,
per la spera del sol ch'ora la scalda;
e passa il mare, onde conduce copia
di nebbia tal, che, s'altro non la sturba,
questo emisperio chiude tutto e salda;
e poi si solve, e cade in bianca falda
di fredda neve ed in noiosa pioggia,
onda l'aere s'attrista tutto e piagne:
e Amor, che sue ragne
ritira in alto pel vento che poggia,
non m'abbandona; sì è bella donna
questa crudel che m'è data per donna.

Fuggito è ogne augel che 'l caldo segue
del paese d'Europa, che non perde
le sette stelle gelide unquemai;
e li altri han posto a le lor voci triegue
per non sonarle infino al tempo verde,
se ciò non fosse per cagion di guai;
e tutti li animali che son gai

The travelling wind which stirs the air rises from the Ethiopian
sand, heated now by the sun's sphere; and crosses the sea whence it
gathers such abundance of mist, that, if no other thing opposes, it
shuts off and binds this hemisphere; and then yields, and falls in
white drift of cold snow and in dreary rain, at which the air grows
altogether sad and weeps: and Love, who draws his nets on high
because of the powerful wind, does not leave me; so beautiful is this
cruel woman who has been given to me as mistress.

Every bird that follows the heat has fled from the land of Europe
which never once is rid of the seven frozen stars; the others have
imposed a truce upon their voices so that they will not ring out until
the green time, except for some grief; and all the animals that are

di lor natura, son d'amor disciolti,
però che 'l freddo lor spirito ammorta:
e 'l mio più d'amor porta;
chè li dolzi pensier' non mi son tolti
nè mi son dati per volta di tempo,
ma donna li mi dà c'ha picciol tempo.

Passato hanno lor termine le fronde
che trasse fuor la virtù d'Ariete
per ardonare il mondo, e morta è l'erba;
ramo di foglia verde a noi s'asconde
se non se in lauro, in pino o in abete
o in alcun che sua verdura serba;
e tanto è la stagion forte ed acerba,
c'ha morti li fioretti per le piagge,
li quai non poten tollerar la brina:
e la crudele spina
però Amor di cor non la mi tragge;
per ch'io son fermo di portarla sempre
ch'io sarò in vita, s'io vivesse sempre.

gay by nature are freed from loving because the cold deadens their spirit: and mine bears greater love; for sweet thoughts are not taken from me, nor are they given me by the changing of season, but a woman who has been short time in the world gives them to me.

Leaves which the power of the Ram brought forth to deck the world have passed their date, and the grass is dead; every green-leafed branch is hidden from us except in laurel, or in pine, or in fir, or in other tree that keeps its greenness; and so strong and bitter is the season, that it has killed the little flowers along the banks, which cannot bear the frost: and yet Love does not draw the cruel thorn from my heart; so I am determined to bear it for as long as there is life in me, should I live for ever.

Versan le vene le fummifere acque
per li vapor' che la terra ha nel ventre,
che d'abisso li tira suso in alto;
onde cammino al bel giorno mi piacque
che ora è fatto rivo, e sarà mentre
che durerà del verno il grande assalto;
la terra fa un suol che par di smalto,
e l'acqua morta si converte in vetro
per la freddura che di fuor la serra:
e io de la mia guerra
non son però tornato un passo a retro,
nè vo' tornar; chè se 'l martiro è dolce,
la morte de' passar ogni altro dolce.

Canzone, or che sarà di me ne l'altro
dolce tempo novello, quando piove
amore in terra da tutti li cieli,
quando per questi geli
amore è solo in me, e non altrove?
Saranne quello ch'è d'un uom di marmo,
se in pargoletta fia per core un marmo.

The streams run with smoke-laden waters because of the steam the earth has in its bowels, which it draws out from the abyss into upper air; so that a path that I was glad to walk on when days were fair, has become a torrent, and will be one while the great onslaught of winter last; the earth has a surface that seems enamel, and the dead water changes to glass because of the cold which grips it from without: and I have not drawn back one step from this war of mine, nor want to draw back; for if suffering is sweet, death must surpass every other sweetness.

My song, what will become of me in the sweet new season when love rains upon the earth from every heaven, if love lives in me now, in spite of all these frosts, and nowhere else? I shall become a man of marble, if in a girl there is a heart of marble.

Al poco giorno e al gran cerchio d'ombra
son giunto, lasso! ed al bianchir de' colli,
quando si perde lo color ne l'erba;
e 'l mio disio però non cangia 'l verde,
si è barbato ne la dura petra
che parla e sente come fosse donna.

Similmente questa nova donna
si sta gelata come neve a l'ombra;
che non la move, se non come petra,
il dolce tempo che riscalda i colli
e che li fa tornar di bianco in verde
perchè li copre di fioretti e d'erba.

Quand'ella ha in testa una ghirlanda d'erba
trae de la mente nostra ogn'altra donna;
perche si mischia il crespo giallo e l' verde
sì bel, ch'Amor lì viene a stare a l'ombra,
che m'ha serrato intra piccioli colli
più forte assai che la calcina petra.

I HAVE come to a short day and a great arc of shadow, alas! and to
the hill's whitening when colour vanishes from the grass; and my
desire does not, for this, change its green, it is so rooted in the hard
stone that speaks and hears as if it were a woman.

Likewise this heaven-born woman remains frozen like snow in
the shade; for she is not moved, unless as a stone is, by the sweet
time which warms the hills and makes them turn from white to
green so that it may cover them with little flowers and plants.

When she has a grass garland upon her head, she draws our mind
from every other woman, because she mingles the waving yellow
and the green in such lovely wise that Love comes to stand in their
shadow, he who has locked me between small hills much more
firmly than lime locks stone.

La sua bellezza ha più vertù che petra,
e 'l colpo suo non può sanar per erba;
ch'io son fuggito per piani e per colli,
per poter scampar da cotal donna;
e dal suo lume non mi può far ombra
poggio nè muro mai, nè fronda verde.

Io l'ho veduta già vestita a verde
sì fatta, ch'ella avrebbe messo in petra
l'amor ch'io porto pur a la sua ombra;
ond'io l'ho chesta in un bel prato d'erba,
innamorata com'anco fu donna,
e chiuso intorno d'altissimi colli.

Ma ben ritorneranno i fiumi a' colli
prima che questo legno molle e verde
s'infiammi, come suol far bella donna,
di me; che mi torrei dormire in petra
tutto il mio tempo e gir pascendo l'erba,
sol per veder do' suoi panni fann'ombra.

Her beauty has more virtue than precious stones, and the wound
she gives is not to be cured by herb; for I have fled by plain and hill
to be able to escape from such a woman, and neither mound nor
wall nor green foliage can ever give me shade from her light.

I have seen her dressed in green, so fashioned that she would
have inspired a stone with the love I bear her very shadow; so that
I have wished her on a fair meadow of grass, surrounded by highest
hills, as much in love as ever woman was.

But well may the rivers return to the hills before this soft green
wood catches fire, as fair woman is wont to, for my sake; so that I
would choose to sleep out my life on hard stone and go about feeding on grass, only to look where her garments cast shade.

Quandunque i colli fanno più nera ombra,
sotto un bel verde la giovane donna
la fa sparer, com'uom petra sott'erba.

Così nel mio parlar voglio esser aspro
com'è ne li atti questa bella petra,
la qual ognora impetra
maggior durezza e più natura cruda,
e veste sua persona d'un diaspro
tal, che per lui, o perch'ella s'arretra,
non esce di faretra
saetta che già mai la colga ignuda:
ed ella ancide, e non val ch'om si chiuda
nè si dilunghi da' colpi mortali,
che, com'avesser ali,
giungono altrui e spezzan ciascun'arme;
sì ch'io non so da lei nè posso atarme.

Every time the hills cast blackest shade, it makes this young woman disappear amid fair green, as a man hides a precious stone in grass.

In my speech I wish to be as harsh as this lovely stone-girl is in her actions, who every moment grows more stonelike in hardness and rough nature, and clothes her person in adamant so that, because of this, or because she makes away, no arrow ever comes from quiver that can pierce her naked: and she kills, and it does not avail a man to close himself in, or fly from the mortal blows, which, as if they had wings, reach one and shatter every weapon; so that I know not how to defend myself from her, nor can I.

Non trovo scudo ch'ella non mi spezzi
nè loco che dal suo viso m'asconda;
chè, come fior di fronda,
così de la mia mente tien la cima:
cotanto del mio mal par che si prezzi,
quanto legno di mar che non lieva onda;
e 'l peso che m'affonda
è tal che non potrebbe adequar rima.
Ahi angosciosa e dispietata lima
che sordamente la mia vita scemi,
perchè non ti ritemi
sì di rodermi il core a scorza a scorza,
com'io di dire altrui chi ti dà forza?

Chè più mi triema il cor qualora io penso
di lei in parte ov'altri li occhi induca,
per tema non traluca
lo mio penser di fuor sì che si scopra,
ch'io non fo de le morte, che ogni senso
co li denti d'Amor già mi manduca;
ciò è che 'l pensier bruca
la lor vertù sì che n'allenta l'opra.
E m'ha percosso in terra, e stammi sopra

I find no shield which she does not shatter, nor place where I can
hide from her face; as, like the flower above the leaves, she holds
the topmost of my mind: she seems to heed my misfortune, as
much as a ship does a mild sea; and the weight which forces me
down is such that no rhyme could equal it. Ah agonizing and pitiless trap that deafly wears out my life, why do you not keep from
eating my heart skin by skin, as I refrain from telling anyone who
gives you power?

For my heart trembles more when I think of her, in a place where
I can be seen by others – for fear that my thought may shine
through and betray itself – than I tremble at death, which already
gnaws every nerve of mine with the teeth of Love; that is, the
thought devours their strength, so that their action falters. Love
has struck me to the ground and stands above me, holding the

con quella spada ond'elli ancise Dido,
Amore, a cui io grido
merzè chiamando, e umilmente il priego;
ed el d'ogni merzè par messo al niego.

Egli alza ad ora ad or la mano, e sfida
la debole mia vita, esto perverso,
che disteso a riverso
mi tiene in terra d'ogni guizzo stanco:
allor mi surgon ne la mente strida;
e 'l sangue, ch'è per le vene disperso,
fuggendo corre verso
lo cor, che 'l chiama: ond'io rimango bianco.
Elli mi fiede sotto il braccio manco
sì forte, che 'l dolor nel cor rimbalza:
allor dico: «S'elli alza
un'altra volta, Morte m'avrà chiuso
prima che 'l colpo sia disceso giuso.»

Così vedess'io lui fender per mezzo
lo core a la crudele che 'l mio squatra!
poi non mi sarebb'atra
la morte, ov'io per sua bellezza corro:

sword with which he slew Dido, and to him I cry for mercy, and
humbly pray; and he seems to be set on denying me every mercy.

Every now and then this perverse one, who keeps me on my
back upon the ground, too tired to twist, raises his hand, and chal-
lenges my weak life: then cries rise in my mind; and the blood
which is sent out through my veins comes in a rush to the heart,
which calls it; and I am left white. He wounds me under my left
arm so violently, that the pain starts up in my heart again: then I
say: 'If he raises his hand once more, Death will have gathered me
before the blow has descended.'

O might I see Love strike right through the heart of that cruel
one who quarters mine! then the death to which I run for sake of
her beauty would not be black to me: as she, that thieving, deadly

chè tanto dà nel sol quanto nel rezzo
questa scherana micidiale e latra.
Ohmè, perchè non latra
per me, com'io per lei, nel caldo borro?
chè tosto griderei: «Io vi soccorro»;
e fare' l volentier, sì come quelli
che ne' biondi capelli
ch'Amore per consumarmi increspe e dora
metterei mano, e piacere' le allora.

S'io avessi le belle trecce prese,
che fatte son per me scudiscio e ferza,
pigliandole anzi terza,
con esse passerei vespero e squille:
e non sarei pietoso nè cortese,
anzi farei com'orso quando scherza;
e se Amor me ne sferza,
io mi vendicherei di più di mille.
Ancor ne li occhi, ond'escon le faville
che m'infiammano il cor, ch'io porto anciso,
guarderei presso e fiso,
per vendicar lo fuggir che mi face;
e poi le renderei con amor pace.

murderess, inflicts as much by daylight as by dark. O, why does she
not yelp for me, as I for her, in the hot abyss? for I would quickly
shout: 'I'll help you'; and I'd do it willingly; as some men would,
so would I thrust my hand in the fair hair that Love has waved and
gilded to consume me, and then she would find me pleasant.

If I had once caught hold of the lovely locks which have become
both switch and whip for me, taking them before matins I would
spend evensong and midnight with them: and I would not be spar-
ing or kind, rather I would act like a bear when it is playful; and if
love now whips me with them, I would avenge myself more than a
thousand-fold. I would gaze, fixedly and close, into the eyes, from
which come the sparks that burn my heart, which I bear dead within
me, to avenge myself for her shunning me; and then with love I
would give her peace again.

Canzon, vattene dritto a quella donna
che m'ha ferito il core e che m'invola
quello ond'io ho più gola,
e dàlle per lo cor d'una saetta;
chè bell'onor s'acquista in far vendetta.

TRE donne intorno al cor mi son venute,
e seggonsi di fore;
chè dentro siede Amore,
lo quale è in segnoria de la mia vita.
Tanto son belle e di tanta vertute,
che 'l possente segnore,
dico quel ch'è nel core,
a pena del parlar di lor s'aita.
Ciascuna par dolente e sbigottita,
come persona discacciata e stanca,
cui tutta gente manca
e cui vertute nè beltà non vale.
Tempo fu già nel quale,
secondo il lor parlar, furon dilette;
or sono a tutti in ira ed in non cale.
Queste così solette

My song, go straight to that woman who has wounded my heart
and who robs me of what I most hunger for, and thrust an arrow
through her heart; for fine honour is won in taking revenge.

THREE women have come about my heart and sit outside it; for
Love sits within who has lordship of my life. The women are so
lovely and of such dignity, that the powerful lord, I mean he who
is in my heart, can scarcely bring himself to speak to them. Each
seems to be grieving and bewildered, like a hunted, weary person
who lacks all followers, and to whom worth and beauty are of no
avail. There was once a time when by their converse they were
found delightful; now they are scorned by everyone and dis-
regarded. So these women, deserted in this way, have come as if

venute son come a casa d'amico;
che sanno ben che dentro è quel ch'io dico.

Dolesi l'una con parole molto,
e 'n su la man si posa
come succisa rosa;
il nudo braccio, di dolor colonna,
sente l'oraggio che cade dal volto;
l'altra man tiene ascosa
la faccia lagrimosa:
discinta e scalza, e sol di sè par donna.
Come Amor prima per la rotta gonna
la vide in parte che il tacere è bello,
egli, pietoso e fello,
di lei e del dolor fece dimanda.
«Oh di pochi vivanda,»
rispose in voce con sospiri mista,
«nostra natura qui a te ci manda:
io, che son la più trista,
son suora a la tua madre, e son Drittura;
povera, vedi, a panni ed a cintura.»

to a friend's house; for they well know that he is within of whom I have spoken.

One sorrows much in her words, and rests her head upon her hand like a fresh-cut rose; the bare arm, column to grief, feels the downpour from her face; the other hand keeps her weeping face hidden: loosely girt and barefoot, and only in herself seeming woman. When Love first saw through her torn skirt that part of her that it is courteous to be silent about, he asked her, pitying and indignant, about herself and her grief. 'O food of the few,' she replied in a voice mixed with sighs, 'our nature brings us to you: I, who am the saddest, am sister to your mother, and am Right; poor, as you see, in dress and girdle.'

Poi che fatta si fu palese e conta,
doglia e vergogna prese
lo mio segnore, e chiese
chi fosser l'altre due ch'eran con lei.
E questa, ch'era sì di pianger pronta,
tosto che lui intese,
più nel dolor s'accese,
dicendo: «A te non duol de gli occhi miei?»
Poi cominciò: «Si come saper dei,
di fonte nasce il Nilo picciol fiume
quivi dove 'l gran lume
toglie a la terra del vinco la fronda:
sovra la vergin onda
genera' io costei che m'è da lato
e che s'asciuga con la treccia bionda.
Questo mio bel portato
mirando sè ne la chiara fontana,
generò questa che m'è piu lontana.»

Fenno i sospiri Amore un poco tardo;
e poi con gli occhi molli,
che prima furon folli,
salutò le germane sconsolate.
E po' che prese l'uno e l'atro dardo,

When she had revealed and made herself known, my lord was
seized by grief and shame, and asked who were the other two who
were with her. And this woman, who was so possessed by weeping,
as soon as she heard him, waxed angrier in sorrow, and said: 'Does
it not hurt you to see me weep?' Then she began: 'As you must
know, the Nile is born, as a little river, from a spring where the
great light denies the earth the osier's leaf: by the virgin wave I
gave birth to her who is by my side and who dries herself with her
own fair hair. This lovely offspring of mine, gazing at herself in
the clear fountain, begot her who is further away from me.'

Sighs made Love falter a little; and then with wet eyes, that first
had been carefree, he greeted the disconsolate descendants. And
when he had taken up one and the other dart he said: 'Raise up

disse: «Drizzate i colli;
ecco l'armi ch'io volli;
per non usar, vedete, son turbate.
Larghezza e Temperanza, e l'altre nate
del nostro sangue, mendicando vanno.
Però, se questo è danno,
piangano gli occhi e dolgasi la bocca
de li uomini a cui tocca,
che sono a' raggi di cotal ciel giunti;
non noi, che semo de l'eterna rocca:
chè, se noi siamo or punti,
noi pur saremo, e pur tornerà gente,
che questo dardo farà star lucente.»

E io, che ascolto nel parlar divino
consolarsi e dolersi
così alti dispersi
l'esiglio che m'è dato onor mi tegno:
chè, se giudizio o forza di destino
vuol pur che 'l mondo versi
i bianchi fiori in persi,
cader co' buoni è pur di lode degno.
E se non che de gli occhi miei 'l bel segno

your heads: here are the weapons that I wanted; they are in disorder, you see, for lack of use. Liberality and Temperance, and the others born of our blood, go about begging. But, if this is harmful, let the men weep and speak sadly whom it concerns, who have seen the light of such a day; we need not grieve who are of the eternal rock: for, if we are now afflicted, we shall still live on, and people will be found again who will make this dart shine.'

And I, who listen to such noble refugees, lamenting and consoling themselves, hold the banishment that has been meted to me, an honour: for, if judgement or the power of fate is still to make the world turn its white flowers to red, to fall with the good is still worthy of praise. And if it were not that my eyes are denied their

per lontananza m'è tolto dal viso
che m'have in foco miso,
lieve mi conterei ciò che m'è grave.
Ma questo foco m'have
già consumato sì l'ossa e la polpa,
che Morte al petto m'ha posto la chiave.
Onde, s'io ebbi colpa,
più lune ha volto il sol poi che fu spenta,
se colpa muore perchè l'uom si penta.

Canzone, a' panni tuoi non ponga uom mano,
per veder quel che bella donna chiude:
bastin le parti nude;
lo dolce pome a tutta gente niega,
per cui ciascun man piega.
Ma s'elli avvien che tu alcun mai trovi
amico di virtù, ed e' ti priega,
fatti di color novi,
poi li ti mostra; e 'l fior, ch'è bel di fori,
fa disiar ne li amorosi cori.

fair mark by distance, and this puts me in the fire, I would consider
what is grievous something slight. But this fire has already so de-
voured my flesh and bones, that Death has put its key to my breast.
So that, if I had a share of blame, the sun has brought on many
moons since it was expiated, if blame dies because a man repents.

My song, let no man lay a hand on your clothes, to see what
lovely woman hides: let the bare parts suffice; the sweet fruit to
which every hand stretches, deny to every one. But if it chance that
you ever find one who is a friend to virtue, and he begs you, put
on new colours, and show yourself to him; and make the flower,
which is the beauty of flowers, be desired in loving hearts.

Canzone, uccella con le bianche penne;
canzone, caccia con li neri veltri,
che fuggir mi convenne,
ma far mi poterian di pace dono.
però nol fan che non san quel che sono:
camera di perdon savio uom non serra,
che 'l perdonare è bel vincer di guerra.

FRANCESCO PETRARCA

Voi ch'ascoltate in rime sparse il suono
di quei sospiri ond'io nudriva il core
in sul mio primo giovenile errore,
quand'era in parte altr'uom da quel ch'i' sono;
del vario stile in ch'io piango e ragiono
fra le vane speranze e 'l van dolore,
ove sia chi per prova intenda amore,
spero trovar pietà, non che perdono.

My song, bird with the white feathers, song, hunt with the black harehounds whom I should rather flee, but they could make me a gift of peace. But they do not do it, for they do not know what manner of man I am: a wise man does not lock the door of pardon, for to pardon is a fine victory in war.

You who hear in my scattered rhymes the sound of those sighs on which I fed my heart in my first youthful mistake, when I was in part another man from the one I am now; for the varied manner in which I weep and reflect there, amid vain hopes and vain grief, I hope to have pity, not only pardon, from whosoever by experience knows love.

Ma ben veggio or sì come al popol tutto
favola fui gran tempo: onde sovente
di me medesmo meco mi vergogno:
e del mio vaneggiar vergogna è 'l frutto,
e 'l pentirsi, e 'l conoscer chiaramente
che quanto piace al mondo è breve sogno.

La gola e 'l sonno e l'oziose piume
hanno del mondo ogni vertù sbandita;
ond'è dal corso suo quasi smarrita
nostra natura, vinta dal costume.
Ed è sì spento ogni benigno lume
del ciel, per cui s'informa umana vita,
che per cosa mirabile s'addita
chi vol far d'Elicona nascer fiume.

Qual vaghezza di lauro? qual di mirto?
«Povera e nuda vai, Filosofia,»
dice la turba al vil guadagno intesa.
Pochi compagni avrai per l'altra via;
tanto ti prego più, gentile spirto:
non lassar la magnanima tua impresa.

But I see clearly today how I was the talk of everyone for a long time, and for this often, within me, I grow ashamed of myself: and I see how shame is the fruit of my having strayed, and repentance, and the clear knowledge that whatever the world loves is a brief dream.

Gluttony and dullness and slothful couches have banished every virtue from the world; so that our nature, overcome by habit, has all but lost the way. And all the kindly lights, by which human life is quickened, are so extinguished in heaven, that he who wishes to lead a stream from Helicon is pointed out as a marvel.

Such desire for laurels? such desire for myrtle? 'Philosophy, you go along poor and naked,' say the crowd, bent on vile gain. You will have few companions on the other road; I beg you so much the more, gentle spirit, not to turn from your great-hearted undertaking.

Movesi il vecchierel canuto e bianco
del dolce loca ov'ha sua età fornita,
e da la famigliuola sbigottita
che vede il caro padre venir manco;
indi traendo poi l'antiquo fianco
per l'estreme giornate di sua vita,
quanto più pò col buon voler s'aita,
rotto da gli anni e dal camino stanco:

e viene a Roma, seguendo 'l desio,
per mirar la sembianza di Colui
ch'ancor lassù nel ciel vedere spera.
Così, lasso! talor vo cercand'io,
donna, quanto è possibile, in altrui
la disiata vostra forma vera.

Mille fiate, o dolce mia guerrera,
per aver co' begli occhi vostri pace,
v'aggio profferto il cor; ma a voi non piace
mirar sì basso con la mente altera:

The poor old man, grizzled and white, leaves the sweet place
where he has always kept himself, and leaves his frightened family
who see their dear father failing. Then dragging his aged limbs
through the last days of life, broken by the years and weary of
journeying, he takes what help he can from a good will;

and comes to Rome, pursuing his desire, to see the likeness of
Him whom he hopes to see above in heaven once more. So, alas!
do I sometimes go seeking, my lady, as far as I may, your desired
true form in others.

A thousand times, o my sweet warrior, to have peace with your
lovely eyes, I have offered you my heart; but you do not care, with
your proud mind, to look so low: and if perchance some other

e se di lui fors'altra donna spera,
vive in speranza debile e fallace:
mio, perchè sdegno ciò ch'a voi dispiace,
esser non può giammai così com'era.

Or s'io lo scaccio, ed e' non trova in voi
nell'esilio infelice alcun soccorso,
nè sa star sol, nè gire ov'altri 'l chiama
poria smarrire il suo natural corso;
che grave colpa fia d'ambeduo noi,
e tanto più di voi, quanto più v'ama.

S o l o e pensoso i più deserti campi
vo mesurando a passi tardi e lenti,
e gli occhi porto per fuggire intenti
ove vestigio uman l'arena stampi.
Altro schermo non trovo che mi scampi
dal manifesto accorger de le genti;
perchè ne gli atti d'allegrezza spenti
di fuor si legge com'io dentro avampi:

women should hope for that heart of mine, she lives in hope that is
weak and false: it can never be as it was, since I despise what does
not please you.

Now if I expel my heart, and it does not find any refuge in its
unhappy exile in you, nor knows how to live alone, nor to go
where others call, it might wander from its natural course; which
will be a grave offence in both of us, and more so in you, since it
loves you the more.

A l o n e and thoughtful, I go pacing the most deserted fields with
slow hesitant steps, and I am watchful so as to flee from any place
where human traces mark the sand. I find no other defence that
protects me from the open awareness of people; because they
can see from without, in my actions bereft of joy, how I inwardly
flame:

sì ch'io mi credo omai che monti e piagge,
e fiumi e selve sappian di che tempre
sia la mia vita, ch'è celata altrui.
Ma pur sì aspre vie nè sì selvagge
cercar non so ch'Amor non venga sempre
ragionando con meco, ed io con lui.

NON al suo amante più Diana piacque
quando, per tal ventura, tutta ignuda
la vide in mezzo delle gelid'acque;
ch'a me la pastorella alpestra e cruda,
posta a bagnar un leggiadretto velo,
ch'a l'aura il vago e biondo capel chiuda;
tal che mi fece or quand'egli arde il cielo,
tutto tremar d'un amoroso gelo.

PADRE del Ciel, dopo i perduti giorni,
dopo le notti vaneggiando spese
con quel fero desio ch'al cor s'accese
mirando gli atti per mio mal sì adorni;

so that now I believe that mountains and banks, and rivers and woods know what the tenour of my life is, which is hidden from others. And yet I cannot find any paths so harsh or wild that Love will not always come, talking with me the while, and I with him.

DIANA did not please her lover more when, by such a chance, he saw her naked in the midst of icy waters, than I was pleased by the hard mountain shepherdess, set there to wash a graceful veil that binds that lovely fair hair from the breeze; such that she made me tremble with an amorous chill, now when the heavens burn.

FATHER of Heaven, after the lost days, after the nights spent in straying with that fierce desire that burned in my heart when I looked upon those lineaments so lovely to my harm, may it please

piacciati omai, col tuo lume, ch'io torni
ad altra vita ed a più belle imprese;
sì ch'avendo le reti indarno tese,
il mio duro avversario se ne scorni.

Or volge, Signor mio, l'undecim'anno
ch'i' fui sommesso al dispietato giogo,
che sopra i più soggetti è più feroce.
Miserere del mio non degno affanno;
riduci i pensier vaghi a miglior luogo;
rammenta lor com'oggi fosti in croce.

Nova angeletta sovra l'ale accorta
scese dal cielo in sulla fresca riva
là ond'io passava sol per mio destino.
Poi che senza compagna e senza scorta
mi vide, un laccio che di seta ordiva,
tese fra l'erba ond'è verde il camino.
Allor fui preso; e non mi spiacque poi;
sì dolce lume uscìa degli occhi suoi.

you now, by your light, that I should turn to another life and
nobler endeavours; so that my hard adversary, having stretched his
nets in vain, may be discomfited.

Now the eleventh year comes round, my Lord, since I was bent
under the pitiless yoke which is crueller to the more submissive.
Have mercy on my unworthy suffering; bring back my wandering
thoughts to a better place; remind them how today you were on
the cross.

A wondrous angel borne on rapid wing came down from heaven
upon the fresh bank where I was passing alone, to my fate. When
she saw I was without fair companion or guide, she stretched a
noose she had wound of silk, in the grass with which the path was
green. Then was I taken; nor did it displease me after; so sweet a
light issued from her eyes.

CHIARE, fresche e dolci acque,
ove le belle membra
pose colei che sola a me par donna;
gentil ramo, ove piacque
(con sospir mi rimembra)
a lei di fare al bel fianco colonna;
erba e fior, che la gonna
leggiadra ricoverse
con l'angelico seno;
aere sacro sereno,
ov'Amor co' begli occhi il cor m'aperse:
date udienzia insieme
alle dolenti mie parole estreme.

S'egli è pur mio destino
(e il cielo in ciò s'adopra)
ch'Amor quest'occhi lagrimando chiuda,
qualche grazia il meschino
corpo fra voi ricopra,
e torni l'alma al proprio albergo ignuda.
La morte fia men cruda

CLEAR, fresh, and sweet waters, where she who alone to me seems woman rested her lovely limbs; gentle trunk, of which she liked (as I remember with sighs) to make a column for her lovely side; grass and flower, which the gay dress covered as well as the heavenly bosom; holy calm air, where Love opened my heart with those lovely eyes: give hearing all together to my last grieving words.

If it is my destiny (and heaven works for this) that Love should close these eyes even while they weep, may some kindness inter my miserable body in your midst, and may my soul return naked to its own abode. Death will be less cruel if I can go forward with

se questa spene porto
a quel dubbioso passo;
che lo spirito lasso
non poria mai in più riposato porto
nè 'n più tranquilla fossa
fuggir la carne travagliata e l'ossa.

Tempo verrà ancor forse,
ch'all'usato soggiorno
torni la fera bella e mansueta;
e là 'v'ella mi scorse
nel bendetto giorno,
volga la vista desiosa e lieta,
cercandomi; et, o pietà!
già terra infra le pietre
vedendo, Amor l'inspiri
in guisa che sospiri
sì dolcemente che mercè m'impetre,
e faccia forza al Cielo,
asciugandosi gli occhi col bel velo.

this hope to that uncertain pass; as my weary spirit could never fly from my troubled flesh and bones to a more restful haven or a quieter grave.

Perhaps a time will come again when this mild and lovely fierce one may come back to her accustomed haunt; and there, where she noticed me upon that blessed day, may turn her happy eager face to look for me; and, o pity! seeing me already earth among the stones, Love may inspire her to sigh so softly that she will obtain mercy for me, and have her way with Heaven, drying those eyes with that lovely veil.

Da' be' rami scendea
(dolce nella memoria)
una pioggia di fior sovra 'l suo grembo;
ed ella si sedea
umile in tanta gloria,
coverta già dell'amoroso nembo.
Qual fior cadea sul lembo,
qual su le trecce bionde,
ch'oro forbito e perle
eran quel dì a vederle;
qual si posava in terra, e qual su l'onde;
qual con un vago errore
girando, parea dir: qui regna Amore.

Quante volte diss'io
allor pien di spavento:
costei per fermo nacque in Paradiso!
Così carco d'obblio
il divin portamento
e 'l volto e le parole e 'l dolce riso
m'aveano, e sì diviso

From the lovely branches there came down (sweet in memory)
a rain of flowers into her lap, and she sat modest amid so great glory,
covered now by the loving shower. A flower fell upon her hem,
another on her fair hair which seemed polished gold and pearl that
day; one rested on the ground, and another upon the wave; one,
in charmed flight, turning as it fell, seemed to say: here Love
reigns.

How many times did I say then full of fear: she was born, for
certain, in Paradise! Her divine bearing and face and words had
so weighted me with forgetfulness and cut me off from the true

dall'immagine vera,
ch'i' dicea sospirando:
qui come venn'io, o quando?
credendo esser in Ciel, non là dov'era.
Da indi in qua mi piace
quest'erba sì, ch'altrove non ho pace.

Se tu avessi ornamenti quant' hai voglia,
potresti arditamente
uscir del bosco e gir infra la gente.

ITALIA mia, benchè 'l parlar sia indarno
alle piaghe mortali
che nel bel corpo tuo sì spesse veggio,
piacemi almen ch'e' miei sospir sian quali
spera 'l Tevero e l'Arno,
e 'l Po, dove doglioso e grave or seggio.
Rettor del ciel, io cheggio
che la pietà che ti condusse in terra,
ti volga al tuo diletto almo paese:
vedi, Signor cortese,
di che lievi cagion che crudel guerra;
e i cor, che 'ndura e serra

image of things that I said sighing: how did I come here, or when? believing myself in Heaven, not where I really was. From that time forth this grass has so pleased me that I find peace in no other place.

[Song], if you had as much ornament as you have desire, you could leave the wood boldly and go among people.

MY Italy, although talking cannot heal the mortal wounds that I see so frequent in your fair body, I am glad that at least my sighs are such as Tiber and the Arno and the Po (where I now sit sorrowful and heavy) hope for. Governor of Heaven, I ask that the pity which brought you upon earth may turn you now to your beloved kindly country. See, gracious Lord, how cruel a war from how

Marte superbo e fero,
apri tu, Padre, e 'ntenerisci e snoda;
ivi fa che 'l tuo vero
(qual io mi sia) per la mia lingua s'oda.

Voi, cui Fortuna ha posto in mano il freno
delle belle contrade,
di che nulla pietà par che vi stringa,
che fan qui tante pellegrine spade?
Perchè 'l verde terreno
del barbarico sangue si depinga?
Vano error vi lusinga;
poco vedete, e parvi veder molto;
che 'n cor venale amor cercate o fede.
Qual più gente possede,
colui è più da' suoi nemici avvolto.
O diluvio raccolto
di che deserti strani
per inondar i nostri dolci campi!
Se dalle proprie mani
questo n'avven, or che fia che ne scampi?

slight causes: and do you open, Father, and soften and free the
hearts that proud, fierce Mars hardens and holds fast: there let your
truth be heard (whatever I may be) from my tongue.

O you, in whose hands Fortune has put the bridle of the fair
regions, no pity of which seems to restrain you, what are so many
alien swords doing here? Why is the green earth painted with bar-
barian blood? A vain mistake is deluding you; little you see and
think you see a lot; since you look for love and faith in mercenary
hearts. He who possesses most people is most surrounded by his
enemies. O deluge borne here from what foreign deserts to flood
our pleasant fields! If this comes about by our own hands, who will
there be, then, to save us?

Ben provide Natura al nostro stato
quando dell'Alpi schermo
pose fra noi e la tedesca rabbia;
ma 'l desir cieco e 'ncontra 'l suo ben fermo
s'è poi tanto ingegnato,
ch'al corpo sano ha procurato scabbia.
Or dentro ad una gabbia
fere selvagge e mansuete gregge
s'annidan sì che sempre il miglior geme:
ed è questo del seme,
per più dolor, del popol senza legge,
al qual, come si legge,
Mario aperse sì 'l fianco,
che memoria dell'opra anco non langue,
quando, assetato e stanco,
non più bevve del fiume acqua, che sangue.

Nature provided excellently for our state when she placed the shield of the Alps between us and the German rage: but blind desire, set against its own good, has now devised so well that it has brought sores to the healthy body. Now, in the one cage, wild beasts and submissive flocks couch, so that the better has always to weep: and this is the doing, to our greater grief, of the descendants of that lawless people* whose side, as we read, was laid open by Marius so savagely that the memory of the deed has not languished, when, tired and thirsty, he did drink water from the river so much as blood.

---

* The Teutones.

Cesare taccio, che per ogni piaggia
fece l'erbe sanguigne
di lor vene, ove 'l nostro ferro mise.
Or par, non so per che stelle maligne,
che 'l Cielo in odio n'aggia:
vostra mercè cui tanto si commise:
vostre voglie divise
guastan del mondo la più bella parte.
Qual colpa, qual giudicio o qual destino,
fastidire il vicino
povero; e le fortune afflitte e sparte
perseguire; e 'n disparte
cercar gente, e gradire
che sparga 'l sangue e venda l'alma a prezzo?
Io parlo per ver dire,
non per odio d'altrui nè per disprezzo.

I keep silent about Caesar who, on every shore where he took our arms, made the grass bloody from their veins. Now it seems, I know not by what evil stars, that Heaven hates us: thanks to you to whom so much has been committed: your divided wills lay waste the fairest part of the world. What guilt, what judgement, or what destiny, drives you to worry your poor neighbour, and to hunt out his threatened and scattered goods, and recruit your soldiers from foreign countries, and be glad that blood should be shed, and the soul traded for a price? I talk to speak the truth, and not from hate or contempt of others.

Nè v'accorgete ancor, per tante prove,
del bavarico inganno,
che, alzando 'l dito, con la morte scherza?
Peggio è lo strazio, al mio parer, che 'l danno.
Ma 'l vostro sangue piove
più largamente; ch'altr'ira vi sferza.
Dalla mattina a terza
di voi pensate, e vederete come
tien caro altrui chi tien sè così vile.
Latin sangue gentile,
sgombra da te queste dannose some:
non far idolo un nome
vano, senza soggetto:
che 'l furor di lassù, gente ritrosa,
vincerne d'intelletto,
peccato è nostro e non natural cosa.

And are you not yet made aware, by such repeated experience, of the deceit of the Bavarians who raise a finger and toy with death? The dishonour, as I see it, is worse than the harm. But your blood rains more widely; as a different anger whips you on. Take thought of yourselves from matins to the third hour, and you will see how dear the man holds others who holds himself so vile. Noble Latin blood, shake from yourself these hurtful burdens: do not make an idol of an empty, groundless name: that the fury from up there, a backward people, overcomes us in intelligence is our failing and nothing natural.

Non è questo 'l terren ch'i' toccai pria?
Non è questo 'l mio nido,
ove nudrito fui sì dolcemente?
Non è questa la patria in ch'io mi fido,
madre benigna e pia,
che copre l'uno e l'altro mio parente?
Per Dio, questo la mente
talor vi mova; e con pietà guardate
le lagrime del popol doloroso,
che sol da voi riposo,
dopo Dio, spera: e, pur che voi mostriate
segno alcun di pietate,
virtù contra furore
prenderà l'arme; e fia 'l combatter corto;
che l'antico valore
nell'italici cor non è ancor morto.

Signor, mirate come 'l tempo vola,
e sì come la vita
fugge, e la morte n'è sovra le spalle.
Voi siete or qui: pensate alla partita;
chè l'alma ignuda e sola
conven ch'arrive a quel dubbioso calle.
Al passar questa valle,

Is this not the ground I first touched? Is not this my nest, where I was so sweetly nurtured? Is this not the native land in which I trust, kind, devout mother, who covers both parents of mine? In God's name, let this sometimes move your minds; look with pity upon the tears of the sorrowful people who, after God, hope for rest from you alone: and, as long as you show some sign of pity, virtue will take arms against fury; and the fighting shall be brief; for the ancient valour is not yet dead in Italian hearts.

My Lords, see how time is winging, and how life flies, and death is at our shoulders. You are now here: think of your leave-taking; for the soul must needs reach that uncertain pass, naked and alone.

piacciavi porre giù l'odio e lo sdegno,
venti contrari alla vita serena;
e quel che 'n altrui pena
tempo si spende, in qualche atto più degno,
o di mano o d'ingegno,
in qualche bella lode,
in qualche onesto studio si converta:
così quaggiù si gode,
e la strada del ciel si trova aperta.

Canzone, io t'ammonisco
che tua ragion cortesemente dica;
perchè fra gente altera ir ti conviene,
e le voglie son piene
già dell'usanza pessima ed antica
del ver sempre nemica.
Proverai tua ventura
fra magnanimi pochi, a chi 'l ben piace:
di' lor: chi m'assicura?
I 'vo gridando: pace, pace, pace.

To go through this valley, may it please you to lay down hate and disdain, adverse winds for the life of calm; and let the time which is being spent in causing others pain be turned to some worthier deed of hand or mind, to some fine, praiseworthy thing, to some just endeavour; in this way one rejoices here below, and finds the way to heaven open.

My song, I charge you that you give out your meaning courteously, because you must go among proud people; and minds are now full of the worst ancient prejudices, always the enemy of truth. You will take your chance among the magnanimous few, who love the good. Say to them: Who will champion me? I keep crying: peace, peace, peace.

Dɪ pensier in pensier, di monte in monte
mi guida Amor; ch'ogni segnato calle
provo contrario alla tranquilla vita.
Se 'n solitaria piaggia, rivo o fonte,
se 'n fra duo poggi siede ombrosa valle,
ivi s'acqueta l'alma sbigottita;
e, com'Amor la 'nvita,
or ride or piagne or teme or s'assicura:
e 'l volto che lei segue, ov'ella il mena,
si turba e rasserena,
ed in un esser picciol tempo dura;
onde alla vista uom di tal vita esperto
diria: questi arde, e di suo stato è incerto.

Per alti monti e per selve aspre trovo
qualche riposo; ogni abitato loco
è nemico mortal degli occhi miei.
A ciascun passo nasce un pensier novo
della mia donna, che sovente in gioco
gira il tormento ch'i' porto per lei;
et appena vorrei

Fʀᴏᴍ thought to thought, from mountain to mountain Love leads me; since I find every marked path hostile to the life of quiet. If there is a stream or fountain on a lonely slope, if, between two hills, lies a shady vale, there the frightened soul calms itself: and, as Love bids, now laughs, now weeps, now fears, now is assured: and my face which follows the soul, wherever it leads, is disturbed and clears, and stays little time in the one state; so that a man learned in such a life would say on seeing me: This one burns, and is uncertain of his fortune.

In high mountains and in wild woods I find some rest; each inhabited place is the mortal enemy of my eyes. With each pace some new thought of my mistress is born, which often turns the torment I bear for her to joy; and as soon as I would change my sweet and

cangiar questo mio viver dolce amaro,
ch'i' dico: forse ancor ti serva Amore
ad un tempo migliore;
forse a te stesso vile, altrui se' caro:
et in questa trapasso sospirando:
Or potrebb'esser vero? or come? or quando?

Ove porge ombra un pino alto od un colle,
talor m'arresto, e pur nel primo sasso
disegno con la mente il suo bel viso.
Poi ch'a me torno, trovo il petto molle
della pietate; ed allor dico: ahi lasso,
dove se' giunto; ed onde se' diviso!
Ma mentre tener fiso
posso al primo pensier la mente vaga,
e mirar lei, ed obbliar me stesso,
sento Amor sì da presso
che del suo proprio error l'alma s'appaga:
in tante parti e sì bella la veggio,
che se l'error durasse, altro non cheggio.

bitter life, then I say: perhaps Love is still preserving you for a better time; perhaps, though hateful to yourself, you are dear to another: and, sighing the while, I go on: But could this be true? but how? but when?

Where a tall pine tree or a hill offers shade, sometimes I stop, and on the nearest stone trace mentally her lovely face. When I come to myself again, I find my breast wet from tenderness; and then I say: Alas, what have you come to, and what have you left behind? But as long as I can keep my mind steadily upon that first thought, and gaze on her and forget myself, I feel Love so closely that my mind is ravished by its own delusion. I see her in so many places and her so lovely, that were the deception to last, I ask nothing more.

I' l'ho più volte (or chi fia che mel creda?)
nell'acqua chiara e sopra l'erba verde
veduta viva, e nel troncon d'un faggio,
e 'n bianca nube sì fatta che Leda
avria ben detto che sua figlia perde,
come stella che 'l Sol copre col raggio:
e quanto in più selvaggio
loco mi trovo e 'n più deserto lido,
tanto più bella il mio pensier l'adombra.
Poi quando il vero sgombra
quel dolce error, pur lì medesmo assido
me freddo, pietra morta in pietra viva,
in guisa d'uom che pensi e pianga e scriva.

Ove d'altra montagna ombra non tocchi,
verso 'l maggior e 'l più spedito giogo,
tirar mi suol un desiderio intenso:
indi i miei danni a misurar con gli occhi
comincio, e 'ntanto lagrimando sfogo
di dolorosa nebbia il cor condenso,
allor ch'i miro e penso,

I have many times (now who will believe me?) seen her vividly
in clear water or on green grass, and in the trunk of a beech tree
and on a white cloud, so fashioned that Leda would have surely
said that her daughter is eclipsed, like a star that the Sun obscures
with its rays: and the wilder the place, the lonelier the strand where
I happen to be, so much the lovelier does my thought shadow her
forth. Then when the truth clears away that sweet deception, still I
sit there the same, sit cold, dead stone on living stone, like a man
who thinks and weeps and writes.

An intense desire continually draws me to the loftiest, most
advantageous crest which the shadow of other mountains does not
touch. From there I begin to judge my sufferings with my eyes,
and weep then, and ease the heart, oppressed by a sorrowful mist,
when I see and think what a space separates me from that lovely

quanta aria dal bel viso mi diparte,
che sempre m'è sì presso e sì lontano.
Poscia fra me pian piano:
Che fai tu lasso? forse in quella parte
or di tua lontananza si sospira:
ed in questo pensier l'alma respira.

Canzone, oltra quell'alpe,
là dove 'l ciel è più sereno e lieto,
mi rivedrai sovr'un ruscel corrente,
ove l'aura si sente
d'un fresco ed odorifero laureto.
Ivi è 'l mio cor, e quella che 'l m'invola:
qui veder puoi l'immagine mia sola.

IN qual parte del ciel, in qual idea
era l'esempio, onde Natura tolse
quel bel viso leggiadro, in ch'ella volse
mostrar qua giù quanto lassù potea?
Qual ninfa in fonti, in selve mai qual dea,
chiome d'oro sì fino a l'aura sciolse?
Quando un cor tante in sè vertuti accolse?
Ben che la somma è di mia morte rea.

face, which is always so near to me and so far. Then softly to my-self: What are you doing, wretch? Perhaps over there she sighs for your being far away: and in this thought the soul breathes.

My song, beyond that mount, where the sky is clearer and more glad, you will see me again by a running stream where the breeze smells of a fresh and fragrant laurel grove. There is my heart, and she who steals it from me: here you can see only my effigy.

IN what part of heaven, in what celestial form was the original from which Nature took that glad, lovely face by which it wanted to show down here how much on high could be created? What nymph in fountain, or in the woods what goddess, ever loosed to the breeze hair of such fine gold? When did a heart gather into itself so many virtues? Although their sum is guilty of my death.

Per divina bellezza indarno mira
chi gli occhi de costei già mai non vide
come soavemente ella gli gira;
non sa come Amor sana, e come ancide,
chi non sa come dolce ella sospira,
e come dolce parla, e dolce ride.

Or che 'l ciel e la terra e 'l vento tace,
e le fere e gli augelli il sonno affrena,
notte 'l carro stellato in giro mena,
e nel suo letto il mar senz'onda giace;
veggio, penso, ardo, piango; e chi mi sface
sempre m'è innanzi per mia dolce pena:
guerra è 'l mio stato, d'ira e di duol piena;
e sol di lei pensando ho qualche pace.

Così sol d'una chiara fonte viva
move 'l dolce e l'amaro ond'io mi pasco;
una man sola mi risana e punge.
E perchè 'l mio martir non giunga a riva,
mille volte il dì moro e mille nasco;
tanto dalla salute mia son lunge.

He looks in vain for divine beauty who never saw the eyes of
this fair as she gently turns them; nor does he know how Love
heals and kills who does not know how sweetly she sighs, and how
sweetly talks, and sweetly laughs.

Now that the heavens and the earth and the wind is silent, and the
wild beasts and the birds are bridled by sleep, night leads its starry
car upon its round, and, without one wave, the sea lies in its bed;
I see, think, burn, and weep; and she who is my undoing is always
before me to my sweet pain: my state is one of war, full of rage and
grief; and only in thinking of her do I have some peace.

So from one clear and living fountain the sweet and the bitter
move upon which I feed; one single hand heals and pierces me. And
so that my suffering may not come to shore, I die a thousand times
each day, a thousand I am born; so far am I from my salvation.

Pien d'un vago pensier, che mi desvia
da tutti gli altri, e fammi al mondo ir solo,
ad or ad or a me stesso m'involo,
pur lei cercando che fuggir devria:
e veggiola passar sì dolce e ria,
che l'alma trema per levarsi a volo;
tal d'armati sospir conduce stuolo
questa bella d'Amor nemica e mia.

Ben, s'io non erro, di pietate un raggio
scorgo fra 'l nubiloso altero ciglio,
che 'n parte rasserena il cor doglioso:
allor raccolgo l'alma, e poi ch'i' aggio
di scovrirle il mio mal preso consiglio,
tanto le ho a dir che 'ncominciar non oso.

Per mezz'i boschi inospiti e selvaggi
onde vanno a gran rischio uomini et arme,
vo securo io; chè non pò spaventarme
altri che 'l Sol ch'à d'Amor vivo i raggi.

Full of one fond thought that separates me from all other men,
and makes me go through the world alone, from time to time I am
rapt out of myself, while I look for her whom I should fly from.
And I see her go by so sweet and deadly that my soul trembles to
take flight, she leads such a troop of armed sighs with her, this
beautiful enemy of Love and mine.

Truly, if I am not mistaken, I make out a ray of pity coming
from that high cloudy brow which in part brightens my sad heart.
Then I summon up my soul again, and when I am about to reveal
my ill-advised choice to her, I have so much to tell her that I do not
dare begin.

Through the heart of inhospitable, wild woods where men with
arms go at great risk, I go secure; for nothing can frighten me but
that Sun which draws its living rays from Love. And I go singing

E vo cantando (o penser miei non saggi!)
lei che 'l ciel non poria lontana farme;
ch'i' l'ho negli occhi; e veder seco parme
donne e donzelle, e sono abeti e faggi!

Parme d'udirla, udendo i rami e l'ôre
e le frondi e gli augei lagnarsi, e l'acque
mormorando fuggir per l'erba verde.
Raro un silenzio, un solitario orrore
d'ombrosa selva mai tanto mi piacque;
se non che dal mio Sol troppo si perde.

O CAMERETTA, che già fosti un porto
a le gravi tempeste mie diurne,
fonte se' or di lagrime notturne,
che 'l dì celate per vergogna porto.
O letticciuol, che requie eri e conforto
in tanti affanni, di che dogliose urne
ti bagna Amor, con quelle mani eburne,
solo ver' me crudeli a sì gran torto!

(o my foolish thoughts!) her whom heaven cannot make distant
from me; for I have her in my eyes; and seem to see women and
girls with her, and they are firs and beech-trees!

I seem to hear her, hearing the branches and the breeze and the
leaves and the birds complaining, and the waters murmuring as they
flee through the green grass. Rarely did a silence, a lonely awfulness
of shady woodland so please me; except that too much of my Sun
is meanwhile lost.

O LITTLE room that were once a harbour from those severe daily
tempests of mine, you are now a fount of nightly tears which by
day I bear hid for shame. O little bed that were repose and comfort
in so many torments, from what sorrowful urns does Love bathe
you, with those ivory hands that are cruel to me alone – so wrongly!

Nè pur il mio secreto, e 'l mio riposo
fuggo, ma più me stesso, e 'l mio pensèro,
che, seguendol talor, levommi a volo;
e 'l vulgo, a me nemico, et odioso
(chi 'l pensò mai?), per mio refugio chero:
tal paura ho di ritrovarmi solo.

Rotta è l'alta Colonna e 'l verde Lauro
che facean ombra al mio stanco pensero;
perdut'ho quel che ritrovar non spero
dal borea all'austro, o dal mar indo al mauro.
Tolto m'hai, Morte, il mio doppio tesauro,
che mi fea viver lieto e gire altero;
e ristorar nol può terra nè impero,
nè gemma oriental nè forza d'auro.

I do not flee from privacy and rest, but rather from myself and
my own thoughts which, when I used to follow them, sometimes
raised me to flight; and I desire the crowd, hostile and hateful to me
(who would ever have thought it?), for my refuge: so great a fear
have I of being alone again.

Shattered is the high column * and the green Laurel † which
cast shade for my tired thoughts; I have lost what I do not hope to
find again from Boreas to Auster, from the Indian sea to the
Mauritanian. You have taken my double treasure from me, Death,
which made me go about so lightsome and proud; and the earth
cannot, nor empire, nor eastern gem, nor power of gold, make good
my loss.

---

* his protector, Colonna;   † his lady, Laura
(who had both died shortly before)

Ma se consentimento è di destino,
che poss'io più se no aver l'alma trista,
umidi gli occhi sempre e 'l viso chino?
O nostra vita, ch'è sì bella in vista,
com' perde agevolmente in un mattino
quel che 'n molt'anni a gran pena s'acquista!

GLI occhi di ch'io parlai sì caldamente,
e le braccia e le mani e i piedi e 'l viso
che m'avean sì da me stesso diviso
e fatto singular dall'altra gente;
le crespe chiome d'or puro lucente,
e 'l lampeggiar dell'angelico riso
che solean far in terra un paradiso,
poca polvere son, che nulla sente.

Ed io pur vivo; onde mi doglio e sdegno,
rimaso senza 'l lume ch'amai tanto,
in gran fortuna e 'n disarmato legno.
Or sia qui fine al mio amoroso canto:
secca è la vena dell'usato ingegno,
e la cetera mia rivolta in pianto.

But if this is with the consent of fate, what can I do but bear a sad soul, wet eyes and bent head for ever? O our life which is so fair outwardly, how easily does it lose in a morning what in many years with great struggling is gained!

THE eyes of which I so warmly spoke, and the arms and the hands and the feet and the face which had so separated me from myself, and marked me out from other people; the waving hair of pure and shining gold, and the flashing of the angelic smile which used to make a paradise on earth, are now a little dust which feels no mortal thing.

And yet I live; at which I grieve and despise myself, left as I am without the light I so loved, in a great storm, in a disabled ship. Now let there be here an end to my loving song: dry is the vein of accustomed skill, and my lyre all turned to weeping.

Levommi il mio pensèr in parte ov'era
quella ch'io cerco, e non ritrovo in terra:
ivi, fra lor che 'l terzo cerchio serra,
la rividi più bella, e meno altera.
Per man mi prese, e disse: in questa spera
sarai ancor meco, se 'l desir non erra;
i' so' colei che ti die' tanta guerra,
e compie' mia giornata inanzi sera.

Mio ben non cape in intelletto umano:
te solo aspetto, e quel che tanto amasti
e là giuso è rimaso, il mio bel velo.
Deh, perchè tacque ed allargò la mano?
Ch'al suon de' detti sì pietosi e casti
poco mancò ch'io non rimasi in cielo.

Quel rosignuol che sì soave piagne
forse suoi figli o sua cara consorte,
di dolcezza empie il cielo e le campagne
con tante note sì pietose e scorte;

My thoughts raised me to a place where was she whom I seek and
find no more on earth: there, among those whom the third circle
encloses, I saw her again, more lovely and less proud. She took me
by the hand, and said: you will be with me again in this sphere, if
my desire is not misled; I am she who inflicted such war upon you,
and who completed my day before evening.

My goodness is not compassed by human understanding: you
alone I wait for, and, what you so much loved that stays below, my
lovely veil. O, why did she go silent and open her hand? For at the
sound of words so pitying and pure little more was wanted for me
to have stayed in heaven.

That nightingale that is so softly weeping perhaps for its children
or its dear mate, fills the heavens and the fields with the sweetness of
so many pitiful and brilliant notes, and all night, it seems, accom-

e tutta notte par che m'accompagne
e mi rammente la mia dura sorte:
ch'altri che me non ho di cui mi lagne;
che 'n Dee non credev'io regnasse Morte.

O che lieve è ingannar chi s'assecura!
Que' duo bei lumi, assai più che 'l Sol chiari,
chi pensò mai veder far terra oscura?
Or conosch'io che mia fera ventura
vuol che vivendo e lagrimando impari
come nulla quaggiù diletta e dura.

Li angeli eletti e l'anime beate
cittadine del cielo, il primo giorno
che Madonna passò, le fur intorno
piene di maraviglia e di pietate.
Che luce è questa, qual nova beltate?
dicean tra lor; perch'abito sì adorno
dal mondo errante a quest'alto soggiorno
non salì mai in tutta questa etate.

panies me, and reminds me of my hard fate: for I have none for
whom to grieve but myself; because I did not believe that Death
could reign in Goddesses.

O how easy it is, the deceiving of one who feels secure! Who
would ever have thought to see two lovely lights, clearer far than
the sun, become dark earth? Now I know that my savage fate is to
make me learn, living and weeping, that nothing here below delights and lasts.

THE chosen angels and the blessed souls, citizens of heaven, on
the first day that my lady passed, gathered about her full of wonder
and deference. What light is this, and what new beauty? they said
to one another: since never in this age did so fair a form mount
from the wandering earth to this high rest.

Ella contenta aver cangiato albergo,
si paragona pur coi più perfetti;
e parte ad or ad or si volge a tergo
mirando s'io la seguo, e par ch'aspetti:
ond'io voglie e pensier tutti al ciel ergo;
perch'io l'odo pregar pur ch'i' m'affretti.

I' vo piangendo i miei passati tempi
i quai posi in amar cosa mortale,
senza levarmi a volo, avend'io l'ale
per dare forse di me non bassi esempi.
Tu, che vedi i miei mali indegni ed empi,
re del cielo, invisibile, immortale,
soccorri all'alma disviata e frale,
e 'l suo difetto di tua grazia adempi:

sì che, s'io vissi in guerra ed in tempesta,
mora in pace et in porto; e se la stanza
fu vana, almen sia la partita onesta.
A quel poco di viver che m'avanza
ed al morir degni esser tua man presta.
Tu sai ben che 'n altrui non ho speranza.

She, happy to have changed her abode, stands equal with the most perfect; and meanwhile, from time to time, she turns and looks back to see if I am following her, and it seems that she is waiting: so that I raise all my thoughts and wishes heavenwards; because I hear her praying that I should hasten.

I keep weeping over my past which I spent in loving a mortal thing, without lifting myself to flight, although I had wings to give perhaps no mean proof of myself. You, who see my unworthy and wicked ills, king of heaven, unseen, everlasting, help this soul, lost and frail, and make good its infirmity with your grace:

so that, if I have lived in war and tempest, I may die in peace and in port; and, if my sojourn was vain, my leave taking at least may be just. May your hand deign to be near in that little of life which is left to me and in my death. You know full well that I place no hope in any other being.

FAZIO DEGLI UBERTI

Io guardo i crespi e li biondi capelli,
de’ quali ha fatto per me rete Amore;
d’un fil di perle e quando d’un bel fiore
per me’ pigliare i’ trovo che gli adesca.
E poi riguardo dentro gli occhi belli,
che passan per li miei dentro dal core
con tanto vivo e lucente splendore,
che propriamente par che d’un sol esca.
Virtù mostra che in lor ognor più cresca,
ond’io, che sì leggiadri star gli veggio,
così fra me sospirando ragiono:
– Ohmè! perchè non sono
a solo a sol con lei ov’io la cheggio?
sì ch’io potessi quella treccia bionda
disfarla a onda a onda
e far de’ suoi begli occhi a miei due specchi,
che lucon sì che non trovan parecchi.

I LOOK upon her fair and waving locks, of which Love has made
a net for me; I find that to catch me more easily he sometimes
baits it with a string of pearls and sometimes with a fine flower.
And then I look into her lovely eyes, which pass through mine into
my heart, with a splendour so bright and vivid that it really seems
to come from a sun. They show a goodness that grows in them constantly, so that I, to whom they are so comely, say to myself with
sighs: ‘Oh! why am I not alone with her, alone where I wish to be?
so that I may undo that fair head of hair wave by wave, and make
her eyes two mirrors to mine, so shining as not to meet their
equal.’

Poi guardo l'amorosa e bella bocca,
la spaziosa fronte e 'l vago piglio
e i bianchi denti, il dritto naso e 'l ciglio
pulito e brun, tal che dipinto pare.
E 'l vago mio pensier allor mi tocca
dicendo: – Vedi allegro dar di piglio
dentro a quel labbro sottile e vermiglio,
dov'ogni dolce e saporito pare!
E odi suo vezzoso ragionare
quanto ben mostra, morbida e pietosa,
e come 'l suo parlar parte e divide.
Vedi, quand'ella ride
che passa per diletto ogn'altra cosa! –
Così di quella bocca il pensier mio
mi sprona, perchè io
non ho nel mondo cosa ch'io non desse
a tal ch'un sì con buon voler dicesse.

Poi guardo la sua svelta e bianca gola
com'esce ben delle spalle e del petto;
il mento tondo, fesso, piccioletto,
tal che più bel con l'occhio non disegno.

Then I look at her beautiful loving mouth, her broad forehead
and fond expression, white teeth, straight nose, and comely brown
eyebrows, such that they seem painted. And an amorous thought
then recurs to me with these words: 'Think how gladdening it
would be to catch fast within that fine, scarlet lip, where every
sweetness and savour seems to be. And listen to her charming
speech, how well it sounds, soft and compassionate, and how she
breaks and orders her talk. See, when she laughs, how she surpasses
every other thing in delight!' In this way my thought, playing
about her mouth, spurs me on, for I possess nothing in this world
that I would not give so that it might say 'yes' with a good will.

Then I look at her slender, white throat and the exquisite way it
rises from her shoulders and her bosom; her round chin, small and
dimpled, such that the eye can discern no better. And that thought

E quel pensier che sol per lei m'invola
mi dice: – Vedi allegro e bel diletto
aver quel collo fra le braccia stretto
e fare in quella gola un picciol segno! –
Poi soppragiunge e dice: – Apri lo ingegno;
se le parti di fuor son così belle,
l'altre che den valer che dentro copre!
chè sol per le belle opre,
che fanno in ciel il sole e l'altre stelle
dentro da lor si crede 'l paradiso.
Dunque, se miri fiso
pensar ben dei ch'ogni terren piacere
si trova dove tu non puoi vedere.

Poi guardo i bracci suoi distesi e grossi,
la bianca mano morbida e pulita,
le belle lunghe e sottilette dita
vaghe di quello anel che l'un tien cinto.
E 'l mio pensier mi dice: – Or se tu fossi
dentro a que' bracci, fra quella partita,
tanto diletto avrebbe la tua vita,
che dir per me non si potrebbe il quinto.
Vedi ch'ogni suo membro par dipinto,

which puts me in ecstasy for her sake alone says to me: – Think of
the fine, gay delight of having that neck tight in your arms and of
making a little mark on that throat! Then it goes on and says:
'Stir your imagination; if the outward parts are so lovely, how rare
must be the others which she hides! for paradise is believed to be
beyond the sun and other stars simply because of the lovely effect
that these have in heaven. So, if you gaze steadily, you will think
that every earthly bliss lies where your eye cannot go.'

Then I look at her full and rounded arms, the hand, white, soft,
and fine, the lovely, long slender fingers heightened by the ring
which holds one of them in its circlet. And my thought says: 'Now
if you were in those arms, in their embrace, your life would know
such joy that I could not express the hundredth part of it. See how
every one of her limbs seems painted shapely and large as is right for

formoso e grande quanto a lei s'avviene,
con un colore angelico di perla;
graziosa a vederla
e disdegnosa dove si convene,
umile e vergognosa e temperata;
e sempre a virtù guata,
e in fra' suoi be' costumi un atto regna
che d'ogni riverenza la fa degna.

Soave va a guisa di pavone,
diritta sopra sè com'una grua;
guarda che propriamente ben par sua
quant'esser può donnesca leggiadria.
– E se ne vuoi veder viva ragione, –
dice il pensier – guardi la mente tua
ben fissamente allor ch'ella s'indua
con donna che leggiadra e bella sia:
chè, come par che fugga e vada via
dinanzi al sole ogni altra chiarezza,
così costei ogni adornezza isface.
Vedi se ella piace
ch'amore è tanto quanto sua bellezza

her, with an angelic hue of pearl; pleasant in her bearing and scorn-
ful when it is seemly, humble and shy and mild; and she looks constantly to virtue, and a grace reigns in her fine ways that makes her
worthy of every deference.'

Soft she walks in the manner of a peacock, holding herself upright as the crane does; see how everything of womanly gaiety
seems hers by right. 'And if you wish to see the living proof of this,'
my thought says, 'keep your attention on her when she is with a
woman who is beautiful and gay: for, as every other brightness
seems to fly and vanish before the sun, so does this fair vanquish
every other beauty. Judge if she is pleasant when love is no more

e la somma bontà che in lei si trova.
Quel ch'a lei piace e giova
è sol d'onesta e di gentil usanza,
chè sol in suo ben far prende speranza.

Canzon, tu puoi ben dir sicuramente
che, poi ch'al mondo bella donna nacque,
nessun mai non piacque
generalmente quanto fa costei;
perchè si trova in lei
biltà di corpo e d'anima bontade,
fuor che le manca un poco di pietade.

GIOVANNI BOCCACCIO

VETRO son fatti i fiumi, ed i ruscelli
gli serra di fuor ora la freddura;
vestiti son i monti e la pianura
di bianca neve e nudi gli arbuscelli,
l'erbette morte, e non cantan gli uccelli
per la stagion contraria a lor natura;
borea soffia, ed ogni creatura
sta chiusa per lo freddo ne' sua ostelli.

than her beauty and the excelling good which is in her. What she
likes and indulges is always honest and seemly, and she puts her
hope solely in acting rightly.'

My song, you can say with certainty that since beautiful woman
was born into the world, none has found such universal favour as
this one has, because in her there is both beauty of body and goodness of soul, only she somewhat lacks sympathy.

THE rivers have turned to glass, and the cold now locks the streams
from without; the mountains and the plains are clad in white snow,
and the trees are bare, the grass dead, and the birds do not sing because of the season inimical to their nature; the north wind blows,
and every creature stays, because of the cold, shut fast in its abode.

Ed io, dolente, solo ardo ed incendo
in tanto foco, che quel di Vulcano
a rispetto non è una favilla;
e giorno e notte chiero, a giunta mano,
alquanto d'acqua il mio signor, piangendo,
nè ne posso impetrar sol una stilla.

In morte del Petrarca

OR sei salito, caro signor mio,
nel regno, al quale ancor salire aspetta
ogn'anima da Dio a quell'eletta,
nel suo partir di questo mondo rio;
or se' colà, dove spesso il desio
ti tirò già per veder Lauretta,
or sei dove la mia bella Fiammetta
siede con lei nel cospetto di Dio.

Or con Sennuccio e con Cino e con Dante
vivi, sicuro d'eterno riposo,
mirando cose da noi non intese.
Deh, s'a grado ti fui nel mondo errante,
tirami drieto a te, dove gioioso
veggia colei che pria d'amor m'accese.

And I alone, grieving, burn and flame so fiercely, that Vulcan's
fire was not a spark to this one of mine; and day and night I beg,
with joined hands, weeping the while, for a little water from my
lord, nor can I procure one single drop.

Upon the Death of Petrarch

NOW have you gone up, my dear lord, to the realm whither every
soul chosen by God for that honour, trusts to ascend on leaving this
wicked world: now you are where your desire drew you frequently
in the past, to see Laura, now you are where my lovely Fiammetta
sits with her in the sight of God.

Now you live with Sennuccio and Cino and Dante, sure of
eternal rest, looking on things not comprehended by us. O, if I was
pleasant to you in the wandering world, draw me after you, where,
glad, I might see her who first fired me with love.

Dal «Decameron»

(Giornata II)

Amor, s'io posso uscir de' tuoi artigli,
appena creder posso
che alcuno altro uncin mai più mi pigli.

Io entrai giovanetta en la tua guerra,
quella credendo somma e dolce pace,
e ciascuna mia arme posi in terra,
come sicuro chi si fida face;
tu, disleal tiranno aspro e rapace,
tosto mi fosti addosso
con le tue armi e co' crudel roncigli.

Poi, circondata dalle tue catene,
a quel che nacque per la morte mia,
piena d'amare lagrime e di pene
presa mi desti, ed hammi in sua balìa;
ed è sì cruda la sua signoria,
che già mai non l'ha mosso
sospir nè pianto alcun che m'assottigli.

From the 'Decameron'

(The Second Day)

Love, if I can get free from your claws, I can hardly imagine any
other hook will ever take me.

I went into your war when young, thinking it would be the
highest peace and sweet, and laid every one of my arms on the
ground, as confidently as one who trusts; dishonourable, harsh, and
thieving tyrant, you seized upon me immediately with your arms
and cruel hooks.

Then, wound in your chains, you gave me captive, full of tears
and griefs, to him who was born for my death, and he has me in
thrall; and his lordship is so brutal that he has never once been
moved by any of the sighing or weeping that wastes me.

Li prieghi miei tutti glien porta il vento:
nullo n'ascolta nè ne vuole udire;
per che ognora cresce il mio tormento,
onde 'l viver m'è noi' nè so morire;
deh! dolgati, signor, del mio languire;
fa' tu quel ch'io non posso:
dalmi legato dentro a' tuoi vincigli.

Se questo far non vuogli, almeno sciogli
i legami annodati da speranza;
deh! io ti priego, signor, che tu vogli:
chè, se tu 'l fai, ancor porto fidanza
di tornar bella qual fu mia usanza,
ed il dolor rimosso,
di bianchi fiori ornarmi e di vermigli.

FRANCO SACCHETTI

Di poggio in poggio e di selva in foresta,
come falcon che da signor villano
di man si leva e fugge di lontano,

The wind bears all my prayers to him: he will not hear or consider them; thus my anguish increases all the time, so that to live is tedious, nor can I die; o grieve, my lord, for my languishing; effect what I cannot: deliver him to me in your bonds.

If you will not do this, at least free me from the ties knotted by hope; oh I beg you, my lord, be pleased to: for, if you do, I feel sure I shall become beautiful again, as I used to be, and when sorrow has been taken from me, I shall deck myself with white flowers and with crimson ones.

From hill to hill and from wood to forest, like a falcon which springs up from the hand of an uncouth master and flees far,

lasso, men vo, ben ch'io non sia disciolto,
donne, partir volendo da colui
che vi dà forza sovra i cor altrui.

Ma, quando pelegrina esser più crede
da lui mia vita, più presa si vede.

LA neve e 'l ghiaccio e' venti d'oriente,
la fredda brina e l'alta tramontana
cacciata hanno de' boschi suo' Diana.

Perch'ella vide secche l'erbe e' fiori,
volar le fronde e spogliar la foresta,
coverta s'ha col vel la bionda testa,

ed è venuta al loco ov'ella nacque,
dove più ch'altra donna sempre piacque.

– O VAGHE montanine pasturelle,
donde venite sì legiadre e belle?

wearied, I go on, though I am not freed, ladies, even while I wish
to leave him who gives you power over the hearts of men.

But when my life believes itself most remote from him, it sees it
is most taken.

THE snow and the ice and the east winds, the cold hoar-frost and
the high north wind have chased Diana from her woods.

Because she sees the grass withered, and withered the flowers, the
leaves flying and the forest bared, she has covered her fair head with
a veil,

and she has come to the place where she was born, where she
always delighted more than other woman.

'O DELIGHTING mountain shepherdesses, whence do you come
so gay and fair?'

Qual'è il paese dove nate sète,
che sì bel frutto più che gli altri aduce?
Creature d'Amor vo' mi parete,
tanto la vostra vista addorna luce!
Nè oro nè argento in voi riluce,
e, mal vestite, parete angiolelle. –

– No' stiamo in alpe, presso ad un boschetto;
povera capannetta è 'l nostro sito:
col padre e con la madre in picciol letto
torniam la sera dal prato fiorito,
dove natura si ha sempre nodrito,
guardando il dì le nostre peccorelle. –

– Assa' si de' doler vostra bellezza,
quando tra monti e valli la mostrate;
chè non è terra di sì grande altezza
dove non foste degne ed onorate.
Deh ditemi se voi vi contentate
di star ne' boschi così poverelle. –

'What country were you born in, that brings forth fruit so much lovelier than the others? You seem to me creatures of love, your aspect is so enhanced with light. No gold or silver shines on you, and, poorly dressed, you seem angels.'

'We stay in the mountains, near a little wood; our dwelling is a poor hut: in the evening we go back to our father and mother to share a little bed, from the flowering meadow where Nature has ever cared for us, while we watch our sheep by day.'

'Much is your beauty to be lamented, when you show it amid mountains and valleys; for there is no earthly place of so great height but you would be worthy and honoured there. O tell me if you are content to stay so poor in the woods.'

– Più si contenta ciascuna di noi
andar drieto le mandre a la pastura
che non farebbe qual fosse di voi
d'andar a feste dentro a vostre mura.
Richezza non cerchiam, nè più ventura
che balli e canti e fiori e ghirlandelle. –

Ballata, s'i' fosse come già fui,
diventerei pastore e montanino;
e prima ch'io il dicesse altrui,
sarei al loco di costor vicino;
ed or direi – Biondella! – ed or – Martino! –
seguendo sempre dove andasson elle.

MATTEO BOIARDO

Nè più dolce a' nostri ochi il ciel sfavilla
de lumi adorno che la notte inchina,
nè il vago tremolar de la marina
al sol nascente lucida e tranquilla;
nè quella stella che de su ne stilla
fresca rogiada a l'ora matutina,
nè in giazio terso nè in candida brina
ragio di sol che sparso resintilla;

'Each of us is happier following the flocks to pasture than anyone of you would be to go to a feast within your walls. We do not
look for riches, nor other excitement than dances and songs and
flowers and garlands.'

Song, if I were as once I was, I would become a shepherd and a
highlander, and before I told anyone of it, I would be living near
their place; and now I would say – Whitey! – and now – Martin! –
always following where they went.

HEAVEN does not sparkle more sweetly to our eyes when it is fair
with lights that the night brings low, nor the charmed trembling of
the waves, clear and calm in the rising sun; nor that star which
drops the fresh dew at the morning hour, nor a ray from the sun
that, refracted, dazzles on gleaming ice or white hoar-frost;

nè tanto el veder nostro a sè retira
qual cosa più gentile et amorosa
su nel ciel splende, on qua giù in terra spira:
quanto la dolce vista e graziosa
de quei begli occhi che Amor volve e gira;
e chi no il crede, de mirar non li osa.

G I À vidi uscir di l'onde una matina
il sol di ragi d'òr tutto iubato,
e di tal luce in facia colorato,
che ne incendeva tutta la marina.
E vidi la rogiada matutina
la rosa aprir d'un color sì infiamato,
che ogni luntan aspetto avria stimato
che un foco ardesse ne la verde spina.

E vidi a la stagion prima e novella
uscir la molle erbetta, come sòle
aprir le foglie ne la prima etate.
E vidi una ligiadra donna e bella
su l'erba coglier rose al primo sole
e vincer queste cose di beltate.

nor does anything more gracious and enamouring shine in heaven or breathe upon earth that draws our gaze as does the sweet and blissful look of those lovely eyes which Love turns this way and that; and whoever doubts this, has not dared to look upon them.

I HAVE seen the sun rising from the waves one morning, maned all with gold, and complexioned with such light that he set all the waves on fire. And I have seen the morning dew bring the rose to open with so flaming a colour that any distant eye would have judged a fire to be burning upon the green thorn.

And I have seen the soft grass spring in the new and early season, as it is wont to open its blades in its first days. And I saw a woman, gay and fair, going over the grass, gathering roses in the first sunlight and overcoming all these things in beauty.

Ecco la pastorella mena al piano
la bianca torma ch'è sotto sua guarda,
vegendo il Sol calare, e l'ora tarda,
e fumar l'alte ville di luntano.
Erto se leva lo aratore insano,
e il giorno fugitivo intorno guarda,
e scioglie il iugo a' bovi, che non tarda,
per gire al suo riposo a mano a mano.

Et io soletto, sanza alcun sogiorno,
de' mei pensier co' il Sol sosta non have,
e con le stelle a sospirar ritorno.
Dolce affanno d'amor, quanto èi suave:
chè io non poso la notte e non al giorno,
e la fatica eterna non me è grave!

LORENZO DE MEDICI

Donne belle, io ho cercato
lungo tempo del mio core.
Ringraziato sie tu, Amore,
ch'io l'ho pure alfin trovato.

Now the shepherdess leads the white troop that is in her keeping down to the plain, for she sees the sun declining, and the hour late, and the high country-houses sending up their smoke in the distance. The bent ploughman lifts himself straight and tall, and looks about at the day that flees, and frees his oxen from the yoke that he may not be late in returning to his rest.

And I alone, without any refuge, have no respite from my thoughts with the sun, and come to sigh again with the stars. Sweet unrest of love, how mild you are: for I rest neither by night nor by day, and the eternal travail does not weigh on me!

FAIR ladies, I have searched a long time for my heart. You are to be thanked, Love, for my finding it at long last.

Egli è forse in questo ballo
chi il mio cor furato avìa:
hallo seco, e sempre arallo,
mentre fia la vita mia:
ella è sì benigna e pia,
ch'ella arà sempre il mio core.
Ringraziato sie tu, Amore,
ch'io l'ho pure alfin trovato.

Donne belle, io v'ho da dire
come il mio cor ritrovai:
quand'io me 'l sentii fuggire,
in più luoghi ricercai:
poi duo begli occhi guardai,
dove ascoso era il mio core.
Ringraziato sie tu, Amore,
ch'io l'ho pure alfin trovato.

Che si viene a questa ladra,
che il mio cor m'ha così tolto?
Com'ell'è bella e leggiadra,
come porta amor nel volto!

Perhaps the one who had stolen my heart is in this dance: she
has it with her and will have it as long as my life lasts: she is so
kindly and tender, that she will always have my heart. You are to
be thanked, Love, for my finding it at long last.

Fair ladies, I must tell you how I found my heart again: when I
felt it escaping from me, I search for it in many places: then I looked
into two lovely eyes where my heart was hidden. You are to be
thanked, Love, for my finding it at long last.

What does this fair thief deserve, who has taken my heart like
this? How fair and gay she is, and how love shows in her face!

Non sia mai il suo cor sciolto,
ma sempre arda col mio core,
Ringraziato sie tu, Amore,
ch'io l'ho pure alfin trovato.

Questa ladra, o Amor, lega,
o col furto insieme l'ardi:
non udir s'ella ti priega;
fa' che gli occhi no li guardi:
ma, se hai saette e dardi,
fa' vendetta del mio core.
Ringraziato sie tu, Amore,
ch'io l'ho pure alfin trovato.

Canzona di Bacco

QUANT'è bella giovinezza,
che si fugge tuttavia!
Chi vuol esser lieto, sia:
di doman non c'è certezza.

Quest'è Bacco e Arianna
belli, e l'un dell'altro ardenti:
perchè 'l tempo fugge e 'nganna,
sempre insieme stan contenti.

Never let her heart be freed, but let it always burn with mine. You are to be thanked, Love, for my finding it at long last.

Bind this fair thief, o Love, and let her burn with what she has stolen: don't listen if she pleads; watch you do not look into her eyes: but if you have arrows and darts, avenge my heart. You are to be thanked, Love, for my finding it at last.

Song for Bacchus

How lovely youth is that ever flies! Let him be glad who will be: there is no certainty in tomorrow.

This is Bacchus and Ariadne, fair, and each burning for the other: because time flies and deceives, they always stay together in

Queste ninfe ed altre genti
sono allegre tuttavia.
Chi vuol esser lieto, sia:
di doman non c'è certezza.

Questi lieti satiretti
delle ninfe innamorati,
per caverne e per boschetti
han lor posto cento agguati:
or da Bacco riscaldati,
ballon, salton tuttavia.
Chi vuol esser lieto, sia:
di doman non c'è certezza.

Queste ninfe hanno anco caro
da lor essere ingannate:
non può fare a Amor riparo
se non gente rozze e 'ngrate:
ora insieme mescolate
suonon, canton tuttavia.
Chi vuol esser lieto, sia:
di doman non c'è certezza.

happiness. These nymphs and other people are always merry. Let
him be glad who will be: there is no certainty in tomorrow.

These glad little satyrs are in love with the nymphs, and have
laid a hundred ambushes for them in caves and woods: now, heated
by Bacchus, they keep up their dancing and their leaping. Let him
be glad who will be: there is no certainty in tomorrow.

These nymphs would fain be tricked by them: no one can guard
against Love but uncouth, ungrateful people: now mingling together, they play instruments and sing always. Let him be glad who
will be: there is no certainty in tomorrow.

Questa soma che vien drieto
sopra l'asino, è Sileno:
così vecchio è ebbro e lieto,
già di carne e d'anni pieno:
se non può star ritto, almeno
ride e gode tuttavia.
Chi vuol esser lieto, sia:
di doman non c'è certezza.

Mida vien dopo costoro:
ciò che tocca, oro diventa.
E che giova aver tesoro,
s'altri poi non si contenta?
Che dolcezza vuoi che senta
chi ha sete tuttavia?
Chi vuol esser lieto, sia:
di doman non c'è certezza.

Ciascun apra ben gli orecchi:
di doman nessun si paschi;
oggi sian, giovani e vecchi,
lieti ognun, femmine e maschi;
ogni tristo pensier caschi,
facciam festa tuttavia.
Chi vuol esser lieto, sia:
di doman non c'è certezza.

This load who comes behind them upon an ass is Silenus: so old
and drunk and glad, and full, by now, of years and meat: if he cannot stand upright, at least he laughs and has enjoyment still. Let
him be glad who will be: there is no certainty in tomorrow.

Midas comes after these: whatever he touches turns to gold.
What point is there in having treasure, if it does not make you
happy? What sweet pleasure do you imagine a man has who is
always thirsty? Let him be glad who will be: there is no certainty in
tomorrow.

Let every one open their ears wide: let no one feed on tomorrow;
let every one, young and old, women and men, be glad this very
day; banish every sad thought, let us keep perpetual holiday. Let
him be glad who will be: there is no certainty in tomorrow.

Donne e giovinetti amanti,
viva Bacco e viva Amore!
Ciascun suoni, balli e canti!
Arda di dolcezza il core!
Non fatica, non dolore!
Quel c'ha esser, convien sia.
Chi vuol esser lieto, sia;
di doman non c'è certezza.

ANGELO POLIZIANO

Canzona

UDITE, selve, mie dolce parole,
poi che la ninfa mia udir non vole.

La bella ninfa è sorda al mio lamento
e 'l suon di nostra fistula non cura:
di ciò si lagna il mio cornuto armento,
nè vuol bagnare il grifo in acqua pura,
nè vuol toccar la tenera verdura;
tanto del suo pastor gl'incresce e dole.
Udite, selve, mie dolce parole.

Woman and young lovers, long live Bacchus and long live Love! Let each one play, and dance, and sing! Let the heart burn with sweetness! Neither labour, nor grief! What is to happen needs must be. Let him be glad who will be; there is no certainty in tomorrow.

Song

HEAR, woods, my sweet words, since my nymph will not hear them.
The lovely nymph is deaf to my lament and does not care for the sound of our pipe: and so my horned flock languishes, nor will they put their mouths to pure water, nor wish to touch the tender grass; so do they suffer and grieve for their shepherd.
Hear, woods, my sweet words.

Ben si cura l'armento del pastore:
la ninfa non si cura dello amante;
la bella ninfa che di sasso ha il core,
anzi di ferro, anzi l'ha di diamante:
ella fugge da me sempre d'avante,
come agnella dal lupo fuggir sòle.
Udite, selve, mie dolce parole.

Digli, zampogna mia, come via fugge
cogli anni insieme la bellezza snella;
e digli come il tempo ne distrugge,
nè l'età persa mai si rinnovella:
digli che sappi usar suo' forma bella,
chè sempre mai non son rose e viole.
Udite, selve, mie dolce parole.

Portate, venti, questi dolci versi
dentro all'orecchie della ninfa mia:
dite quant'io per lei lacrime versi,
e lei pregate che crudel non sia:
dite che la mia vita fugge via
e si consuma come brina al sole.

The flock feels deeply for the shepherd: the nymph does not feel
for her lover; the lovely nymph who has a heart of stone, of iron
rather, no, rather of diamond: she always runs from before me, as
lamb is wont to run from wolf.
   Hear, woods, my sweet words.
   Tell her, my pipe, that slim loveliness flies with the years; and
tell her how time destroys us, and a lost time of life is never renewed: tell her that she should know how to use her lovely form,
for roses and violets are not for eternity.
   Hear, woods, my sweet words.
   Bear, winds, these sweet numbers to the ears of my nymph: tell
her how many tears I shed for her, and beg her not to be cruel: tell
her my life flies from me and is consumed like hoar-frost in the sun.

Udite, selve, mie dolce parole;
poichè la ninfa mia udir non vole.

Baccanale

Oɢɴᴜɴ segua, Bacco, te!
Bacco Bacco, eù oè!

Chi vuol bever, chi vuol bevere,
vegna a bever, vegna qui.
Voi imbottate come pevere.
Io vo' bever ancor mì.
Gli è del vino ancor per tì.
Lassa bever prima a me.
Ognun segua, Bacco, te.

Io ho vòto già il mio corno:
dammi un po' il bottazo in qua.
Questo monte gira intorno,
e 'l cervello a spasso va.
Ognun corra in qua e in là,
come vede fare a me;
ognun segua, Bacco, te.

Hear, woods, my sweet words; since my nymph will not hear them.

Bacchanal

Lᴇᴛ each one follow you, Bacchus! Bacchus Bacchus, yuh yeh!
Whoever wants to drink, whoever wants to drink, let him come and drink, let him come here. You swallow like big funnels. I want to drink, me as well. There is wine for you as well. Let me drink first. Let each one follow you, Bacchus.
I have already emptied my horn: give me the flask over here for a moment. This mountain is wheeling round, and my brain has gone for a spin. Everyone run here and there, as you see me doing; let each one follow you, Bacchus.

I' mi moro già di sonno.
Son io ebra, o sì o no?
Star più ritti i piè non ponno.
Voi siet'ebrie, ch'io lo so.
Ognun facci com'io fo:
ognun succi come me:
ognun segua, Bacco, te.

Ognun gridi Bacco Bacco,
e pur cacci del vin giù:
poi con suoni farem fiacco.
Bevi tu, e tu, e tu.
I' non posso ballar più.
Ognun gridi eù, oè;
ognun segua, Bacco, te.
Bacco Bacco, eù oè!

I' MI trovai, fanciulle, un bel mattino
di mezo maggio in un verde giardino.

I am already dying of tiredness. Am I drunk, say yes or no? My feet cannot hold me upright any longer. You are drunk, that I know. Everyone do as I do: everyone swill like me: everyone follow you, Bacchus.

Everyone cry Bacchus, Bacchus, and still toss the wine back. Then we will get feebler and feebler with our noise. You drink, and you, and you. I can dance no longer. Everyone shout yuh yeh! everyone follow you, Bacchus. Bacchus Bacchus, yuh yeh!

I FOUND myself, maidens, one fine morning in the middle of May, in a green garden.

Eran d'intorno violette e gigli
fra l'erba verde, vaghi fior novelli
azzurri gialli candidi e vermigli:
ond'io porsi la mano a côr di quelli
per adornar e' mie' biondi capelli
e cinger di grillanda el vago crino.
I' mi trovai, fanciulle ...

Ma poi ch'i' ebbi pien di fiori un lembo,
vidi le rose e non pur d'un colore:
io corsi allor per empier tutto el grembo,
perch'era sì soave il loro odore
che tutto mi senti' destar el core
di dolce voglia e d'un piacer divino.
I' mi trovai, fanciulle ...

I' posi mente: quelle rose allora
mai non vi potre' dir quant'eran belle:
quale scoppiava della boccia ancora;
qual'erano un po' passe e qual novelle.
Amor mi disse allor: – Va', cô' di quelle
che più vedi fiorite in sullo spino. –
I' mi trovai, fanciulle ...

Around me in the green grass were violets and lilies and other
lovely new flowers, blue, yellow, white, and crimson: so that I
stretched out my hand to pluck them to deck my fair hair and to
crown my beloved's locks with a garland. I found myself,
maidens. ...

But when I had a skirt-fold full of flowers, I saw roses, and not
of a single colour: I ran then to fill all my lap, because they smelt so
sweetly that my heart came quite awake with soft desire and a
divine pleasure. I found myself, maidens. ...

I took thought: I could never tell you how lovely those roses
were then: some were still bursting from the bud; others were
slightly overblown, and some, quite new. Love said to me then:
'Go, gather those which you see flowering most perfectly upon the
thorn.' I found myself, maidens. ...

Quando la rosa ogni suo' foglia spande,
quando è più bella, quando è più gradita;
allora è buona a mettere in ghirlande,
prima che sua belleza sia fuggita:
sicchè, fanciulle, mentre è più fiorita,
coglian la bella rosa del giardino.
I' mi trovai, fanciulle …

Io ti ringrazio, Amore,
d'ogni pena e tormento,
e son contento · omai d'ogni dolore.

Contento son di quanto ho mai sofferto,
Signor, nel tuo bel regno;
poi che per tua merzè sanza mio merto
m'hai dato un sì gran pegno,
poi che m'hai fatto degno
d'un sì beato riso,
che 'n paradiso · n'ha portato il core.
Io ti ringrazio, Amore.

When the rose stretches every petal, when it is most lovely,
when it is most pleasant; then is it good for putting in a garland,
before its beauty be fled: so, maidens, let us gather the fair rose of
the garden while its bloom is perfect. I found myself, maidens. …

I THANK you, Love, for every pain and torment, and am happy
now for your every sorrow.

I am happy for what I have suffered, Lord, in your fine kingdom;
since in your generosity, without my deserving it, you have given
me so great a pledge, since you have made me worthy of so blessed
a smile that it has carried my heart away to paradise. I thank you,
Love.

In paradiso el cor n'hanno portato
que' begli occhi ridenti,
ov'io ti vidi, Amore, star celato
con le tue fiamme ardenti.
O vaghi occhi lucenti
che 'l cor tolto m'avete,
onde traete · sì dolce valore?
Io ti ringrazio, Amore.

I' ero già della mia vita in forse:
madonna in bianca vesta
con un riso amoroso mi soccorse,
lieta bella et onesta:
dipinta avea la testa
di rose e di viole,
gli occhi che 'l sole · avanzan di splendore.
Io ti ringrazio, Amore.

Those lovely eyes have carried my heart away to paradise, where
I saw you, Love, hidden in your glowing flames. O shining eyes
that have taken my heart, whence do you draw such sweet power?
I thank you, Love.

I doubted for my life: my lady dressed in white saved me with a
loving smile, happy, fair, and modest, she: her hair was decked
with roses and violets, her eyes surpassed the sun in brightness. I
thank you, Love.

Ben venga maggio
e 'l gonfalon selvaggio:

Ben venga primavera
che vuol l'uom s'innamori.
E voi, donzelle, a schiera
con li vostri amadori,
che di rose e di fiori
vi fate belle il maggio,

venite alla frescura
delli verdi arbuscelli.
Ogni bella è sicura
fra tanti damigelli;
chè le fiere e gli uccelli
ardon d'amore il maggio.

Chi è giovane e bella
deh non sie punto acerba,
chè non si rinnovella
l'età, come fa l'erba:
nessuna stia superba
all'amadore il maggio.

Welcome May and its wild banner.
Welcome spring that desires man to fall in love. And you, maidens, in a crowd with your lovers, who make yourselves lovely with roses and other flowers in May, come to the cool shade of the green bushes. Every fair is safe among so many youths; for beasts and birds burn with love in May.
She who is young and beautiful, oh do not let her be harsh, for this age does not renew itself as does the grass: let none be proud with her lover in May.

Ciascuna balli e canti
di questa schiera nostra.
Ecco che i dolci amanti
van per voi, belle, in giostra:
qual dura a lor si mostra
farà sfiorire il maggio.

Per prender le donzelle
si son gli amanti armati.
Arrendetevi, belle,
a' vostri innamorati;
rendete e' cuor furati,
non fate guerra il maggio.

Chi l'altrui core invola
ad altrui doni el core.
Ma chi è quel che vola?
È l'angiolel d'amore,
che viene a fare onore
con voi, donzelle, al maggio.

Let each one of this our band sing and dance. See, your sweet lovers go to the joust for your sakes, you fair: she who shows herself hard to them makes the May shed its bloom.

The loving youths are armed to win the maidens. Surrender yourselves, you fair, to your lovers. Give back the hearts you have robbed, do not wage war in May.

Let the one who has stolen a heart from another give hers in exchange. But who is that flying there? It is the angel of love who comes to do honour with you, my maidens, to the May.

Amor ne vien ridendo
con rose e gigli in testa,
e vien di voi caendo.
Fategli, o belle, festa.
Qual sarà la più presta
a dargli e' fior del maggio?

Ben venga il peregrino.
Amor, che ne comandi?
Che al suo amante il crino
ogni bella ingrillandi;
chè le zitelle e grandi
s'innamoran di maggio.

LUDOVICO ARIOSTO

Capitolo VIII

O più che 'l giorno a me lucida e chiara,
dolce, gioconda, aventurosa notte,
quanto men ti sperai tanto più cara.

Stelle a furti d'amor soccorrer dotte,
che minuisti il lume, nè per vui
mi fur l'amiche tenebre interrotte.

Love comes here laughing, crowned with roses and lilies, and comes seeking you. Greet him merrily, you fair. Who will be quickest to give him the May-flower?

Welcome to the traveller. Love, what is your bidding? That every fair put a garland about the head of her love; that girls and grown women fall in love in May.

Poem in Terza Rima – VIII

O MORE shining and glad than the day to me, sweet, glad, fortunate night, so much the dearer as I little expected you.

Stars learned in helping love's own thefts that dimmed your light, not by you were the friendly shades broken.

Sonno propizio, che lasciando dui
vigili amanti soli, così oppresso
avevi ogn'altro, che invisibil fui.

Benigna porta, che con sì sommesso
e con sì basso suon mi fusti aperta,
ch'a pena ti sentì chi t'era presso.

O mente ancor di non sognar incerta,
quando abbracciar da la mia dea mi vidi,
e fu la mia con la sua bocca inserta.

O benedetta man, ch'indi mi guidi;
o cheti passi che m'andate inanti;
o camera, che poi così m'affidi.

O complessi iterati, che con tanti
nodi cingete i fianchi, il petto, il collo,
che non ne fan più l'edere o li acanti.

Bocca ove ambrosia libo nè satollo
mai ne ritorno; o dolce lingua, o umore,
per cui l'arso mio cor bagno e rimollo.

Timely sleep, that leaving two wide-awake lovers alone, had so
overcome everyone else, that I was invisible.

Kindly door, that were opened with so subdued and low a sound,
that he who was close to you hardly heard.

O mind still uncertain if it dreamed or not, when I saw myself
clasped by my goddess, and my mouth was enclosed in hers.

O blessed hand, that next lead me; o quiet steps that proceed me,
o room, that then so secure me.

O repeated embraces, that bind hips, breast, neck, with so many
twinings that ivy or acanthus have fewer.

Mouth, whence I sup ambrosia, nor ever come away satiate; o
soft tongue, o dewiness, in which I bathe and soften my burnt heart
again.

Fiato, che spiri assai più grato odore
che non porta da l'indi o da sabei
fenice al rogo, in che s'incende e more.

O letto, testimon de' piacer miei;
letto cagion ch'una dolcezza io gusti,
che non invidio il lor nettare ai dèi.

O letto donator de' premi giusti,
letto, che spesso in l'amoroso assalto
mosso, distratto ed agitato fusti.

Voi tutti ad un ad un, ch'ebbi de l'alto
piacer ministri, avrò in memoria eterna,
e quanto è il mio poter, sempre vi esalto.

Nè piu debb'io tacer di te, lucerna,
che con noi vigilando, il ben ch'io sento
vuoi che con gli occhi ancor tutto discerna.

Per te fu dupplicato il mio contento;
nè veramente si può dire perfetto
uno amoroso gaudio a lume spento.

Breath, that inhale far more pleasant fragrance than the phoenix on his pyre, on which he flames and dies, yields among Indians or Sabaeans.

O bed, witness to my pleasures; bed, cause of my tasting a sweetness such that I do not envy the gods their nectar.

O bed, giver of just rewards, bed, which was often moved, ruffled, and shaken by the loving tussle.

All of you, one by one, shall I keep in everlasting memory as ministers of my high pleasure, and I praise you as much as in my power.

Nor should I keep more silent about you, lantern, that, staying awake with us, desire that my eyes should perceive the good I know.

My happiness was doubled through you; nor can love enjoyed by extinguished light be truly said to be perfect.

Quanto più giova in sì suave effetto,
pascer la vista or de li occhi divini,
or de la fronte, or de l'eburneo petto;

mirar le ciglia e l'aurei crespi crini,
mirar le rose in su le labbra sparse,
porvi la bocca e non temer de' spini;

mirar le membra, a cui non può uguagliarse
altro candor e giudicar mirando
che le grazie del ciel non vi fur scarse,

e quando a un senso satisfar, e quando
all'altro e sì che ne fruiscan tutti,
e pur un sol non ne lasciar in bando!

Deh! perche son d'amor sì rari i frutti?
deh! perche del gioir sì brieve il tempo?
perche sì lunghi e senza fine i lutti?

Perchè lasciasti, ohimè, così per tempo
invida Aurora, il tuo Titone antico,
e del partir m'accelerasti il tempo?

How much more it adds, in such sweet action, to feed the gaze
upon the divine eyes, her forehead, her ivory bosom;
    look upon her brow and hair of curling gold, look on the roses
shed upon her lips, put your mouth there, and fear no thorns;
    look upon her limbs, which no other whiteness can equal and
think as you look that heaven's graces were never wanting there,
    and now indulge one sense, and now another and in such a style
that all have play, and not even one stays banished!
    O why are the fruits of love so rare? o why the time for enjoy-
ing them so short? why so long and endless are our griefs?
    Why, envious Dawn, ah me! did you leave your ancient
Tithonus so promptly, and speed my time of parting?

Ti potess'io, come ti son nemico,
nocer così! Se 'l tuo vecchio t'annoia,
chè non ti cerchi un più giovane amico?

e vivi, e lascia altrui viver in gioia!

MICHELANGELO BUONARROTI

(Su di uno schizzo del David al Louvre – 1502)

DAVITTE colla fromba
e io coll'arco
Michelagniolo.
Rott'è l'alta colonna.

QUANTO si gode, lieta e ben contesta
di fior, sopra crin d'or d'una, ghirlanda,
che l'altro innanzi l'uno all'altro manda,
come che 'l primo sia a baciar la testa!
Contenta è tutto il giorno quella vesta
che serra 'l petto e poi par che si spanda,
e quel d'oro filato si domanda
le guance e 'l collo di toccar non resta.

If only I could hurt you like that, for I am your enemy! If your old man bores you, why not find a younger lover?
and live, and let live in joy!

(On a sketch for his 'David' in the Louvre, dated 1502)

DAVID with the sling and I with the bow, Michelangelo. Broken is the high column.

HOW the garland rejoices, happy and finely woven with flowers, on the golden hair of this woman, as it puts another flower forward, then one before that, as if all might be first to kiss her head. That dress is contented all the day, binding that bosom and, lower, spreading out, and that lace of gold asks for those cheeks and does not cease to touch the neck.

Ma più lieto quel nastro par che goda,
dorato in punta, con sì fatte tempre,
che preme e tocca il petto, ch'egli allaccia.
E la schietta cintura, che s'annoda,
mi par dir seco: qui vo' stringer sempre!
Or che farebber dunque le mie braccia!

QUA si fa elmi di calici e spade,
e 'l sangue di Cristo si vend'a giumelle,
e croce e spine son lance e rotelle,
e pur da Cristo pazienza cade.
Ma non c'arrivi più 'n queste contrade,
che n'andre' 'l sangue suo 'nsin alle stelle,
poscia ch'a Roma gli vendon la pelle,
e ecci d'ogni ben chiuse le strade.

But happier still that ribbon, gilded at the edge, so finely tempered, that presses and touches the bosom which it entwines. And the shapely girdle which, fastened, seems to say to itself: here would I clasp for ever! Then what would my arms do!

HERE they make helmets and swords from chalices, and sell the blood of Christ by the cup-full, and cross and thorns are lances and shields, and still patience descends on us from Christ. But let him come no more in these parts, for his blood would spurt up to the stars, since at Rome they sell his skin, and the ways to every good are closed to us.

S'i' ebbi ma' voglia a perder tesauro,
per ciò che qua opra da me è partita,
e puo' quel nel manto che Medusa in Mauro;
ma se alto in cielo è povertà gradita,
qual fia di nostro stato il gran restauro,
s'un altro segno ammorza l'altra vita?

> finis.
> Vostro Miccelangniolo in Turchia

Dimmi, di grazia, Amor, se gli occhi mei
veggono 'l ver della beltà, c'aspiro,
o s'io ho dentro, allor che, dov'io miro,
veggo scolpito il viso di costei.
Tu 'l de' saper, po' che tu vien con lei
a torm'ogni mia pace, ond'io m'adiro;
nè vorre' manco un minimo sospiro
nè men ardente foco chiederei.

If ever I had the desire to lose what is precious, for all work has gone from me here, he in the mantle can do what the Medusa did in Mauritania; but if poverty finds favour in high heaven, what will be the great remedy for our state, if this other ensign smothers the other life?

> finish.
> Your Michelangelo in Turkey

TELL me, Love, I pray, if my eyes see the truth of the beauty to which I aspire, or if I have it within me, since, where I look, I see her face engraved. You must know, because you come with her to rob me of every moment of peace, at which I rage; not that I would want one sigh the less, nor would ask for a less blazing fire.

La beltà, che tu vedi, è ben da quella,
ma cresce, poi c'a miglior loco sale,
se per gli occhi mortali all'alma corre.
Quivi si fa divina, onesta e bella,
com'a sè simil vuol cosa immortale.
Questa e non quella a gli occhi tuo' precorre.

O HIMÈ, ohimè, ch'i' son tradito
da' giorni mie' fugaci e dallo specchio,
che 'l ver dice a ciascun, che fiso 'l guarda!
Così n'avvien, chi troppo al fin ritarda,
com'ho fatt'io, che 'l tempo m'è fuggito,
si trova come me 'n un giorno vecchio.
Nè mi posso pentir, nè m'apparecchio,
nè mi consiglio con la morte appresso.
Nemico di me stesso,
inutilmente i pianti e sospir verso,
che non è danno pari al tempo perso.

The beauty which you see comes really from her, but grows
when it ascends to a higher place – if it should pass through mortal
eyes to the soul. There it becomes divine, pure, and lovely in the
likeness of the immortal part that wishes it so. This latter is the
beauty that goes before your eyes, not the first one.

ALAS, alas, for I am betrayed by my fleeting days and by the mirror, that tells the truth to each one who looks on it fixedly! So does
it befall whoever puts off too much to the end, as I have done, for
my time has flown, he finds himself, like me, old in a day. Nor can I
repent, nor make ready, nor can I take counsel of myself with death
near. My own self's enemy, I uselessly pour forth tears and sighs,
for there is no harm like time lost.

Ohimè, Ohimè, pur reiterando
vo 'l mio passato tempo e non ritrovo
in tutto un giorno che sia stato mio!
Le fallaci speranza e 'l van desio,
piangendo, amando, ardendo e sospirando
(c'affetto alcun mortal non mi è più nuovo)
m'hanno tenuto, ond'il conosco e provo:
lontan certo dal vero,
or con periglio pero;
chè 'l breve tempo m'è venuto manco,
nè saria ancor, se s'allungasse, stanco.

I' vo lasso, ahimè, nè so ben dove;
anzi temo, ch'il veggio, e 'l tempo andato
me 'l mostra, nè mi val che gli occhi chiuda.
Or che 'l tempo la scorza cangia e muda,
la morte e l'alma insieme ognor fan prove,
la prima e la seconda, del mio stato.
E s'io non sono errato
(che Dio 'l voglia ch'io sia!)
l'eterna pena mia
nel mal libero inteso oprato vero
veggio, Signor, nè so quel ch'io mi spero.

Alas, Alas, I keep going over my past time and do not find in the whole of it one day that has been mine! False hopes and empty desire, weeping, loving, longing, and sighing (for no human feeling is any longer new to me) have possessed me, so that I know and feel this: certainly far from truth, I perish now in danger; for our short time of life has dwindled for me, nor would I weary of those things, if it could be prolonged.

I go on wearily, alas, nor do I well know where; rather I am afraid for I see it, and departed time points it, nor does it serve for me to close my eyes. Now that time has changed and transformed its bark, death, the first and second, and the soul struggle together constantly for my being. And if I am not in error (God grant that I am), I see eternal suffering for me in the truth I understood and wantonly abused, nor do I know what I have to hope for.

SE nel volto per gli occhi il cor si vede,
altro segno non ho più manifesto
della mia fiamma; adunque basti or questo,
Signor mio caro, a domandar mercede.
Forse lo spirto tuo, con maggior fede
ch'i' non credo, che sguarda il foco onesto,
che m'arde, fia di me pietoso e presto,
come grazia c'abbonda a chi ben chiede.

O felice quel dì, se questo è certo!
Fermisi in un momento il tempo e l'ore,
il giorno e 'l sol nella su' antica traccia,
acciò ch'i' abbi, e non già per mio merto,
il desiato mio dolce signore
per sempre nell'indegne e pronte braccia.

IF the heart is seen in one's face, in one's eyes, I have no more evident sign of my heart's flame; therefore let this suffice you now,
my dear Lord, as a request for recompense. Perhaps your spirit,
with greater faith than I think, looking on the pure fire which burns
me, will be pitying, and speedily, towards me, as grace abounds to
him who prays earnestly.

O happy that day, if this is certain! Let time and the hours stop
in one moment, day and the sun in his ancient track, so that I may
have, and not, certainly, for my worthiness, my sweet longed-for
lord for ever in my unworthy and ready arms.

I' T'HO comprato, ancor che molto caro,
un po' di non so che, che sa di buono,
perc'a l'odor la strada spesso imparo.
Ovunque tu ti sia, dovunqu'i' sono,
senz'alcun dubbio ne son certo e chiaro.
Se da me ti nascondi, i' tel perdono.
Portando 'l, dove vai, sempre con teco,
ti troverei, quand'io fossi ben cieco.

IN me la morte, in te la vita mia.
Tu distingui e concedi e parti il tempo;
quanto vuo', breve e lungo è il viver mio.

Felice son nella tua cortesia.
Beata l'alma, ove non corre tempo,
per te s'è fatta a contemplare Dio.

I HAVE bought you, at great expense, it is true, a little something, which smells sweetly, because I often come to know a street by its scent. Wherever you may be, wherever I am, I am certain and clear about that now, without one doubt. If you hide from me, I forgive you. Carrying this with you always, as you go about, I would find you if I were quite blind.

IN me death, in you my life. You mark and grant and separate time; as you wish, short or long is the pace of my life.

Happy am I in your courtesy. Blessed the soul in which time does not run. By you, it is made to look upon God.

VEGGIO nel tuo bel viso, Signor mio,
quel che narrar mal puossi in questa vita.
L'anima della carne ancor vestita,
con esso è già più volte ascesa a Dio.
E se 'l vulgo malvagio, isciocco e rio
di quel che sente altrui segna e addita,
non è l'intensa voglia men gradita,
l'amor, la fede e l'onesto desio.

A quel pietoso fonte, onde siam tutti,
s'assembra ogni beltà che qua si vede,
più c'altra cosa alle persone accorte;
nè altro saggio abbiam, nè altri frutti
del cielo in terra; e chi v'ama con fede
trascende a Dio, e fa dolce la morte.

O NOTT', o dolce tempo, benchè nero,
con pace ogn'opra sempr'al fin assalta.
Ben ved'e ben intende chi t'esalta,
e chi t'onor', ha l'intellett'intero.

I SEE in your fair face, my Lord, what can ill be told in this life.
Your soul has already ascended many times to God, still clothed in
the flesh, and with that face. And if the malicious, foolish, evil
throng marks and points out what others feel, the burning will is
not less pleasing, nor the love, the faith, the honest desire.

Every beauty that is seen here recalls, more than other things,
that fount of pity, whence we all come, to feeling people; nor do
we have other earnest, nor other fruit of heaven upon this earth;
and he who loves you with faith ascends to God, and sees death as
sweet.

O NIGHT, o sweet time, in spite of blackness, you overcome each
labour with peace in the end. He who praises you sees and understands clearly, and he has a sound judgement who does you

Tu mozzi e tronchi ogni stanco pensiero,
chè l'umid'ombra ogni quiet'appalta,
e dall'infirma parte alla più alta
in sogno spesso porti, ov'ire spero.

O ombra del morir, per cui si ferma
ogni miser', a l'alma, al cor nemica,
ultimo degli afflitti e buon rimedio;
tu rendi sana nostra carn'inferma,
rasciugh'i pianti, e posi ogni fatica,
e furi a chi ben vive ogn'ir'e tedio.

Non vider gli occhi miei cosa mortale,
allor che ne' bei vostri intera pace
trovai, ma dentro, ov'ogni mal dispiace,
chi d'amor l'alma a sè simil m'assale:
e se creata a Dio non fosse eguale,
altro che 'l bel di fuor, c'agli occhi piace,
più non vorria; ma perch'è si fallace,
trascende nella forma universale.

honour. You break and cut short every tired thought, since dank
shade dispenses every quiet; and often in dream you bear us from
the lowest part to the highest, where I hope to go.

O shadow of dying, for whom each affliction, the enemy of soul
and heart, is suspended, last and good remedy of the miserable;
you make our weak flesh whole, dry our tears, and lay every effort
to rest, and steal anger and tedium from him who lives well.

My eyes saw no mortal thing, when I found utter peace in your fine
eyes, but saw within, where every evil is unwelcome, him who
attacks my soul – his likeness – with love: and if that were not
created in the image of God, I would no longer desire other than
the outward beauty which pleases the eye; but because this is
fallacious, it loses itself in the form of universal beauty.

Io dico, c'a chi vive quel che muore
quetar non può desir, nè par s'aspetti
l'eterno al tempo, ove altri cangia il pelo.
Voglia sfrenata il senso è, non amore,
che l'alma uccide; e 'l nostro fa perfetti
gl'amici qui, ma più per morte in cielo.

Non ha l'ottimo artista alcun concetto
c'un marmo solo in sè non circoscriva
col suo soverchio; e solo a quello arriva
la man che ubbidisce all'intelletto.
Il mal ch'io fuggo, e 'l ben ch'io mi prometto,
in te, Donna leggiadra, altera e diva,
tal si nasconde; e perch'io più non viva,
contraria ho l'arte al disiato effetto.

Amor dunque non ha, nè tua beltate,
o durezza, o fortuna, o gran disdegno,
del mio mal colpa, o mio destino o sorte,
se dentro del tuo cor morte e pietate
porti in un tempo, e che 'l mio basso ingegno
non sappia, ardendo, trarne altro che morte.

I say that what dies cannot still the desire of him who is living,
nor does eternity appear to wait upon time, where the skin of
beings changes. The senses lead, not to love, but to unbridled desire
that kills the soul; and our love makes perfect friendships here, but
more perfect still, through death, in heaven.

The best artist has not one idea that a piece of marble, still unworked, does not contain within itself; and that conception is
realized only by the hand that obeys the judgement. The evil I fly
from, and the good I promise myself are likewise hid in you, gay,
proud, divine Lady; and, so that I die, my art is opposed to the
desired result.

So love is not to blame for my plight, nor your beauty, nor the
hardness of things, nor chance, nor great scorn, nor is my destiny
or fate, if within your heart you bear at the one time death and pity,
and my miserable wit does not know, though burning, how to draw
anything from you but death.

Sì come per levar, Donna, si pone
in pietra alpestra e dura
una viva figura,
che là più cresce, u' più la pietra scema;
tal alcun'opre buone,
per l'alma, che pur trema,
cela il soverchio della propria carne
con l'inculta sua cruda e dura scorza.
Tu pur dalle mie streme
parti puo' sol levarne,
ch'in me non è di me voler nè forza.

Ben può talor col mio 'rdente desio
salir la speme, e non essere fallace;
chè s'ogni nostro affetto al ciel dispiace,
a che fin fatto avrebbe il mondo Iddio?
Qual più giusta cagion dell'amart'io
è, che dar gloria a quella eterna pace,
onde pende il divin, che di te piace,
e c'ogni cor gentil fa casto e pio?

Lady, just as one supposes a living figure to be in hard alpine stone, so as to draw it out, and it gradually grows as the stone flakes away; so the surface of our own flesh with its unworked, rough, hard skin, hides deeds worthy of the soul that trembles the while. And you can draw these from my outward parts, you alone, as in me there is neither will nor strength of mine.

My hope can sometimes ascend with my burning desire, and not be false; for if every one of our desires is unacceptable to heaven, to what end did God make the world? What more righteous cause have I for loving you, than to glorify that eternal peace (from which what is divine and pleases in you comes) that makes every heart chaste and holy?

Fallace speme ha sol l'amor, che muore
con la beltà, c' ogni momento scema,
ond'è soggetta al variar d'un bel viso.
Dolce è ben quella in un pudico core
che per cangiar di scorza o d'ora strema
non manca, e qui caparra il paradiso.

I' FU', già son molt'anni, mille volte
ferito e morto, non che vinto e stanco,
da te, mia colpa; e or col capo bianco,
riprenderò le tue promesse stolte?
Quante volte ha' legate, e quant'isciolte
le triste membra, e sì spronato il fianco,
c'appena posso ritornar meco, anco,
bagnando il petto con lacrime molte!

Di te mi dolgo, Amor, con teco parlo,
sciolto da tue lusinghe, a che bisogna
prender l' arco crudel, tirare a voto?
Al legno incenerato sega o tarlo
o dietro a un correndo è gran vergogna
c'ha perso e ferma ogni destrezza e moto.

Only that love is tainted with false hope that dies with beauty which lessens every moment, for, in this way, it is subject to the changing of a fair face. Sweet is that love in an innocent heart which does not fail for altering of feature or the last hour, and it has earnest paradise here.

I WAS, many years since, wounded and annihilated a thousand times, not simply conquered and wearied, by you, my failing; and now when I have white hairs, shall I take up your promises again? How many times have you bound, and how many, freed these sad limbs, and so spurred this side, that I can scarce come to myself yet, though bathing my breast with many tears!

I complain of you, Love, I am talking to you, freed as I am from your lures: why must you take up your cruel bow and shoot wildly? For saw or wood-worm to attack burnt wood, or to go running after one who has lost all nimbleness and speed, is a most shameful thing.

DEH fàmmiti vedere in ogni loco!
Se da mortal bellezza arder mi sento,
appresso al tuo mi sarà foco ispento,
e io nel tuo sarò, com'ero, in foco.
Signor mio caro, i' te sol chiamo e 'nvoco
contro l'inutil mio cieco tormento:
tu sol puo' rinnovarmi fuora e drento
le voglie, e 'l senno, e 'l valor lento e poco;

tu desti al tempo ancor quest'alma diva,
e 'n questa spoglia ancor fragil' e stanca
l'incarcerasti, e con fiero destino.
Che poss'io altro, che così non viva?
Ogni ben senza te, Signor, mi manca;
il cangiar sorte è sol poter divino.

PASSA per gli occhi al core in un momento
qualunque obbietto di beltà lor sia,
e per sì larga e sì capace via,
c'a mille non si chiude, non c'a cento,

O MAKE me see you in every place! If I feel myself burn for mortal beauty, mine will be a dead fire when yours approaches, and in yours I will be, as I have been, on fire. Dear my Lord, I call and invoke you alone against my fruitless, blind torment: you alone can renew for me, without and within, my desires and judgement and my little tardy worth;

you gave to time this soul, though divine, and imprisoned it in this form, though frail and tired, with a savage destiny. What more can I do, so that I may not live like this? Every good without you, Lord, is held from me; to change fate is a power solely divine.

ANY feature of beauty that comes before my eyes passes through them in an instant to my heart, and by so broad and capacious a way, that it is not closed to a thousand, far less a hundred, of every

d'ogni età, d'ogni sesso: ond'io pavento,
carco d'affanni, e più di gelosia;
nè fra sì vari volti so qual sia
c'anzi morte mi die 'ntero contento.

S'un ardente desir mortal bellezza
ferma del tutto, non discese insieme
dal ciel con l'alma; è dunque umana voglia.
Ma se pass'oltre, Amor, tuo nome sprezza,
c'altro die cerca; e di quel più non teme
c'a lato vien contro sì bassa spoglia.

LA forza d'un bel viso a che mi sprona?
C'altro non è c'al mondo mi diletti:
ascender vivo fra gli spirti eletti,
per grazia tal, c'ogn'altra par men buona.
Se ben col fattor l'opra sua consuona,
che colpa vuol giustizia ch'io n'aspetti,
s'i' amo, anz'ardo, e per divin concetti,
onoro e stimo ogni gentil persona?
....

age, each sex: so that I am afraid, burdened with weariness and
more with jealousy, nor do I know which might be the face among
so many different ones that would give me complete happiness
before death.

If mortal beauty quite arrests a burning desire, that beauty did
not come down from heaven with the soul; the desire is therefore
human. But if it goes beyond, then, Love, it scorns your name,
since it seeks another day; and does not fear what comes at its side
for so base a prize.

WHAT does the power of a beautiful face spur me to? For there is
nothing else in the world that delights me: to ascend living among
the blessed spirits, by such access of grace, that every other seems
less good. If the work is in harmony with its maker, what blame
does justice keep in store for me, if I love, no, burn, and honour
and value every gentle being, for divine thoughts?

L'ALMA, inquieta e confusa, in sè non trova
altra cagion c'alcun grave peccato
mal conosciuto, onde non è celato
all'immensa pietà, c'a' miser giova.
I' parlo a te, Signor, c'ogni mia prova,
fuor del tuo sangue, non fa l'uom beato:
miserere di me, da ch'io son nato
a la tua legge; e non fia cosa nuova.

NON può, Signor mio car, la fresca e verde
età sentir, quant'a l'ultimo passo
si cangia gusto, amor, voglie e pensieri.
Più l'alma acquista, ove più 'l mondo perde;
l'arte e la morte non van bene insieme:
che convien più, che di me dunque speri?

GIUNTO è già 'l corso della vita mia,
con tempestoso mar per fragil barca,
al comun porto, ov'a render si varca
conto e ragion d'ogn'opra trista e pia.

THE uneasy, troubled soul finds no cause for its state but some
heavy sin, ill recognized, though not for that concealed from the
immense Pity that the miserable need.
   I speak to you, Lord, – no experience of mine can attain bliss,
without your blood: have mercy upon me, since I am born to your
law; and there is to be no new way.

OUR fresh, green age cannot, my dear Lord, know how much
taste, love, wishes, and thoughts change at our final step. The soul
gains more, the more it loses the world; art and death do not go
well together: what else is needed, what then do you hope from
me?

THE course of my life has now brought me, through a stormy sea,
in a frail ship, to the common port, where one crosses over to
account for every miserable and every holy work. So that I now

Onde l'affettuosa fantasia,
che l'arte mi fece idol'e monarca,
conosco or ben, com'era d'error carca,
e quel c'a mal suo grado ogn'uom desia.

Gli amorosi pensier, già vani e lieti,
che fien'or, s'a due morti m'avvicino?
D'una so 'l certo, e l'altra mi minaccia.
Nè pinger nè scolpir fia più che quieti
l'anima volta a quell'Amor divino
c'aperse, a prender noi, 'n croce le braccia.

GL'INFINITI pensier mie', d'error pieni,
ne gli ultim'anni della vita mia
restringer si dovrien 'n un sol, che sia
guida agli eterni suo' giorni sereni.
Ma che poss'io, Signor, s'a me non vieni
con l'usata ineffabil cortesia?
....

see how utterly mistaken was the fond imagining that made art an
idol and a king for me, and know what, to his own harm, each man
desires.

What will become, now, of thoughts of love, once light and gay,
if I draw near to two deaths? I know the certainty of one, and the
other threatens me. There shall be no more painting, no more
making sculpture to calm the soul turned to that divine Love that
opened arms upon the cross, to take us.

MY infinite thoughts, full of confusion, should be narrowed down
to one in the last years of my life, one which can be my guide to
eternal, unclouded days.

But what can I do, Lord, if you do not come to me with your
familiar ineffable courtesy?

Le favole del mondo m'hanno tolto
il tempo dato a contemplare Iddio,
nè sol le grazie sue poste in oblio,
ma con lor, più che senza, a peccar volto.
Quel c'altri saggio, me fa cieco e stolto,
e tardi a riconoscer l'error mio.
Manca la speme, e pur cresce 'l desio,
che da te sia dal proprio amor disciolto.

Ammezzami la strada c'al ciel sale,
Signor mio caro, e a quel mezzo solo
salir m'è di bisogno la tua 'ita.
Mettimi in odio quanto 'l mondo vale,
e quante sue bellezze onoro e colo,
c'anzi morte caparri eterna vita.

Scarco d'un'importuna e greve salma,
Signor mio caro, e dal mondo disciolto,
qual fragil legno a te stanco rivolto
da l'orribil procella in dolce calma.

The idle tales of the world have robbed me of the time I was given to know God, nor have they only thrust his gracious gifts into oblivion, but, with them, rather than without, have turned me to sinning. What makes others wise makes me blind and stupid, and slow to acknowledge my error. Hope fails me, and yet the desire to be freed from self-love by you, God, grows.

Cut by half for me the road that climbs to heaven, my dear Lord, and for that half alone I shall need your help to climb. Make me hate what has value in the world, and those of its beauties that I honour and serve, so that before death I may have earnest of eternal life.

Relieved of a demanding and heavy burden, my dear Lord, and freed from the world, I turn to you, wearied, like a frail ship from the fearful storm, towards sweet calm. The thorns and the nails and

Le spine e i chiodi, e l'una e l'altra palma
col tuo benigno, umil, pietoso volto
prometton grazia di pentirsi molto,
e speme di salute a la trist'alma.

Non mirin con giustizia i tuo' sant'occhi
il mio passato, e 'l castigato orecchio
non tenda a quello il tuo braccio severo.
Tuo sangue sol mie colpe lavi e tocchi,
e più affondi, quant'i' sono più vecchio,
di pronta aita e di perdono intero.

VITTORIA COLONNA

Vivo su questo scoglio orrido e solo,
quasi dolente augel che 'l verde ramo
e l'acqua pura abborre; e a quelli ch'amo
nel mondo ed a me stessa ancor m'involo,
perchè espedito al sol che adoro e colo
vada il pensiero. E sebben quanto bramo
l'ali non spiega, pur quando io 'l richiamo
volge dall'altre strade a questa il volo.

the palm of one and the other hand, with your kindly, humble,
pitying face, promise the grace of great repentance, and hope of
salvation to the sad soul.

Do not let your holy eyes look upon my past in judgement, and
do not let your cruelly offended ear make you stretch an arm in
anger against me. Let your blood only wash and touch upon my
faults, and let it go the deeper, bringing ready aid and complete
pardon, as I am so much the older.

I LIVE upon this fearful, lonely rock, like a sorrowing bird that
shuns green branch and clear water; and I take myself away from
those I love in this world and from my very self, so that my thoughts
may go speedily to him, the sun I adore and worship. And although
they do not try their wings as much as I wish, yet when I call them
back, they turn their flight from other paths to this one.

E 'n quel punto che giunge lieto e ardente
là 've l'invio, sì breve gioia avanza
qui di gran lunga ogni mondan diletto.
Ma se potesse l'alta sua sembianza
formar, quant'ella vuol, l'accesa mente,
parte avrei forse qui del ben perfetto.

QUAL digiuno augellin, che vede ed ode
batter l'ali alla madre intorno, quando
gli reca il nutrimento, ond'egli, amando
il cibo e quella, si rallegra e gode,
e dentro al nido suo si strugge e rode
per desio di seguirla anch'ei volando,
e la ringrazia in tal modo cantando
che par ch'oltre 'l poter la lingua snode;

tal io qualor il caldo raggio e vivo
del divin sole, onde nutrisco il core,
più dell'usato lucido lampeggia,
muovo la penna spinta dall'amore
interno; e senza ch'io stessa m'avveggia
di quel ch'io dico, le sue lodi scrivo.

And at the instant they reach, glad and fervent, the place I send them to, their joy, so brief, greatly surpasses any worldly delight. But if they could recreate his high aspect, as the kindled mind desires, I would perhaps here have a part in perfect good.

LIKE a hungry fledgling, who sees and hears his mother beating her wings about her, when she brings him back nourishment, so that he, who loves the food and her, rejoices and is glad, and, confined in his nest, chafes and rages with the desire to follow her, flying himself, and thanks her by singing in such style that his tongue seems loosened beyond its power;
so do I sometimes, when the warm and living ray of the divine sun whence I nourish my heart flashes with more than usual clearness, move my pen urged by inward love; and write his praises without noting myself what I say.

GASPARA STAMPA

Io non v'invidio punto, angeli santi,
le vostre tante glorie e tanti beni,
e que' disir di ciò che braman pieni,
stando voi sempre a l'alto Sire avanti;
perchè i diletti miei son tali e tanti,
che non posson capire in cor terreni,
mentr'ho davanti i lumi almi e sereni,
di cui conven che sempre scriva e canti.

E come in ciel gran refrigerio e vita
dal volto Suo solete voi fruire,
tal io qua giù da la beltà infinita.
In questo sol vincete il mio gioire,
che la vostra è eterna e stabilita,
e la mia gloria può tosto finire.

Per le saette tue, Amor, ti giuro,
e per la tua possente e sacra face,
che, se ben questa m'arde e 'l cor mi sface,
e quelle mi feriscon, non mi curo;

I don't envy you in the least, holy angels, your so many glories
and blessings, and those longings for what, fully enjoyed, is still
desired, you being always in the presence of our exalted Lord; because my joys are of such a kind and so numerous, as not to be
compassed by earthly hearts, while I have before me those kindly,
serene eyes, of which I must needs write and sing always.

And as you are wont to cull great refreshment and life from His
face in heaven, so do I here below, from his infinite beauty. In this
alone do you surpass my delight, that your glory is eternal and
founded, and mine can speedily end.

By your arrows, Love, I swear, and by your mighty, sacred torch,
that, although the one burn me and waste my heart, and the others
wound, I do not mind; however far you go into the past or the

quantunque nel passato e nel futuro
qual l'une acute, e qual l'altra vivace,
donne amorose, e prendi qual ti piace,
che sentisser giamai nè fian, nè furo;

perchè nasce virtù da questa pena,
che 'l senso del dolor vince ed abbaglia,
sì che o non duole, o non si sente appena.
Quel, che l'anima e 'l corpo mi travaglia,
è la temenza ch'a morir mi mena,
che 'l foco mio non sia foco di paglia.

Io son da l'aspettar ormai sì stanca,
sì vinta dal dolor e dal disio,
per la sì poca fede e molto oblio
di chi del suo tornar, lassa, mi manca,
che lei, che 'l mondo impalidisce e 'mbianca
con la sua falce e dà l'ultimo fio,
chiamo talor per refrigerio mio,
sì 'l dolor del mio petto si rinfranca.

future, there never was, nor will be, loving women, and take which-
ever one you will, to feel the first sharp, and the second devouring,
as I do;

for a virtue is born of this pain of mine that overcomes and dazes
the sense of suffering, so that it does not hurt, or is hardly felt.
That – and it tortures soul and body – is the fear which leads me
towards death, lest my fire should be a blaze of straw.

I AM by now so tired from waiting, so beaten by grief and desire, because of the so little faith and great forgetfulness of him who denies
me, weary as I am, his return, that I call on the presence, who makes
the world pale and whiten with her sickle, and extorts the last
penalty, to relieve me, so strongly does the grief wake in my
bosom.

Ed ella si fa sorda al mio chiamare
schernendo i miei pensier fallaci e folli,
come sta sordo anch'egli al suo tornare.
Così col pianto, ond'ho gli occhi miei molli,
fo pietose quest'onde e questo mare;
ed ei si vive lieto ne' suoi colli.

O GRAN valor d'un cavalier cortese,
d'aver portato fin in Francia il core
d'una giovane incauta, ch'Amore
a lo splendor de' suoi begli occhi prese!
Almen m'aveste le promesse attese
di temprar con due versi il mio dolore,
mentre, signor, a procacciarvi onore
tutte le voglie avete ad una intese.

I' ho pur letto ne l'antiche carte
che non ebber a sdegno i grandi eroi
parimenti seguir Venere e Marte.
E del re, che seguite, udito ho poi
che queste cure altamente comparte,
ond'è chiar dagli espèri ai lidi eoi.

And she becomes deaf to my cries, despising my fond and foolish
thoughts, as he stays deaf to the thought of his returning. So with
tears which keep my eyes wet, I make these waves and this sea pitiful; and he lives happy among his hills.

O RARE bravery of a gentle knight to have carried away, right
into France, the heart of an unwary young woman whom Love
took with the shining of his fine eyes! If you had only kept your
promises to mitigate my grief with two lines, while, sir, you keep
all your desires bent to one, to win honour for yourself.

I have, however, read in antique pages that the great heroes did
not scorn to follow Venus and Mars equally. And I have since heard
of the king whom you follow, that he divides his cares between
these in exalted style, for which he is renowned from the western to
the eastern world.

O NOTTE, a me più chiara é più beata
che i più beati giorni ed i più chiari,
notte degna da' primi e da' più rari
ingegni esser, non pur de ma, lodata;
tu de le gioie mie sola sei stata
fida ministra; tu tutti gli amari
de la mia vita hai fatto dolci e cari,
resomi in braccio lui che m'ha legata.

Sol mi mancò che non divenni allora
la fortunata Alcmena, a cui stè tanto
più de l'usato a ritornar l'aurora.
Pur così bene io non potrò mai tanto
dir di te, notte candida, ch'ancora
da la materia non sia vinto il canto.

O TANTE indarno mie fatiche sparse,
o tanti indarno miei sparsi sospiri,
o vivo foco, o fè, che, se ben miri,
di tal null'altra mai non alse ed arse,

O NIGHT, more clear and blest for me than the clearest, most blessed days, night worthy to be praised by the first, the finest wits, not only by me; you alone have been the trustful minister of my joys; you have made all the bitters of my life sweet and dear, giving me into the arms of him who has bound me.

All that was lacking was for me then to have become lucky Alcmena, for whom the dawn delayed to return so much longer than its wont. Yet I can never speak so much good of you, fair night, that my song would not be surpassed by its theme.

O MY labours poured out in vain, o my so many vainly poured out sighs, o living fire, o faith, which, if I see aright, never chilled, nor

o carte invan vergate e da vergarse
per lodar quegli ardenti amati giri,
o speranze ministre de' disiri,
a cui premio più degno dovea darse,

tutte ad un tratto ve ne porta il vento,
poi che da l'empio mio signore stesso
con queste proprie orecchie dir mi sento
che tanto pensa a me, quanto m'è presso,
e partendo, si parte in un momento
ogni membranza del mio amor da esso.

RIMANDATEMI il cor, empio tiranno,
ch'a sì gran torto avete ed istraziate,
e di lui e di me quel proprio fate,
che le tigri e i leon di cerva fanno.
Son passati otto giorni, a me un anno,
ch'io non ho vostre lettere od imbasciate,
contra le fè che voi m'avete date,
o fonte di valor, conte, e d'inganno.

burned any other woman in such a way, o papers vainly scored, and to be scored, in praise of those burning, beloved eyes, o hopes ministering to desires, to which a worthy prize should have been given,
    all of you are carried away in a moment by the wind, since I have heard with these ears of mine my wicked lord himself say that he thinks of me, being near, and when he leaves, every memory of my love leaves him in an instant.

SEND back my heart, wicked tyrant, which you have and tear so wrongly, and do to it and me just what tigers and lions do to hinds. Eight days have passed, a year to me, in which I have had no letters or messages from you, contrary to the vow you made me, o count, spring of valour and deceit.

Credete ch'io sia Ercol o Sansone
a poter sostener tanto dolore,
giovane e donna e fuor d'ogni ragione,
massime essendo qui senza 'l mio core
e senza voi a mia difensione,
onde mi suol venir forza e vigore?

Io non veggio giamai giunger quel giorno,
ove nacque Colui che carne prese,
essendo Dio, per scancellar l'offese
del nostro padre al suo Fattor ritorno,
che non mi risovenga il modo adorno,
col quale, avendo Amor le reti tese
fra due begli occhi ed un riso, mi prese:
occhi, ch'or fan da me lunge soggiorno;

e de l'antico amor qualche puntura
io non senta al desire ed al cor darmi,
sì fu la piaga mia profonda e dura.
E, se non che ragion pur prende l'armi
e vince il senso, questa acerba cura
sarebbe or tal che non potrebbe aitarmi.

Do you think I am Hercules or Samson to bear so much grief, I, young and a woman and out of my wits, above all since I am here without my heart and without you to defend me, you, from whom strength and vigour are wont to reach me?

I NEVER see that day return when He was born, who put on flesh, although God, come to us again to wipe away our father's wicked acts against his Maker, without remembering the compelling way in which Love, spreading his net between two fine eyes and a smile, caught me: eyes that now sojourn far from me;
and without feeling the old love give some prick to my desires and my heart, so deep and severe was my wound. And, if reason did not take up arms and conquer feeling, that bitter care would even now be such that reasoning could not help me.

La piaga, ch'io credea che fosse salda
per la omai molta assenzia e poco amore
di quell'alpestro ed indurato core,
freddo più che di neve fredda falda,
si desta ad or ad ora e si riscalda,
e gitta ad or ad or sangue ed umore;
sì che l'alma si vive anco in timore,
ch'esser devrebbe omai sicura e balda.

Nè, perchè cerchi aggiunger novi lacci
al collo mio, so far che molto o poco
quell'antico mio nodo non m'impacci.
Si suol pur dir che foco scaccia foco;
ma tu, Amor, che 'l mio martir procacci,
fai che questo in me, lassa, or non ha loco.

TORQUATO TASSO

Ecco mormorar l'onde
e tremolar le fronde
a l'aura mattutina e gli arboscelli,
e sovra i verdi rami i vaghi augelli
cantar soavemente
e rider l'oriente:

The wound, which I believed to be healed by the now continued
absence and slight love of that flinty, hardened heart, colder than
cold sheet of snow, wakes from time to time, and grows warm, and
spurts, from time to time, with blood and moistness; so that my
soul still lives in fear, when it should now be safe and confident.

Nor can I in any way put new bonds to my neck, without that
early knot's hindering me more or less. They often say that fire
drives away fire; but you, Love, who seek my martyrdom, pre-
vent this happening in me, weary though I be.

Now the waves murmur and leaves and bushes tremble in the
morning breeze, and above the green branches enamoured birds
sing softly and the east smiles: now the dawn already shows and is

ecco già l'alba appare
e si specchia nel mare,
e rasserena il cielo
e le campagne imperla il dolce gelo,
e gli alti monti indora.
O bella e vaga Aurora.
L'aura è tua messaggera, e tu de l'aura
ch'ogni arso cor ristaura.

ORE, fermate il volo
nel lucido oriente,
mentre se 'n vola il ciel rapidamente;
e, carolando intorno
a l'alba mattutina
ch'esce da la marina,
l'umana vita ritardate e 'l giorno.
E voi, Aure veloci,
portate i miei sospiri
là dove Laura spiri
e riportate a me sue chiare voci,
sì che l'ascolti io solo,
sol voi presenti e 'l signor nostro Amore,
Aure soavi ed Ore.

mirrored in the sea, and the sky grows clear and the mild frost decks
the fields with pearls and the high mountains with gold. O lovely,
eager Dawn. The breeze is your messenger, and you are hers,
who freshens every parched heart.

HOURS, halt your flight in the shining east, while heaven flies
quickly on; and, dancing about the first light, as it comes up from
the waves, slow human life and the day. And you, swift Breezes,
bear my sighs where Laura breathes and carry back to me her own
clear words, so that I may listen to them alone, with only you
present and our lord Love, sweet Breezes and Hours.

LA giovinetta scorza,
ch'involge il tronco e i rami
d'un verde lauro, Amor vuol ch'io sempre ami;
e le tenere fronde,
fra cui vaghi concenti
fan gli augelletti al mormorar de' venti;
e l'ombra fresca e lieta
che da le foglie acerbe
cade co' dolci sonni in grembo a l'erbe.
Quivi le rete asconde,
nè 'n parte più secreta,
stanco di saettare, Amor s'acqueta.

GIAMMAI più dolce raggio
non spiega il sole in un fiorito maggio
di quel che le tue rose e i tuoi ligustri
fa sì chiari ed illustri;
nè caggiono giammai la state e 'l verno,
tal c'hai l'aprile eterno:
perpetua primavera hai nel bel viso
e 'l sol è il dolce riso.

LOVE invites me to love for ever the tender bark that enwraps a green laurel's trunk and branches; and the young foliage from which the birds make harmony to the wind's murmuring; and the fresh and happy shade that falls from the unripened leaves upon the grass's lap with soft slumbers. There Love hides his nets, nor is there a more secluded place where, tired of shooting his arrows, he is soothed.

THE sun in a flowering May never shed a sweeter light than the one which makes your roses and may-flowers so clear and brilliant; nor do they ever fall in summer or winter, so that you have an eternal April: you have perpetual spring in your face and your soft smile is the sun.

VITA de la mia vita,
tu mi somigli pallidetta oliva
o rosa scolorita;
nè di beltà sei priva,
ma in ogni aspetto tu mi sei gradita,
o lusinghiera o schiva;
e se mi segui o fuggi
soavemente mi consumi e struggi.

O VIA più bianca e fredda
di lei che spesso fa parer men belle
col suo splendor le stelle;
turba il suo puro argento
o nube o pioggia o vento,
nulla il tuo bel candore e i vaghi giri.
S'in me tu lieta giri
sia la mia vita un sogno ed io contento.

LIFE of my life, you seem like the pallid olive to me, or the faded
rose; nor are you charmless, but you are pleasant to me, however
you appear, flattering or shy; and whether you follow or fly, softly
you consume and unmake me.

O WHITER and colder far than her who often makes the stars less
fair with her shining; a cloud or rain or wind dims her pure silver,
nothing, your lovely whiteness and your fairest eyes. If you turn
glad to me, my life can be a dream and I be happy.

SIEPE, che gli orti vaghi
e me da me dividi,
sì bella rosa in te giammai non vidi
com'è la donna mia
bella, amorosa e pia;
e mentr'io stendo sovra te la mano
la mi stringe pian piano.

MENTRE angoscia e dolore
e spavento e timore
sono intorno al mio core afflitto e stanco,
vestitevi di bianco,
o miei negri pensieri:
del candor de la fede,
ch'ove s'uccide più forte rinasce,
siano le vostre fasce.
O miei fidi guerrieri,
su, su, veloci e pronti
prendete i passi ed ingombrate i monti.

HEDGE, that separate the fair orchards and me from myself, I never saw so lovely a rose in you, as lovely, fond, and holy as my lady is; and while I stretch my hand over you, she presses it softly.

WHILE anguish and grief and terror and anxiety are about my tired afflicted heart, clothe yourselves in white, o black thoughts of mine: let your robes be of the whiteness of the faith, which with killing is more strongly reborn. O my trusty warriors, up, up, quick and ready, take the passes and throng the mountains.

QUAL rugiada o qual pianto
quai lacrime eran quelle
che sparger vidi dal notturno manto
e dal candido volto de le stelle?
E perchè seminò la bianca luna
di cristalline stelle un puro nembo
a l'erba fresca in grembo?
Perchè ne l'aria bruna
s'udian, quasi dolendo, intorno intorno
gir l'aure insino al giorno?
Fur segni forse de la tua partita,
vita de la mia vita?

Io v'amo sol perchè voi siete bella,
e perchè vuol mia stella,
non ch'io speri da voi, dolce mio bene,
altro che pene.

E se talor de gli occhi miei mostrate
aver qualche pietate,
io non spero da voi del pianger tanto
altro che pianto.

WHAT dew or what weeping, what tears were those that I saw scattered from night's mantle and the pallid face of the stars? And why did the white moon sow a pure cloud of crystalline stars in the lap of the fresh grass? Why were the breezes heard swirling around in the dusky air, as if complaining, until daylight? Were they signs perhaps of your leaving, life of my very life?

I LOVE you simply because you are fair, and my star wishes it, not that I hope for anything from you, my sweet life, but woes.

And if you show pity sometimes for my eyes, I do not hope for anything but weeping for so much weeping.

Nè, perchè udite i miei sospiri ardenti
che per voi spargo a i venti,
altro spera da voi questo mio core
se non dolore.

Lasciate pur ch'io v'ami e ch'io vi miri
e che per voi sospiri,
chè pene pianto e doglia è sol mercede
de la mia fede.

Fummo un tempo felici
io amante ed amato,
voi amata ed amante in dolce stato.
Poi d'amante nemica
voi diveniste, ed io
volsi in disdegno il giovanil desio.
Sdegno vuol ch'io ve'l dica,
sdegno che nel mio petto
tien viva l'onta del mio don negletto;
e le fronde ne svelle
del vostro lauro; or secche e già sì belle.

Nor, because you hear my burning sighs, that for you I give out
to the winds, does this heart of mine hope for anything from you
but sorrow.

Let me still love you and look on you and sigh for you, since
woes, weeping, and sorrow is all the reward I have for loyalty.

We were once happy, I loving and beloved, you beloved and
loving, in a sweet state. Then you became love's enemy, and I
changed my youthful passion into scorn. Scorn demands that I tell
you this, scorn that in my breast keeps fresh the shame of my neglected offering; and tears the leaves from your laurel; now dry and
once so beautiful.

A la Signora Duchessa di Ferrara

SPOSA regal, già la stagion ne viene
che gli accorti amatori a' balli invita,
e ch'essi a' rai di luce alma gradita
vegghian le notti gelide e serene.
Del suo fedel già le secrete pene
ne' casti orecchi è di raccorre ardita
la verginella, e lui tra morte e vita
soave inforsa e 'n dolce guerra il tiene.
Suonano i gran palagi e i tetti adorni
di canto; io sol di pianto il carcer tetro
fo risonar. Questa è la data fede?
Son questi i miei bramati alti ritorni?
Lasso! dunque prigion, dunque ferètro
chiamate voi pietà, Donna, e mercede?

To Her Grace the Duchess of Ferrara

ROYAL bride, now the season is coming round which invites attentive lovers to dances, and in which they charm the chill, clear nights in the rays of kindly, pleasing light. The young virgin dares to tell now the secret pangs of her lover to chaste ears, and softly leaves him doubtful between life and death and keeps him in sweet warfare.

The great palaces, the ornamented roofs resound with song; alone I make this dark prison echo with weeping. Is this the faith you plighted? Are these my longed-for, high deserts? Alas! then, Lady, you call a prison, pity, a coffin, then, recompense?

A Guglielmo Gonzaga, Duca di Mantova

SIGNOR, nel precipizio ove mi spinse
Fortuna, ognor più caggio in ver' gli abissi,
nè quinci ancora alcun mio prego udissi,
nè volto di pietà per me si pinse.
Ben veggio il sol, ma qual talora il cinse
oscuro velo in tenebroso eclissi;
e veggio in cielo i lumi erranti e fissi:
ma chi d'atro pallor così li tinse?
Or dal profond oscuro a te mi volgo
e grido: – A me, nel mio gran caso indegno,
dammi, che puoi, la destra e mi solleva;
ed a quel peso vil che sì l'aggreva
sottraggi l'ale del veloce ingegno,
e volar mi vedrai lunge dal volgo. –

To Guglielmo Gonzaga, Duke of Mantua

SIR, down the precipice over which Fortune thrust me, I fall and deeper fall towards the abyss, nor has anyone hearkened to my prayer up till now, nor has a face coloured with pity for me. Indeed I see the sun, but as he is when a dark veil wraps him in shadowy eclipse; and I see the fixed and wandering stars in heaven: but who has stained them like that with gloomy pallor?

Now from the dark depths I turn to you and cry: Give me, you who can, your right hand in my great, unworthy plight, and raise me; and draw the wing of swift invention from under the vile weight that crushes it, and you will see me fly far from the crowd.

In morte di Margherita Bentivoglio

Non è questo un morire,
immortal Margherita,
ma un passar anzi tempo a l'altra vita;
nè de l'ignota via
duol ti scolori o tema,
ma sol pietà per la partenza estrema.
Di noi pensosa e pia,
di te lieta e sicura,
t'accommiati dal mondo, anima pura.

Al Signor Gaspare Micinelli

Quando fioriva io già di fama e d'anni,
scriver bramai con sì purgati inchiostri
ne l'alta patria tua, fra pompe ed ostri
che ristorasser d'aspro esilio i danni;
or, perch'uom cinto di purpurei panni
lodi miei versi e li rilegga e mostri,
non me n'appago e bramo ombrosi chiostri
ov'io faccia a la morte illustri inganni.

On the Death of Margherita Bentivoglio

This is not a dying, immortal Margaret, but a passing before your time to another life; nor may grief or fear at the unknown way make you pale, but only pity for the final parting. Troubled and compassionate for our sake, happy and sure for your own, you bid the world good-bye, pure soul.

To Signor Gaspare Micinelli

When I flourished in fame and years, I longed to write with such purified inks in your exalted country, among the pomp and purple that might repay bitter exile's losses; now, I am not satisfied if a man clad in princely robes should praise my lines and read them again and show them, and I long for shady cloisters where I might cheat death in illustrious style.

Gasparro, oh foss'io pur ne' vostri monti
tra' novi alberghi e le memorie antiche
di color che gran pregio ebber ne l'armi,
che forse canterei sì gravi carmi
a me medesmo ed a le Muse amiche
che farei scorno a molti illustri e conti!

Al Padre Don Angelo Grillo

Io sparsi ed altri miete: io pur inondo
pianta gentil, cultor non forse indegno,
ed altri i frutti coglie, e me 'n disdegno,
ma per timore il duol nel petto ascondo.
Io porto il peso, io solco il mar profondo,
altri n'han la merce: chi giusto regno
così governa? o chi sarà sostegno
s'in terra caggio o tra gli scogli affondo?

O that I were, Gasparro, among your mountains, among new abodes and the old memories of those who were greatly skilled in arms, for I should perhaps utter, then, songs of such weight to myself and the befriending Muses that I would shame many high and renowned ones!

To Father Don Angelo Grillo

I SOWED and others reap: I still water a gentle plant, a perhaps not unworthy husbandman, and others seize on the fruit, myself disdaining, but for fear I hide my grief within my bosom. I bear the weight, I furrow the deep sea, others have the merchandise: who governs a lawful kingdom so? or who will be my prop if I fall to the ground or sink among rocks?

E mentre pur m'attempo e d'anno in anno
sento le forze in me più stanche e dome,
non sono eguali al dolor mio le glorie,
nè verdeggia in Parnaso a queste chiome
sacrato lauro: e, perchè arroge al danno,
son tromba muta a mille altrui vittorie.

Ad un buffone del Duca Alfonso II

SIGNOR, storta di Palla e tremebondo
cannon di Marte e turbine e tempesta,
di cui temendo di tremar non resta
Tifeo là sotto, onde ne squassa il pondo,
così armatura senza pari al mondo
il zoppo fabro di sua man ti vesta,
e la sua moglie un par di corna in testa
gli ponga, accesa del tuo amor giocondo:

And while still I age, and from year to year feel the powers in
me more weary and more subdued, glories are not equal to my
sorrow, nor does a consecrated laurel spring green upon Parnassus
for these locks: and, to aggravate the harm, I am the mute trumpet
of a thousand victories by others.

To a Clown of Duke Alfonso II's

SIR, scimitar of Pallas and trembling cannon of Mars and whirl-
wind and tempest, fearing which, Typheus does not stop quaking
there below, so that his load shakes – may the limping smith clothe
you in such armour, unparalleled in the world, and his wife, on fire
with joyful love of you, place a pair of horns upon his head:

opra col tuo signor, che si disserri
la mia prigione, o tu con un fendente
manda in pezzi le porte e i catenacci:
così n'andremo in fra la Marzia gente,
tu tutto armato, io sol con gli spallacci,
fra noi le penne accomunando e i ferri.

*Loda il Signor Luigi Camoens, il Quale ha scritto un poema
in lingua Spagnola de' Viaggi del Vasco*

Vasco, le cui felici, ardite antenne
incontro al sol che ne riporta il giorno
spiegâr le vele e fêr colà ritorno
ov'egli par che di cader accenne,
non più di te per aspro mar sostenne
quel che fece al Ciclope oltraggio e scorno,
nè chi turbò l'Arpie nel suo soggiorno,
nè die più bel subietto a colte penne.

work upon your lord, that my prison be unbolted, or do you
with a downward cut send doors and horrid chains into pieces; so
we shall go among the Martian folk, you, completely armed, I with
shoulder-plates alone, sharing equally between us the feathers and
the irons.

*He Praises Signor Luigi Camoens, who Has Written a Long Poem
in Spanish about the Voyages of Vasco da Gama*

Vasco, whose happy, daring masts spread sails towards the sun
which brings us new day, and returned where it appears to hint
of falling, not more was borne on the harsh sea by him who insulted
and mocked the Cyclops, or who roused the Harpy in her den, nor
did this give fairer subject for learned quill.

Ed or quella del colto e buon Luigi
tant'oltre stende il glorioso volo,
ch'i tuoi spalmati legni andar men lunge:
ond'a quelli a cui s'alza il nostro polo
ed a chi ferma in contra i suoi vestigi
per lui del corso tuo la fama aggiunge.

O BELLA età de l'oro,
non già perchè di latte
se 'n corse il fiume e stillò mèle il bosco;
non perchè i frutti loro
diêr da l'aratro intatte
le terre, e gli angui errâr senz'ira o tosco;
non perchè nuvol fosco
non spiegò allor suo velo,
ma in primavera eterna
ch'ora s'accende e verna,
rise di luce e di sereno il cielo;
nè portò peregrino
o merce o guerra a gli altrui lidi il pino.

And now that of learned, good Luigi draws out its glorious
flight so surpassingly, that your caulked hulls did not go as far:
so that the fame of your journey reaches, through him, both those
above whom our pole is raised and those who gaze on the signs of
the opposite one.

O LOVELY age of Gold, not because the river ran with milk and
the wood dripped honey; not because the earth, untouched by the
plough, gave forth its fruits, and the snakes came and went without
hate or poison; nor because dark cloud did not spread its veil, but
the sky, which now burns and freezes, laughed with light and clearness; nor bark bore pilgrim or goods or war to foreign strands.

Mal sol perchè quel vano
nome senza soggetto,
quell'idolo d'errori, idol d'inganno,
quel che da 'l volgo insano
onor poscia fu detto,
che di nostra natura il feo tiranno,
non mischiava il suo affanno
fra le liete dolcezze
de l'amoroso gregge;
nè fu sua dura legge
nota a quell'alme in libertate avvezze;
ma legge aurea e felice
che Natura scolpì: *S'ei piace, ei lice.*

Allor tra fiori e linfe
traen dolci carole
gli Amoretti senz'archi e senza faci;
sedean pastori e ninfe,
meschiando a le parole
vezzi e susurri, ed a i susurri i baci
strettamente tenaci;

But only because that vain name without substance, that idol of
errors, idol of deception (what was later called honour by the sense-
less crowd, which made it the tyrant of our nature) did not mingle
its wearisomeness with the gay pleasures of the amorous flock; nor
was its hard law known to those souls charmed with liberty; only
a golden, happy law that Nature engraved: *What you desire to do,
you may.*

Then Cupids, without bows or torches, carolled softly among
flowers and plants; shepherds and nymphs sat mixing caresses and
whispers with their words, and kisses with their whispers, tightly

la verginella ignude
scopria le fresche rose,
ch'or tien ne 'l velo ascose,
e le poma de 'l seno acerbe e crude;
e spesso in fiume o in lago
scherzar si vide con l'amata il vago.

Tu prima, Onor, velasti
la fonte de i diletti,
negando l'onde a l'amorosa sete:
tu a' begli occhi insegnasti
di starne in sè ristretti,
e tener lor bellezze altrui secrete:
tu raccogliesti in rete
le chiome a l'aura sparte:
tu i dolci atti lascivi
festi ritrosi e schivi,
a i detti il fren ponesti, a i passi l'arte:
opra è tua sola, o Onore,
che furto sia quel che fu don d'Amore.

clinging; the young virgin displayed her fresh roses nakedly which she now keeps hidden by a veil, and the small, unsweetened apples of her breasts; and often was the lover seen to play with the beloved in river or in lake.

You first, Honour, veiled the fountain of delights, denying its waves to amorous thirst; you taught lovely eyes to stay contracted to themselves, and keep their beauties concealed from others, you gathered in a net the tresses scattered to the wind: you made the sweet, lascivious acts, shy and shameful, and forced a bridle upon words, and art on simple walking: this work is yours alone, o Honour, that what was Love's gift should become robbery.

E son tuoi fatti egregi
le pene e i pianti nostri.
Ma tu, d'Amore e di Natura donno,
tu domator de' regi,
che fai tra questi chiostri
che la grandezza tua capir non ponno?
Vattene, e turba il sonno
a gl'illustri e potenti:
noi qui negletta e bassa
turba, senza te lassa
viver ne l'uso de l'antiche genti.
Amiam, chè non ha tregua
con gli anni umana vita, e si dilegua.

Amiam: chè 'l Sol si muore e poi rinasce;
a noi sua breve luce
s'asconde, e 'l sonno eterna notte adduce.

And your boasted deeds are our pains and tears. But you, lord
of Love and Nature, you governor of kings, what are you doing in
these alleys that cannot contain your greatness? Be gone, and
trouble the sleep of the famous and the powerful: leave us here, a
low, neglected crowd, to live without you, in the manner of ancient
peoples. Let us love, for human life makes no truce with the years,
and dwindles away.

Let us love: for the sun dies and then is born again; from us he
hides his brief light, and eternal night brings sleep.

GIORDANO BRUNO

Amor, per cui tant'alto il ver discerno,
ch'apre le porte di diamante e nere,
per gli occhi entra il mio nume; e per vedere
nasce, vive, si nutre, ha regno eterno.
Fa scorger quanto ha il ciel, terra ed inferno,
fa presenti d'assenti effigie vere,
repiglia forze, e, trando dritto, fere,
e impiaga sempre il cuor, scopre ogni interno.

Adunque, volgo vile, al vero attendi;
porgi l'orecchio al mio dir non fallace;
apri, apri, se puoi, gli occhi, insano e bieco.
Fanciullo il credi, perchè poco intendi;
perchè ratto ti cangi, ei par fugace;
per esser orbo tu, lo chiami cieco.

E chi m'impenna, e chi mi scalda il core,
chi non mi fa temer fortuna o morte,
chi le catene ruppe e quelle porte,
onde rari son sciolti ed escon fore?

Love, by whom I distinguish the truth so remote and high, who opens the black and adamantine gates, enters my spirit through my eyes; and is born to see; lives, is fed, has eternal reign for this. He calls into being all that heaven, earth, and hell contain, he causes true copies of the absent to be present, summons up powers and, hurling straight, strikes, wounds the heart ever, and discovers every inward.

Therefore, base throng, look to the truth; incline your ears to my not false speech; open, open, if you can, your eyes, cross-grained and mad as you are. You believe him a child, because you understand so little; because you change rapidly, he seems elusive; as you are eyeless, you call him blind.

And who is to fledge me, and who warm my heart, who not make me fear chance or death, who broke the chains and those gates, whence few are freed and go forth? Ages, years, months, days, and

L'etadi, gli anni, i mesi, i giorni e l'ore,
figlie ed armi del tempo, e quella corte
a cui nè ferro, nè diamante è forte,
assicurato m'han dal suo furore.

Quindi l'ali sicure a l'aria porgo,
ne temo intoppo di cristallo o vetro;
ma fendo i cieli, e a l'infinito m'ergo.
E mentre dal mio globo agli altri sorgo,
e per l'eterio campo oltre penetro,
quel ch'altri lungi vede, lascio al tergo.

MAI fia che de l'amor io mi lamente
senza del qual non voglio esser felice;
sia pur ver che per lui penoso stente,
non vo' non voler quel che sì me lice.
Sia chiar o fosco il ciel, fredd' o ardente,
sempr'un sarò ver l'unica fenice.
Mal può disfar altro destin o sorte
quel nodo che non può sciorre la morte.

hours, daughters and weapons of time, and that assembly for whom
not iron or diamond is durable, have made me safe from his fury.

So that I stretch my wings to the air, nor fear barrier of crystal or
glass; but cut the heavens, and rise to the infinite. And as from my
globe I ascend to others, and penetrate higher into the ethereal field,
what others see as distant I leave behind my back.

NEVER shall it come about that I complain of love without which
I do not wish to be happy; it may be true that for its sake I struggle
painfully, I still do not want not to want what is granted me thus.
Let the heavens be clear or dark, cold or burning, I shall always be
the same towards the only phoenix. Ill can any other destiny or fate
undo that knot which death itself cannot loose.

Al cor, al spirto, a l'alma
non è piacer, o libertade, o vita,
qual tanto arrida, giove e sia gradita,
qual più sia dolce, graziosa ed alma,
ch'il stento, giogo e morte,
ch'ho per natura, voluntade e sorte.

Unico augel del sol, vaga Fenice,
ch'appareggi col mondo gli anni tui
quai colmi ne l'Arabia felice,
tu sei che fuste, io son quel che non fui.
Io per caldo d'amor muoio infelice,
ma te ravviv' il sol co' raggi sui.
Tu bruggi 'n un, ed io in ogni loco;
io da Cupido, hai tu da Febo il foco.

Hai termini prefissi
di lunga vita, e io ho breve fine,
che pronto s'offre per mille ruine;
nè so quel che vivrò, nè quel che vissi:
me cieco fato adduce,
tu certo torni a riveder tua luce.

There is no pleasure, liberty, life, that so smiles on, serves and is pleasant, that is sweeter, more pleasant, and kinder, to my heart, my spirit, my soul, than the hardship, yoke, and death, that I have by nature, will, and fate.

Only bird of the sun, fair Phoenix, who equal the world's years with your own, which you live out in Araby the blest, you are what you were, I am what I was not. I die unhappy from heat of love, but the sun revives you with his rays. You burn in one, and I, in every place; I have my fire from Cupid, you from Phoebus.

You have fixed term of long life, and I have a short course which readily yields itself in a thousand different ruinings; nor do I know what I shall live out, nor what I have lived: blind fate leads me, you return surely to see your light again.

Annosa quercia, che gli rami spandi
a l'aria, e fermi le radici 'n terra;
nè terra smossa, nè gli spirti grandi
che da l'aspro Aquilon il ciel disserra,
nè quanto fia ch'il vern' orrido mandi,
dal luogo ove stai salda, mai ti sferra;
mostri della mia fè ritratto vero,
qual smossa mai strani accidenti fero.

Tu medesmo terreno
mai sempre abbracci, fai colto e comprendi,
e di lui per le viscere distendi
radici grate al generoso seno:
i' ad un solo oggetto
ho fisso il spirto, il senso e l'intelletto.

TOMMASO CAMPANELLA

Modo di filosofare

Il mondo è il libro dove il Senno eterno
scrisse i propri concetti, e vivo tempio
dove, pingendo i gesti e 'l proprio esempio,
di statue vive ornò l'imo e 'l superno;

Aged oak, who spread your branches to the air, and set your roots
in earth; neither tremor of earth, nor the great powers which the
North wind looses from the skies, nor whatever the hateful winter
sends, ever dislodges you from the spot where you rise firm; you
stand as the true image of my faith, which catastrophes never
moved.

You ever and always embrace the same soil, make it fruitful and
bind it, and through its bowels thrust roots welcome to the generous breast: I have spirit, senses, and intellect constant to one end.

The Way of Progressing in Philosophy

The world is the book where eternal Wisdom wrote its own ideas,
and the living temple where, depicting its own acts and likeness, it
decorated the height and the depth with living statues; so that every

perch'ogni spirto qui l'arte e 'l governo
leggere e contemplar, per non farsi empio,
debba, e dir possa: – Io l'universo adempio,
Dio contemplando a tutte cose interno. –

Ma noi, strette alme a' libri e tempii morti,
copiati dal vivo con più errori,
gli anteponghiamo a magistero tale.
O pene, del fallir fatene accorti,
liti, ignoranze, fatiche e dolori:
deh torniamo, per Dio, all'originale!

Gli uomini son giuoco di Dio e degli Angeli

Nel teatro del mondo ammascherate
l'alme da' corpi e dagli effetti loro,
spettacolo al supremo consistoro
da natura, divina arte, apprestate,
fan gli atti e detti tutte a chi son nate;
di scena in scena van, di coro in coro;
si veston di letizia e di martòro,
dal comico fatal libro ordinate.

spirit, to guard against profanity, should read and contemplate here art and government, and each should say: 'I fill the universe, seeing God in all things.'

But we, souls bound to books and dead temples, copied with many mistakes from the living, place these things before such instruction. O ills, quarrels, ignorance, labours, pains, make us aware of our falling away: o, let us, in God's name, return to the original!

Men Are the Sport of God and His Angels

Masked upon the stage of the world by bodies and their properties, our souls, prepared by nature, divine art, for their performance before the highest council, go through the actions and pronounce the words which they were born to; from scene to scene, from interlude to interlude, clothe themselves in gladness and suffering, as ordained by the fateful comedy-book.

Nè san, nè ponno, nè vogliono fare,
nè patir altro che 'l gran Senno scrisse,
di tutte lieto, per tutte allegrare;
quando, rendendo, al fin di giuochi e risse,
le maschere alla terra, al cielo, al mare,
in Dio vedrem chi meglio fece e disse.

Contro Cupido

SON tremila anni omai che 'l mondo cole
un cieco Amore, c'ha la faretra e l'ale;
ch'or di più è fatto sordo, e l'altrui male,
privo di caritate, udir non vuole.
D'argento è ingordo, e a brun vestirsi suole,
non più nudo fanciul schietto e leale,
ma vecchio astuto; e non usa aureo strale,
poichè fur ritrovate le pistole,

Nor do they know, nor can they, nor wish to do, or suffer other
than what great Wisdom, pleased with all, has written to make all
glad; when, at the end of games and disputes, their masks restored
to earth, sky, sea, we shall see in God who best wrought and who
best spoke.

Against Cupid

IT is now three thousand years since the world first worshipped
Love that is blind, with his arrows and his wings; who now, in
addition, has been made deaf, and will not, in his lack of all charity,
hear of another's misfortune. He is gluttonous of silver, and accustomed to dress in brown, no longer a plain and loyal naked child,
but a cunning old man; and he does not use a golden arrow, since
pistols were contrived,

ma carbon, solfo, vampa, tuono e piombo,
che di piaghe infernali i corpi ammorba,
e sorde e losche fa l'avide menti.
Pur dalla squilla mia sento un rimbombo:
– Cedi, bestia impiagata, sorda ed orba,
al saggio Amor dell'anime innocenti –

Al carcere

COME va al centro ogni cosa pesante
dalla circonferenza, e come ancora
in bocca al mostro che poi la devora,
donnola incorre timente e scherzante;
così di gran scienza ognuno amante,
che audace passa dalla morta gora
al mar del vero, di cui s'innamora,
nel nostro ospizio alfin ferma le piante.

but coal, sulphur, flame, thunder, and lead, which infects bodies with hellish wounds, and makes greedy minds deaf and unseeing. Yet I hear an echo to my alarm: 'Yield, beast, scarred, deaf, and blind, to the wise Love of innocent souls.'

To His Prison

As every heavy thing travels from circumference to centre, and as, too, the timorous and playful weasel runs into the mouth of the monster that then devours it, so every lover of great knowledge, who boldly passes from the dead pond to the sea of truth, with which he falls in love, fixes his feet at last in our abode.

Ch'altri l'appelli antro di Polifemo,
palazzo altri d'Atlante, e chi di Creta
il laberinto, e chi l'inferno estremo,
che qui non val favor, saper, nè pietà,
io ti so dir; del resto, tutto tremo,
ch'è rocca sacra a tirannia segreta.

Di sè stesso

Sciolto e legato, accompagnato e solo,
gridando cheto, il fiero stuol confondo:
folle all'occhio mortal del basso mondo,
saggio al Senno divin dell'alto polo.
Con vanni in terra oppressi al ciel men volo,
in mesta carne d'animo giocondo;
e, se talor m'abbassa il grave pondo,
l'ale pur m'alzan sopra il duro suolo.

Which some call Polyphemus's cavern, others, Atlas's palace,
and some, the Cretan labyrinth, and some, uttermost hell – I can
tell you that here favour, knowledge or piety have no power; for
the rest, I tremble utterly, for this is a citadel sacred to hidden
tyranny.

On Himself

Freed and bound, accompanied and alone, quiet and shouting, I
confound the savage throng: mad to the mortal eye of this low
world, wise to the divine Wisdom of the high pole. With my
pinions crushed to earth I fly to heaven, a joyful spirit in sad flesh;
and, if at times the heavy burden bows me, my wings still raise me
above the hard ground.

La dubbia guerra fa le virtù conte.
Breve è verso l'eterno ogn'altro tempo,
e nulla è più leggier ch'un grato peso.
Porto dell'amor mio l'imago in fronte,
sicuro d'arrivar lieto per tempo
ove io senza parlar sia sempre inteso.

Giudizio sopra Dante, Tasso e Petrarca

TASSO, i leggiadri e graziosi detti
de' duoi maggior della tosca favella
dilettan ben, perchè la vesta è bella,
onora l'esquisiti alti concetti;
ma via più giova il fuoco de' lor petti,
onde nell'alma a virtù non rubella
nasce il soave ardor e la fiammella
ch'è propria dei ben nati spirti eletti.

Doubtful warfare makes virtues known. Short is every other time before eternity, and nothing is lighter than a pleasing load. I bear the image of my love upon my forehead, sure of arriving happily, in good time, where without speaking I shall be ever understood.

His Estimate of Dante, Tasso, and Petrarch

TASSO, the graceful and easy expressions of the two greatest of the Tuscan tongue give much delight, because the garment is fair and does honour to the high, exquisite thoughts; but far more profitable is the fire in their bosoms, from which springs, in the soul not hostile to virtue, that spark and sweet burning which is proper to well-born, chosen spirits.

Voi gli aggiungete e trapassate in dire,
ma il cor per l'ale vostre ancor non sente
ergersi al Ciel, e punger da giuste ire.
Deh! quando fuor della smarrita gente
ci sentirem dal vostro stil rapire
al degno oggetto dell'umana gente?

*Dalla « Lamentevole orazione profetale dal profondo della
fossa dove stava incarcerato »*

A TE tocca, o Signore,
se invan non m'hai creato,
d'esser mio salvatore.
Per questo notte e giorno
a te lagrimo e grido.
Quando ti parrà ben ch'io sia ascoltato?
Più parlar non mi fido,
chè i ferri c'ho d'intorno,
ridonsi e fanmi scorno
del mio invano pregare,
degli occhi secchi e del rauco esclamare.

You equal and surpass them in expression, but the heart does not
yet feel itself lifted to heaven on your wings, nor pricked with
righteous anger. Oh! when will we feel ourselves snatched by your
art from the erring throng to humankind's worthy end?

*From 'Prophetic Prayer of Lament from the Depth of the Pit in
Which He Was Imprisoned'*

IT is for you, o Lord, if you have not created me in vain, to prove
my saviour. For this I weep and cry to you night and day. When
will it seem good to you that I should be heard? I do not trust myself to say more, for the irons I have about me laugh and mock me
for praying in vain, for my dried-up eyes and hoarse exclaiming.

*Dalle «Orazioni tre in salmodia metafisicale
congiunte insieme»*

OMNIPOTENTE Dio, benchè del fato
invittissima legge e lunga pruova
d'esser non sol mie' prieghi invano sparsi,
ma al contrario esauditi, mi rimuova
dal tuo cospetto, io pur torno ostinato,
tutti gli altri rimedi avendo scarsi.
Che s'altro Dio potesse pur trovarsi,
io certo per aiuto a quel n'andrei.
Nè mi si potria dir mai ch'io fosse empio,
se da te, che mi scacci in tanto scempio,
a chi m'invita mi rivolgerei.
Deh, Signor, io vaneggio; aita, aita!
pria che del Senno il tempio
divenga di stoltizia una meschita.

*

BEN so che non si trovano parole
che muover possan te a benivolenza
di chi *ab aeterno* amar non destinasti;
chè 'l tuo consiglio non ha penitenza,

*From 'Three Prayers in Metaphysical Psalm-form
Joined Together'*

ALMIGHTY God, although the unconquerable law of fate, and long
experience not simply of my prayers' being poured forth in vain,
but of their being taken in contrary sense, banish me from your
sight, I still return obstinately, since all other remedies are not
enough for me. For if there were, say, another God, certainly I
would go to him for help. Nor could anyone ever say I was wicked,
if I turned from you who thrust me into such destruction to one
who welcomes me. O, Lord, I wander; help! help! before the
temple of Wisdom becomes a mosque of foolishness.

WELL do I know that no words are to be found that will move
you to benevolence towards one whom you did not destine for
your love from all eternity; for your counsel is without remorse,

nè può eloquenza di mondane scuole
piegarti a compassion, se decretasti
che 'l mio composto si disfaccia e guasti
fra miserie cotante ch'io patisco.
E se sa tutto il mondo il mio martoro,
il ciel, la terra, e tutti i figli loro;
perchè a te, che lo fai, l'istoria ordisco?
E s'ogni mutamento è qualche morte,
Tu, Dio immortal ch'io adoro,
come ti muterai a cangiar mia sorte?

*

Io pur ritorno a dimandar mercede,
dove 'l bisogno e 'l gran dolor mi caccia.
Ma non ho tal retorica nè voce,
ch'a tanto tribunal poi si confaccia.
Nè poca carità, nè poca fede,
nè la poca speranza è che mi nuoce.
E se, com'altri insegna, pena atroce

nor can the eloquence of worldly assemblies bend you to pitying,
if you decreed that my mixed being is to be unmade and to waste
among the many miseries I suffer. And if the whole world knows
of my martyrdom, heaven, earth, and all their children; why do I
rehearse the tale to you who have caused this? And if every change
is something of a death, You, immortal God whom I adore, how
will you change so as to alter my fate?

STILL I come back to ask for mercy, where need and great grief
hunts me. But I have not the eloquence or voice that would be
fitting then for such a jury. Nor is it little charity, nor little faith,
nor little hope that obstructs me. And if, as some teach, there is

che l'anima pulisca e renda degna
della tua grazia, si ritrova al mondo,
non han l'alpe cristallo così mondo,
ch'alla mia puritade si convegna.
Cinquanta prigioni, sette tormenti
passai, e pur son nel fondo;
e dodici anni d'ingiurie e di stenti.

*

Io, con gli amici pur sempre ti scuso
ch'altro secolo in premio a tuo' riserbi,
e che i malvagi in sè sieno infelici,
sempre affligendo gli animi superbi
sdegno, ignoranza e sospetto rinchiuso;
e che di lor fortune traditrici
traboccan sempre al fine. Ma gli amici,
se, quelii dentro, e noi di fuor, siamo
tutti meschini, chieggon la cagione,
che fa nel nostro mal tue voglie buone;

unspeakable pain in the world which cleanses the soul and makes it
worthy of your grace, the alps have not crystal so clean as would
be needed for my purifying. Fifty prisons, seven torturings, have I
passed through and still am I in the depths; after twelve years of
humiliations and sufferings.

I STILL excuse you constantly with friends, saying that you keep
another world for your own, and that the wicked are unhappy in
themselves, as disdain, ignorance, and close-kept suspicion continually afflict proud minds; and they are always overwhelmed in
the end by their own treacherous fortune. But my friends ask why,
if we are all miserable, those others inwardly, we in an outward
way, your good designs should be effected through our wicked-

che se gli altri enti, e noi, figli d'Adamo,
doveamo trasmutarci a ben del tutto
di magione in magione,
perchè non fai tal muta senza lutto?

*

SE mi sciogli, io far scuola ti prometto
di tutte nazioni
a Dio liberator, verace e vivo,
s'a cotanto pensier non è disdetto
il fine a cui mi sproni;
gl'idoli abbatter, far di culto privo
ogni dio putativo
e chi di Dio si serve, e a Dio non serve;
por di ragione il seggio e lo stendardo
contra il vizio codardo;
a libertà chiamar l'anime serve,
umiliar le proterve.
Nè a tetti, ch'avvilisce
fulmine o belva, dir canzon novelle,
per cui Sion languisce.
Ma tempio farò il cielo, altar le stelle.

ness; for if other creatures and we, children of Adam, must be
transformed from stage to stage for the good of all, why do you not
bring about such change without our lamenting?

IF you free me, I promise to make all nations into a school for
true and living God the liberator, if so daring a thought is not to
be denied the fulfilment to which you spur me; to throw down the
idols, deprive every imaginary god of worship and him who makes
God serve his own purposes, and is of no service to God; raise the
seat and banner of reason against cowardly vice; call enslaved souls
to freedom, humble the froward. Nor sing new psalms, for which
Sion is faint, under roofs that lightning or beast may spoil. But I
shall make the heavens your temple, your altar the stars.

Dispregio della Morte

QUANTE prende dolcezze e meraviglie
l'anima, uscendo dal gravante e cieco
nostro terreno speco!
Snella per tutto il mondo e lieta vola,
riconosce l'essenze, e vede seco
gli ordini santi e l'eroica famiglia,
che la guida e consiglia,
e come il primo Amor tutti consola,
e quanti mila n'ha una stella sola.

*

MIRANDO 'l mondo e le delizie sacre
e quanti onor a Dio fan gli almi spirti,
comincerai stupirti
come Egli miri pur la nostra terra
picciola, nera, brutta e, più vo' dirti,
dove ha tante biastemme orrende ed acre,
che par che si dissacre;
dove sta l'odio, la morte e la guerra,
e l'ignoranza troppo più l'afferra.

Scorn at Death

HOW much sweetness and wonder seizes on the soul, when it comes out from this heavy, blinded cave of ours! Clean and glad it flies through all the universe, recognizes the essences of things, and sees by its side the orders of saints and the heroic family, which guide and counsel it, and how first Love comforts all, and how many spirits a single star holds.

LOOKING on the universe and its holy joys and how many tributes the benign spirits pay to God, you will begin to be amazed that He can look on our little, black, ugly earth, and – I shall say more to you – in which there are so many terrifying and bitter evils, that it seems to lose all sacredness; where hate, death, and war are found, and ignorance, infinitely greater, grips it.

*Canzone a Berillo di pentimento desideroso di confessione
ecc. fatta nel Caucaso*

SIGNORE, troppo peccai, troppo, il conosco;
Signor, più non m'ammiro
del mio atroce martìro.
Nè le mie abbominevoli preghiere
di medicina, ma di mortal tosco
fur degne. Ahi, stolto e losco!
Dissi: – Giudica, Dio, – non – Miserere. –
Ma l'alta tua benigna sofferenza,
per cui più volte non mi fulminasti,
mi dà qualche credenza
che perdonanza alfin mi riserbasti.

*

Io mi credevo Dio tener in mano,
non seguitando Dio,
ma l'argute ragion del senno mio,
    che a me ed a tanti ministrâr la morte.
Benchè sagace e pio, l'ingegno umano
divien cieco e profano,
se pensa migliorar la comun sorte,

*Song of Repentance for Beryl (Don Brigo of Pavia) with the Desire
to be Confessed, etc., Composed in the 'Caucasus'*

LORD, too much I sinned, too much, I know; Lord, I no longer
wonder at my appalling torment. Nor were my loathsome prayers
worthy of balm, but of deadly poison. Ah! foolish and darkened! I
said: Judge, God, – not – Have mercy. But your high kindly
patience, thanks to which, many times, you have not blasted me,
gives me some assurance that you have reserved pardon for me at
the last.

I BELIEVED I held God in my hand, though not following God,
but the subtle reasonings of my intellect, that to me and so many
have dealt death. Although wise and pious, human wit becomes
blind and profane, if it thinks to better the common fate before you,

pria che mostrarti a' sensi suoi, Dio vero,
e mandarlo ed armarlo non ti degni,
come tuo messaggiero,
di miracoli e prove e contrassegni.

*

TARDI, Padre, ritorno al tuo consiglio,
tardi il medico invoco;
tanto aggravato, il morbo non dà loco.
Quanto più alzar vo' gli occhi al tuo splendore,
più mi sento abbagliar, gravarmi il ciglio.
Poi con fiero periglio
dal lago inferior tento uscir fuore
con quelle forze che non ho, meschino.
Meschino me, per me stesso perduto,
chè l'aiuto divino,
che sol salvarmi può, bramo e rifiuto!

*

MERTI non ho per quelli gran peccata,
che contra te ho commesso,
Madre di Cristo, e voi che state appresso,

true God, see fit to reveal yourself to its faculties, and send it and
arm it as your messenger, with miracles and proofs and signs.

LATE, father, I come back for your counsel, late I summon the
doctor; so worsened the disease that it does not yield. The more
I wish to raise my eyes to your brightness, the more I feel dazzled,
my eyelids weighing. Then, to my fierce danger, I try to get out of
the bottommost lake with those powers that, wretch, I do not possess. Wretch that I am, lost thanks to myself, since I desire and
refuse the divine aid which alone can save me!

I HAVE no merit, thanks to those great sins which I have committed against you, Mother of Christ, and you who are near her,

spirti beati, abitator del lume,
che 'l mondo adempie, e sol la terra ingrata
ancor non ha purgata,
prego contra ragion, contra il costume,
ch'al vostro capital fiero inimico
impetrate da lui qualche perdono,
ch' a' peccator fu amico;
poichè tra gli empi il maggior empio io sono.

GIOVAN BATTISTA MARINO

Donna che si lava le gambe

Sovra basi d'argento in conca d'oro
io vidi due colonne alabastrine
dentro linfe odorate e cristalline
franger di perle un candido tesoro.
O (dissi) del mio mal posa e ristoro,
di Natura e d'Amor mète divine,
stabilite per ultimo confine
ne l'Oceano de le dolcezze loro.

blessed spirits, inhabitants of the light which fills the world, and has not cleansed the ungrateful earth alone; I pray unreasonably, against use, for you to beg some pardon for your fierce major enemy from him who was the friend of sinners; because among the wicked, the greatest one am I.

Woman Washing Her Legs

In a shell of gold upon silver base I saw two columns of alabaster amid perfumed and crystal currents breaking a white treasure of pearls. O (I said) resting-place and balm of my suffering, divine ends of Nature and Love, set as the utmost bounds in the Ocean of their own delights.

Fossi Alcide novel, chè i miei trofei
dove mai non giungesse uman desio
traspiantandovi in braccio erger vorrei.
O stringer, qual Sanson, vi potess'io,
chè col vostro cader dolce darei
tomba a la morte e morte al dolor mio.

Dafne in Lauro

DEH, perchè fuggi, o Dafne,
da chi ti segue ed ama,
e fuor che i tuoi begli occhi altro non brama?
Se' molle ninfa? o duro tronco forse
di questo alpestro monte,
rigida e sorda a chi ti prega e chiama?
Ma se tu tronco sei,
come al fuggir le piante hai così pronte?
Come non sai fermarti ai preghi miei?
Così dicea, ma scorse
in vero tronco allor cangiata Apollo
la bella fuggitiva
fermarsi immobilmente in su la riva.

Might I be a new Alcides, for, taking you up in my arms, I
would raise my trophies where human desire had never reached. Or
might I crush you together, like Samson, for I would give death a
tomb with your sweet fall and death to my grief.

Daphne into Laurel

O WHY do you flee, o Daphne, from him who follows and loves
you, and desires nothing other than your lovely eyes? Are you a
soft nymph? or perhaps a hard tree-trunk of this flinty mountain-
side, unbending and deaf to him who begs and calls you? But if you
are a trunk, why are your feet so ready to flee? How can you not
stay for my entreaties? So Apollo was speaking, but he saw then
the lovely fugitive, changed into a real trunk, stay unmovingly
upon the bank.

Fede rotta

Sovra l'umida arena
de le latine sponde
di propria man Tirrena
queste parole un dì scriver vid'io:
Mirzio è sol l'amor mio.
Ahi fu ben degna di sì fral parola,
crudel, l'arena sola; onde poi l'onde
e del Tebro in un punto e de l'oblio
Mirzio, ch'era il tu'amore,
radessero dal lido e dal tuo core.

Bella schiava

Nera sì, ma se' bella, o di Natura
fra le belle d'Amor leggiadro mostro.
Fosca è l'alba appo te; perde e s'oscura
presso l'ebeno tuo l'avorio e l'ostro.
Or quando, or dove il mondo antico o il nostro
vide sì viva mai, sentì sì pura
o luce uscir di tenebroso inchiostro,
o di spento carbon nascere arsura?

Broken Vows

On the damp sands of the Italian shore, I saw Tirrena with her own
hand writing these words one day: Mirtius is my only love. Ah,
cruel fair, the sand alone was fit for words so frail; since the waves
of the Tiber and forgetfulness at the one instant erased Mirtius,
who was your love, from the beach and from your heart.

Beautiful Slave

Black, yes, but you are beautiful, or a graceful monster of
Nature's among Love's beauties. The dawn is gloomy where you
are; ivory and hue of rose fade and are darkened beside your ebony.
When or where did the ancient world, or ours, see so living, feel so
pure a light come from shady ink, or burning spring from burnt-
out coal?

Servo di chi m'è serva, ecco ch'avvolto
porto di bruno laccio il core intorno,
che per candida man non fia mai sciolto.
Là 've più ardi, o Sol, sol per tuo scorno
un sole è nato; un Sol, che nel bel volto
porta la notte ed ha negli occhi il giorno.

Dipartita

Già fuor de l'onde il Sol sferza i destrieri,
ecco del mio partir l'ora che giunge;
Lilla, intanto, s'Amor ne scalda e punge,
sieno i fidi sospir nostri corrieri.
E come per incogniti sentieri
con Aretusa Alfeo si ricongiunge,
così mentre vivranno i corpi lunge,
a visitarsi tornino i pensieri.

Slave of her who is slave to me, look, I bear a dusky noose round my heart that will never be loosed by white hand. Where you most burn, o Sun, a sun has been born for your sole shaming; a sun that wears night upon her face, and in her eyes has day.

Leave-taking

ALREADY the sun whips his coursers from the waves, and now the hour of my leave-taking arrives; Lilla, the while, if Love warms and pricks us on, let our faithful sighs be our messengers. And as by unknown ways Alpheus joins himself with Arethusa again, so while our bodies live far apart, let our thoughts come back to visit one another.

Spesso due stelle in ciel destre e felici,
se ben per vario sito il corso fanno,
scontrarsi almen con lieti aspetti amici.
E due piante talor divise stanno,
ma sotterra però con le radici
se non co' rami, a ritrovar si vanno.

L'amore incostante

(al Signor Marcello Sacchetti)

CHI vuol veder, Marcello,
Proteo d'amor novello,
novel camaleonte,
a me giri la fronte,
ch'ognor pensier volgendo,
forme diverse e color vari apprendo.

Già defender non oso
il mio fallo amoroso;
anzi l'error confesso,
la colpa accuso io stesso:

Often two stars, nimble and happy in heaven, even though they take their way through different parts, have met at least with glad and loving look. And two plants often stand separate, but move to find one another again, if not with their branches, still with their roots underground.

Inconstant Love

(to Signor Marcello Sacchetti)

WHOEVER cares to see a Proteus of new love, Marcello, a new chameleon, let him turn his eyes on me, for, as my thoughts come back to this subject at all times, so do I embrace different forms and various colours.

I do not in the least dare defend my amorous failing; rather I confess my being wrong, and charge myself with the fault: but

ma chi fia che raccoglia
sul corso fren de la sfrenata voglia?

Chi d'un cupido amante
il desir vaneggiante
o circoscrive o lega,
che si move e si piega
lieve più ch'alga o fronda
che tremi in ramo a l'aura, in lido a l'onda?

Non ha sol un oggetto
il mio bramoso affetto:
cento principi e cento
trov' io del mio tormento;
sempre che vada o miri,
sempre ho nove cagioni ond'io sospiri.

Ogni beltà, ch'io veggia,
il cor mi tiranneggia;
d' ogni cortese sguardo
subito avampo ed ardo.
Lasso! ch'a poco a poco
son fatto esca continua ad ogni foco.

who is there who can catch the bridle of the unbridled will as it
careers?

Who can circumscribe or bind the wandering desire of a covet-
ous lover which moves and bends lightly as seaweed or leaf trembles
on the branch in the breeze, by the seashore in the wave?

My burning affection has not just a single object: I find a hundred
causes for torment and a hundred more; as long as I go or look
about, I always have new reasons for sighing.

Every beauty I see dominates my heart; I flame and burn instantly at each kind look. Alas! I gradually grow to be unfailing
fuel for every fire.

Quante forme repente
offre l'occhio a la mente,
tante son lacci ed ami
perch'io vie più sempr'ami:
or per una languisco,
or per altra mi struggo e 'ncenerisco.

Me la fresca beltate,
me la più tarda etate
infiamma e punge e prende:
quella però m'incende
con le grazie e co' lumi,
questa con gli atti gravi e co' costumi.

L'una per la sua pura
semplicetta natura,
l'altra per l'altra parte
de l'ingegno e de l'arte,
egualmente mi piace
e la rozza bellezza e la sagace.

Usi fregiarsi: i fregi
chi fia che non appregi?
Vada inculta e sprezzata,
sol di se stessa ornata:

The sudden forms the eye offers to the mind are so many traps and hooks to make me love much more and more: now I languish for one woman, now for another am destroyed and turned to ashes.

Fresh beauty or maturer age inflame and spur and take me: the former sets me on fire with her graces and her eyes, the latter with her stately gestures and her ways.

The first for her pure simple nature, the other for the other endowment of wit and art, – the uncultivated beauty and the wise one please me equally.

Let a woman be in the habit of tricking herself out: who will not appreciate her ornaments? Let her be unsophisticated and

quella schiettezza adoro,
quella sua povertate è mio tesoro.

O vezzosa e lasciva,
o ritrosetta e schiva,
quella mi fa sperare
che sia tal qual appare,
questa il pensier lusinga
ch'ami d'esser amata e che s'infinga.

Colei, perchè si vede
che di statura eccede:
costei, perchè mi sembra
più sciolta ne le membra:
preso di doppio nodo,
ambedue fra me stesso ammiro e lodo.

Gota bianca e vermiglia
m'alletta a maraviglia;
pallido e smorto volto
sovente il cor m'ha tolto:
ma s'ama ancor talora
bruno ciglio, occhio oscuro e guancia mora.

negligent, adorned only with herself: I adore that directness, that poverty of hers is my treasure.

Let her be winning and lascivious, or shy and backward, the first makes me hope she will be as she seems, the second gives me the flattering idea that she loves to be loved and pretends.

This one, because she is seen to be of uncommon height; that one because she seems more supple of limb: taken in a double knot, I admire and praise each to myself.

A white and crimson cheek delights me wonderfully; a pale, white face has often claimed my heart: but dusky brow, dark eye and swarthy cheek are also to be loved at times.

O crin d'or biondo e terso
tra vivi fior cosperso,
che si confonda e spieghi,
leggiadra man disleghi,
scorger parmi in quell'atto
de l'Aurora purpurea il bel ritratto;

o chiome altra mi mostri
del color degl'inchiostri,
raccolte o pur cadenti
sovra due stelle ardenti,
l'assomiglio non meno
della Notte tranquilla al bel sereno.

Se ride un'angeletta,
quel suo viso è saetta;
se piange, a la mia vita
quel suo pianto è ferita;
se non piange nè ride,
senza stral, senza piaga ancor m'uccide.

Ninfa ch'or alta, or grave,
snoda voce soave
soavemente, e cria

Let a carefree hand unbind a head of gleaming fair hair, clustering, smooth, loosed about living flowers, I seem to see in that action
the fair portrait of the rose-hued Dawn;
    or let another show me hair as black as ink, gathered up or fall-
ing above two burning stars, I compare her no less to the lovely
calm of quiet Night.
    If an angelic little creature laughs, that face of hers is an arrow;
if she weeps, her weeping is a wound in my life; if she neither weeps
nor laughs, without arrow, or wound, she still kills me.
    A nymph who looses her soft voice softly, now high, now deep,

angelica armonia,
chi fia che non invoglie
a baciar quella bocca, onde la scioglie?

Ove fra lieta schiera
fanciulla lusinghiera
batta con dite argute
dolci fila minute,
qual alma non fia vaga
d'aver da man sì dotta e laccio e piaga?

Veder per piagge o valli
giovinetta che balli,
in vago abito adorno
portar con arte intorno
il piede e la persona;
e qual rustico cor non imprigiona?

Se m'incontro in bellezza
a star tra l' coro avvezza
de le nove sirene
di Pindo e d'Ippocrene,
con gli sguardi e co' carmi
può ferirmi in un punto e può sanarmi.

and utters angelic harmonies, who is there who does not have the
desire to kiss that mouth whence she frees her voice?

Where an alluring girl in a gay company strikes the sweet, fine
cords with subtle fingers, what soul would not desire to be caught
and wounded by so expert a hand?

See a young girl dancing by bank or valley, graceful in a fair
dress, who skilfully whirls body and foot; and what rustic heart
does she not imprison?

If I meet a beauty that can take her place beside the nine sirens
of Pindus and Hippocrene, with her looks and songs she can wound
me and, at the same time, heal me.

Havvi donna gentile
ch'al ciel alza il mio stile.
Costei, ch'ama il mio canto,
amo e bramo altrettanto,
e stato cangerei
sol per esserle in sen co' versi miei.

Altra, qualor mi legge,
mi riprende e corregge.
Allor convien ch'io dica:
– O pur l'avessi amica,
o soggiacer felice
a sì bella maestra e correttrice!

Insomma, e queste e quelle
per me tutte son belle,
di tutte arde il desio.
Marcello, or, s'avess'io
mill'alme e mille cori,
sarei nido capace a tanti amori?

There is a courteous lady who extols my style to heaven. Her who loves my song I love and desire as much, and I would change my nature to be in her bosom with my poems.

Another, when she reads me, reproves and corrects me. Then must I needs say: 'O might I yet have her as lover, – o happy submission to so lovely a teacher and corrector!'

In short, these ones and those, they are all beautiful to me, my desire burns for them all. Now, Marcello, if I had a thousand souls and a thousand hearts, would I be a nest large enough for so many loves?

PIETRO METASTASIO

La Libertà

GRAZIE agl' inganni tuoi,
alfin respiro, o Nice;
alfin d'un infelice
ebber gli Dei pietà:
   sento da' lacci suoi,
sento che l'alma è sciolta;
non sogno questa volta,
non sogno libertà.

Mancò l'antico ardore,
e son tranquillo a segno,
che in me non trova sdegno
per mascherarsi amor.
   Non cangio più colore
quando il tuo nome ascolto;
quando ti miro in volto
più non mi batte il cor.

Liberty

THANKS to your deceits, at last I can breathe, o Nice; at last the
Gods have had pity upon an unfortunate man: I feel that my soul
is freed from its snares; I am not dreaming this time, I am not
dreaming of liberty.

   The old ardour has failed, and I am so calm that love does not
find any scorn in me to mask itself with. I no longer change colour
when I hear your name; when I look you in the face, my heart no
longer quickens.

Sogno, ma te non miro
sempre ne' sogni miei;
mi desto, e tu non sei
il primo mio pensier.

 Lungi da te m'aggiro,
senza bramarti mai;
son teco, e non mi fai
nè pena, nè piacer.

Di tua beltà ragiono,
nè intenerir mi sento;
i torti miei rammento,
e non mi so sdegnar.

 Confuso più non sono
quando mi vieni appresso;
col mio rivale istesso
posso di te parlar.

Volgimi il guardo altero,
parlami in volto umano;
il tuo disprezzo è vano,
è vano il tuo favor.

 Chè più l'usato impero
quei labbri in me non hanno;
quegli occhi più non sanno
la via di questo cor.

I dream but I do not see you constantly in my dreams; I wake,
and you are not my first thought. I go about in places far removed
from you without ever wishing for you; I am with you, and it gives
me neither pain nor joy.

I speak of your beauty, nor feel myself melting; I recall my misfortunes, and cannot be offended. I am no longer confused when
you approach me; I can talk of you to my rival himself.

Turn your haughty look on me, speak to me with kind face;
your contempt is vain, and vain, your favour. For those lips no
longer have their accustomed sway over me; those eyes no longer
know the way to this heart.

Quel che or m'alletta o spiace,
se lieto o mesto or sono,
già non è più tuo dono,
già colpa tua non è:
  che senza te mi piace
la selva il colle il prato;
ogni soggiorno ingrato
m'annoia ancor con te.

Odi, s'io son sincero:
ancor mi sembri bella,
ma non mi sembri quella
che paragon non ha:
  e (non t'offenda il vero)
nel tuo leggiadro aspetto
or vedo alcun difetto,
che mi parea beltà.

Quando lo stral spezzai,
(confesso il mio rossore)
spezzar m'intesi il core,
mi parve di morir.
  Ma, per uscir di guai,
per non vedersi oppresso,
per riacquistar se stesso
tutto si può soffrir.

What delights or displeases me, if I am merry or sad, is no longer
your gift, nor your fault: for without you I take pleasure in wood
and hill and meadow; even with you every joyless place is tedious.

Listen, to judge if I am sincere: you still strike me as beautiful,
but you do not seem the woman who has no equal: and (do not be
offended by the truth) I now see in your glad face some blemishes
which I once took for beauties.

When I broke off the arrow, I felt my heart breaking, (I confess
my blushes), I seemed to be dying. But we can suffer anything to
free ourselves from woes, to see ourselves no longer tyrannized, to
repossess ourselves.

Nel visco, in cui s'avvenne
quell' augellin talora,
lascia le penne ancora,
ma torna in libertà:
　poi le perdute penne
in pochi dì rinnova;
cauto divien per prova,
nè più tradir si fa.

So che non credi estinto
in me l'incendio antico,
perchè sì spesso il dico,
perchè tacer non so.
　Quel naturale istinto,
Nice, a parlar mi sprona,
per cui ciascun ragiona
de' rischi che passò.

Dopo il crudele cimento
narra i passati sdegni,
di sue ferite i segni
mostra il guerrier così.
　Mostra così contento
schiavo, che uscì di pena,
la barbara catena
che strascinava un dì.

In the lime where it has chanced to come, the little bird sometimes leaves even feathers, but returns to liberty: then grows its
lost feathers again in a few days; becomes wary from experience,
and does not let itself be betrayed another time.

I know you do not think the old flame dead in me, because I say
it so often, because I do not know how to keep silent. The natural
instinct which makes every one dwell on risks they have escaped –
that, Nice, spurs me to talk.

After the cruel danger we tell of threats that are past, the warrior
in this way shows the marks of his wounds. In this way the slave,
who has escaped from pain, happily shows the barbarous chain
which he once dragged.

Parlo, ma sol parlando
me soddisfar procuro:
parlo, ma nulla io curo
che tu mi presti fe';
    parlo, ma non dimando
se approvi i detti miei,
nè se tranquilla sei
nel ragionar di me.

Io lascio un'incostante,
tu perdi un cor sincero:
non so di noi primiero
chi s'abbia a consolar.
    So che un sì fido amante
non troverà più Nice;
che un'altra ingannatrice
è facile a trovar.

Nel comporre l' Olimpiade

SOGNI e favole io fingo; e pure in carte
mentre favole e sogni orno e disegno,
in lor, folle ch'io son, prendo tal parte,
che del mal che inventai piango e mi sdegno.

I speak, but in speaking have satisfaction myself alone: I speak, but do not in the least care that you should credit what I say; I speak, but do not ask if you approve my words, nor if you are calm in talking of me.

I leave an inconstant heart, you lose a sincere one: I do not know which of us will be first to be consoled. I know that Nice will never again find so faithful a lover; that it is easy to find another deceiving woman.

While Writing the Olympiad

DREAMS and fables I fashion; and even while I sketch and elaborate fables and dreams upon paper, fond as I am, I so enter into them that I weep and am offended at ills I invent. But am I wiser

Ma forse, allor che non m'inganna l'arte,
più saggio sono? È l'agitato ingegno
forse allor più tranquillo? O forse parte
da più salda cagion l'amor, lo sdegno?

Ah! che non sol quelle ch'io canto o scrivo
favole son; ma quanto temo e spero,
tutto è menzogna, e delirando io vivo.
Sogno della mia vita è il corso intero.
Deh tu, Signor, quando a destarmi arrivo,
fa' ch'io trovi riposo in sen del vero.

UGO FOSCOLO

Di sè stesso

PERCHÈ taccia il rumor d'una catena,
di lagrime, di speme, e d'amor vivo,
e di silenzi; chè pietà mi affrena
se con lei parlo, o di lei penso o scrivo.
Tu sol mi ascolti, o solitario rivo,
ove ogni notte Amor seco mi mena,
qui affido il pianto e i miei danni descrivo,
qui tutta verso del dolor la piena.

when art does not deceive me? Is my disturbed mind perhaps calmer then? Or does love and scorn perhaps spring from firmer cause?

Ah, not only what I sing and write are fables; but what I fear and hope for, all is falsehood, and I live in a feverishness. The whole course of my life has been dream. O Lord, let me find rest in the bosom of truth, when finally I come to wake.

On Himself

So that the stirring of a chain may be silent, I live on tears, on hope, on love, and silences; for tenderness restrains me, if I speak with her, or think or write of her. You alone listen to me, o lonely stream, where every night Love leads me in his company, here I confide my tears and declare my sufferings, and here pour out the fullness of my grief.

E narro come i grandi occhi ridenti
arsero d'immortal raggio il mio core,
come la rosea bocca, e i rilucenti
odorati capelli, ed il candore
delle divine membra, e i cari accenti
m'insegnarono alfin pianger d'amore.

Alla sua donna lontana

MERITAMENTE, però ch'io potei
abbandonarti, or grido alle frementi
onde che batton l'alpi, e i pianti miei
sperdon sordi del Tirreno i venti.
Sperai, poichè mi han tratto uomini e Dei
in lungo esilio fra spergiure genti
dal bel paese ove or meni sì rei,
me sospirando, i tuoi giorni fiorenti,
sperai che il tempo, e i duri casi, e queste
rupi ch' io varco anelando, e le eterne,
ov'io qual fiera dormo, atre foreste,
sarien ristoro al mio cor sanguinente;
Ahi, vota speme! Amor fra l'ombre inferne
seguirammi immortale, onnipotente.

And tell how those great laughing eyes burnt my heart with an immortal ray, how the rose-like mouth, and the shining fragrant locks, and the whiteness of the divine limbs, and the dear cadence taught me at last to weep for love.

To His Distant Love

RIGHTLY, since I could leave you, do I now cry to the trembling waves that beat upon the Alps, and the Tyrrhenian winds deafly scatter my lament. I hoped, after men and Gods dragged me into long exile among peoples self-betrayed from the fair region where you so poorly pass your Florentine days, sighing for me, I hoped that time, and hardships, and these rocks which I cross panting, and the eternal black forests where I sleep like a wild beast, that these might mean comfort to my bleeding heart. Ah, empty hope! Love will follow me amid the infernal shades immortal, all-powerful.

Il proprio ritratto

SOLCATA ho fronte, occhi incavati intenti;
crin fulvo, emunte guance, ardito aspetto;
labbri tumidi, arguti, al riso lenti,
capo chino, bel collo, irsuto petto;
membra esatte; vestir semplice eletto;
ratti i passi, il pensier, gli atti, gli accenti:
prodigo, sobrio; umano, ispido, schietto;
avverso al mondo, avversi a me gli eventi.

Mesto i più giorni e solo; ognor pensoso,
alle speranze incredulo e al timore;
il pudor mi fa vile; e prode l'ira;
cauta in me parla la ragion; ma il core,
ricco di vizi e di virtù, delira –
Morte, tu mi darai fama e riposo.

Alla sera

FORSE perchè della fatal quiete
tu sei l'immago a me sì cara vieni,
o sera! E quando ti corteggian liete
le nubi estive e i zeffiri sereni,

Self-portrait

MY brow is furrowed, my eyes, sunk and intense; hair, tawny,
cheeks, colourless, look, bold; thick, well-drawn lips, slow to
laughter, bent head, fine neck, my chest, hairy; compact limbs;
choice and simple style of dress; quick in step, in thought, in act, in
speech: prodigal and sober; kindly and bristling, open; hostile to
the world, events are hostile to me.

Melancholy most days, and alone; constantly thoughtful; doubting before hopes and fears; fine modesty makes me craven; and
anger, brave; reason speaks cautioning me, but my heart, rich in
vices and virtues, raves – Death, you will give me fame and rest.

To Evening

PERHAPS because you are the image of that fatal quiet your coming is so dear to me, o evening! When the summer clouds and calm

e quando dal nevoso aere inquiete
tenebre e lunghe all'universo meni
sempre scendi invocata, e le secrete
vie del mio cor soavemente tieni.

Vagar mi fai co' miei pensier su l'orme
che vanno al nulla eterno; e intanto fugge
questo reo tempo, e van col lui le torme
delle cure onde meco egli si strugge;
e mentre io guardo la tua pace, dorme
quello spirto guerrier ch'entro mi rugge.

A Zacinto

N è più mai toccherò le sacre sponde
ove il mio corpo fanciulletto giacque,
Zacinto mia, che te specchi nell'onde
del greco mar da cui vergine nacque
Venere, e fea quelle isole feconde
col suo primo sorriso, onde non tacque
le tue limpide nubi, e le tue fronde
l'inclito verso di colui che l'acque

breezes woo you, and again when from the snowy air you bring
long and troubled shades to the world, you always come down as
one prayed for, and gently follow out the secret ways of my heart.

You make me linger in thought, upon the paths that go towards
eternal nothingness; and, meanwhile, this evil time flies, and with it
go the swarms of cares in which it wastes itself and me; and as I
look upon your peace, that warrior spirit which roars in me is
sleeping.

To Zante

NEVER more shall I touch the sacred shores where my infant body
lay, my Zante, who look at yourself in the mirror of the Greek
waves from which the virgin Venus rose to life, and made these
islands fertile with her first smile; so that the renowned verse does
not pass over in silence your sereneclouds and leafiness, the verse of

cantò fatali ed il diverso esiglio
per cui bello di fama e di sventura
baciò la sua petrosa Itaca Ulisse.
Tu non altro che il canto avrai del figlio,
o materna mia terra; a noi prescrisse
il fato illacrimata sepoltura.

In morte del fratello Giovanni

UN dì, s'io non andrò sempre fuggendo
di gente in gente, mi vedrai seduto
su la tua pietra, o fratel mio, gemendo
il fior dei tuoi gentili anni caduto.
La madre or sol, suo dì tardo traendo,
parla di me col tuo cenere muto:
ma io deluse a voi le palme tendo;
e se da lunge i miei tetti saluto,
sento gli avversi Numi, e le secrete
cure che al viver tuo furon tempesta,
e prego anch'io nel tuo porto quiete.
Questo di tanta speme oggi mi resta!
Straniere genti, l'ossa mie rendete
allora al petto della madre mesta.

him who sang the fatal waters and the various exile through which, lovely with fame and misfortune, Ulysses came to kiss his rocky Ithaca. You will not have more than the song of your child, o my mother earth; for us fate has ordained an unwept sepulchre.

Upon the Death of His Brother John

ONE day, if I am not to keep fleeing from people to people, you will see me seated upon your stone, o my brother, weeping for the fallen flower of your generous years. Our mother alone now, drawing out her late day, speaks to your dumb ashes of me: but I stretch out vain hands to you both; and if from afar I hail the roofs of home, I am aware of the hostile Gods, and the secret cares which were a tempest to your life, and I too pray for quietness in your haven. This is what is left to me today of so much hope! Foreign peoples, give back my bones then to the bosom of my sad mother.

A Luigia Pallavicini caduta da cavallo

I BALSAMI beati
per te le Grazie apprestino,
per te i lini odorati
che a Citerea porgeano
quando profano spino
le punse il piè divino,

quel dì che insana empiea
il sacro Ida di gemiti,
e col crine tergea,
e bagnava di lagrime
il sanguinoso petto
al ciprio giovinetto.

Or te piangon gli Amori,
te fra le Dive liguri
Regina e Diva! e fiori
votivi all'ara portano
d'onde il grand'arco suona
del figlio di Latona.

To Luigia Pallavicini Who Fell from Her Horse

LET the Graces make ready the blessed oils for you, for you the scented garments that they held out for Venus when a profane thorn pricked her foot divine,

that day when distractedly she filled sacred Ida with her moaning, and wiped with her hair, and bathed with her tears the bloody breast of the Cypriot youth.

Now the Cupids weep for you, you Queen and Goddess among the Ligurian Goddesses! and bear offerings of flowers to the altar from whence the great bow of Latona's son rings out.

E te chiama la danza
ove l'aure portavano
insolita fragranza,
allor che a' nodi indocile
la chioma al roseo braccio
ti fu gentile impaccio.

Tal nel lavacro immersa,
che fiori, dall'inachio
clivo cadendo, versa,
Palla i dall'elmo liberi
crin sulla man che gronda
contien fuori dell'onda.

Armoniosi accenti
dal tuo labbro volavano,
e dagli occhi ridenti
traluceano di Venere
i disdegni e le paci,
la speme, il pianto, e i baci.

And the dance calls for you, to which the breezes came with rare fragrance when, untamed by its knots, your hair formed a gentle impediment to your rosy arm.

Just as when Pallas, immersed in the bath that fills with the stream pouring from the Inachian cliff, holds her hair, free of the helmet, out of the water with dripping hand.

Loving accents flew from your lips, and in your laughing eyes shone the scorn and the peace of Venus, the hope, the weeping, and the kisses.

Deh! perchè hai le gentili
forme e l'ingegno docile
volto a studi virili?
Perchè non dell'Aonie
seguivi, incauta, l'arte,
ma i ludi aspri di Marte?

Invan presaghi i venti
il polveroso agghiacciano
petto e le reni ardenti
dell'inquieto alipede,
ed irritante il morso
accresce impeto al corso.

Ardon gli sguardi, fuma
la bocca, agita l'ardua
testa, vola la spuma,
ed i manti volubili
lorda, e l'incerto freno,
ed il candido seno;

O why have you turned your gentle form and mild understanding to manly pursuits? Why did you follow, rash one, not the
Aonian arts but the rough games of Mars?

Vainly prophetic the winds froze the dusty chest and the burning
haunches of the restless wingèd steed, and the bit, chafing, gave
greater impulse to its career.

Its glances burn, its mouth steams, the high head shakes, the
foam flies, and streaks the flowing skirts, and the uncertain bridle,
and the white bosom;

e il sudor piove, e i crini
sul collo irti svolazzano,
suonan gli antri marini
allo incalzato scalpito
della zampa che caccia
polve e sassi in sua traccia.

Già dal lito si slancia
sordo ai clamori e al fremito;
già già fino alla pancia
nuota . . . e ingorde si gonfiano
non più memori l'acque
che una Dea da lor nacque.

Se non che il re dell'onde
dolente ancor d'Ippolito
surse per le profonde
vie del tirreno talamo,
e respinse il furente
col cenno onnipotente.

and sweat rains down, and the mane flutters on the bristling neck, the ocean caves resound to the hurried beating of the hoof that spurns dust and stones from its track.

Already it throws itself from the shore deaf to the cries and the shuddering; now, now up to the belly it swims ... and the waters swell, as if they gorged their fill, no longer mindful that a Goddess was born from them.

But, no, the king of the waves, still grieving for Hippolytus, rose from the deep paths of the Tyrrhenian bed, and threw back the furious beast with an all-powerful sign.

Quei dal flutto arretrosse
ricalcitrando e, orribile!
sovra l'anche rizzosse;
scuote l'arcion, te misera
su la petrosa riva
strascinando mal viva.

Pèra chi osò primiero
discortese commettere
a infedele corsiero
l'agil fianco femineo,
e aprì con rio consiglio
nuovo a beltà periglio!

Chè or non vedrei le rose
del tuo volto sì languide,
non le luci amorose
spiar ne' guardi medici
speranza lusinghiera
della beltà primiera.

It drew back from the surge, trampling backwards and, horror!
reared up; it shakes the saddle and drags you, unfortunate one,
scarce alive, over the stony beach.

May he perish who first was unmannerly enough to dare to en-
trust the soft female side to faithless steed, and, with evil counsel,
uncover a new danger to beauty.

For now I would not see the roses of your face so lifeless, nor
your loving eyes search the doctor's looks for a flattering hope of
your first beauty.

Di Cintia il cocchio aurato
le cerve un dì traevano,
ma al ferino ululato
per terrore insanirono,
e dalla rupe etnea
precipitâr la Dea.

Gioian d'invido riso
le abitatrici olimpie,
perchè l'eterno viso,
silenzioso e pallido,
cinto apparia d'un velo
ai conviti del cielo:

ma ben piansero il giorno
che dalle danze efesie
lieta facea ritorno
fra le devote vergini,
e al ciel salia più bella
di Febo la sorella.

One day the hinds were drawing the golden coach of Diana, but
they went mad with terror at the wild beasts' howling, and hurled
the Goddess from the Etnean cliff.

The female dwellers on Olympus rejoiced with envious smile,
because the immortal face, silent and pale, was veiled when she
appeared before the guests of heaven:

but they sorely wept the day she returned happy to the Ephesian
dances among the dedicated virgins, and the sister of Phoebus rose
more lovely in heaven.

De' Sepolcri

(A Ippolito Pindemonte)

DEORUM MANIUM IURA SANCTA
SUNTO (XII TAB.)

ALL'OMBRA de' cipressi e dentro l'urne
confortate di pianto è forse il sonno
della morte men duro? Ove più il Sole
per me alla terra non fecondi questa
bella d'erbe famiglia e d'animali,
e quando vaghe di lusinghe innanzi
a me non danzeran l'ore future,
nè da te, dolce amico, udrò più il verso
e la mesta armonia che lo governa,
nè più nel cor mi parlerà lo spirto
delle vergini Muse e dell'Amore,
unico spirto a mia vita raminga,
qual fia ristoro a' dì perduti un sasso
che distingua le mie dalle infinite
ossa che in terra e in mar semina morte?

On Tombs

(To Ippolito Pindemonte)

LET THE RIGHTS OF THE DIVINE SHADES
BE HELD SACRED (XII TAB)

IN the shade of cypresses and within urns comforted by weeping is
the sleep of death perhaps less hard? When for me the sun no longer
makes the earth fertile with this fair family of plants and animals,
and when future hours will not dance before me, lovely with vain
promise, and when I shall not hear your verse, sweet friend, nor the
sad harmony that sways it, nor in my heart will the spirit any longer
speak of the virgin Muses and of love, only spirit of my wandering
life, what recompense for days lost will a stone be that may mark
out my bones from the infinite number that death sows on land and

Vero è ben, Pindemonte! Anche la Speme,
ultima Dea, fugge i sepolcri; e involve
tutte cose l'obblio nella sua notte;
e una forza operosa le affatica
di moto in moto; e l'uomo e le sue tombe
e l'estreme sembianze e le reliquie
della terra e del ciel traveste il tempo.

Ma perchè pria del tempo a sè il mortale
invidierà l'illusion che spento
pur lo sofferma al limitar di Dite?
Non vive ei forse anche sotterra, quando
gli sarà muta l'armonia del giorno,
se può destarla con soavi cure
nella mente de' suoi? Celeste è questa
corrispondenza d'amorosi sensi,
celeste dote è negli umani; e spesso
per lei si vive con l'amico estinto
e l'estinto con noi, se pia la terra
che lo raccolse infante e lo nutriva,
nel suo grembo materno ultimo asilo

in the sea? True it is indeed, Pindemonte! Even Hope, the last of
goddesses, flies from graves; and oblivion wraps all things in its
night; and a busy force wears them from one movement to the next;
and time disguises man and his tombs and last appearances and the
relics of earth and sky.

But why, before time, will mortal man deny himself the illusion
which him, though dead, still arrests on the threshold of the under-
world? Does he perhaps not live even below ground, when day's
harmony is silent to him, if he can awaken it with sweet cares in
the minds of his own? Heavenly is this meeting of tender feelings,
a heavenly gift to humans; and often through it we live with the
departed friend and the departed with us, if reverently the earth
which received him as a child and fed him, keeps his relics sacred

porgendo, sacre le reliquie renda
dall'insultar de' nembi e dal profano
piede del vulgo, e serbi un sasso il nome,
e di fiori odorata arbore amica
le ceneri di molli ombre consoli.

Sol chi non lascia eredità d'affetti
poca gioia ha dell'urna; e se pur mira
dopo l'esequie, errar vede il suo spirto
fra 'l compianto de' templi acherontei,
o ricovrarsi sotto le grandi ale
del perdono d'Iddio: ma la sua polve
lascia alle ortiche di deserta gleba
ove nè donna innamorata preghi,
nè passeggier solingo oda il sospiro
che dal tumulo a noi manda Natura.

Pur nuova legge impone oggi i sepolcri
fuor de' guardi pietosi, e il nome a' morti
contende. E senza tomba giace il tuo
sacerdote, o Talìa, che a te cantando
nel suo povero tetto educò un lauro
con lungo amore, e t'appendea corone;

from the assault of lightning and the profane feet of the crowd,
offering a last refuse in its motherly lap, and if a stone retains his
name, and a fragrant tree, kind with flowers, consoles his ashes with
soft shade.

Only he who leaves no inheritance of affection has little joy in
urns; and if he should look beyond funeral rites, he sees his spirit
wandering amid the general weeping of Acherontian temples, or
stealing under the great wings of the pardon of God: but his dust
he leaves to the nettles of the desert where no loving woman prays,
nor lonely traveller hears the sigh that Nature sends to us from the
tomb.

Yet a new law today sets graves beyond pitying glances, and to
the dead denies their name. And your priest, o Thalia, lies without
sepulchre, he, who singing to you in his poor dwelling, raised up a
laurel with enduring love, and hung crowns to you there; and you,

e tu gli ornavi del tuo riso i canti
che il lombardo pungean Sardanapàlo,
cui solo è dolce il muggito de' buoi
che dagli antri abduàni e dal Ticino
lo fan d'ozi beato e di vivande.
O bella Musa, ove sei tu? Non sento
spirar l'ambrosia, indizio del tuo Nume,
fra queste piante ov'io siedo e sospiro
il mio tetto materno. E tu venivi
e sorridevi a lui sotto quel tiglio
ch'or con dimesse frondi va fremendo
perchè non copre, o Dea, l'urna del vecchio
cui già di calma era cortese e d'ombre.
Forse tu fra plebei tumuli guardi
vagolando, ove dorma il sacro capo
del tuo Parini? A lui non ombre pose
tra le sue mura la città, lasciva
d'evirati cantori allettatrice,
non pietra, non parola; e forse l'ossa
col mozzo capo gl'insanguina il ladro
che lasciò sul patibolo i delitti.

with your laughter, enriched the songs in which he struck the
Lombard Sardanapalus, who only hearkens to the lowing, that
comes from the Abduan hollows and the Ticino, of cattle that
make him blissful with ease and feasting. O fair Muse, where are
you? I do not scent the ambrosia exhaled, which is sign of your
presence, here where I sit among these plants and sigh for my
mother's house. And you would come and smile upon him under
that lime-tree which now with downcast, leafy boughs keeps shiver-
ing, because it does not cover, o Goddess, the urn of that old man
to whom it was once generous in giving calm and shade. Perhaps,
wandering among humble graves, you look for the spot where
sleeps the sacred head of your Parini? This city, the whorish nurse
of unmanned singers, gave him no shade within its walls, no stone,
no word; and perhaps the thief who parted from his crimes upon
the scaffold, now stains, with the blood of his severed head, those

Senti raspar fra le macerie e i bronchi
la derelitta cagna ramingando
su le fosse e famelica ululando;
e uscir del teschio, ove fuggìa la Luna,
l'upupa e svolazzar su per le croci
sparse per la funerea campagna,
e l'immonda accusar col luttuoso
singulto i rai di che son pie le stelle
alle obbliate sepolture. Indarno
sul tuo poeta, o Dea, preghi rugiade
dalla squallida notte. Ahi! su gli estinti
non sorge fiore, ove non sia d'umane
lodi onorato e d'amoroso pianto.

Dal dì che nozze e tribunali ed are
dier alle umane belve essere pietose
di sè stesse e d'altrui, toglieano i vivi
all'etere maligno ed alle fere
i miserandi avanzi che Natura
con veci eterne a sensi altri destina.

bones. You hear the stray bitch, that roams over the burial pits
and howls from hunger, scraping among the rubble and undergrowth; and hear the owl, that flies out from the skull where it
shunned the moon, and glides among the crosses scattered over
the funereal scene, defiled bird, with mournful sob, cry out against
the rays which the stars in pity shed on forgotten graves. Vainly,
ò Goddess, do you pray for dews to descend upon your poet from
the dismal night. Ah! no flower rises over the deceased, unless it is
honoured by human praise and tears of love.

From the day that marriage and law courts and altars bade human
animals be tender of themselves and of one another, the living took
those remains, which Nature with constant varying destines for
other purposes, from the corrupting atmosphere and from wild
beasts. Tombs were the testimony of past glories, and the altar

Testimonianza a' fasti eran le tombe,
ed are a' figli e uscian quindi i responsi
de' domestici Lari, e fu temuto
su la polve degli avi il giuramento:
religion che con diversi riti
le virtù patrie e la pietà congiunta
tradussero per lungo ordine d'anni.
Non sempre i sassi sepolcrali a' templi
fean pavimento; nè agli incensi avvolto
de' cadaveri il lezzo i supplicanti
contaminò; nè le città fur meste
d'effigiati scheletri: le madri
balzan ne' sonni esterrefatte, e tendono
nude le braccia su l'amato capo
del lor caro lattante onde nol desti
il gemer lungo di persona morta
chiedente la venal prece agli eredi
dal santuario. Ma cipressi e cedri
di puri effluvi i zefiri impregnando
perenne verde protendean su l'urne
per memoria perenne, e preziosi
vasi accogliean le lacrime votive.

for a man's sons, and from them came the answers of the household
gods, and an oath sworn upon the dust of ancestors was awful; a
religion which fatherly virtues and wedded devotion transmitted
for a long succession of years. Sepulchral stones did not always
serve as the floors of temples; nor did the stench of corpses surrounded with incense infect those who came to pray; nor were
cities sad with figured skeletons: mothers start terrified in sleep,
and stretch their arms, bare, over the beloved head of their dear
suckling so that the continuous moaning of one dead begging his
heirs to grant him the sanctuary's hireling prayer does not wake her
child. But cypresses and cedars loading the breeze with their
freshness stretched out perennial green over urns in perennial remembrance, and precious vases held the suppliant tears. Friends

Rapian gli amici una favilla al Sole
a illuminar la sotterranea notte,
perchè gli occhi dell'uom cercan morendo
il Sole; e tutti l'ultimo sospiro
mandano i petti alla fuggente luce.
Le fontane versando acque lustrali
amaranti educavano e viole
su la funebre zolla; e chi sedea
a libar latte e a raccontar sue pene
ai cari estinti, una fragranza intorno
sentia qual d'aura de' beati Elisi.
Pietosa insania che fa cari gli orti
de' suburbani avelli alle britanne
vergini dove le conduce amore
della perduta madre, ove clementi
pregaro i Geni del ritorno al prode
che tronca fe' la trionfata nave
del maggior pino, e si scavò la bara.
Ma ove dorme il furor d'inclite geste
e sien ministri al vivere civile
l'opulenza e il tremore, inutil pompa
e inaugurate immagini dell'Orco
sorgon cippi e marmorei monumenti.

stole a spark from the Sun to light the subterranean night, because
the eyes of man in dying search out the Sun; and all breasts send
their last sigh to the light that flies. The fountains pouring waters of
purification raised up amaranths and violets on the turf of the grave;
and whoever sat there to pour out offerings of milk and to tell over
his sorrows to the dear departed, sensed a fragrance around him as
of the air of blessed Elysium. A tender madness, that makes the
gardens of suburban cemeteries dear to British girls, where they are
led by love for a mother lost, where they implored the Fates to be
favourable to the return of the brave man who had the tallest mast
cut from the ship he overcame, and hewed his coffin from it.* But
where the fever for bold deeds sleeps and wealth and fear are the
ministers of civil life, half columns and marble monuments rise as
useless pomp and unpropitious images of Mammon. Already the

* Nelson.

Già il dotto e il ricco ed il patrizio vulgo,
decoro e mente al bello italo regno,
nelle adulate reggie ha sepoltura
già vivo, e i stemmi unica laude. A noi
Morte apparecchi riposato albergo,
ove una volta la fortuna cessi
dalle vendette, e l'amistà raccolga
non di tesori eredità, ma caldi
sensi di liberal carme l'esempio.

A egregie cose il forte animo accendono
l'urne de' forti, o Pindemonte; e bella
e santa fanno al peregrin la terra
che le ricetta. Io quando il monumento
vidi ove posa il corpo di quel grande
che temprando lo scettro a' regnatori
gli allòr ne sfronda, ed alle genti svela
di che lagrime grondi e di che sangue;
e l'arca di colui che nuovo Olimpo
alzò in Roma a' Celesti; e di chi vide

learned and rich and noble mob, the ornament and mind of the fair
Italian kingdom, have their grave still living, in the flattered courts,
and their family crest as their only fame. For us let death prepare a
restful abode, where fortune may at last rest from vengeance, and
let friendship gather no treasure of possessions but the warm
feelings and the example of liberal song.

The urns of the strong fire the strong soul to excelling deeds, o
Pindemonte; and make the earth that is their receptacle lovely and
holy to the pilgrim. When I myself saw the monument where lies
the body of that great man who, even as he strengthened the sceptre
of rulers, took leaves from their laurel, and revealed to peoples with
what tears and with what blood it runs; * and the ark of him who
in Rome raised a new Olympus to the Deities; † and of him who

---

* Machiavelli.　　　　　　† Michelangelo.

sotto l'etereo padiglion rotarsi
più mondi, e il Sole irradiarli immoto,
onde all'Anglo che tanta ala vi stese
sgombrò primo le vie del firmamento;
te beata, gridai, per le felici
aure pregne di vita, e pe' lavacri
che da' suoi gioghi a te versa Apennino!
Lieta dell' aer tuo veste la Luna
di luce limpidissima i tuoi colli
per vendemmia festanti, e le convalli
popolate di case e d'oliveti
mille di fiori al ciel mandano incensi:
e tu prima, Firenze, udivi il carme
che allegrò l'ira al Ghibellin fuggiasco,
e tu i cari parenti e l'idioma
desti a quel dolce di Calliope labbro
che Amore in Grecia nudo e nudo in Roma
d'un velo candidissimo adornando,
rendea nel grembo a Venere Celeste:

saw more worlds turning under the ethereal canopy, and the Sun,
motionless, lighting them,* whence he first cleared the ways of the
firmament for the Englishman who there stretched so great a wing;†
I cried out, you blessed one, for your happy breezes stirring with
life, and for the streams that Apennine pours down to you from her
crests! The moon, glad with your air, clothes your hills, that are
rejoicing for the wine-harvest, with clearest light, and the clustering
valleys peopled with houses and olive groves send up a thousand
flowering incenses: and you first, Florence, heard the song that
lightened the anger of the fugitive Ghibelline,‡ and you gave
parents and speech to that soft lip of Calliope § who, adorning
Love, naked in Greece and naked in Rome, with a veil of the
whitest, restored her to the lap of Heavenly Venus: but more

* Galileo.   † Newton.   ‡ Dante.   § Petrarch.

ma più beata chè in un tempio accolte
serbi l'itale glorie, uniche forse
da che le mal vietate Alpi e l'alterna
onnipotenza delle umane sorti
armi e sostanze t'invadeano ed are
e patria e, tranne la memoria, tutto.
Che ove speme di gloria agli animosi
intelletti rifulga ed all'Italia,
quindi trarrem gli auspici. E a questi marmi
venne spesso Vittorio ad ispirarsi.
Irato a' patri Numi, errava muto
ove Arno è più deserto, i campi e il cielo
desioso mirando; e poi che nullo
vivente aspetto gli molcea la cura,
qui posava l'austero; e avea sul volto
il pallor della morte e la speranza.
Con questi grandi abita eterno: e l'ossa
fremono amor di patria. Ah sì! da quella
religiosa pace un Nume parla:
e nutria contro a' Persi in Maratona
ove Atene sacrò tombe a' suoi prodi,

blessed because you keep, gathered in one temple, Italian glories,
that are unique perhaps, since the ill-contested Alps and the changing omnipotence of human fate have spoiled you of arms and possessions and altars and native land and everything, except memory.
So when hope of glory comes to shine upon daring minds and
upon Italy, from these shall we draw auguries. And to these marble
tombs Vittorio * came often for inspiration. Angry with his country's gods, he would wander silently where the Arno is most barren, and look longingly at the fields and the sky; and when no living sight softened his cares, here the austere man rested; and on his
face there was the pallor of death and hope. He lives eternally with
these great: and his bones tremble with love for his country. Ah,
even so! a deity speaks from that religious peace: and fed the Greek
valour and anger against the Persians at Marathon where Athens

---

* Alfieri.

la virtù greca e l'ira. Il navigante
che veleggiò quel mar sotto l'Eubea,
vedea per l'ampia oscurità scintille
balenar d'elmi e di cozzanti brandi,
fumar le pire igneo vapor, corrusche
d'armi ferree vedea larve guerriere
cercar la pugna; e all'orror de' notturni
silenzi si spandea lungo ne' campi
di falangi un tumulto, e un suon di tube,
e un incalzar di cavalli accorrenti
scalpitanti su gli elmi a' moribondi,
e pianto, ed inni, e delle Parche il canto.

Felice te che il regno ampio de' venti,
Ippolito, a' tuoi verdi anni correvi!
E se il piloto ti drizzò l'antenna
oltre l'isole egee, d'antichi fatti
certo udisti suonar dell'Ellesponto
i liti, e la marea mugghiar portando
alle prode retee l'armi d'Achille
sovra l'ossa d'Ajace: a' generosi
giusta di glorie dispensiera è morte;

consecrated tombs to her brave. The sailor who coasted Euboea
saw through the broad dusk sparks flashing off from helmets and
crashing swords, and pyres reeking with fiery smoke, saw phantom
warriors glaring with steely arms seek out combat; and in the awfulness of the silences of night a tumult of formations spread far into
the plains, and a sound of trumpets, and an urging of horses as they
rushed forward, trampling on the helmets of the dying, and
lamentation, and hymns, and the song of the Fates.

Happy you who travelled the broad reign of the winds, Ippolito,
in your green years! And if the helmsman set the tiller beyond the
Aegean Isles, certainly you heard the shores of the Hellespont resound with ancient deeds, and the surge bellowing as it brought the
arms of Achilles to the Retean beaches, over the tomb of Ajax:
death is the fair bestower of glories to the great-hearted; nor did

nè senno astuto nè favor di regi
all'Itaco le spoglie ardue serbava
chè alla poppa raminga le ritolse
l'onda incitata dagl'inferni Dei.

E me che i tempi ed il desio d'onore
fan per diversa gente ir fuggitivo,
me ad evocar gli eroi chiamin le Muse
del mortale pensiero animatrici.
Siedon custodi de' sepolcri, e quando
il tempo con sue fredde ale vi spazza
fin le rovine, le Pimplee fan lieti
di lor canto i deserti, e l'armonia
vince di mille secoli il silenzio.
Ed oggi nella Tròade inseminata
eterno splende a' peregrini un loco
eterno per la Ninfa a cui fu sposo
Giove, ed a Giove diè Dardano figlio
onde fur Troja e Assàraco e i cinquanta
talami e il regno della giulia gente.

searching wisdom, nor the favour of kings, keep the hard won trophies for the man of Ithaca, for the waves stirred up by the infernal góds took them back from the wandering bark.

And me whom the times and the wish for honour cause to seek refuge among different peoples, let the Muses, the inspirers of mortal thought, summon me to invoke heroes. They sit, the Pimplean sisters,* guardians of sepulchres, and when time, with his cold wings, has shattered even the ruins there, they make deserts glad with their song, and harmony overcomes the silence of a thousand centuries. And today in the unsown Troad, a place shines eternally to pilgrims, eternal because of the Nymph to whom Jove was lord, and she gave to Jove a son, Dardanus, from whom came Troy, Assaracus, and the fifty bridal beds, and the reign of the Giulian

---

* The Muses.

Però che quando Elettra udì la Parca
che lei dalle vitali aure del giorno
chiamava a' cori dell'Eliso, a Giove
mandò il voto supremo: E se, diceva,
a te fur care le mie chiome e il viso
e le dolci vigilie, e non mi assente
premio miglior la volontà de' fati,
la morta amica almen guarda dal cielo
onde d'Elettra tua resti la fama.
Così orando moriva. E ne gemea
l'Olimpio; e l'immortal capo accennando
piovea dai crini ambrosia su la Ninfa
e fe' sacro quel corpo e la sua tomba.
Ivi posò Erittonio, e dorme il giusto
cenere d'Ilo; ivi l'iliache donne
sciogliean le chiome, indarno ahi! deprecando
da' lor mariti l'imminente fato;
ivi Cassandra, allor che il Nume in petto
le fea parlar di Troia il dì mortale,
venne; e all'ombre cantò carme amoroso,
e guidava i nepoti, e l'amoroso
apprendeva lamento a' giovinetti.

people. For when Electra heard one of the Fates calling her from
the living breezes of the day to the courts of Elysium, she sent up
this last prayer to Jove: And if, she said, my tresses and my face
were dear to you and those sweet sleepless nights, and if the will of
the Fates does not grant me a better prize, at least look upon your
dead beloved from heaven so that the fame of your Electra may
survive. So praying, she died. And Olympus wept at it; and the
immortal head bowing rained ambrosia from its locks upon the
Nymph; and made that body sacred and her tomb. There Erich-
tonius rested, and there slept the just ashes of Ilus; there the
Iliachan women would loose their hair, alas, in vain! and cry out
against the impending fate of their husbands: there Cassandra came
when the God in her breast made her speak of Troy's fatal day; and
sang a song of love to the shades, and brought their grandsons, and
taught the loving dirge to these youths. And said, sighing: If ever

E dicea sospirando: Oh se mai d'Argo,
ove al Tidide e di Laerte al figlio
pascerete i cavalli, a voi permetta
ritorno il cielo, invan la patria vostra
cercherete! Le mura opra di Febo
sotto le lor reliquie fumeranno.
Ma i Penati di Troia avranno stanza
in queste tombe; chè de' Numi è dono
servar nelle miserie altero nome.
E voi, palme e cipressi, che le nuore
piantan di Priamo, e crescerete, ahi presto!
di vedovili lagrime innaffiati,
proteggete i miei padri: e chi la scure
asterrà pio dalle devote frondi
men si dorrà di consanguinei lutti
e santamente toccherà l'altare.
Proteggete i miei padri. Un dì vedrete
mendico un cieco errar sotto le vostre
antichissime ombre, e brancolando
penetrar negli avelli, e abbracciar l'urne,
e interrogarle. Gemeranno gli antri
secreti, e tutta narrerà la tomba

heaven allows you to return from Argos where you will graze the horses of Tydides and of the son of Laertes, you will search for your native country in vain! The walls that are the work of Phoebus will smoke under their remains. But the Gods of Troy will be lodged in these tombs; since it is the gift of deities to keep their proud name amid misfortunes. And you, palms and cypresses whom the women of Priam's family plant, and who will grow, soon alas! quickened by widow's tears, protect my ancestors: and whoever shall keep his axe from these dedicated leaves will be less grief-stricken for internecine woes, and he will touch the altar holily. Protect my ancestors. One day you will see a blind beggar wandering under your most ancient shades, and, groping, penetrate them to the burial place, and embrace the urns, and question them. The secret caves will moan, and the tomb relate all, Ilium razed

Ilio raso due volte e due risorto
splendidamente su le mute vie
per far più bello l'ultimo trofeo
ai fatali Pelidi. Il sacro vate,
placando quelle afflitte alme col canto,
i prenci argivi eternerà per quante
abbraccia terre il gran padre Oceano.
E tu onore di pianti, Ettore, avrai
ove fia santo e lagrimato il sangue
per la patria versato, e finchè il Sole
risplenderà su le sciagure umane.

Dai «Frammenti del Carme le Grazie»

ERA più lieta
Urania un dì, quando le Grazie a lei
il gran peplo fregiavano. Con esse
qui Galileo sedeva a spiar l'astro
della loro regina; e il disviava
col notturno rumor l'acqua remota,
che sotto a' pioppi delle rive d'Arno
furtiva e argentea gli volava al guardo.

twice and twice arisen splendidly above the silent ways so as to
make finer the last trophy of the fateful sons of Peleus. The sacred
bard, soothing those tormented souls with song, will immortalize
the Argive princes through as many lands as great father Ocean embraces. And you, Hector, will be honoured in tears wherever they
deem holy and lament blood shed for one's country, and as long as
the Sun shines upon human sorrows.

From 'Fragments of a Hymn to the Graces'

URANIA was happier one day, when the Graces fringed her great
blue robe. With them Galileo sat here to spy out the star of their
queen; and the far water that flew from his gaze, furtive and silver,
under the poplars on the banks of Arno, would draw him away
with its nocturnal sound. Here the dawn, the moon, and the sun

Qui a lui l'alba, la luna e il sol mostrava,
gareggiando di tinte, or le severe
nubi su la cerulea alpe sedenti,
or il piano che fugge alle tirrene
Nereidi, immensa di città e di selve
scena e di templi e d'arator beati,
or cento colli, onde Appennin corona
d'ulivi e d'antri e di marmoree ville
l'elegante città, dove con Flora
le Grazie han serti e amabile idioma.

*

Già del piè, delle dita, e dell'errante
estro, e degli occhi vigili alle corde
ispirata sollecita le note
che pingon come l'armonia diè moto
agli astri, all'onda eterea e alla natante
terra per l'oceano, e come franse
l'uniforme creato in mille volti
co' raggi e l'ombre e il ricongiunse in uno,

displayed for him, vying in their hues, now the stern clouds sitting
on the sky-blue mountain, now the plain that flies towards the
Tyrrhenian Nereids, vast scene of cities and woods and temples and
blessed ploughmen, now a hundred hills, with which the Apennine
crowns, with olives and caves and marble villas, the shapely city,
where with Flora the Graces have garlands and a delightful speech.

ALREADY with her foot, her fingers, and wandering fire, and with
her eyes watchful of the strings, inspired she summons the notes
that depict how harmony gave motion to the stars, to the ethereal
wave and to the earth coming forth from the ocean, and how it
broke the created whole into a thousand aspects with light and
shade, and reassembled them into one, and gave sounds to the air

e i suoni all'aere, e diè i colori al sole,
e l'alterno continuo tenore
alla fortuna agitatrice e al tempo;
sì che le cose dissonanti insieme
rendan concento d'armonia divina
e innalzino le menti oltre la terra.
Come quando più gaio Euro provòca
sull'alba il queto Lario, e a quel sussurro
canta il nocchiero e allegransi i propinqui
liuti, e molle il flauto si duole
d'innamorati giovani e di ninfe
su le gondole erranti; e dalle sponde
risponde il pastorel con la sua piva:
per entro i colli rintronano i corni
terror del cavriol, mentre in cadenza
di Lecco il malleo domator del bronzo
tuona dagli antri ardenti; stupefatto
perde le reti il pescatore, ed ode.
Tal dell'arpa diffuso erra il concento
per la nostra convalle; e mentre posa
la sonatrice, ancora odono i colli.

*

and colours to the sun, and varying, continuous course to time and
unsettling chance; so that dissonant things together should give out
chords of divine harmony and raise minds beyond the earth. As
when the wind Eurus merrily stirs the quiet Lake of Como at
dawn, and the helmsman sings to that rustling and nearby lutes
rejoice, and the flute, soft, laments for love-sick youths and nymphs
in the wandering gondolas; and from the banks the shepherd
answers with his pipe: from the hills' depth blare the horns that are
the doe's terror, while, rhythmically from Lecco, the hammer,
master of bronze, thunders from the burning caverns; the fisher-
man, amazed, lets slip the net, and listens. So does the harp's sym-
phony wander through our hollow vale; and while the player rests,
the hills still listen.

Io dal mio poggio
quando tacciono i venti fra le torri
della vaga Firenze, odo un Silvano
ospite ignoto a' taciti eremiti
del vicino Oliveto: ei sul meriggio
fa sua casa un frascato, e a suon d'avena
le pecorelle sue chiama alla fonte.
Chiama due brune giovani la sera,
nè piegar erba mi parean ballando.
Esso mena la danza.

*

Spesso per l'altre età, se l'idioma
d'Italia correrà puro a' nepoti,
(è vostro, e voi, deh! lo serbate, o Grazie!)
tento ritrar ne' versi miei la sacra
danzatrice, men bella allor che siede,
men di te bella, o gentile sonatrice,
men amabil di te quando favelli,
o nutrice dell'api. Ma se danza,
vedila! tutta l'armonia del suono
scorre dal suo bel corpo, e dal sorriso

From my hilltop I, when the winds hush among the towers of fairest Florence, hear a Sylvan guest who is unknown to the silent hermits of the nearby Olivet: about noon he makes his house of a green bower, and with the reed's sound, calls the sheep to the fountain. He calls two dark girls in the evening, and they do not seem to bend the grass as they dance. He leads the dance.

Often for other ages, if the speech of Italy is to run pure to our grandchildren (it is yours, and o! do you preserve it, you Graces!), I attempt to trace in my lines the sacred dancer, less lovely when she sits, less lovely than you, o gentle harpist, less loveable than you when you give voice, o nurse of the bees. But if she dances, see her! all the harmony of sound flows from her fair body, and from

della sua bocca; e un moto, un atto, un vezzo,
manda agli sguardi venustà improvvisa.
E chi pinger la può? Mentre a ritrarla
pongo industre lo sguardo, ecco m'elude,
e le carole che lente disegna
affretta rapidissima, e s'invola
sorvolando su' fiori; appena veggio
il vel fuggente biancheggiar fra' mirti.

*

E il velo delle Dee manda improvviso
un suon, qual di lontana arpa, che scorre
sopra i vanni de' Zeffiri soave;
qual venìa dall'Egeo per l'isolette
un'ignota armonia, poi che al reciso
capo e al bel crin d'Orfeo la vaga lira
annodaro scagliandola nell'onde
le delire Baccanti; e sospirando
con l'Ionio propinquo il sacro Egeo
quell'armonia serbava, e l'isolette
stupefatte l'udiro e i continenti.

*

her mouth's smile, and a movement, a gesture, a grace, flashes sudden beauty at the onlookers. And who can paint her? While I fix my gaze intently to draw her, there she slips me, and speeds the circling dance she was slowly weaving, and flies off skimming over the flowers; I scarcely see the fleeting veil whiten among the myrtles.

AND the veil of the Goddesses suddenly gives forth a sound, like that of a distant harp, that softly runs on the wings of Zephyr; as unknown harmony came among the islands from the Aegean, when the raving Bacchantes tied the wondrous lyre to the severed head and fair locks of Orpheus, hurling it into the waves; and the sacred Aegean, sighing with nearby Ionia, kept up that harmony, and the islets, astonished, heard it, and the continents.

DATE candidi giorni a lei che sola,
da che più lieti mi fioriano gli anni,
m'arse divina d'immortale amore.
Sola vive al cor mio cura soave,
sola e secreta spargerà le chiome
sovra il sepolcro mio, quando lontano
non prescrivano i fati anche il sepolcro.
Vaga e felice i balli e le fanciulle
di nera treccia insigni e di sen colmo,
sul molle clivo di Brianza un giorno
guidar la vidi: oggi le vesti allegre
obliò lenta e il suo vedovo coro.
E se alla Luna e all'etere stellato
più azzurro il scintillante Èupili ondeggia,
il guarda avvolta in lungo velo, e plora
col rosignuol, finchè l'Aurora il chiami
a men soave tacito lamento.
A lei da presso il piè volgete, o Grazie,
e nel mirarvi, o Dee, tornino i grandi
occhi fatali al lor natìo sorriso.

GIVE fair days to her who alone, since my years flowered more happily, divine, has burnt my heart with immortal love. She alone lives as a sweet care in my heart, alone and in secret will she shake out her hair upon my tomb, if the fates do not decree that even my tomb should be a distant one. Delighting and happy I saw her lead the dance and maidens who are favoured with black locks and full bosom, on the soft slope of Brianza one day: today she slowly turns from the happy dress and her widowed train. And if the Lake of Pusiano ripples more blue to the moon and the starry ether, she looks on it, wrapped in a long veil, and mourns with the nightingale, until Dawn calls him to less charmed and silent lament. Turn your step near to her, o you Graces, and in seeing you, o Goddesses, let her great fatal eyes light once more with their true-born smile.

GIOVANNI BERCHET

Il trovatore

Va per la selva bruna
solingo il trovator
domato dal rigor
    della fortuna.

La faccia sua sì bella
la disfiorò il dolor;
la voce del cantor
    non è più quella.

Ardea nel suo segreto;
e i voti, i lai, l'ardor
alla canzon d'amor
    fidò indiscreto.

Dal talamo inaccesso
udillo il suo signor:
l'improvido cantor
    tradì se stesso.

The Minstrel

Solitary, the minstrel goes through the dusky wood, cast down by the hardness of fate.

Sorrow has wasted the face that was so handsome; the singer's voice is no longer what it was.

He burned with secret passion; and carelessly, he confided his wishes, his pangs, his heat, in a love-song.

His lord heard him from the secluded wedding-couch: the unwary singer betrayed himself.

Pei dì del giovinetto
tremò alla donna il cor,
ignara fino allor
      di tanto affetto.

E supplice al geloso,
ne contenea il furor:
bella del proprio onor
      piacque allo sposo.

Rise l'ingenua. Blando
l'accarezzò il signor:
ma il giovin trovator
      cacciato è in bando.

De' cari occhi fatali
piu non vedrà il fulgor;
non berrà piu da lor
      l'obblìo de' mali.

Varcò quegli atri muto
ch'ei rallegrava ognor
con gl'inni del valor
      col suo liuto.

The woman's heart trembled for the youth's days; she had not
known so much feeling until then.

And pleading with the jealous man, she restrained his fury: fair
with her own honour, she delighted her husband.

The simple woman laughed. Softly her lord caressed her: but the
young minstrel is banished.

He will no longer look on the lustre of those dear fatal eyes; he
will no more drink forgetfulness of wrongs from them.

He passed through those halls that he would always cheer, playing hymns of bravery on his lute.

Scese, varcò le porte;
stette, guardolle ancor:
e gli scoppiava il cor
  come per morte.

Venne alla selva bruna;
quivi erra il trovator,
fuggendo ogni chiaror
  fuor che la luna.

La guancia sua sì bella
più non somiglia un fior;
la voce del cantor
  non è più quella.

ALESSANDRO MANZONI

Morte di Ermengarda

SPARSA le trecce morbide
sull'affannoso petto,
lenta le palme, e rorida
di morte il bianco aspetto,
giace la pia, col tremolo
sguardo cercando il ciel.

He went down and out through the gates; he stood still, he looked at them again: his heart burst in his bosom as if at the moment of death.

He came to the dusky wood; there the minstrel wanders, flying from every brightness except the moon.

His cheek, once so fair, no longer is like the flower; the singer's voice is no longer what it was.

The Death of Ermengarda

THE soft locks scattered upon the heaving bosom, the hands slow, and the white features dewed with death, the pious girl lies, searching heaven with trembling gaze.

Cessa il compianto: unanime
s'innalza una preghiera:
calata in su la gelida
fronte, una man leggiera
sulla pupilla cerula
stende l'estremo vel.

Sgombra, o gentil, dall'ansia
mente i terrestri ardori;
leva all'Eterno un candido
pensier d'offerta, e muori:
fuor della vita è il termine
del lungo tuo martir.

Tal della mesta, immobile
era quaggiuso il fato:
sempre un obblio di chiedere
che le saria negato;
e al Dio de' santi ascendere,
santa del suo patir.

Ahi! nelle insonni tenebre,
pei claustri solitari,
tra il canto delle vergini,
ai supplicati altari,
sempre al pensier tornavano
gl'irrevocati dì;

The weeping hushes: a general prayer rises: a hand fallen lightly upon the cold forehead, stretches the last veil over her vivid blue eyes.

Clear worldly passions from your troubled mind, o gentle one; raise a pure thought in offering to the Eternal, and die: the end of your long suffering lies beyond life.

Such was the unchanging fate of this sad creature: always to ask for forgetfulness that was denied her; and to ascend to the God of saints, saintly through her forbearance.

Ah! in the unsleeping shadows, through the deserted cloisters, amid the song of the virgins, at the altars implored, those irrevocable days always came back to her;

quando ancor cara, improvvida
d'un avvenir mal fido,
ebbra spirò le vivide
aure del Franco lido,
e tra le nuore Saliche
invidiata uscì:

quando da un poggio aereo,
il biondo crin gemmata,
vedea nel pian discorrere
la caccia affaccendata,
e sulle sciolte redini
chino il chiomato sir;

e dietro a lui la furia
de' corridor fumanti;
e lo sbandarsi, e il rapido
redir dei veltri ansanti;
e dai tentati triboli
l'irto cinghiale uscir;

e la battuta polvere
rigar di sangue, còlto
dal regio stral: la tenera
alle donzelle il volto
volgea repente, pallida
d'amabile terror.

when still beloved, unprepared for a treacherous future, she
eagerly breathed the quickening air of French ground, and went
out, envied, among the Salic brides:

when, bejewelled her fair hair, from an airy height she watched
the flurried chase breaking over the plain, and her long-haired sire
bent over the loose reins;

and behind him the fury of the steaming chargers; and the
ranging and quick grouping of the panting hounds; and the prickly
boar come out from the disturbed undergrowth;

and, struck by the royal shaft, streak the trampled dust with
blood: the tender girl suddenly turned her face to her companions,
pale with a lovable terror.

Oh Mosa errante! oh tepidi
lavacri d'Aquisgrano!
ove, deposta l'orrida
maglia, il guerrier sovrano
scendea del campo a tergere
il nobile sudor!

Come rugiada al cespite
dell'erba inaridita,
fresca negli arsi calami
fa rifluir la vita,
che verdi ancor risorgono
nel temperato albor;

tale al pensier, cui l'empia
virtù d'amor fatica,
discende il refrigerio
d'una parola amica,
e il cor diverte ai placidi
gaudii d'un altro amor.

Ma come il sol che reduce
l'erta infocata ascende,
e con la vampa assidua
l'immobil aura incende,
risorti appena i gracili
steli riarde al suol;

O winding Meuse! o warm springs of Aix-la-Chapelle! where, putting by his fearful coat of mail, the warrior king would come away from the field to cleanse himself of valour's sweat!

As dew makes life flow fresh again in the burnt stalks of a clump of dry grass which rise green again in the mild dawn;

so the refreshment of a friendly word falls upon the thoughts with which love, in its wicked power, tires us, and turns the heart to the calm enjoyment of a different love.

But as the sun that, returning, goes up its fiery slope and kindles the unmoving breeze with its steady flame, burns the newly risen stems back to the ground;

ratto così dal tenue
obblio torna immortale
l'amor sopito, e l'anima
impaurita assale,
e le sviate immagini
richiama al noto duol.

Sgombra, o gentil, dall'ansia
mente i terrestri ardori;
leva all'Eterno un candido
pensier d'offerta, e muori:
nel suol che dee la tenera
tua spoglia ricoprir,

altre infelici dormono,
che il duol consunse; orbate
spose dal brando, e vergini
indarno fidanzate;
madri che i nati videro
trafitti impallidir.

Te dalla rea progenie
degli oppressor discesa,
cui fu prodezza il numero,
cui fu ragion l'offesa,
e dritto il sangue, e gloria
il non aver pietà,

as quickly does slumbering love come back immortal from slight
forgetfulness, and assails the frightened mind, and brings back the
deluding images of the old grief.

Clear worldly passions from your troubled mind, o gentle one;
raise a pure thought in offering to the Eternal, and die; in the
ground which must cover your tender frame,

sleep other unhappy women whom grief consumed; wives be-
reaved by the sword, and virgins vainly betrothed; mothers who
saw their children paling as they were stabbed.

You, the descendant of the evil race of oppressors, for whom
number was bravery; injury, argument; blood, right; and glory,
not to have pity;

te collocò la provida
sventura in fra gli oppressi:
muori compianta e placida;
scendi a dormir con essi:
alle incolpate ceneri
nessuno insulterà.

Muori, e la faccia esanime
si ricomponga in pace;
com'era allor che improvida
d'un avvenir fallace,
lievi pensier virginei
solo pingea. Così

dalle squarciate nuvole
si svolge il sol cadente,
e, dietro il monte, imporpora
il trepido occidente:
al pio colono augurio
di più sereno dì.

you were placed among the oppressed by provident misfortune:
die mourned and calm; go down to sleep with them: no one will
desecrate your blameless ashes.

Die, and let your face, lifeless, be composed again to peace; as it
was when, unprepared for a deceptive future, you simply painted
glad, virgin fancies on the air. So

from the rent clouds the descending sun issues, and reddens the
alarmed east, behind the mountain: sign to the pious crofter of a
calmer day.

GIACOMO LEOPARDI

L'infinito

SEMPRE caro mi fu quest'ermo colle,
e questa siepe, che da tanta parte
dell'ultimo orizzonte il guardo esclude.
Ma sedendo e mirando, interminati
spazi di là da quella, e sovrumani
silenzi, e profondissima quiete
io nel pensier mi fingo; ove per poco
il cor non si spaura. E come il vento
odo stormir tra queste piante, io quello
infinito silenzio a questa voce
vo comparando: e mi sovvien l'eterno,
e le morte stagioni, e la presente
e viva, e il suon di lei. Così tra questa
immensità s'annega il pensier mio:
e il naufragar m'è dolce in questo mare.

The Infinite

IT was always dear to me, this solitary hill, and this hedge which
shuts off the gaze from so large a part of the uttermost horizon.
But sitting and looking out, in thought I fashion for myself endless
spaces beyond, more-than-human silences, and deepest quiet;
where the heart is all but terrified. And as I hear the wind rustling
among these plants, I go on and compare this voice to that infinite
silence: and I recall the eternal, and the dead seasons, and the
present, living one and her sound. So in this immensity my thoughts
drown: and shipwreck is sweet to me in this sea.

La sera del dì di festa

DOLCE e chiara è la notte e senza vento,
e queta sovra i tetti e in mezzo agli orti
posa la luna, e di lontan rivela
serena ogni montagna. O donna mia,
già tace ogni sentiero, e pei balconi
rara traluce la notturna lampa:
tu dormi, che t'accolse agevol sonno
nelle tue chete stanze; e non ti morde
cura nessuna; e già non sai nè pensi
quanta piaga m'apristi in mezzo al petto.
Tu dormi: io questo ciel, che sì benigno
appare in vista, a salutar m'affaccio,
e l'antica natura onnipossente,
che mi fece all'affanno. A te la speme
nego, mi disse, anche la speme; e d'altro
non brillin gli occhi tuoi se non di pianto.
Questo dì fu solenne: or da' trastulli
prendi riposo; e forse ti rimembra
in sogno a quanti oggi piacesti, e quanti
piacquero a te: non io, non già ch'io speri,

The Evening of the Holiday

MILD and clear is the night and without wind, and quietly above
the roofs and among the orchards the moon rests and reveals clear
in the distance every mountain. O my love, every street is already
silent, and only here and there does a night lamp glimmer from the
balconies. You sleep, for easy slumber welcomes you in your quiet
rooms; and no care gnaws you; and certainly you do not know or
guess what a wound you have opened in my breast. You sleep: I
turn to greet this heaven, which in appearance seems so kindly, and
ancient all-powerful nature which made me for pain. To you I deny
hope, nature said to me – even hope; and your eyes shall not shine
from other than tears. This day was a holiday: now you take rest
from games; and perhaps you remember in dream how many liked
you today, how many you liked: but I do not, not that I can hope

al pensier ti ricorro. Intanto io chieggo
quanto a viver mi resti, e qui per terra
mi getto, e grido, e fremo. O giorni orrendi
in così verde etate! Ahi, per la via
odo non lunge il solitario canto
dell'artigian, che riede a tarda notte,
dopo i sollazzi, al suo povero ostello;
e fieramente mi si stringe il core,
a pensar come tutto al mondo passa,
e quasi orma non lascia. Ecco è fuggito
il dì festivo, ed al festivo il giorno
volgar succede, e se ne porta il tempo
ogni umano accidente. Or dov'è il suono
di que' popoli antichi? or dov'è il grido
de' nostri avi famosi, e il grande impero
di quella Roma, e l'armi e il fragorio
che n'andò per la terra e l'oceano?
Tutto è pace e silenzio, e tutto posa
il mondo, e più di lor non si ragiona.
Nella mia prima età, quando s'aspetta
bramosamente il dì festivo, or poscia
ch'egli era spento, io doloroso, in veglia,

it, recur to your mind. Meanwhile I ask how much is left for me to
live, and here upon the ground I throw myself, and cry aloud, and
tremble. O horrible days in so green an age! Ah, I hear on the road,
not far away, the lonely song of the tradesman who returns late at
night, after his amusements, to his poor lodging; and my heart is
fiercely oppressed to think how everything in the world passes, and
leaves almost no trace. Here is the holiday flown, and the normal
day succeeds the festive, and time bears away every human circum-
stance. Where now is the sound of those ancient peoples? Where
now is the fame of our illustrious ancestors, and the great empire of
that Rome, and the arms and the martial noise that went over land
and ocean? All is peace and silence, and the world rests entirely,
and we do not talk of them now. In my earliest years when a holiday is fervently awaited, when once it was passed, I lay, sorrow-

premea le piume; ed alla tarda notte
un canto che s'udia per li sentieri
lontanando morire a poco a poco,
già similmente mi stringeva il core.

Alla luna

O GRAZIOSA luna, io mi rammento
che, or volge l'anno, sovra questo colle
io venia pien d'angoscia a rimirarti:
e tu pendevi allor su quella selva
siccome or fai, che tutta la rischiari.
Ma nebuloso e tremulo dal pianto
che mi sorgea sul ciglio, alle mie luci
il tuo volto apparia, che travagliosa
era mia vita: ed è, nè cangia stile,
o mia diletta luna. E pur mi giova
la ricordanza, e il noverar l'etate
del mio dolore. Oh come grato occorre
nel tempo giovanil, quando ancor lungo
la speme e breve ha la memoria il corso,
il rimembrar delle passate cose,
ancor che triste, e che l'affanno duri!

ful and awake, sunk in my pillow; and in the late night, a song that
was heard in the streets going off, dying little by little, would
oppress my heart in the same way.

To the Moon

FAIR moon, I am reminded that (a year has almost run since then)
I came upon this hill full of anguish to look upon you once more:
and you hung there over that wood as you do now so as to brighten
it all. But your face appeared misty and trembling to my eyes from
the tears which rose at their brim, for troubled was my life: and is,
nor does it change tenour, o my beloved moon. And yet the recalling and telling over the years of my grief helps me. O how pleasantly in youth when hope has still a long course and memory a
short one, does recollection of past things come to us, though they
be sad, and the pain still last!

A Silvia

SILVIA, rimembri ancora
quel tempo della tua vita mortale,
quando beltà splendea
negli occhi tuoi ridenti e fuggitivi,
e tu, lieta e pensosa, il limitare
di gioventù salivi?

Sonavan le quiete
stanze, e le vie dintorno,
al tuo perpetuo canto,
allor che all'opre femminili intenta
sedevi, assai contenta
di quel vago avvenir che in mente avevi.
Era il maggio odoroso: e tu solevi
così menare il giorno.

Io gli studi leggiadri
talor lasciando e le sudate carte,
ove il tempo mio primo
e di me si spendea la miglior parte,
d'in su i veroni del paterno ostello
porgea gli orecchi al suon della tua voce,

To Silvia

SILVIA, do you still remember that time in your mortal life when beauty shone in your laughing, sidelong eyes, and you, gay and thoughtful, mounted the threshold of youth?

The quiet rooms and the streets around hummed to your continual song, when you sat intent upon your womanly work, content with that lovely future you had in mind. It was the scented Maytime: and you used, like this, to pass the day.

Sometimes leaving my pleasant studies and the much-scanned pages where my first years and the best part of myself were spent, from the balconies of my father's house I would strain my ear to

ed alla man veloce
che percorrea la faticosa tela.
Mirava il ciel sereno,
le vie dorate e gli orti,
e quinci il mar da lungi, e quindi il monte.
Lingua mortal non dice
quel ch'io sentiva in seno.

Che pensieri soavi,
che speranze, che cori, o Silvia mia!
Quale allor ci apparia
la vita umana e il fato!
Quando sovviemmi di cotanta speme,
un affetto mi preme
acerbo e sconsolato,
e tornami a doler di mia sventura.
O natura, o natura,
perchè non rendi poi
quel che prometti allor? perchè di tanto
inganni i figli tuoi?

Tu pria che l'erbe inaridisse il verno,
da chiuso morbo combattuta e vinta,
perivi, o tenerella. E non vedevi
il fior degli anni tuoi;

catch the sound of your voice, and of your hand which ran across
the toiling loom. I would look at the clear sky, the gilded streets,
and the gardens, and on this side the sea at a distance, and on that
the mountains. Mortal tongue cannot tell what I felt in my bosom.

What sweet thoughts, what hopes, what hearts, o my Silvia!
How did human life and fate appear to us then! When I am reminded of so much hope, a harsh, disconsolate feeling oppresses
me, and I come again to grieve at my misfortune. O nature, o
nature, why do you not yield afterwards what you promised then?
Why do you deceive your children so much?

You, before winter withered the grass, beset and overcome by
secret disease, you perished, o my tender one. And you did not see

non ti molceva il core
la dolce lode or delle negre chiome,
or degli sguardi innamorati e schivi;
nè teco le compagne ai dì festivi
ragionavan d'amore.

Anche peria fra poco
la speranza mia dolce: agli anni miei
anche negaro i fati
la giovanezza. Ahi come,
come passata sei,
cara compagna dell'età mia nova,
mia lacrimata speme!
Questo è quel mondo? questi
i diletti, l'amor, l'opre, gli eventi
onde cotanto ragionammo insieme?
Questa la sorte delle umane genti?
All'apparir del vero
tu, misera, cadesti: e con la mano
la fredda morte ed una tomba ignuda
mostravi di lontano.

the flower of your years; your heart was not touched by the sweet praise, now of your black hair, now of your loving, shy looks, nor did your friends speak with you of love upon holidays.

My sweet hope also perished in a little while; to my years, too, fate denied youth. Ah, how, how you have passed, dear companion of my early years, my lamented hope? Is this the same world? these the delights, the love, the works, the happenings of which we spoke so much together? This the fate of humankind? At the coming of truth, unfortunate one, you fell: and with your hand pointed in the distance cold death and a naked tomb.

Canto notturno di un pastore errante dell' Asia

CHE fai tu, luna in ciel? dimmi, che fai,
silenziosa luna?
Sorgi la sera, e vai,
contemplando i deserti: indi ti posi.
Ancor non sei tu paga
di riandare i sempiterni calli?
Ancor non prendi a schivo, ancor sei vaga
di mirar queste valli?
Somiglia alla tua vita
la vita del pastore.
Sorge in sul primo albore,
move la greggia oltre pel campo, e vede
greggi, fontane ed erbe;
poi stanco si riposa in su la sera:
altro mai non ispera.
Dimmi, o luna: a che vale
al pastor la sua vita,
la vostra vita a voi? dimmi: ove tende
questo vagar mio breve,
il tuo corso immortale?

Night Song of a Wandering Shepherd of Asia

WHAT are you doing, moon, there in the sky? tell me, what are
you doing, silent moon? You rise in the evening, and go, contemplating deserts: then you rest. Are you not sated with going
over the everlasting paths? Do you not feel a loathing, are you still
eager to look upon these valleys? The shepherd's life is like yours.
He rises at the first dawning, moves his flocks onwards over the
fields, and sees flocks, fountains, and grass; then, tired, towards
evening rests: he never hopes for anything else. Tell me, o moon:
what worth has his life for the shepherd, your life for you? tell me:
where does my brief wandering lead, where, your undying course?

Vecchierel bianco, infermo,
mezzo vestito e scalzo,
con gravissimo fascio in su le spalle,
per montagna e per valle,
per sassi acuti, ed alta rena, e fratte,
al vento, alla tempesta, e quando avvampa
l'ora, e quando poi gela,
corre via, corre, anela,
varca torrenti e stagni,
cade, risorge, e più e più s'affretta,
senza posa o ristoro,
lacero, sanguinoso; infin ch'arriva
colà dove la via
e dove il tanto affaticar fu volto:
abisso orrido, immenso,
ov'ei precipitando, il tutto obblia.
Vergine luna, tale
è la vita mortale.

Nasce l'uomo a fatica,
ed è rischio di morte il nascimento.
Prova pena e tormento
per prima cosa; e in sul principio stesso
la madre e il genitore
il prende a consolar dell'esser nato.

Shrunken old man, white-haired, failing, half-naked, and barefoot, with a most heavy burden upon his shoulders, who runs
through valleys and over mountains, over sharp stones, deep sand,
and brakes, in wind, in storm, when the hour is burning, and when
it freezes – runs on, panting, crosses torrents and marshes, falls
rises again, and hurries more and more, without rest or refreshment, torn and bleeding; until he arrives where the road and all
his travail have led: a horrible, vast abyss into which he falls head-
long, and forgets everything. Virgin moon, such is mortal life.

Man is born to labour, and birth is a risk of death. He experiences
pain and anguish as the first of things; and at the very beginning his
mother and father take to consoling him for being born. Then

Poi che crescendo viene,
l'uno e l'atro il sostiene, e via pur sempre
con atti e con parole
studiasi fargli core,
e consolarlo dell'umano stato:
altro ufficio più grato
non si fa da parenti alla lor prole.
Ma perchè dare al sole,
perchè reggere in vita
chi poi di quella consolar convenga?
Se la vita è sventura,
perchè da noi si dura?
Intatta luna, tale
è lo stato mortale.
Ma tu mortal non sei,
e forse del mio dir poco ti cale.

Pur tu, solinga, eterna peregrina,
che sì pensosa sei, tu forse intendi,
questo viver terreno,
il patir nostro, il sospirar, che sia;
che sia questo morir, questo supremo
scolorar del sembiante,

when he comes to grow, the one and the other support him, and, on and on, ceaselessly, try with words and actions to give him heart, and console him for the human state: no more gratifying service is to be rendered by parents to their children. But why give to the sun, why keep in life one who must then be consoled for it? If life is misfortune, why do we last it out? Inviolate moon, such is the mortal state. But you are not mortal, and perhaps care little for my words.

Yet, lonely, eternal wanderer, who are so thoughtful, perhaps you understand what this earthly life is, our suffering and sighing, and what this dying is, this ultimate fading of the features, and

e perir dalla terra, e venir meno
ad ogni usata, amante compagnia.
E tu certo comprendi
il perchè delle cose, e vedi il frutto
del mattin, della sera,
del tacito, infinito andar del tempo.
Tu sai, tu certo, a qual suo dolce amore
ride la primavera,
a chi giovi l'ardore, e che procacci
il verno co' suoi ghiacci.
Mille cose sai tu, mille discopri,
che son celate al semplice pastore.
Spesso quand'io ti miro
star così muta in sul deserto piano,
che, in suo giro lontano, al ciel confina,
ovver con la mia greggia
seguirmi viaggiando a mano a mano;
e quando miro in cielo arder le stelle;
dico fra me pensando:
a che tante facelle?
Che fa l'aria infinita, e quel profondo
infinito seren? che vuol dir questa
solitudine immensa? ed io che sono?

perishing from the earth, and falling away from every familiar,
loving company. And certainly you understand the why of things,
and see the fruit of morning, of evening, of the silent, endless going
of time. You know, you certainly, to what sweet love of hers
the springtime laughs, whom the heat serves, and what winter with
its ice effects. A thousand things you know, a thousand discover
that are hidden to the simple shepherd. Often when I see you stay
so silently above the empty plain which, in its far sweep, borders on
the sky; or see you follow me with my flock, travelling slow and
steady; and when I look on the stars burning in heaven; in thought
I say to myself: wherefore, so many torches? What does the infinite
air serve, and what the deep infinite sky? What does this boundless
solitude mean? And what am I? So I discuss with myself: both of

Così meco ragiono: e della stanza
smisurata e superba,
e dell'innumerabile famiglia;
poi di tanto adoprar, di tanti moti
d'ogni celeste, ogni terrena cosa,
girando senza posa,
per tornar sempre là donde son mosse;
uso alcuno, alcun frutto
indovinar non so. Ma tu per certo,
giovinetta immortal, conosci il tutto.
Questo io conosco e sento,
che degli eterni giri,
che dell'esser mio frale,
qualche bene o contento
avrà fors'altri; a me la vita è male.

O greggia mia che posi, oh te beata,
che la miseria tua, credo, non sai!
Quanta invidia ti porto!
Non sol perchè d'affanno
quasi libera vai;
ch'ogni stento, ogni danno,
ogni estremo timor subito scordi;
ma più perchè giammai tedio non provi.

the sumptuous and unbounded mansion, and the numberless
family; then, in so much activity, in the so many movements of
every heavenly, every earthly thing, going on without rest, always
coming back to the point from which they were moved, in these I
cannot see any use, any fruit. But you for sure, immortal maiden,
know the sum of all. I know and feel this, that others may have
some profit or contentment from the eternal revolvings, from my
frail being; to me life is evil.

O my flock that rest, o happy you, who, I imagine, do not know
your misery! How much envy I bear you! Not only because you go
nearly free of worry; for you immediately forget every effort,
every blow, every extreme fear; but rather because you never know

Quando tu siedi all'ombra, sovra l'erbe,
tu se' queta e contenta;
e gran parte dell'anno
senza noia consumi in quello stato.
Ed io pur seggo sovra l'erbe, all'ombra,
e un fastidio m'ingombra
la mente, ed uno spron quasi mi punge
sì che, sedendo, più che mai son lunge
da trovar pace o loco.
E pur nulla non bramo,
e non ho fino a qui cagion di pianto.
Quel che tu goda o quanto,
non so già dir; ma fortunata sei.
Ed io godo ancor poco,
o greggia mia, nè di ciò sol mi lagno.
Se tu parlar sapessi, io chiederei:
dimmi: perchè giacendo
a bell'agio, ozioso,
s'appaga ogni animale;
me, s'io giaccio in riposo, il tedio assale?

boredom. When you sit in the shade upon the grass, you are quiet and contented; and you spend untroubled a great part of the year in that state. And yet I sit upon the grass in the shade, and a weariness clouds my mind, and it is as if a spur pricks me so that, sitting as I am, I am farther than ever from finding peace and haven. And yet I desire nothing, and till now have no cause for tears. I cannot even say what it is you enjoy, or how much; but you are lucky. And I continue to enjoy little, o my flock, nor do I sorrow only for this. If you could speak, I would ask you: tell me: why is every animal satisfied lying at dear ease, idle; why if I lie at rest, does tedium assail me?

Forse s'avess'io l'ale
da volar su le nubi,
e noverar le stelle ad una ad una,
o come il tuono errar di giogo in giogo,
più felice sarei, dolce mia greggia,
più felice sarei, candida luna.
O forse erra dal vero,
mirando all'altrui sorte, il mio pensiero:
forse in qual forma, in quale
stato che sia, dentro covile o cuna,
è funesto a chi nasce il dì natale.

Il sabato del villaggio

La donzelletta vien dalla campagna,
in sul calar del sole,
col suo fascio dell'erba; e reca in mano
un mazzolin di rose e di viole,
onde, siccome suole,
ornare ella si appresta
dimani al dì di festa, il petto e il crine.

Perhaps if I had wings to fly above the clouds, and number the stars one by one, or like the thunder roam from crest to crest, I would be happier, my sweet flock, I would be happier, white moon. Or perhaps my thoughts wander from the truth when I look at the fate of others: perhaps in whatever form, in whatever state he may have his being, in den or in cot, the day of birth is gloomy to him who is born.

Saturday in the Village

The girl comes from the country, at the sinking of the sun, with her bundle of grass, and carries in her hand a little bunch of roses and violets with which she is ready to deck her bosom and her hair tomorrow, on the holiday, as is her custom. With neighbours,

Siede con le vicine
su la scala a filar la vecchierella,
incontro là dove si perde il giorno;
e novellando vien del suo buon tempo,
quando al dì della festa ella si ornava,
ed ancor sana e snella
solea danzar la sera intra di quei
ch'ebbe compagni dell'età più bella.
Già tutta l'aria imbruna,
torna azzurro il sereno, e tornan l'ombre
giù da' colli e da' tetti,
al biancheggiar della recente luna.
Or la squilla dà segno
della festa che viene;
ed a quel suon diresti
che il cor si riconforta.
I fanciulli gridando
su la piazzuola in frotta,
e qua e là saltando,
fanno un lieto romore:
e intanto riede alla sua parca mensa,
fischiando, il zappatore,
e seco pensa al dì del suo riposo.

upon the steps, the old woman sits spinning, facing towards where
the light is fading; and goes on talking of her own good season,
when she on holidays, still fresh and supple, would dance the evening away with those youths who were the friends of her fairer age.
Now all the air has darkened, the heavens take on a blue again, and
again the shadows fall from hills and roofs, in the whitening of the
young moon. Now the peal of bells announces the holiday that is
coming, and you would say that at the sound the heart is comforted. The children shouting in the little square in swarms, and
leaping here and there, make a happy din: meanwhile the hoer goes
back whistling to his meagre spread, and thinks in himself of his
day of rest.

Poi quando intorno è spenta ogni altra face,
e tutto l'altro tace,
odi il martel picchiare, odi la sega
del legnaiuol, che veglia
nella chiusa bottega alla lucerna,
e s'affretta, e s'adopra
di fornir l'opra anzi il chiarir dell'alba.

Questo di sette è il più gradito giorno,
pien di speme e di gioia:
diman tristezza e noia
recheran l'ore, ed al travaglio usato
ciascun in suo pensier farà ritorno.

Garzoncello scherzoso,
cotesta età fiorita
è come un giorno d'allegrezza pieno,
giorno chiaro, sereno,
che precorre alla festa di tua vita.
Godi, fanciullo mio; stato soave,
stagion lieta è cotesta.
Altro dirti non vo'; ma la tua festa
ch'anco tardi a venir non ti sia grave.

Then when every other light has gone out, and everything else
is silent, you hear the hammer rapping, hear the saw of the car-
penter who works all night in his closed shop by a lantern, and
hurries, and exerts himself to have the job ready before the lighten-
ing of dawn.

This is the most welcome of seven days, full of hope and joy.
Tomorrow the hours will bring sadness and boredom, and each
will go back in thought to his usual labour.

Mischievous boy, this flowering age of yours is like a day full of
joy, a clear cloudless day which precedes the holiday of your life.
Have enjoyment of it, my son; a sweet state, a happy season, it is.
I do not want to say anything more to you; but may it not weigh
on you that your holiday still delays.

A sè stesso

O R poserai per sempre,
stanco mio cor. Perì l'inganno estremo,
ch'eterno io mi credei. Perì. Ben sento,
in noi di cari inganni,
non che la speme, il desiderio è spento.
Posa per sempre. Assai
palpitasti. Non val cosa nessuna
i moti tuoi, nè di sospiri è degna
la terra. Amaro e noia
la vita, altro mai nulla; e fango è il mondo.
T'acqueta omai. Dispera
l'ultima volta. Al gener nostro il fato
non donò che il morire. Omai disprezza
te, la natura, il brutto
poter, che, ascoso, a comun danno impera,
e l'infinita vanità del tutto.

To Himself

Now you will rest for ever, tired heart of mine. The last deception
has perished which I believed eternal. It has perished. Well do I feel
it, in us has been extinguished not only the hope of dear illusions,
but the desire for them as well. Rest for ever. You have laboured
much. Nothing can repay your stirring, nor is the earth worthy of
sighs. Life is bitterness and tedium, never anything else; and the
world is mud. Be quietened now. Despair for the last time. To
human kind fate has only appointed dying. Scorn nature now, the
brutal power which governs to the universal hurt, and the infinite
vanity of everything.

Coro di morti

SOLA nel mondo eterna, a cui si volve
ogni creata cosa,
in te morte, si posa
nostra ignuda natura;
lieta no, ma sicura
dell'antico dolor. Profonda notte
nella confusa mente
il pensier grave oscura;
alla speme, al desio, l'arido spirto
lena mancar si sente:
così d'affanno e di temenza è sciolto,
e l'età vote e lente
senza tedio consuma.
Vivemmo: e qual di paurosa larva,
e di sudato sogno,
a lattante fanciullo erra nell'alma
confusa ricordanza:
tal memoria n'avanza
del viver nostro: ma da tema è lunge
il rimembrar. Che fummo?
Che fu quel punto acerbo
che di vita ebbe nome?

Chorus of the Dead

DEATH who alone are eternal in this world, to whom every
created thing comes, our naked being rests in you; not happy, but
safe from the ancient grief. Deep night darkens the heavy thought
in the mind confused; the arid spirit feels its will to hope, to desire,
failing: freed thus from anxiety and fear, it spends the empty, slow
ages without weariness. We lived: and as the troubled memory of
frightening spectre and sweated dream haunts the soul of the child
still suckling: so does memory of our life keep with us: but our
remembering is far from fear. What were we? What was that bitter
point that had the name of life? Life is today a dark and awful thing

Cosa arcana e stupenda
oggi è la vita al pensier nostro, e tale
qual de' vivi al pensiero
l'ignota morte appar. Come da morte
vivendo rifuggìa, così rifugge
dalla fiamma vitale
nostra ignuda natura
lieta no, ma sicura,
però ch'esser beato
nega ai mortali e nega a' morti il fato.

La ginestra
o Il fiore del deserto

E gli uomini vollero piuttosto le tenebre
che la luce – Giovanni iii, 19

QUI su l'arida schiena
del formidabil monte
sterminator Vesevo,
la qual null'altro allegra arbor nè fiore,
tuoi cespi solitari intorno spargi,

to our minds, just as unknown death appears to the minds of the living. As our naked nature fled from death while we lived, so it flies from the vital flame now, not happy but safe, because fate denies happiness to the mortal and the dead.

The Broom
or
The Flower of the Desert

And men loved darkness rather
than the light – John iii, 19

HERE upon the arid back of the redoubtable mountain, destroyer Vesuvius, which no other tree or flower cheers, you scatter your

odorata ginestra,
contenta dei deserti. Anco ti vidi
de' tuoi steli abbellir l'erme contrade
che cingon la cittade
la qual fu donna de' mortali un tempo,
e del perduto impero
par che col grave e taciturno aspetto
faccian fede e ricordo al passeggero.
Or ti riveggo in questo suol, di tristi
lochi e dal mondo abbandonati amante,
e d'afflitte fortune ognor compagna.
Questi campi cosparsi
di ceneri infeconde, e ricoperti
dell'impietrata lava,
che sotto i passi al peregrin risona;
dove s'annida e si contorce al sole
la serpe, e dove al noto
cavernoso covil torna il coniglio;
fur liete ville e colti.
E biondeggiar di spiche, e risonaro
di muggito d'armenti;
fur giardini e palagi,

lonely bushes around, fragrant broom, content with deserts. A while ago I saw you beautify with your stems the bare country places that girdle the city which was once the mistress of mortals, and it seems that with their grave and silent look they serve as a testimony and a reminder of that lost empire to the traveller. Now I see you again on this ground, the lover of sad places that are abandoned by the world, and the unfailing companion of adverse fates. These fields that are scattered over with infertile ash and covered with solid lava that resounds to the pilgrim's tread, where nests and twists in the sun the snake, and where the rabbit comes home to his familiar, cave-like burrow, were once happy country houses and cultivated places. And they grew gold with corn, and echoed to the lowing of herds; there were gardens and mansions,

agli ozi de' potenti
gradito ospizio, e fur città famose,
che coi torrenti suoi l'altero monte
dall'ignea bocca fulminando oppresse
con gli abitanti insieme. Or tutto intorno
una ruina involve,
ove tu siedi, o fior gentile, e quasi
i danni altrui commiserando, al cielo
di dolcissimo odor mandi un profumo,
che il deserto consola. A queste piagge
venga colui che d'esaltar con lode
il nostro stato ha in uso, e vegga quanto
è il gener nostro in cura
all'amante natura. E la possanza
qui con giusta misura
anco estimar potrà dell'uman seme,
cui la dura nutrice, ov'ei men teme,
con lieve moto in un momento annulla
in parte, e può con moti
poco men lievi ancor subitamente
annichilare in tutto.
Dipinte in queste rive
son dell'umana gente
«le magnifiche sorti e progressive».

---

the welcome retreat for the leisure of the great, and famous cities
which the proud mountain, thundering with the torrents of its
flaming mouth, crushed along with their inhabitants. Now one
ruin claims everything around the place where you sit, o kindly
flower, and, almost sympathizing for the losses of others, send up
to heaven a perfume of sweetest smell that consoles the desert. Let
him who is accustomed to extol our state come to these slopes and
see how greatly mankind enjoys the care of loving Nature. And
here, too, he will be able to guess rightly the power of humankind which that hard nurse, when we least fear, in a moment, with a
light motion, nullifies in part, and can, with motions scarcely less
light, in no time, annihilate altogether. Displayed upon these banks
are 'the magnificent and progressive destinies of the human race'.

Qui mira e qui ti specchia,
secol superbo e sciocco,
che il calle insino allora
dal risorto pensier segnato innanti
abbandonasti, e volti addietro i passi,
del ritornar ti vanti,
e procedere il chiami.
Al tuo pargoleggiar gl'ingegni tutti
di cui lor sorte rea padre ti fece
vanno adulando, ancora
ch'a ludibrio talora
t'abbian fra sè. Non io
con tal vergogna scenderò sotterra;
ma il disprezzo piuttosto che si serra
di te nel petto mio,
mostrato avrò quanto si possa aperto:
bench'io sappia che obblio
preme chi troppo all'età propria increbbe.
Di questo mal, che teco
mi fia comune, assai finor mi rido.
Libertà vai sognando, e servo a un tempo
vuoi di novo il pensiero,

Here look and here see yourself mirrored, proud, foolish century,
that have abandoned the path, leading forward till now, of new-
risen thought, and turned your steps backwards, and boast of the
regression, and call it advancing. To your babbling all gifted souls,
whose evil fate has given them you for a father, pay tribute even
although sometimes they hold you in scorn among themselves. I
shall not go underground with such shame; but I shall rather have
shown, as much as can be shown openly, the scorn of you which is
locked in my breast, although I know that oblivion presses upon
those who are too hateful to their own age. Much already have I
laughed at this evil which I shall share with you. You keep dreaming of Liberty and you want thought to be once more the slave of

sol per cui risorgemmo
dalla barbarie in parte, e per cui solo
si cresce in civiltà, che sola in meglio
guida i pubblici fati.
Così ti spiacque il vero
dell'aspra sorte e del depresso loco
che natura ci diè. Per questo il tergo
vigliaccamente rivolgesti al lume
che il fe palese: e, fuggitivo, appelli
vil chi lui segue, e solo
magnanimo colui
che sè schernendo o gli altri, astuto o folle,
fin sopra gli astri il mortal grado estolle.

Uom di povero stato e membra inferme,
che sia dell'alma generoso ed alto,
non chiama sè nè stima
ricco d'or nè gagliardo,
e di splendida vita o di valente
persona infra la gente
non fa risibil mostra;

a single age, thought by which alone we have risen a little above
barbarism, and by which alone one grows in civilization, and which
alone guides public destinies for the best. So unpleasant have
proved the truths of the hard fate and the low place that nature gave
you. Because of this you have turned your backs cravenly on the
light which made them clear, and fleeing you call coward him who
follows it, and great-hearted only him who, mocking himself or
others, in cunning or foolishness, extols the human state above the
stars.

Always a creature of scant power and weak limbs, a man who is
also generous and exalted of soul does not boast or value himself
for being lusty or rich in gold, and does not make a laughable show
of splendid life or strength among people; but lets himself appear

ma sè di forza e di tesor mendico
lascia parer senza vergogna, e noma
parlando, apertamente, e di sue cose
fa stima al vero uguale.
Magnanimo animale
non credo io già, ma stolto,
quel che nato a perir, nutrito in pene,
dice, a goder son fatto,
e di fetido orgoglio
empie le carte, eccelsi fati e nove
felicità, quali il ciel tutto ignora,
non pur quest'orbe, promettendo in terra
a' popoli che un'onda
di mar commosso, un fiato
d'aura maligna, un sotterraneo crollo
distrugge sì, ch'avanza
a gran pena di lor la rimembranza.
Nobil natura è quella
ch'a sollevar s'ardisce
gli occhi mortali incontra
al comun fato, e che con franca lingua,
nulla al ver detraendo,
confessa il mal che ci fu dato in sorte,
e il basso stato e frale;

beggared of strength and treasure, and talks of this openly, and
gives a value that is the true one to his possessions. I do not at all
believe him a great-hearted creature who, born to perish, nourished
in pains, says, I was made to have enjoyment, and fills pages with
noisome pride, promising exalted fortunes and new happinesses,
unknown to heaven, far less this world, to peoples whom a wave
of the sea aroused, a breath of pestilent wind, a subterranean col-
lapse so destroys that the memory of them hardly remains. His is a
noble nature who dares to raise mortal eyes against the common
fate, and who, with free tongue, not detracting anything from the
truth, attests the evil and the low weak state that has been given tò
us as destiny; that nature which shows itself great and strong in

quella che grande e forte
mostra sè nel soffrir, nè gli odii e l'ire
fraterne, ancor più gravi
d'ogni altro danno, accresce
alle miserie sue, l'uomo incolpando
del suo dolor, ma dà la colpa a quella
che veramente è rea, che de' mortali
è madre in parto ed in voler matrigna.
Costei chiama inimica; e incontro a questa
congiunta esser pensando,
siccom'è il vero, ed ordinata in pria
l'umana compagnia,
tutti fra sè confederati estima
gli uomini, e tutti abbraccia
con vero amor, porgendo
valida e pronta ed aspettando aita
negli alterni perigli e nelle angosce
della guerra comune. Ed alle offese
dell'uomo armar la destra, e laccio porre
al vicino ed inciampo,
stolto crede così qual fora in campo
cinto d'oste contraria, in sul più vivo
incalzar degli assalti,

suffering, and does not add to its miseries with hates and anger against brother men (things clearly graver than every other ill), blaming man for its grief, but gives the blame to her who is truly evil, who is the mother of humankind in bearing them, and their stepmother in feelings. He calls her enemy; and considering the human brotherhood to be, first of all, ordered and united against her, as is true, he deems all men to be allies, and embraces all with true love, offering sincere and ready help, and expecting as much, in the successive perils and anguishes of the common war. And to take up arms to the hurt of man, and to set snares and obstacles for his neighbour, he thinks as foolish an action as it would be on the battlefield, surrounded by a hostile army, in the most desperate moment of attack, to begin fierce struggles with friends, while

gl'inimici obbliando, acerbe gare
imprender con gli amici,
e sparger fuga e fulminar col brando
infra i proprii guerrieri.
Così fatti pensieri
quando fien, come fur, palesi al volgo,
e quell'orror che primo
contra l'empia natura
strinse i mortali in social catena,
fia ricondotto in parte
da verace saper, l'onesto e il retto
conversar cittadino,
e giustizia e pietade, altra radice
avranno allor che non superbe fole,
ove fondata probità del volgo
così star suole in piede
qual star può quel ch'ha in error la sede.

Sovente in queste rive,
che, desolate, a bruno
veste il flutto indurato, e par che ondeggi,
seggo la notte; e su la mesta landa
in purissimo azzurro
veggo dall'alto fiammeggiar le stelle,

enemies are forgotten, and to spread flight and descend with the
sword among one's own warriors. When thoughts of this kind are, as
they were, revealed to the crowd, together with the horror that first
drew mortals together in a social chain against unholy Nature, then
shall the honest and upright intercourse of the city be brought back,
in part, by right knowledge, and justice and piety will then have
another root than that of proud follies, upon which the established
morality of the vulgar is used to stand, as well as that may stand
which is founded upon error.

Often upon these slopes which, abandoned as they are, the solid
flow clothes in brown, and, it seems, still undulates, I sit at night
and, upon the sad waste, see the stars that flame from purest blue,

cui di lontan fa specchio
il mare, e tutto di scintille in giro
per lo voto seren brillare il mondo.
E poi che gli occhi a quelle luci appunto,
ch'a lor sembrano un punto,
e son immense in guisa
che un punto a petto a lor son terra e mare
veracemente; a cui
l'uomo non pur, ma questo
globo ove l'uomo è nulla,
sconosciuto è del tutto; e quando miro
quegli ancor più senz'alcun fin remoti
nodi quasi di stelle,
ch'a noi paion qual nebbia, a cui non l'uomo
e non la terra sol, ma tutte in uno,
del numero infinite e della mole,
con l'aureo sole insiem, le nostre stelle
o son ignote, o così paion come
essi alla terra, un punto
di luce nebulosa; al pensier mio
che sembri allora, o prole
dell'uomo? E rimembrando
il tuo stato quaggiù, di cui fa segno
il suol ch'io premo; e poi dall'altra parte,

mirrored from afar by the sea, and see the world all shining with sparks that turn through empty heaven. And then I focus my eyes on those lights that seem a point to them, and are so huge that the sea and the land compared to them are, in reality, a point; to which not only man, but this globe where man is nothing, is completely unknown; and when I gaze at those knots, almost, of stars which are even more, are infinitely remote, which to us seem like a mist, and to which, not only man or the earth, but all the sum of our stars, infinite in number and size, together with the golden sun are either unknown, or appear a point of misty light as those knots themselves do to the earth, what do you seem in my judgement then, o children of men? And when I remember your condition here below, which the ground I press on testifies; and then, on the

che te signora e fine
credi tu data al Tutto, e quante volte
favoleggiar ti piacque, in questo oscuro
granel di sabbia, il qual di terra ha nome,
per tua cagion, dell'universe cose
scender gli autori, e conversar sovente
co' tuoi piacevolmente, e che i derisi
sogni rinnovellando, ai saggi insulta
fin la presente età, che in conoscenza
ed in civil costume
sembra tutte avanzar; qual moto allora,
mortal prole infelice, o qual pensiero
verso te finalmente il cor m'assale?
No so se il riso o la pietà prevale.

Come d'arbor cadendo un picciol pomo,
cui là nel tardo autunno
maturità senz'altra forza atterra,
d'un popol di formiche i dolci alberghi
cavati in molle gleba
con gran lavoro, e l'opre,
e le ricchezze ch'adunate a prova

other hand, that you believe you have been appointed master and
end of All, and how often you like to tell tales of the authors of
universal things, how they come down upon this unknown grain
of sand called the earth on your account, and often speak with you
pleasantly; and when I remember too, that, renewing these laughable dreams, you insult the wise right to the present age, which
seems to surpass all others in knowledge and social usage; what
feeling, then, or what thought for you, assails my heart, o unhappy
humankind? I do not know if laughter or pity predominates.

As a little apple which ripeness, with no other aid, brings to
earth in the late autumn, falls, crushes, lays waste, and covers at one
and the same moment the sweet mansions of a people of ants which
had been hollowed out of the soft loam with great labour, and their
works and their riches which the industrious tribe, vying with one

con lunga affaticar l' assidua gente
avea provvidamente al tempo estivo,
schiaccia, diserta e copre
in un punto; così d'alto piombando,
dall'utero tonante
scagliata al ciel profondo,
di ceneri e di pomici c di sassi
notte e ruina, infusa
di bollenti ruscelli,
o pel montano fianco
furiosa tra l'erba
di liquefatti massi
e di metalli e d'infocata arena
scendendo immensa piena,
le cittadi che il mar là su l'estremo
lido aspergea, confuse
e infranse e ricoperse
in pochi istanti: onde su quelle or pasce
la capra, e città nove
sorgon dall'altra banda, a cui sgabello
son le sepolte, e le prostrate mura
l'arduo monte al suo piè quasi calpesta.
Non ha natura al seme
dell'uom più stima o cura

another, with long fatigue, had gathered in the summertime, so
were the cities which the sea washed, on its very edge, shattered
and covered over in a few minutes by a night and ruin of ashes,
pumice, stones, in molten streams, which, shot up to far heaven
from the thundering womb, rained down from on high, or by the
huge overflowing of liquified masses, of metals and burning sand,
which came down the mountain side furiously through the grass: so
that over those cities now browses the goat, and new cities rise
opposite which have for their seat the buried and prostrate walls
that the mountain almost tramples at its foot. Nature has no more
regard or care for the seed of man than for the ant: and if the mas-

ch'alla formica: e se più rara in quello
che nell'altra è la strage,
non avvien ciò d'altronde
fuor che l'uom sue prosapie ha men feconde.

Ben mille ed ottocento
anni varcàr poi che spariro, oppressi
dall'ignea forza, i popolati seggi,
e il villanello intento
ai vigneti che a stento in questi campi
nutre la morta zolla e incenerita,
ancor leva lo sguardo
sospettoso alla vetta
fatal, che nulla mai fatta più mite
ancor siede tremenda, ancor minaccia
a lui strage ed ai figli ed agli averi
lor poverelli. E spesso
il meschino in sul tetto
dell'ostel villereccio, alla vagante
aura giacendo tutta notte insonne,
e balzando più volte, esplora il corso
del temuto bollor, che si riversa
dall'inesausto grembo
su l'arenoso dorso, a cui riluce

sacre of the one is less frequent than that of the other, this happens
for no other reason than that man is less fertile in offspring.

Full a thousand and eight hundred years have passed away since
the peopled places disappeared, crushed by fiery might, and the
peasant busy at his vine which the dead and ashy soil of these fields
barely nourishes, still lifts his eyes suspiciously to the fatal peak
that, not for a moment milder, still sits awesome, still threatens destruction to him and his children and their poor little possessions.
And often the wretch lying sleepless in the wandering breeze upon
the roof of his rustic dwelling, jumps up repeatedly and scans the
course of the fearful molten lava which pours from the unexhausted
womb on to the sandy sides, and its light is reflected in the bay of

di Capri la marina
e di Napoli il porto e Mergellina.
E se appressar lo vede, o se nel cupo
del domestico pozzo ode mai l'acqua
fervendo gorgogliar, desta i figliuoli,
desta la moglie in fretta, e via, con quanto
di lor cose rapir posson, fuggendo,
vede lontan, l'usato
suo nido, e il picciol campo,
che gli fu dalla fame unico schermo,
preda al flutto rovente,
che crepitando giunge, e inesorato
durabilmente sopra quei si spiega.

Torna al celeste raggio
dopo l'antica obblivion l'estinta
Pompei, come sepolto
scheletro, cui di terra
avarizia o pietà rende all'aperto;
e dal deserto foro
diritto infra le file
de' mozzi colonnati il peregrino
lunge contempla il bipartito giogo

Capri, and the port of Naples; and Mergellina. And if he sees it
approaching, or if he ever hears the water gurgling feverishly in
the gloom of the household well, he wakes his children, he hur-
riedly wakes his wife, and, fleeing with as much of their belongings
as they can snatch up, he sees from safe distance his accustomed nest
and the little field which was his only shield against hunger, fall
prey to the white-hot tide that arrives crackling and, relentless,
spreads over these things durably.

After ancient obliteration lifeless Pompeii returns to daylight
like a buried skeleton that the greed of land or piety gives back to
the air; and from the deserted forum the pilgrim gazes for long
where, rising between the lines of truncated columns, he sees the

e la cresta fumante,
ch'alla sparsa ruina ancor minaccia.
E nell'orror della secreta notte
per li vacui teatri,
per li templi deformi e per le rotte
case, ove i parti il pipistrello asconde,
come sinistra face
che per voti palagi atra s'aggiri,
corre il baglior della funerea lava,
che di lontan per l'ombre
rosseggia e i lochi intorno intorno tinge.
Così, dell'uomo ignara e dell'etadi
ch'ei chiama antiche, e del seguir che fanno
dopo gli avi i nepoti,
sta natura ognor verde, anzi procede
per sì lungo cammino
che sembra star. Caggiono i regni intanto,
passan genti e linguaggi: ella nol vede:
e l'uom d'eternità s'arroga il vanto.

divided peak and the smoking summit which still threaten the scattered ruin. And in the horror of the secret night, through the empty theatres, and the deformed temples and broken houses where the bat conceals its young, the glow of the deathly lava hastens like an evil torch circling blackly through vacant palaces, and from afar reddens through the shades, and stains all the places about. So, heedless of man and the ages which he calls ancient, and of the way in which the youngest generation follow their ancestors, Nature keeps green at all times, rather goes forward by so long a road that it seems to stand still. Meanwhile kingdoms fall, races and languages pass away: she does not see this: and man usurps the boast of eternity.

E tu, lenta ginestra,
che di selve odorate
queste campagne dispogliate adorni,
anche tu presto alla crudel possanza
soccomberai del sotterraneo foco,
che ritornando al loco
già noto, stenderà l'avaro lembo
su tue molli foreste. E piegherai
sotto il fascio mortal non renitente
il tuo capo innocente:
ma non piegato insino allora indarno
codardamente supplicando innanzi
al futuro oppressor; ma non eretto
con forsennato orgoglio inver le stelle,
nè sul deserto, dove
e la sede e i natali
non per voler ma per fortuna avesti;
ma più saggia, ma tanto
meno inferma dell'uom, quanto le frali
tue stirpi non credesti
o dal fato o da te fatte immortali.

And you, slow bush of broom, that deck these bare country places with fragrant copses, you too will soon fall to the cruel power of the subterranean fire, which, coming again to its known limit, will stretch its rapacious hem over your soft forests. And you will bend your innocent head beneath the mortal burden without struggling; but a head that has not been bent in cowardly supplication, vainly, before the coming oppressor; nor raised with vainglorious pride towards the stars, nor over the desert where you sprang and grew not by choosing to, but by chance. But you will have been wiser and so much the less infirm than man, as you did not believe your frail kind made immortal by fate or by yourself.

GIUSEPPE GIUSTI

La guigliottina a vapore

HANNO fatto nella China
una macchina a vapore
per mandar la guigliottina:
questa macchina in tre ore
fa la testa a cento mila
           messi in fila.

L'instrumento ha fatto chiasso,
e quei preti han presagito
che il paese passo passo
sarà presto incivilito;
rimarrà come un babbeo
           l'Europeo.

L'imperante è un uomo onesto;
un po' duro, un po' tirato,
un po' ciuco, ma del resto
ama i sudditi e lo Stato,
e protegge i bell'ingegni
           de' suoi regni.

The Steam-driven Guillotine

THEY have made a steam engine in China to power the guillotine: this machine in three hours looks after the heads of a hundred thousand, queueing in a line.

The instrument has caused a stir, and the local priests have predicted that the country will soon, step by step, be civilized; the European will meantime seem a dunce.

The Emperor is an honest man, a little hard, a little stingy, a little stupid, but, for the rest, he loves his subjects and the State, and he patronizes the brilliant minds of his dominions.

V' era un popolo ribelle
che pagava a malincuore
i catasti e le gabelle:
il benigno imperatore
ha provato in quel paese
    quest'arnese.

La virtù dell'istrumento
ha fruttato una pensione
a quel boia di talento,
col brevetto d'invenzione,
e l'ha fatto Mandarino
    di Pekino.

Grida un frate: oh! bella cosa!
gli va dato anco il battesimo.
ah perchè, (dice al Canosa
un Tiberio in diciottesimo),
questo genio non m'è nato
    nel Ducato!

There was a rebellious people who payed taxes and import duty with an ill-will: the kindly emperor has tried this apparatus in that country.

The worth of the instrument has produced a pension for that talented executioner, with patent rights for his invention, and has made him a Mandarin of Peking.

A friar shouts: Oh! What a fine thing! He is also to be baptized. Ah why, (says a thumbnail Tiberius* to Canosa†), wasn't this genius born in my Duchy!

---

  * The Duke of Modena.   † His minister.

La chiocciola

V I V A la chiocciola,
viva una bestia
che unisce il merito
alla modestia.
Essa all'astronomo
e all'architetto
forse nell'animo
destò il concetto
del cannocchiale,
e delle scale:
> viva la chiocciola,
> caro animale.

Contenta ai comodi
che Dio la fece,
può dirsi il Diogene
della sua spece.
Per prender aria
non passa l'uscio;
nelle abitudini
del proprio guscio
sta persuasa
e non intasa:
> viva la chiocciola
> bestia da casa.

The Snail

LONG live the snail, long live a beast that unites merit with modesty. It perhaps suggested to the astronomer and the architect the telescope and the spiral staircase. Long live the snail, dear animal.

Content with the comforts which God provided, it could be called the Diogenes of its species. To take the air it doesn't step across its threshold; it is confirmed in the habits of its own shell and does not catch colds: long live the snail, household beast.

Di cibi estranei
acre prurito
svegli uno stomaco
senza appetito:
essa, sentendosi
bene in arnese,
ha gusto a rodere
del suo paese
tranquillamente
l'erba nascente:
    viva la chiocciola,
    bestia astinente.

Nessun procedere
sa colle buone,
e più d'un asino
fa da leone.
Essa al contrario,
bestia com'è,
tira a proposito
le corna a sè;
non fa l'audace,
ma frigge e tace:
    viva la chiocciola,
    bestia di pace.

Let the piquancy of exotic foods stimulate a stomach without appetite: the snail feels itself in good shape and likes to nibble the springing grass of its home country: long live the snail, abstemious beast.

No one knows how to get on with kindness and so every one acts like a lion rather than an ass. The snail, on the contrary, draws its horns in just at the right moment; it does not go in for daring, but splutters and is silent: long live the snail, peaceful beast.

Natura, varia
ne' suoi portenti,
la privilegia
sopra i viventi
perchè (carnefici,
sentite questa)
le fa rinascere
perfin la testa;
cosa mirabile,
ma indubitabile;
 viva la chiocciola,
 bestia invidiabile.

Gufi dottissimi,
che predicate
e al vostro simile
nulla insegnate;
e, voi, girovaghi,
ghiotti, scapati,
padroni idrofobi,
servi arrembati,
prego a cantare
l'intercalare:
 viva la chiocciola,
 bestia esemplare.

Nature, that varies in its prodigies, has favoured the snail more
than ordinary living beings, because (listen to this, you execu-
tioners) she makes even its head grow again; a wonderful thing, but
not to be doubted: long live the snail, enviable beast.

Most learned owls who preach and teach your neighbour nothing; and you, scavengers, gluttons, numbskulls, rabid masters,
brokendown servants, I beg you to sing the refrain: long live the
snail, exemplary beast.

Sant'Ambrogio

VOSTRA Eccellenza, che mi sta in cagnesco
per que' pochi scherzucci di dozzina,
e mi gabella per anti-tedesco
perche metto le birbe alla berlina,
o senta il caso avvenuto di fresco
a me, che girellando, una mattina
càpito in Sant'Ambrogio di Milano,
in quello vecchio, là, fuori di mano.

M'era compagno il figlio giovinetto
d'un di que' capi un po' pericolosi,
di quel tal Sandro, autor d'un romanzetto,
ove si tratta di Promessi Sposi. ...
Che fa il nesci, Eccellenza? o non l'ha letto?
Ah, intendo: il suo cervel, Dio lo riposi,
in tutt'altre faccende affaccendato,
a questa roba è morto e sotterrato.

Entro, e ti trovo un pieno di soldati,
di que' soldati settentrionali,
come sarebbe Boemi e Croati,
messi qui nella vigna a far da pali:

The Church of Sant'Ambrogio

YOUR Excellency, who is cross with me for those few trifling little jokes of mine, and labels me for anti-German because I pillory rogues, oh listen to this experience which recently fell to me when, wandering around one morning, I happened to enter Sant'Ambrogio, the old one, there, out of the way.

I was accompanied by the young son of one of those slightly dangerous brains, of that certain Sandro, author of a little novel which deals with The Betrothed. ... Why look as if you know nothing about it, Excellency? or haven't you read it? Oh, I understand: your brain, God rest it, is busied with quite different business, and is dead and buried to stuff of this kind.

I go in, and I find a full house of soldiers, those northern soldiers, likely to be Bohemians and Croats, stuck here in the vineyard

difatto se ne stavano impalati,
come sogliono in faccia a' generali,
co' baffi di capecchio e con que' musi,
davanti a Dio, diritti come fusi.

Mi tenni indietro; chè, piovuto in mezzo
di quella maramaglia, io non lo nego
d' aver provato un senso di ribrezzo,
che lei non prova in grazia dell'impiego.
Sentiva un'afa, un alito di lezzo;
scusi, Eccellenza, mi parean di sego,
in quella bella casa del Signore,
fin le candele dell'altar maggiore.

Ma, in quella che s'appresta il sacerdote
a consacrar la mistica vivanda,
di subita dolcezza mi percuote
su, di verso l'altare, un suon di banda.
Dalle trombe di guerra uscian le note
come di voce che si raccomanda,
d'una gente che gema in duri stenti
e de' perduti beni si rammenti.

to serve as poles: in fact they stood planted there as they do normally before a general, with their tow moustaches and those faces
of theirs, before God, straight as spindles.

I kept back; for, when I landed in among that mob, I don't deny
it, I experienced a sense of revulsion, which you don't experience
thanks to your job. My nostrils were assailed by a mugginess, a
faint stink; 'beg your pardon, Excellency, but even the candles on
the great altar seemed of suet in that fine house of God.

But at the moment when the priest makes ready to consecrate the
mystic food, the music of a band, from up near the altar, struck me
with instant sweetness. Notes came from the war-trumpets that
were like the pleading voice of a people who groan in hardship and
remember lost possessions.

Era un coro del Verdi; il coro a Dio
là de' Lombardi miseri, assetati;
quello: *O Signore, dal tetto natìo,*
che tanti petti ha scossi e inebriati.
Qui cominciai a non esser più io;
e, come se que' còsi diventati
fossero gente della nostra gente,
entrai nel branco involontariamente.

Che vuol ella, Eccellenza, il pezzo è bello,
poi nostro, e poi sonato come va:
e coll'arte di mezzo, e col cervello
dato all' arte, l'ubbie si buttan là.
Ma, cessato che fu, dentro, bel bello,
io ritornava a star come la sa;
quand'eccoti per farmi un altro tiro,
da quelle bocche che parean di ghiro,

un cantico tedesco, lento lento,
per l'aer sacro a Dio mosse le penne:
era preghiera, e mi parea lamento,
d'un suono grave, flebile, solenne,

It was a chorus by Verdi; that chorus to God sung by the Lom-
bards, thirsting and sorrowful; that: *O Lord, from the houses where
we were born,* which has shaken and filled so many bosoms. At this
point I began to be myself no longer; and, as if those objects had
become people of our people, I entered involuntarily into the
crowd.

What's surprising, Excellency, the piece is a fine one, then ours,
and then played as it should be: and when art comes between, and
when the mind is given to art, prejudices are thrown aside. But
when it had finished, gradually in myself I came again to feel you
know how; when, there, to play me another trick, from those
mouths like those of dormice,

a German song slowly, slowly moved its wings through that air
sacred to God: it was a prayer and it seemed a lament to me, one
of earnest, plaintive, solemn tone, such that I keep hearing it in

tal, che sempre nell'anima lo sento;
e mi stupisco che in quelle cotenne,
in quei fantocci esotici di legno,
potesse l'armonia fino a quel segno.

Sentia, nell'inno, la dolcezza amara
de' canti uditi da fanciullo: il core,
che da voce domestica gl'impara,
ce li ripete i giorni del dolore:
un pensier mesto della madre cara,
un desiderio di pace e d'amore,
uno sgomento di lontano esilio,
che mi faceva andare in visibilio.

E, quando tacque, mi lasciò pensoso
di pensieri più forti e più soavi.
– Costor, dicea tra me, re pauroso
degl'italici moti e degli slavi,
strappa a' lor tetti, e qua, senza riposo,
schiavi gli spinge, per tenerci schiavi;
gli spinge di Croazia e di Boemme,
come mandre a svernar nelle Maremme.

my soul; and I marvel that in those squareheads, in those out-
landish, wooden puppets, harmony could achieve so much.

I heard, in the hymn, the bitter sweetness of songs listened to in
childhood: the heart, which learns them from a familiar voice, sings
them over in days of sorrow: a sad thought of our dear mother, a
desire for peace and love, dismay at distant exile, which melted me.

And when it hushed, it left me thinking stronger, sweeter
thoughts. These men, I said to myself, are snatched from their
homes by a king afraid of Italian and Slav stirrings, and are forced
here, without pause, as slaves to keep us slaves; he drives them
from Croatia and Bohemia as flocks are driven to winter in the
Maremma.

A dura vita, a dura disciplina,
muti, derisi, solitari stanno,
strumenti ciechi d'occhiuta rapina,
che lor non tocca e che forse non sanno:
e quest'odio, che mai non avvicina
il popolo lombardo all'alemanno,
giova a chi regna dividendo, e teme
popoli avversi affratellati insieme.

Povera gente! lontana da' suoi,
in un paese, qui, che le vuol male,
chi sa che, in fondo all'anima, po' poi,
non mandi a quel paese il principale!
Gioco che l'hanno in tasca come noi. –
Qui, se non fuggo, abbraccio un caporale,
colla su' brava mazza di nocciolo,
duro e piantato lì come un piolo.

Living a hard life, subject to hard discipline, they remain silent, mocked at, and alone, blind instruments of keen-eyed rapine, which does not fall to them and which they perhaps do not know of. And this hate which never lets the Lombard people approach the German, serves the purposes of a king who reigns by dividing, and who fears hostile peoples banded in brotherliness.

Poor souls! far from their own, in a country, here, that wishes them harm, who knows but that they, deep down, would have the emperor at the devil! I bet they loathe him as we do. – At this point, if I do not fly, I shall embrace a corporal with his brave hazel staff, standing there stiff and rooted as a stake.

GIOSUÈ CARDUCCI

Pianto antico

L'ALBERO a cui tendevi
la pargoletta mano,
il verde melograno
da' bei vermigli fior,

nel muto orto solingo
rinverdì tutto or ora
e giugno lo ristora
di luce e di calor.

Tu fior de la mia pianta
percossa e inaridita,
tu de l'inutil vita
estremo unico fior,

sei ne la terra fredda,
sei ne la terra negra;
nè il sol più ti rallegra
nè ti risveglia amor.

Ancient Lament

THE tree to which you stretched your baby hand, the green
pomegranate-tree with its fine scarlet flowers,
    has just grown green again in the deserted, silent courtyard and
June is reviving it with light and heat.
    You, flower of my stricken, dried-up plant, you the last only
flower of my useless life,
    you are in the cold earth, you are in the black earth, nor does the
sun any longer delight, nor can love wake you.

Il comune rustico

O CHE tra faggi e abeti erma su i campi
smeraldini la fredda orma si stampi
al sole del mattin puro e leggero,
o che foscheggi immobile nel giorno
morente su le sparse ville intorno
a la chiesa che prega o al cimitero

che tace, o noci de la Carnia, addio!
Erra tra i vostri rami il pensier mio
sognando l'ombre d'un tempo che fu.
Non paure di morti ed in congreghe
diavoli goffi con bizzarre streghe,
ma del comun la rustica virtù

accampata a l'opaca ampia frescura
veggo ne la stagion de la pastura
dopo la messa il giorno de la festa.
Il consol dice, e poste ha pria le mani
sopra i santi segnacoli cristiani:
— Ecco, io parto fra voi quella foresta

The Country Community

WHETHER between beech-trees and firs your cold imprint be left,
lone upon the emerald fields in the sun of pure and lightsome morning, or it gloom motionless in the day that dies upon the scattered
dwellings around the praying church or the cemetery that
    is silent, farewell, o walnut-trees of Carnia! My thoughts roam
among your branches, dreaming of the shades of a time that is gone.
Not fears of the dead or gross devils leagued with fantastic witches
do I see, but the rustic virtue of the community
    displayed in the dim and spreading chill in the season of pastur-
age, after mass on a holiday. The Consul says, and first he has laid
his hands upon the sacred Christian symbols: 'There, I divide
among you that forest

d'abeti e pini ove al confin nereggia.
E voi trarrete la mugghiante greggia
e la belante a quelle cime là.
E voi, se l'unno o se lo slavo invade,
eccovi, o figli, l'aste, ecco le spade,
morete per la nostra libertà. –

Un fremito d'orgoglio empieva i petti,
ergea le bionde teste; e de gli eletti
in su le fronti il sol grande feriva.
Ma le donne piangenti sotto i veli
invocavan la Madre alma de' cieli.
Con la man tesa il console seguiva:

– Questo, al nome di Cristo e di Maria,
ordino e voglio che nel popol sia. –
A man levata il popol dicea Sì.
E le rosse giovenche di su 'l prato
vedean passare il piccolo senato,
brillando su gli abeti il mezzodí.

of firs and pines where it blackens at the edge. And you will take
the lowing herd and the bleating one to those peaks there. And if
the Hun or the Slav invades, here, my sons, is the spear, here are
swords for you, you will die for your liberty.'

A shiver of pride possessed their breasts, it raised the fair heads,
and the sun struck upon the foreheads of the chosen. But the women
weeping beneath their veils, called upon the kindly mother of the
heavens. With outstretched hand the Consul continued:

'This, in the name of Christ and Mary, I order and desire should
have effect among the people.' With raised hands the people said,
So let it be. And the young red heifers on the meadow saw the little
senate pass, as noon shone upon the firs.

Alla stazione in una mattina d'autunno

O H quei fanali come s'inseguono
accidiosi là dietro gli alberi,
tra i rami stillanti di pioggia
sbadigliando la luce su 'l fango!

Flebile, acuta, stridula fischia
la vaporiera da presso. Plumbeo
il cielo e il mattino d'autunno
come un grande fantasma n'è intorno.

Dove e a che move questa, che affrettasi
a' carri foschi, ravvolta e tacita
gente? a che ignoti dolori
o tormenti di speme lontana?

Tu pur pensosa, Lidia, la tessera
al secco taglio dài de la guardia,
e al tempo incalzante i begli anni
dài, gl'istanti gioiti e i ricordi.

At the Station, One Morning in Autumn

O H T H O S E lamps how drearily they succeed one another behind
the trees, amid branches dripping with rain, their light yawning
upon the ground!

Near at hand the train whistles desolate, sharp, shrilling. Leaden,
the sky, and the autumn morning is like a great phantom around us.

Where and to what end do these people, muffled and silent, hurry-
ing to dark coaches, move? to what unknown griefs? to what torment of distant hopes?

You Lydia, thoughtful also, give your ticket to the dry clipping
of the collector, and give your lovely years, moments enjoyed,
memories, to hastening time.

Van lungo il nero convoglio e vengono
incappucciati di nero i vigili,
come ombre; una fioca lanterna
hanno, e mazze di ferro: ed i ferrei

freni tentati rendono un lugubre
rintocco lungo: di fondo a l'anima
un'eco di tedio risponde
doloroso, che spasimo pare.

E gli sportelli sbattuti al chiudere
paion oltraggi: scherno par l'ultimo
appello che rapido suona:
grossa scroscia su' vetri la pioggia.

Già il mostro, conscio di sua metallica
anima, sbuffa, crolla, ansa, i fiammei
occhi sbarra; immane pe 'l buio
gitta il fischio che sfida lo spazio.

Va l'empio mostro; con traino orribile
sbattendo l'ale gli amor miei portasi.
Ahi, la bianca faccia e 'l bel velo
salutando scompar ne la tènebra.

The guards come and go along the black train, hooded in black,
like shades; they have a dim lantern and iron hammers, and the
    iron brakes, tested, respond with a long funereal ring: from the
soul's depth an echo of tedium, lamenting answers, that seems a
start of agony.
    And the carriage-doors slammed shut seem outrages: the last
call that sounds briefly, mockery: the rain beats large upon the
window.
    Already the monster, conscious of its metallic soul, snorts,
shakes, pants, bares its flaming eyes; huge through the gloom, it
hurls its whistle, challenging space.
    The evil monster goes: wings flurrying, it carries away my loves
with its horrible carriages. Ah, the white face and lovely veil disappear, even as they bid farewell, into the shadows.

O viso dolce di pallor roseo,
o stellanti occhi di pace, o candida
tra' floridi ricci inchinata
pura fronte con atto soave!

Fremea la vita nel tepid'aere,
fremea l'estate quando mi arrisero;
e il giovine sole di giugno
si piacea di baciar luminoso

in tra i riflessi del crin castanei
la molle guancia: come un'aureola
più belli del sole i miei sogni
ricingean la persona gentile.

Sotto la pioggia, tra la caligine
torno ora, e ad esse vorrei confondermi;
barcollo com'ebro, e mi tocco,
non anch'io fossi dunque un fantasma.

Oh qual caduta di foglie, gelida,
continua, muta, greve, su l'anima!
io credo che solo, che eterno,
che per tutto nel mondo è novembre.

O soft face of rose-like paleness, o eyes brimming with peace, o
white, pure forehead bent in sweet grace between luxuriant locks!
  Life trembled in the warm air, the summer trembled, when they
smiled on me, and the young sun of June was glad to kiss with light
the soft cheek amid the auburn lustre of the hair: my dreams,
lovelier than the sun, encircled the gentle form, too, as if with a
halo.
  Under the rain, in the mist, I now go back, and I would be glad
to lose myself in them; I stagger like a drunkard, and touch myself
for fear I too might be a phantom.
  O such a fall of leaves, icy, incessant, silent, grievous, upon the
soul! I believe that only, that eternally, for everything in the world,
it is November.

Meglio a chi 'l senso smarrì de l'essere,
meglio quest'ombra, questa caligine:
io voglio, io voglio adagiarmi
in un tedio che duri infinito.

Mezzogiorno alpino

N EL gran cerchio de l'alpi, su 'l granito
squallido e scialbo, su' ghiacciai candenti,
regna sereno intenso ed infinito
nel suo grande silenzio il mezzodì.

Pini ed abeti senza aura di venti
si drizzano nel sol che gli penètra,
sola garrisce in picciol suon di cetra
l'acqua che tenue tra i sassi fluì.

Congedo

F IOR tricolore,
tramontano le stelle in mezzo al mare
e si spengono i canti entro il mio core.

Luckier he whose senses desert him, better this shadow, this mist; I want, I want to drift in a tedium that stretches infinite.

Alpine Morning

IN the great circle of the alps, upon the discoloured, pale granite, upon the burning glaciers, noon reigns serene, intense and infinite in its great silence.

Pines and firs untouched by breath of wind rise straight in the sun that penetrates them, only the water that runs thin among the stones protests with the small sound of a lute.

Salute in Farewell

THREE-COLOURED flower, the stars go down into the midst of the sea and the songs die within my heart.

321

GIOVANNI PASCOLI

Allora

ALLORA ... in un tempo assai lunge
felice fui molto; non ora:
ma quanta dolcezza mi giunge
da tanta dolcezza d'allora!

Quell'anno! per anni che poi
fuggirono, che fuggiranno,
non puoi, mio pensiero, non puoi,
portare con te, che quell'anno!

Un giorno fu quello, ch'è senza
compagno, ch'è senza ritorno;
la vita fu van parvenza
sì prima sì dopo quel giorno!

Un punto! ... così passeggero,
che in vero passò non raggiunto,
ma bello così, che molto ero
felice, felice, quel punto!

At that Time

AT that time ... in a most distant time I was very happy; not
now: but how much sweetness comes to me from so much sweetness then!

That year! through all the years that later fled, that will fleet
away, you cannot, my thoughts, you cannot bear with you anything but that year!

It was a day that is without fellow, that is without return; life
was an empty appearance, equally, before and after that day!

A point! ... so passing, that in truth it passed by unattained, but
so lovely that I was happy, very happy, at that point!

Romagna

a Severino

SEMPRE un villaggio, sempre una campagna
mi ride al cuore (o piange), Severino:
il paese ove, andando, ci accompagna
l'azzurra vision di San Marino:

sempre mi torna al cuore il mio paese
cui regnarono Guidi e Malatesta,
cui tenne pure il Passator cortese,
re della strada, re della foresta.

Là nelle stoppie dove singhiozzando
va la tacchina con l'altrui covata,
presso gli stagni lustreggianti, quando
lenta vi guazza l'anatra iridata,

oh! fossi io teco; e perderci nel verde,
e di tra gli olmi, nido alle ghiandaie,
gettarci l'urlo che lungi si perde
dentro il meridiano ozio dell'aie;

The Romagna

to Severino

EVER a village, ever a stretch of countryside laughs at my heart (or
weeps), o Severino: the country where, as we go, we are accompanied by the blue vision of San Marino:
   ever my homeland comes back to my heart where Guidi and
Malatesta reigned, which courteous Passator also held, he, king of
the road, and king of the forest.
   There among the stubble where the turkey-hen goes wheezing
with a brood not her own, near the shining ponds, where the many-
gleaming duck paddles slow,
   oh! might I be with you; and we, lose ourselves in the green,
and from among the elms, the jays' nest, send up the shout which
loses itself in the noon ease of the barn-yards;

mentre il villano pone dalle spalle
gobbe la ronca e afferra la scodella,
e 'l bue rumina nelle opache stalle
la sua laboriosa lupinella.

Da' borghi sparsi le campane in tanto
si rincorron coi lor gridi argentini:
chiamano al rezzo, alla quiete, al santo
desco fiorito d'occhi di bambini.

Già m'accoglieva in quelle ore bruciate
sotto ombrello di trine una mimosa,
che fioria la mia casa ai dì d'estate
co' suoi pennacchi di color di rosa;

e s'abbracciava per lo sgretolato
muro un folto rosaio a un gelsomino;
guardava il tutto un pioppo alto e slanciato,
chiassoso a giorni come un biricchino.

Era il mio nido: dove, immobilmente,
io galoppava con Guidon Selvaggio
e con Astolfo; o mi vedea presente
l'imperatore nell'eremitaggio.

while the farmhand takes the pruning-fork from his humped
shoulders and grasps the bowl, and the ox chews its monotonous
cud in the dim stalls.

From the scattered hamlets, meanwhile, the bells mingle their
silvery shouts: they call to repose, to quiet, to the pious table
decked with the flowers of children's eyes.

Once a mimosa welcomed me under a trailing umbrella in those
burnt hours, a mimosa which decorated my house in summer days
with its pink tassels;

and a thick rose-bush embraced a jasmine through the crumbling wall; a poplar, tall and slender, noisy by day as a cheeky boy,
looked upon the whole scene.

It was my nest: where, without moving, I galloped with Guidon
Selvaggio and with Astolfo; or saw before me the emperor in the
hermitage.

E mentre aereo mi poneva in via
con l'ippogrifo pel sognato alone,
o risonava nella stanza mia
muta il dettare di Napoleone;

udia tra i fieni allor allor falciati
de' grilli il verso che perpetuo trema,
udiva dalle rane dei fossati
un lungo interminabile poema.

E lunghi, e interminati, erano quelli
ch'io meditai, mirabili a sognare:
stormir di frondi, cinguettìo d'uccelli,
risa di donne, strepito di mare.

Ma da quel nido, rondini tardive,
tutti tutti migrammo un giorno nero;
io, la mia patria or è dove si vive;
gli altri son poco lungi; in cimitero.

Così più non verrò per la calura
tra que' tuoi polverosi biancospini,
ch'io non ritrovi nella mia verzura
del cuculo ozioso i piccolini,

And while, aloft, I rode with the hippogriff on the way to the
dreamed-of ring of light, or the sayings of Napoleon echoed in my
noiseless room;

I heard from the hay-fields, cut just then, the cicadas' verse that
endlessly trembles, heard a long, unending poem from the frogs in
the ditches.

And long, and without end, were those which I brooded on,
wonderful things to dream: rustling of leaves, birds' twittering,
women's laughter, roar of the sea.

But from that nest, late swallows, we all, all migrated one black
day; for me, homeland now is where one lives; the others are not
far removed; in the churchyard.

So I shall no longer come in the heat between your dusty haw-
thorns, lest I should find, in my green places, the younglings of the
idle cuckoo,

Romagna solatìa, dolce paese,
cui regnarono Guidi e Malatesta,
cui tenne pure il Passator cortese,
re della strada, re della foresta.

Orfano

LENTA la neve fiocca, fiocca, fiocca.
Senti: una zana dondola pian piano.
Un bimbo piange, il piccol dito in bocca;
canta una vecchia, il mento sulla mano.
La vecchia canta: Intorno al tuo lettino
c'è rose e gigli, tutto un bel giardino.
Nel bel giardino il bimbo s'addormenta.
La neve fiocca lenta, lenta, lenta ...

Novembre

GEMMEA l'aria, il sole così chiaro
che tu ricerchi gli albicocchi in fiore,
e del prunalbo l'odorino amaro
            senti nel cuore ...

---

sunny Romagna, sweet homeland, where Guidi and Malatesta ruled, which courteous Passator also held, he, king of the road and king of the forest.

Orphan

SLOWLY the snow is flaking, flaking, flaking. Listen: a cradle is rocking gently. A child cries, a small finger in its mouth; there is an old woman singing, her chin upon her hand. The old woman is singing: Around your bed there are roses and lilies, a whole lovely garden. In the lovely garden the child is falling asleep. The snow is flaking slowly, slowly, slowly ...

November

GEM-LIKE the air, the sun so clear that you look for the apricots' blossoming, and smell in your heart the bitterish scent of the whitethorn ...

Ma secco è il pruno, e le stecchite piante
di nere trame segnano il sereno,
e vuoto il cielo, e cavo al piè sonante
              sembra il terreno.

Silenzio, intorno: solo, alle ventate,
odi lontano, da giardini ed orti,
di foglie un cader fragile. È l'estate,
              fredda, dei morti.

La voce

C'È una voce nella mia vita,
che avverto nel punto che muore;
    voce stanca, voce smarrita,
col tremito del batticuore:

voce d'una accorsa anelante,
che al povero petto s'afferra
    per dir tante cose e poi tante,
ma piena ha la bocca di terra:

But the thornbush is dry, and the stick-like plants mark the heavens with black designs, and empty is the sky, and the earth seems hollow, echoing to the step.

Silence, around: only, in the wind's quickening, you hear in the distance, from orchard and garden, a brittle falling of leaves. It is the summer, cold, of the dead.

The Voice

THERE is a voice in my life, which I make out just as it dies; a tired voice, a voice lost, with the tremor of my heart-beat:

voice panting from its haste, that clutches the poor breast to say so many things and so many more, but that mouth is full of earth:

tante tante cose che vuole
ch'io sappia, ricordi, sì ... sì ...
ma di tante tante parole
non sento che un soffio ... Zvanì ...

Quando avevo tanto bisogno
di pane e di compassione,
che mangiavo solo nel sogno,
svegliandomi al primo boccone;

una notte, su la spalletta
del Reno, coperta di neve,
dritto e solo (passava in fretta
l'acqua brontolando, Si beve?);

dritto e solo, con un gran pianto
d'aver a finire così,
mi sentii d'un tratto daccanto
quel soffio di voce ... Zvanì ...

Oh! la terra, com'è cattiva!
la terra, che amari bocconi!
ma voleva dirmi, io capiva:
— No ... no ... Di' le devozioni!

---

so many things that it wants me to know and remember, like
this ... like that ... but of so many, many words I hear only a
breath ... Johnnie ...

When I was in such need of bread and pity, which I ate only in
dream, waking at the first mouthful;

one night, on the snow-covered edge of the Reno, I, upright and
alone (the river passed mumbling, will you drink?);

upright and alone, weeping bitterly to have to end like this, I
suddenly heard at my side that breathing voice ... Johnnie ...

Oh! how wicked the earth is! the earth, what bitter mouthfuls!
but it wanted to say to me, I understood: 'No ... no. ... Say your
prayers!

Le dicevi con me pian piano,
con sempre la voce più bassa:
   la tua mano nella mia mano:
ridille! vedrai che ti passa.

   Non far piangere piangere piangere
(ancora!) chi tanto soffrì!
   il tuo pane, prega il tuo angelo
che te lo porti ... Zvanì ... –

   Una notte dalle lunghe ore
(nel carcere!), che all'improvviso
   dissi – Avresti molto dolore,
tu, se non t'avessero ucciso,

   ora, o babbo! – che il mio pensiero,
dal carcere, con un lamento,
   vide il babbo nel cimitero,
le pie sorelline in convento:

   e che agli uomini, la mia vita,
volevo lasciargiela lì ...
   risentii la voce smarrita
che disse in un soffio ... Zvanì ...

'You used to say them with me quietly with a voice that fell
lower and lower: your hand in my hand: say them again! you will
see that this will pass from you.
   'Do not make her weep, weep, weep (still!) who suffered so
much! beg your angel to bring you your bread ... Johnnie ...'
   On a night of long hours (in prison!), when suddenly I said,
'You would have grieved much, now, if they had not killed you,
o father!' when my thoughts, from prison, saw, with woe, my
father in the cemetery, my devout little sisters in the convent:
   and when I wished to leave my life to men there ... I heard the
lost voice again which said breathingly ... Johnnie ...

Oh! la terra come è cattiva!
non lascia discorrere, poi!
   Ma voleva dirmi, io capiva:
– Piuttosto di' un requie per noi!

   Non possiamo nel camposanto
più prendere sonno un minuto,
   chè sentiamo struggersi in pianto
le bimbe che l'hanno saputo!

   Oh! la vita mia che ti diedi
per loro, lasciarla vuoi qui?
   qui, mio figlio? dove non vedi
chi uccise tuo padre ... Zvanì? –

   Quante volte sei rivenuta
nei cupi abbandoni del cuore,
   voce stanca, voce perduta,
col tremito del batticuore:

   voce d'una accorsa anelante
che ai poveri labbri si tocca
   per dir tante cose e poi tante;
ma piena di terra ha la bocca:

Oh! how wicked the earth is! do not let it be spoken of, then!
But you wanted to say to me, I understood: 'Rather say a requiem
for us!

'We cannot take our rest in the churchyard a moment, for we
hear our daughters who witnessed our end, wasting themselves in
weeping.

'Oh! do you want to lay down here that life of mine I gave you
for them? Here, my son? Where you do not see who killed your
father ... Johnnie?'

How many times have you returned in the dark surrenders of
my heart, tired voice, voice lost, with the tremor of my heart-
beat:

voice panting from its haste, which touches the poor lips to say
so many things and so many more; but that mouth is full of earth:

la tua bocca! con i tuoi baci,
già tanto accorati a quei dì!
   a quei dì beati e fugaci
che aveva i tuoi baci Zvanì!

che m'addormentavano gravi
campane col placido canto,
   e sul capo biondo che amavi,
sentivo un tepore di pianto!

che ti lessi negli occhi, ch'erano
pieni di pianto, che sono
   pieni di terra, la preghiera
di vivere e d'essere buono!

Ed allora, quasi un comando,
no, quasi un compianto, t'uscì
   la parola che a quando a quando
mi dici anche adesso ... Zvanì ...

your mouth! with your kisses, so distressed even in the old days! in those blessed and fleeting days when Johnnie knew your kisses!

for heavy bells would lay me asleep with their peaceful song, and on the fair head which you loved, I would feel the warmth of tears!

for I read in your eyes which were full of tears, which now are full of earth, the prayer to live and be good!

And then, like a command, no, almost a voiced regret, the word escaped from you, which at times you say to me even now ... Johnnie ...

Il gelsomino notturno

E s'APRONO i fiori notturni
nell'ora che penso a' miei cari.
Sono apparse in mezzo ai viburni
le farfalle crepuscolari.

Da un pezzo si tacquero i gridi:
là sola una casa bisbiglia.
Sotto l'ali dormono i nidi,
come gli occhi sotto le ciglia.

Dai calici aperti si esala
l'odore di fragole rosse.
Splende un lume là nella sala.
Nasce l'erba sopra le fosse.

Un'ape tardiva sussurra
trovando già prese le celle.
La Chiocetta per l'aia azzurra
va col suo pigolìo di stelle.

Per tutta la notte s'esala
l'odore che passa col vento.

The Jasmine at Night

AND the flowers of night open, in the hour that I think of those
dear to me. The twilight butterflies have appeared among the
viburnums.

For a while now the cries have ceased: only over there a house
whispers. Nests sleep under wings, like eyes under eyelids.

The scent of red strawberries is breathed up from open chalices.
A light shines there in the room. Grass springs above ditches.

A late bee murmurs finding the cells already taken. The Hen
goes through the blue barnyard followed by her chirping of stars.

All through the night a scent rises that passes with the wind. The

Passa il lume su per la scala;
brilla al primo piano: s'è spento ...

È l'alba: si chiudono i petali
un poco gualciti; si cova,
dentro l'urna molle e segreta,
non so che felicità nuova.

L'ora di Barga

AL mio cantuccio, donde non sento
se non le reste brusir del grano,
il suon dell'ore viene col vento
dal non veduto borgo montano:
suono che uguale, che blando cade,
come una voce che persuade.

Tu dici, È l'ora; tu dici, È tardi,
voce che cadi blanda dal cielo.
Ma un poco ancora lascia che guardi
l'albero, il ragno, l'ape, lo stelo,
cose ch'han molti secoli o un anno
o un'ora, e quelle nubi che vanno.

___

light passes up the stairs: shines out from the first floor: is extinguished ...

It is dawn: the petals close, slightly crumpled; there nests in the
soft and secret urn some new happiness, I cannot say what.

Time at Barga

To my corner, from which I hear nothing but the bearded grain's
rustling, the ringing of the hours comes from the unseen mountain
hamlet: a sound that falls even, falls mild, like a voice persuading.

You say, It is time; you say, It is late, voice that falls mild from
heaven, but let me look a little longer on the tree, the spider, the
bee, the stem, things that have many centuries in them, or a year,
or an hour, and those clouds that pass.

333

Lasciami immoto qui rimanere
fra tanto moto d'ale e di fronde;
e udire il gallo che da un podere
chiama, e da un altro l'altro risponde,
e, quando altrove l'anima è fissa,
gli strilli d'una cincia che rissa.

E suona ancora l'ora, e mi manda
prima un suo grido di meraviglia
tinnulo, e quindi con la sua blanda
voce di prima parla e consiglia,
e grave grave grave m'incuora:
mi dice, È tardi; mi dice, È l'ora.

Tu vuoi che pensi dunque al ritorno
voce che cadi blanda dal cielo!
Ma bello è questo poco di giorno
che mi traluce come da un velo!
Lo so ch'è l'ora, lo so ch'è tardi;
ma un poco ancora lascia che guardi.

Let me stay here, unmoving amid so much movement of wing
and leaf; and hear the cock that calls from one farm, and from
another, the other answers, and, when the soul is elsewhere intent,
the shrilling of a tomtit that quarrels.

And the hour rings out again, and addresses me first with its
tinkling voice of wonder, and then with its former mild voice
speaks and advises and ponderously encourages me: it says to me,
It is late; it says to me, It is time.

You want me then to think of my return, voice that falls mild
from heaven! But this little part of the day that shines through to
me as if from behind a veil is beautiful! I know it is time, I know it
is late; but let me stay and watch a little longer.

Lascia che guardi dentro il mio cuore,
lascia ch'io viva del mio passato;
se c'è sul bronco sempre quel fiore,
s'io trovi un bacio che non ho dato!
Nel mio cantuccio d'ombra romita
lascia ch'io pianga su la mia vita!

E suona ancora l'ora, e mi squilla
due volte un grido quasi di cruccio,
e poi, tornata blanda e tranquilla,
mi persuade nel mio cantuccio:
è tardi! è l'ora! Sì, ritorniamo
dove son quelli ch'amano ed amo.

GABRIELE D'ANNUNZIO

Canto del sole

Ecco, e la glauca marina destasi
fresca a' freschissimi favonii; palpita:
ella sente nel grembo
gli amor verdi de l'alighe.

Let me look into my heart. Let me live over my past, to see if there is still that flower upon the tree-stump, if I find a kiss that I have not given! Let me weep over my life from my corner of lonely shade.

And the hour rings again, and a cry almost as of annoyance shakes me with sound twice, and then grown mild and peaceful again, persuades me in my corner: it is late! it is time! Then, let us go back where there are those who love and whom I love.

Song of the Sun

Look, the green sea wakes fresh to freshest breezes; it trembles: it feels in its lap the green loves of the seaweeds.

Sente: la sfiorano a torme i queruli
gabbiani, simili da lunge passano
le fulve e nere vele
pe'l gran sole cullandosi;

e in ampia cerchia ne l'acqua i floridi
poggi specchiantisi paiono imagini
di piramidi vinte
dal trionfo de l'edere.

Thàlatta! thàlatta! Volino, balzino
su su dal giovine core, zampillino
i tuoi brevi pirrichii,
o divino Asclepiade!

O Mare, o glorià, forza d'Italia,
alfin da' liberi tuoi flutti a l'aure
come un acciar temprata
la Giovinezza sfolgori!

Romanza

Dolcemente muor Febbraio
in un biondo suo colore.
Tutta a 'l sol, come un rosaio,
la gran piazza aulisce in fiore.

It feels: the querulous sea-gulls skim it in crowds, similar, in the distance, pass ochre and black sails rocked in the great sun;
and in the broad circle of the water the flowering hills, mirrored, seem images of pyramids overcome in the ivy's triumph.

Thalatta! thalatta! let your short numbers fly, spring from the youthful heart, let them go spurting upwards, o divine Asclepiades!

O Sea, o glory, strength of Italy, at last from your free surges let Youth flash out like tempered steel to the wind!

Romance

Sweetly dies February in a fairness of its own. All in the sun the great square in flower sends up fragrance like a rose-garden.

Dai novelli fochi accesa,
tutta a l' sol, la Trinità
su la tripla scala ride
ne la pia serenità.

L'obelisco pur fiorito
pare, quale un roseo stelo;
in sue vene di granito
ei gioisce, a mezzo il cielo.

Ode a piè de l'alta scala
la fontana mormorar,
vede a 'l sol l'acque croscianti
ne la barca scintillar.

In sua gloria la Madonna
sorridendo benedice
di su l'agile colonna
lo spettacolo felice.

Cresce il sole per la piazza
dilagando in copia d'or.
È passata la mia bella
e con ella va il mio cuor.

Lit by the new fires, all in the sun, the Trinity laughs above its
triple stair-way in the holy clearness.

The obelisque, too, seems to have flowered like a rose-coloured
stalk; it glories in its veins of granite amid the heavens.

It hears at the foot of the high stair-way the fountain murmuring, it sees the water pouring in the sun, flashing in the boat.

In her glory the Virgin Mary, smiling from the slender column,
bestows a blessing on the happy sight.

The sun grows, flooding the square with abundance of gold. My
fair one has passed and with her goes my heart.

A una torpediniera nell' Adriatico

NAVIGLIO d'acciaio, diritto veloce guizzante
bello come un'arme nuda,
vivo palpitante
come se il metallo un cuore terribile chiuda;

tu che solo al freddo coraggio dell'uomo t'affili
come l'arme su la cote,
e non soffri i vili
su la piastra ardente del ponte che il fremito scote;

messaggero primo di morte sul mar guerreggiato,
franco vèlite del mare,
tu passi, – e il tuo fato
io seguo nel flutto guardando la scìa luccicare.

Crollan dal ciel sommo valanghe di nubi difformi
fra colonne alte di raggi;
trapassano a stormi
a stormi gli uccelli radendo con gridi selvaggi;

To a Torpedo-boat in the Adriatic

SHIP of steel, straight, swift, flashing, lovely as a naked weapon,
alive, quivering as if the metal enclosed a terrible heart;
　　you who are edged only by man's cold courage like the weapon
upon the whetstone, and do not tolerate cowards on the burning
walk of the bridge which the trembling shakes;
　　first messenger of death on the contested sea, free ranger of the
sea, you pass – and I follow your fate, watching the wake glittering
in the surge.
　　Phalanxes of misshapen cloud crumble from highest heaven between tall columns of rays; flock after flock of birds skim past with
wild cries;

sotto la bufera cinereo là verso Ancona
l'Adriatico s'oscura:
se di lungi tuona,
il rombo rimbomba giù giù per la cupa calura.

Fa schermo la nube. Ma l'occhio dell'anima scorge
oltremare in lontananza
la città che sorge
alta sul suo golfo splendendo a la nostra speranza,

da tutte le torri splendendo nell'unica fede:
«Sempre a te! Sempre la stessa!»
poi che ancora crede,
la triste sorella domata, a la nostra promessa.

E un'ombra s'allunga, s'aggrava su l'acque (io la scorgo
con un brivido interrotto
crescere, nel gorgo
livido una macchia far come di sangue corrotto);

under the squall the Adriatic darkens to ashen there towards
Ancona: if it thunders in the distance, the rumble re-echoes down,
down through the dark sultriness.

The clouds form a shield. But the soul's eye makes out across the
sea in the distance the city which rises high above its gulf, shining
out to our hope,

from all its towers shining in the one faith: 'Always yours!
Always the same!' since our sad, captive sister still believes in our
promise.

And a shadow stretches, weighs upon the water (I perceive it
growing with an intermittent shudder, making a clot as of bad
blood in the glaring abyss),

s'allunga da Lissa remota a la riva materna.
Ecco, appar Faa di Bruno.
«Sarà dunque eterna
la vergogna?» E ascolta. «Nessun risponde, nessuno?»

Tu, tu, o naviglio d'acciaio, veloce guizzante
bello come un'arme nuda,
vivo palpitante
come se il metallo un cuore terribile chiuda;

tu che solo al freddo coraggio dell'uomo t'affili
come l'arme su la cote,
e non soffri i vili
su la piastra ardente del ponte che il fremito scote;

messaggero primo di morte sul mar guerreggiato,
franco vèlite del mare,
oh rispondi! Il fato
è certo; e a quel Giorno s'accendono i fochi su l'are.

it makes from far Lissa towards the mother shore. And now, Faa
di Bruno appears. 'Will the shame last for ever?' And he listens.
'Does no one answer, no one?'
You, you, o ship of steel, straight, swift, flashing, lovely as a
naked weapon, alive, quivering as if the metal enclosed a terrible
heart;
you who are edged only by man's cold courage like the weapon
upon the whetstone, and do not tolerate cowards on the burning
walk of the bridge which the trembling shakes;
first messenger of death on the contested sea, free ranger of the
sea, oh answer! Fate is certain; and the fires are lit upon the altars
for that day.

Assisi

Assisi, nella tua pace profonda
l'anima sempre intesa alle sue mire
non s'allentò; ma sol si finse l'ire
del Tescio quando il greto aspro s'inonda.

Torcesi la riviera sitibonda
che è bianca del furor del suo sitire.
Come fiamme anelanti di salire,
sorgon gli ulivi dalla torta sponda.

A lungo biancheggiar vidi, nel fresco
fiato della preghiera vesperale,
le tortuosità desiderose.

Anche vidi la carne di Francesco,
affocata dal dèmone carnale,
sanguinar su le spine delle rose.

Assisi

Assisi, in your deep peace the soul, ever intent upon its own
ends, did not slacken; but the flowing of the Tescio when the
rough river-bed floods was only imagined.

The thirsty course twists, white with the fury of its thirst. Like
flames panting to ascend, the olives rise on the twisted bank.

In the distance I saw the ardent twistings whitening in the fresh
breath of the evening prayer.

I saw, too, the flesh of Francis, flamed hectic by the fleshly demon,
bleeding on the roses' thorns.

Bocca d'Arno

Bocca di donna mai mi fu di tanta
soavità nell'amorosa via
(se non la tua, se non la tua, presente)
come la bocca pallida e silente
del fiumicel che nasce in Falterona.
Qual donna s'abbandona
(se non tu, se non tu) sì dolcemente
come questa placata correntìa?
Ella non canta,
e pur fluisce quasi melodìa
all'amarezza.

    Qual sia la sua bellezza
    io non so dire,
    come colui che ode
    suoni dormendo e virtudi ignote
    entran nel suo dormire.

Le saltano all'incontro i verdi flutti,
schiumanti di baldanza,
con la grazia dei giovini animali.
In catena di putti
non mise tanta gioia Donatello,

Mouth of the Arno

Woman's mouth to me was never of such soft charm in the ways of love (if not yours, if not yours, which is here) as the pale and silent mouth of the little river that is born in Falterona. What woman gives herself (if not you, if not you) so sweetly as this stilled current? It does not sing and yet flows almost a melody to bitterness.

What its beauty is I cannot say, like one who hears sounds in sleep and unknown powers enter into his slumber.

Towards it leap the green surges, foaming with vigour, with the grace of young animals. Donatello did not put such joy into a chain

fervendo il marmo sotto lo scalpello,
quando ornava le bianche cattedrali.
Sotto ghirlande di fiori e di frutti
svolgeasi intorno ai pergami la danza
infantile, ma non sì fiera danza
come quest'una.

  V'è creatura alcuna
  che in tanta grazia
  viva ed in sì perfetta
  gioia, se non quella lodoletta
  che in aere si spazia?

Forse l'anima mia, quando profonda
sè nel suo canto e vede la sua gloria
forse l'anima tua, quando profonda
sè nell'amore e perde la memoria
degli inganni fugaci in che s'illuse
ed anela con me l'alta vittoria.
Forse conosceremo noi la piena
felicità dell'onda
libera e delle forti ali dischiuse
e dell'inno selvaggio che si sfrena.
Adora e attendi!

of little angels, the marble feverish under his chisel, when he decorated the white cathedrals. The infant dance went round trellises, under garlands of flowers and fruit, but not so proud a dance as this one.

Is there any creature that lives in such grace, in so perfect a joy, unless it be that little lark that soars in air?

Perhaps my soul, when, deep in its own song, it sees its glory — perhaps your soul, when it enters deeply into love and loses remembrance of the fleeting deceptions in which it was caught and pants with me in high victory. Perhaps we shall know the full happiness of the free wave and of the strong, opened wings and of the wild hymn that is loosed. Adore and watch!

Adora, adora, e attendi!
Vedi? I tuoi piedi
nudi lascian vestigi
di luce, ed a' tuoi occhi prodigi
sorgon dall'acque. Vedi?

Grandi calici sorgono dall'acque,
di non so qual leggiere oro intessuti.
Le nubi i monti i boschi i lidi l'acque
trasparire per le corolle immani
vedi, lontani e vani
come in sogni paesi sconosciuti.
Farfalle d'oro come le tue mani
volando a coppia scoprono su l'acque
con meraviglia i fiori grandi e strani,
mentre tu fiuti
l'odor salino.
    Fa un suo gioco divino
    l'Ora solare,
    mutevole e gioconda
    come la gola d'una colomba
    alzata per cantare.

Adore, adore, and watch! Do you see? Your naked feet are leaving tracks of light, and they rise from the water to your miraculous eyes. Do you see?

Great goblets rise up from the water, filigreed with indescribable fine gold. You see the clouds, mountains, woods, the shores, the waters shining through huge petals, far-off and transitory as unknown countries in dream. Golden butterflies like your hands discover with wonder, as they fly over the water in couples, the great strange flowers, while you breathe in the salt smell.

The hour of the sun plays its divine game, changeful and pleased like a dove's throat stretched to sing.

Sono le reti pensili. Talune
pendon come bilance dalle antenne
cui sostengono i ponti alti e protesi
ove l'uom veglia a volgere la fune;
altre pendono a prua dei palischermi
trascorrendo il perenne
specchio che le rifrange; e quando il sole
batte a poppa i navigli, stando fermi
i remi, un gran fulgor le trasfigura:
grandi calici sorgono dall'acque,
gigli di foco.

  Fa un suo divino gioco
  la giovine Ora
  che è breve come il canto
  della colomba. Godi l'incanto,
  anima nostra, e adora!

La pioggia nel pineto

TACI. Su le soglie
del bosco non odo
parole che dici
umane; ma odo

They are the hanging nets. Some hang like scales from the rods
fixed to the high platforms stretched out above the stream, where
the man watches to pull in the twine; others hang from the prows
of fishing-boats, crossing the evergreen mirror that refracts them;
and when the sun beats down on the sterns of the boats, the oars at
rest, a great radiance transfigures them; great goblets rise from the
waters, lilies of fire.

 The young Hour, short as the song of the dove, plays divinely.
Enjoy the charm, our soul, and adore!

The Rain in the Pine-wood

HUSH. On the edge of the wood I do not hear human words that
you are saying; but I hear newer words which far-off drops and

parole più nuove
che parlano gocciole e foglie
lontane.
Ascolta. Piove
dalle nuvole sparse.
Piove su le tamerici
salmastre ed arse,
piove su i pini
scagliosi ed irti,
piove su i mirti
divini,
su le ginestre fulgenti
di fiori accolti,
su i ginepri folti
di coccole aulenti,
piove su i nostri volti
silvani,
piove su le nostre mani
ignude,
su i nostri vestimenti
leggieri,
su i freschi pensieri
che l'anima schiude
novella,
su la favola bella
che ieri
t'illuse, che oggi m'illude,
o Ermione.

leaves are speaking. Listen. It is raining from the scattered clouds. It rains on the salty, burnt tamarinds, on the rough, prickly pines, on the divine myrtles, on the broom flashing with clustered flowers, on the junipers thick with odorous berries, it rains upon our wood-wild faces, it rains on our naked hands, on our light clothes, on the fresh thoughts which the soul, renewed, discloses, on the lovely fable that yesterday beguiled you, that today beguiles me, o Hermione.

Odi? La pioggia cade
su la solitaria
verdura
con un crepitìo che dura
e varia nell'aria
secondo le fronde
più rade, men rade.
Ascolta. Risponde
al pianto il canto
delle cicale
che il pianto australe
non impaura,
nè il ciel cinerino.
E il pino
ha un suono, e il mirto
altro suono, e il ginepro
altro ancora, stromenti
diversi
sotto innumerevoli dita.
E immersi
noi siam nello spirto
silvestre,
d'arborea vita viventi;
e il tuo volto ebro
è molle di pioggia
come una foglia,

Do you hear? The rain is falling on the lonely greenery with a rustling that keeps on and varies in the air according as the leaves are more spaced or less spaced. Listen. The song of the cicada answers the weeping, the song that the westering lament does not awe, nor the ashen sky. And the pine has one sound, and the myrtle another sound, and the juniper another again, different instruments under numberless fingers. And we are plunged in the forest's spirit, living with a tree-like life; and your exulting face is soft with rain

e le tue chiome
auliscono come
le chiare ginestre,
o creatura terrestre
che hai nome
Ermione.

Ascolta, ascolta. L'accordo
delle aeree cicale
a poco a poco
più sordo
si fa sotto il pianto
che cresce;
ma un canto vi si mesce
più roco
che di laggiù sale,
dall'umida ombra remota.
Più sordo e più fioco
s'allenta, si spegne.
Sola una nota
ancor trema, si spegne,
risorge, trema, si spegne.
Non s'ode voce del mare.
Or s'ode su tutta la fronda
crosciare
l' argentea pioggia
che monda,

like a leaf, and your locks are fragrant like the shining broom, o
earthly creature who are named Hermione.

Listen, listen. The harmony of the airy cicadas is growing gradually duller under the weeping that increases; but a song enters, a
hoarser one that rises from down there, from the far damp shade.
Duller and weaker it dwindles, it fades. Only a note still trembles,
fades, rises again, trembles, fades. We do not hear the voice of the
sea. Now on all the leaves we hear the silver rain beating that

il croscio che varia
secondo la fronda
più folta, men folta.
Ascolta.
La figlia dell'aria
è muta; ma la figlia
del limo lontana,
la rana,
canta nell'ombra più fonda,
chi sa dove, chi sa dove!
E piove su le tue ciglia,
Ermione.

Piove su le tue ciglia nere
sì che par tu pianga
ma di piacere; non bianca
ma quasi fatta virente,
par da scorza tu esca.
E tutta la vita è in noi fresca
aulente,
il cuor nel petto è come pesca
intatta,
tra le palpebre gli occhi
son come polle tra l'erbe,
i denti negli alvèoli
son come mandorle acerbe.

cleanses, the beating that varies according as the leaves are more close, less close. Listen. The daughter of the air is mute, but the distant daughter of the swamp, the frog, sings in the deepest shadow, who knows where, who knows where! And it rains upon your eyelashes, Hermione.

It rains upon your black eyelashes so that you seem to weep but from pleasure; not white, but almost made green, you seem to come out from bark. And all life is fresh, odorous, in us, the heart in our breasts like an untouched peach, the eyes in their eyelids like rivulets in grass, the teeth in their gums like ripening almonds. And we go

E andiam di fratta in fratta,
or congiunti or disciolti
(e il verde vigor rude
ci allaccia i mallèoli
c'intrica i ginocchi)
chi sa dove, chi sa dove!
E piove su i nostri volti
silvani,
piove su le nostre mani
ignude,
su i nostri vestimenti
leggieri,
su i freschi pensieri
che l'anima schiude
novella,
su la favola bella
che ieri
m'illuse, che oggi t'illude,
o Ermione.

I pastori

SETTEMBRE, andiamo. È tempo di migrare.
Ora in terra d'Abruzzi i miei pastori
lascian gli stazzi e vanno verso il mare:

from thicket to thicket, now joined, now separate (and the rough green vigour traps our ankles, entangles our knees) who knows where, who knows where! And it rains upon our woodwild faces, it rains on our naked hands, on our light clothes, on the fresh thoughts which the soul, renewed, discloses, on the lovely fable that yesterday beguiled me, that today beguiles you, o Hermione.

The Shepherds

SEPTEMBER, let us go. It is time to migrate. Now in the land of the Abruzzi my shepherds leave the huts and go towards the sea: they

scendono all'Adriatico selvaggio
che verde è come i pascoli dei monti.

Han bevuto profondamente ai fonti
alpestri, che sapor d'acqua natìa
rimanga ne' cuori esuli a conforto,
che lungo illuda la lor sete in via.
Rinnovato hanno verga d'avellano.

E vanno pel tratturo antico al piano,
quasi per un erbal fiume silente,
su le vestigia degli antichi padri.
O voce di colui che primamente
conosce il tremolar della marina!

Ora lungh'esso il litoral cammina
la greggia. Senza mutamento è l'aria.
Il sole imbionda sì la viva lana
che quasi dalla sabbia non divaria.
Isciacquìo, calpestìo, dolci romori.

Ah perchè non son io co' miei pastori?

go down to the wild Adriatic which is green like the mountain pastures.

They have drunk deep at alpine springs, so that the taste of native water may remain in exile hearts as a comfort, to charm their thirst for long upon the way. They have renewed their staffs of hazel.

And they go along the ancient drove-path to the plain, as if by a grassy, silent river, upon the traces of the early fathers. O voice of him who first knows the trembling of the sea!

Now on the shore at its side marches the flock. The air is without motion. The sun so gilds the living wool that it hardly differs from the sand. Sea-washing, trampling, sweet sounds.

Ah why am I not with my shepherds?

DINO CAMPANA

La chimera

NON so se tra roccie il tuo pallido
Viso m'apparve, o sorriso
Di lontananze ignote
Fosti, la china eburnea
Fronte fulgente o giovine
Suora de la Gioconda:
O delle primavere
Spente, per i tuoi mitici pallori
O Regina o Regina adolescente:
Ma per il tuo ignoto poema
Di voluttà e di dolore
Musica fanciulla esangue,
Segnato di linea di sangue
Nel cerchio delle labbra sinuose,
Regina de la melodia:
Ma per il vergine capo
Reclino, io poeta notturno
Vegliai le stelle vivide nei pelaghi del cielo,
Io per il tuo dolce mistero
Io per il tuo divenir taciturno,

The Chimera

I DO not know if your pale face appeared to me among the rocks, or if you were the smile of distances unknown, your bent ivory forehead flashing, o young sister of the Gioconda: o Queen of dead springtimes for your mythical palenesses, o youthful queen: but for your unknown poem of voluptuousness and grief, music, bloodless girl, marked with a line of blood in the round of sinuous lips, Queen of melody: but for your virgin head bent, I, poet of the night, watched out the vivid stars in the deeps of the sky, I for your soft mystery, I for your becoming silent, do not know if the

Non so se la fiamma pallida
Fu dei capelli il vivente
Segno del suo pallore,
Non so se fu un dolce vapore,
Dolce sul mio dolore,
Sorriso di un volto notturno:
Guardo le bianche rocce le mute fonti dei venti
E l'immobilità dei firmamenti
E i gonfii rivi che vanno piangenti
E l'ombre del lavoro umano curve là sui poggi algenti
E ancora per teneri cieli lontane chiare ombre correnti
E ancora ti chiamo ti chiamo Chimera.

L'invetriata

LA sera fumosa d'estate
Dall'alta invetriata mesce chiarori nell'ombra
E mi lascia nel cuore un suggello ardente.
Ma chi ha (sul terrazzo sul fiume si accende una lampada)
    chi ha
A la Madonnina del Ponte chi è chi è che ha acceso la
    lampada? – c'è

pale flame was the tresses' living sign of her paleness, I do not know
if it was a soft mist, soft upon my grief, smile of a face of night. I
look at the white rocks, the dumb fountains of the wind, and the
immobility of firmaments and the swollen streams that pass weeping and the shadows of human labour curved there on icy heights
and still, through tender heavens, far lucid shades running, and still
I call you, I call you Chimera.

The Skylight

THE smoky evening of summer from the high skylight mixes
brightnesses with shade and leaves a burning seal upon my heart.
But who has (on the terrace on the river a lamp is being lit) who
has, for the little Madonna of the Bridge, who is it, who is it that

Nella stanza un odor di putredine: c'è
Nella stanza una piaga rossa languente.
Le stelle sono bottoni di madreperla e la sera si veste di
    velluto:
E tremola la sera fatua: è fatua la sera e tremola ma c'è
Nel cuore della sera c'è,
Sempre una piaga rossa languente.

La sera di fiera

Il cuore stasera mi disse: non sai?
La rosabruna incantevole
Dorata da una chioma bionda:
E dagli occhi lucenti e bruni colei che di grazia imperiale
Incantava la rosea
Freschezza dei mattini:
E tu seguivi nell' aria
La fresca incarnazione di un mattutino sogno:
E soleva vagare quando il sogno
E il profumo velavano le stelle
(Che tu amavi guardar dietro i cancelli
Le stelle le pallide notturne):

has lit the lamp? There is an odour of decay in the room, there is
in the room a red and drooping wound. The stars are buttons of
mother of pearl and the evening dresses in velvet. The spirited
evening trembles: it is spirited, the evening, and trembling but
there is in the heart of the evening there is, always a red and drooping wound.

The Evening of the Fair

My heart said to me this evening: do you not know? The charming rose-and-dark girl gilded with fair hair: and with shining brown
eyes, she who with imperial grace charmed the rose-like freshness
of the mornings: and you followed the fresh incarnation of a morning dream through the air: and she would wander when dream and
perfume veiled the stars (for you loved to watch beyond the iron-
gates the stars the pallid night-times): she who used to pass silently

Che soleva passare silenziosa
E bianca come un volo di colombe
Certo è morta: non sai?
Era la notte
Di fiera della perfida Babele
Salente in fasci verso un cielo affastellato un paradiso di
    fiamma
In lubrici fischi grotteschi
E tintinnare d'angeliche campanelle
E gridi e voci di prostitute
E pantomime d'Ofelia
Stillate dall'umile pianto delle lampade elettriche
....
Una canzonetta volgaruccia era morta
E mi aveva lasciato il cuore nel dolore
E me ne andavo errando senz'amore
Lasciando il cuore mio di porta in porta:
Con Lei che non è nata eppure è morta
E mi ha lasciato il cuore senz'amore:
Eppure il cuore porta nel dolore:
Lasciando il cuore mio di porta in porta.

and white as a flight of doves, certainly she's dead: do you not know? It was the night of the fair of treacherous Babel towering in clusters towards a gathered heaven, a paradise of flames, in lewd whistlings grotesquely, and tinkling of angelic bells and shouts and cries of prostitutes and burlesques of Ophelia distilled from the humble weeping of electric bulbs. A vulgarish song was dead and had left my heart in grief, and I wandered on without love, leaving my heart at this door and the next one: with Her who is not born and yet is dead who has left my heart without love: yet she takes my heart to grief: leaving my heart in this door and the next one.

Giardino autunnale

AL giardino spettrale al lauro muto
De le verdi ghirlande
A la terra autunnale
Un ultimo saluto!
A l'aride pendici
Aspre arrossate nell'estremo sole
Confusa di rumori
Rauchi grida la lontana vita:
Grida al morente sole
Che insanguina le aiole.
S'intende una fanfara
Che straziante sale: il fiume spare
Ne le arene dorate: nel silenzio
Stanno le bianche statue a capo i ponti
Volte: e le cose già non sono più.
E del fondo silenzio come un coro
Tenero e grandioso
Sorge ed anela in alto al mio balcone:
E in aroma d'alloro,
In aroma d'alloro acre languente,
Tra le statue immortali nel tramonto
Ella m'appar, presente.

Autumnal Garden

To the ghostly garden, to the dumb laurel with the green garlands, to the autumnal earth, a last farewell! To the hard, barren
slopes, reddened in the final sun, distant life cries in a confusion of
harsh noises: it cries to the dying sun that has stained the flowerbeds
with blood. A blast of trumpets, rising and tearing is heard: the
river vanishes in the gilded sands: in the silence white statues stand,
turned at the ends of bridges: and former things are no more. And
from the distance silence like a chorus, tender and majestic, rises
and breathes on high at my balcony: and in the odour of laurel, in
the bitter, failing smell of laurel, from between the statues immortal
in the sunset she appears to me, present.

Firenze

(Uffizi)

ENTRO dei ponti tuoi multicolori
L'Arno presago quietamente arena
E in riflessi tranquilli frange appena
Archi severi tra sfiorir di fiori.

....

Azzuro l'arco dell'intercolonno
Trema rigato tra i palazzi eccelsi:
Candide righe nell'azzurro: persi
Voli: su bianca gioventù in colonne.

Vecchi versi

(San Petronio, Bologna)

....
....
....
....

LE rosse torri altissime ed accese
Dentro dell'azzurrino tramonto commosso di vento
Vegliavano dietro degli alti palazzi le imprese
Gentili del serale animamento

Florence

(The Uffizi)

BETWEEN your many-coloured bridges the Arno, prophetic, is quietly silting, and in calm reflections hardly breaks the strict arches in the space when flowers are deflowered.

..... *Blue, the arch joining the columns trembles, limned between exalted palaces: white lines on the blue: lost flights: over white youth on columns.*

Old Lines

(San Petronio, Bologna)

.... THE red and glowing towers so tall in the blue twilight disturbed by wind watched the kindly purposes of the evening animation behind high palaces.

....
....
Esse parlavano lievi e tacevano: gli occhi levati
Invan seguendo la scìa sconosciuta nell'aria
De le parole rotte che il vicendevole vento
Diceva per un'ansia solitaria.

Bastimento in viaggio

L'ALBERO oscilla a tocchi nel silenzio.
Una tenue luce bianca e verde cade dall'albero.
Il cielo limpido all'orizzonte, carico verde e dorato dopo
    la burrasca.
Il quadro bianco della lanterna in alto
Illumina il segreto notturno: dalla finestra
Le corde dall'alto a triangolo d'oro
E un globo bianco di fumo
Che non esiste come musica
Sopra del cerchio coi tocchi dell'acqua in sordina.

.... They spoke low and went silent: upturned eyes vainly followed the unknown wake in the air of broken words which the intermittent wind spoke for a lonely anxiety.

Ship under Way

THE mast swings, beat for beat, in the silence. A faint white and green light falls from the mast. The sky clear to the horizon, loaded green and gilt after the squall. The white square of the ship's light on high illuminates the night's secret: from the window the ropes from above in a gold triangle and a globe white with smoke which does not exist like music above the circle with the muted beating of the water.

Quattro liriche per S.A.

i. I piloni fanno il fiume più bello

I PILONI fanno il fiume più bello
E gli archi fanno il cielo più bello
Negli archi la tua figura.
Più pura nell'azzurro è la luce d'argento
Più bella la tua figura.
Più bella la luce d'argento nell'ombre degli archi
Più bella della bionda Cerere la tua figura.

ii. Sul più illustre paesaggio

Sul più illustre paesaggio
Ha passeggiato il ricordo
Col vostro passo di pantera
Sul più illustre paesaggio
Il vostro passo di velluto
E il vostro sguardo di vergine violata
Il vostro passo silenzioso come il ricordo
Affacciata al parapetto
Sull'acqua corrente
I vostri occhi forti di luce.

Four Lyrics for S.A.

i. The Piers of the Bridge make the River more Beautiful

THE piers of the bridge make the river more beautiful and its
arches make the sky more beautiful – in the arches the form of
you – purer on the blue is the silver light – more beautiful the form
of you – more beautiful the silver light in the shade of the arches –
more beautiful than fair Ceres the form of you.

ii. On the most Illustrious Landscape

On the most illustrious landscape memory has walked with your
panther step – on the most illustrious landscape your velvet step
and the look you have, of a virgin violated – your silent step like
the memory – you, turned to the parapet above the flowing water,
your eyes strong with light.

iii. Vi amai nella città dove per sole

Vi amai nella città dove per sole
Strade si posa il passo illanguidito
Dove una pace tenera che piove
A sera il cuor non sazio e non pentito
Volge a un'ambigua primavera in viole
Lontane sopra il cielo impallidito.

iv. In un momento

In un momento
Sono sfiorite le rose
I petali caduti
Perchè io non potevo dimenticare le rose
Le cercavamo insieme
Abbiamo trovato delle rose
Erano le sue rose erano le mie rose
Questo viaggio chiamavamo amore
Col nostro sangue e colle nostre lagrime facevamo le rose
Che brillavano un momento al sole del mattino

---

iii. I Loved You in the City where ... in Deserted ...

I loved you in the city where the languid step lingers in deserted streets, where a tender peace which rains down at evening turns the heart, not filled and not repentant, to a dubious spring in violet distances above the paler sky.

iv. In a Moment

In a moment the roses have shed their bloom, the petals fallen, because I could not forget the roses. We looked for them together: we found roses: they were her roses, were my roses. This journey we called love. With our blood and our tears we made the roses which shone a moment in the morning sun. We ruined their bloom

Le abbiamo sfiorite sotto il sole tra i rovi
Le rose che non erano le nostre rose
Le mie rose le sue rose

P.S. E così dimenticammo le rose.

.

Firenze vecchia

Ho visto il tuo palazzo palpitare
Di mille fiamme in una sera calda
O Firenze, il magnifico palazzo.
Già la folla à riempito la gran piazza
E vocia verso il suo palazzo vecchio
E beve la sua anima maliarda.
La confraternità di buona morte
Porta una bara sotto le tue mura:
Questo m'allieta questo m'assicura
Della tua forza di contro alla morte:
Non bruciano le tue feree midolla
I tempi nuovi e non l'amaro agreste
Delle tue genti: in ricordanze in feste
L'aspero sangue sotto a te ribolla.

under the sun, among the briars, the roses which were not our roses
– my roses, her roses.
    P.S. And so we forgot the roses.

Old Florence

I saw your palace throb with a thousand flames on a warm evening, o Florence, your magnificent palace. The crowd has already
filled the great square and shouts towards its old palace and drinks
its witching soul. The Fraternity of the Good Death bear a coffin
beneath your walls: this gladdens me, this assures me of your
strength against death: new times do not burn your iron marrow,
nor the rough hardness of your peoples: in rememberings, in cele-
brations the crude blood seethes in you. Iron, blood, flame, it is

O ferro o sangue o fiamma è tutto fuoco
Che brucia la viltà dentro le vene!
A te dai petti e dalle gole piene,
Di gioia e forza un'inesausta polla!

Una strana zingarella

Tu sentirai le rime scivolare
In cadenza nel caldo della stanza
Sopra al guanciale pallida a sognare
Ti volgerai, di questa lenta danza
Magnetica il sussurro a respirare.
La luna stanca è andata a riposare
Gli ulivi taccion, solo un ubriaco
Che si stanca a cantare e ricantare:
Tu magra e sola con i tuoi capelli
Sei restata. Nel cielo a respirare
Stanno i tuoi sogni. Volgiti ed ascolta
Nella notte gelata il mio cantare
Sulle tue spalle magroline e gialle
I capelli vorrei veder danzare

one fire that burns the vileness in our veins! To you from breasts
and from full throats, an unfailing stream of joy and strength!

A Strange Gipsy

You will feel my rhymes slipping in cadence in the warmth of
the room, you will turn to dream upon the wan pillow, to breathe
the whisper of this slow, magnetic dance. The tired moon has gone
to rest, the olives are silent, only a drunkard wears himself out,
singing and singing again: you, thin and alone, your hair towards
me, have stayed. Your dreams are hovering in the sky, to breathe.
Turn and listen to my singing in the chilled night. I want to see
your hair dance on your skinny yellow shoulders. You are as pure

Sei pura come il suono e senza odore
Un tuo bacio è acerbetto e sorridente
E doloroso, e l'occhio è rilucente
È troppo bello, l'occhio è perditore.
Sicuramente tu non sai cantare
Ma la vocetta deve essere acuta
E perforante come il violino
E sorridendo deve pizzicare
Il cuore. I tuoi capelli sulle spalluccine?
Ami i profumi? E perchè vai vestita
Di sangue? Ami le chiese?
No tu temi i profumi. Il corpiccino
È troppo fine e gli occhi troppo neri
Oh se potessi vederti agitare
La tua animuccia tagliente tremare
E i tuoi occhi lucenti arrotondare
Mentre il santo linfatico e canoro
Che dovevi tentare
Spande in ginocchio nuvole d'incenso
Ringraziando il Signore
E non lo puoi amare
Christus vicisti

as sound and without scent. A kiss of yours is bitterish and smiling
and sorrowful, and your eye is sparkling, is too lovely, your eye is
perdition. Certainly you won't sing well, but your little voice must
be sharp and piercing like a violin, and, as you smile, must pluck at
the heart. Your hair on your thin shoulders? Do you love perfume?
And why do you go dressed in blood? Do you love churches? No;
you are afraid of perfume. Your little body is too slight and your
eyes, too dark. O if I could see you shake, your cutting little soul
tremble, and your shining eyes grow round, while the sonorous,
pale saint whom you had to tempt kneels and scatters clouds of incense, thanking the Lord, and you cannot love him. *Christus*

L'avorio del crocifisso
Vince l'avorio del tuo ventre
Dalla corona non sì dolce e gloriosa
Nera increspata movente
Nell'ombra grigia vertiginosa
E tu piangi in ginocchio per terra colle mani
    sugli occhi
E i tuoi piedi lunghi e brutti
Allargati per terra come zampe
D'una bestia ribelle e mostruosa.
Che sapore avranno le tue lacrimucce?
Un poco di fuoco? Io vorrei farne
Un diadema fantastico e portarlo
Sul mio capo nell'ora della morte
Per udirmi parlare in confidenza
I demonietti dai piedi forcuti.
Povera bimba come ti calunnio
Perchè hai i capelli tragici
E ti vesti di rosso e non odori.

vicisti. The ivory of the crucifix surpasses the ivory of your belly –
from the crown, not so sweet and glorious, black waving moving
in the grey whirling shade – And you weep kneeling on the earth,
your hands over your eyes, and your long ugly feet splayed on
the earth like the paws of some monstrous, defiant beast. What taste
will your little tears have? A touch of fire? I would like to make a
fantastic diadem of them and wear it on my head at the hour of my
death to hear the little demons with cloven hooves, speak to me in
confidence. Poor child, how I wrong you with words, because you
have tragic hair, and you dress in red, and have no scent.

Donna genovese

Tu mi portasti un po' d'alga marina
Nei tuoi capelli, ed un odor di vento,
Che è corso di lontano e giunge grave
D'ardore, era nel tuo corpo bronzino:
– Oh la divina
Semplicità delle tue forme snelle –
Non amore non spasimo, un fantasma,
Un'ombra della necessità che vaga
Serena e ineluttabile per l'anima
E la discioglie in gioia, in incanto serena
Perchè per l'infinito lo scirocco
Se la possa portare.
Come è piccolo il mondo e leggero nelle tue mani!

GIUSEPPE UNGARETTI

Agonia

Morire come le allodole assetate
sul miraggio

Woman of Genoa

You brought me a little seaweed in your hair, and the breath of a wind, that has come from afar and arrives heavy with sultriness, was in your bronzed body: – oh the divine simplicity of your clean limbs – not love, not sudden unrest, a phantom, a shadow of the necessity which wanders calm and inescapable through the soul and melts it in joy, calm in its spell so that the hot wind can bear it away through the infinite. How small the world is, and light, in your hands!

Agony

To die like thirst-stricken larks close upon the mirage

O come la quaglia
passato il mare
nei primi cespugli
perchè di volare
non ha più voglia

Ma non vivere di lamento
come un cardellino accecato

Veglia

UN'INTERA nottata
buttato vicino
a un compagno
massacrato
con la sua bocca
digrignata
volta al plenilunio
con la congestione
delle sue mani
penetrata
nel mio silenzio
ho scritto
lettere piene d'amore

Non sono mai stato
tanto
attaccato alla vita

Or like the quail, once the sea is past, in the first bushes, because it has no more wish to fly.

But not to live on lament like a blinded finch.

Watch

A WHOLE night, thrown down beside a friend who has been slaughtered, with his grinning mouth turned to the full moon, with the convulsion of his hands reaching into my silence, I have written letters full of love.

I have never been so attached to life.

I fiumi

MI tengo a quest'albero mutilato
abbandonato in questa dolina
che ha il languore
di un circo
prima o dopo lo spettacolo
e guardo
il passaggio quieto
delle nuvole sulla luna

Stamani mi sono disteso
in un'urna d'acqua
e come una reliquia
ho riposato

L'Isonzo scorrendo
mi levigava
come un suo sasso

Ho tirato su
le mie quattr'ossa
e me ne sono andato
come un acrobata
sull'acqua

Rivers

I LEAN upon this wounded tree abandoned in this depression that
has the listlessness of a circus before or after the show, and I look
at the clouds quietly passing over the moon.

This morning I stretched out in an urn of water and like a relic
I lay there.

The Isonzo running by polished me like one of its stones.

I took upon me my own four limbs and went away like an acro-
bat over the water .

Mi sono accoccolato
vicino ai miei panni
sudici di guerra
e come un beduino
mi sono chinato a ricevere
il sole

Questo è l'Isonzo
e qui meglio
mi sono riconosciuto
una docile fibra
dell'universo

Il mio supplizio
è quando
non mi credo
in armonia

Ma quelle occulte
mani
che m'intridono
mi regalano
la rara
felicità

Ho ripassato
le epoche
della mia vita

Questi sono
i miei fiumi

I squatted down beside my clothes, filthy with war, and like a
Beduin bent my head to receive the sun.

This is the Isonzo and here, best of all, I know myself a pliant
thread in the universe.

My torture is when I do not think myself in harmony.

But those hidden hands which work me grant me rare happiness.

I have gone through the ages of my life.

These are my rivers.

Questo è il Serchio
al quale hanno attinto
duemil'anni forse
di gente mia campagnola
e mio padre e mia madre

Questo è il Nilo
che mi ha visto
nascere e crescere
e ardere d'inconsapevolezza
nelle estese pianure

Questa è la Senna
e in quel suo torbido
mi sono rimescolato
e mi sono conosciuto

Questi sono i miei fiumi
contati nell'Isonzo

Quest è la mia nostalgia
che in ognuno
mi traspare
ora ch'è notte
che la mia vita mi pare
una corolla
di tenebre

This is the Serchio from which they have drawn for two thousand years perhaps, my country people, both my father and my mother.

This is the Nile which has seen me be born and grow and burn with unknowingness in the stretching plains.

This is the Seine and in that murkiness it has I have been stirred and have known myself.

These are my rivers told over in the Isonzo.

This is my nostalgia which in each of them shines through to me now that it is night and my life appears a flower of shadows.

Mattina

M'ILLUMINO
d'immenso

Nostalgia

QUANDO
la notte è a svanire
poco prima di primavera
e di rado
qualcuno passa

Su Parigi s'addensa
un oscuro colore
di pianto

In un canto
di ponte
contemplo
l'illimitato silenzio
di una ragazza
tenue

Le nostre
malattie
si fondono

E come portati via
si rimane

Morning

I FILL with light of immensity.

Nostalgia

WHEN the night is about to pass away a little before spring and
rarely does anyone pass
  Upon Paris there gathers an unclear colour of weeping.
  At the corner of a bridge I reflect upon the limitless silence of a
slender girl.
  Our sicknesses run together
  And we remain as if carried away.

In memoria

S I chiamava
Moammed Sceab

Discendente
di emiri di nomadi
suicida
perchè non aveva più
Patria

Amò la Francia
e mutò nome

Fu Marcel
ma non era Francese
e non sapeva più
vivere
nella tenda dei suoi
dove si ascolta la cantilena
del Corano
gustando un caffè

E non sapeva
sciogliere
il canto
del suo abbandono

In Memory

H E was called Mohammed Sceab.

A descendant of the emirs of the nomads, a suicide because he no longer had a native land.

He loved France and changed his name.

He was Marcel but he was not French and he no longer knew how to live in the tent of his own where they listen to the singsong of the Koran, sipping coffee.

And he did not know how to loose the song of his abandonment.

L'ho accompagnato
insieme alla padrona dell'albergo
dove abitavamo
a Parigi
dal numero 5 della rue des Carmes
appassito vicolo in discesa

Riposa
nel camposanto d'Ivry
sobborgo che pare
sempre
in una giornata
di una
decomposta fiera

E forse io solo
so ancora
che visse.

Quiete

L' UVA è matura, il campo arato,

Si stacca il monte dalle nuvole.

I accompanied him together with the proprietress of the hotel
where we lived at Paris, from number 5 rue des Carmes, faded little
downhill alley.
He rests in the cemetery of Ivry, a suburb that always has the
look of a broken-up fair,
And perhaps I alone still know that he lived.

Quiet

THE grapes are ripe, the field, ploughed,
The mountain detaches itself from the clouds.

Sui polverosi specchi dell'estate
Caduta è l'ombra,

Tra le dita incerte
Il loro lume è chiaro
E lontano.

Colle rondini fugge
L'ultimo strazio.

Sera

Appiè dei passi della sera
Va un'acqua chiara
Colore dell'uliva,

E giunge al breve fuoco smemorato

Nel fumo ora odo grilli e rane,

Dove tenere tremano erbe.

On the dusty mirrors of summer the shadow has fallen.
Between uncertain fingers their light is clear and distant.
With the swallows flies the last tearing pain.

Evening

At the foot of the evening's passes clear water runs by, olive-coloured,
And reaches the brief fire without memory.
In the smoke I hear now crickets and frogs,
Where the grass trembles tenderly.

La pietà

SONO un uomo ferito.

E me ne vorrei andare
E finalmente giungere,
Pietà, dove si ascolta
L'uomo che è solo con sè.

Non ho che superbia e bontà.

E mi sento esiliato in mezzo agli uomini.

Ma per essi sto in pena.

Non sarei degno di tornare in me?

Ho popolato di nomi il silenzio.

Ho fatto a pezzi cuore e mente
Per cadere in servitù di parole?

Regno sopra fantasmi.

O foglie secche,
Anima portata qua e là ...

Pity

I AM a wounded man.

And I would go away and finally come, Pity, where the man who is alone with himself is heard.

I have only pride and goodness.

And I feel exiled among men.

But for them I am in torment.

Would I not be worthy to come to myself again?

I have peopled silence with names.

Have I shattered heart and mind to fall into bondage to words?

I rule over ghosts.

O dry leaves, soul borne here and there. ...

No, odo il vento e la sua voce
Di bestia immemorabile.

Dio, coloro che t'implorano
Non ti conoscono più che di nome?

M'hai discacciato dalla vita.

Mi discaccerai dalla morte?

Forse l'uomo è anche indegno di sperare.

Anche la fonte del rimorso è secca?

Il peccato che importa,
Se alla purezza non conduce più.

La carne si ricorda appena
Che una volta fu forte.

È folle e usata, l'anima.

Dio, guarda la nostra debolezza.

Vorremmo una certezza.

No, I hear the wind and its voice, an immemorial beast's.
God, do those who implore you no longer know you but by
name?
You have thrust me away from life.
Will you thrust me from death?
Perhaps man is not even fit for hope.
Is the fountain of remorse dry also?
What does sin matter if it no longer leads to purity.
The flesh scarce remembers that once it was strong.
Mad and unregenerate is the soul.
God, look upon our weakness.
We would have a certainty.

Di noi nemmeno più ridi?

E compiangici dunque, crudeltà.

Non ne posso più di stare murato
Nel desiderio senza amore.

Una traccia mostraci di giustizia.

La tua legge qual'è?

Fulmina le mie povere emozioni,
Liberami dall'inquietudine.

Sono stanco di urlare senza voce.

2

Malinconiosa carne
Dove una volta pullulò la gioia,
Occhi socchiusi del risveglio stanco,
Tu vedi, anima troppo matura,
Quel che sarò, caduto nella terra?

È nei vivi la strada dei defunti,

Do you not even laugh at us any longer?
Weep for us then, cruelty.
I can no longer bear being walled-up in desire without love.
Show us a sign of justice.
What is your law?
Blast my poor feelings, free me from restlessness.
I am tired of howling voicelessly.

Melancholy flesh, where joy once teemed, eyes half-opened in
tired awakening, do you see, my too mature soul, what I shall be,
fallen to earth?
The road of the deceased is among the living,

Siamo noi la fiumana d'ombre.

Sono esse il grano che ci scoppia in sogno,

Loro è la lontananza che ci resta,

E loro è l'ombra che dà peso ai nomi.

La speranza d'un mucchio d'ombra
E null'altro è la nostra sorte?

E tu non saresti che un sogno, Dio?

Almeno un sogno, temerari,
Vogliamo ti somigli.

È parto della demenza più chiara.

Non trema in nuvole di rami
Come passeri di mattina
Al filo delle palpebre.

In noi sta e langue, piaga misteriosa.

We are the great river of shades.
They are the grain which breaks open in dream,
Theirs is the distance which keeps with us,
And theirs is the shadow which gives weight to names.
The hope of a mound of shadow and nothing else, is that our fate?
And you would prove nothing but a dream, God?
We want you, rashly, to be at least like a dream.
It is the offspring of clearest insanity.
It does not tremble in the clouds of branches like sparrows at morning on the thread of eyelids.
It stays and worsens in us, a mysterious wound.

3

La luce che ci punge
È un filo sempre più sottile.

Più non abbagli tu, se non uccidi?

Dammi questa gioia suprema.

4

L'uomo, monotono universo,
Crede allargarsi i beni
E dalle sue mani febbrili
Non escono senza fine che limiti.

Attaccato sul vuoto
Al suo filo di ragno,
Non teme e non seduce
Se non il proprio grido.

Ripara il logorio alzando tombe.
E per pensarti, Eterno,
Non ha che le bestemmie.

The light which pricks us is a thread that is each time more slender.
Can you not dazzle more, without killing?
Give me this supreme joy.

Man, monotonous universe, believes he pours blessings on himself and from his feverish hands nothing but limitations endlessly come.
Tied to the void by his spider thread, he does not fear and does not compel anything except his own cry.
He covers up his wasting away by raising tombs, and to think of you, Eternal One, he has no words but blasphemies.

Tutto ho perduto

TUTTO ho perduto dell'infanzia
E non potrò mai più
Smemorarmi in un grido.

L'infanzia ho sotterrato
Nel fondo delle notti
E ora, spada invisibile,
Mi separa da tutto.

Di me rammento che esultavo amandoti,
Ed eccomi perduto
In infinito delle notti.

Disperazione che incessante aumenta
La vita non mi è più,
Arrestata in fondo alla gola,
Che una roccia di gridi.

I Have Lost Everything

I HAVE lost everything of childhood and I shall no longer be
able to lose memory in a cry.

I have buried childhood in the deep of nights and now it divides
me, invisible sword, from everything.

Of myself I recall that I gloried in loving you, and here I am,
lost in infinity of nights.

Despair endlessly growing, life, stuck in my throat, is now no
more than a rock of cries.

Da «Giorno per giorno»

PASSA la rondine e con essa estate,
E anch'io, mi dico, passerò …
Ma resti dell'amore che mi strazia
Non solo segno un breve appannamento
Se dall'inferno arrivo a qualche quiete …

*

NON più furori reca a me l'estate,
Nè primavera i suoi presentimenti;
Puoi declinare, autunno,
Con le tue stolte glorie:
Per uno spoglio desiderio, inverno
Distende la stagione più clemente! …

Non gridate più

CESSATE d'uccidere i morti,
Non gridate più, non gridate
Se li volete ancora udire,
Se sperate di non perire.

From 'Day by Day'

THE swallow passes and with it summer, and I too, I tell myself,
shall pass. … But do not let a brief darkening remain as the sole
sign of the love that tears me, if I am to come from hell to some
calm. …

SUMMER no longer brings me furies, nor spring its presagings;
you can decline, autumn, with your stupid glories: for a bared
desire, winter stretches out the mildest season! …

Do Not Cry Out Any More

STOP killing the dead, do not cry out any more, do not cry out
if you want to hear them still, if you hope not to perish.

Hanno l'impercettibile sussurro,
Non fanno più rumore
Del crescere dell'erba,
Lieta dove non passa l'uomo.

EUGENIO MONTALE

Falsetto

ESTERINA, i vent'anni ti minacciano,
grigiorosea nube
che a poco a poco in sè ti chiude.
Ciò intendi e non paventi.
Sommersa ti vedremo
nella fumèa che il vento
lacera o addensa, violento.
Poi dal fiotto di cenere uscirai
adusta più che mai,
proteso a un'avventura più lontana
l'intento viso che assembra
l'arciera Diana.
Salgono i venti autunni,
t'avviluppano andate primavere;
ecco per te rintocca
un presagio nell'elisie sfere.

Theirs is the imperceptible whisper, they make no more sound
than the grass growing, happily where no man passes.

Falsetto

DEAR HESTER, twenty years of age threaten you, a grey and
flushing cloud that little by little takes you into itself. You understand this and are not afraid. We shall see you going under the
smokiness which the wind tears or curdles in its violence. Then you
will emerge from the flood of ashes more scorched than ever, your
rapt face lifted to a more distant adventure, seeming the huntress
Diana. Twenty autumns rise, departed springtimes wind you
about; there, a prophecy sounds for you among the heavenly

Un suono non ti renda
qual d'incrinata brocca
percossa!; io ti prego sia
per te concerto ineffabile
di sonagliere.

La dubbia dimane non t'impaura.
Leggiadra ti distendi
sullo scoglio lucente di sale
e al sole bruci le membra.
Ricordi la lucertola
ferma sul masso brullo;
te insidia giovinezza,
quella il lacciòlo d'erba del fanciullo.
L'acqua è la forza che ti tempra,
nell'acqua ti ritrovi e ti rinnovi:
noi ti pensiamo come un'alga, un ciottolo,
come un'equorea creatura
che la salsedine non intacca
ma torna al lito più pura.

Hai ben ragione tu! Non turbare
di ubbie il sorridente presente.
La tua gaiezza impegna già il futuro
ed un crollar di spalle

spheres. Let it be no sound of a cracked jug being struck!; I pray that for you it will be an ineffable melody of little bells.

Doubtful tomorrow doesn't frighten you. Glad you stretch out on the rock shining with salt, and burn your limbs in the sun. Remember the lizard motionless on the naked boulder; youth lies in wait for you, and for him, the boy's grass noose. The water is the force that tries you, in the water you find and renew yourself: and we think of you as a sea-plant, a pebble, some marine creature whom the saltiness does not corrode, but who comes purer to shore.

How right you are! Do not disturb the smiling present with misgivings. Your gaiety already involves the future and a shrug of

dirocca i fortilizi
del tuo domani oscuro.
T'alzi e t'avanzi sul ponticello
esiguo, sopra il gorgo che stride:
il tuo profilo s'incide
contro uno sfondo di perla.
Esiti a sommo del tremulo asse,
poi ridi, e come spiccata da un vento
t'abbatti fra le braccia
del tuo divino amico che t'afferra.

Ti guardiamo noi, della razza
di chi rimane a terra.

MERIGGIARE pallido e assorto
presso un rovente muro d'orto,
ascoltare tra i pruni e gli sterpi
schiocchi di merli, frusci di serpi.

Nelle crepe del suolo o su la veccia
spiar le file di rosse formiche
ch'ora si rompono ed ora s'intrecciano
a sommo di minuscole biche.

your shoulders throws down the citadels of your dark tomorrow.
You rise and advance along the slender springboard above the
shouting whirlpool; your profile is engraved upon a pearly ground.
You hesitate upon the trembling plank, then laugh, and as if
snatched off by the wind, throw yourself into your divine lover's
arms and he holds you.

We watch you, we who belong to the race of those who are
earth-bound.

To laze at noon, pale and abstracted, by a white-hot garden wall,
to listen to clicking of blackbirds and snakes' rustling among the
thorns and the undergrowth.

To make out the files of red ants in the cracks in the ground or
upon the weeds, breaking order and then twining together on top
of their miniature ricks.

Osservare tra frondi il palpitare
lontano di scaglie di mare
mentre si levano tremuli scricchi
di cicale dai calvi picchi.

E andando nel sole che abbaglia
sentire con triste meraviglia
com'è tutta la vita e il suo travaglio
in questo seguitare una muraglia
che ha in cima cocci aguzzi di bottiglia.

PORTAMI il girasole ch'io lo trapianti
nel mio terreno bruciato dal salino,
e mostri tutto il giorno agli azzurri specchianti
del cielo l'ansietà del suo volto giallino.

Tendono alla chiarità le cose oscure,
si esauriscono i corpi in un fluire
di tinte: queste in musiche. Svanire
è dunque la ventura delle venture.

To observe through leaves the far pulsing of the scales of the sea
while the wavering screech of cicadas rises from the bare summits.
   And as you walk in the dazzling sun to feel with sad wonder how
life and its struggle is in this following a high wall that has broken
bits of bottle along its top.

BRING me the sunflower so that I can transplant it to my ground
that is burnt with the sea-salt, and show the anxiety of its yellowed
face all day to the mirroring blues of the sky.
   Obscure things tend towards clearness, bodies consume themselves in a flowing of shades: these in music. To vanish is then the
chance of chances.

Portami tu la pianta che conduce
dove sorgono bionde trasparenze
e vapora la vita quale essenza;
portami il girasole impazzito di luce.

Da « Mediterraneo »

ANTICO, sono ubriacato dalla voce
ch'esce dalla tue bocche quando si schiudono
come verdi campane e si ributtano
indietro e si disciolgono.
La casa delle mie estati lontane,
t'era accanto, lo sai,
là nel paese dove il sole cuoce
e annuvolano l'aria le zanzare.
Come allora oggi in tua presenza impietro,
mare, ma non più degno
mi credo del solenne ammonimento
del tuo respiro. Tu m'hai detto primo
che il piccino fermento
del mio cuore non era che un momento
del tuo; che mi era in fondo

Bring me the plant which leads to where the sunny depths rise
and life evaporates like spirit; bring me the sunflower maddened
with the light.

From 'Mediterranean'

ANCIENT one, I am drunken with the voice that escapes from
your mouths when they lift clear like green bells and throw themselves back and break up. The home of my far-away summers was
by your side, as you know, there in the country where the sun
broils and mosquitoes cloud the air. Just as then today I am stilled
by your presence, my sea, but no longer think myself worthy of the
grave warning that you breathe. You were first to tell me that the
tiny seething of my heart was simply an impulse of yours; that in

la tua legge rischiosa: esser vasto e diverso
e insieme fisso:
e svuotarmi così d'ogni lordura
come tu fai che sbatti sulle sponde
tra sùgheri alghe asterie
le inutili macerie del tuo abisso.

*

DISSIPA tu se lo vuoi
questa debole vita che si lagna,
come la spugna il frego
effimero di una lavagna.
M'attendo di ritornare nel tuo circolo,
s'adempia lo sbandato mio passato.
La mia venuta era testimonianza
di un ordine che in viaggio mi scordai,
giurano fede queste mie parole
a un evento impossibile, e lo ignorano.
Ma sempre che traudii
la tua dolce risacca su le prode
sbigottimento mi prese
quale d'uno scemato di memoria
quando si risovviene del suo paese.

---

my depth of being there was your perilous law: to be vast, mani-
fold, and yet, to be bound: and so to clear myself of every filthiness
as you do who dash upon the shores among cork-fragments, seaweed, starfishes, the fruitless rubbish of your void.

OBLITERATE, if you want to, this weak life with its complaining,
as the sponge does the ephemeral stroke upon a blackboard. I am
waiting to re-enter your circle, let my broken-up past be fulfilled.
My coming was witness to an order which I forgot upon my journey, my words swear allegiance to an impossible event and do not
know it. But always when I half-heard your gentle surf upon the
shore, alarm seized me as it does someone of weak memory when
he recalls his home. Having learnt my lesson, not so much from

Presa la mia lezione
più che dalla tua gloria
rabida, dall'ansare
che quasi non dà suono
di qualche tuo meriggio desolato,
a te mi rendo in umiltà. Non sono
che favilla d'un tirso. Bene lo so, bruciare,
questo, non altro, è il mio significato.

Delta

LA vita che si rompe nei travasi
secreti a te ho legata:
quella che si dibatte in sè e par quasi
non ti sappia, presenza soffocata.

Quando il tempo s'ingorga alle sue dighe
la tua vicenda accordi alla sua immensa,
ed affiori, memoria, più palese
dall'oscura regione ove scendevi,
come ora, al dopopioggia, si riaddensa
il verde ai rami, ai muri il cinabrese.

your raving glory, as from that panting, which hardly makes a
sound, on some deserted afternoon of yours, I give myself up to
you in humility. I am no more than a spark from a signal light. Well
do I know it, to burn, this and nothing else, is the significance I am
to have.

Delta

I BIND that life which breaks off in secret transfusings to you:
the life that contends with itself and seems almost not to know you,
stifled presence.

When time floods high against its dykes, you attune your fortune to its huge one, and rise, memory of mine, clearer from the
dim region where you descended, as now, in the after-rain, the
green once more intensifies upon the branches, and on the walls
their wash of red.

Tutto ignoro di te fuor del messaggio
muto che mi sostenta sulla via:
se forma esisti o ubbìa nella fumea
d'un sogno t'alimenta
la riviera che infebbra, torba, e scroscia
incontro alla marea.

Nulla di te nel vacillar dell'ore
bigie o squarciate da un vampo di solfo
fuori che il fischio del rimorchiatore
che dalle brume approda al golfo.

Mottetto

Lo sai: debbo riperderti e non posso.
Come un tiro aggiustato mi sommuove
ogni opera, ogni grido e anche lo spiro
salino che straripa
dai moli e fa l'oscura primavera
di Sottoripa.

I do not know anything about you except for the mute message which supports me on my way: whether you exist as a shade, or whether the shore which goes feverish, troubled, and crashes with the rising tide, nourishes you, a delusion, in the haze of a dream.

Nothing of you in the wavering of the hours, grey or rent by a sulphur flame, except the hooting of the tug as, from the mists, it comes to harbour in the gulf.

Motet

You know: I have to lose you again and I can't. Like a well-aimed shot, every action, every cry startles me, and even the salt breath that overflows the harbour-wall and makes the uncertain spring of Sottoripa.

Paese di ferrame e alberature
a selva nella polvere del vespro.
Un ronzìo lungo viene dall'aperto,
strazia com'unghia ai vetri. Cerco il segno
smarrito, il pegno solo ch'ebbi in grazia
da te.
       E l'inferno è certo.

Dora Markus

F U dove il ponte di legno
mette a Porto Corsini sul mare alto
e rari uomini, quasi immoti, affondano
o salpano le reti. Con un segno
della mano additavi all'altra sponda
invisibile la tua patria vera.
Poi seguimmo il canale fino alla darsena
della città, lucida di fuliggine,
nella bassura dove s'affondava
una primavera inerte, senza memoria.

Place of iron and ship-masts in a forest amid the dust of evening.
A long hum comes from the open, unbearable as nails on glass. I
look for the lost-sight-of sign, the only pledge you granted me.
    And hell-fire is certain.

Dora Markus

I T was where the wooden pier thrusts out on the high sea at Porto
Corsini and a few men, almost unmoving, drop and hoist up the
nets. With a wave of your hand you pointed towards your true
native land on the invisible opposite shore. Then we followed the
canal right to the basin of the town, shining with soot, in the flat
landscape where a motionless spring was sinking, without
memories.

E qui dove un'antica vita
si screzia in una dolce
ansietà d'Oriente,
le tua parole iridavano come le scaglie
della triglia moribonda.

La tua irrequietudine mi fa pensare
agli uccelli di passo che urtano ai fari
nelle sere tempestose:
è una tempesta anche la tua dolcezza,
turbina e non appare,
e i suoi riposi sono anche più rari.
Non so come stremata tu resisti
in questo lago
d'indifferenza ch'è il tuo cuore; forse
ti salva un amuleto che tu tieni
vicino alla matita delle labbra,
al piumino, alla lima: un topo bianco,
d'avorio; e così esisti!

2

Ormai nella tua Carinzia
di mirti fioriti e di stagni,
china sul bordo sorvegli
la carpa che timida abbocca

And here where an old life is variegated in a soft oriental anxiety,
your words flashed a rainbow like the scales on the dying sea-fish.

Your restlessness makes me think of birds of passage dashing
themselves against lighthouses on stormy evenings: your sweetness itself is a tempest, whirling and not showing, and its pauses are
even rarer. I do not know how you resist, though spent, in this lake
of indifference which is your heart; perhaps some charm saves you,
one you keep near your lipstick, your powder-puff, your nail-file:
a white mouse, in ivory; and so you subsist!

2

Now in your Carinzia of flowering myrtles and ponds, bent upon
the brink you watch the carp gaping timidly, or follow in the lime-

o segui sui tigli, tra gl'irti
pinnacoli le accensioni
del vespro e nell'acque un avvampo
di tende da scali e pensioni.

La sera che si protende
sull'umida conca non porta
col palpito dei motori
che gemiti d'oche e un interno
di nivee maioliche dice
allo specchio annerito che ti vide
diversa una storia di errori
imperturbati e la incide
dove la spugna non giunge.

La tua leggenda, Dora!
Ma è scritta già in quegli sguardi
di uomini che hanno fedine
altere e deboli in grandi
ritratti d'oro e ritorna
ad ogni accordo che esprime
l'armonica guasta nell'ora
che abbuia sempre più tardi.

trees, the kindling of early night between the ragged pinnacles and in the water a blazing of awnings from the quays and lodging-houses.

The evening that stretches out over the humid basin brings, with the throbbing of motors, only the geese's crying and an interior of snow-white porcelain tells the blackened mirror, that sees you changed, a story of cool mistakes and engraves it where the sponge cannot reach.

Your legend, Dora! But it is already written in the looks of those men who have high-set, weak whiskers in large golden portraits and it recurs with each chord that the broken harmonica articulates in the moment of darkening, later and later.

È scritta là. Il sempreverde
alloro per la cucina
resiste, la voce non muta,
Ravenna è lontana, distilla
veleno una fede feroce.
Che vuole da te? Non si cede
voce, leggenda o destino. ...
Ma è tardi, sempre più tardi.

La Casa dei doganieri

Tu non ricordi la casa dei doganieri
sul rialzo a strapiombo sulla scogliera:
desolata t'attende dalla sera
in cui v'entrò lo sciame dei tuoi pensieri
e vi sostò irrequieto.

Libeccio sferza da anni le vecchia mura
e il suono del tuo riso non è più lieto:
la bussola va impazzita all'avventura
e il calcolo dei dadi più non torna.
Tu non ricordi; altro tempo frastorna
la tua memoria; un filo s'addipana.

It is written there. The evergreen laurel survives for the kitchen,
the voice does not change, Ravenna is far away, a ferocious faith
distils poison. What does it want of you? Voice, legend, or destiny
are not to be surrendered. But it is late, always later.

The Shore-watchers' House

You don't remember the shore-watchers' house on the cliff sheer
above the rocky coast: it waits for you unhappily since the night
the swarm of your thoughts came there and stayed without peace.

South winds have lashed the old walls for years and the sound
of your laugh is no longer gay: the compass turns crazily, at ran-
dom, and the guess about the dice is no longer lucky. You don't
recall; another time prevents your memory; a thread is wound.

Ne tengo ancora un capo; ma s'allontana
la casa e in cima al tetto la banderuola
affumicata gira senza pietà.
Ne tengo un capo; ma tu resti sola
nè qui respiri nell'oscurità.

Oh l'orizzonte in fuga, dove s'accende
rara la luce della petroliera!
Il varco è qui? (Ripullula il frangente
ancora sulla balza che scoscende …)
Tu non ricordi la casa di questa
mia sera. Ed io non so chi va e chi resta.

Eastbourne

«Dio salvi il re» intonano le trombe
da un padiglione erto su palafitte
che aprono il varco al mare quando sale
a distruggere peste
umide di cavalli nella sabbia
del litorale.

I still hold an end of it; but the house recedes and the blackened weathervane on top of its roof spins pitilessly. I hold an end of it; but you stay alone and do not breathe here in the dark.

Oh the retreating sky-line where the tanker's light flares rarely! Is this the crossing point? (The breakers still seethe at the crumbling height …) You don't remember the house of this my evening. And I do not know who leaves and who stays.

Eastbourne

'God save the king', the brass band intones from a pavilion built high on piles that open a passage to the sea when it rises to destroy the marks of horse-hooves damp in the sand upon the shoreline.

Freddo un vento m'investe
ma un guizzo accende i vetri
e il candore di mica delle rupi
ne risplende.

Bank Holiday ... Riporta l'onda lunga
della mia vita
a striscio, troppo dolce sulla china.
Si fa tardi. I fragori si distendono,
si chiudono in sordina.

Vanno su sedie a ruote i mutilati,
li accompagnano cani dagli orecchi
lunghi, bimbi in silenzio o vecchi. (Forse
domani tutto parrà un sogno.)
                                    E vieni
tu pure voce prigioniera, sciolta
anima ch'è smarrita,
voce di sangue, persa e restituita
alla mia sera.

Come lucente muove sui suoi spicchi
la porta di un albergo
– risponde un'altra e le rivolge un raggio –

A chilling wind assails me but a glimmer lights the windows and
with it the white of mica shines in the cliffs.

Bank Holiday. ... It brings back the long drawn wave of my life
glidingly, too pleasant in its lapse. It grows late. The crashes resound more widely, but end in a mutedness.

Upon their wheel-chairs invalids pass, attended by long eared
dogs, silent children, or the old. (Perhaps tomorrow all this will
be like a dream.) And you too come, imprisoned voice, soul set
free who have strayed, lost voice of blood restored to my own
evening.

As, flashing light from its leaves, a hotel door revolves – another answers, sending back a ray – a roundabout disturbs me that

m'agita un carosello che travolge
tutto dentro il suo giro; ed io in ascolto
(«mia patria!») riconosco il tuo respiro,
anch'io mi levo e il giorno è troppo folto.

Tutto apparirà vano: anche la forza
che nella sua tenace ganga aggrega
i vivi e i morti, gli alberi e gli scogli
e si svolge da te, per te. La festa
non ha pietà. Rimanda
il suo scroscio la banda, si dispiega
nel primo buio una bontà senz'armi.

Vince il male. . . . La ruota non s'arresta.

Anche tu lo sapevi, luce-in-tenebra.

Nella plaga che brucia, dove sei
scomparsa al primo tocco delle campane, solo
rimano l'acre tizzo che già fu
Bank Holiday.

within its track overturns all: and I intently listening ('my country!') know your breathing, I too rise up and the day is far too crowded.

Everything will seem empty, even the force which unites in its untiring hold the living and the dead, trees and rocks, and is moved by you, for you. The holiday is without mercy. The band puts away its clamour, in the first dusk a goodness without armament unfolds.

Evil conquers. . . . The wheel will not stop.

You knew this too, light-in-darkness.

In that burning streak, where you have vanished at the bells' first note, only the acrid brand is left that once was Bank Holiday.

Corrispondenze

Or che in fondo un miraggio
di vapori vacilla e si desperde,
altro annunzia, tra gli alberi, la squilla
del picchio verde.

La mano che raggiunge il sottobosco
e trapunge la trama
del cuore con le punte dello strame,
è quella che matura incubi d'oro
a specchio delle gore
quando il carro sonoro
di Bassareo riporta folli mùgoli
di arieti sulle toppe arse dei colli.

Torni anche tu, pastora senza greggi,
e siedi sul mio sasso?
Ti riconosco; ma non so che leggi
oltre i voli che svariano sul passo.
Lo chiedo invano al piano dove una bruma
èsita tra baleni e spari su sparsi tetti,
alla febbre nascosta dei diretti
nella costa che fuma.

Correspondences

Now that in the distance a mirage of vapours wavers and is scattered, the drumming of the green woodpecker, among the trees, announces something different.

The hand that reaches the undergrowth and pierces through the heart's web with the littered points is the one that nurses portents of gold in the mirror of ponds when the rumbling car of Bacchus brings back wild yells of rams from burnt patches in the hills.

Are you coming back too, shepherdess without flocks, and will you sit on my stone? I recognize you; but do not know what you read beyond the flights that weave over the pass. I vainly ask the plain where a haze lingers among flashes and shots upon the scattered roofs, ask the hidden fever of expresses in the coast that steams.

La primavera hitleriana

Nè quella ch'a veder lo sol si gira ...
(Dante(?) a Giovanni Querini)

F OLTA la nuvola bianca delle falene impazzite
turbina intorno agli scialbi fanali e sulle spallette,
stende a terra una coltre su cui scricchia
come su zucchero il piede; l'estate imminente sprigiona
ora il gelo notturno che capiva
nelle cave segrete della stagione morta,
negli orti che da Maiano scavalcano a questi renai.

Da poco sul corso è passato a volo un messo infernale
tra un alala di scherani, un golfo mistico acceso
e pavesato di croci a uncino l'ha preso e inghiottito,
si sono chiuse le vetrine, povere
e inoffensive benchè armate anch'esse
di cannoni e giocattoli di guerra,
ha sprangato il beccaio che infiorava
di bacche il muso dei capretti uccisi,
la sagra dei miti carnefici che ancora ignorano il sangue
s'è trasformata in un sozzo trescone d'ali schiantate,

Hitler Spring

Nor her whom to see the sun turns ...
(Dante(?) to Giovanni Querini)

DENSE the white cloud of moths, maddened, whirls about the dim
lamps and parapets, spreads a sheet on the earth that crackles like
sugar underfoot; the nearing summer liberates now the nightly chill
that was held in the secret quarries of the dead season, in the orchards that from Maiano slither down to these sand-banks.

A short while ago on the main-street a hellish messenger flashed
past amid the chanting of henchmen, a mystic gulf, alight and
bannered with hooked crosses, took and swallowed him, the shop-
windows are shuttered, poor and harmless, though armed, even
they, with cannons and toys of war, the butcher has put up bars, he
who used to decorate the young goats' heads with berries, the rite
of mild killers who still do not know blood, has been transformed

di larve sulle golene e l'acqua seguita a rodere
le sponde e più nessun è incolpevole.

Tutto per nulla, dunque? – e le candele
romane, a San Giovanni, che sbiancavano lente
l'orizzonte, ed i pegni e i lunghi addii
forti come un battesimo nella lugubre attesa
dell'orda (ma un gemma rigò l'aria stillando
sui ghiacci e le riviere dei tuoi lidi,
gli angeli di Tobia, i sette, la semina
dell'avvenire) e gli eliotropi nati
dalle tue mani – tutto arso e succhiato
da un polline che stride come il fuoco
e ha punto di sinibbio …

                    Oh la piagata
primavera è pur festa se raggela
in morte questa morte! Guarda ancora
in alto, Clizia, è la tua sorte, tu
che il non mutato amor mutata serbi,
fino a che il cieco sole che in te porti

---

into a sickening reel of crushed wings, of larva upon the mud-flats
and the water keeps gnawing the banks and no one now is blameless.

All for nothing, then? – and the roman candles, at Saint John's
day, that slowly paled the skyline, and the tokens and the long fare-
wells strong as a baptism in the mournful waiting of the horde (but
a gem streaked the air, scattering on the ice, and the shores of your
coastline, Tobias's angels, the seven, the seed of the future) and the
heliotropes born from your hands – all burnt and sucked dry by a
pollen that hisses like fire, and has the sharpness of driving snow.

Oh the wounded springtime is still holiday if it freezes this death
in death! Look up again, Clizia, it is your fate, you who, though
changed, keep your love unchanged, until the blind sun you bear

si abbàcini nell'Altro e si distrugga
in Lui per tutti. Forse le sirene, i rintocchi
che salutano i mostri nella sera
della loro tregenda si confondono già
col suono che slegato dal cielo, scende, vince –
col respiro d'un'alba che domani per tutti
si riaffacci, bianca ma senz'ali
di raccapriccio, ai greti arsi del sud ...

Lungomare

Il soffio cresce, il buio è rotto a squarci,
e l'ombra che tu mandi sulla fragile
palizzata s'arriccia. Troppo tardi

se vuoi esser te stessa! Dalla palma
tonfa il sorcio, il baleno è sulla miccia,
sui lunghissimi cigli del tuo sguardo.

in you is dazzled in the Other and is destroyed in Him for everyone. Perhaps the sirens, the tolling bells that greet the monsters on
the evening of their witches' Sabbath are already mingling with the
sound that, unloosed from heaven, descends, conquers, – with
the breathing of a dawn that tomorrow, for everyone, breaks again,
white, but without wings of horror, over the scorched wadis of the
south. ...

Sea-front

The blowing strengthens, the dark is torn to rags, and the shadow
which you cast upon the light fencing crinkles. Too late
    if you want to be yourself! The rat has thudded down from
the palm-tree, the lightning is playing about the fuse, about the
long, long eyelashes of your gaze.

Su una lettera non scritta

Per un formicolìo d'albe, per pochi
fili su cui s'impigli
il fiocco della vita e s'incollani
in ore e in anni, oggi i delfini a coppie
capriolano coi figli? Oh ch'io non oda
nulla di te, ch'io fugga dal bagliore
dei tuoi cigli. Ben altro è sulla terra.

Sparir non so nè riaffacciarmi; tarda
la fucina vermiglia
della notte, la sera si fa lunga,
la preghiera è supplizio e non ancora
tra le rocce che sorgono t'è giunta
la bottiglia dal mare. L'onda, vuota,
si rompe sulla punta, a Finisterre.

On a Letter Never Written

For a swarming of dawns, for a few wires upon which the loose
wool of life is caught and looped into hours and years, today are
the dolphins in pair cavorting with their children? Oh that I might
hear nothing of you, might fly from the lightning of your brow.
Far other is upon the earth.

I cannot vanish, nor turn my face again; the red furnace of the
night is lingering, the evening drawing out, prayer is torture, and
not yet among rocks that jut has the bottle from the sea come to
you. The wave breaks, emptily, upon the headland, at Finisterre.

Giorno e notte

ANCHE una piuma che vola può disegnare
la tua figura, o il raggio che gioca a rimpiattino
tra i mobili, il rimando dello specchio
di un bambino, dai tetti. Sul giro delle mura
strascichi di vapore prolungano le guglie
dei pioppi e giù sul trespolo s'arruffa il pappagallo
dell'arrotino. Poi la notte afosa
sulla piazzola, e i passi, e sempre questa dura
fatica di affondare per risorgere eguali
da secoli, o da istanti, d'incubi che non possono
ritrovare la luce dei tuoi occhi nell'antro
incandescente; e ancora le stesse grida e i lunghi
pianti sulla veranda
se rimbomba improvviso il colpo che t'arrossa
la gola e schianta l'ali o perigliosa
annunziatrice dell'alba
e si destano i chiostri e gli ospedali
a un lacerìo di trombe ...

Day and Night

EVEN a feather gliding by can sketch your shape, or the ray which
plays hide-and-seek among the furniture, the reflection of the
child's mirror, from the roofs. Upon the circuit of the walls streaks
of smoke prolong the spires of poplars and below, upon the trestle,
the knife-grinder's parrot ruffles its feathers. Then the sultry night
upon the little square, and the footsteps, and ever this hard struggle
to sink only to rise unchanged for centuries, moments, of nightmares
which cannot find the light of your eyes again in the glowing cave;
and still the same cries and the drawn-out weeping on the verandah
if the shot suddenly echoes that makes your throat flush and shat-
ters your wings, o dangerous messenger of dawn, and the cloisters
and the hospitals awake at a rending of trumpets. ...

Vento sulla mezzaluna

Il grande ponte non portava a te.
T'avrei raggiunta anche navigando
nelle chiaviche, a un tuo comando. Ma
già le forze, col sole sui cristalli
delle verande, andavano stremandosi.

L'uomo che predicava sul Crescente
mi chiese «Sai dov'è Dio?» Lo sapevo
e glielo dissi. Scosse il capo. Sparve
nel turbine che prese uomini e case
e li sollevò in alto, sulla pece.

Edimburgo. 1948

L'ombra della magnolia

L'ombra della magnolia giapponese
si sfoltisce or che i bocci paonazzi
sono caduti. Vibra intermittente
in vetta una cicala. Non è più
il tempo dell'unisono vocale,

Wind in the Crescent

The great bridge did not lead to you. I would have reached you
navigating the sewers at a command from you. But already my
powers were, with the sun on the verandah windows, gradually
spending themselves.

The man preaching on the Crescent asked me 'Do you know
where God is?' I did, and told him. He shook his head. He vanished
in the whirling wind that snatched up men and houses and lifted
them on high, upon pitch blackness.

Edinburgh, 1948

The Magnolia's Shade

The shade of the Japanese magnolia is thinned out now that the
purplish buds have fallen. A cicada quivers at intervals from the
height. It is no longer the time of the unison of voices, Clizia, the

Clizia, il tempo del nume illimitato
che divora e rinsangua i suoi fedeli.
Spendersi era più facile, morire
al primo batter d'ale, al primo incontro
col nemico, un trastullo. Comincia ora
la via più dura: ma non te consunta
dal sole e radicata, e pure morbida
cesena che sorvoli alta le fredde
banchine del tuo fiume, – non te fragile
fuggitiva cui zenit nadir cancro
capricorno rimasero indistinti
perchè la guerra fosse in te e in chi adora
su te le stimme del tuo Sposo, flette
il brivido del gelo .... Gli altri arretrano
e piegano. La lima che sottile
incide tacerà, la vuota scorza
di chi cantava sarà presto polvere
di vetro sotto i piedi, l'ombra è livida, –
è l'autunno, è l'inverno, è l'oltrecielo
che ti conduce e in cui mi getto, cèfalo
saltato in secco al novilunio.

Addio.

time of the limitless deity who devours his faithful and restores
them with blood again. To be consumed was easier, dying at the
first flutter of a wing, at the first encounter with the enemy, a game.
Now the harder way begins: but not you, consumed by the sun
and rooted and yet a tender thrush who fly high above the cold
wharves of your river, the shiver of frost does not bend you, frail
fugitive, for whom zenith nadir cancer capricorn remained undistin-
guished so that the war might be in you and in who adores upon
you the marks of your Bridegroom. ... The others fall back, and
buckle. The file which finely cuts its way will be silenced, the
empty shell of him who sang will soon be a powder of glass underfoot, the shadow is livid, it is autumn, it is winter, it is the beyond
which leads you and into which I throw myself, sea-fish jumped
clear of the water under the new moon.

Farewell.

L'anguilla

L'ANGUILLA, la sirena
dei mari freddi che lascia il Baltico
per giungere ai nostri mari,
ai nostri estuari, ai fiumi
che risale in profondo, sotto la piena avversa,
di ramo in ramo e poi
di capello in capello, assottigliati,
sempre più addentro, sempre più nel cuore
del macigno, filtrando
tra gorielli di melma finchè un giorno
una luce scoccata dai castagni
ne accende il guizzo in pozze d'acquamorta,
nei fossi che declinano
dai balzi dell'Appennino alla Romagna;
l'anguilla, torcia, frusta,
freccia d'Amore in terra
che soli i nostri botri o i disseccati
ruscelli pirenaici riconducono
a paradisi di fecondazione;
l'anima verde che cerca
vita dove là solo
morde l'arsura e la desolazione,

The Eel

THE eel, the siren of cold seas that leaves the Baltic to reach our seas, our estuaries, the rivers which, deep down, it follows upwards. under the opposing spate, from branch to branch, from tendril to tendril, thinned down, ever more inland, ever more into the heart of rock, slipping through little channels of slime, until one day the light glancing from chestnut-trees illuminates its streak in the stagnant pools, in the hollows that go down from the steeps of the Apennines to the Romagna; the eel, torch, lash, arrow of Love upon earth, which our gullies and fiery, dried-up streams alone lead back to paradises of fertility; the green soul that looks for life in places where only heat and desolation gnaw, the spark which says every-

la scintilla che dice
tutto comincia quando tutto pare
incarbonirsi, bronco seppellito,
l'iride breve gemella
di quella che incastoni in mezzo ai cigli
e fai brillare intatta in mezzo ai figli
dell'uomo, immersi nel tuo fango, puoi tu
non crederla sorella?

SE t'hanno assomigliato
alla volpe sarà per la falcata
prodigiosa, pel volo del tuo passo
che unisce e divide, che sconvolge
e rinfranca il selciato (il tuo terrazzo,
le strade presso il Cottolengo, il prato,
l'albero che ha il mio nome ne vibrano
felici, umili e vinti) – o forse solo
per l'onda luminosa che diffondi
dalle mandorle tenere degli occhi,
per l'astuzia dei tuoi pronti stupori,
per lo strazio
di piume lacerate che può dare
la tua mano d'infante in una stretta;

thing begins when everything seems blackened, a buried stump, the brief rainbow, twin-sister to the one which you set in the middle of your eye, and let shine in the midst of the sons of men, sunk in your mud, – can you not believe her a sister?

IF they have likened you to the fox, it will be for the miraculous leap, for the flight of your step that draws together and divides, that turns up and freshens the gravel (your balcony, the streets near the Cottolengo, the meadow, the tree that has my name quiver with it, happy, humble, and defeated) – or perhaps only for the luminous wave that you shed from the tender almonds of your eyes, for the shrewdness of your quick amazements, for the hurt of torn feathers that your child's hand can give in a clasp; if they have likened you

se t'hanno assomigliato
a un carnivoro biondo, al genio perfido
delle fratte (e perchè non all'immondo
pesce che dà la scossa, alla torpedine?)
è forse perchè i ciechi non ti videro
sulle scapole gracili le ali,
perchè i ciechi non scorsero il presagio
della tua fronte incandescente, il solco
che vi ho graffiato a sangue, croce cresima
incantesimo jattura voto vale
perdizione e salvezza; se non seppero
crederti più che donnola o che donna,
con chi dividerò la mia scoperta,
dove seppellirò l'oro che porto,
dove la brace che in me stride quando,
lasciandomi, ti volgi dalle scale?

Per album

Ho cominciato anzi giorno
a buttar l'amo per te (lo chiamavo «il lamo»).

to a fair carnivore, to the treacherous genius of the undergrowth
(and why not to the unclean fish that gives the shock, the torpedo-
fish?) it is perhaps because the blind did not see the wings on your
fine shoulder-blades, because the blind did not make out the omen
of your glowing forehead, the groove that I have scratched there in
blood, cross, chrism, enchantment, misfortune, prayer meaning
perdition and salvation; if they did not know how to think of you
as more than weasel or woman, whom can I share my discovery
with, where shall I bury the gold I bear, where the live coal that
rages in me when, leaving me, you turn from the stairs?

For an Album

I BEGAN before daylight to cast my hook for you (I called it
by a nickname, 'I-love-her'). But no flash of a tail could I catch

Ma nessun guizzo di coda
scorgevo nei pozzi limosi,
nessun vento veniva col tuo indizio
dai colli monferrini,
Ho continuato il mio giorno
sempre spiando te, larva girino
frangia di rampicante francolino
gazzella zebù ocàpi
nuvola nera grandine
prima della vendemmia, ho spigolato
tra i filari inzuppati senza trovarti.
Ho proseguito fino a tardi
senza sapere che tre cassettine
— SABBIA SODA SAPONE; la piccionaia
da cui partì il tuo volo: da una cucina, —
si sarebbero aperte per me solo.
Così sparisti nell'orizzonte incerto.
Non c'è pensiero che imprigioni il fulmine
ma chi ha veduto la luce non se ne priva.
Mi stesi al piede del tuo ciliegio, ero
già troppo ricco per contenerti viva.

in the muddy wells, no wind came with a sign of you from the hills
of Monferrato. I went on with my day, always watching for you
larva, tadpole, creeper-fringe, ptarmigan, gazelle, zebu, okapi,
black cloud, hailstone, before the wine-harvest I went gleaning
among the soaking rows without finding you. I carried on till late
without knowing that three containers — SAND, SODA, SOAP, the
pigeon-house from which you took flight, from a kitchen, — were
to be opened for me alone. So you vanished on the uncertain sky-
line. There is no thought to capture lightning, but he who has seen
the light will not be robbed of it. I stretched out at the foot of your
cherry-tree, I was already far too rich to hold you living.

SALVATORE QUASIMODO

Vento a Tìndari

TÌNDARI, mite ti so
fra larghi colli pensile sull'acque
dell'isole dolci del dio,
oggi m'assali
e ti chini in cuore.

Salgo vertici aerei precipizi,
assorto al vento dei pini,
e la brigata che lieve m'accompagna
s'allontana nell'aria,
onda di suoni e amore,
e tu mi prendi
da cui male mi trassi
e paure d'ombre e di silenzi,
rifugi di dolcezze un tempo assidue
e morte d'anima.

A te ignota è la terra
ove ogni giorno affondo
e segrete sillabe nutro:

Wind at Tindari

TINDARI, I know you to be mild between broad hills, over-
hanging the waters of the sweet islands of the god, today you
assail me and bend within my heart.

I climb peaks, airy precipices, intent on the wind from the pines,
and the troop that gaily keep me company go off into the air, wave
of sounds and love, and you take me from whom I wrongly drew
myself away, and fears of shadows and silences, retreats of blessed-
ness once unfailing, and death of soul.

The land is unknown to you where each day I go deep and feed

altra luce ti sfoglia sopra i vetri
nella veste notturna,
e gioia non mia riposa
sul tuo grembo.

Aspro è l'esilio,
e la ricerca che chiudevo in te
d'armonia oggi si muta
in ansia precoce di morire;
e ogni amore è schermo alla tristezza,
tacito passo nel buio
dove mi hai posto
amaro pane a rompere.

Tìndari serena torna;
soave amico mi desta
che mi sporga nel cielo da una rupe
e io fingo timore a chi non sa
che vento profondo m'ha cercato.

Strada di Agrigentum

Là dura un vento che ricordo acceso
nelle criniere dei cavalli obliqui
in corsa lungo le pianure, vento

secret syllabry: other light bares you, in your night dress, and joy
not mine lies in your lap.

Harsh is exile, and my search for harmony which ended in you
is changed today into early anxiety at dying; and every love is a
shield against sadness, muted step in the gloom where you have
placed me to break bitter bread.

Tindari, come back serene; sweet friend, wake me that I may
lift myself from a rock to heaven and I pretend fear for whoever
does not know what deep wind has searched me.

Street in Agrigentum

THERE a wind endures that I remember afire in the manes of the
slanting horses racing over the plains, wind that soils and gnaws

che macchia e rode l'arenaria e il cuore
dei telamoni lugubri, riversi
sopra l'erba. Anima antica, grigia
di rancori, torni a quel vento, annusi
il delicato muschio che riveste
i giganti sospinti giù dal cielo.
Come sola allo spazio che ti resta!
E più t'accori s'odi ancora il suono
che s'allontana largo verso il mare
dove Espero già striscia mattutino:
il marranzano tristemente vibra
nella gola al carraio che risale
il colle nitido di luna, lento
tra il murmure d'ulivi saraceni.

Antico inverno

DESIDERIO delle tue mani chiare
nella penombra della fiamma:
sapevano di rovere e di rose;
di morte. Antico inverno.

---

the sandstone and the heart of the gloomy statued columns, thrown back upon the earth. Ancient soul, grey with resentment, go back to that wind, breathe in the fine scent of moss that clothes the giants thrown down by heaven. How lonely in the space that is still yours! And you are the more stricken, if you hear the sound that goes off far towards the sea which Hesperus already streaks with morning. The jew's harp sadly quivers in the carter's mouth as he goes up the hill that is clean with moonlight, slow amid the murmur of saracenic olives.

Ancient Winter

DESIRE of your clear hands in the half light of the flame: they smelt of oakwood and roses; of death. Ancient winter.

Cercavano il miglio gli uccelli
ed erano sùbito di neve;
così le parole:
un po' di sole, una raggiera d'angelo,
e poi la nebbia; e gli alberi,
e noi fatti d'aria al mattino.

Imitazione della gioia

Dove gli alberi ancora
abbandonata più fanno la sera,
come indolente
è svanito l'ultimo tuo passo,
che appare appena il fiore
sui tigli e insiste alla sua sorte.

Una ragione cerchi agli affetti,
provi il silenzio nella tua vita.
Altra ventura a me rivela
il tempo specchiato. Addolora
come la morte, bellezza ormai
in altri volti fulminea.
Perduto ho ogni cosa innocente,
anche in questa voce, superstite
a imitare la gioia.

The birds looked for their grain and were suddenly of snow;
similarly words; a little sun, an angel's glory, and then the mist;
and the trees, and us made of air in the morning.

Imitation of Joy

Where the trees make the evening even more abandoned, how
languidly your last step has vanished, as the flower just shows
on the linden tree and insists upon its fate.

You search a motive for feelings, experience silence in your life.
Mirrored time reveals a different adventure to me. Beauty now
flashing in other faces makes me sad, like death. I have lost every
innocent thing, even in this voice, surviving to imitate joy.

411

Ed è sùbito sera

OGNUNO sta solo sul cuor della terra
trafitto da un raggio di sole:
ed è sùbito sera.

Oboe sommerso

AVARA pena, tarda il tuo dono
in questa mia ora
di sospirati abbandoni.

Un òboe gelido risillaba
gioia di foglie perenni,
non mie, e smemora;

in me si fa sera:
l'acqua tramonta
sulle mie mani erbose.

Ali oscillano in fioco cielo,
làbili: il cuore trasmigra
ed io son gerbido,

e i giorni una maceria.

And in No Time it's Evening

EACH one stands alone on the heart of the earth pierced through
by a ray of sunlight: and in no time it's evening.

Sunken Oboe

GRASPING pain, delay your gift in this my hour of longed-for
abandon.
   An icy oboe rephrases joy of evergreen leaves, not mine, and
takes away memory;
   in me it is evening: the water fades upon my grassy hands.
   Wings waver in dim heaven changefully: the heart migrates and
I am untilled,
   and the days a heap of rubble.

Lettera alla madre

«MATER *dulcissima*, ora scendon le nebbie,
il Naviglio urta confusamente sulle dighe,
gli alberi si gonfiano d'acqua, bruciano di neve;
non sono triste nel Nord: non sono
in pace con me, ma non aspetto
perdono da nessuno, molti mi devono lacrime
da uomo a uomo. So che non stai bene, che vivi
come tutte le madri dei poeti, povera
e giusta nella misura d'amore
per i figli lontani. Oggi sono io
che ti scrivo.» Finalmente, dirai, due parole
di quel ragazzo che fuggì di notte, con un mantello corto
e alcuni versi in tasca. Povero, così pronto di cuore,
lo uccideranno un giorno in qualche luogo.
«Certo, ricordo, fu da quel grigio scalo
di treni lenti che portavano mandorle e arance,
alla foce dell'Imera, il fiume pieno di gazze,
di sale, d'eucalyptus. Ma ora ti ringrazio,
questo voglio, dell'ironia che hai messo
sul mio labbro mite come la tua.

Letter to my Mother

'MATER dulcissima, now the mists come down, the canal of the
Naviglio thrusts vaguely against its banks, the trees swell with
water, burn with snow; I am not sad in the North, am not at peace
with myself, but do not expect pardon from any one, many owe
me tears as from man to man. I know you are not well, that you live
like all the mothers of poets, poor and perfect in the measure of
their love for far-off sons. Today it is I who am writing to you.'
At last, you will say, two words from the boy who fled by night
in a short cape, a few lines in his pocket. Poor thing, so open-
hearted, they'll kill him one day in some place. 'Certainly, I remember, it was from that grey yard of slow trains that bore almonds
and oranges to the estuary of the Imera, the river full of magpies,
salt, eucalyptus. But now I thank you, I want to, for the irony which
you laid upon my lip as mild as yours. That smile has saved me from

Quel sorriso m'ha salvato da pianti e da dolori.
E non importa se ora ho qualche lacrima per te,
per tutti quelli che come te aspettano,
e non sanno che cosa. Ah, gentile morte,
non toccare l'orologio in cucina che batte sopra il muro,
tutta la mia infanzia è passata sullo smalto
del suo quadrante, su quei fiori dipinti:
non toccare le mani, il cuore dei vecchi.
Ma forse qualcuno risponde? O morte di pietà,
morte di pudore. Addio, cara, addio, mia
dulcissima mater.»

O miei dolci animali

ORA l'autunno guasta il verde ai colli,
o miei dolci animali. Ancora udremo,
prima di notte, l'ultimo lamento
degli uccelli, il richiamo della grigia
pianura che va incontro a quel rumore
alto di mare. E l'odore di legno
alla pioggia, l'odore delle tane,
com'è vivo qui fra le case,
fra gli uomini, o miei dolci animali.

---

weeping and from griefs. And it does not matter if I have some
tears for you now, for all those who, like you, await and do not
know what. O kind death, do not touch the clock in the kitchen
ticking upon the wall. All my childhood has passed on the enamel
of its face, on those painted flowers. Do not touch the hands, the
hearts of the old. Perhaps some one will answer? O death of mercy,
death of shame. Goodbye, dear, goodbye, my dulcissima mater.'

O My Sweet Animals

Now autumn spoils the green of hills, o my sweet animals. We
shall hear again, before nightfall, the final lament of the birds, the
call of the grey plain that goes towards that high noise of the sea.
And the smell of wood in the rain, the smell of the hollows, how
keen it is here between the houses, among men, o my sweet animals.

Questo volto che gira gli occhi lenti,
questa mano che segna il cielo dove
romba un tuono, sono vostri, o miei lupi,
mie volpi bruciate dal sangue.
Ogni mano, ogni volto, sono vostri.
Tu mi dici che tutto è stato vano,
la vita, i giorni corrosi da un'acqua
assidua, mentre sale dai giardini
un canto di fanciulli. Ora lontani,
dunque, da noi? Ma cedono nell'aria
come ombre appena. Questa la tua voce.
Ma forse io so che tutto non è stato.

Dalla Rocca di Bergamo Alta

HAI udito il grido del gallo nell'aria
di là dalle murate, oltre le torri
gelide d'una luce che ignoravi,
grido fulmineo di vita, e stormire
di voci dentro le celle, e il richiamo
d'uccello della ronda avanti l'alba.
E non hai detto parole per te:
eri nel cerchio ormai di breve raggio:

This face that slowly turns its eyes about, this hand that marks the heavens where a peal of thunder resounds, are yours, o my wolves, my foxes burnt with blood. Every hand, every face is yours. You tell me everything has been in vain, life, the days worn away by a steady flow of water, while from the garden rises a singing of children. Perhaps far from us now? But they yield in the air like shadows, if as much. This your voice. But perhaps I know everything has not been.

From the Castle-rock of High Bergamo

YOU heard the cry of the cock in the air beyond the walls, beyond the towers icy with a light you were not aware of, a cry startling with life, and the murmur of voices from the cells, and the cry of the sentinel bird before dawn. And you said nothing for yourself: you were now in the orbit of short rays: and the antelope and the

e tacquero l'antilope e l'airone
persi in un soffio di fumo maligno,
talismani d'un mondo appena nato.
E passava la luna di febbraio
aperta sulla terra, ma a te forma
nella memoria, accesa al suo silenzio.
Anche tu fra i cipressi della Rocca
ora vai senza rumore; e qui l'ira
si quieta al verde dei giovani morti,
e la pietà lontana è quasi gioia.

heron were silent, lost in a gust of malignant smoke, magic em-
blems of a world all but unborn. And the February moon passed
openly above the earth, but to you, a form in memory, lit with its
own silence. You too are going now, between the cypresses of the
Fortress, without sound; and here anger is made quiet by the green
of the young dead, and distant pity is almost joy.

INDEX OF FIRST LINES